Rocket Robinson and the Pharaoh's Fortune

for Charlie, Violet, and Jennifer

Please direct all inquiries to:

BoilerRoom Studios
2149 W. Giddings Ave.
Chicago, IL 60625

www.rocketrobinson.com

ISBN: 978-0-9893655-0-5

Library of Congress Control Number: 2013910122

Printed in the United States of America

Rocket Robinson
and the Pharaoh's Fortune

Sean O'Neill

BOILERROOM
STUDIOS

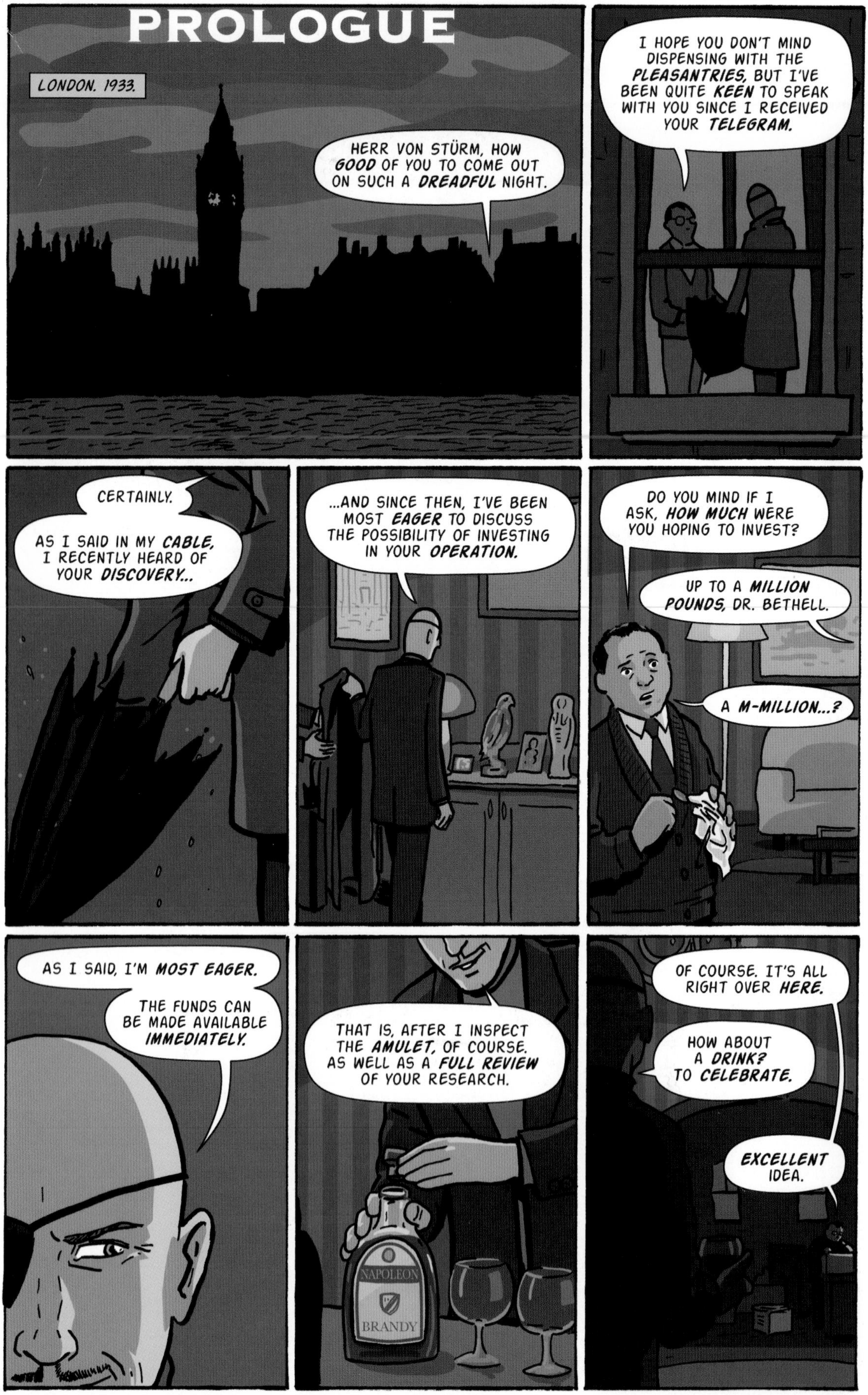
PROLOGUE
LONDON. 1933.
HERR VON STÜRM, HOW GOOD OF YOU TO COME OUT ON SUCH A DREADFUL NIGHT.
I HOPE YOU DON'T MIND DISPENSING WITH THE PLEASANTRIES, BUT I'VE BEEN QUITE KEEN TO SPEAK WITH YOU SINCE I RECEIVED YOUR TELEGRAM.
CERTAINLY.
AS I SAID IN MY CABLE, I RECENTLY HEARD OF YOUR DISCOVERY...
...AND SINCE THEN, I'VE BEEN MOST EAGER TO DISCUSS THE POSSIBILITY OF INVESTING IN YOUR OPERATION.
DO YOU MIND IF I ASK, HOW MUCH WERE YOU HOPING TO INVEST?
UP TO A MILLION POUNDS, DR. BETHELL.
A M-MILLION...?
AS I SAID, I'M MOST EAGER.
THE FUNDS CAN BE MADE AVAILABLE IMMEDIATELY.
THAT IS, AFTER I INSPECT THE AMULET, OF COURSE. AS WELL AS A FULL REVIEW OF YOUR RESEARCH.
NAPOLEON
BRANDY
OF COURSE. IT'S ALL RIGHT OVER HERE.
HOW ABOUT A DRINK? TO CELEBRATE.
EXCELLENT IDEA.

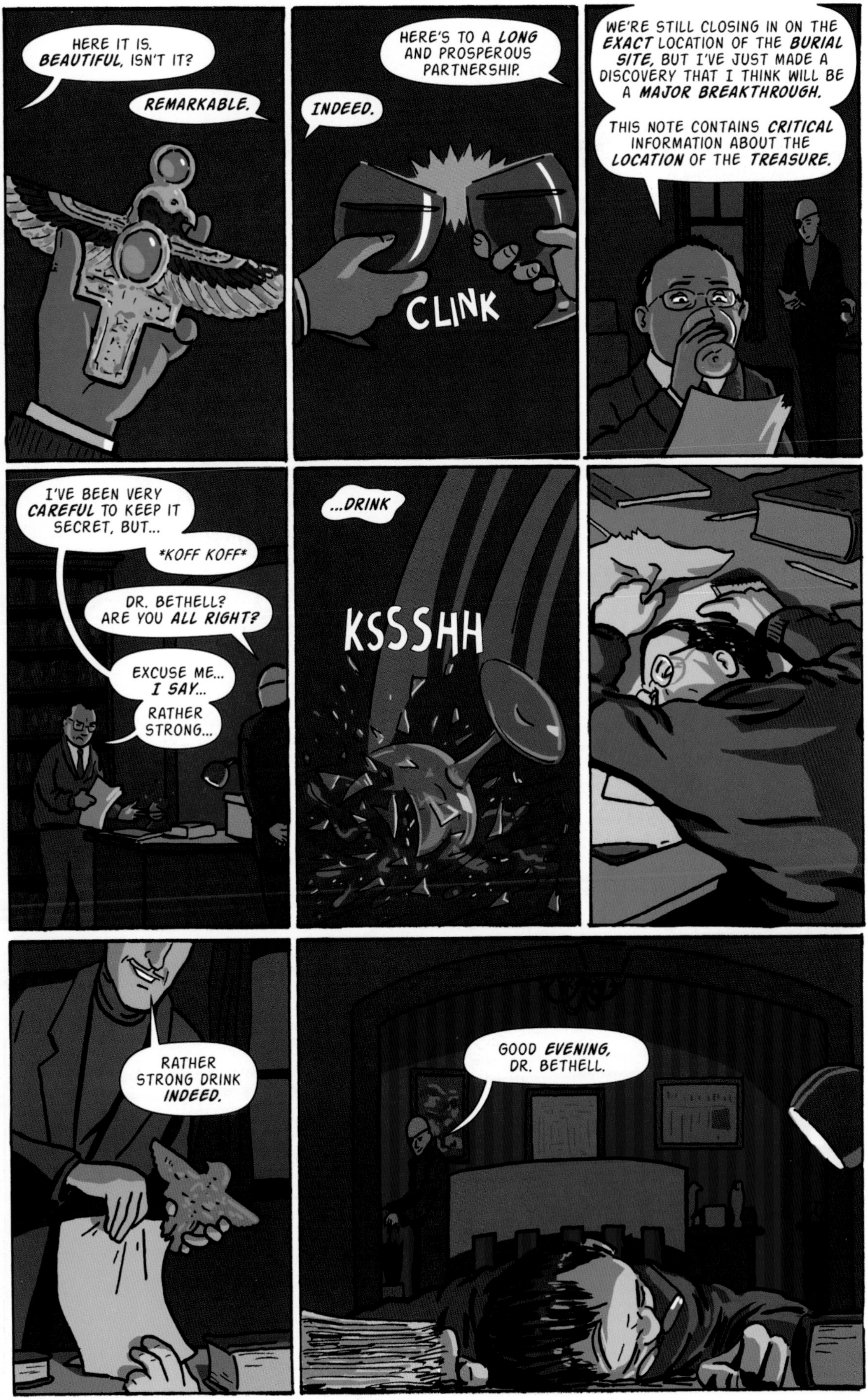
HERE IT IS. BEAUTIFUL, ISN'T IT?
REMARKABLE.
HERE'S TO A LONG AND PROSPEROUS PARTNERSHIP.
INDEED.
CLINK
WE'RE STILL CLOSING IN ON THE EXACT LOCATION OF THE BURIAL SITE, BUT I'VE JUST MADE A DISCOVERY THAT I THINK WILL BE A MAJOR BREAKTHROUGH.
THIS NOTE CONTAINS CRITICAL INFORMATION ABOUT THE LOCATION OF THE TREASURE.
I'VE BEEN VERY CAREFUL TO KEEP IT SECRET, BUT...
KOFF KOFF
DR. BETHELL? ARE YOU ALL RIGHT?
EXCUSE ME... I SAY...
RATHER STRONG...
...DRINK
KSSSHH
RATHER STRONG DRINK INDEED.
GOOD EVENING, DR. BETHELL.

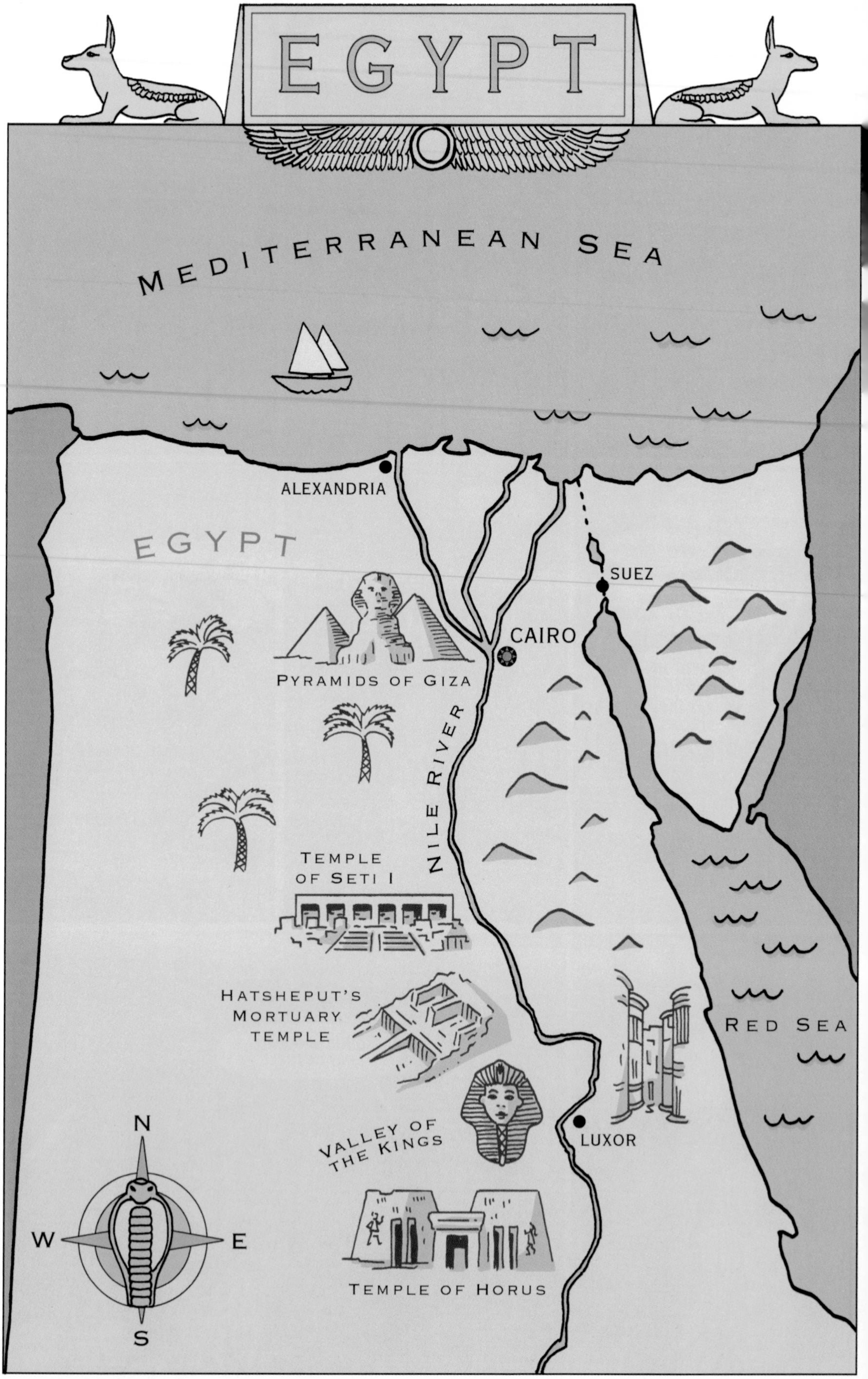
EGYPT
MEDITERRANEAN SEA
ALEXANDRIA
EGYPT
SUEZ
CAIRO
PYRAMIDS OF GIZA
NILE RIVER
TEMPLE OF SETI I
HATSHEPUT'S MORTUARY TEMPLE
RED SEA
VALLEY OF THE KINGS
LUXOR
N
W
E
S
TEMPLE OF HORUS

CHAPTER ONE

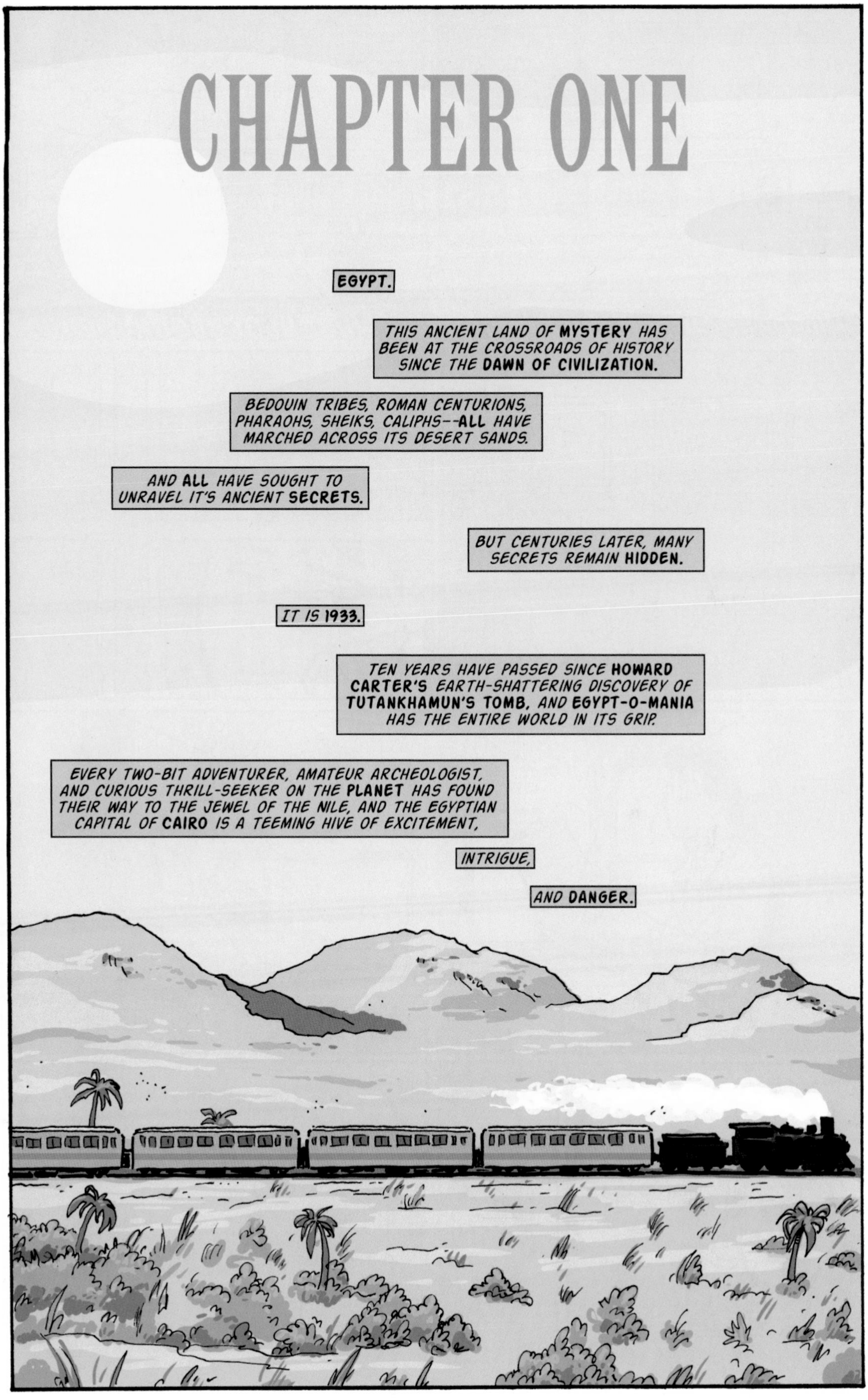
EGYPT.
THIS ANCIENT LAND OF MYSTERY HAS BEEN AT THE CROSSROADS OF HISTORY SINCE THE DAWN OF CIVILIZATION.
BEDOUIN TRIBES, ROMAN CENTURIONS, PHARAOHS, SHEIKS, CALIPHS--ALL HAVE MARCHED ACROSS ITS DESERT SANDS.
AND ALL HAVE SOUGHT TO UNRAVEL IT'S ANCIENT SECRETS.
BUT CENTURIES LATER, MANY SECRETS REMAIN HIDDEN.
IT IS 1933.
TEN YEARS HAVE PASSED SINCE HOWARD CARTER'S EARTH-SHATTERING DISCOVERY OF TUTANKHAMUN'S TOMB, AND EGYPT-O-MANIA HAS THE ENTIRE WORLD IN ITS GRIP.
EVERY TWO-BIT ADVENTURER, AMATEUR ARCHEOLOGIST, AND CURIOUS THRILL-SEEKER ON THE PLANET HAS FOUND THEIR WAY TO THE JEWEL OF THE NILE, AND THE EGYPTIAN CAPITAL OF CAIRO IS A TEEMING HIVE OF EXCITEMENT,
INTRIGUE,
AND DANGER.

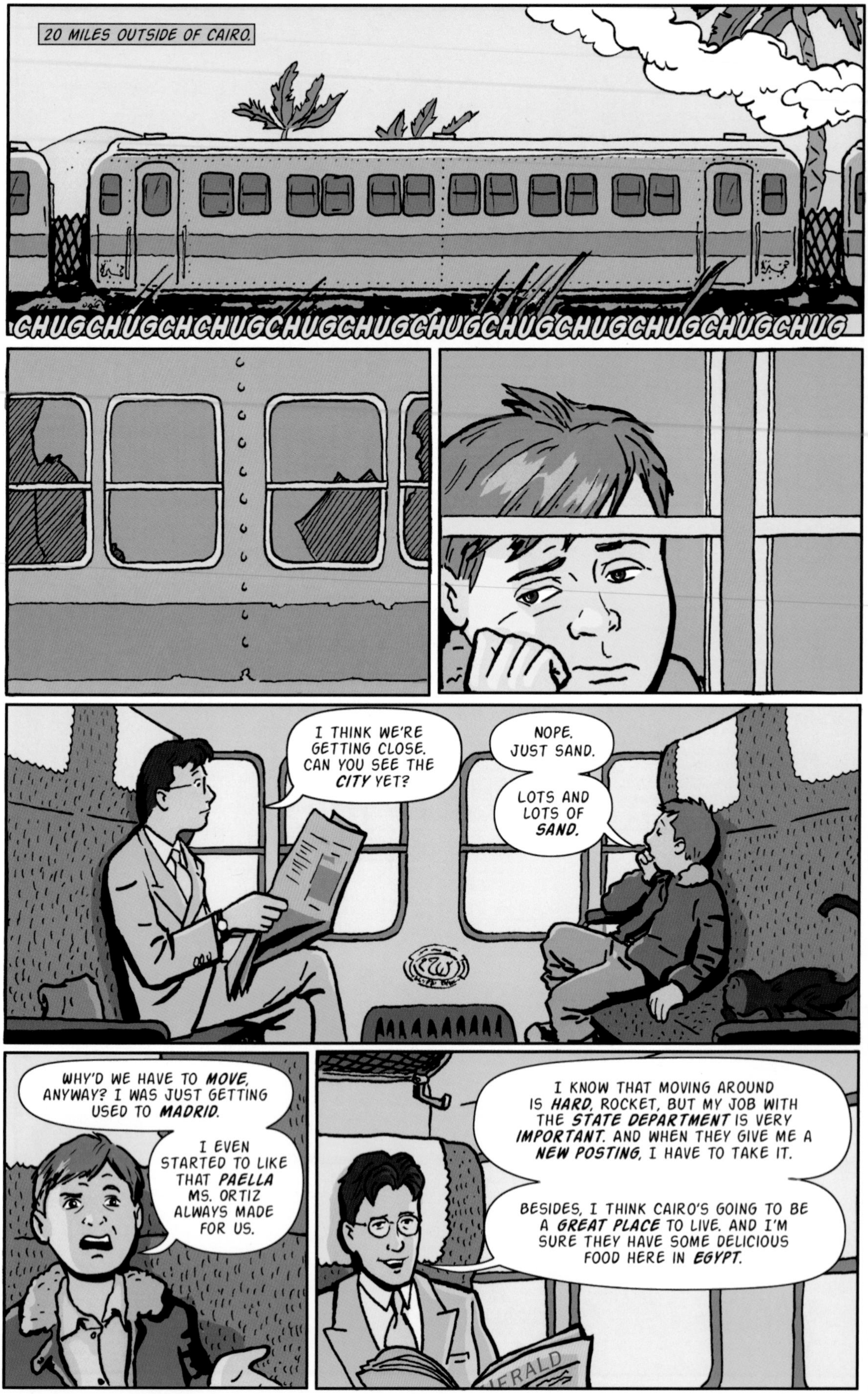
20 MILES OUTSIDE OF CAIRO.
CHUGCHUGCHCHUGCHUGCHUGCHUGCHUGCHUGCHUGCHUGCHUG
I THINK WE'RE GETTING CLOSE. CAN YOU SEE THE CITY YET?
NOPE. JUST SAND.
LOTS AND LOTS OF SAND.
WHY'D WE HAVE TO MOVE, ANYWAY? I WAS JUST GETTING USED TO MADRID.
I EVEN STARTED TO LIKE THAT PAELLA MS. ORTIZ ALWAYS MADE FOR US.
I KNOW THAT MOVING AROUND IS HARD, ROCKET, BUT MY JOB WITH THE STATE DEPARTMENT IS VERY IMPORTANT. AND WHEN THEY GIVE ME A NEW POSTING, I HAVE TO TAKE IT.
BESIDES, I THINK CAIRO'S GOING TO BE A GREAT PLACE TO LIVE. AND I'M SURE THEY HAVE SOME DELICIOUS FOOD HERE IN EGYPT.
HERALD

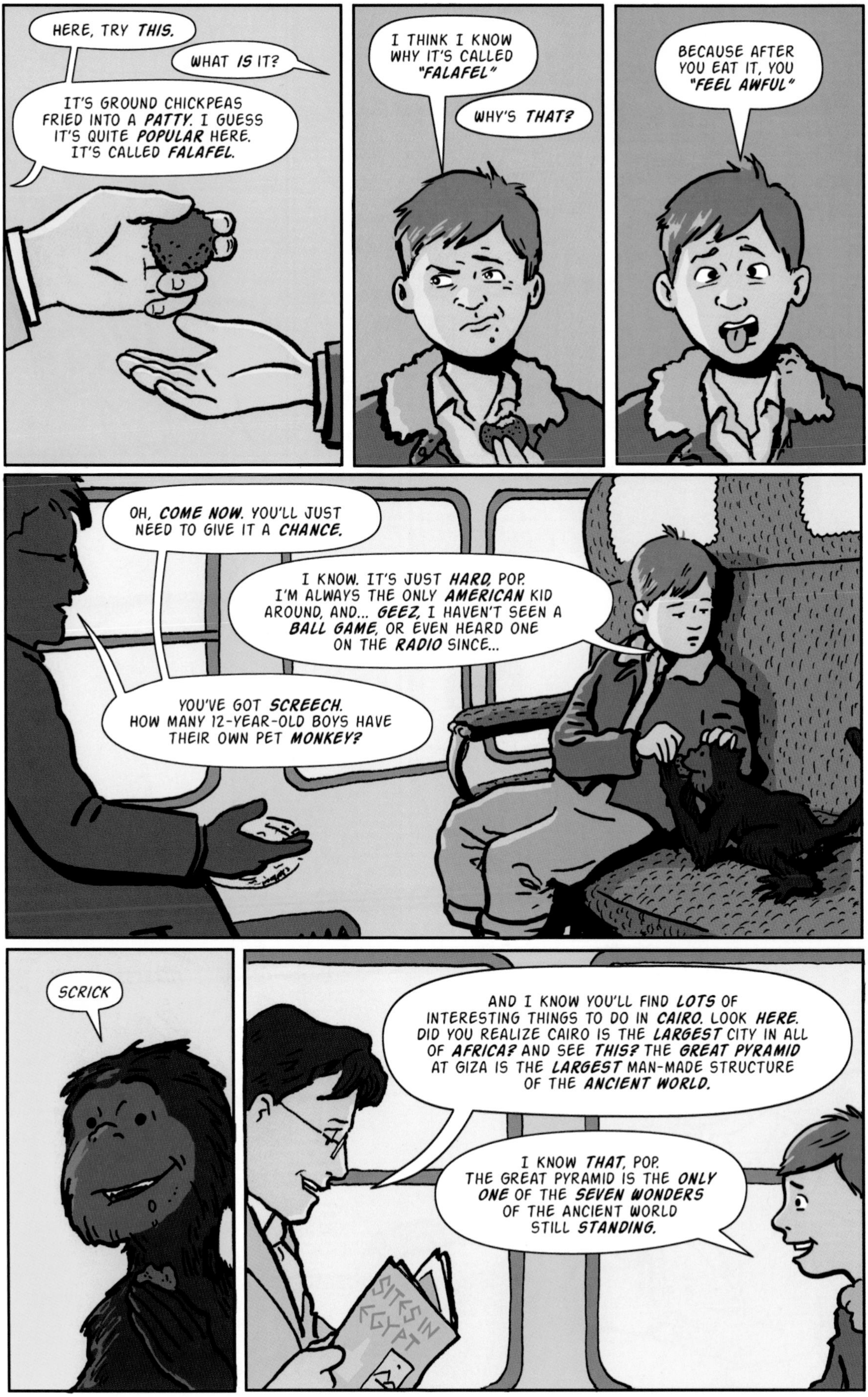
HERE, TRY THIS.
WHAT IS IT?
IT'S GROUND CHICKPEAS FRIED INTO A PATTY. I GUESS IT'S QUITE POPULAR HERE. IT'S CALLED FALAFEL.
I THINK I KNOW WHY IT'S CALLED "FALAFEL"
WHY'S THAT?
BECAUSE AFTER YOU EAT IT, YOU "FEEL AWFUL"
OH, COME NOW. YOU'LL JUST NEED TO GIVE IT A CHANCE.
I KNOW. IT'S JUST HARD, POP. I'M ALWAYS THE ONLY AMERICAN KID AROUND, AND... GEEZ, I HAVEN'T SEEN A BALL GAME, OR EVEN HEARD ONE ON THE RADIO SINCE...
YOU'VE GOT SCREECH. HOW MANY 12-YEAR-OLD BOYS HAVE THEIR OWN PET MONKEY?
SCRICK
AND I KNOW YOU'LL FIND LOTS OF INTERESTING THINGS TO DO IN CAIRO. LOOK HERE. DID YOU REALIZE CAIRO IS THE LARGEST CITY IN ALL OF AFRICA? AND SEE THIS? THE GREAT PYRAMID AT GIZA IS THE LARGEST MAN-MADE STRUCTURE OF THE ANCIENT WORLD.
I KNOW THAT, POP. THE GREAT PYRAMID IS THE ONLY ONE OF THE SEVEN WONDERS OF THE ANCIENT WORLD STILL STANDING.
SITES IN EGYPT

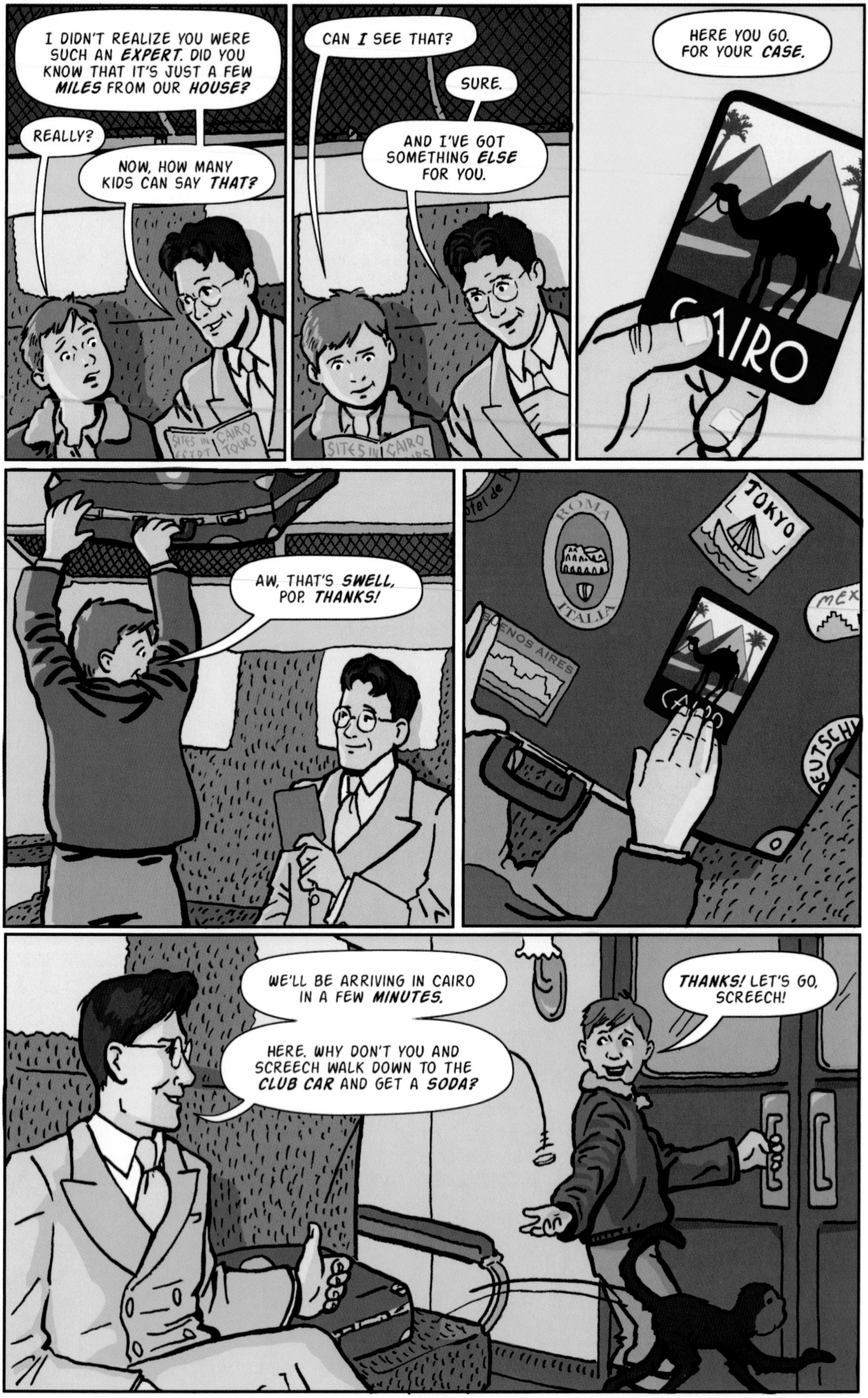

I DIDN'T REALIZE YOU WERE SUCH AN **EXPERT.** DID YOU KNOW THAT IT'S JUST A FEW **MILES** FROM OUR **HOUSE?**
REALLY?
NOW, HOW MANY KIDS CAN SAY **THAT?**
SITES IN EGYPT
CAIRO TOURS
CAN **I** SEE THAT?
SURE.
AND I'VE GOT SOMETHING **ELSE** FOR YOU.
HERE YOU GO. FOR YOUR **CASE.**
CAIRO
AW, THAT'S **SWELL,** POP. **THANKS!**
ROMA
ITALIA
TOKYO
BUENOS AIRES
CAIRO
WE'LL BE ARRIVING IN CAIRO IN A FEW **MINUTES.**
HERE. WHY DON'T YOU AND SCREECH WALK DOWN TO THE **CLUB CAR** AND GET A **SODA?**
THANKS! LET'S GO, SCREECH!

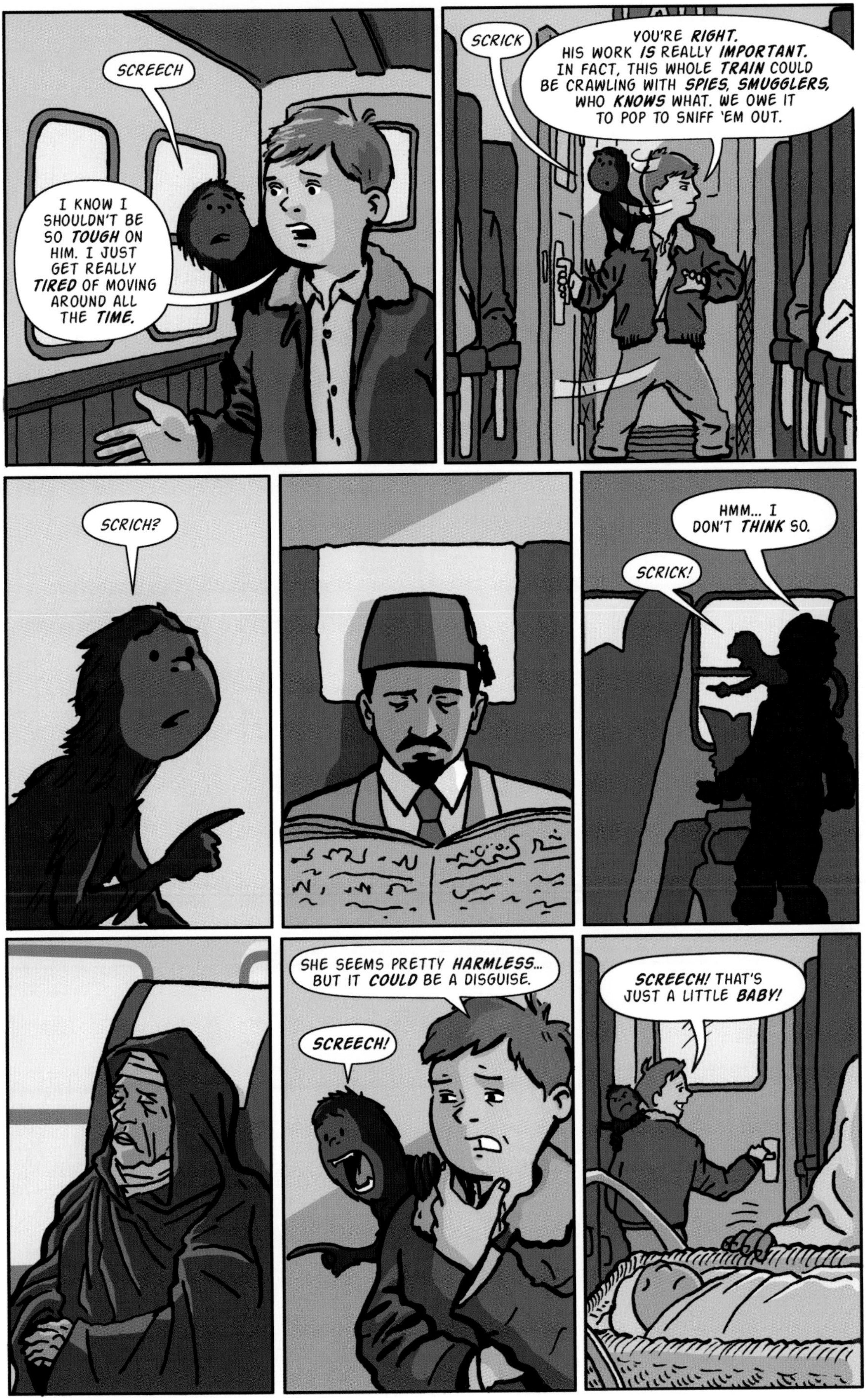
SCREECH
I KNOW I SHOULDN'T BE SO TOUGH ON HIM. I JUST GET REALLY TIRED OF MOVING AROUND ALL THE TIME.
SCRICK
YOU'RE RIGHT. HIS WORK IS REALLY IMPORTANT. IN FACT, THIS WHOLE TRAIN COULD BE CRAWLING WITH SPIES, SMUGGLERS, WHO KNOWS WHAT. WE OWE IT TO POP TO SNIFF 'EM OUT.
SCRICH?
HMM... I DON'T THINK SO.
SCRICK!
SHE SEEMS PRETTY HARMLESS... BUT IT COULD BE A DISGUISE.
SCREECH!
SCREECH! THAT'S JUST A LITTLE BABY!

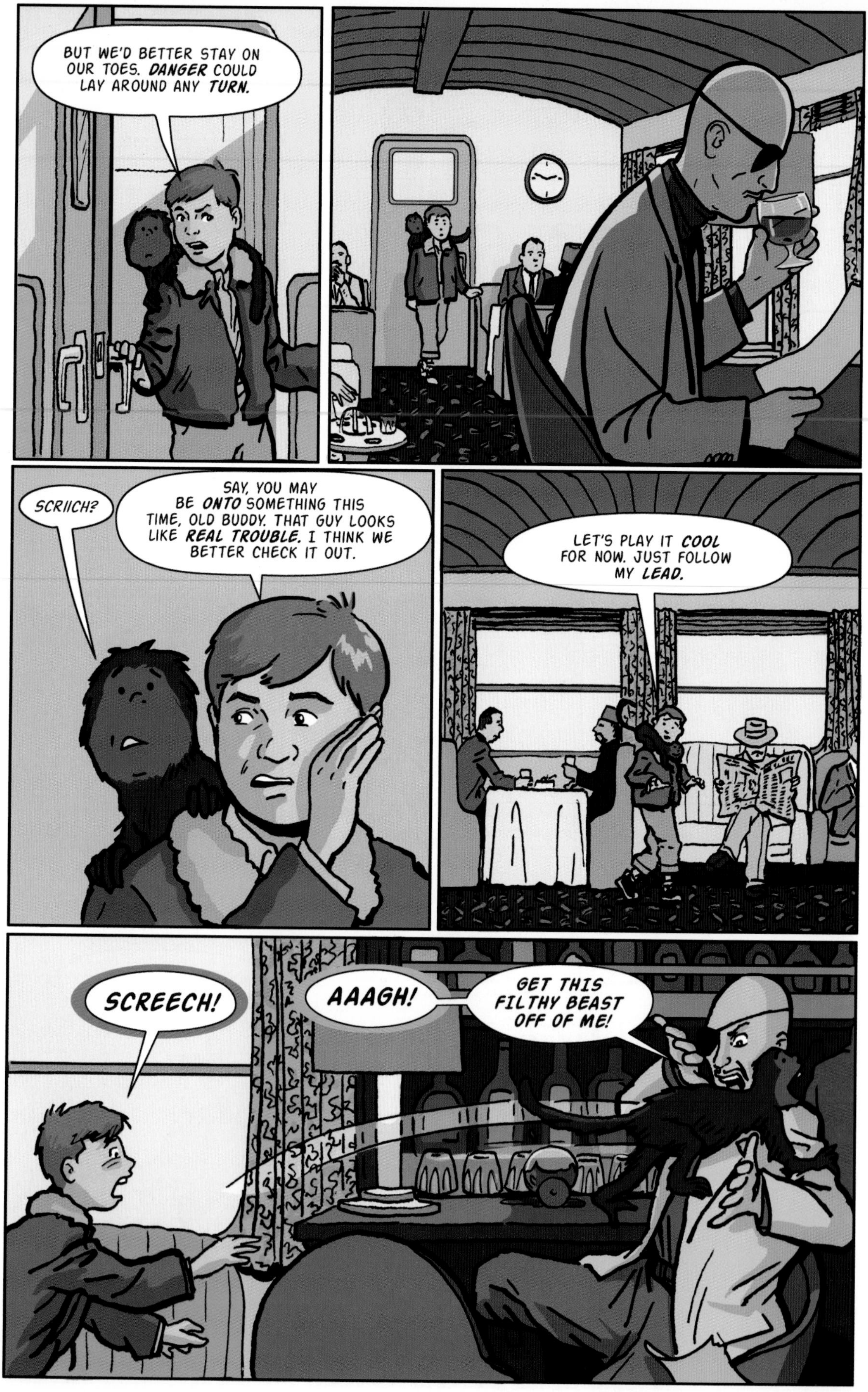
BUT WE'D BETTER STAY ON OUR TOES. DANGER COULD LAY AROUND ANY TURN.
SCRIICH?
SAY, YOU MAY BE ONTO SOMETHING THIS TIME, OLD BUDDY. THAT GUY LOOKS LIKE REAL TROUBLE. I THINK WE BETTER CHECK IT OUT.
LET'S PLAY IT COOL FOR NOW. JUST FOLLOW MY LEAD.
SCREECH!
AAAGH!
GET THIS FILTHY BEAST OFF OF ME!

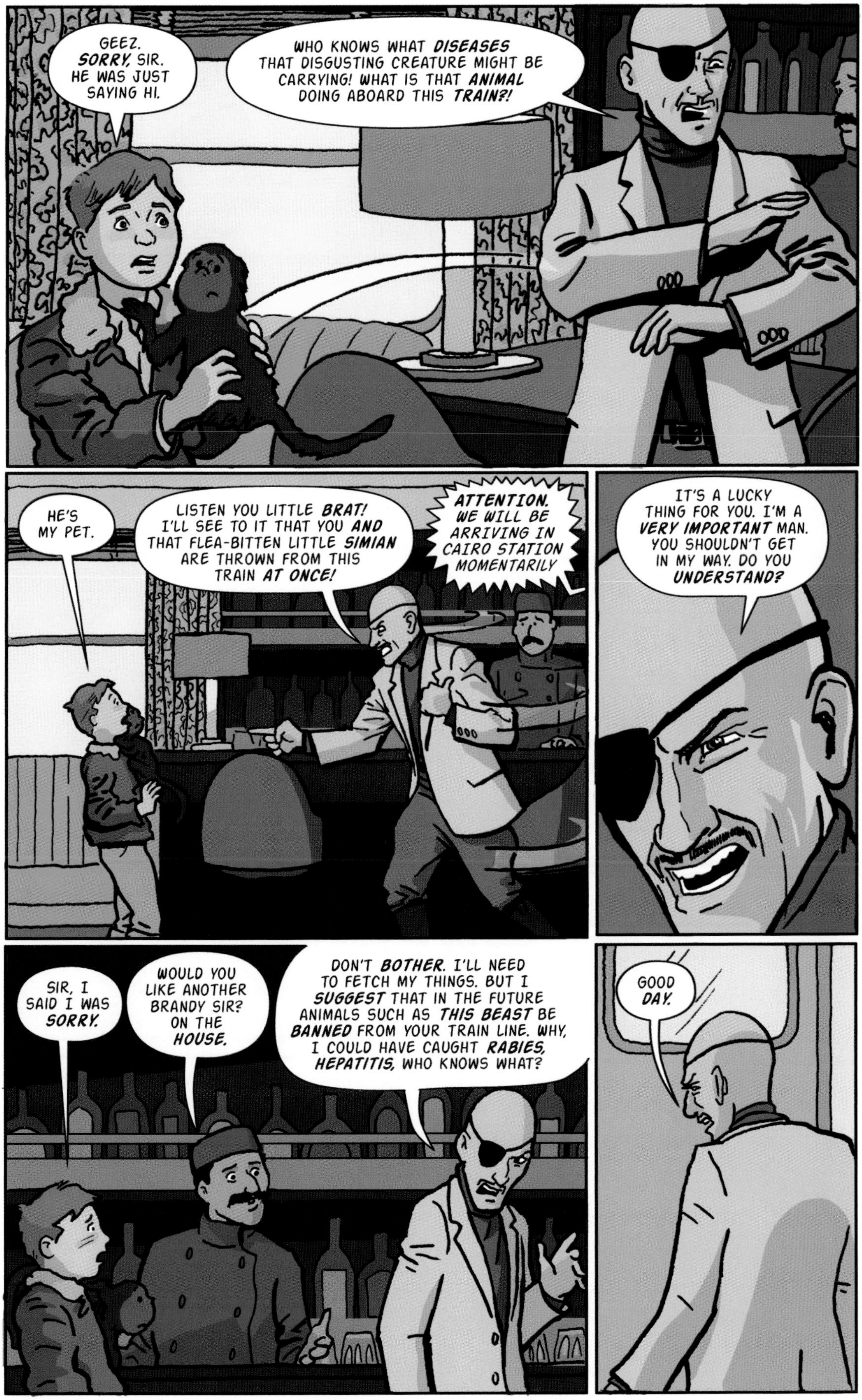
GEEZ. SORRY, SIR. HE WAS JUST SAYING HI.
WHO KNOWS WHAT DISEASES THAT DISGUSTING CREATURE MIGHT BE CARRYING! WHAT IS THAT ANIMAL DOING ABOARD THIS TRAIN?!
HE'S MY PET.
LISTEN YOU LITTLE BRAT! I'LL SEE TO IT THAT YOU AND THAT FLEA-BITTEN LITTLE SIMIAN ARE THROWN FROM THIS TRAIN AT ONCE!
ATTENTION. WE WILL BE ARRIVING IN CAIRO STATION MOMENTARILY
IT'S A LUCKY THING FOR YOU. I'M A VERY IMPORTANT MAN. YOU SHOULDN'T GET IN MY WAY. DO YOU UNDERSTAND?
SIR, I SAID I WAS SORRY.
WOULD YOU LIKE ANOTHER BRANDY SIR? ON THE HOUSE.
DON'T BOTHER. I'LL NEED TO FETCH MY THINGS. BUT I SUGGEST THAT IN THE FUTURE ANIMALS SUCH AS THIS BEAST BE BANNED FROM YOUR TRAIN LINE. WHY, I COULD HAVE CAUGHT RABIES, HEPATITIS, WHO KNOWS WHAT?
GOOD DAY.

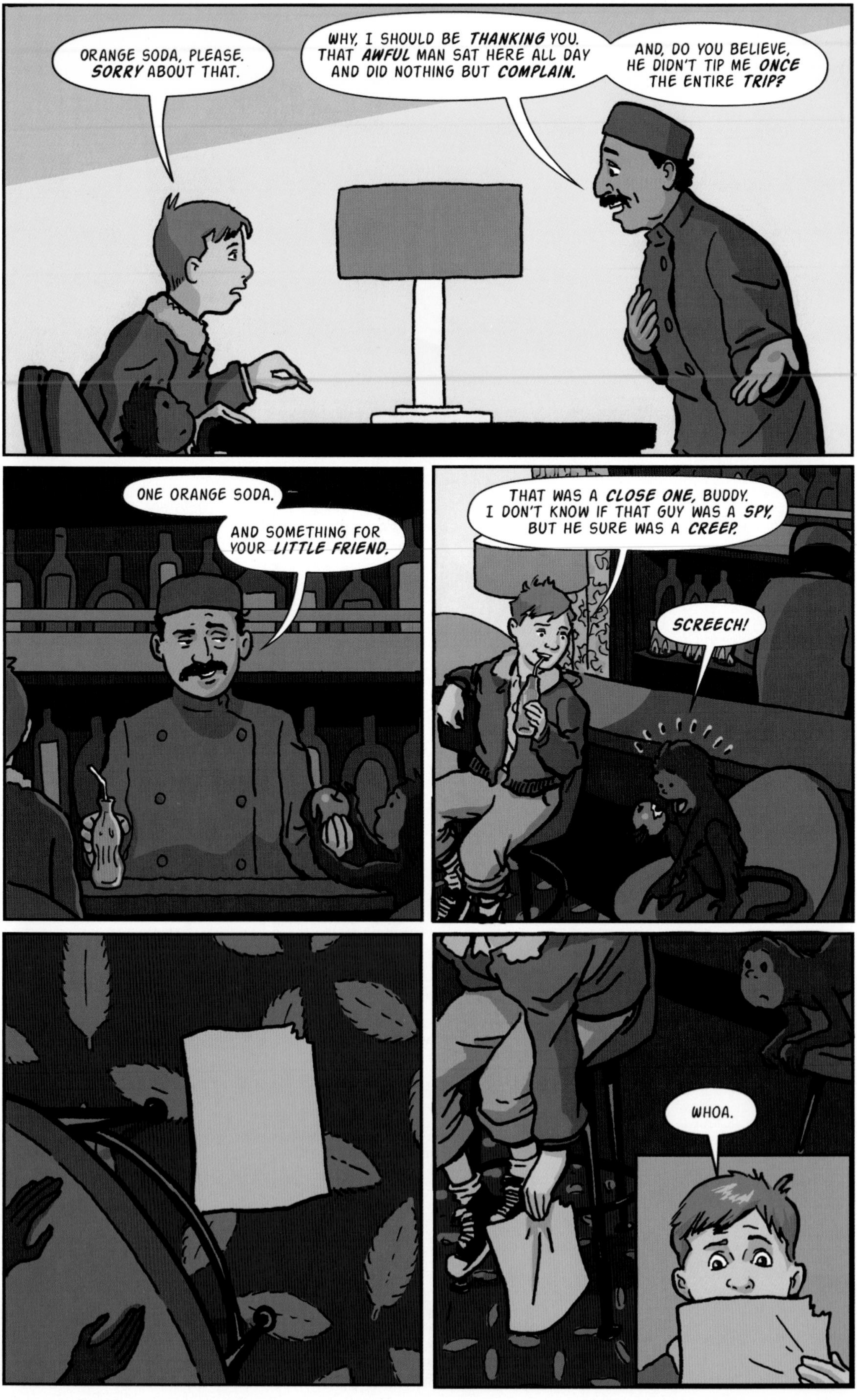
ORANGE SODA, PLEASE. SORRY ABOUT THAT.
WHY, I SHOULD BE THANKING YOU. THAT AWFUL MAN SAT HERE ALL DAY AND DID NOTHING BUT COMPLAIN.
AND, DO YOU BELIEVE, HE DIDN'T TIP ME ONCE THE ENTIRE TRIP?
ONE ORANGE SODA.
AND SOMETHING FOR YOUR LITTLE FRIEND.
THAT WAS A CLOSE ONE, BUDDY. I DON'T KNOW IF THAT GUY WAS A SPY, BUT HE SURE WAS A CREEP.
SCREECH!
WHOA.

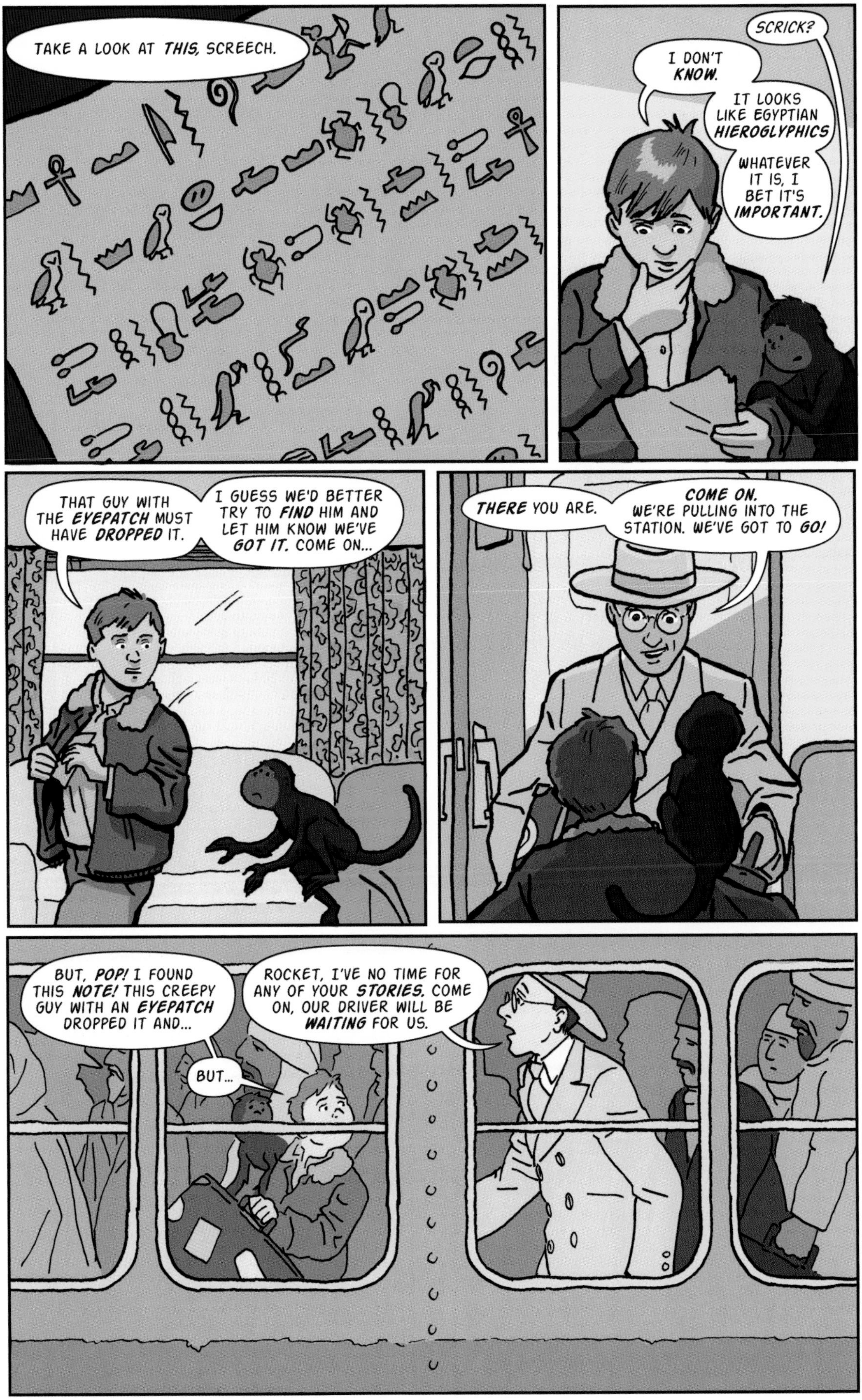
TAKE A LOOK AT THIS, SCREECH.
I DON'T KNOW.
SCRICK?
IT LOOKS LIKE EGYPTIAN HIEROGLYPHICS
WHATEVER IT IS, I BET IT'S IMPORTANT.
THAT GUY WITH THE EYEPATCH MUST HAVE DROPPED IT.
I GUESS WE'D BETTER TRY TO FIND HIM AND LET HIM KNOW WE'VE GOT IT. COME ON...
THERE YOU ARE.
COME ON. WE'RE PULLING INTO THE STATION. WE'VE GOT TO GO!
BUT, POP! I FOUND THIS NOTE! THIS CREEPY GUY WITH AN EYEPATCH DROPPED IT AND...
ROCKET, I'VE NO TIME FOR ANY OF YOUR STORIES. COME ON, OUR DRIVER WILL BE WAITING FOR US.
BUT...

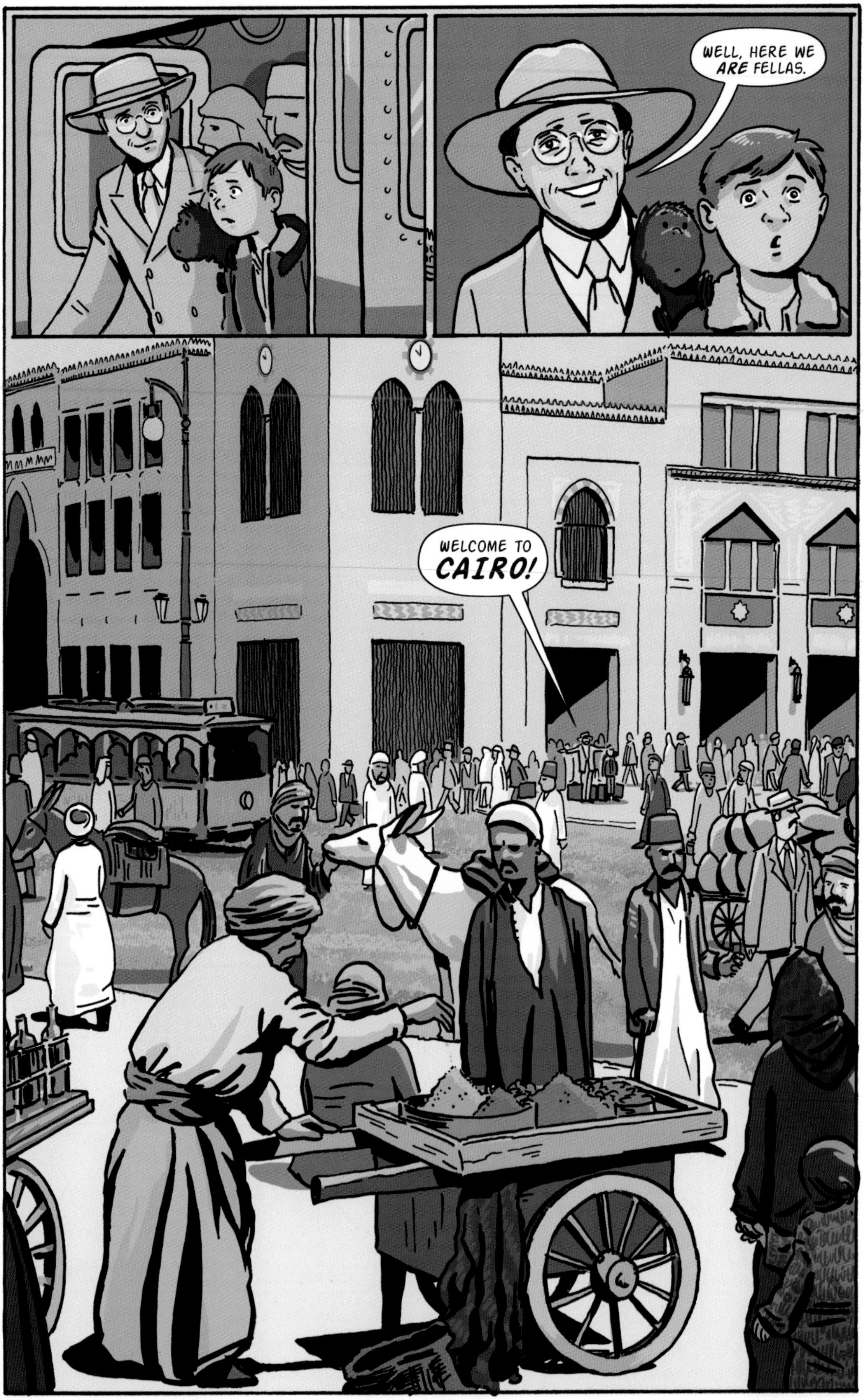
WELL, HERE WE *ARE* FELLAS.
WELCOME TO **CAIRO!**

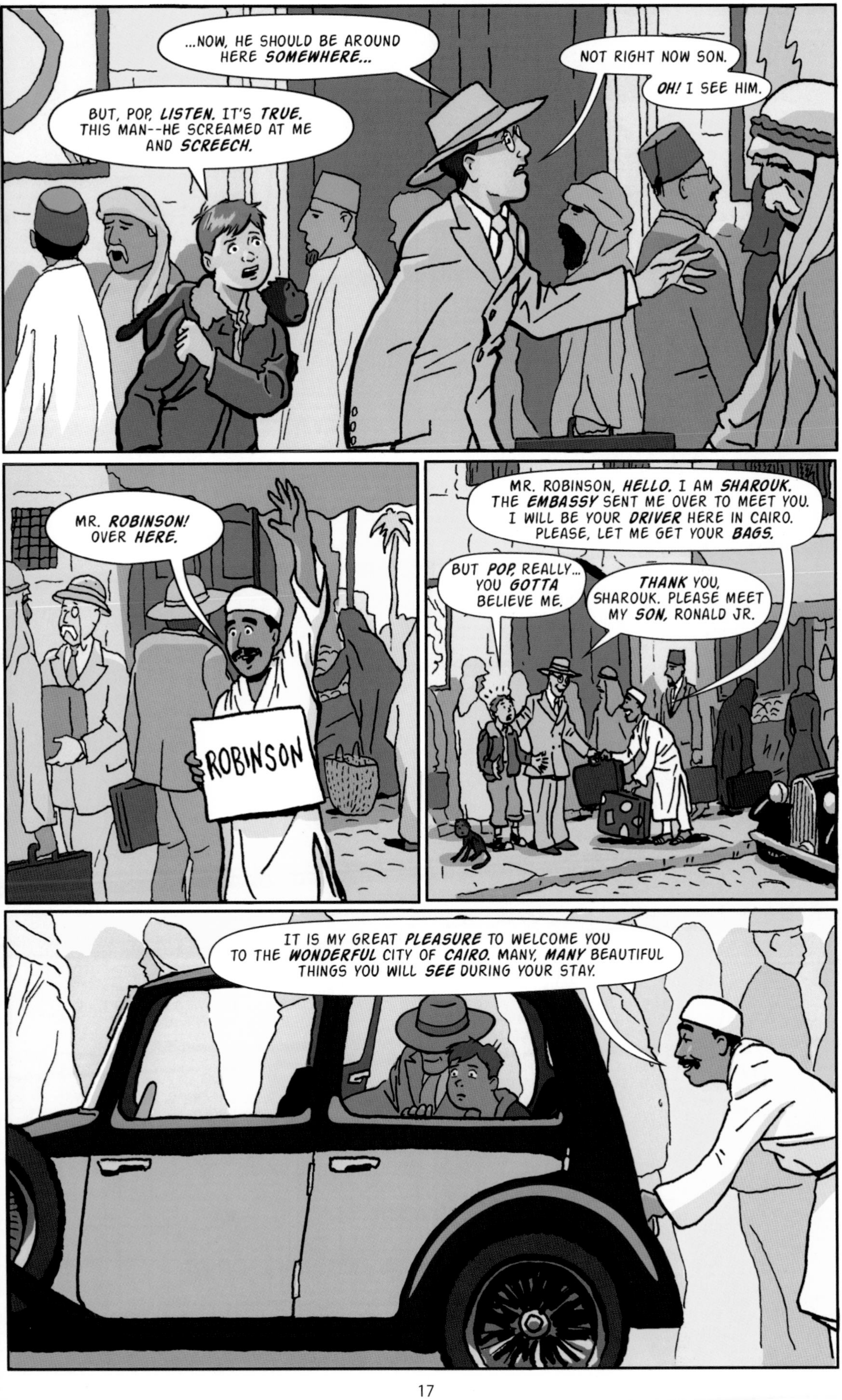
...NOW, HE SHOULD BE AROUND HERE SOMEWHERE...
BUT, POP, LISTEN. IT'S TRUE. THIS MAN--HE SCREAMED AT ME AND SCREECH.
NOT RIGHT NOW SON.
OH! I SEE HIM.
MR. ROBINSON! OVER HERE.
ROBINSON
MR. ROBINSON, HELLO. I AM SHAROUK. THE EMBASSY SENT ME OVER TO MEET YOU. I WILL BE YOUR DRIVER HERE IN CAIRO. PLEASE, LET ME GET YOUR BAGS.
THANK YOU, SHAROUK. PLEASE MEET MY SON, RONALD JR.
BUT POP, REALLY... YOU GOTTA BELIEVE ME.
IT IS MY GREAT PLEASURE TO WELCOME YOU TO THE WONDERFUL CITY OF CAIRO. MANY, MANY BEAUTIFUL THINGS YOU WILL SEE DURING YOUR STAY.

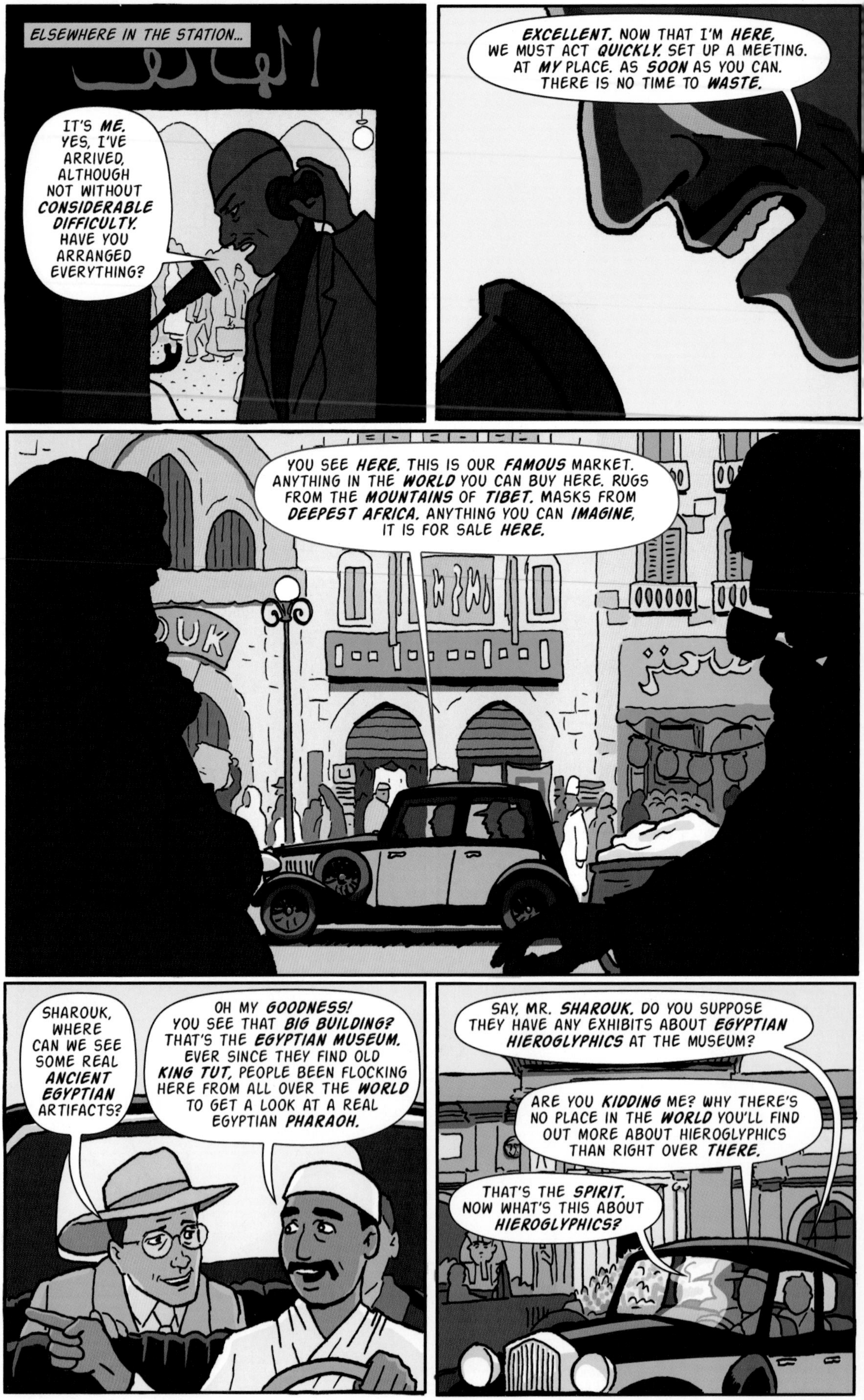

ELSEWHERE IN THE STATION...
IT'S ME. YES, I'VE ARRIVED, ALTHOUGH NOT WITHOUT CONSIDERABLE DIFFICULTY. HAVE YOU ARRANGED EVERYTHING?
EXCELLENT. NOW THAT I'M HERE, WE MUST ACT QUICKLY. SET UP A MEETING. AT MY PLACE. AS SOON AS YOU CAN. THERE IS NO TIME TO WASTE.
YOU SEE HERE. THIS IS OUR FAMOUS MARKET. ANYTHING IN THE WORLD YOU CAN BUY HERE. RUGS FROM THE MOUNTAINS OF TIBET. MASKS FROM DEEPEST AFRICA. ANYTHING YOU CAN IMAGINE, IT IS FOR SALE HERE.
SHAROUK, WHERE CAN WE SEE SOME REAL ANCIENT EGYPTIAN ARTIFACTS?
OH MY GOODNESS! YOU SEE THAT BIG BUILDING? THAT'S THE EGYPTIAN MUSEUM. EVER SINCE THEY FIND OLD KING TUT, PEOPLE BEEN FLOCKING HERE FROM ALL OVER THE WORLD TO GET A LOOK AT A REAL EGYPTIAN PHARAOH.
SAY, MR. SHAROUK. DO YOU SUPPOSE THEY HAVE ANY EXHIBITS ABOUT EGYPTIAN HIEROGLYPHICS AT THE MUSEUM?
ARE YOU KIDDING ME? WHY THERE'S NO PLACE IN THE WORLD YOU'LL FIND OUT MORE ABOUT HIEROGLYPHICS THAN RIGHT OVER THERE.
THAT'S THE SPIRIT. NOW WHAT'S THIS ABOUT HIEROGLYPHICS?

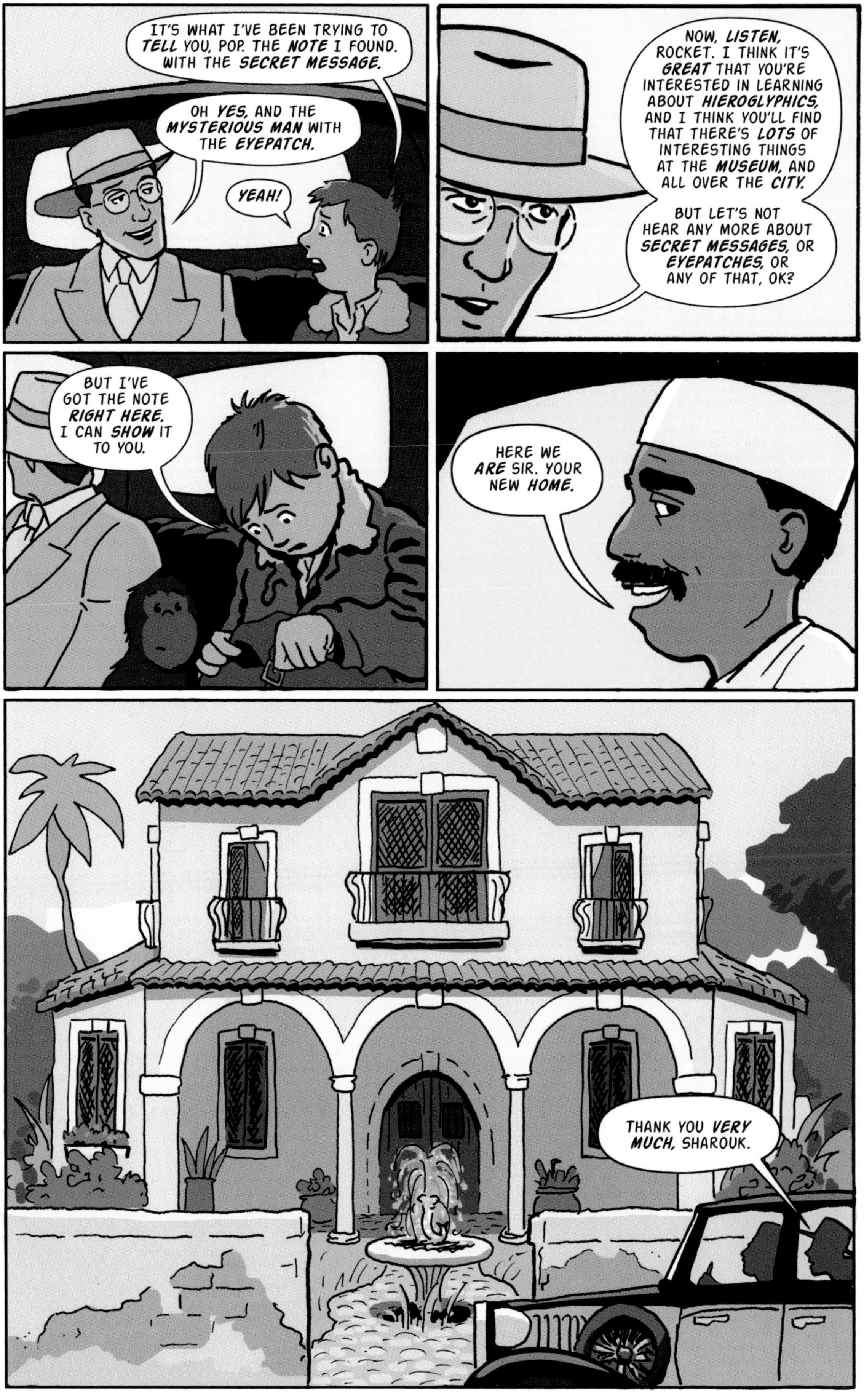
IT'S WHAT I'VE BEEN TRYING TO TELL YOU, POP. THE NOTE I FOUND. WITH THE SECRET MESSAGE.
OH YES, AND THE MYSTERIOUS MAN WITH THE EYEPATCH.
YEAH!
NOW, LISTEN, ROCKET. I THINK IT'S GREAT THAT YOU'RE INTERESTED IN LEARNING ABOUT HIEROGLYPHICS, AND I THINK YOU'LL FIND THAT THERE'S LOTS OF INTERESTING THINGS AT THE MUSEUM, AND ALL OVER THE CITY.
BUT LET'S NOT HEAR ANY MORE ABOUT SECRET MESSAGES, OR EYEPATCHES, OR ANY OF THAT, OK?
BUT I'VE GOT THE NOTE RIGHT HERE. I CAN SHOW IT TO YOU.
HERE WE ARE SIR. YOUR NEW HOME.
THANK YOU VERY MUCH, SHAROUK.

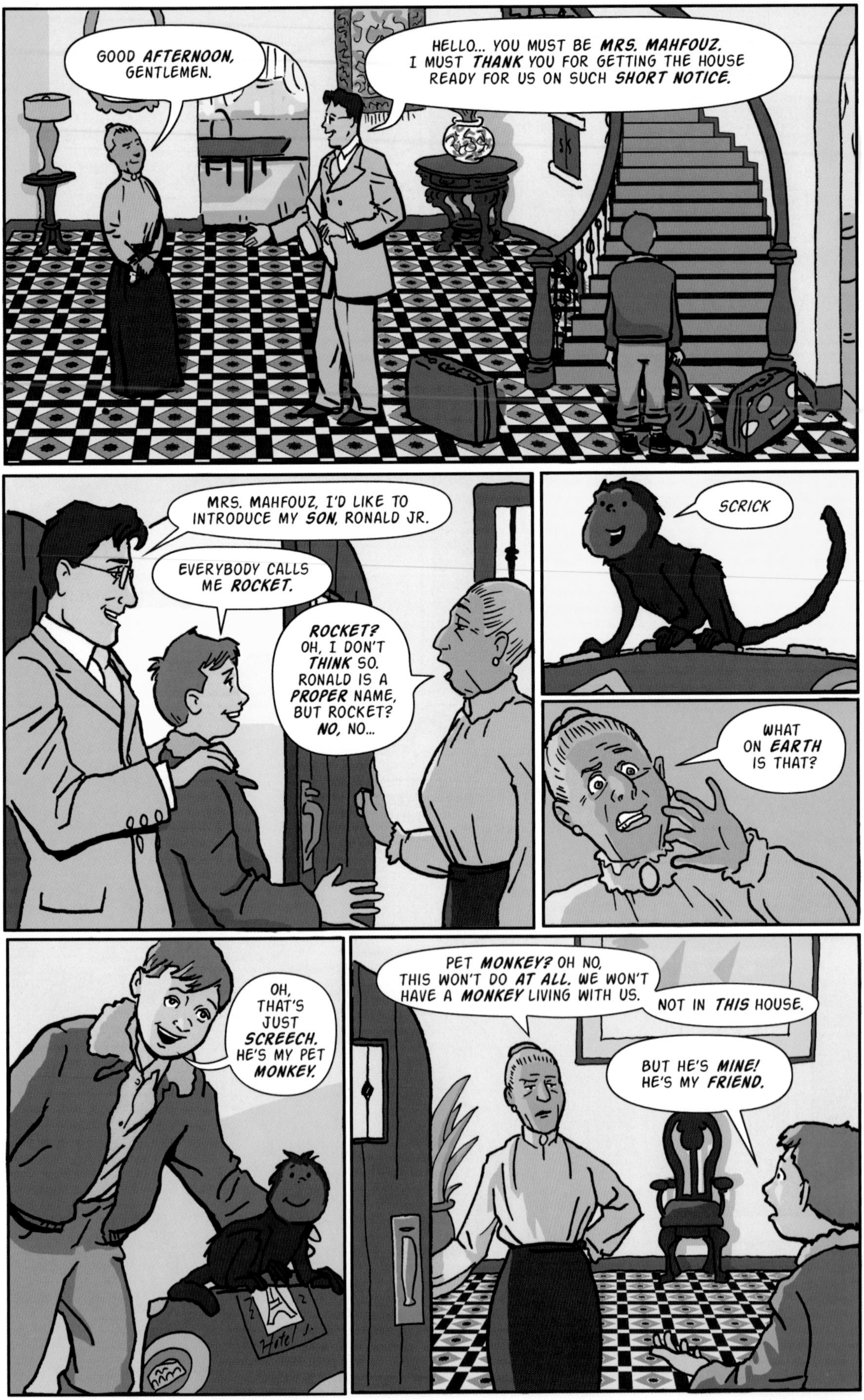
GOOD AFTERNOON, GENTLEMEN.
HELLO... YOU MUST BE MRS. MAHFOUZ. I MUST THANK YOU FOR GETTING THE HOUSE READY FOR US ON SUCH SHORT NOTICE.
MRS. MAHFOUZ, I'D LIKE TO INTRODUCE MY SON, RONALD JR.
EVERYBODY CALLS ME ROCKET.
ROCKET? OH, I DON'T THINK SO. RONALD IS A PROPER NAME, BUT ROCKET? NO, NO...
SCRICK
WHAT ON EARTH IS THAT?
OH, THAT'S JUST SCREECH. HE'S MY PET MONKEY.
PET MONKEY? OH NO, THIS WON'T DO AT ALL. WE WON'T HAVE A MONKEY LIVING WITH US.
NOT IN THIS HOUSE.
BUT HE'S MINE! HE'S MY FRIEND.

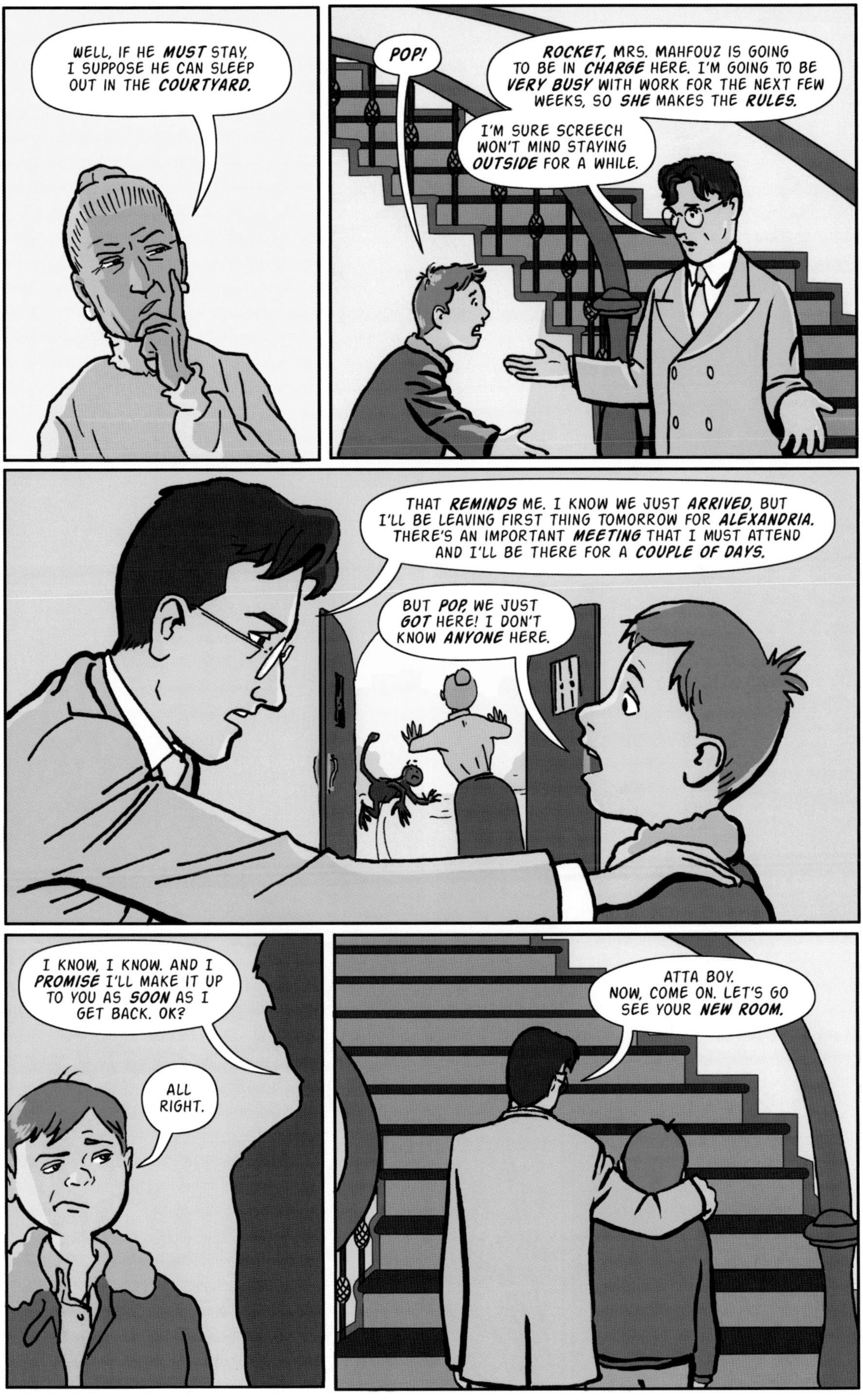
WELL, IF HE MUST STAY, I SUPPOSE HE CAN SLEEP OUT IN THE COURTYARD.
POP!
ROCKET, MRS. MAHFOUZ IS GOING TO BE IN CHARGE HERE. I'M GOING TO BE VERY BUSY WITH WORK FOR THE NEXT FEW WEEKS, SO SHE MAKES THE RULES.
I'M SURE SCREECH WON'T MIND STAYING OUTSIDE FOR A WHILE.
THAT REMINDS ME. I KNOW WE JUST ARRIVED, BUT I'LL BE LEAVING FIRST THING TOMORROW FOR ALEXANDRIA. THERE'S AN IMPORTANT MEETING THAT I MUST ATTEND AND I'LL BE THERE FOR A COUPLE OF DAYS.
BUT POP, WE JUST GOT HERE! I DON'T KNOW ANYONE HERE.
I KNOW, I KNOW. AND I PROMISE I'LL MAKE IT UP TO YOU AS SOON AS I GET BACK. OK?
ALL RIGHT.
ATTA BOY. NOW, COME ON. LET'S GO SEE YOUR NEW ROOM.

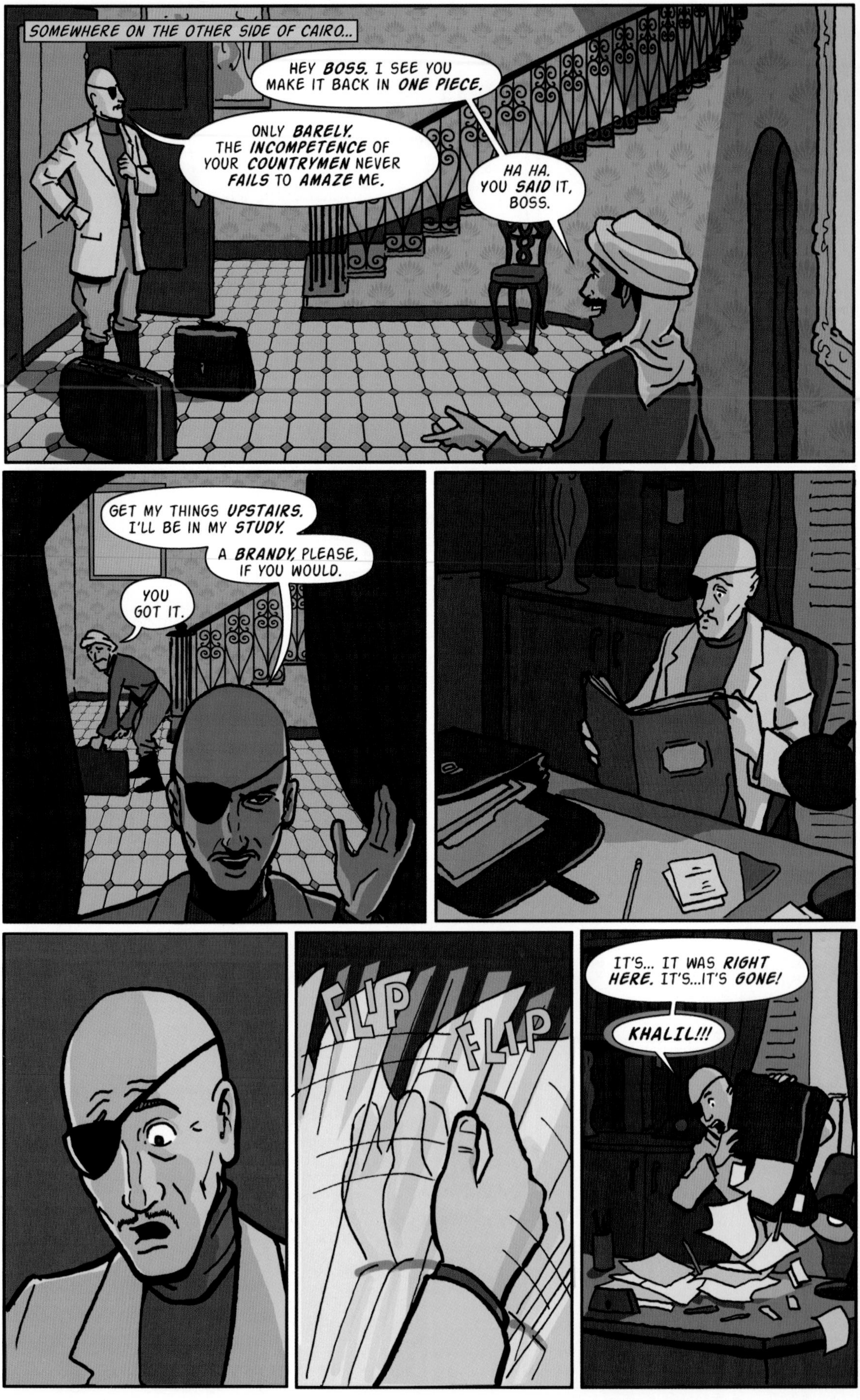
SOMEWHERE ON THE OTHER SIDE OF CAIRO...
HEY BOSS. I SEE YOU MAKE IT BACK IN ONE PIECE.
ONLY BARELY. THE INCOMPETENCE OF YOUR COUNTRYMEN NEVER FAILS TO AMAZE ME.
HA HA. YOU SAID IT, BOSS.
GET MY THINGS UPSTAIRS. I'LL BE IN MY STUDY.
A BRANDY, PLEASE, IF YOU WOULD.
YOU GOT IT.
FLIP
FLIP
IT'S... IT WAS RIGHT HERE. IT'S...IT'S GONE!
KHALIL!!!

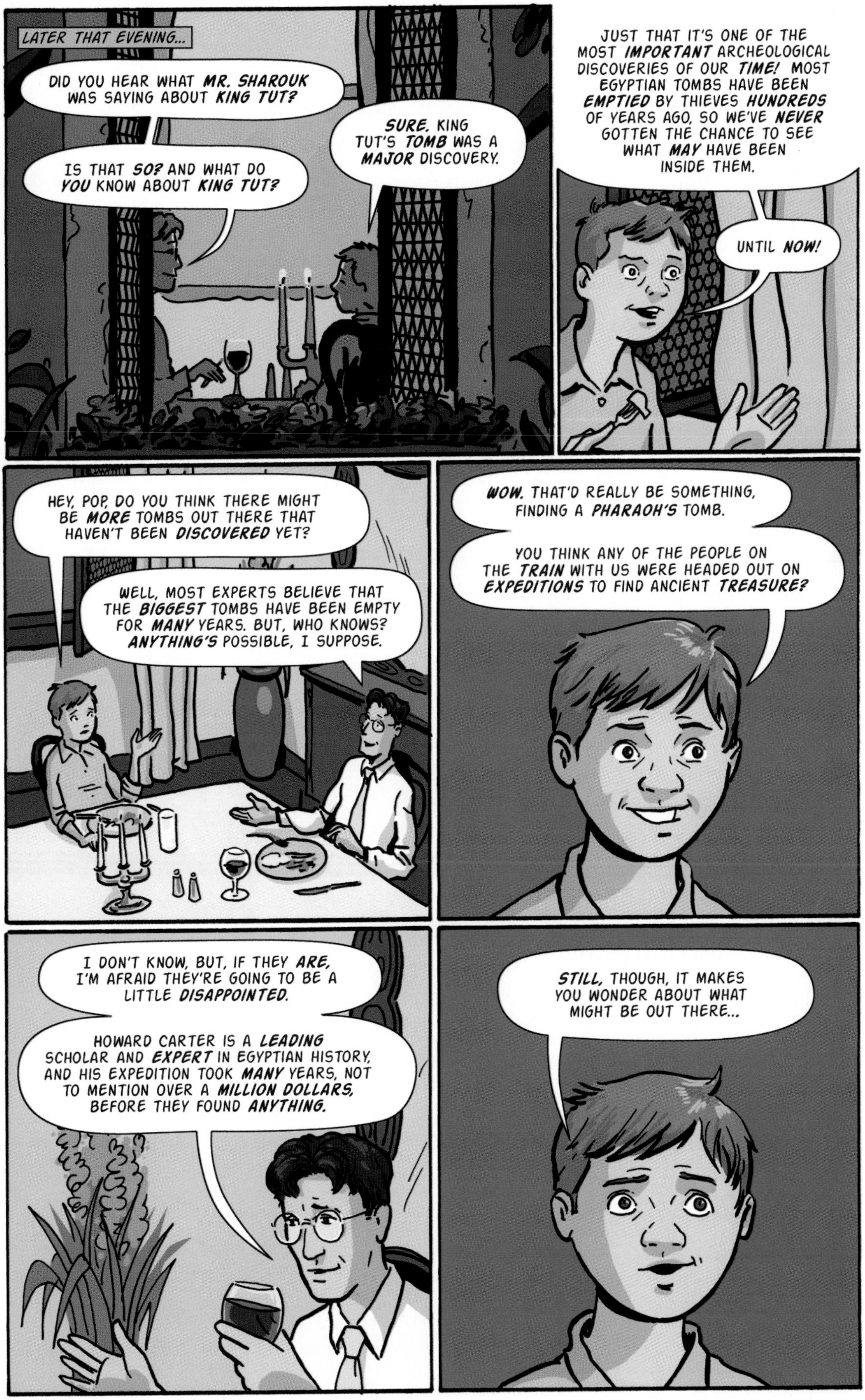
LATER THAT EVENING...
DID YOU HEAR WHAT MR. SHAROUK WAS SAYING ABOUT KING TUT?
IS THAT SO? AND WHAT DO YOU KNOW ABOUT KING TUT?
SURE. KING TUT'S TOMB WAS A MAJOR DISCOVERY.
JUST THAT IT'S ONE OF THE MOST IMPORTANT ARCHEOLOGICAL DISCOVERIES OF OUR TIME! MOST EGYPTIAN TOMBS HAVE BEEN EMPTIED BY THIEVES HUNDREDS OF YEARS AGO, SO WE'VE NEVER GOTTEN THE CHANCE TO SEE WHAT MAY HAVE BEEN INSIDE THEM.
UNTIL NOW!
HEY, POP, DO YOU THINK THERE MIGHT BE MORE TOMBS OUT THERE THAT HAVEN'T BEEN DISCOVERED YET?
WELL, MOST EXPERTS BELIEVE THAT THE BIGGEST TOMBS HAVE BEEN EMPTY FOR MANY YEARS. BUT, WHO KNOWS? ANYTHING'S POSSIBLE, I SUPPOSE.
WOW. THAT'D REALLY BE SOMETHING, FINDING A PHARAOH'S TOMB.
YOU THINK ANY OF THE PEOPLE ON THE TRAIN WITH US WERE HEADED OUT ON EXPEDITIONS TO FIND ANCIENT TREASURE?
I DON'T KNOW, BUT, IF THEY ARE, I'M AFRAID THEY'RE GOING TO BE A LITTLE DISAPPOINTED.
HOWARD CARTER IS A LEADING SCHOLAR AND EXPERT IN EGYPTIAN HISTORY, AND HIS EXPEDITION TOOK MANY YEARS, NOT TO MENTION OVER A MILLION DOLLARS, BEFORE THEY FOUND ANYTHING.
STILL, THOUGH, IT MAKES YOU WONDER ABOUT WHAT MIGHT BE OUT THERE...

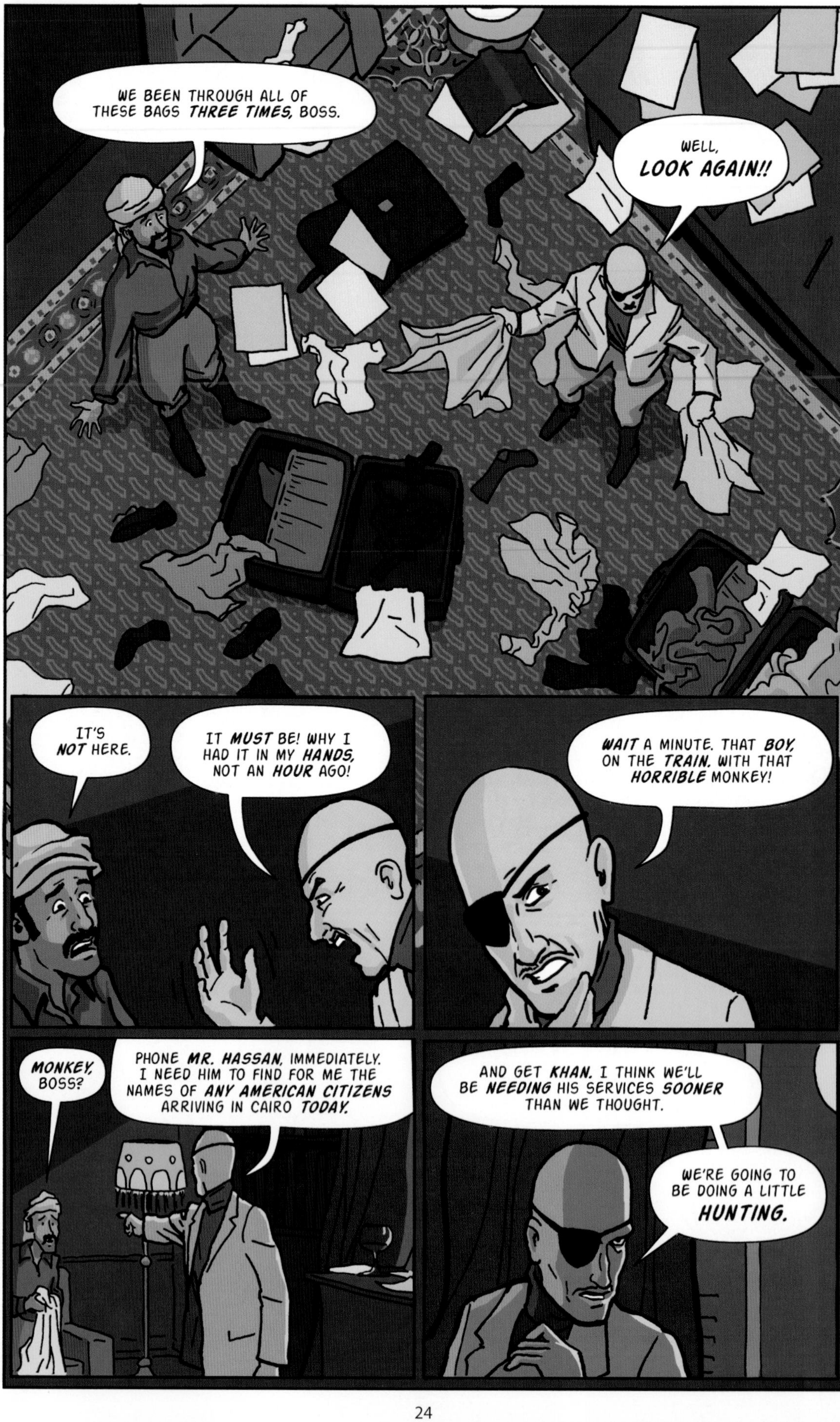
WE BEEN THROUGH ALL OF THESE BAGS THREE TIMES, BOSS.
WELL, LOOK AGAIN!!
IT'S NOT HERE.
IT MUST BE! WHY I HAD IT IN MY HANDS, NOT AN HOUR AGO!
WAIT A MINUTE. THAT BOY, ON THE TRAIN. WITH THAT HORRIBLE MONKEY!
MONKEY, BOSS?
PHONE MR. HASSAN, IMMEDIATELY. I NEED HIM TO FIND FOR ME THE NAMES OF ANY AMERICAN CITIZENS ARRIVING IN CAIRO TODAY.
AND GET KHAN. I THINK WE'LL BE NEEDING HIS SERVICES SOONER THAN WE THOUGHT.
WE'RE GOING TO BE DOING A LITTLE HUNTING.

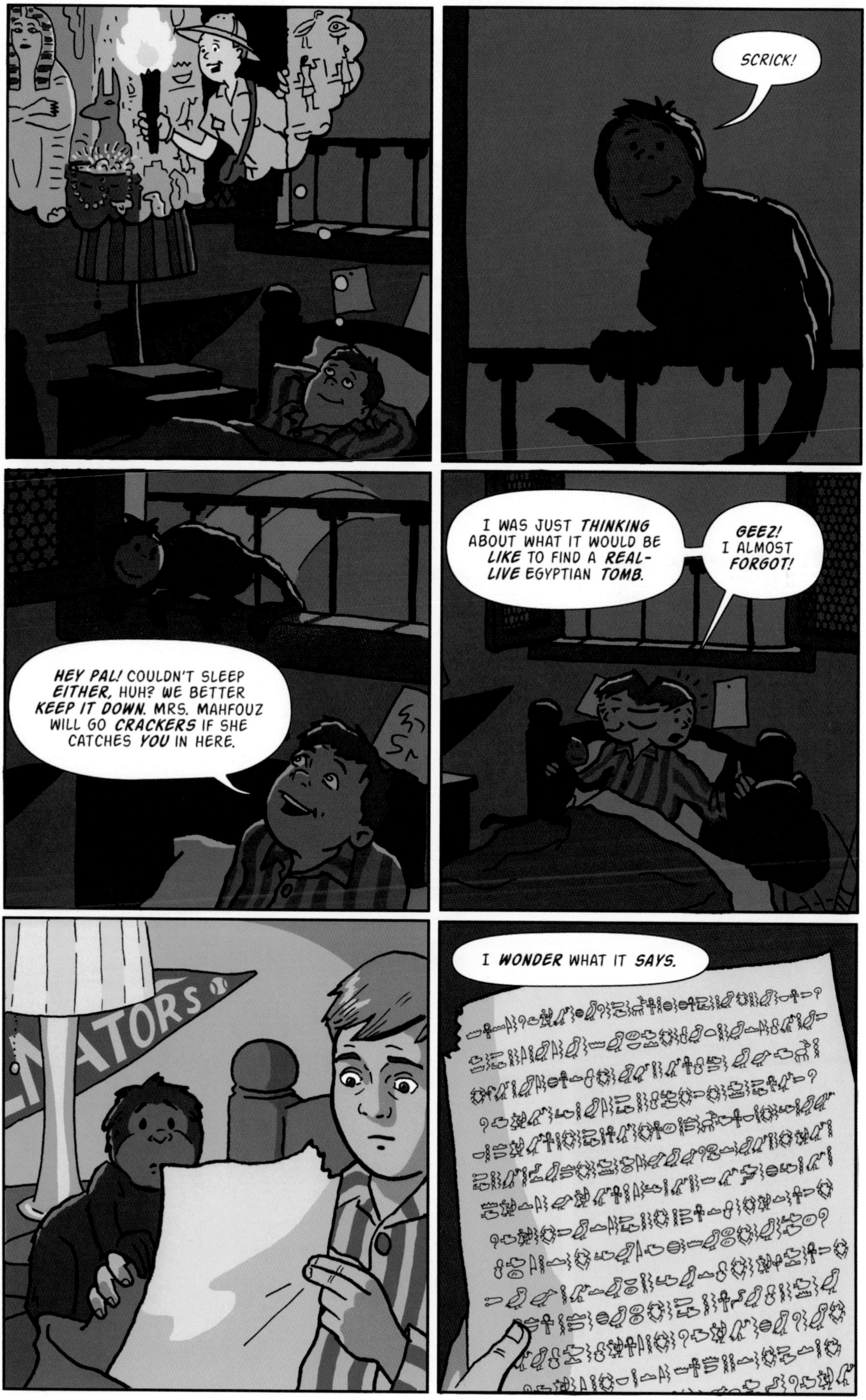
SCRICK!
HEY PAL! COULDN'T SLEEP EITHER, HUH? WE BETTER KEEP IT DOWN. MRS. MAHFOUZ WILL GO CRACKERS IF SHE CATCHES YOU IN HERE.
I WAS JUST THINKING ABOUT WHAT IT WOULD BE LIKE TO FIND A REAL-LIVE EGYPTIAN TOMB.
GEEZ! I ALMOST FORGOT!
ATORS
I WONDER WHAT IT SAYS.

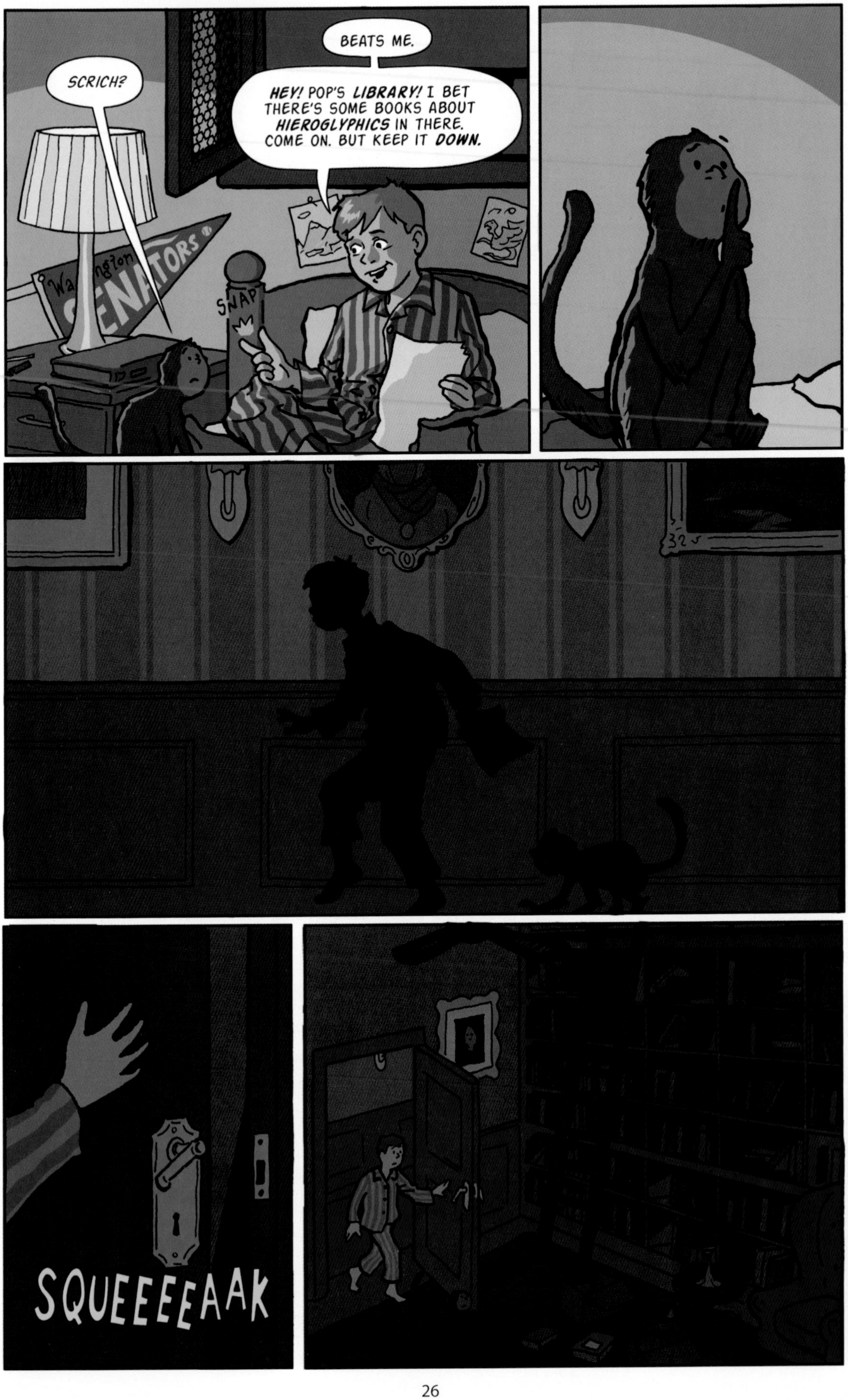

SCRICH?
BEATS ME.
HEY! POP'S LIBRARY! I BET THERE'S SOME BOOKS ABOUT HIEROGLYPHICS IN THERE. COME ON. BUT KEEP IT DOWN.
Washington SENATORS
SNAP
SQUEEEEEAAK

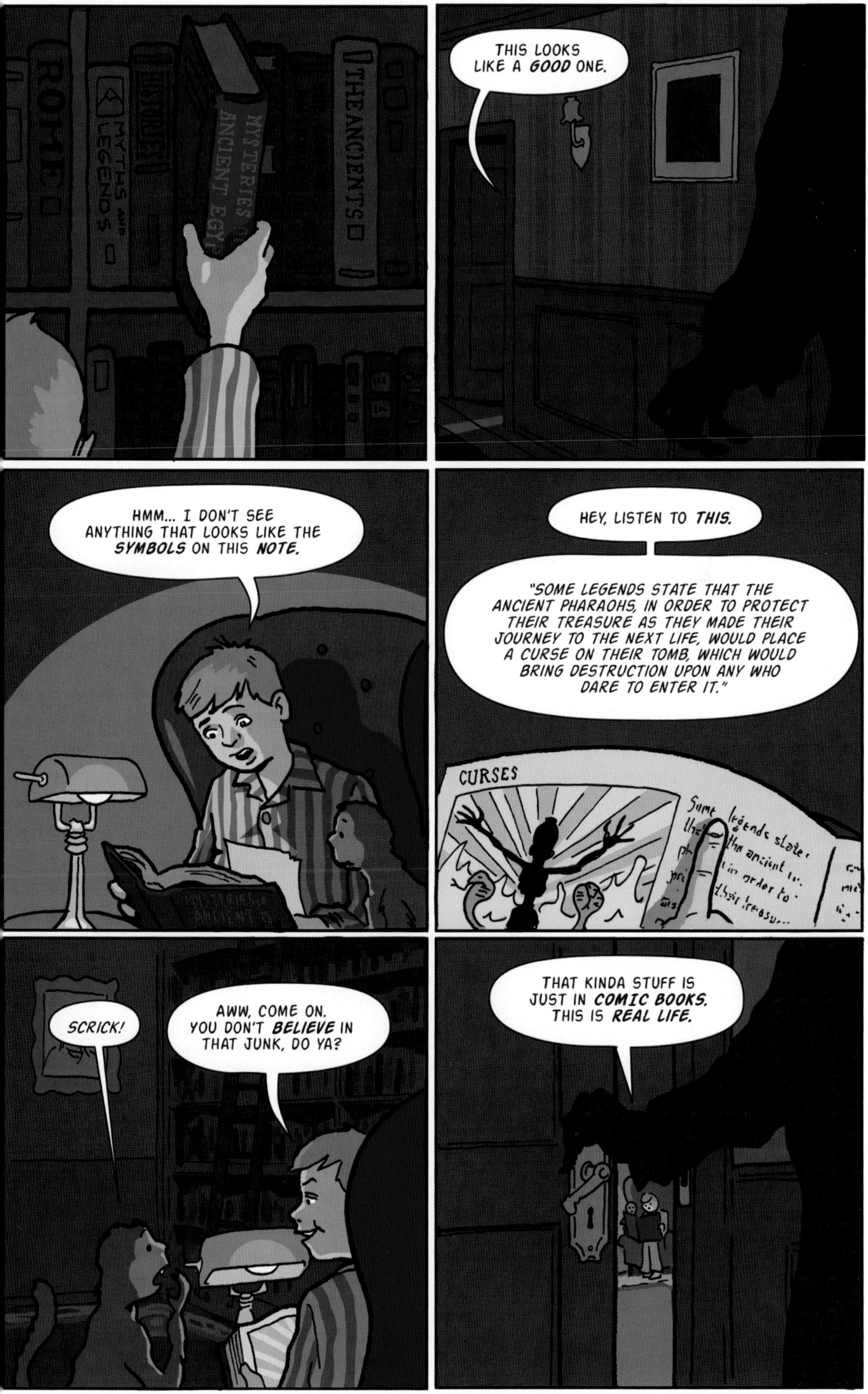
ROME
MYTHS AND LEGENDS
HISTORY
MYSTERIES ANCIENT EGY
THE ANCIENTS
THIS LOOKS LIKE A GOOD ONE.
HMM... I DON'T SEE ANYTHING THAT LOOKS LIKE THE SYMBOLS ON THIS NOTE.
HEY, LISTEN TO THIS.
"SOME LEGENDS STATE THAT THE ANCIENT PHARAOHS, IN ORDER TO PROTECT THEIR TREASURE AS THEY MADE THEIR JOURNEY TO THE NEXT LIFE, WOULD PLACE A CURSE ON THEIR TOMB, WHICH WOULD BRING DESTRUCTION UPON ANY WHO DARE TO ENTER IT."
CURSES
SCRICK!
AWW, COME ON. YOU DON'T BELIEVE IN THAT JUNK, DO YA?
THAT KINDA STUFF IS JUST IN COMIC BOOKS. THIS IS REAL LIFE.

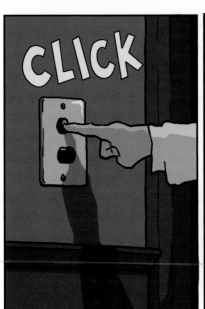

CLICK

AAAAAAAAAHHHH!

MY *GOODNESS!* RONALD! WHAT ON *EARTH* ARE YOU DOING UP AT THIS *HOUR?* AND THAT *MONKEY* WITH YOU, IN YOUR FATHER'S *LIBRARY!*

SORRY MRS. MAHFOUZ. I COULDN'T *SLEEP.*

COME ON NOW. OFF TO *BED* WITH YOU.

AND *OUT* YOU GO!

I'LL FIGURE OUT WHAT THIS MEANS. *SOMEHOW.*

JOURNAL

CHAPTER TWO

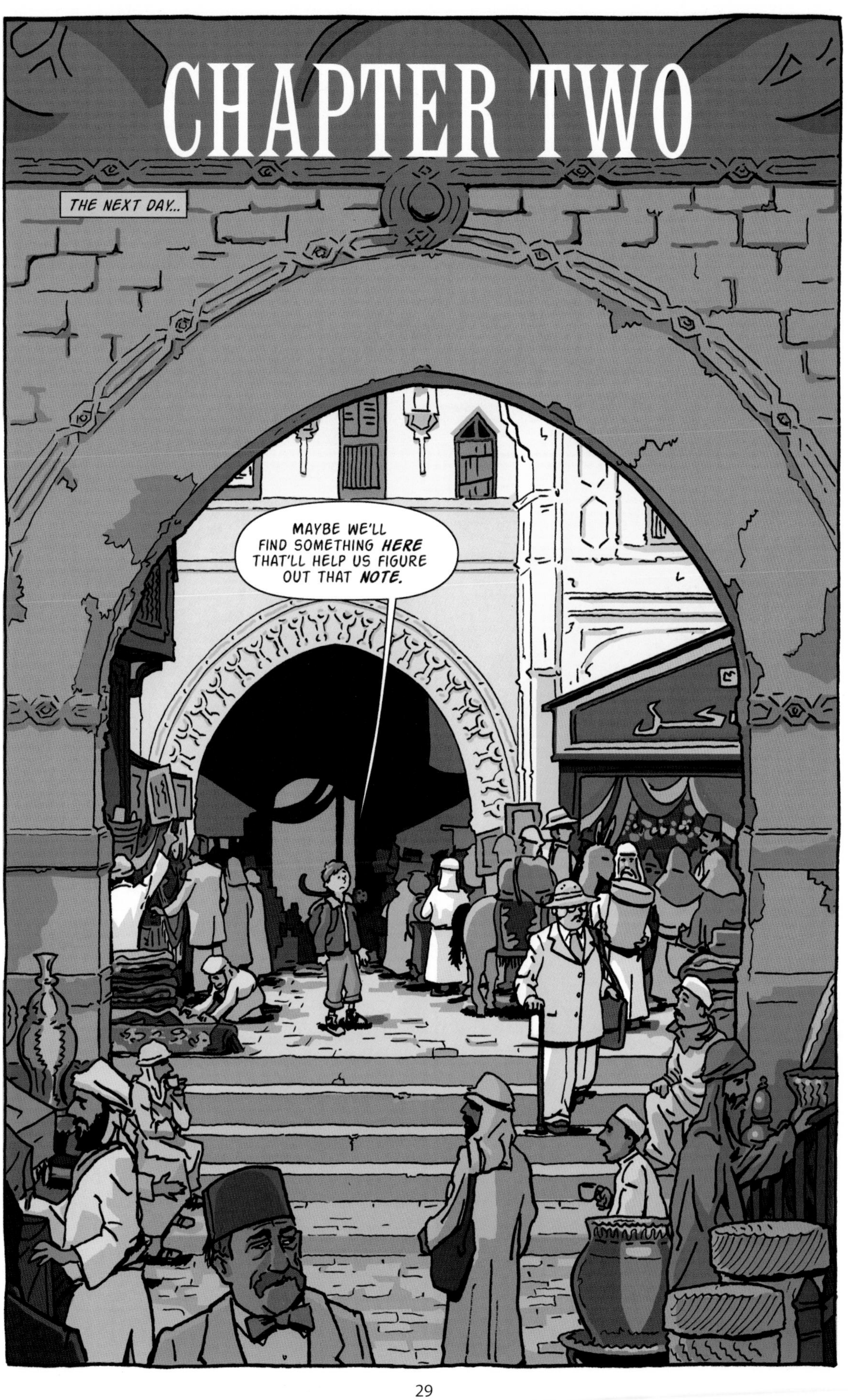
THE NEXT DAY...
MAYBE WE'LL FIND SOMETHING HERE THAT'LL HELP US FIGURE OUT THAT NOTE.

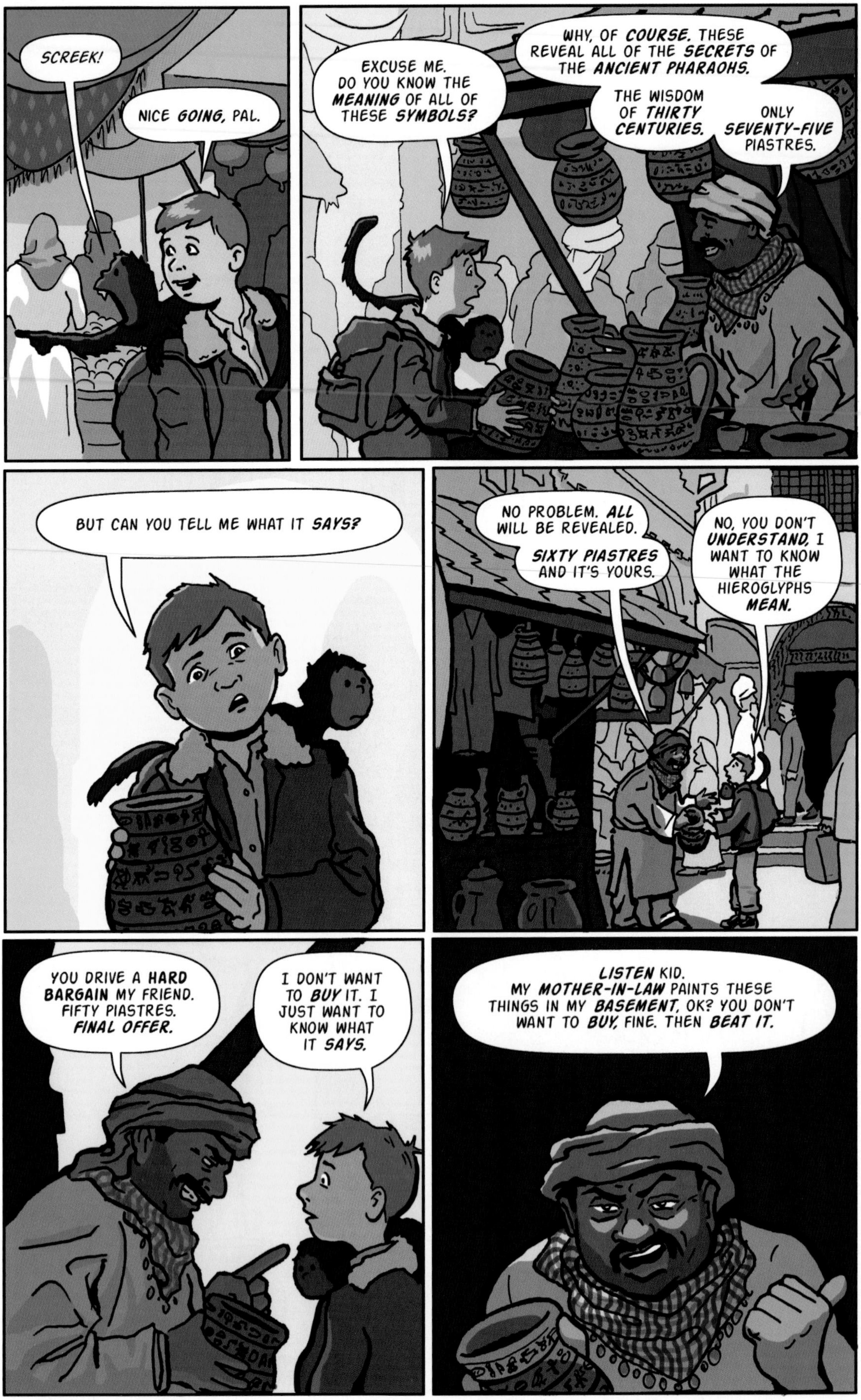

SCREEK!
NICE GOING, PAL.
EXCUSE ME. DO YOU KNOW THE MEANING OF ALL OF THESE SYMBOLS?
WHY, OF COURSE. THESE REVEAL ALL OF THE SECRETS OF THE ANCIENT PHARAOHS.
THE WISDOM OF THIRTY CENTURIES.
ONLY SEVENTY-FIVE PIASTRES.
BUT CAN YOU TELL ME WHAT IT SAYS?
NO PROBLEM. ALL WILL BE REVEALED.
SIXTY PIASTRES AND IT'S YOURS.
NO, YOU DON'T UNDERSTAND, I WANT TO KNOW WHAT THE HIEROGLYPHS MEAN.
YOU DRIVE A HARD BARGAIN MY FRIEND. FIFTY PIASTRES. FINAL OFFER.
I DON'T WANT TO BUY IT. I JUST WANT TO KNOW WHAT IT SAYS.
LISTEN KID. MY MOTHER-IN-LAW PAINTS THESE THINGS IN MY BASEMENT, OK? YOU DON'T WANT TO BUY, FINE. THEN BEAT IT.

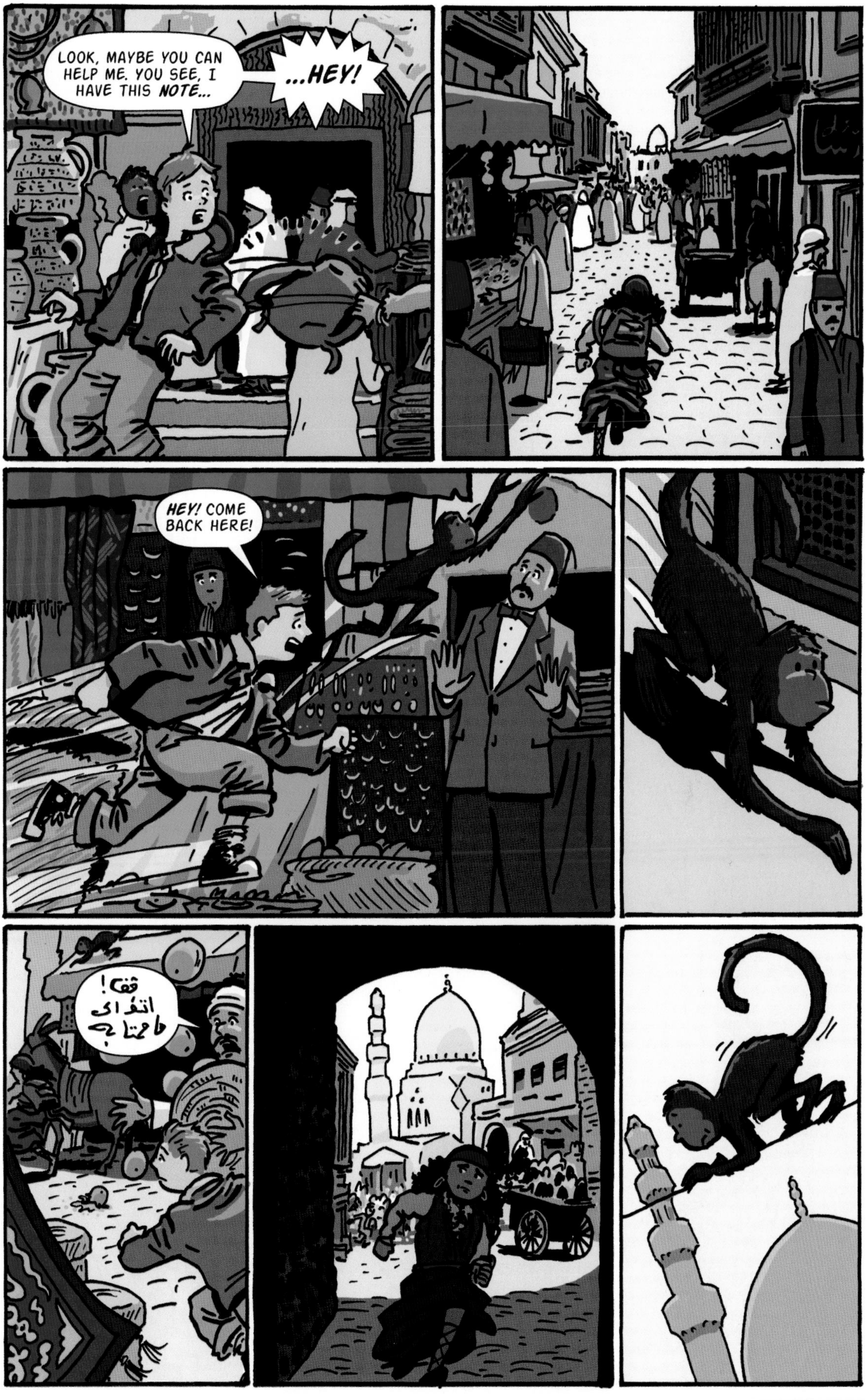
LOOK, MAYBE YOU CAN HELP ME. YOU SEE, I HAVE THIS *NOTE*...
...HEY!
HEY! COME BACK HERE!
قف!

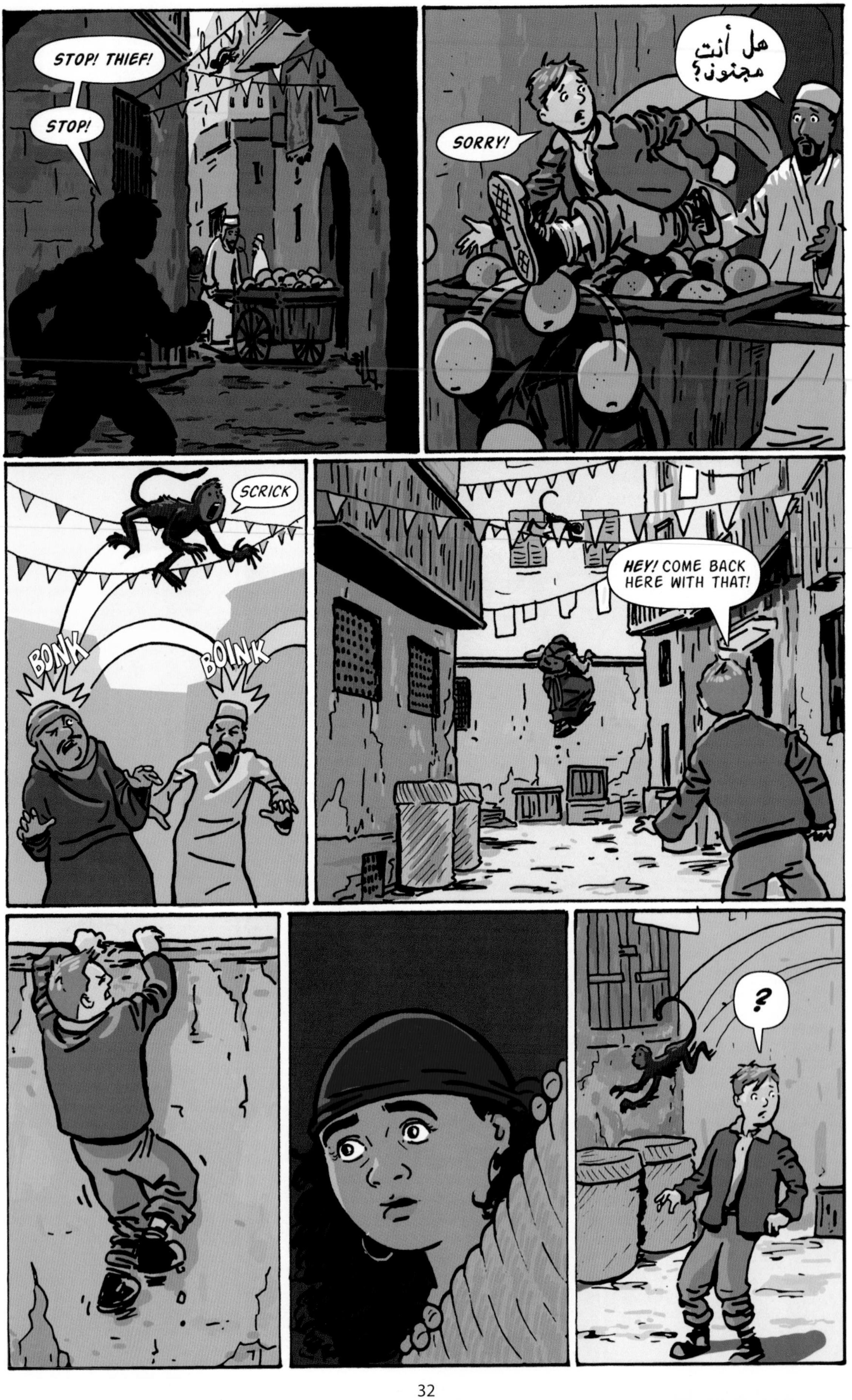
STOP! THIEF!
STOP!
هل أنت مجنون؟
SORRY!
SCRICK
BONK
BOINK
HEY! COME BACK HERE WITH THAT!
?

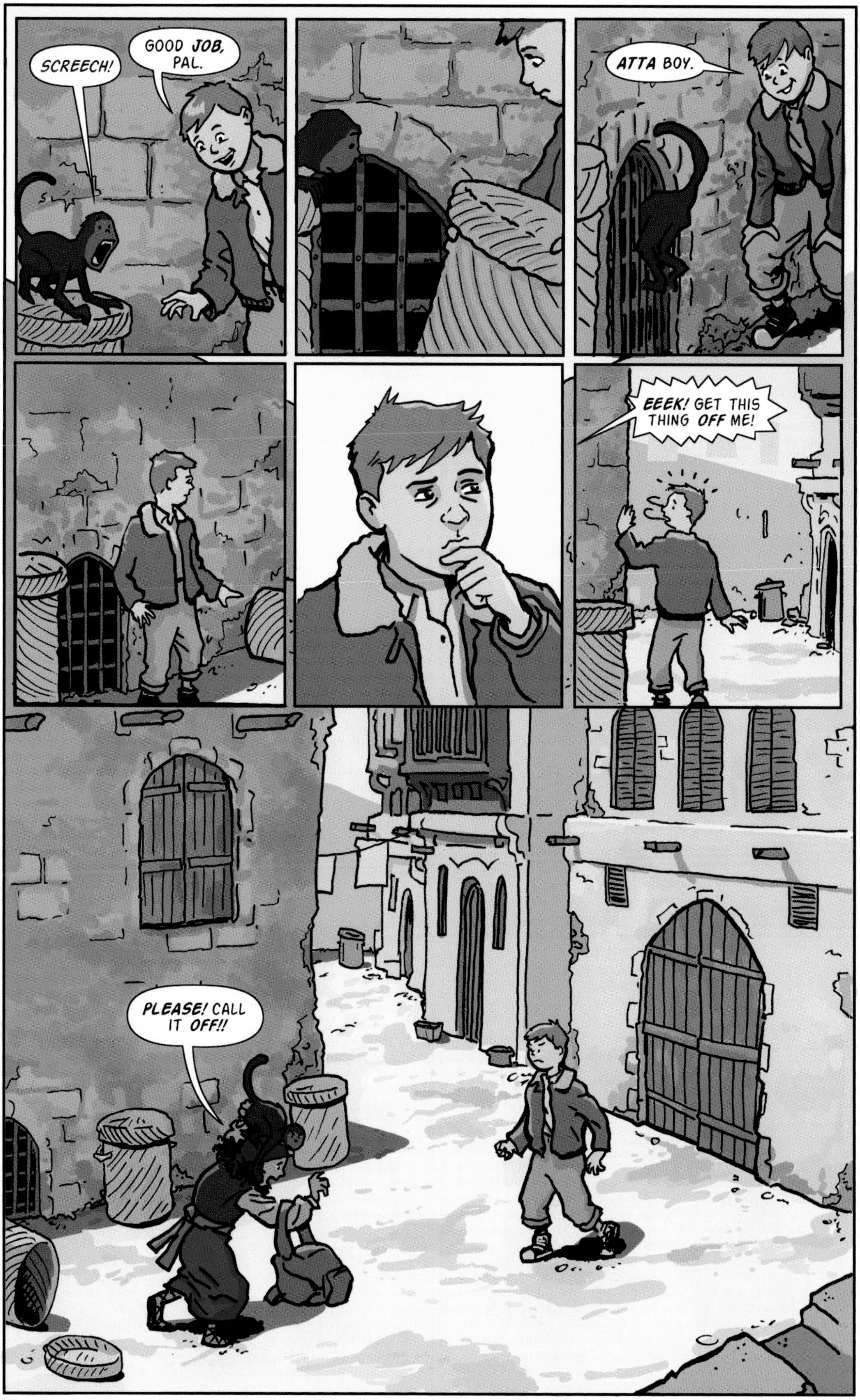
SCREECH!
GOOD JOB, PAL.
ATTA BOY.
EEEK! GET THIS THING OFF ME!
PLEASE! CALL IT OFF!!

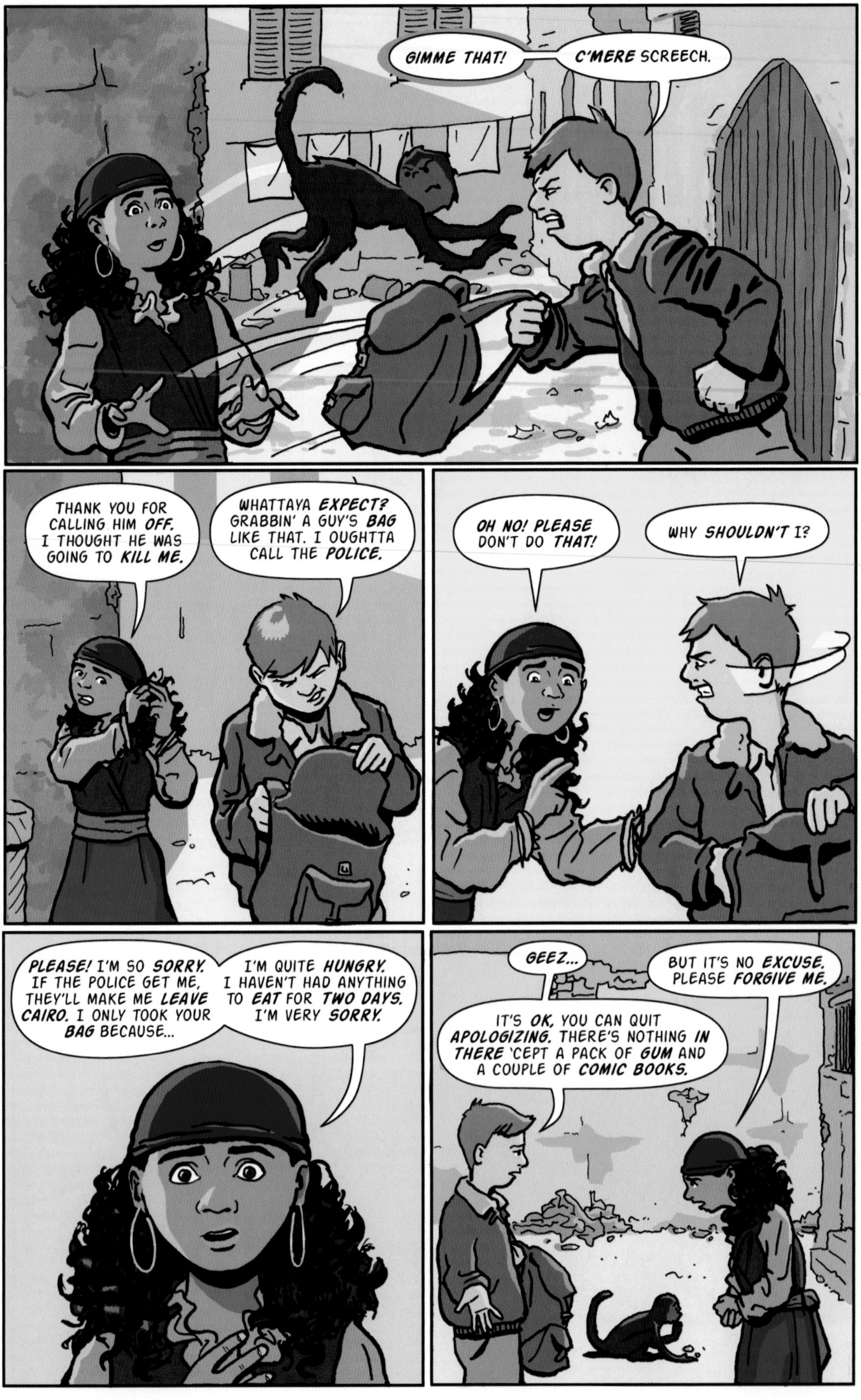
GIMME THAT!
C'MERE SCREECH.
THANK YOU FOR CALLING HIM OFF. I THOUGHT HE WAS GOING TO KILL ME.
WHATTAYA EXPECT? GRABBIN' A GUY'S BAG LIKE THAT. I OUGHTTA CALL THE POLICE.
OH NO! PLEASE DON'T DO THAT!
WHY SHOULDN'T I?
PLEASE! I'M SO SORRY. IF THE POLICE GET ME, THEY'LL MAKE ME LEAVE CAIRO. I ONLY TOOK YOUR BAG BECAUSE...
I'M QUITE HUNGRY. I HAVEN'T HAD ANYTHING TO EAT FOR TWO DAYS. I'M VERY SORRY.
GEEZ...
BUT IT'S NO EXCUSE. PLEASE FORGIVE ME.
IT'S OK, YOU CAN QUIT APOLOGIZING. THERE'S NOTHING IN THERE 'CEPT A PACK OF GUM AND A COUPLE OF COMIC BOOKS.

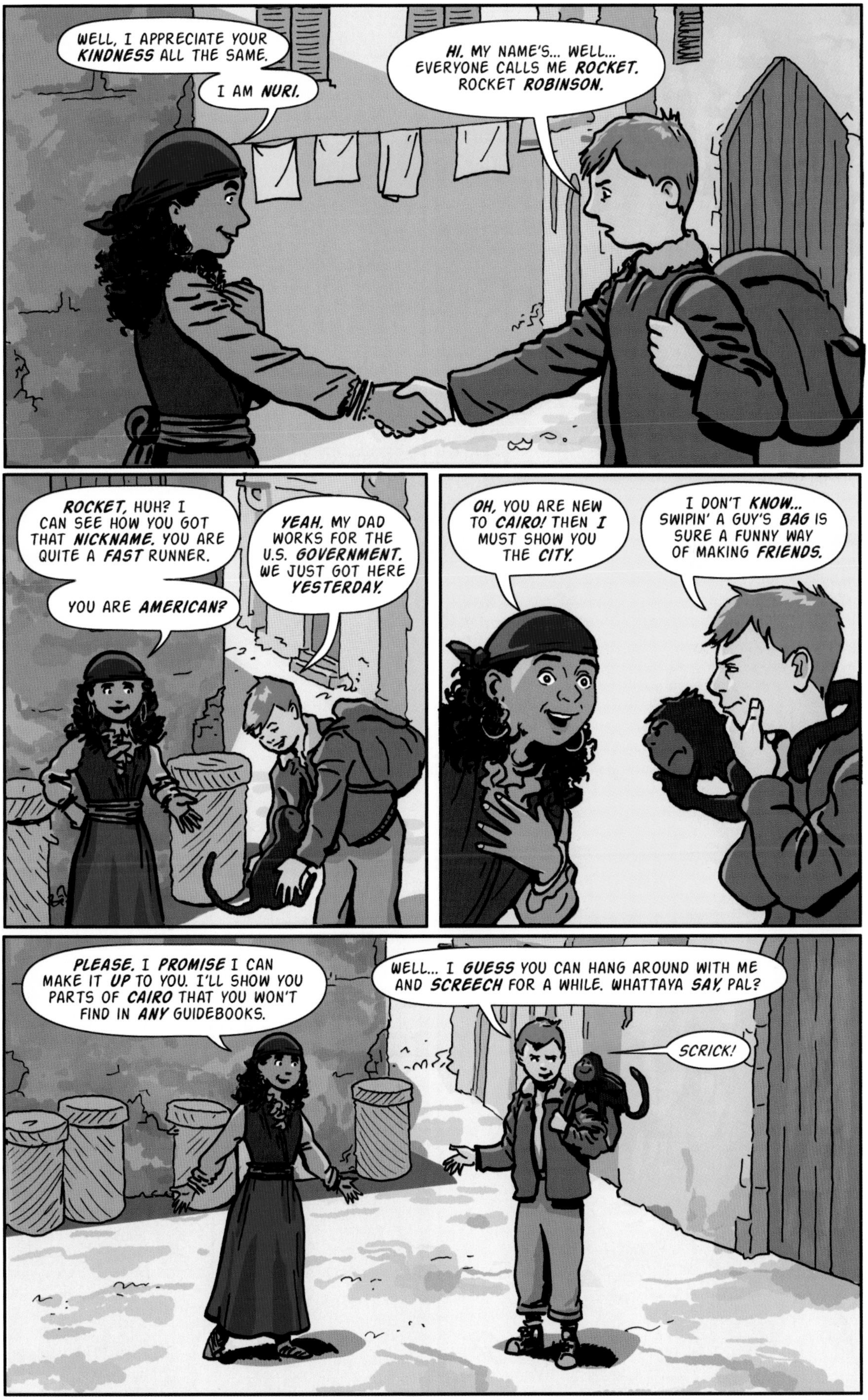
WELL, I APPRECIATE YOUR KINDNESS ALL THE SAME.
I AM NURI.
HI. MY NAME'S... WELL... EVERYONE CALLS ME ROCKET. ROCKET ROBINSON.
ROCKET, HUH? I CAN SEE HOW YOU GOT THAT NICKNAME. YOU ARE QUITE A FAST RUNNER.
YOU ARE AMERICAN?
YEAH. MY DAD WORKS FOR THE U.S. GOVERNMENT. WE JUST GOT HERE YESTERDAY.
OH, YOU ARE NEW TO CAIRO! THEN I MUST SHOW YOU THE CITY.
I DON'T KNOW... SWIPIN' A GUY'S BAG IS SURE A FUNNY WAY OF MAKING FRIENDS.
PLEASE. I PROMISE I CAN MAKE IT UP TO YOU. I'LL SHOW YOU PARTS OF CAIRO THAT YOU WON'T FIND IN ANY GUIDEBOOKS.
WELL... I GUESS YOU CAN HANG AROUND WITH ME AND SCREECH FOR A WHILE. WHATTAYA SAY, PAL?
SCRICK!

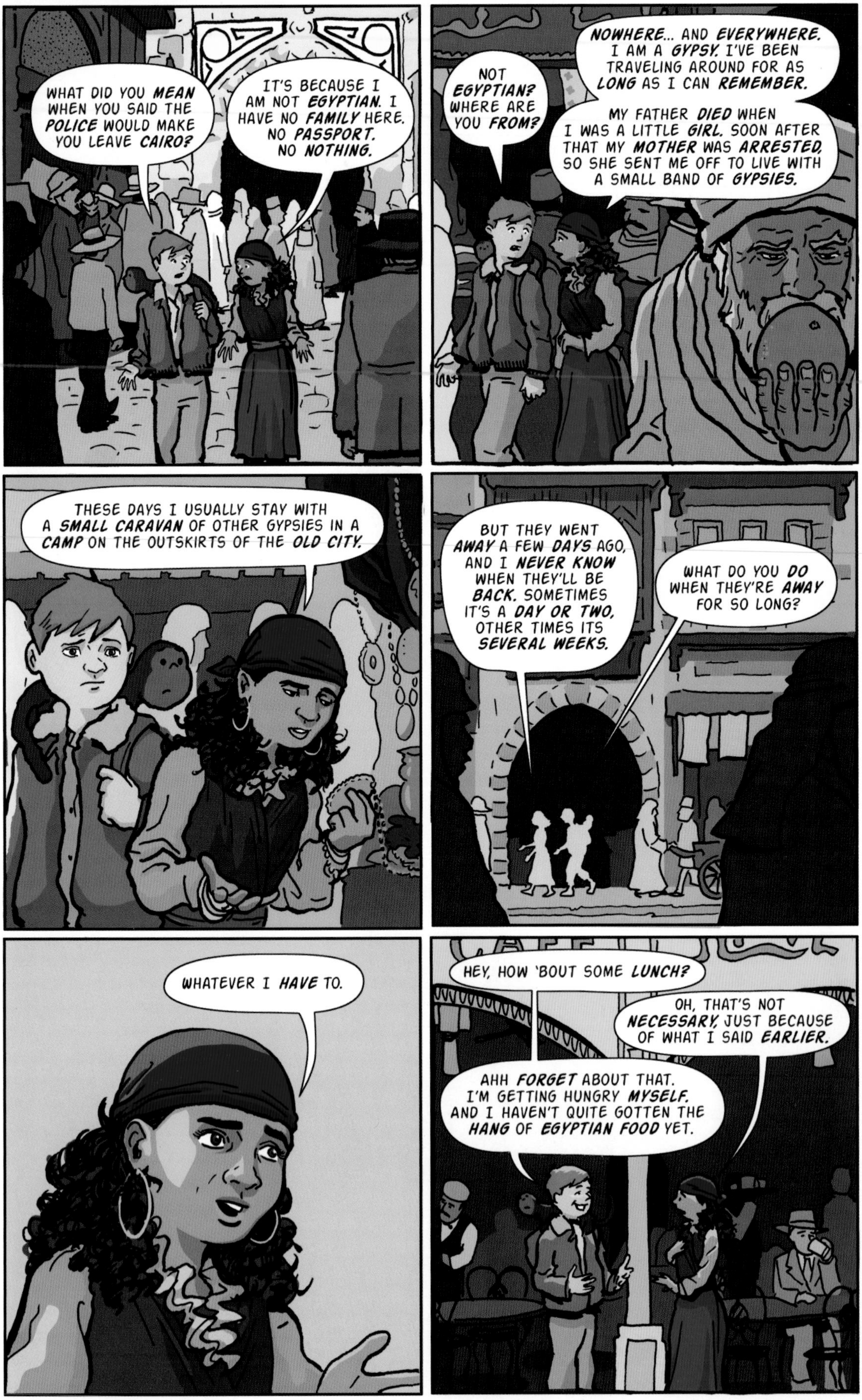
WHAT DID YOU MEAN WHEN YOU SAID THE POLICE WOULD MAKE YOU LEAVE CAIRO?
IT'S BECAUSE I AM NOT EGYPTIAN. I HAVE NO FAMILY HERE. NO PASSPORT. NO NOTHING.
NOT EGYPTIAN? WHERE ARE YOU FROM?
NOWHERE... AND EVERYWHERE. I AM A GYPSY. I'VE BEEN TRAVELING AROUND FOR AS LONG AS I CAN REMEMBER.
MY FATHER DIED WHEN I WAS A LITTLE GIRL. SOON AFTER THAT MY MOTHER WAS ARRESTED, SO SHE SENT ME OFF TO LIVE WITH A SMALL BAND OF GYPSIES.
THESE DAYS I USUALLY STAY WITH A SMALL CARAVAN OF OTHER GYPSIES IN A CAMP ON THE OUTSKIRTS OF THE OLD CITY.
BUT THEY WENT AWAY A FEW DAYS AGO, AND I NEVER KNOW WHEN THEY'LL BE BACK. SOMETIMES IT'S A DAY OR TWO, OTHER TIMES ITS SEVERAL WEEKS.
WHAT DO YOU DO WHEN THEY'RE AWAY FOR SO LONG?
WHATEVER I HAVE TO.
HEY, HOW 'BOUT SOME LUNCH?
OH, THAT'S NOT NECESSARY, JUST BECAUSE OF WHAT I SAID EARLIER.
AHH FORGET ABOUT THAT. I'M GETTING HUNGRY MYSELF. AND I HAVEN'T QUITE GOTTEN THE HANG OF EGYPTIAN FOOD YET.

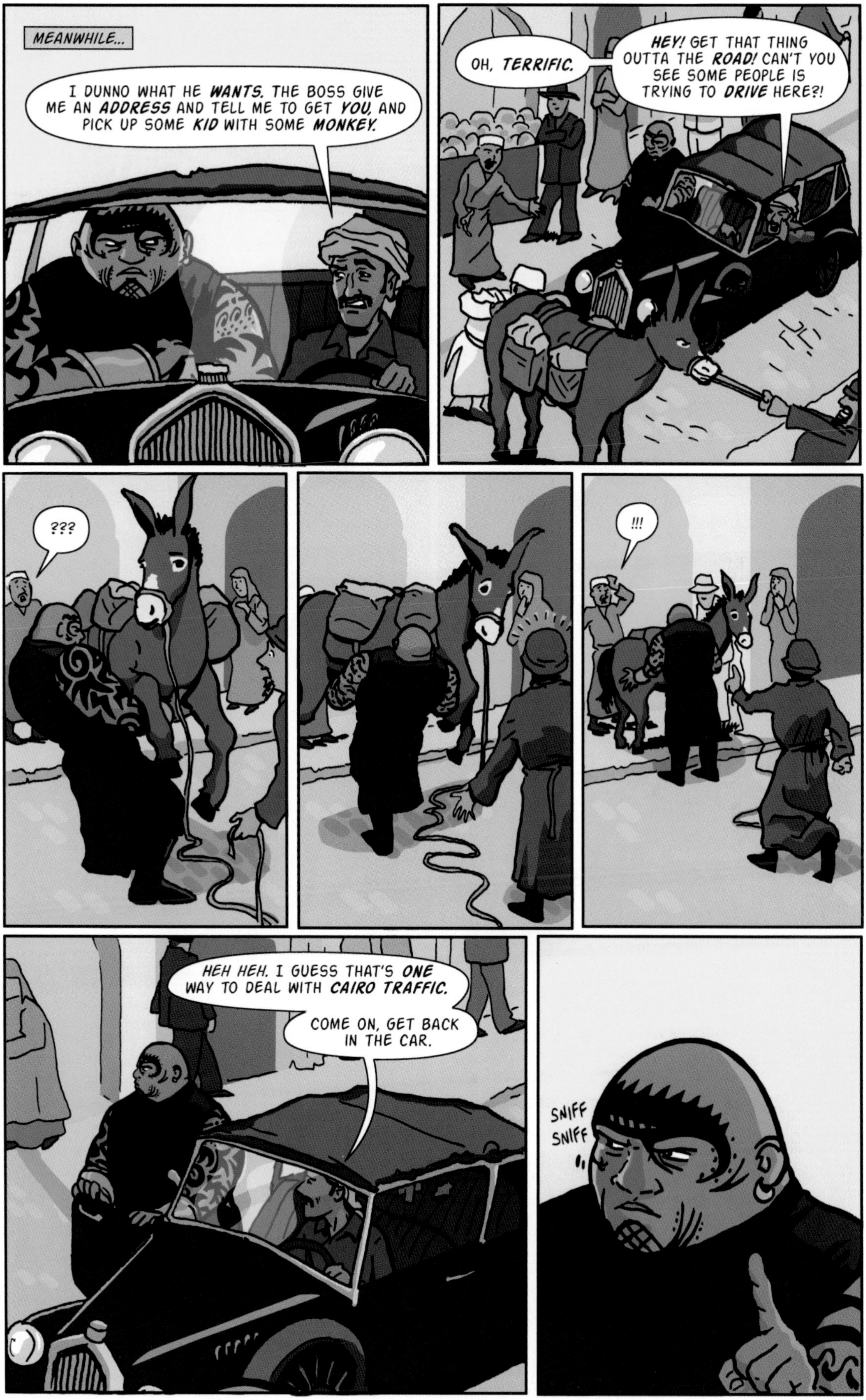
MEANWHILE...
I DUNNO WHAT HE WANTS. THE BOSS GIVE ME AN ADDRESS AND TELL ME TO GET YOU, AND PICK UP SOME KID WITH SOME MONKEY.
OH, TERRIFIC.
HEY! GET THAT THING OUTTA THE ROAD! CAN'T YOU SEE SOME PEOPLE IS TRYING TO DRIVE HERE?!
???
!!!
HEH HEH. I GUESS THAT'S ONE WAY TO DEAL WITH CAIRO TRAFFIC.
COME ON, GET BACK IN THE CAR.
SNIFF SNIFF

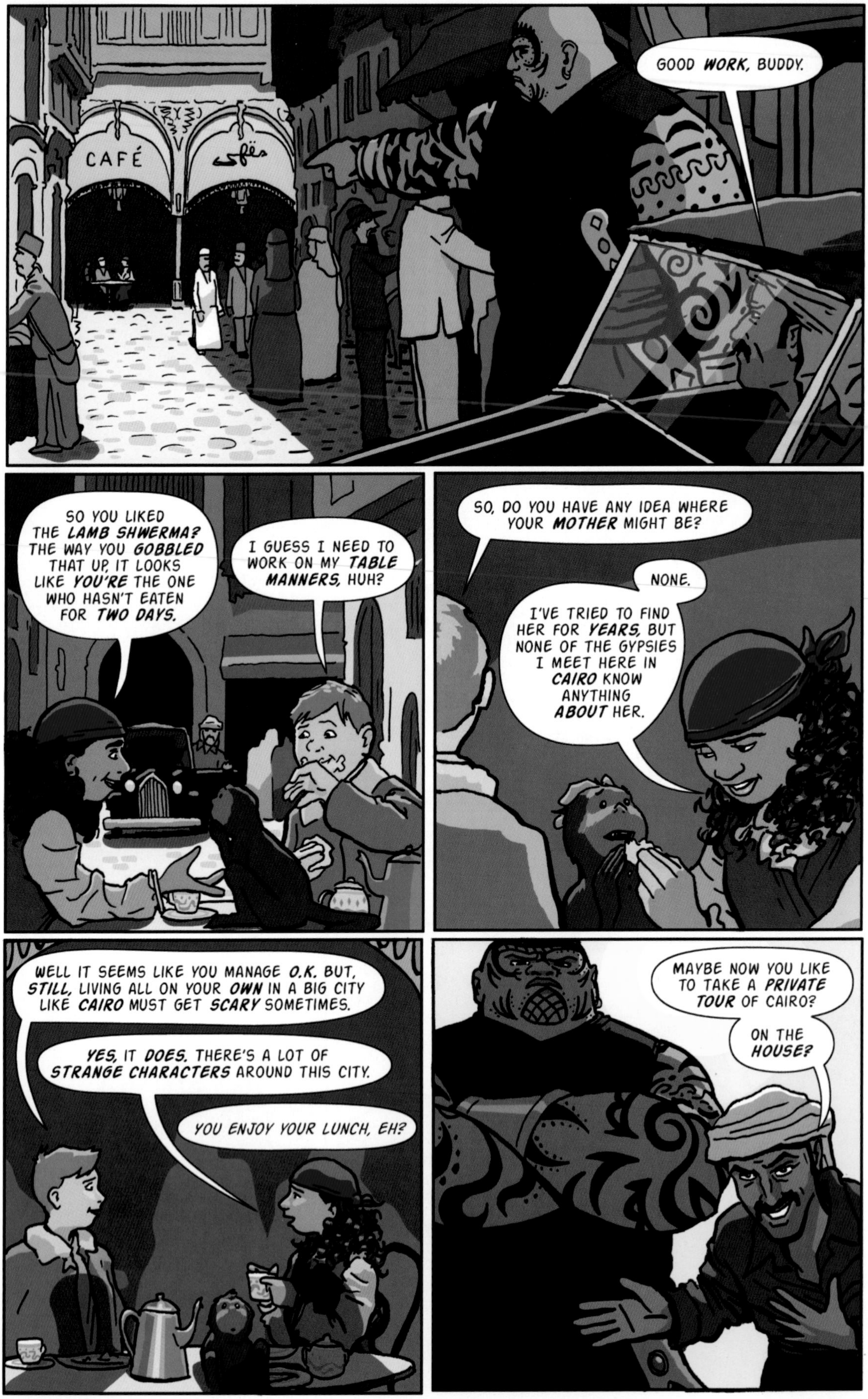
CAFÉ
GOOD WORK, BUDDY.
SO YOU LIKED THE LAMB SHWERMA? THE WAY YOU GOBBLED THAT UP, IT LOOKS LIKE YOU'RE THE ONE WHO HASN'T EATEN FOR TWO DAYS.
I GUESS I NEED TO WORK ON MY TABLE MANNERS, HUH?
SO, DO YOU HAVE ANY IDEA WHERE YOUR MOTHER MIGHT BE?
NONE.
I'VE TRIED TO FIND HER FOR YEARS, BUT NONE OF THE GYPSIES I MEET HERE IN CAIRO KNOW ANYTHING ABOUT HER.
WELL IT SEEMS LIKE YOU MANAGE O.K. BUT, STILL, LIVING ALL ON YOUR OWN IN A BIG CITY LIKE CAIRO MUST GET SCARY SOMETIMES.
YES, IT DOES. THERE'S A LOT OF STRANGE CHARACTERS AROUND THIS CITY.
YOU ENJOY YOUR LUNCH, EH?
MAYBE NOW YOU LIKE TO TAKE A PRIVATE TOUR OF CAIRO?
ON THE HOUSE?

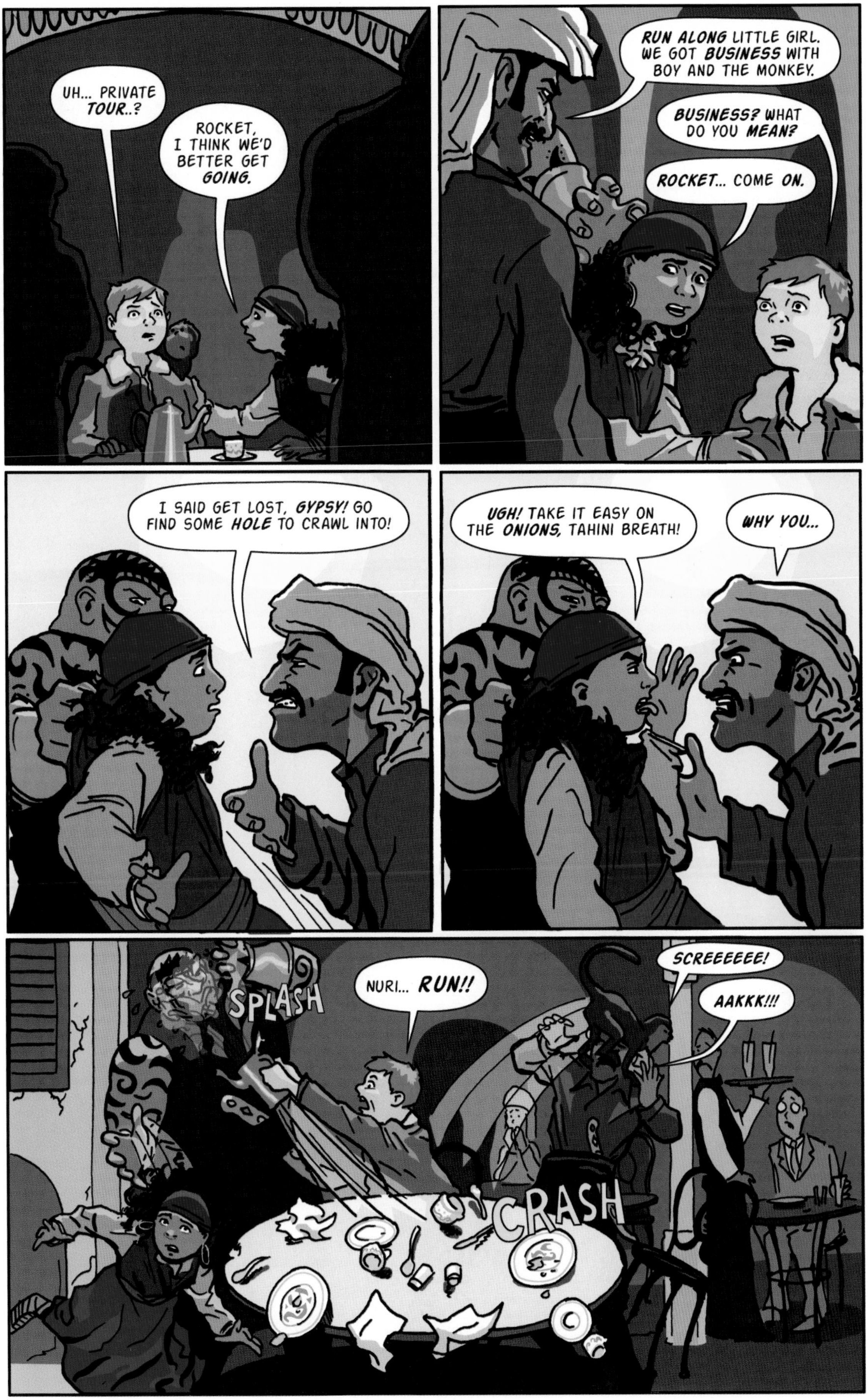
UH... PRIVATE TOUR..?
ROCKET, I THINK WE'D BETTER GET GOING.
RUN ALONG LITTLE GIRL. WE GOT BUSINESS WITH BOY AND THE MONKEY.
BUSINESS? WHAT DO YOU MEAN?
ROCKET... COME ON.
I SAID GET LOST, GYPSY! GO FIND SOME HOLE TO CRAWL INTO!
UGH! TAKE IT EASY ON THE ONIONS, TAHINI BREATH!
WHY YOU...
SPLASH
NURI... RUN!!
SCREEEEEEE!
AAKKK!!!
CRASH

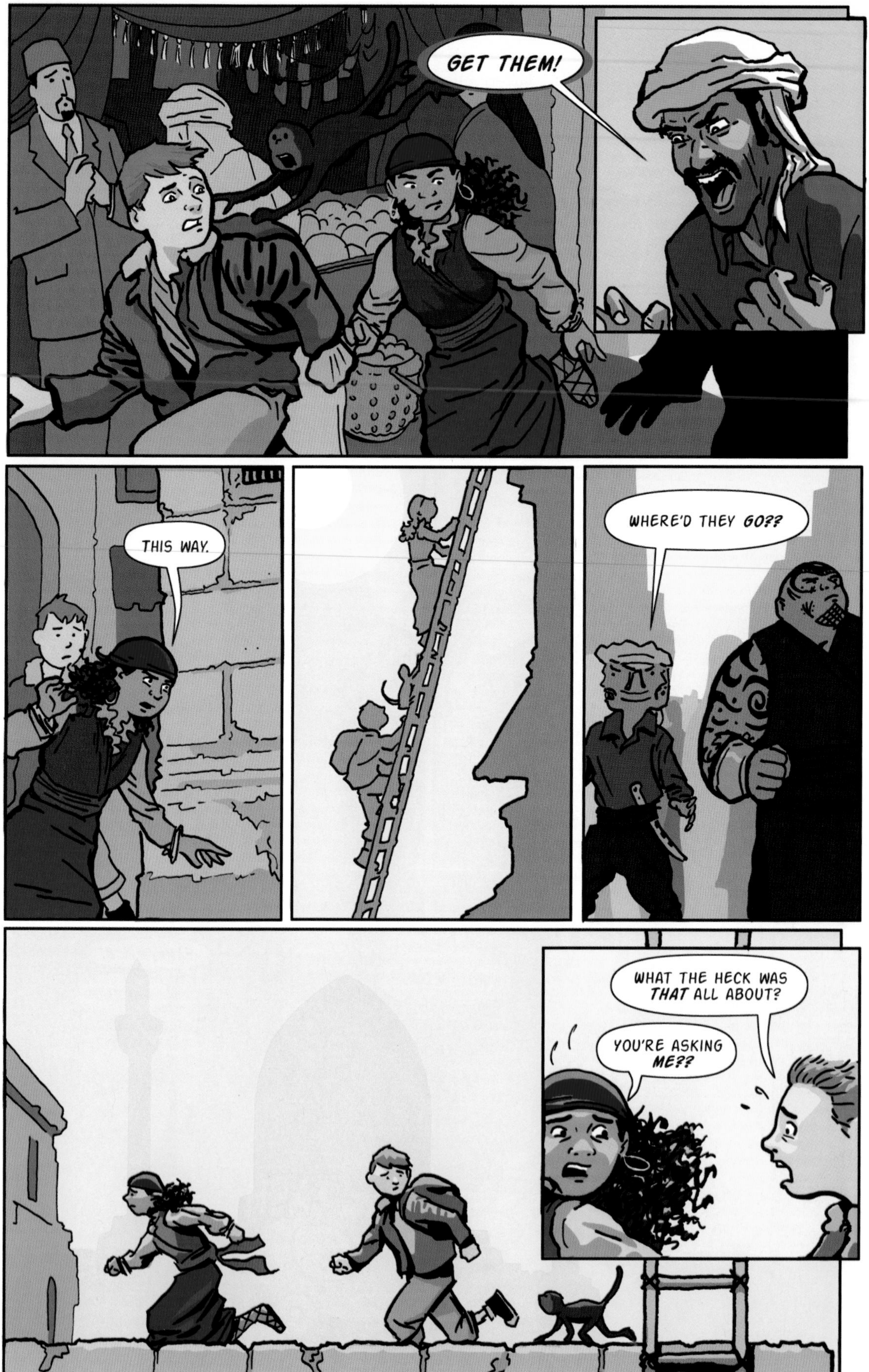
GET THEM!
THIS WAY.
WHERE'D THEY GO??
WHAT THE HECK WAS THAT ALL ABOUT?
YOU'RE ASKING ME??

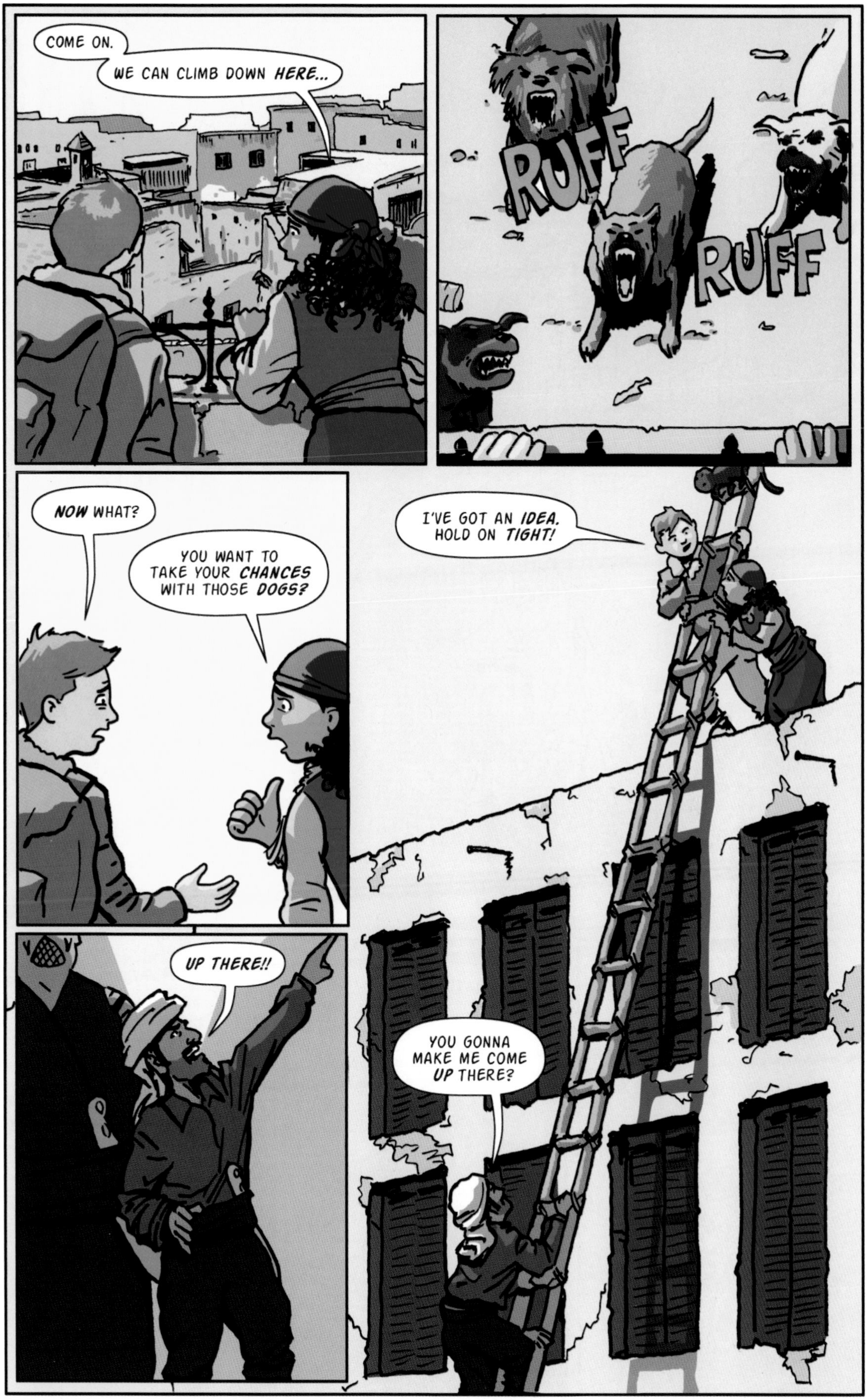
COME ON.
WE CAN CLIMB DOWN HERE...
RUFF
RUFF
NOW WHAT?
YOU WANT TO TAKE YOUR CHANCES WITH THOSE DOGS?
UP THERE!!
I'VE GOT AN IDEA. HOLD ON TIGHT!
YOU GONNA MAKE ME COME UP THERE?

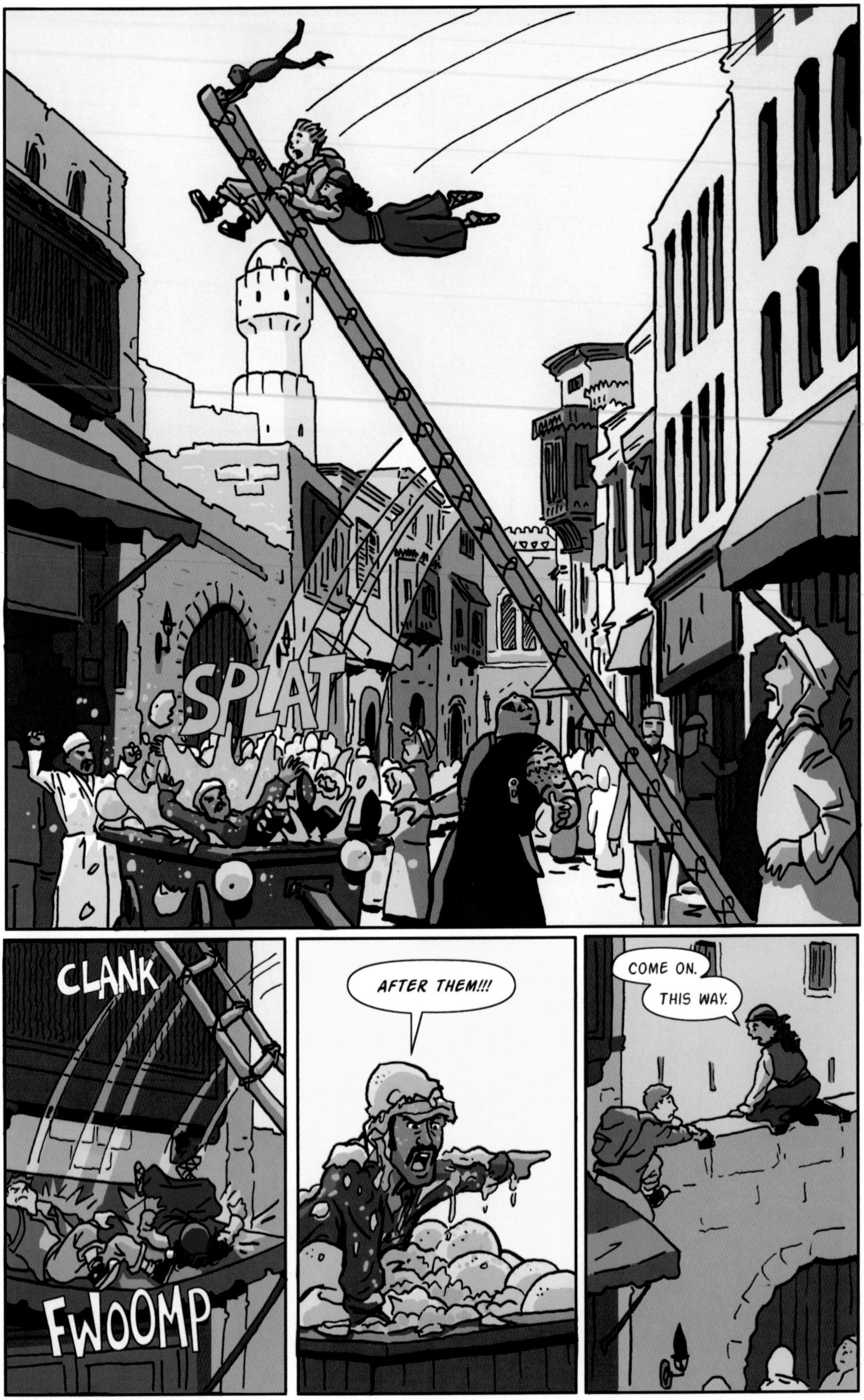
SPLAT
CLANK
FWOOMP
AFTER THEM!!!
COME ON.
THIS WAY.

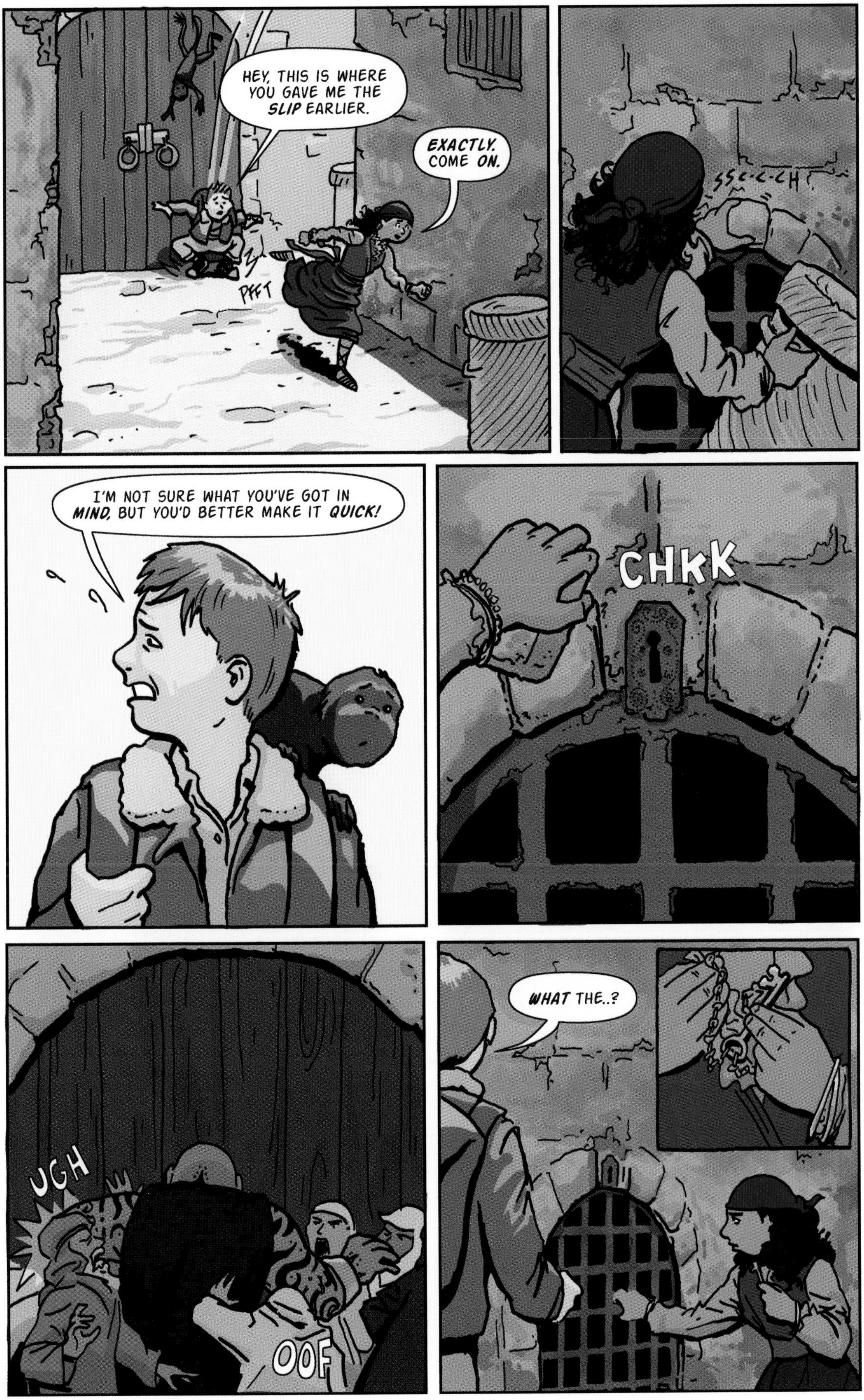
HEY, THIS IS WHERE YOU GAVE ME THE *SLIP* EARLIER.
PFFT
EXACTLY. COME *ON.*
SSC-C-CH
I'M NOT SURE WHAT YOU'VE GOT IN *MIND,* BUT YOU'D BETTER MAKE IT *QUICK!*
CHKK
UGH
OOF
WHAT THE..?

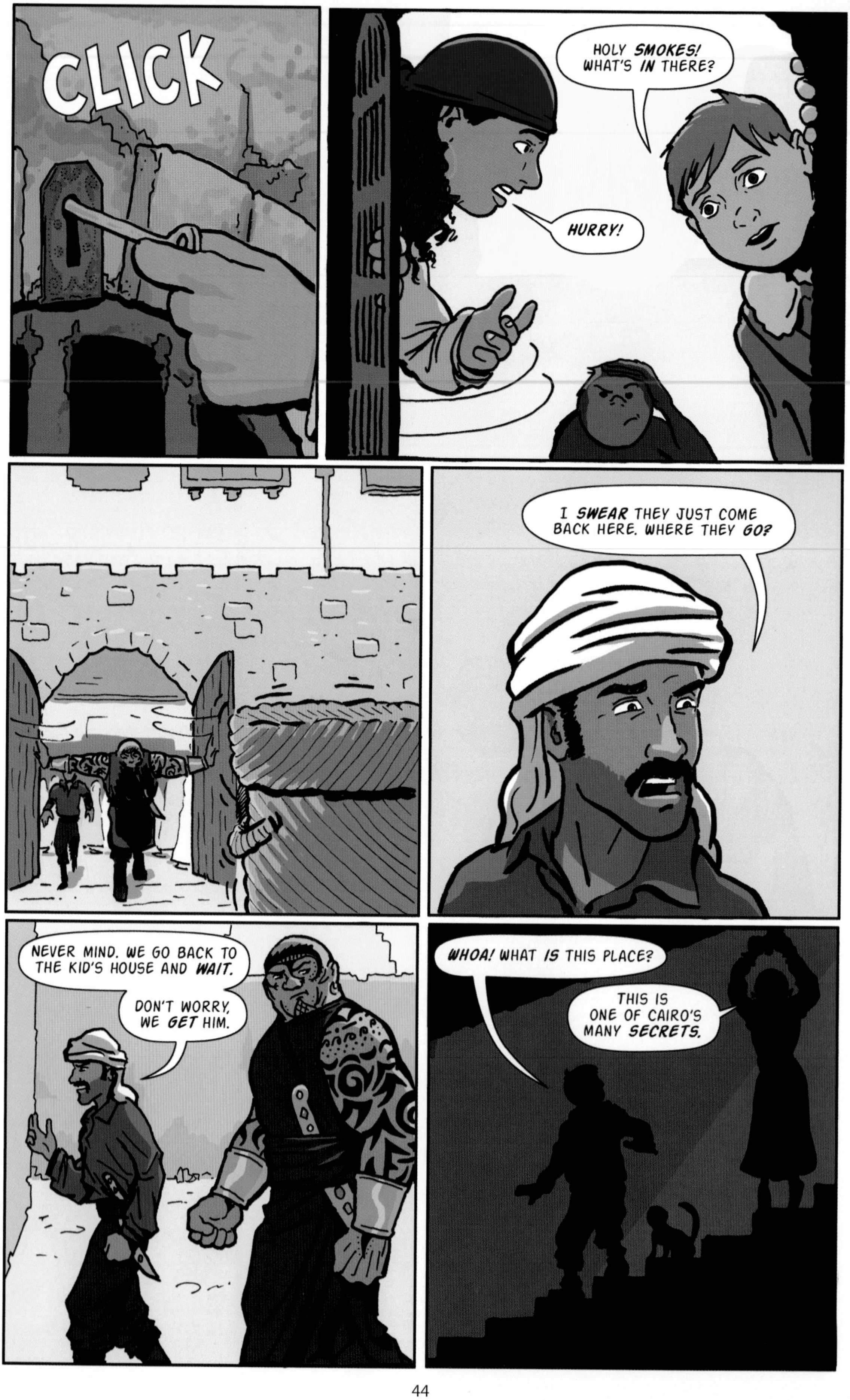
CLICK
HOLY SMOKES! WHAT'S IN THERE?
HURRY!
I SWEAR THEY JUST COME BACK HERE. WHERE THEY GO?
NEVER MIND. WE GO BACK TO THE KID'S HOUSE AND WAIT.
DON'T WORRY, WE GET HIM.
WHOA! WHAT IS THIS PLACE?
THIS IS ONE OF CAIRO'S MANY SECRETS.

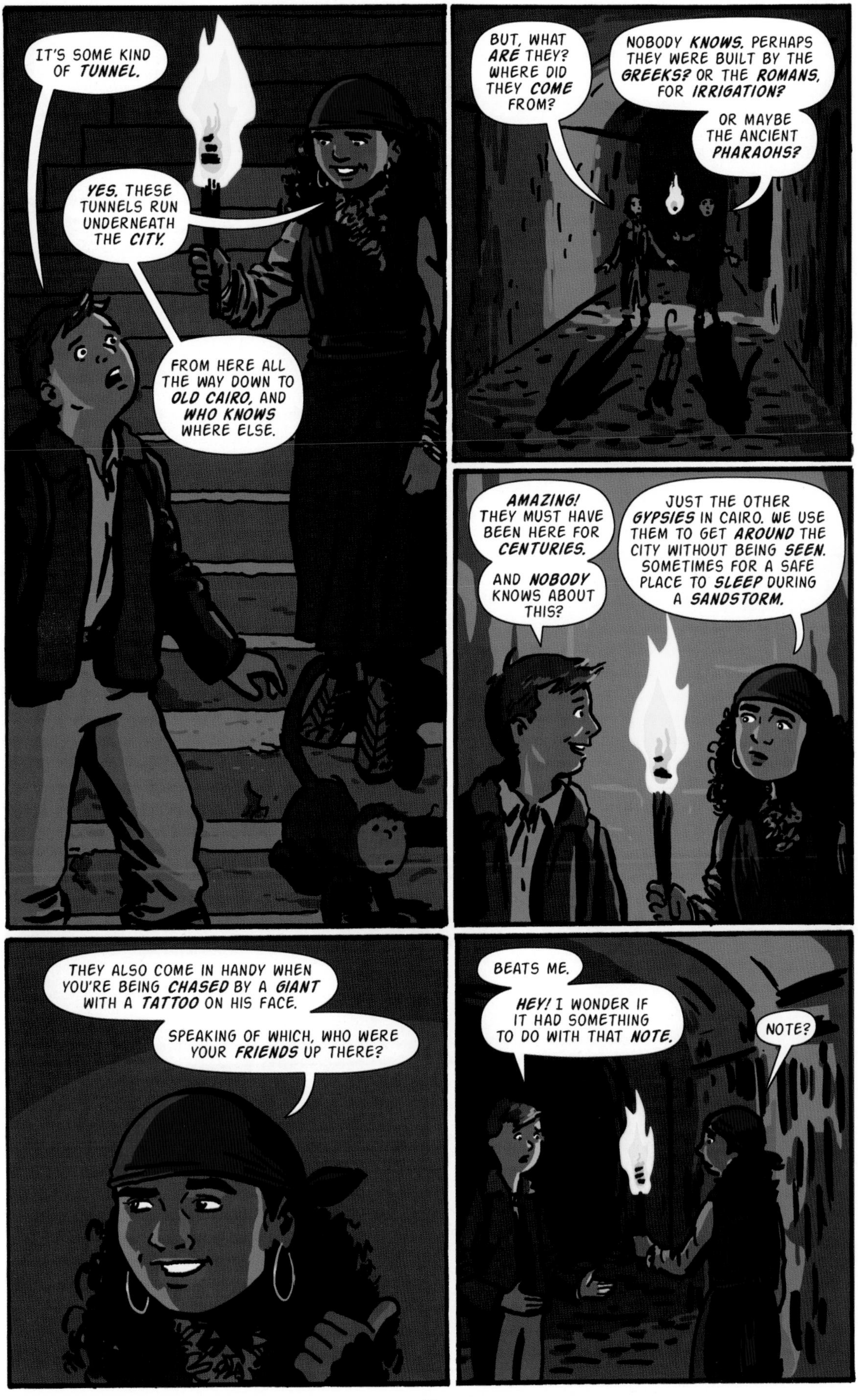
IT'S SOME KIND OF TUNNEL.
YES. THESE TUNNELS RUN UNDERNEATH THE CITY.
FROM HERE ALL THE WAY DOWN TO OLD CAIRO, AND WHO KNOWS WHERE ELSE.
BUT, WHAT ARE THEY? WHERE DID THEY COME FROM?
NOBODY KNOWS. PERHAPS THEY WERE BUILT BY THE GREEKS? OR THE ROMANS, FOR IRRIGATION?
OR MAYBE THE ANCIENT PHARAOHS?
AMAZING! THEY MUST HAVE BEEN HERE FOR CENTURIES.
AND NOBODY KNOWS ABOUT THIS?
JUST THE OTHER GYPSIES IN CAIRO. WE USE THEM TO GET AROUND THE CITY WITHOUT BEING SEEN. SOMETIMES FOR A SAFE PLACE TO SLEEP DURING A SANDSTORM.
THEY ALSO COME IN HANDY WHEN YOU'RE BEING CHASED BY A GIANT WITH A TATTOO ON HIS FACE.
SPEAKING OF WHICH, WHO WERE YOUR FRIENDS UP THERE?
BEATS ME.
HEY! I WONDER IF IT HAD SOMETHING TO DO WITH THAT NOTE.
NOTE?

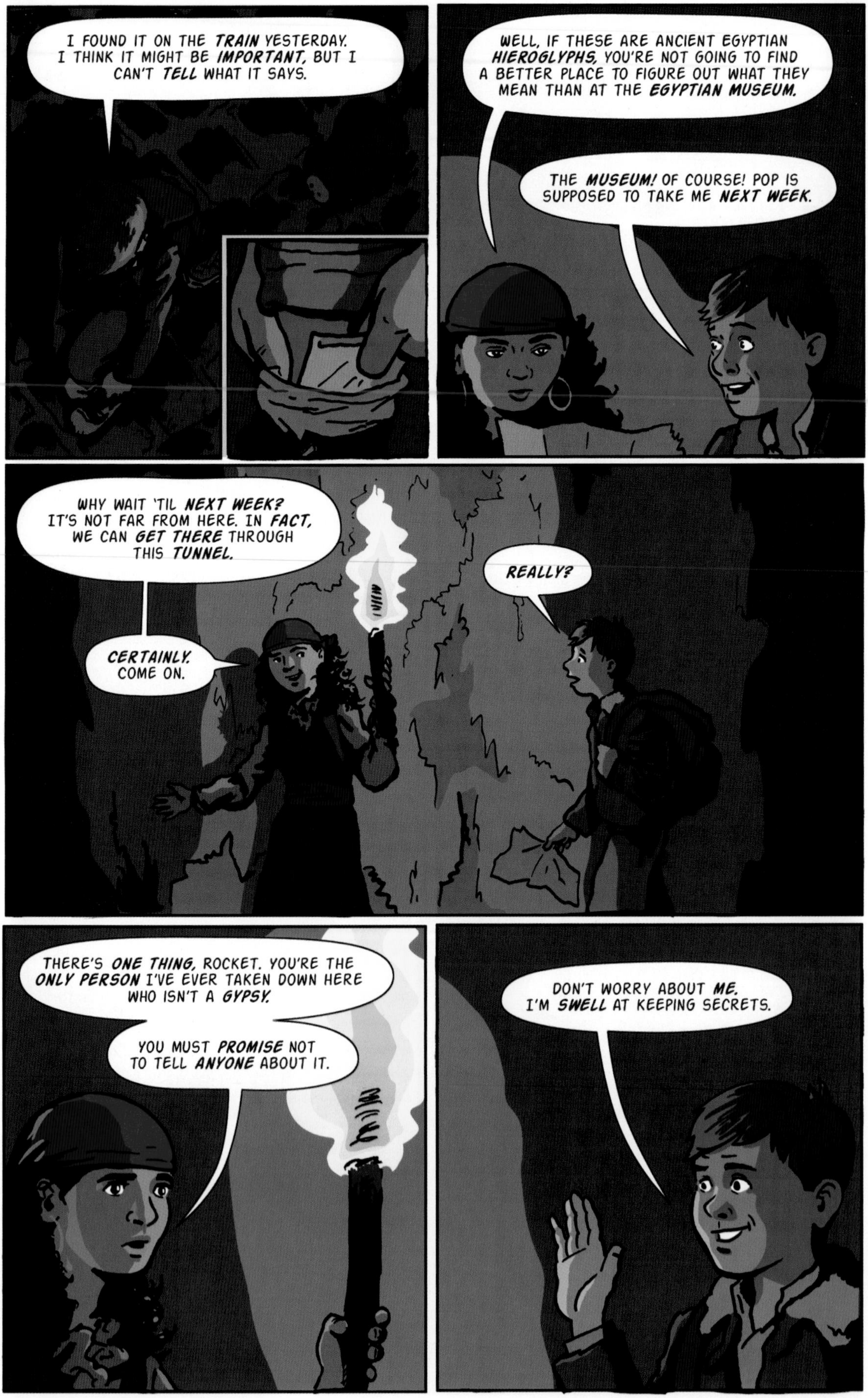
I FOUND IT ON THE TRAIN YESTERDAY. I THINK IT MIGHT BE IMPORTANT, BUT I CAN'T TELL WHAT IT SAYS.
WELL, IF THESE ARE ANCIENT EGYPTIAN HIEROGLYPHS, YOU'RE NOT GOING TO FIND A BETTER PLACE TO FIGURE OUT WHAT THEY MEAN THAN AT THE EGYPTIAN MUSEUM.
THE MUSEUM! OF COURSE! POP IS SUPPOSED TO TAKE ME NEXT WEEK.
WHY WAIT 'TIL NEXT WEEK? IT'S NOT FAR FROM HERE. IN FACT, WE CAN GET THERE THROUGH THIS TUNNEL.
REALLY?
CERTAINLY. COME ON.
THERE'S ONE THING, ROCKET. YOU'RE THE ONLY PERSON I'VE EVER TAKEN DOWN HERE WHO ISN'T A GYPSY.
YOU MUST PROMISE NOT TO TELL ANYONE ABOUT IT.
DON'T WORRY ABOUT ME. I'M SWELL AT KEEPING SECRETS.

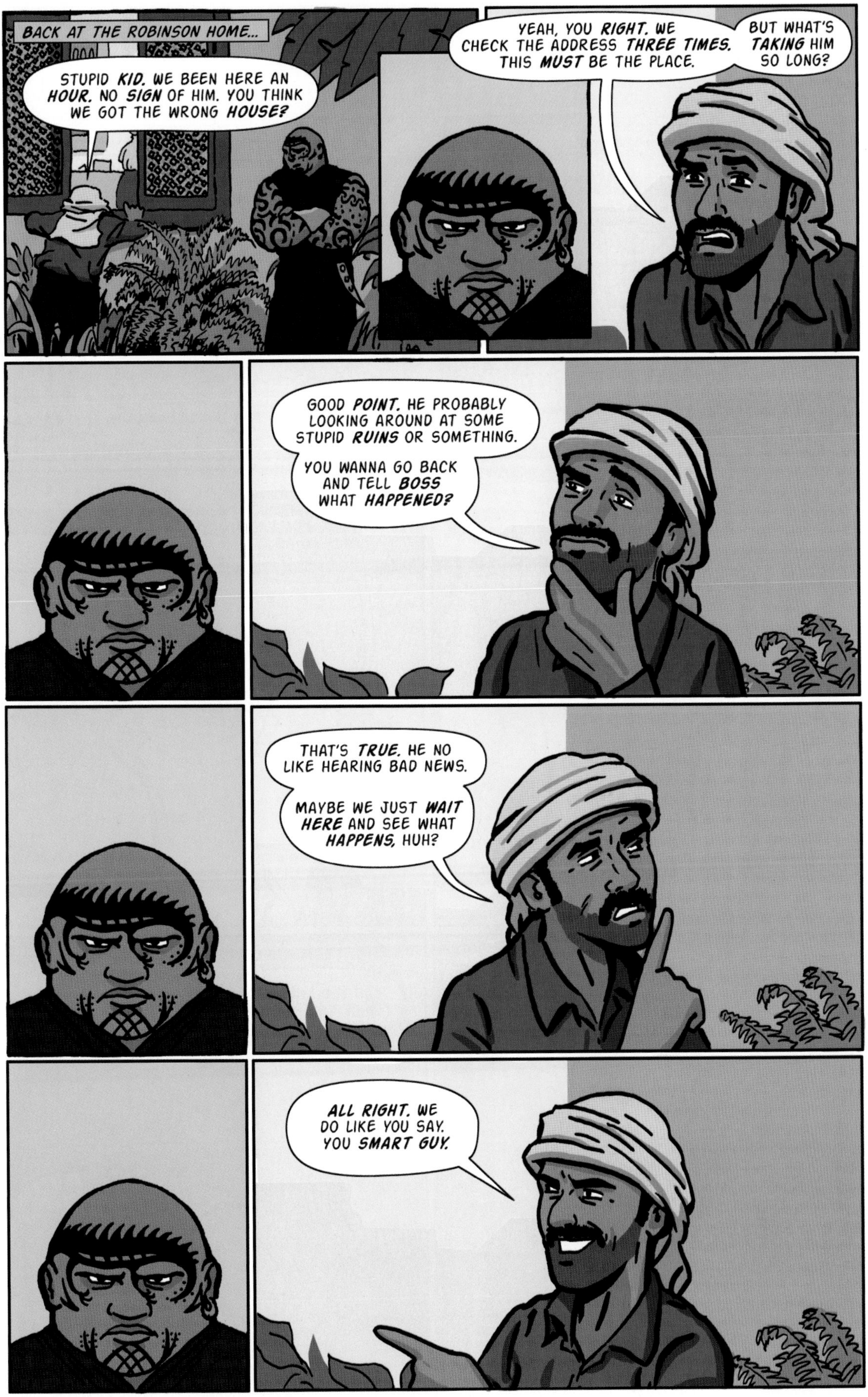
BACK AT THE ROBINSON HOME...
STUPID KID. WE BEEN HERE AN HOUR. NO SIGN OF HIM. YOU THINK WE GOT THE WRONG HOUSE?
YEAH, YOU RIGHT. WE CHECK THE ADDRESS THREE TIMES. THIS MUST BE THE PLACE.
BUT WHAT'S TAKING HIM SO LONG?
GOOD POINT. HE PROBABLY LOOKING AROUND AT SOME STUPID RUINS OR SOMETHING.
YOU WANNA GO BACK AND TELL BOSS WHAT HAPPENED?
THAT'S TRUE. HE NO LIKE HEARING BAD NEWS.
MAYBE WE JUST WAIT HERE AND SEE WHAT HAPPENS, HUH?
ALL RIGHT. WE DO LIKE YOU SAY. YOU SMART GUY.

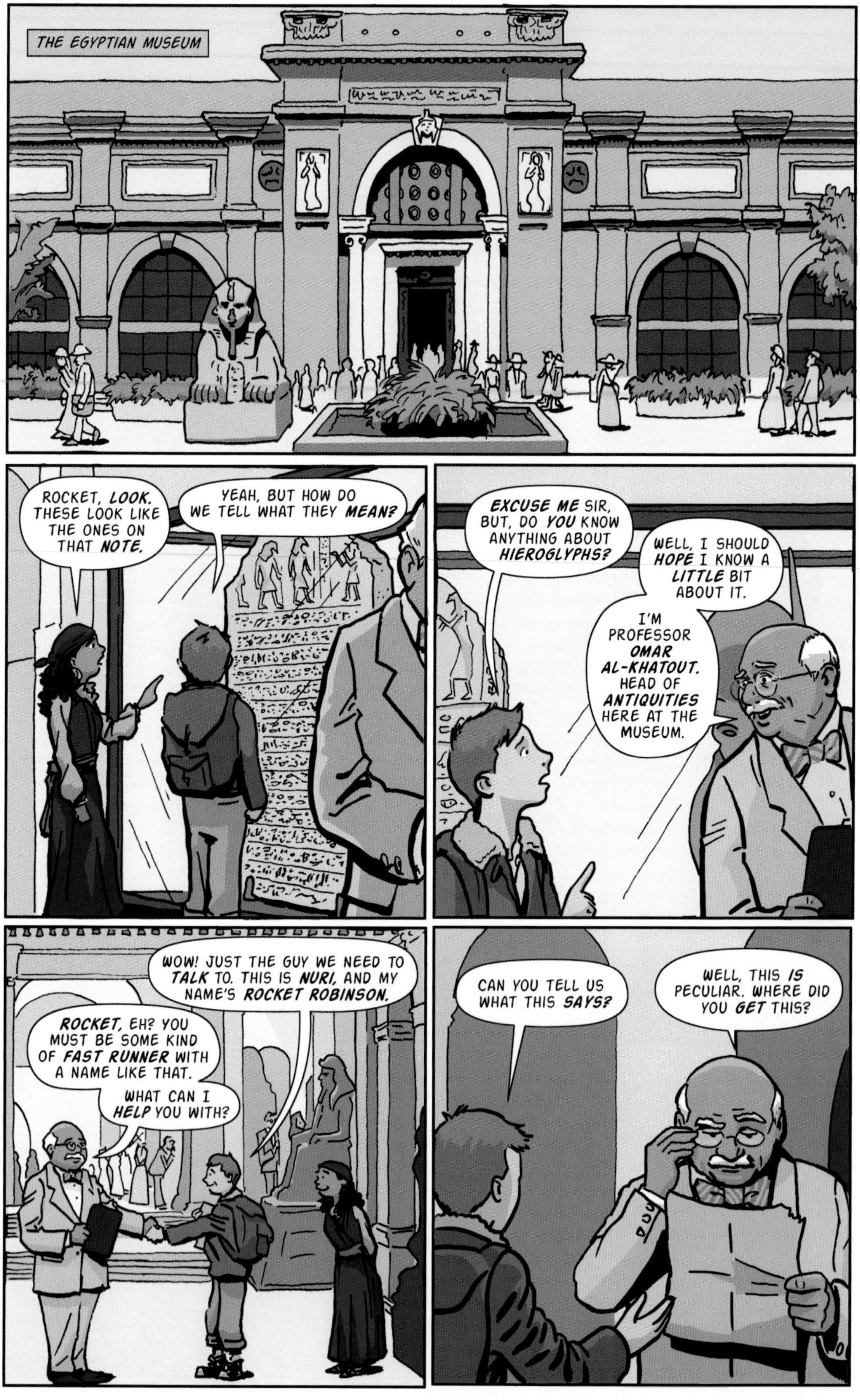
THE EGYPTIAN MUSEUM
ROCKET, LOOK. THESE LOOK LIKE THE ONES ON THAT NOTE.
YEAH, BUT HOW DO WE TELL WHAT THEY MEAN?
EXCUSE ME SIR, BUT, DO YOU KNOW ANYTHING ABOUT HIEROGLYPHS?
WELL, I SHOULD HOPE I KNOW A LITTLE BIT ABOUT IT.
I'M PROFESSOR OMAR AL-KHATOUT. HEAD OF ANTIQUITIES HERE AT THE MUSEUM.
WOW! JUST THE GUY WE NEED TO TALK TO. THIS IS NURI, AND MY NAME'S ROCKET ROBINSON.
ROCKET, EH? YOU MUST BE SOME KIND OF FAST RUNNER WITH A NAME LIKE THAT.
WHAT CAN I HELP YOU WITH?
CAN YOU TELL US WHAT THIS SAYS?
WELL, THIS IS PECULIAR. WHERE DID YOU GET THIS?

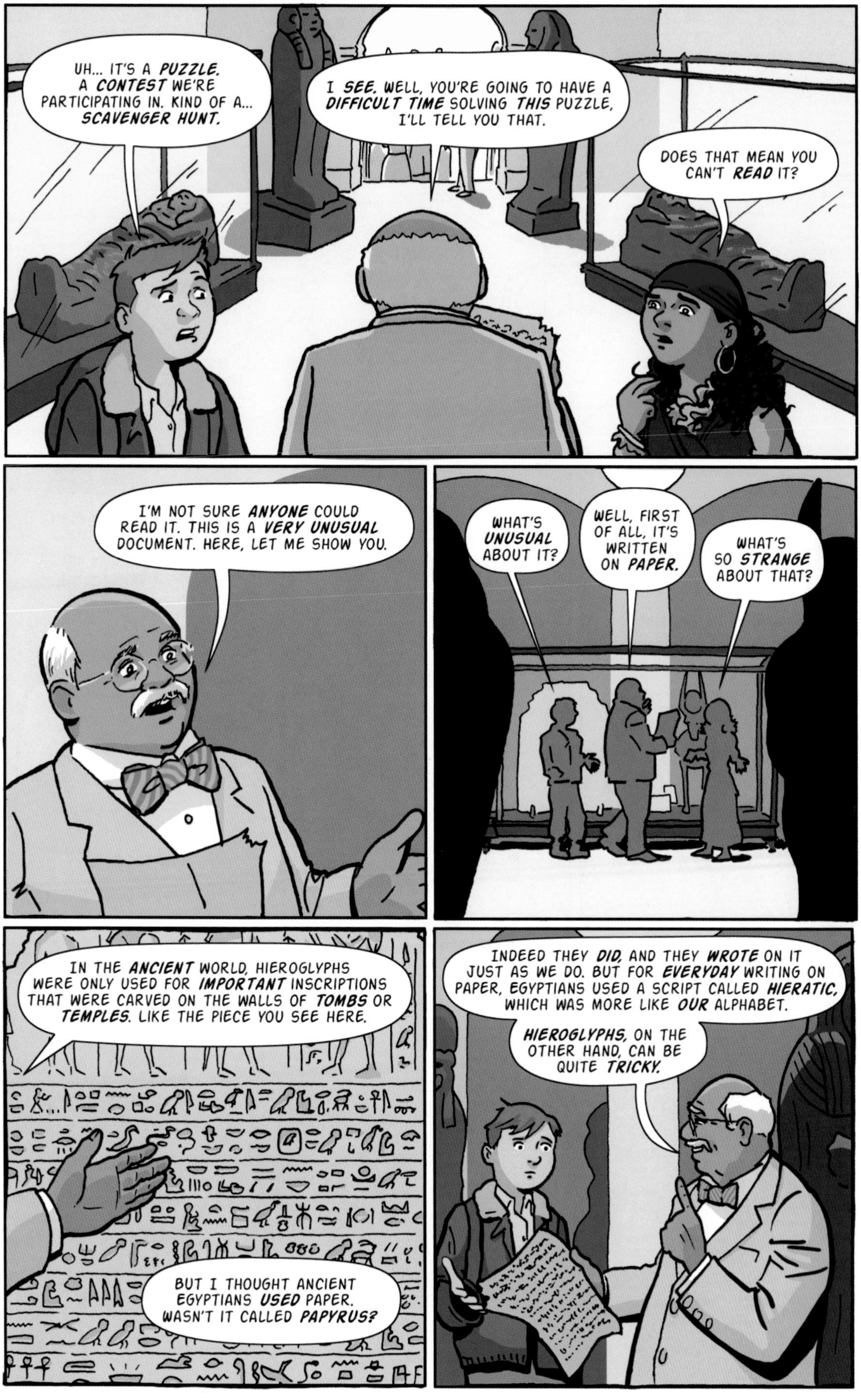
UH... IT'S A PUZZLE. A CONTEST WE'RE PARTICIPATING IN. KIND OF A... SCAVENGER HUNT.
I SEE. WELL, YOU'RE GOING TO HAVE A DIFFICULT TIME SOLVING THIS PUZZLE, I'LL TELL YOU THAT.
DOES THAT MEAN YOU CAN'T READ IT?
I'M NOT SURE ANYONE COULD READ IT. THIS IS A VERY UNUSUAL DOCUMENT. HERE, LET ME SHOW YOU.
WHAT'S UNUSUAL ABOUT IT?
WELL, FIRST OF ALL, IT'S WRITTEN ON PAPER.
WHAT'S SO STRANGE ABOUT THAT?
IN THE ANCIENT WORLD, HIEROGLYPHS WERE ONLY USED FOR IMPORTANT INSCRIPTIONS THAT WERE CARVED ON THE WALLS OF TOMBS OR TEMPLES. LIKE THE PIECE YOU SEE HERE.
BUT I THOUGHT ANCIENT EGYPTIANS USED PAPER. WASN'T IT CALLED PAPYRUS?
INDEED THEY DID, AND THEY WROTE ON IT JUST AS WE DO. BUT FOR EVERYDAY WRITING ON PAPER, EGYPTIANS USED A SCRIPT CALLED HIERATIC, WHICH WAS MORE LIKE OUR ALPHABET.
HIEROGLYPHS, ON THE OTHER HAND, CAN BE QUITE TRICKY.

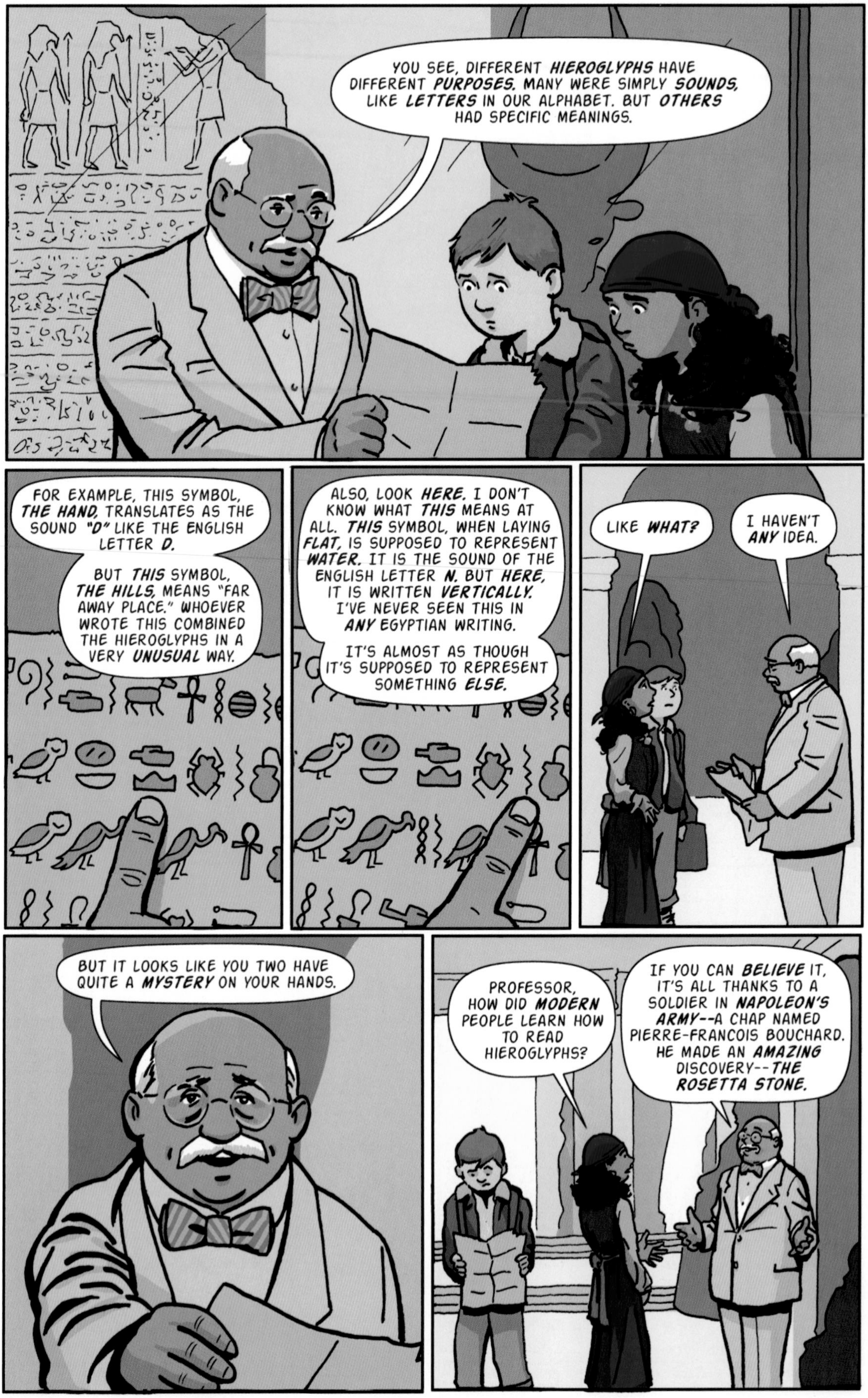
YOU SEE, DIFFERENT HIEROGLYPHS HAVE DIFFERENT PURPOSES. MANY WERE SIMPLY SOUNDS, LIKE LETTERS IN OUR ALPHABET. BUT OTHERS HAD SPECIFIC MEANINGS.
FOR EXAMPLE, THIS SYMBOL, THE HAND, TRANSLATES AS THE SOUND "D" LIKE THE ENGLISH LETTER D.
BUT THIS SYMBOL, THE HILLS, MEANS "FAR AWAY PLACE." WHOEVER WROTE THIS COMBINED THE HIEROGLYPHS IN A VERY UNUSUAL WAY.
ALSO, LOOK HERE. I DON'T KNOW WHAT THIS MEANS AT ALL. THIS SYMBOL, WHEN LAYING FLAT, IS SUPPOSED TO REPRESENT WATER. IT IS THE SOUND OF THE ENGLISH LETTER N. BUT HERE, IT IS WRITTEN VERTICALLY. I'VE NEVER SEEN THIS IN ANY EGYPTIAN WRITING.
IT'S ALMOST AS THOUGH IT'S SUPPOSED TO REPRESENT SOMETHING ELSE.
LIKE WHAT?
I HAVEN'T ANY IDEA.
BUT IT LOOKS LIKE YOU TWO HAVE QUITE A MYSTERY ON YOUR HANDS.
PROFESSOR, HOW DID MODERN PEOPLE LEARN HOW TO READ HIEROGLYPHS?
IF YOU CAN BELIEVE IT, IT'S ALL THANKS TO A SOLDIER IN NAPOLEON'S ARMY--A CHAP NAMED PIERRE-FRANCOIS BOUCHARD. HE MADE AN AMAZING DISCOVERY--THE ROSETTA STONE.

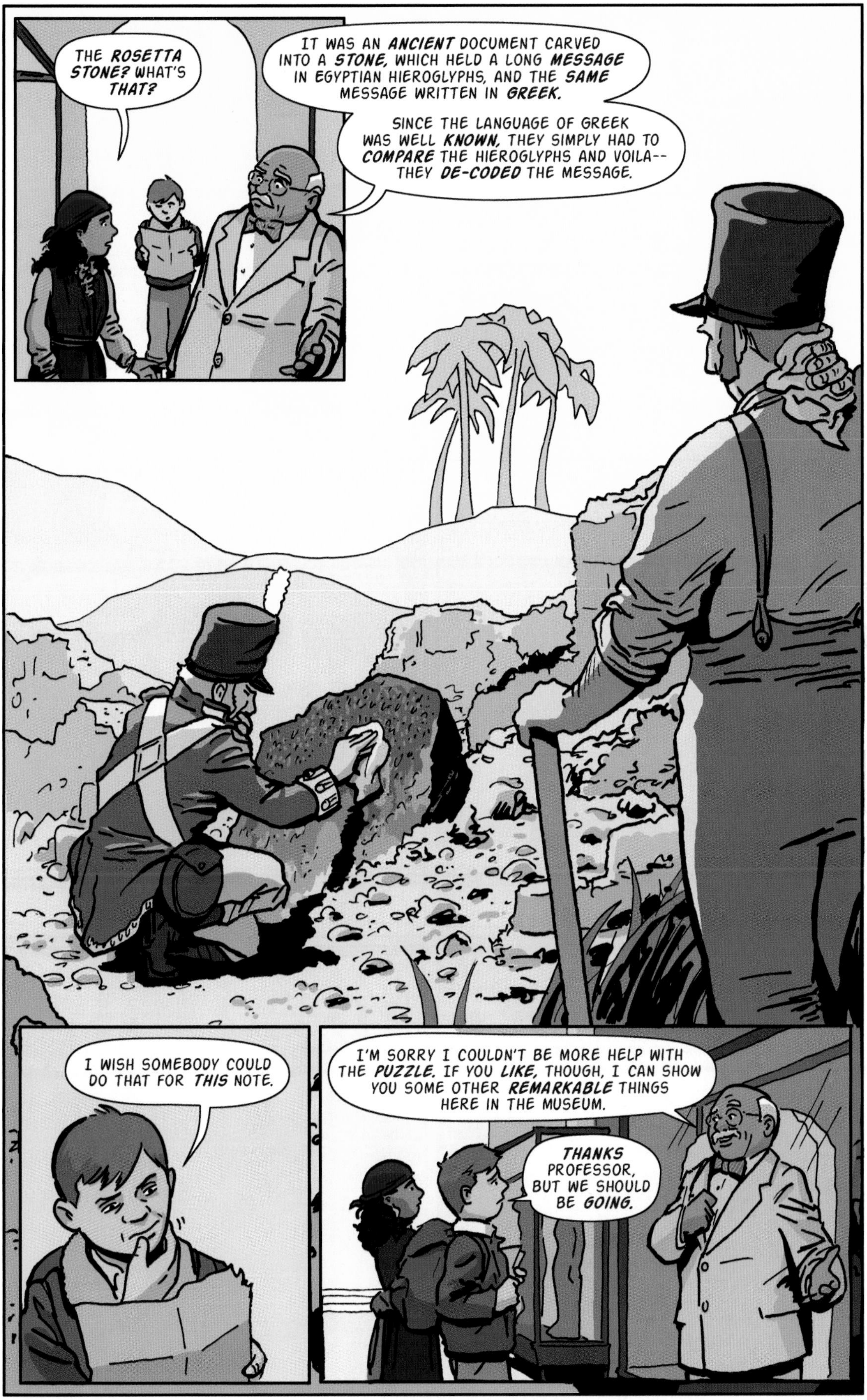
THE ROSETTA STONE? WHAT'S THAT?
IT WAS AN ANCIENT DOCUMENT CARVED INTO A STONE, WHICH HELD A LONG MESSAGE IN EGYPTIAN HIEROGLYPHS, AND THE SAME MESSAGE WRITTEN IN GREEK.
SINCE THE LANGUAGE OF GREEK WAS WELL KNOWN, THEY SIMPLY HAD TO COMPARE THE HIEROGLYPHS AND VOILA-- THEY DE-CODED THE MESSAGE.
I WISH SOMEBODY COULD DO THAT FOR THIS NOTE.
I'M SORRY I COULDN'T BE MORE HELP WITH THE PUZZLE. IF YOU LIKE, THOUGH, I CAN SHOW YOU SOME OTHER REMARKABLE THINGS HERE IN THE MUSEUM.
THANKS PROFESSOR, BUT WE SHOULD BE GOING.

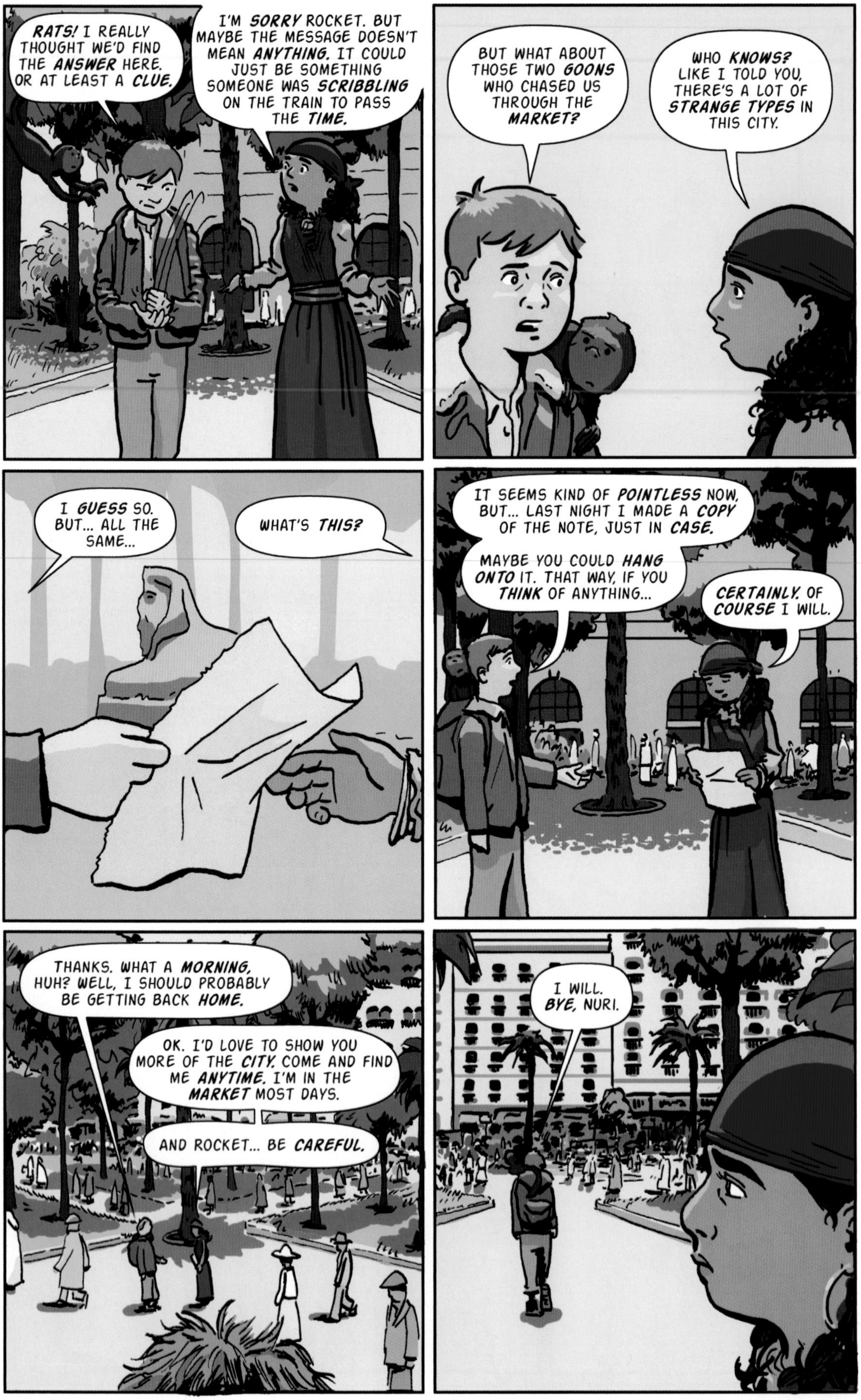
RATS! I REALLY THOUGHT WE'D FIND THE ANSWER HERE. OR AT LEAST A CLUE.
I'M SORRY ROCKET. BUT MAYBE THE MESSAGE DOESN'T MEAN ANYTHING. IT COULD JUST BE SOMETHING SOMEONE WAS SCRIBBLING ON THE TRAIN TO PASS THE TIME.
BUT WHAT ABOUT THOSE TWO GOONS WHO CHASED US THROUGH THE MARKET?
WHO KNOWS? LIKE I TOLD YOU, THERE'S A LOT OF STRANGE TYPES IN THIS CITY.
I GUESS SO. BUT... ALL THE SAME...
WHAT'S THIS?
IT SEEMS KIND OF POINTLESS NOW, BUT... LAST NIGHT I MADE A COPY OF THE NOTE, JUST IN CASE.
MAYBE YOU COULD HANG ONTO IT. THAT WAY, IF YOU THINK OF ANYTHING...
CERTAINLY. OF COURSE I WILL.
THANKS. WHAT A MORNING, HUH? WELL, I SHOULD PROBABLY BE GETTING BACK HOME.
OK. I'D LOVE TO SHOW YOU MORE OF THE CITY. COME AND FIND ME ANYTIME. I'M IN THE MARKET MOST DAYS.
AND ROCKET... BE CAREFUL.
I WILL. BYE, NURI.

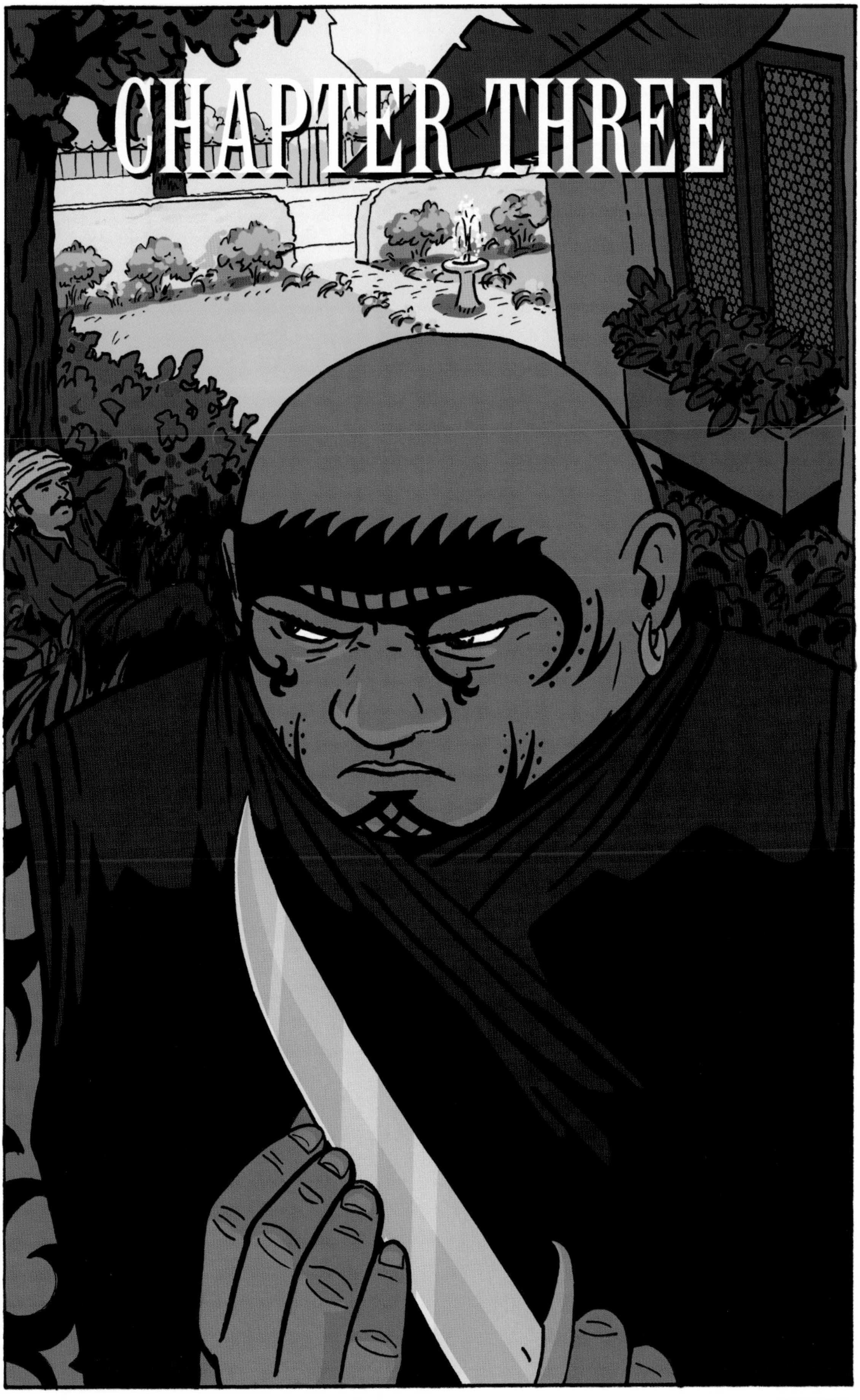
CHAPTER THREE

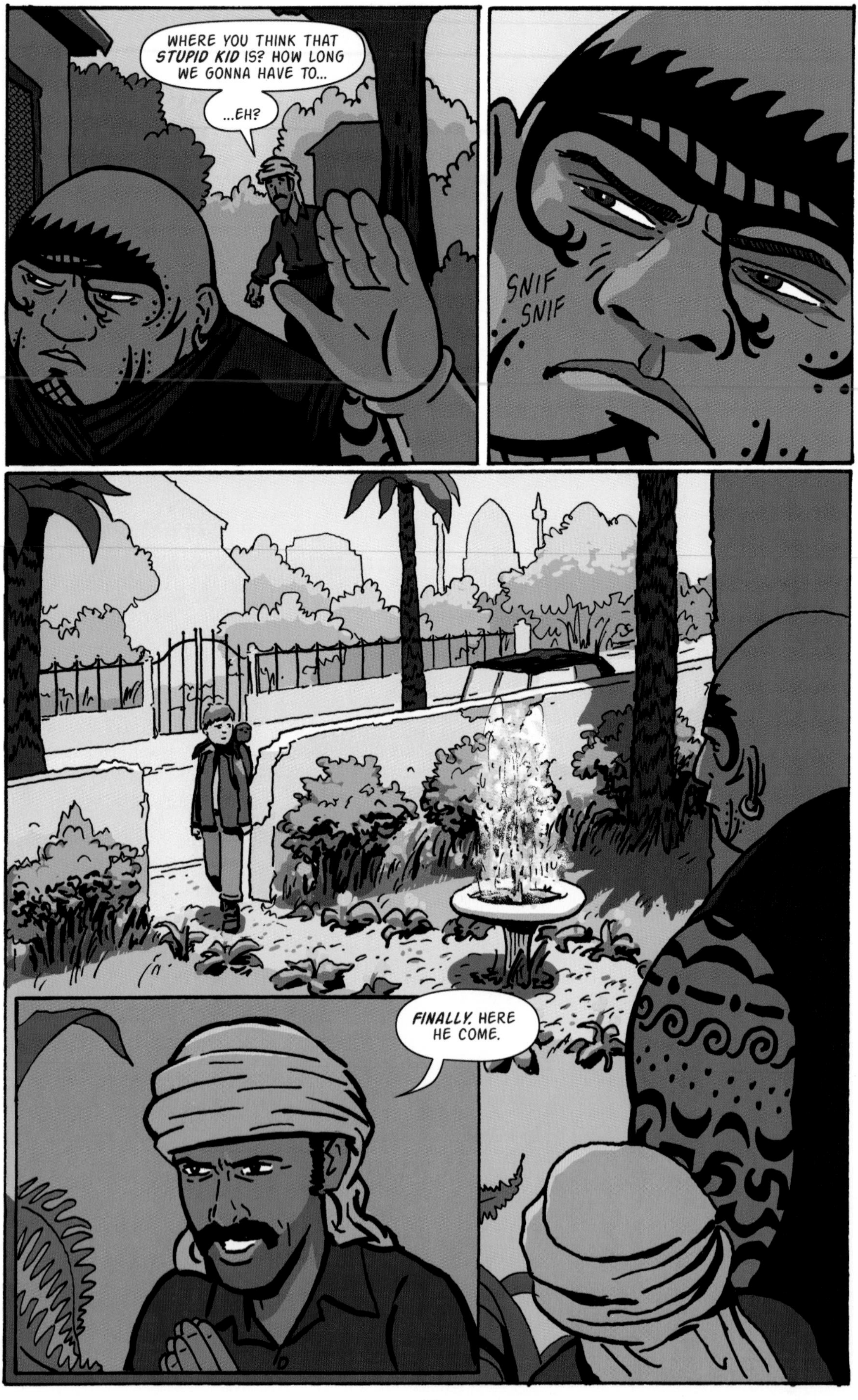
WHERE YOU THINK THAT STUPID KID IS? HOW LONG WE GONNA HAVE TO...
...EH?
SNIF SNIF
FINALLY. HERE HE COME.

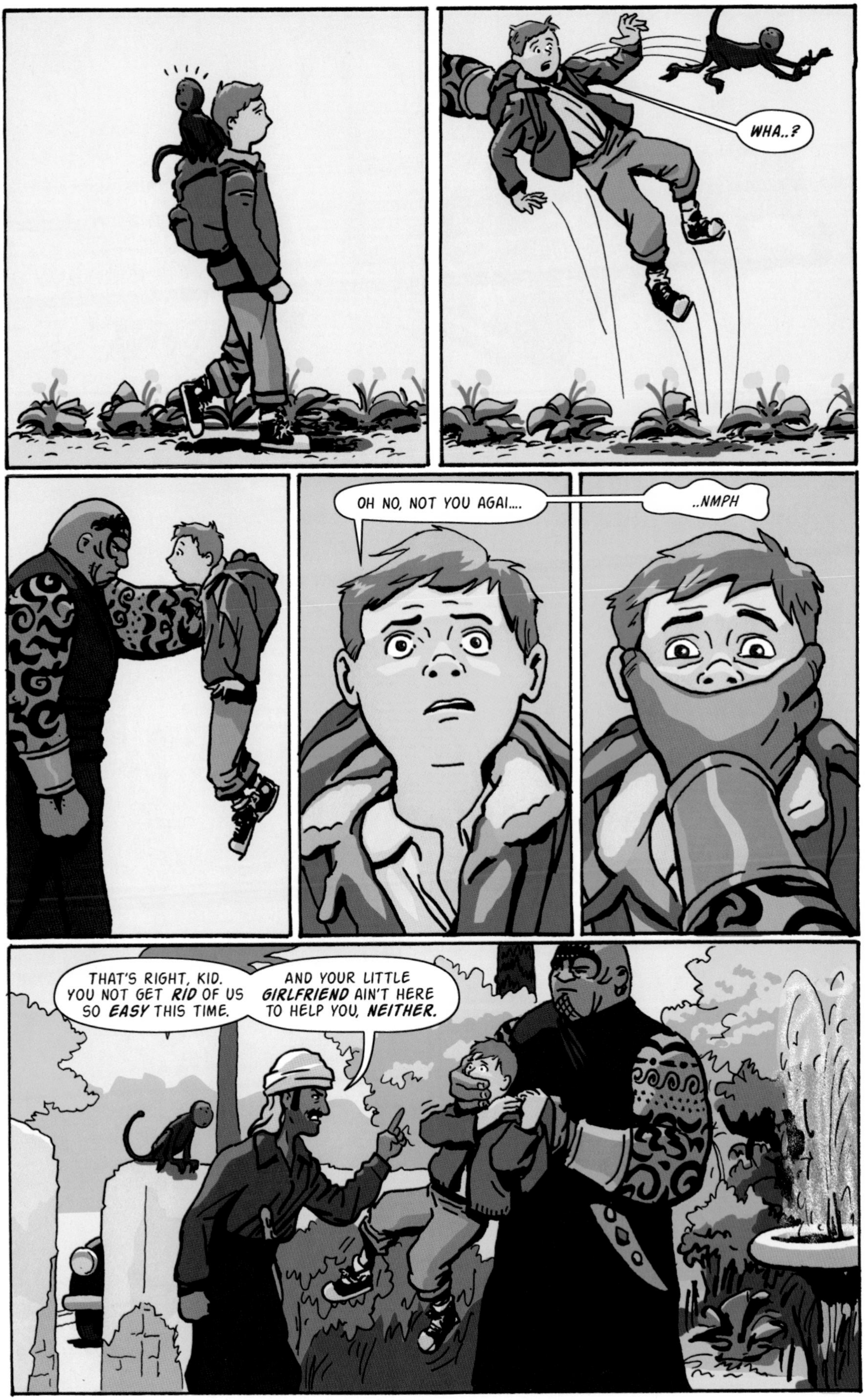
WHA..?
OH NO, NOT YOU AGAI....
..NMPH
THAT'S RIGHT, KID. YOU NOT GET RID OF US SO EASY THIS TIME.
AND YOUR LITTLE GIRLFRIEND AIN'T HERE TO HELP YOU, NEITHER.

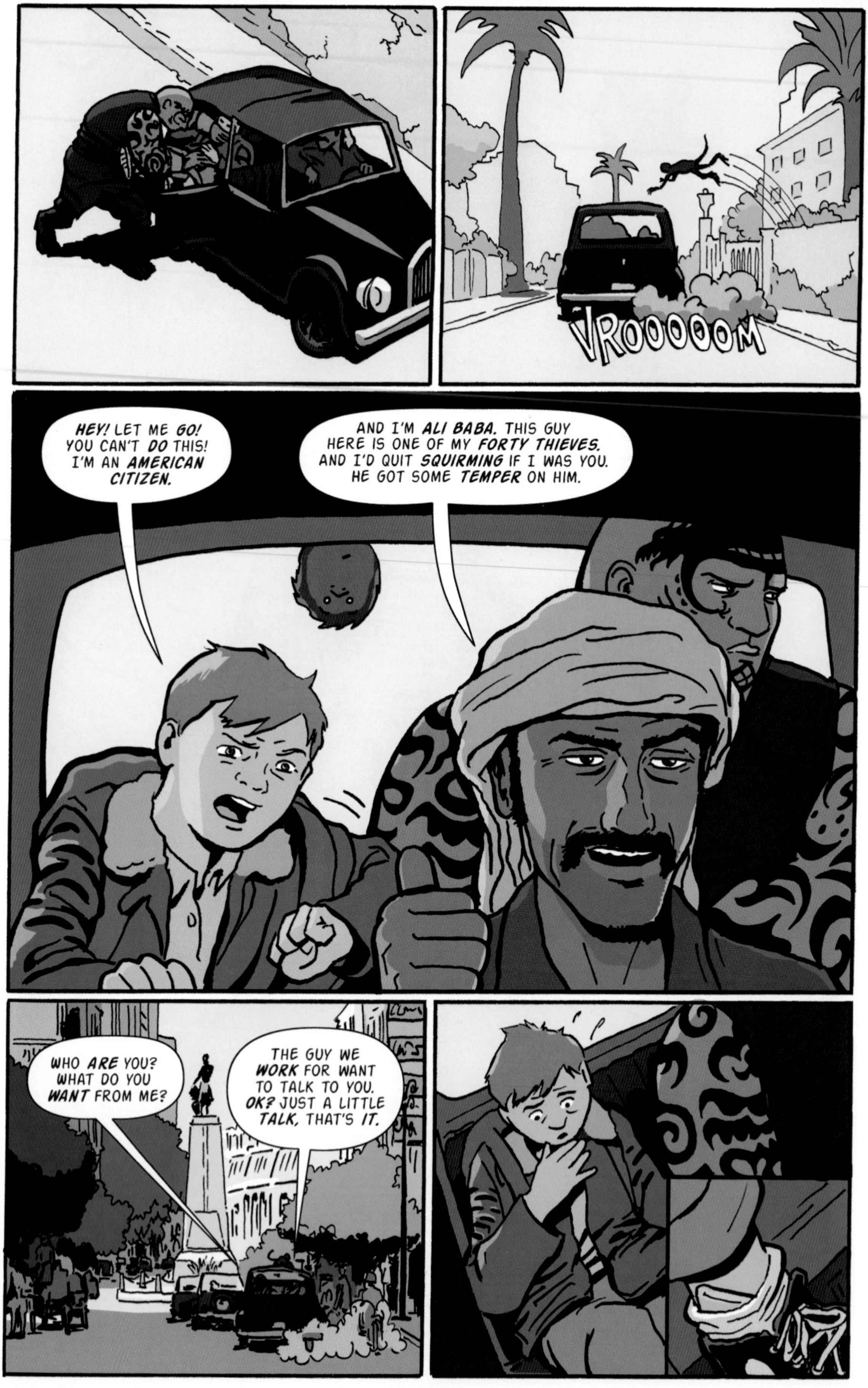
VROOOOOM
HEY! LET ME GO! YOU CAN'T DO THIS! I'M AN AMERICAN CITIZEN.
AND I'M ALI BABA. THIS GUY HERE IS ONE OF MY FORTY THIEVES. AND I'D QUIT SQUIRMING IF I WAS YOU. HE GOT SOME TEMPER ON HIM.
WHO ARE YOU? WHAT DO YOU WANT FROM ME?
THE GUY WE WORK FOR WANT TO TALK TO YOU. OK? JUST A LITTLE TALK, THAT'S IT.

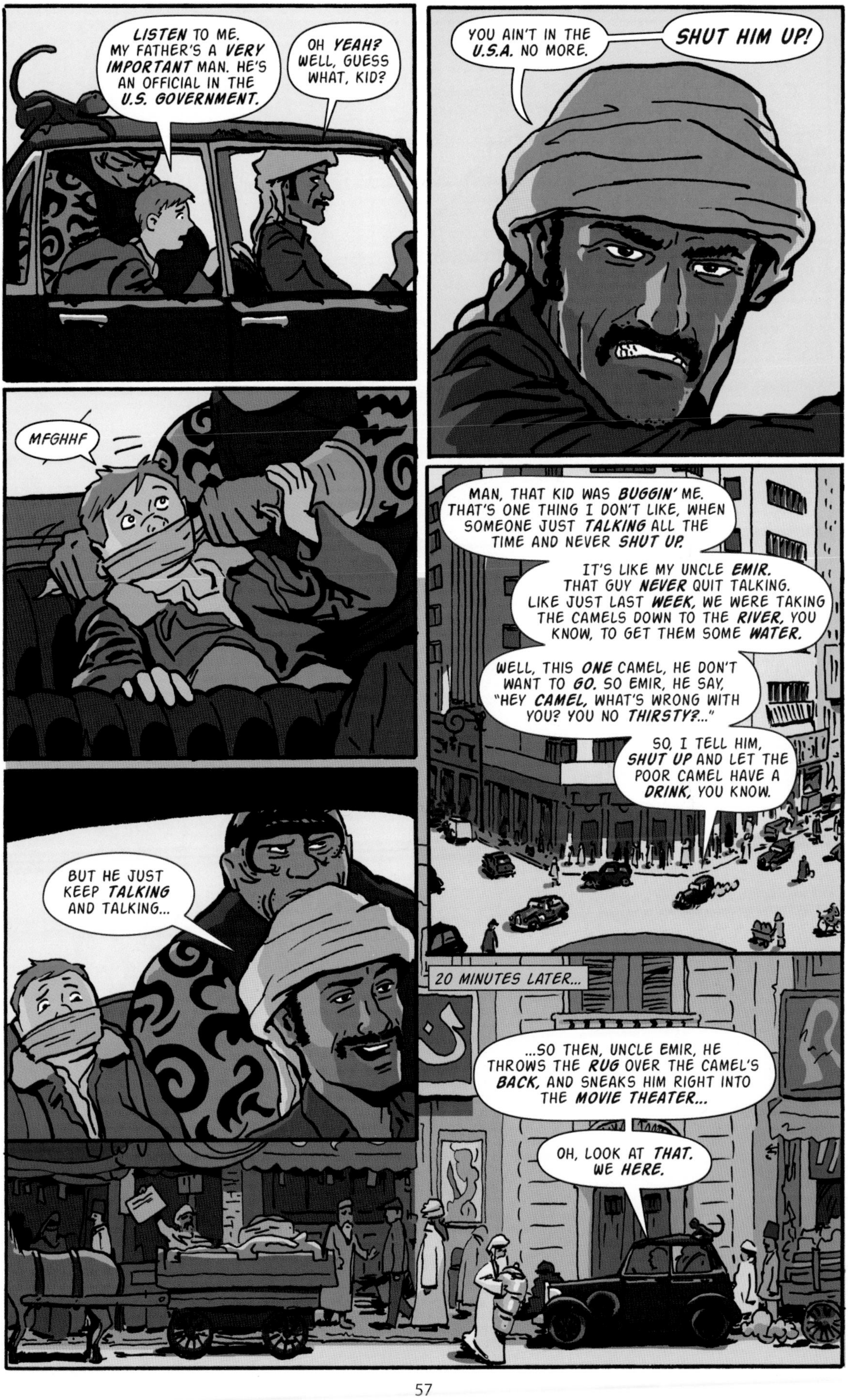
LISTEN TO ME. MY FATHER'S A VERY IMPORTANT MAN. HE'S AN OFFICIAL IN THE U.S. GOVERNMENT.
OH YEAH? WELL, GUESS WHAT, KID?
YOU AIN'T IN THE U.S.A. NO MORE.
SHUT HIM UP!
MFGHHF
MAN, THAT KID WAS BUGGIN' ME. THAT'S ONE THING I DON'T LIKE, WHEN SOMEONE JUST TALKING ALL THE TIME AND NEVER SHUT UP.
IT'S LIKE MY UNCLE EMIR. THAT GUY NEVER QUIT TALKING. LIKE JUST LAST WEEK, WE WERE TAKING THE CAMELS DOWN TO THE RIVER, YOU KNOW, TO GET THEM SOME WATER.
WELL, THIS ONE CAMEL, HE DON'T WANT TO GO. SO EMIR, HE SAY, "HEY CAMEL, WHAT'S WRONG WITH YOU? YOU NO THIRSTY?..."
SO, I TELL HIM, SHUT UP AND LET THE POOR CAMEL HAVE A DRINK, YOU KNOW.
BUT HE JUST KEEP TALKING AND TALKING...
20 MINUTES LATER...
...SO THEN, UNCLE EMIR, HE THROWS THE RUG OVER THE CAMEL'S BACK, AND SNEAKS HIM RIGHT INTO THE MOVIE THEATER...
OH, LOOK AT THAT. WE HERE.

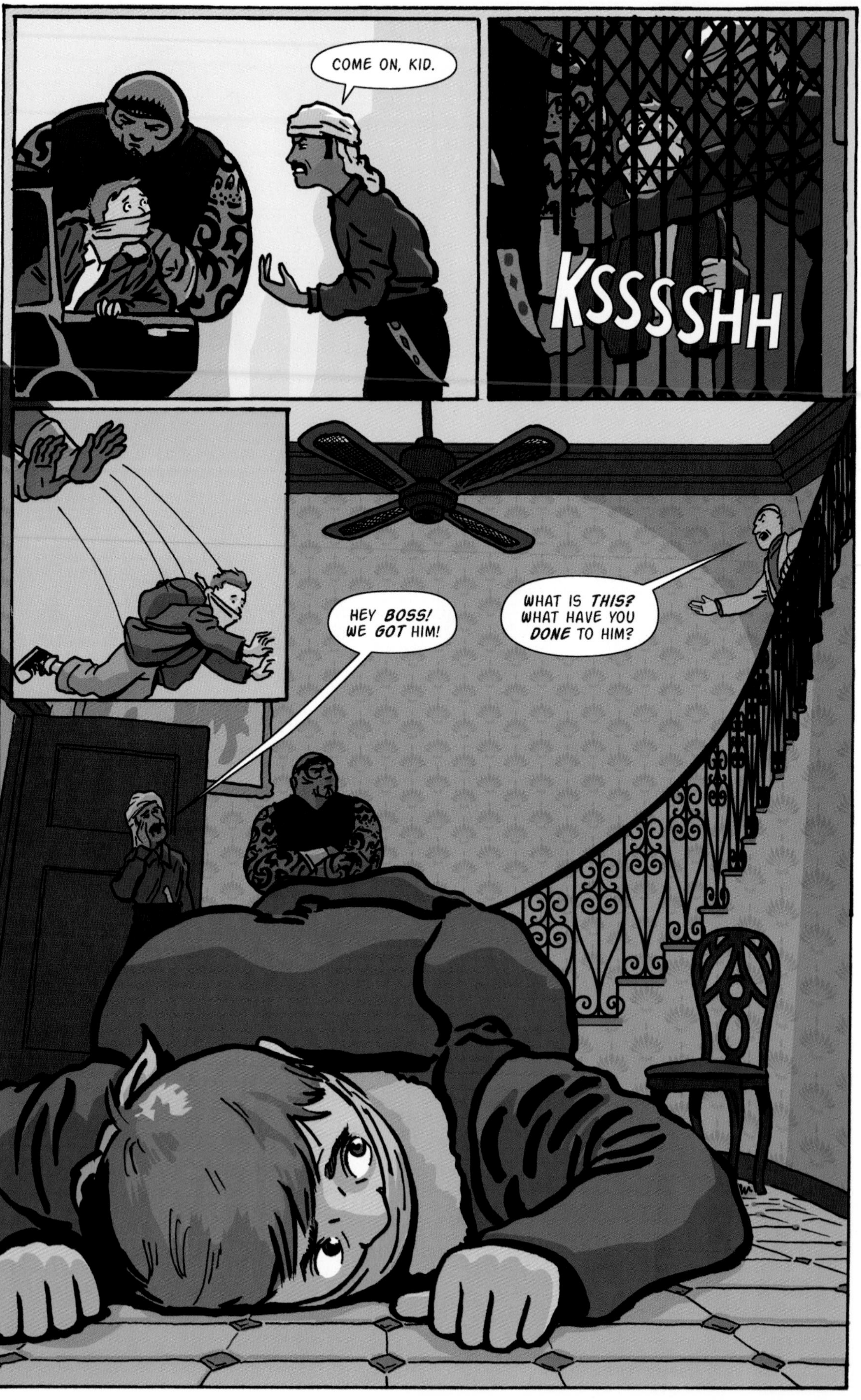
COME ON, KID.
KSSSSHH
HEY BOSS! WE GOT HIM!
WHAT IS THIS? WHAT HAVE YOU DONE TO HIM?

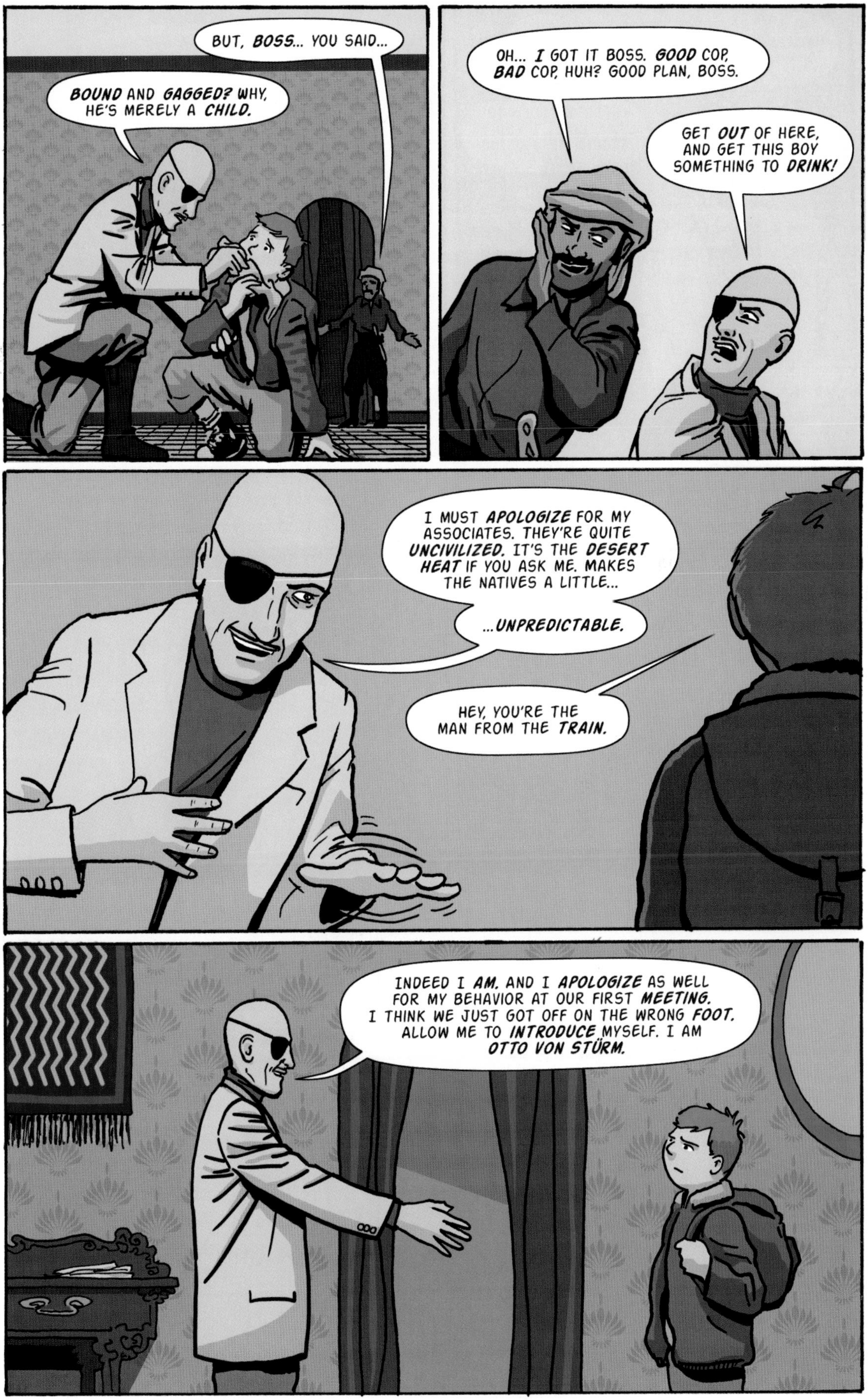
BUT, BOSS... YOU SAID...
BOUND AND GAGGED? WHY, HE'S MERELY A CHILD.
OH... I GOT IT BOSS. GOOD COP, BAD COP, HUH? GOOD PLAN, BOSS.
GET OUT OF HERE, AND GET THIS BOY SOMETHING TO DRINK!
I MUST APOLOGIZE FOR MY ASSOCIATES. THEY'RE QUITE UNCIVILIZED. IT'S THE DESERT HEAT IF YOU ASK ME. MAKES THE NATIVES A LITTLE...
...UNPREDICTABLE.
HEY, YOU'RE THE MAN FROM THE TRAIN.
INDEED I AM. AND I APOLOGIZE AS WELL FOR MY BEHAVIOR AT OUR FIRST MEETING. I THINK WE JUST GOT OFF ON THE WRONG FOOT. ALLOW ME TO INTRODUCE MYSELF. I AM OTTO VON STÜRM.

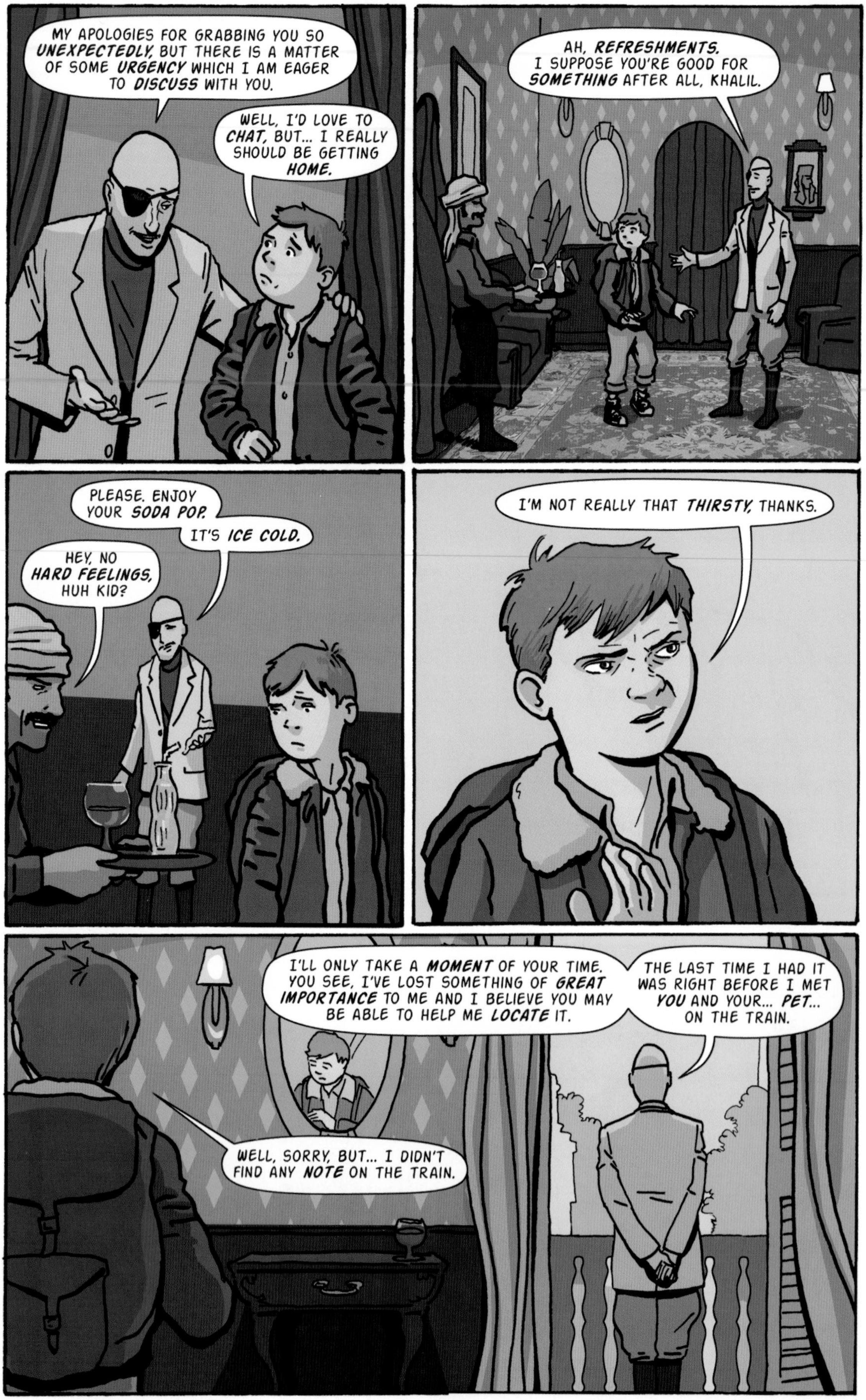
MY APOLOGIES FOR GRABBING YOU SO UNEXPECTEDLY, BUT THERE IS A MATTER OF SOME URGENCY WHICH I AM EAGER TO DISCUSS WITH YOU.
WELL, I'D LOVE TO CHAT, BUT... I REALLY SHOULD BE GETTING HOME.
AH, REFRESHMENTS. I SUPPOSE YOU'RE GOOD FOR SOMETHING AFTER ALL, KHALIL.
PLEASE. ENJOY YOUR SODA POP.
IT'S ICE COLD.
HEY, NO HARD FEELINGS, HUH KID?
I'M NOT REALLY THAT THIRSTY, THANKS.
I'LL ONLY TAKE A MOMENT OF YOUR TIME. YOU SEE, I'VE LOST SOMETHING OF GREAT IMPORTANCE TO ME AND I BELIEVE YOU MAY BE ABLE TO HELP ME LOCATE IT.
THE LAST TIME I HAD IT WAS RIGHT BEFORE I MET YOU AND YOUR... PET... ON THE TRAIN.
WELL, SORRY, BUT... I DIDN'T FIND ANY NOTE ON THE TRAIN.

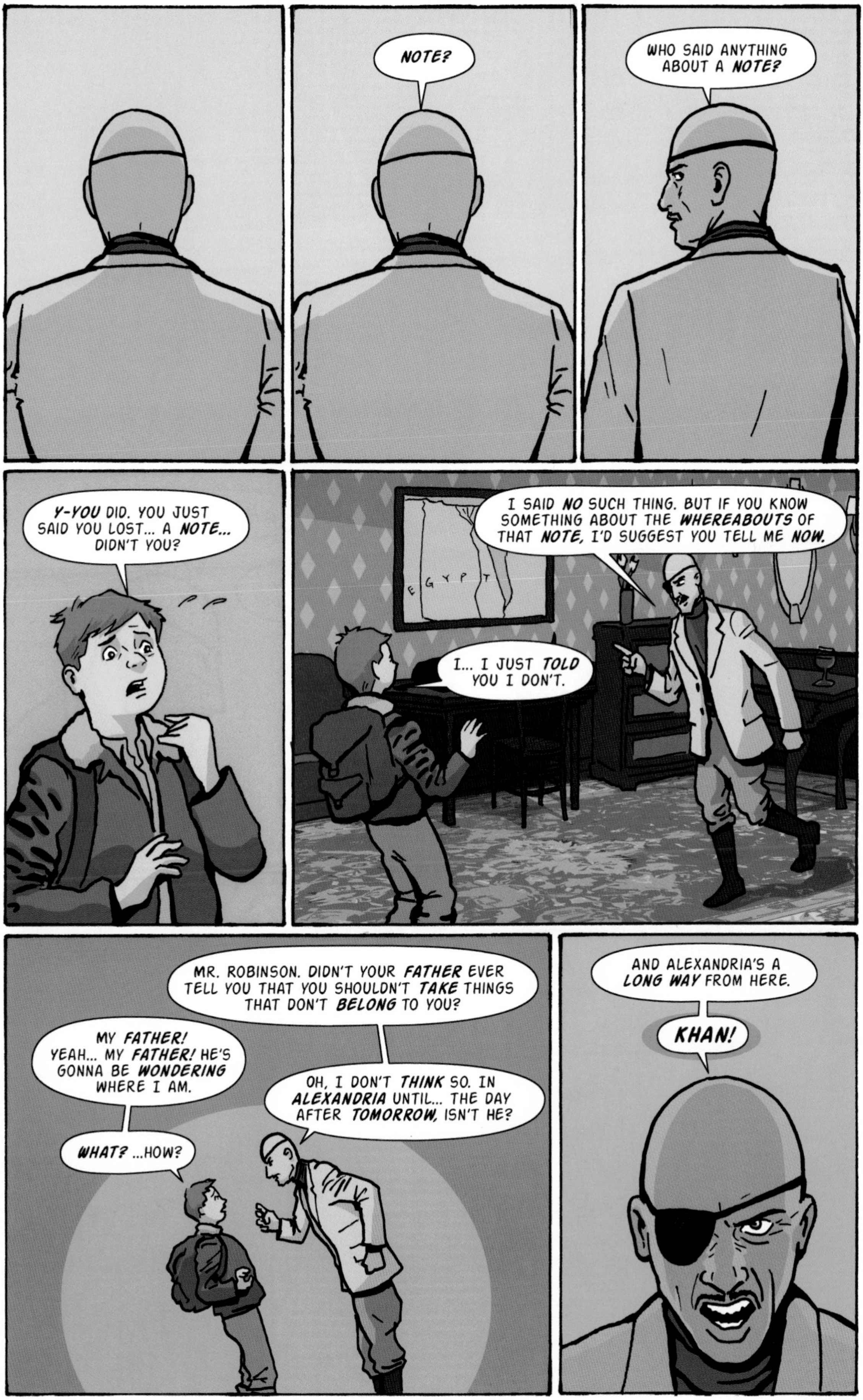
NOTE?
WHO SAID ANYTHING ABOUT A NOTE?
Y-YOU DID. YOU JUST SAID YOU LOST... A NOTE... DIDN'T YOU?
EGYPT
I SAID NO SUCH THING. BUT IF YOU KNOW SOMETHING ABOUT THE WHEREABOUTS OF THAT NOTE, I'D SUGGEST YOU TELL ME NOW.
I... I JUST TOLD YOU I DON'T.
MR. ROBINSON. DIDN'T YOUR FATHER EVER TELL YOU THAT YOU SHOULDN'T TAKE THINGS THAT DON'T BELONG TO YOU?
MY FATHER! YEAH... MY FATHER! HE'S GONNA BE WONDERING WHERE I AM.
OH, I DON'T THINK SO. IN ALEXANDRIA UNTIL... THE DAY AFTER TOMORROW, ISN'T HE?
WHAT? ...HOW?
AND ALEXANDRIA'S A LONG WAY FROM HERE.
KHAN!

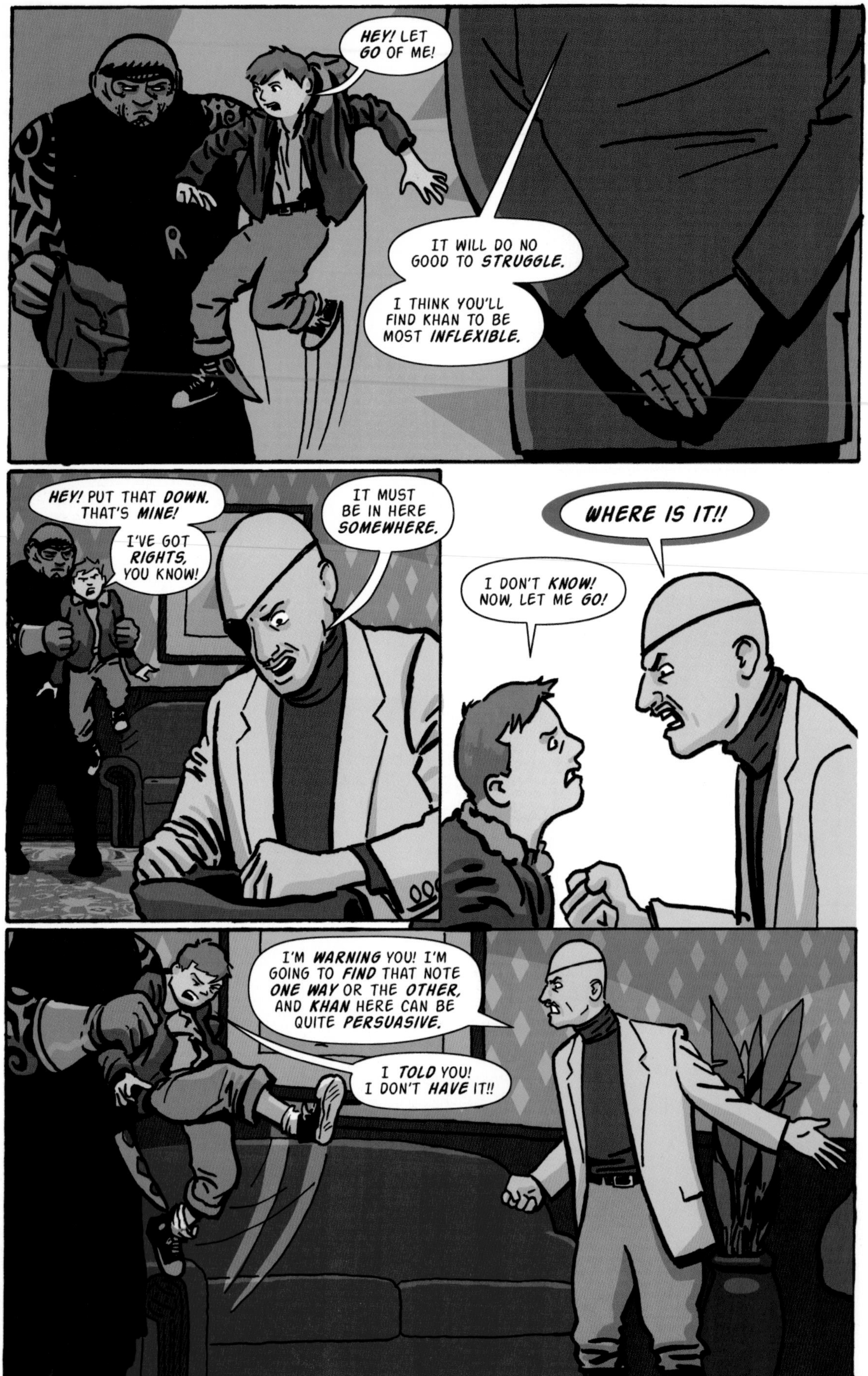
HEY! LET GO OF ME!
IT WILL DO NO GOOD TO STRUGGLE.
I THINK YOU'LL FIND KHAN TO BE MOST INFLEXIBLE.
HEY! PUT THAT DOWN. THAT'S MINE!
I'VE GOT RIGHTS, YOU KNOW!
IT MUST BE IN HERE SOMEWHERE.
WHERE IS IT!!
I DON'T KNOW! NOW, LET ME GO!
I'M WARNING YOU! I'M GOING TO FIND THAT NOTE ONE WAY OR THE OTHER, AND KHAN HERE CAN BE QUITE PERSUASIVE.
I TOLD YOU! I DON'T HAVE IT!!

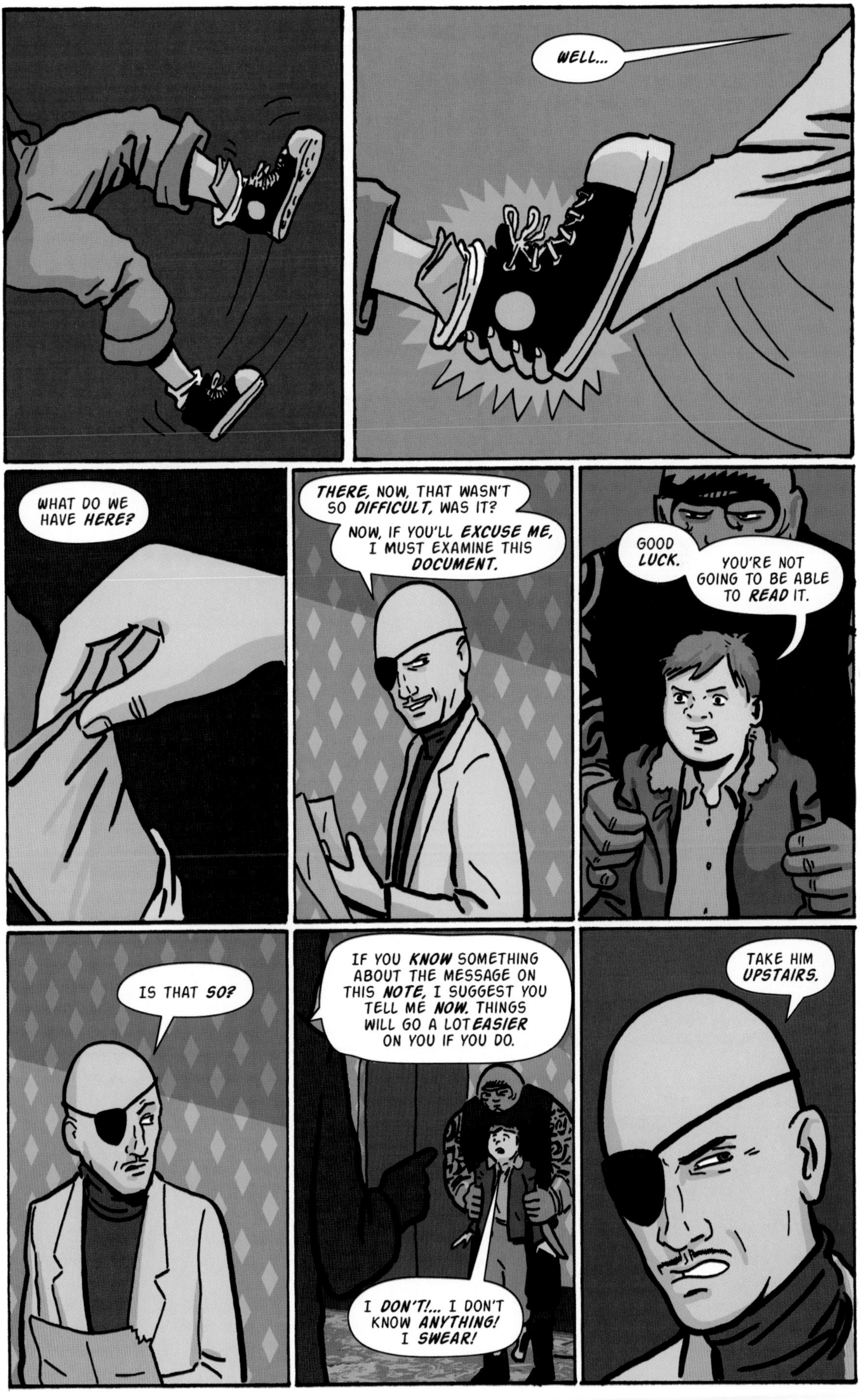
WELL...
WHAT DO WE HAVE HERE?
THERE, NOW, THAT WASN'T SO DIFFICULT, WAS IT?
NOW, IF YOU'LL EXCUSE ME, I MUST EXAMINE THIS DOCUMENT.
GOOD LUCK.
YOU'RE NOT GOING TO BE ABLE TO READ IT.
IS THAT SO?
IF YOU KNOW SOMETHING ABOUT THE MESSAGE ON THIS NOTE, I SUGGEST YOU TELL ME NOW. THINGS WILL GO A LOT EASIER ON YOU IF YOU DO.
I DON'T!... I DON'T KNOW ANYTHING! I SWEAR!
TAKE HIM UPSTAIRS.

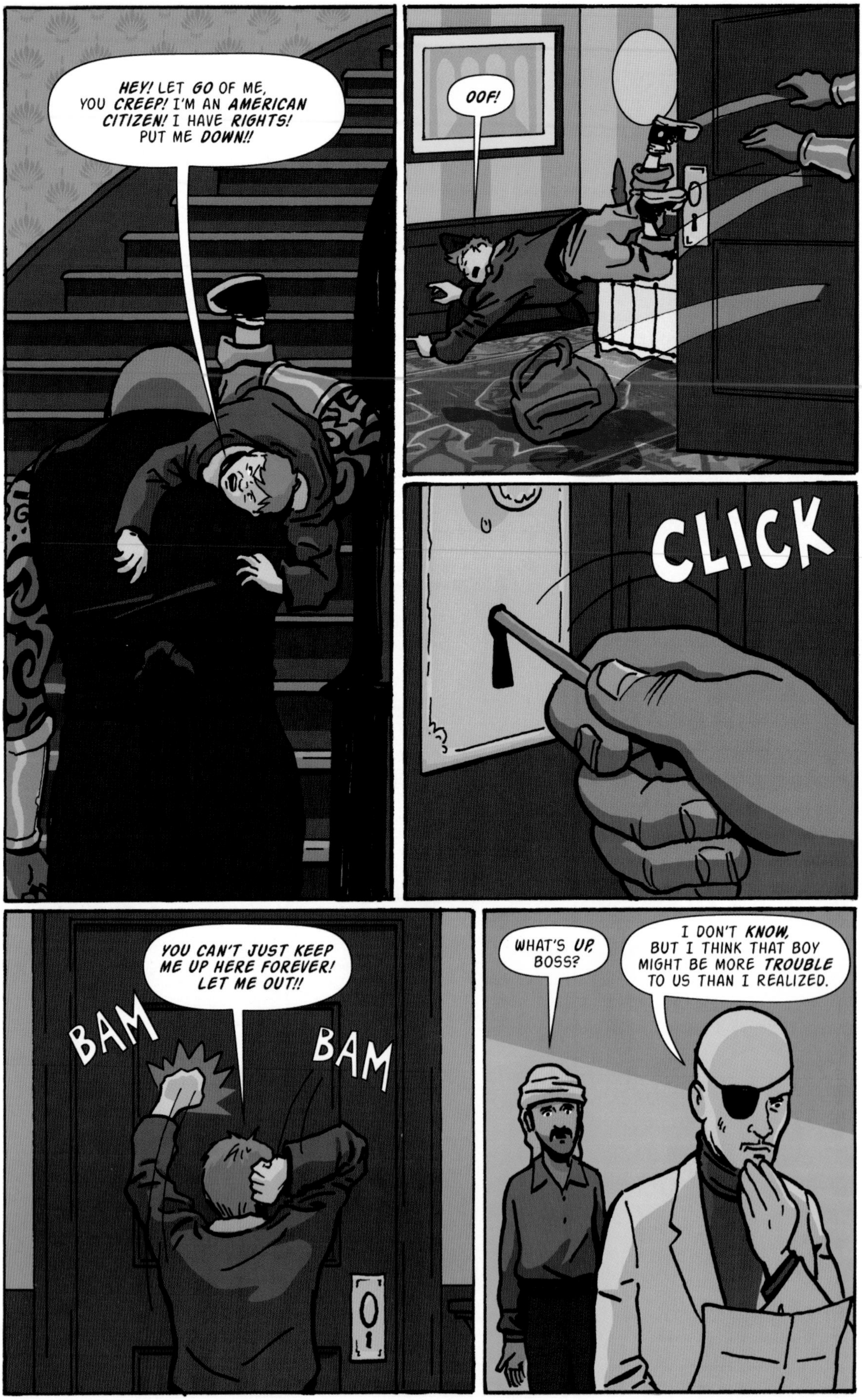
HEY! LET GO OF ME, YOU CREEP! I'M AN AMERICAN CITIZEN! I HAVE RIGHTS! PUT ME DOWN!!
OOF!
CLICK
YOU CAN'T JUST KEEP ME UP HERE FOREVER! LET ME OUT!!
BAM
BAM
WHAT'S UP, BOSS?
I DON'T KNOW, BUT I THINK THAT BOY MIGHT BE MORE TROUBLE TO US THAN I REALIZED.

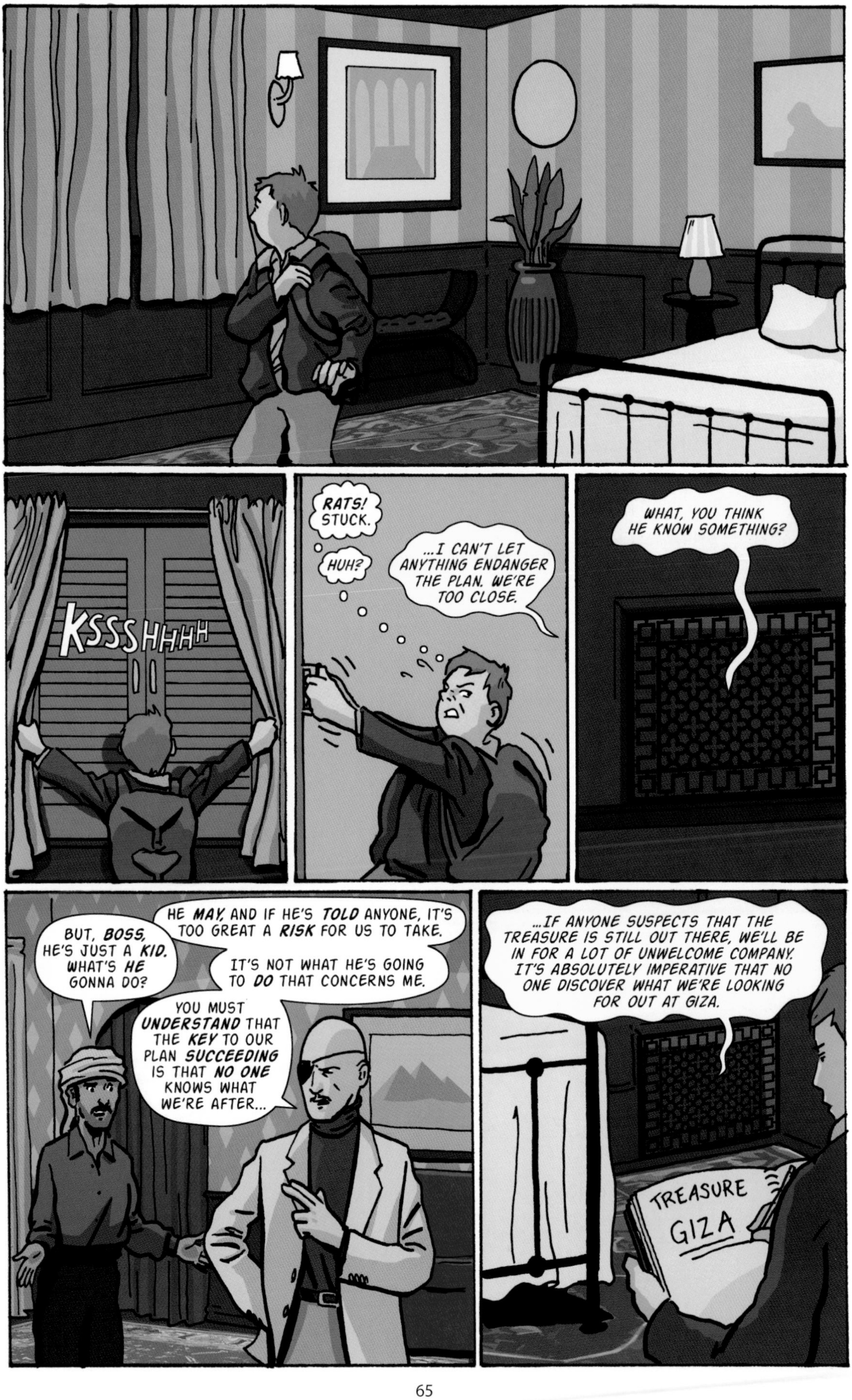
KSSSHHHH
RATS! STUCK.
HUH?
...I CAN'T LET ANYTHING ENDANGER THE PLAN. WE'RE TOO CLOSE.
WHAT, YOU THINK HE KNOW SOMETHING?
BUT, BOSS, HE'S JUST A KID. WHAT'S HE GONNA DO?
HE MAY, AND IF HE'S TOLD ANYONE, IT'S TOO GREAT A RISK FOR US TO TAKE.
IT'S NOT WHAT HE'S GOING TO DO THAT CONCERNS ME.
YOU MUST UNDERSTAND THAT THE KEY TO OUR PLAN SUCCEEDING IS THAT NO ONE KNOWS WHAT WE'RE AFTER...
...IF ANYONE SUSPECTS THAT THE TREASURE IS STILL OUT THERE, WE'LL BE IN FOR A LOT OF UNWELCOME COMPANY. IT'S ABSOLUTELY IMPERATIVE THAT NO ONE DISCOVER WHAT WE'RE LOOKING FOR OUT AT GIZA.
TREASURE
GIZA

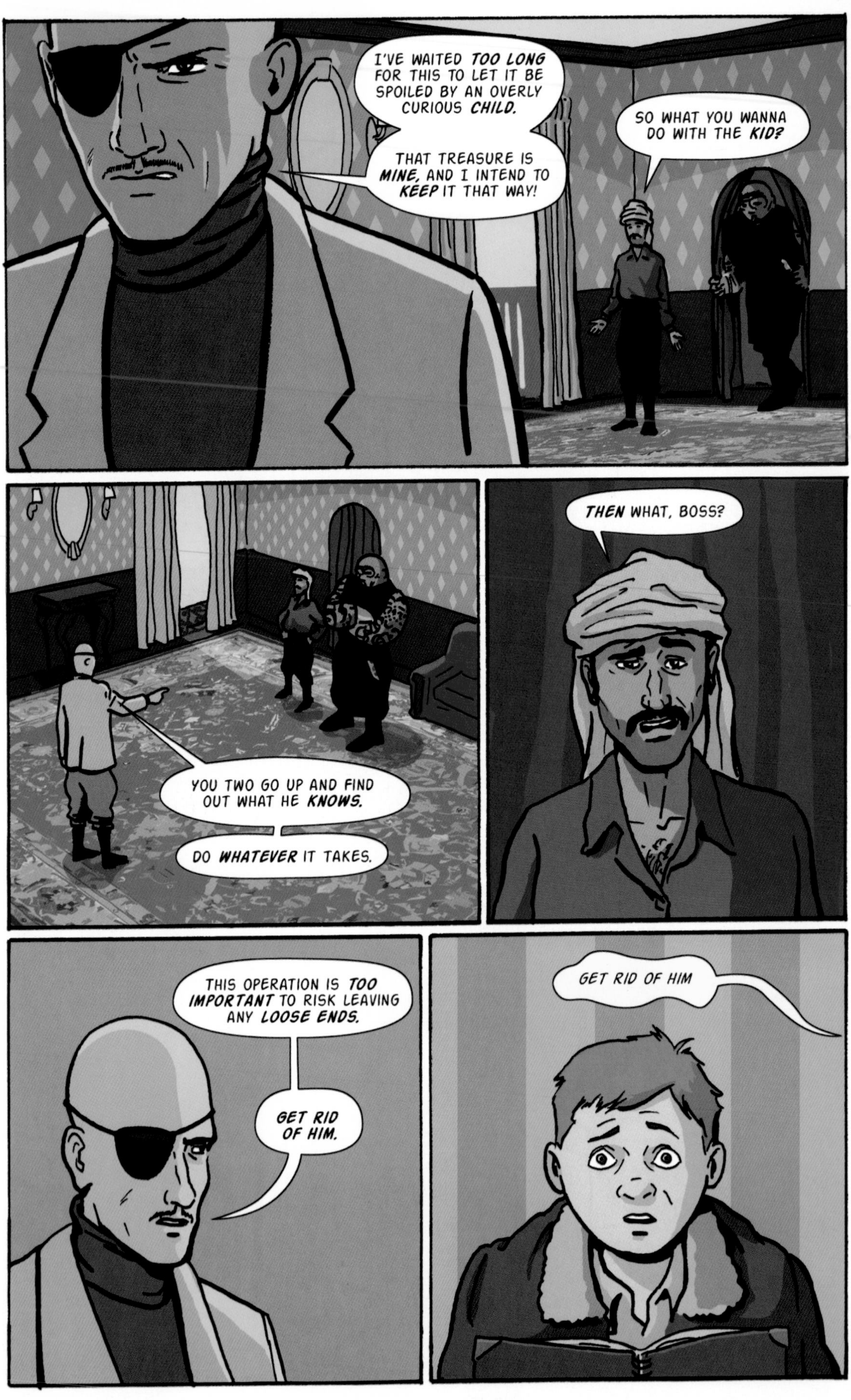
I'VE WAITED TOO LONG FOR THIS TO LET IT BE SPOILED BY AN OVERLY CURIOUS CHILD.
THAT TREASURE IS MINE, AND I INTEND TO KEEP IT THAT WAY!
SO WHAT YOU WANNA DO WITH THE KID?
YOU TWO GO UP AND FIND OUT WHAT HE KNOWS.
DO WHATEVER IT TAKES.
THEN WHAT, BOSS?
THIS OPERATION IS TOO IMPORTANT TO RISK LEAVING ANY LOOSE ENDS.
GET RID OF HIM.
GET RID OF HIM

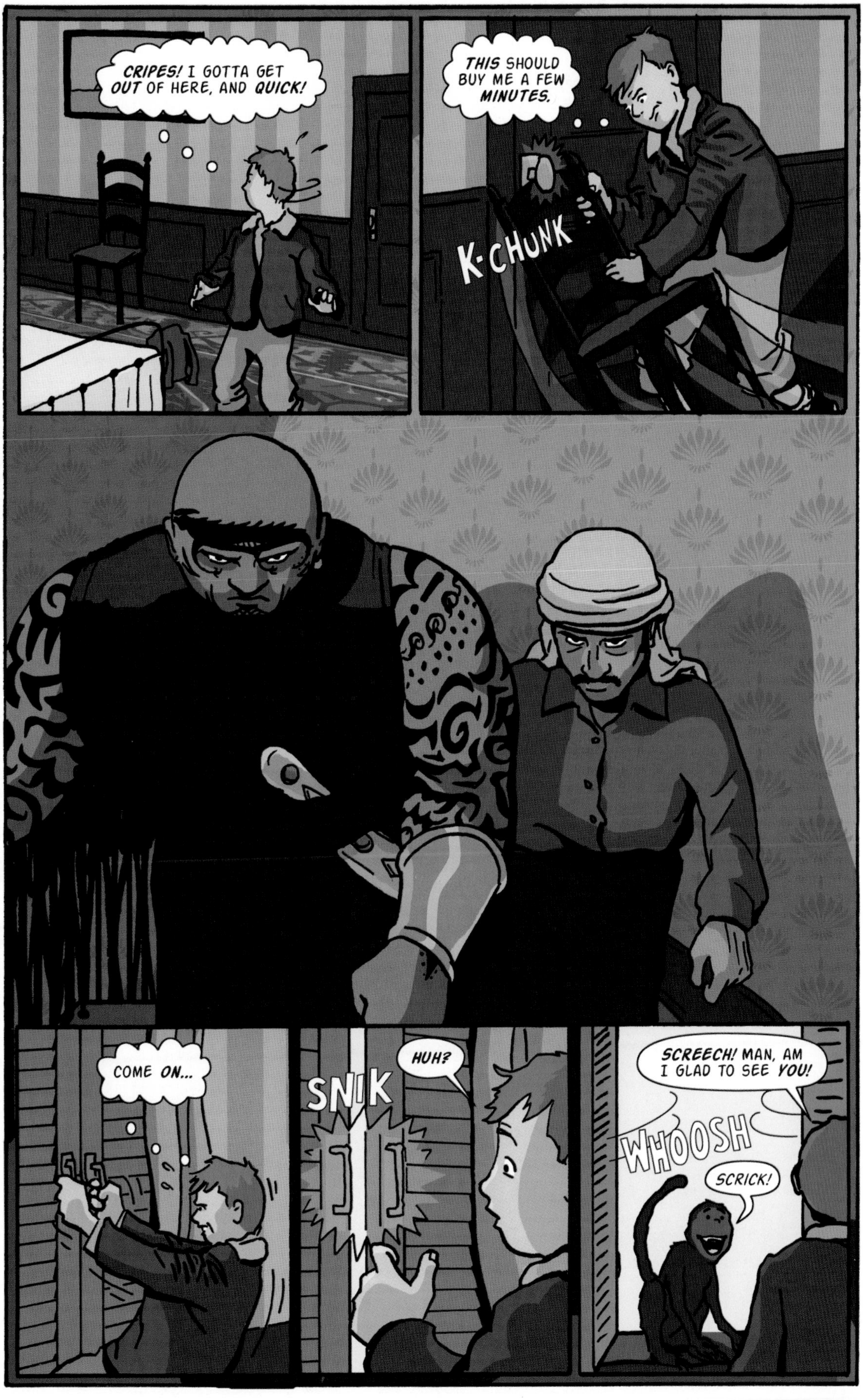
CRIPES! I GOTTA GET OUT OF HERE, AND QUICK!
THIS SHOULD BUY ME A FEW MINUTES.
K-CHUNK
COME ON...
SNIK
HUH?
SCREECH! MAN, AM I GLAD TO SEE YOU!
WHOOSH
SCRICK!

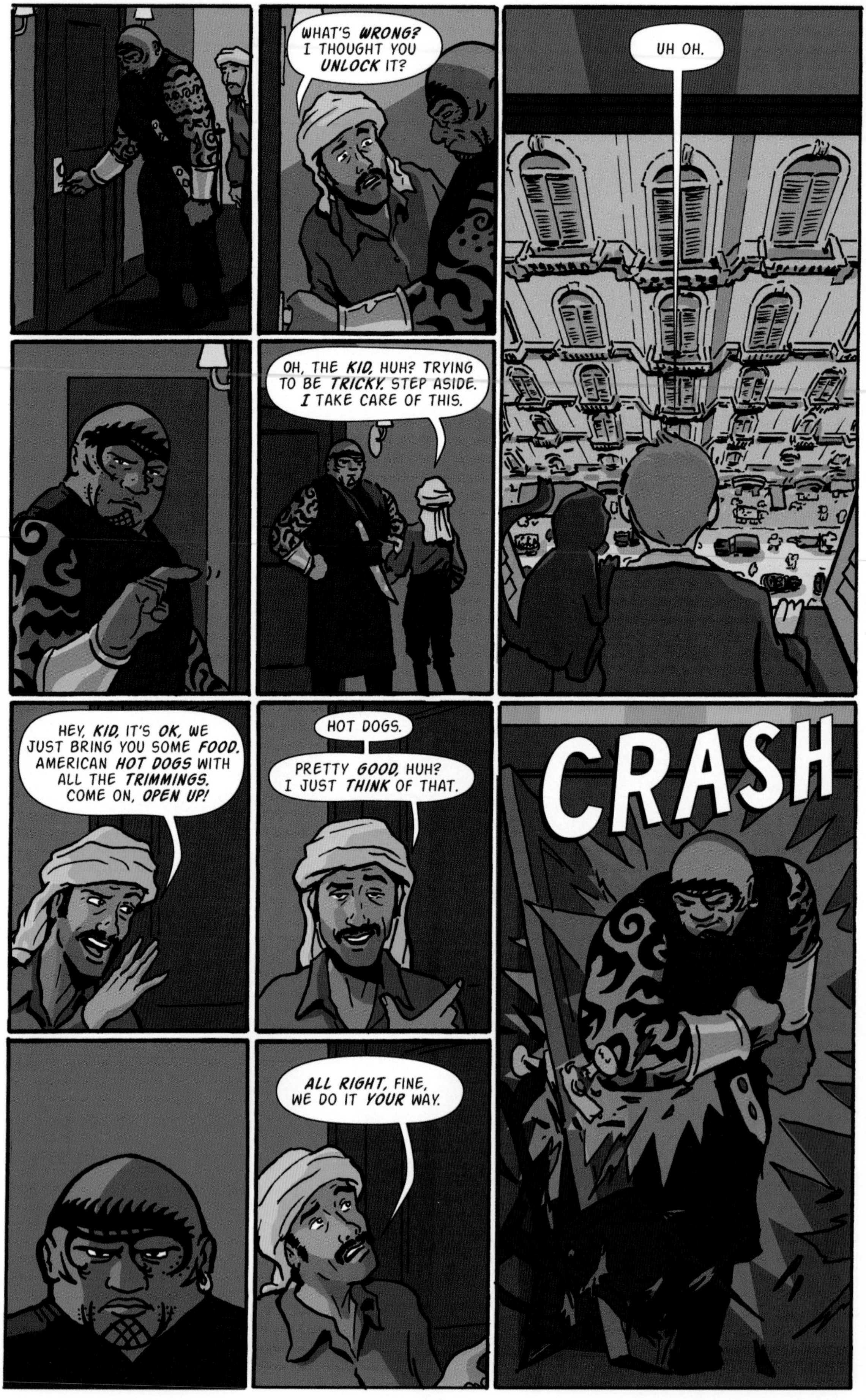
WHAT'S WRONG? I THOUGHT YOU UNLOCK IT?
UH OH.
OH, THE KID, HUH? TRYING TO BE TRICKY. STEP ASIDE. I TAKE CARE OF THIS.
HEY, KID, IT'S OK, WE JUST BRING YOU SOME FOOD. AMERICAN HOT DOGS WITH ALL THE TRIMMINGS. COME ON, OPEN UP!
HOT DOGS.
PRETTY GOOD, HUH? I JUST THINK OF THAT.
CRASH
ALL RIGHT, FINE, WE DO IT YOUR WAY.

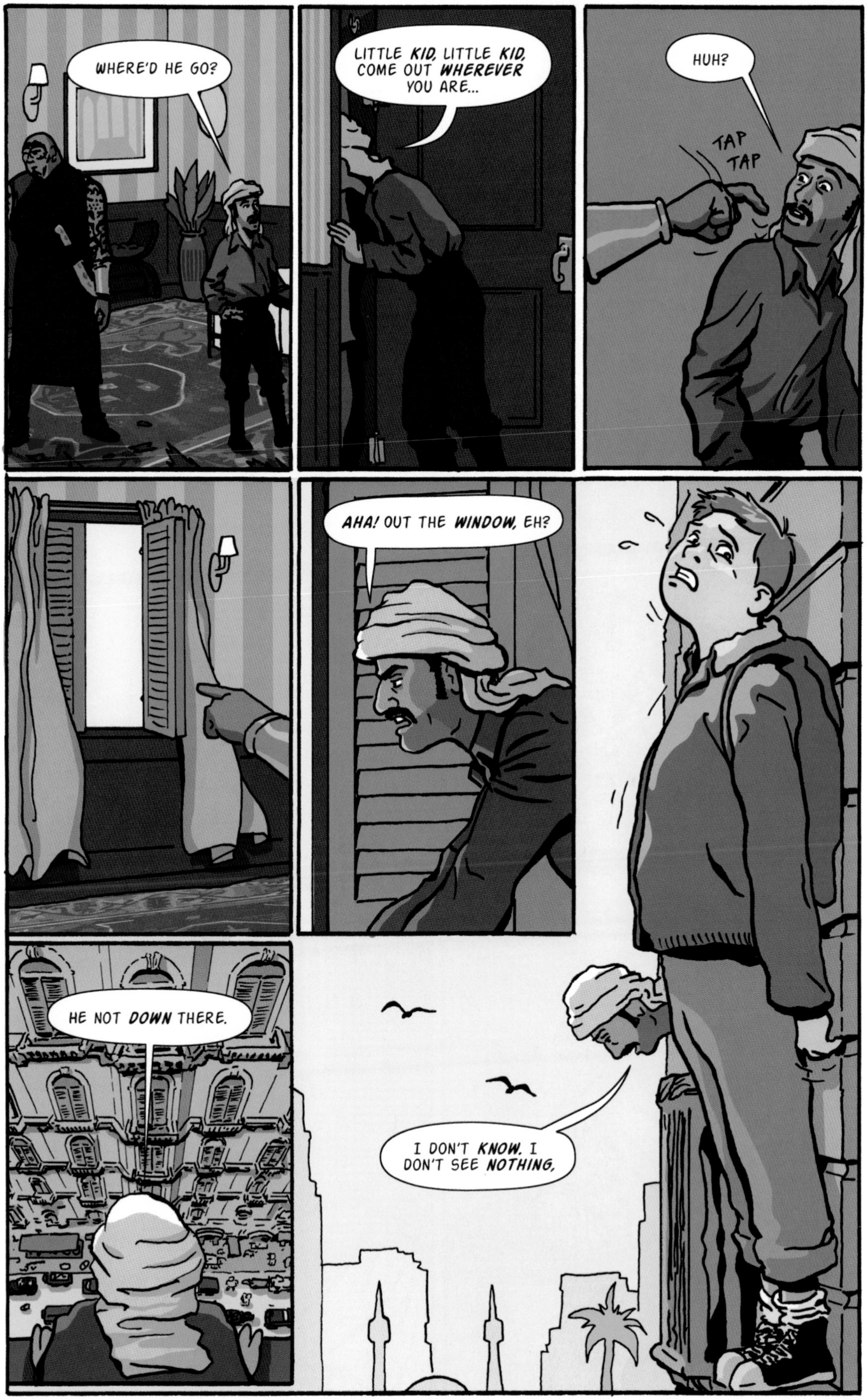

WHERE'D HE GO?
LITTLE KID, LITTLE KID, COME OUT WHEREVER YOU ARE...
HUH?
TAP TAP
AHA! OUT THE WINDOW, EH?
HE NOT DOWN THERE.
I DON'T KNOW. I DON'T SEE NOTHING,

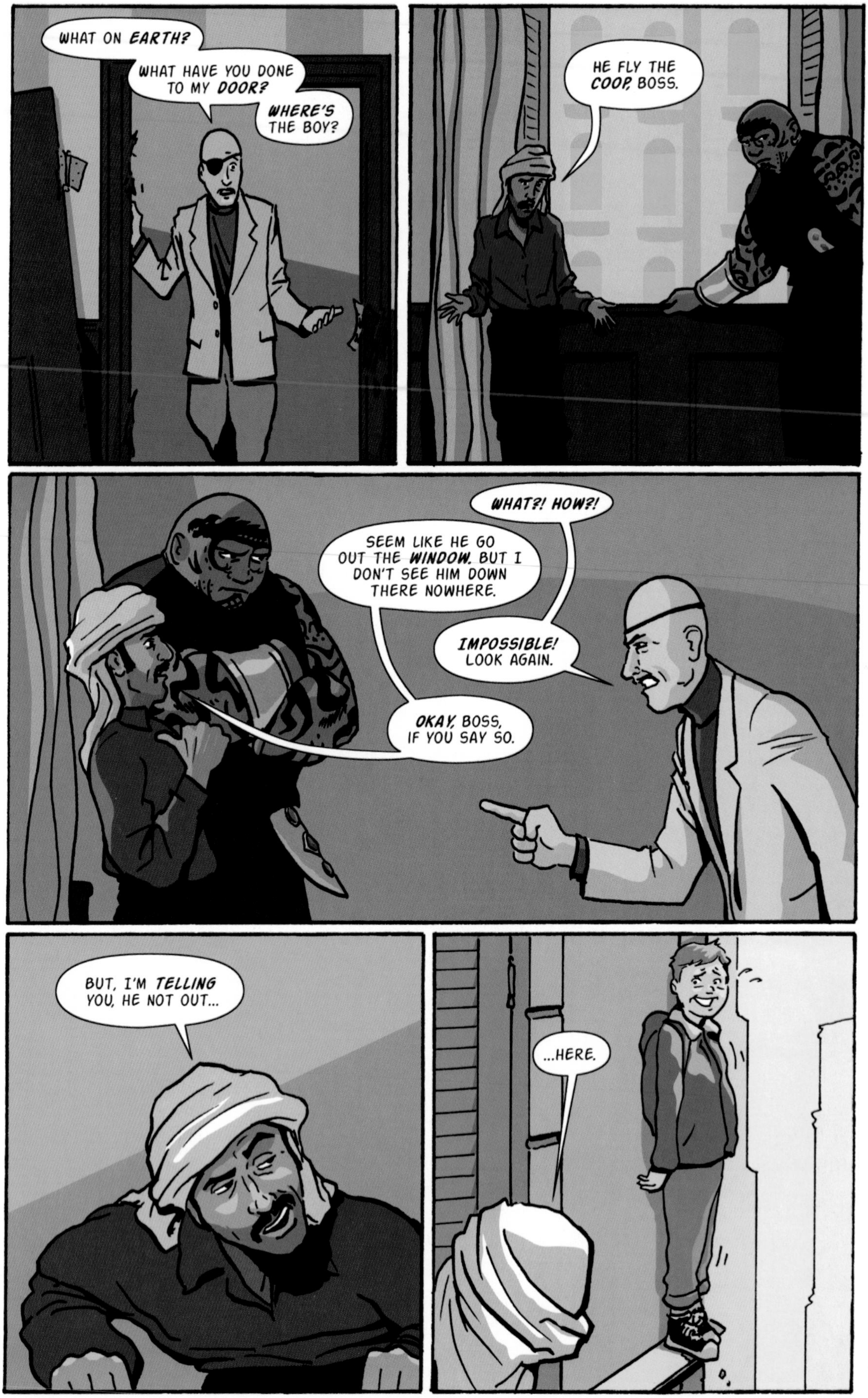
WHAT ON EARTH?
WHAT HAVE YOU DONE TO MY DOOR?
WHERE'S THE BOY?
HE FLY THE COOP, BOSS.
SEEM LIKE HE GO OUT THE WINDOW. BUT I DON'T SEE HIM DOWN THERE NOWHERE.
WHAT?! HOW?!
IMPOSSIBLE! LOOK AGAIN.
OKAY, BOSS, IF YOU SAY SO.
BUT, I'M TELLING YOU, HE NOT OUT...
...HERE.

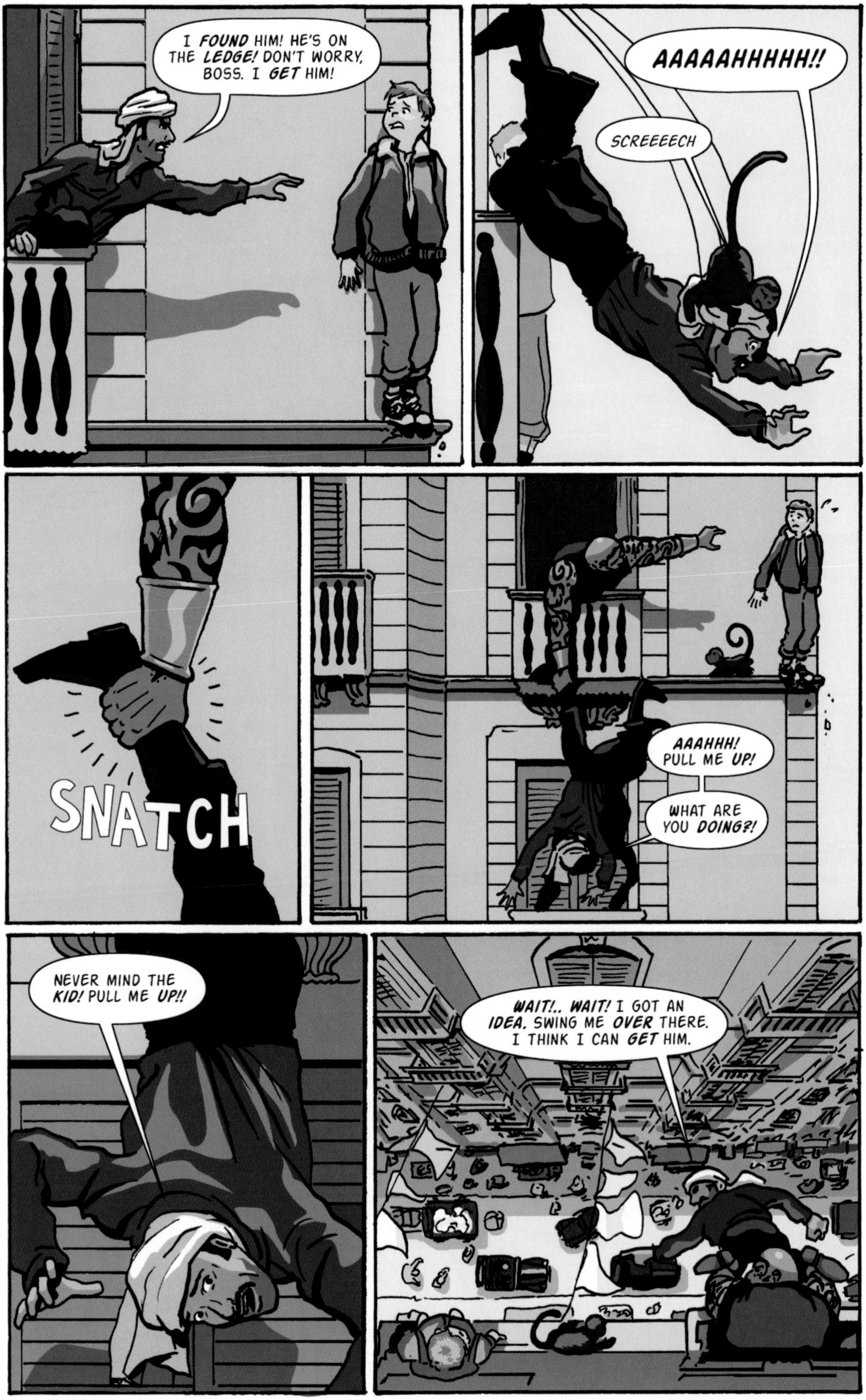
I FOUND HIM! HE'S ON THE LEDGE! DON'T WORRY, BOSS. I GET HIM!
AAAAAHHHHH!!
SCREEEECH
SNATCH
AAAHHH! PULL ME UP!
WHAT ARE YOU DOING?!
NEVER MIND THE KID! PULL ME UP!!
WAIT!.. WAIT! I GOT AN IDEA. SWING ME OVER THERE. I THINK I CAN GET HIM.

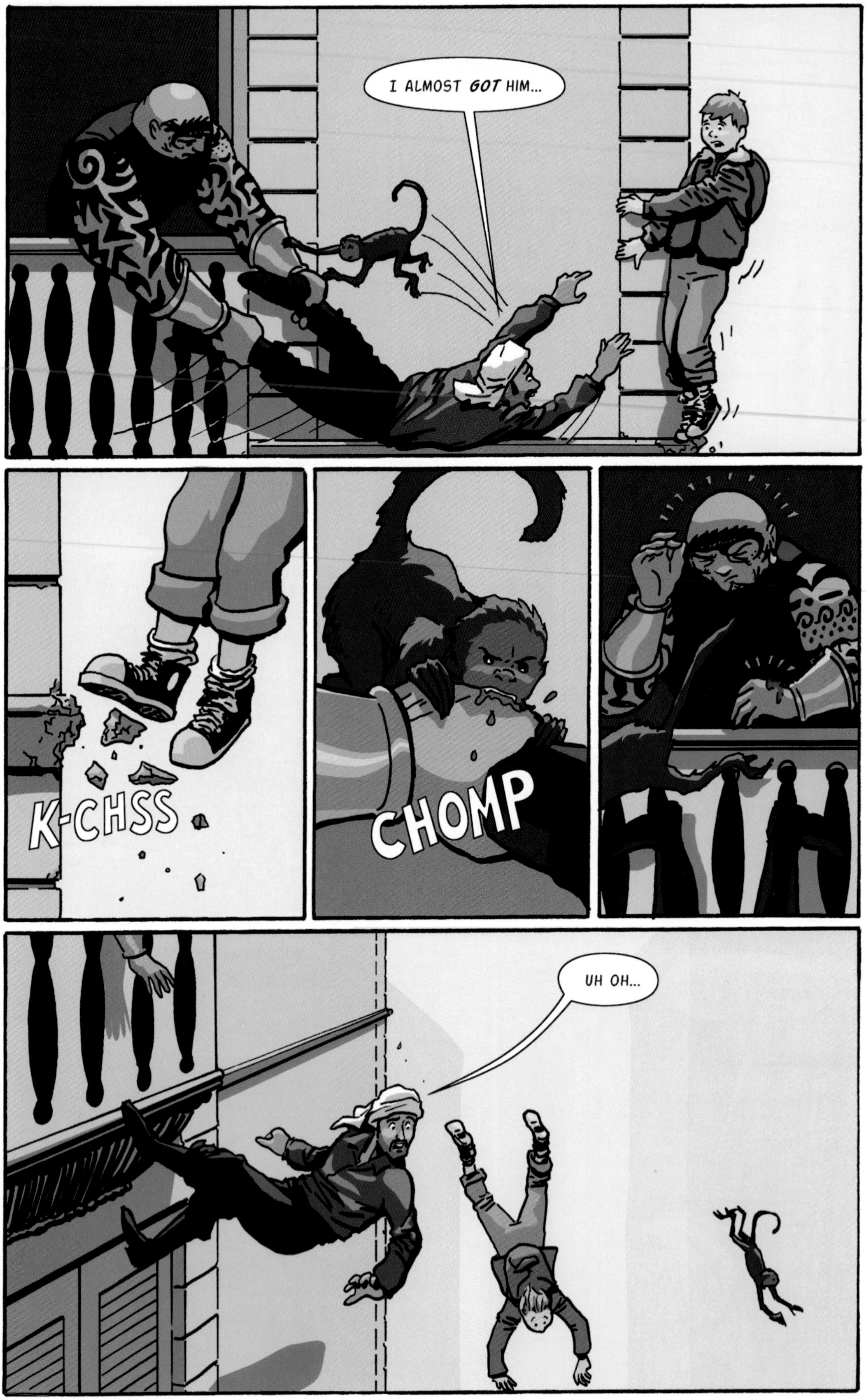
I ALMOST *GOT* HIM...
K-CHSS
CHOMP
UH OH...

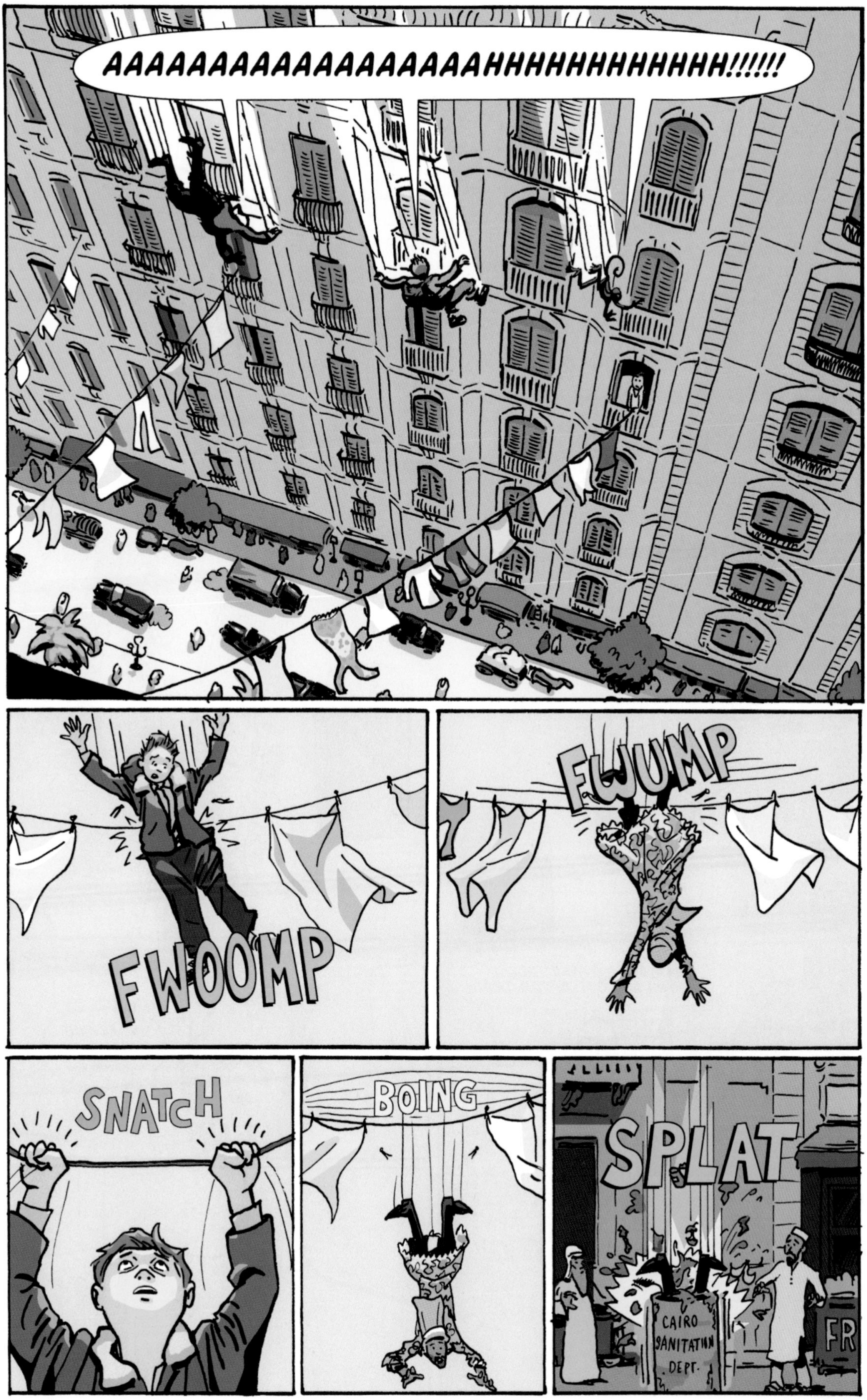
AAAAAAAAAAAAAAAAAAAHHHHHHHHHHHH!!!!!!
FWOOMP
FWUMP
SNATCH
BOING
SPLAT
CAIRO SANITATION DEPT.
FR

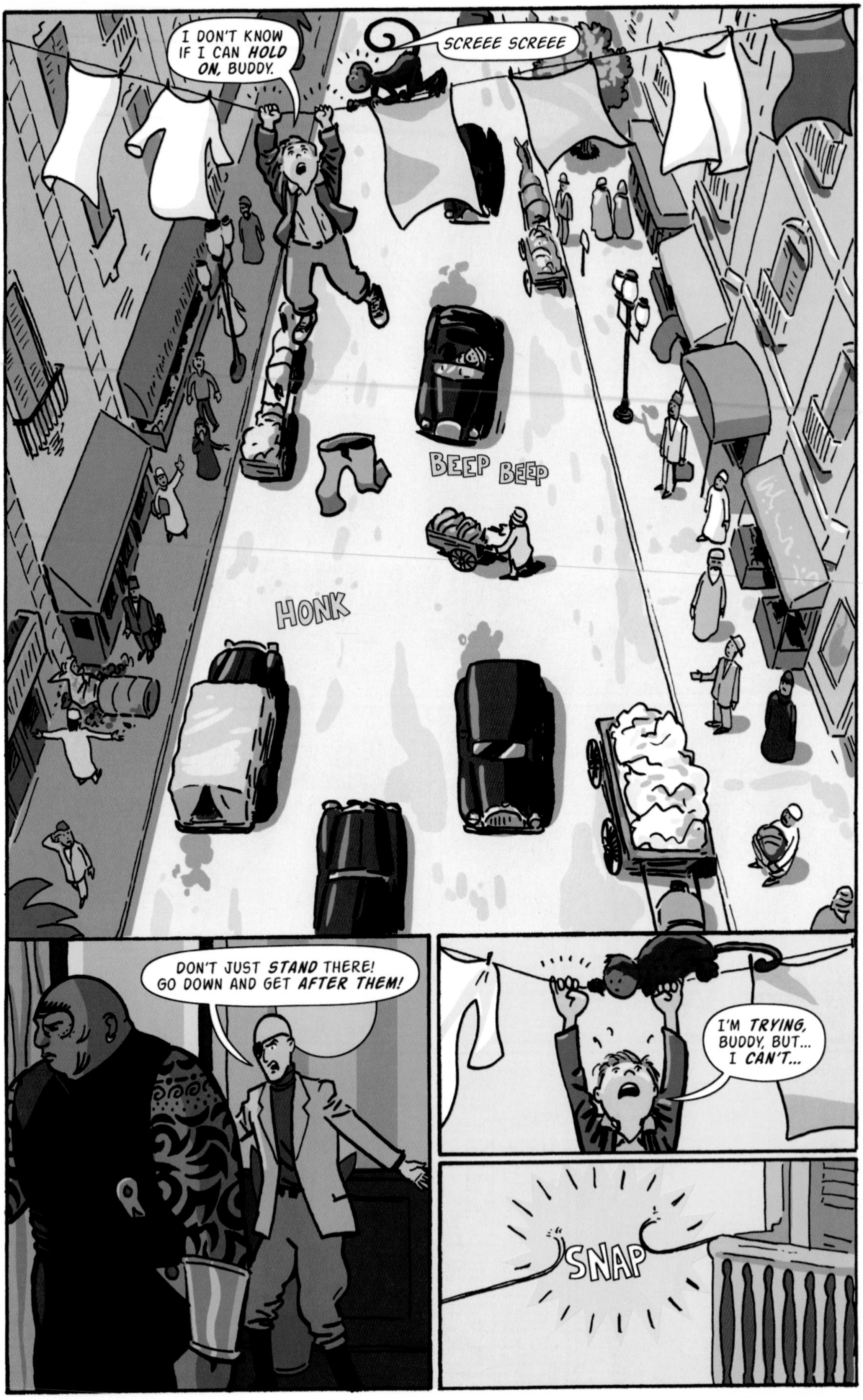
I DON'T KNOW IF I CAN HOLD ON, BUDDY.
SCREEE SCREEE
BEEP BEEP
HONK
DON'T JUST STAND THERE! GO DOWN AND GET AFTER THEM!
I'M TRYING, BUDDY, BUT... I CAN'T...
SNAP

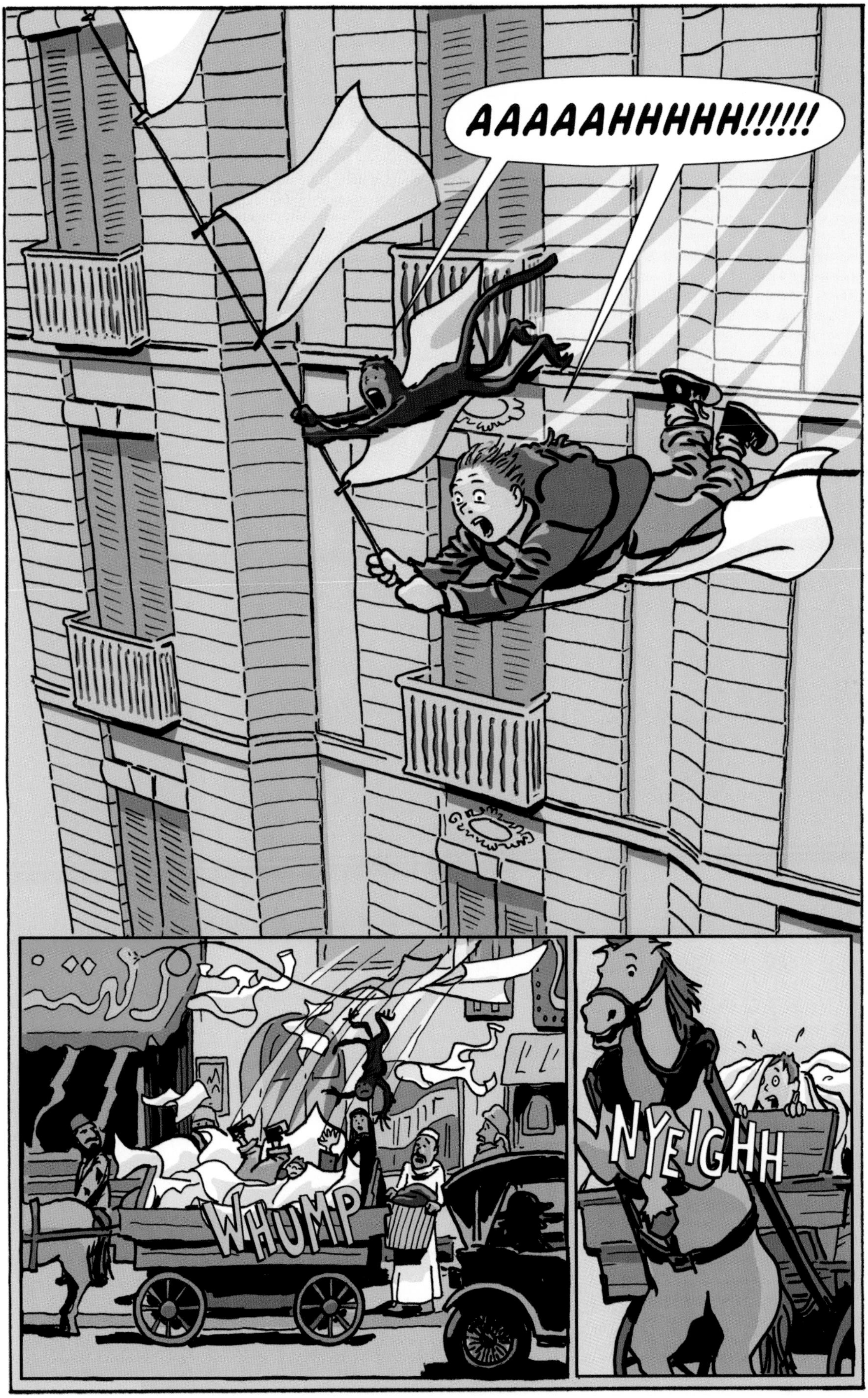
AAAAAHHHHH!!!!!!
WHUMP
NYEIGHH

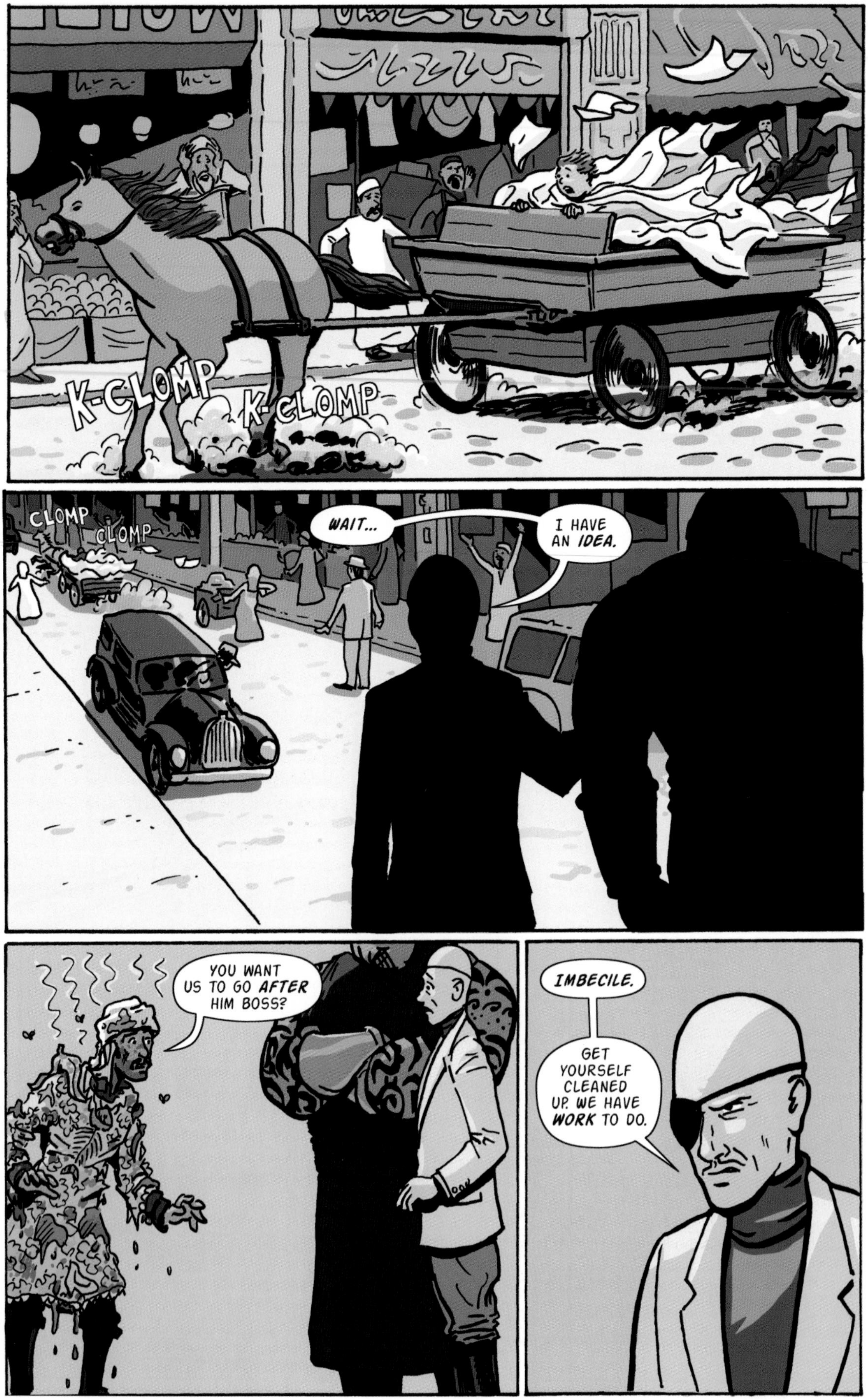
K-CLOMP
K-CLOMP
CLOMP
CLOMP
WAIT...
I HAVE AN IDEA.
YOU WANT US TO GO AFTER HIM BOSS?
IMBECILE.
GET YOURSELF CLEANED UP. WE HAVE WORK TO DO.

CHAPTER FOUR

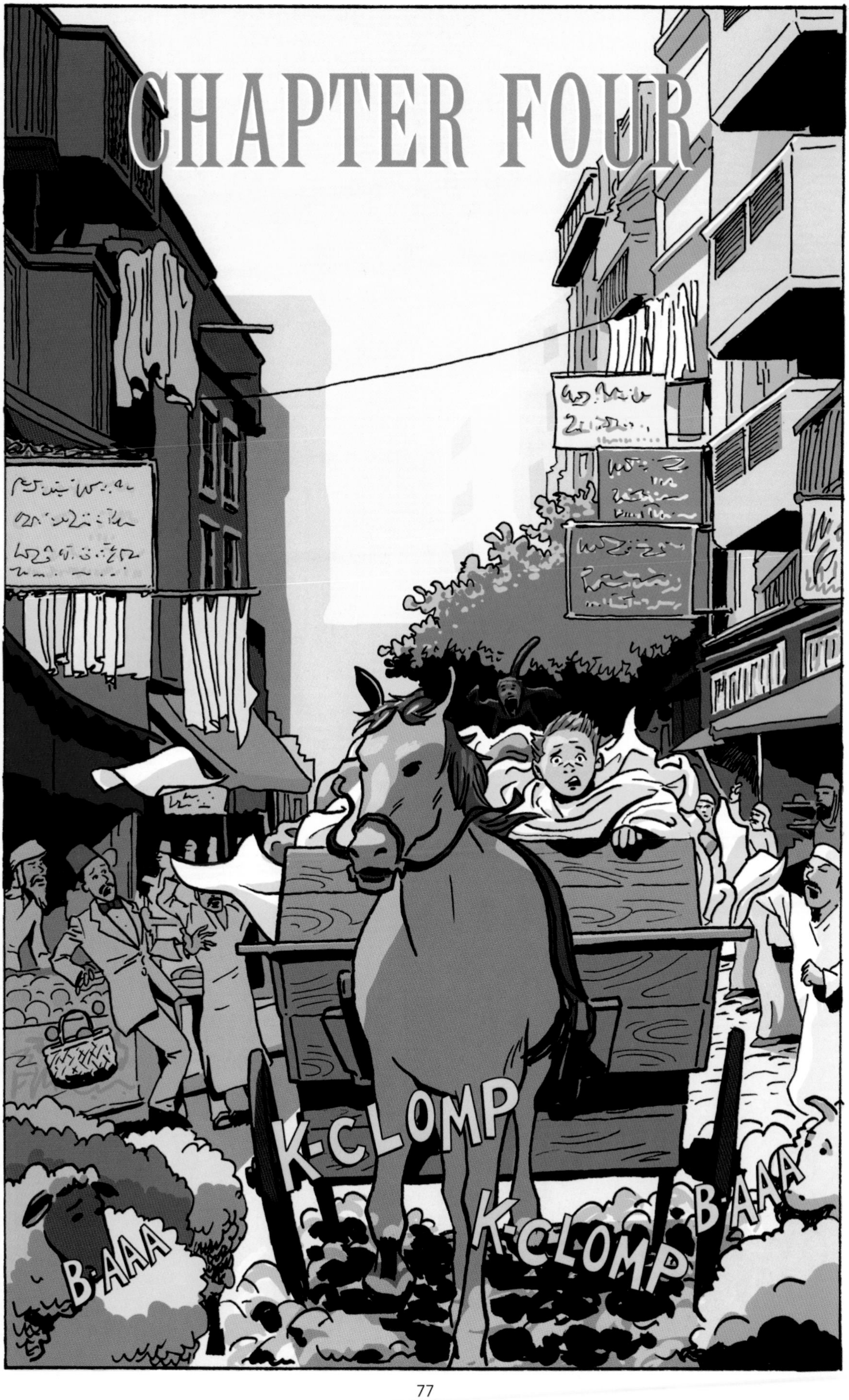
K-CLOMP
K-CLOMP
B-AAA
B-AAA

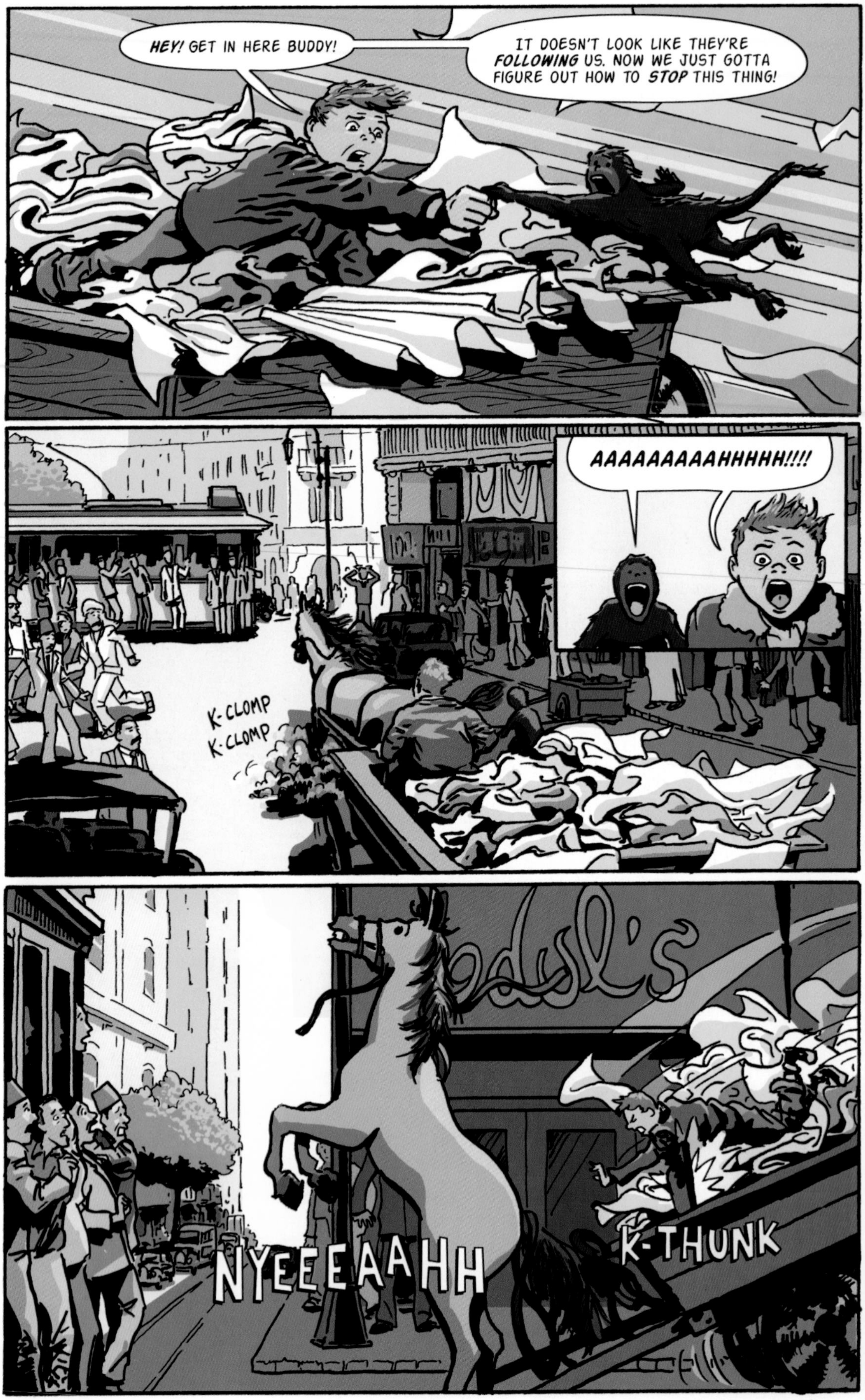
HEY! GET IN HERE BUDDY!
IT DOESN'T LOOK LIKE THEY'RE FOLLOWING US. NOW WE JUST GOTTA FIGURE OUT HOW TO STOP THIS THING!
AAAAAAAAAHHHHH!!!!
K-CLOMP K-CLOMP
NYEEEAAHH
K-THUNK

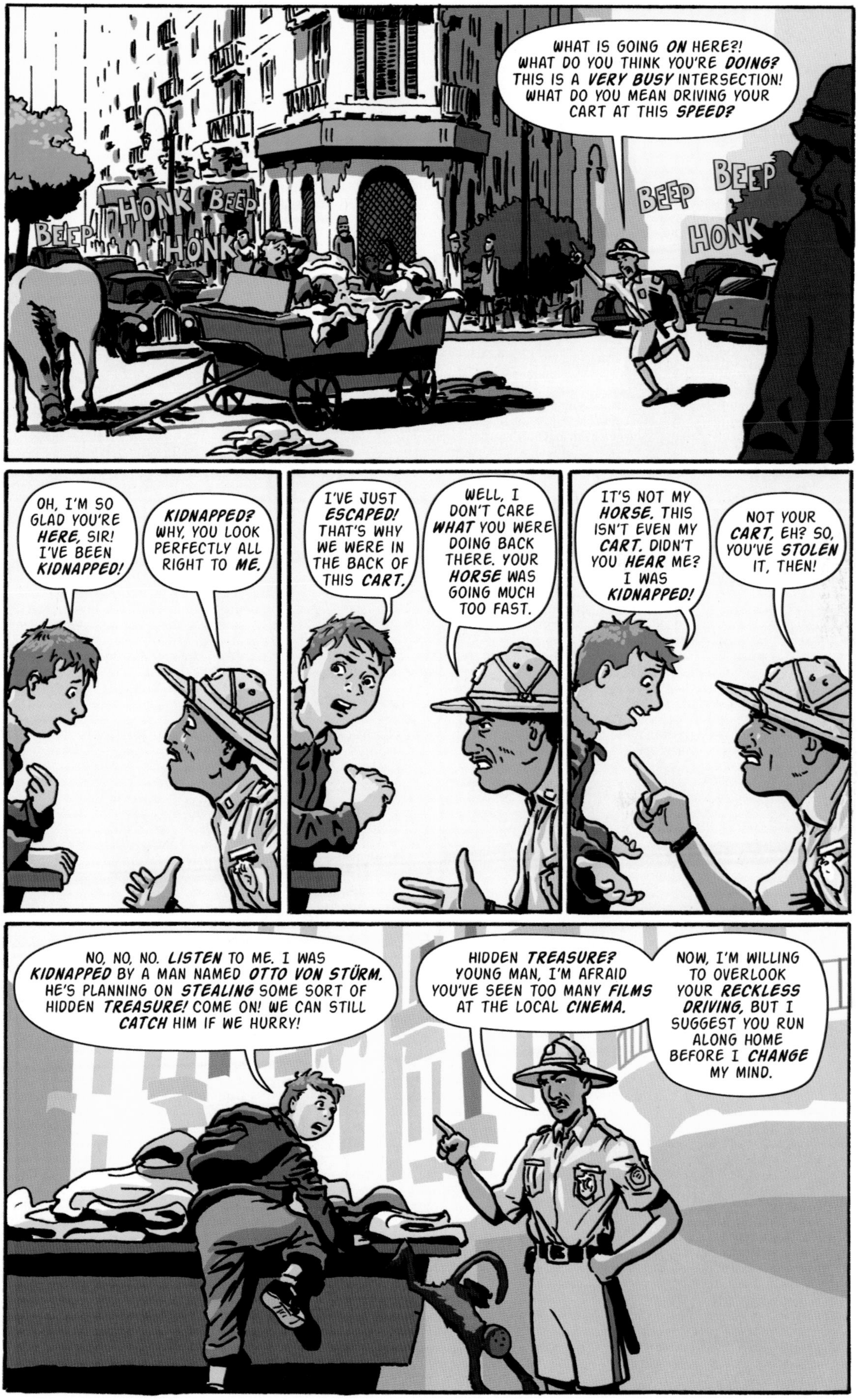
BEEP
HONK
BEEP
HONK
WHAT IS GOING ON HERE?! WHAT DO YOU THINK YOU'RE DOING? THIS IS A VERY BUSY INTERSECTION! WHAT DO YOU MEAN DRIVING YOUR CART AT THIS SPEED?
BEEP
BEEP
HONK
OH, I'M SO GLAD YOU'RE HERE, SIR! I'VE BEEN KIDNAPPED!
KIDNAPPED? WHY, YOU LOOK PERFECTLY ALL RIGHT TO ME.
I'VE JUST ESCAPED! THAT'S WHY WE WERE IN THE BACK OF THIS CART.
WELL, I DON'T CARE WHAT YOU WERE DOING BACK THERE. YOUR HORSE WAS GOING MUCH TOO FAST.
IT'S NOT MY HORSE. THIS ISN'T EVEN MY CART. DIDN'T YOU HEAR ME? I WAS KIDNAPPED!
NOT YOUR CART, EH? SO, YOU'VE STOLEN IT, THEN!
NO, NO, NO. LISTEN TO ME. I WAS KIDNAPPED BY A MAN NAMED OTTO VON STÜRM. HE'S PLANNING ON STEALING SOME SORT OF HIDDEN TREASURE! COME ON! WE CAN STILL CATCH HIM IF WE HURRY!
HIDDEN TREASURE? YOUNG MAN, I'M AFRAID YOU'VE SEEN TOO MANY FILMS AT THE LOCAL CINEMA.
NOW, I'M WILLING TO OVERLOOK YOUR RECKLESS DRIVING, BUT I SUGGEST YOU RUN ALONG HOME BEFORE I CHANGE MY MIND.

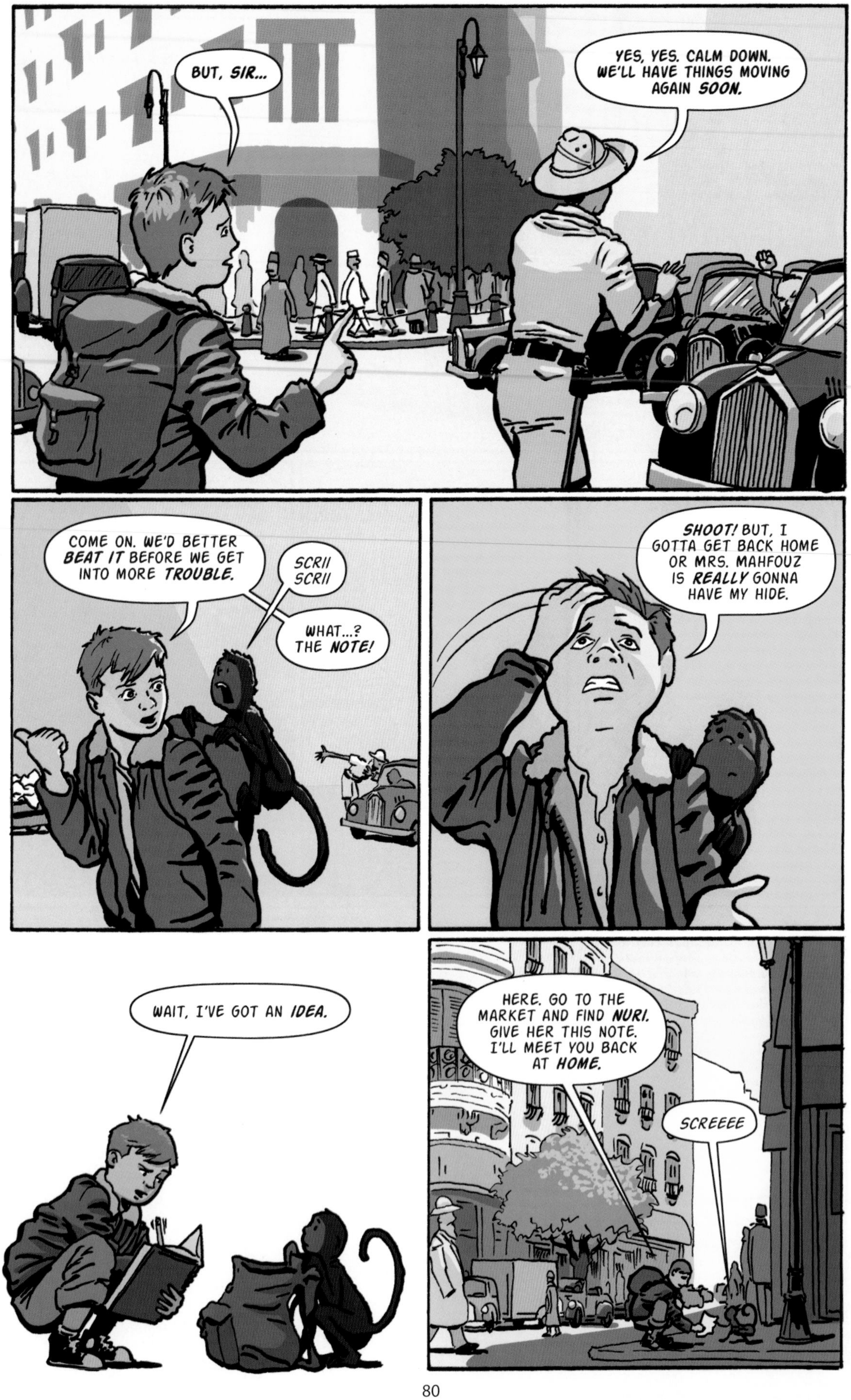
BUT, SIR...
YES, YES. CALM DOWN. WE'LL HAVE THINGS MOVING AGAIN SOON.
COME ON. WE'D BETTER BEAT IT BEFORE WE GET INTO MORE TROUBLE.
SCRII SCRII
WHAT...? THE NOTE!
SHOOT! BUT, I GOTTA GET BACK HOME OR MRS. MAHFOUZ IS REALLY GONNA HAVE MY HIDE.
WAIT, I'VE GOT AN IDEA.
HERE. GO TO THE MARKET AND FIND NURI. GIVE HER THIS NOTE. I'LL MEET YOU BACK AT HOME.
SCREEEE

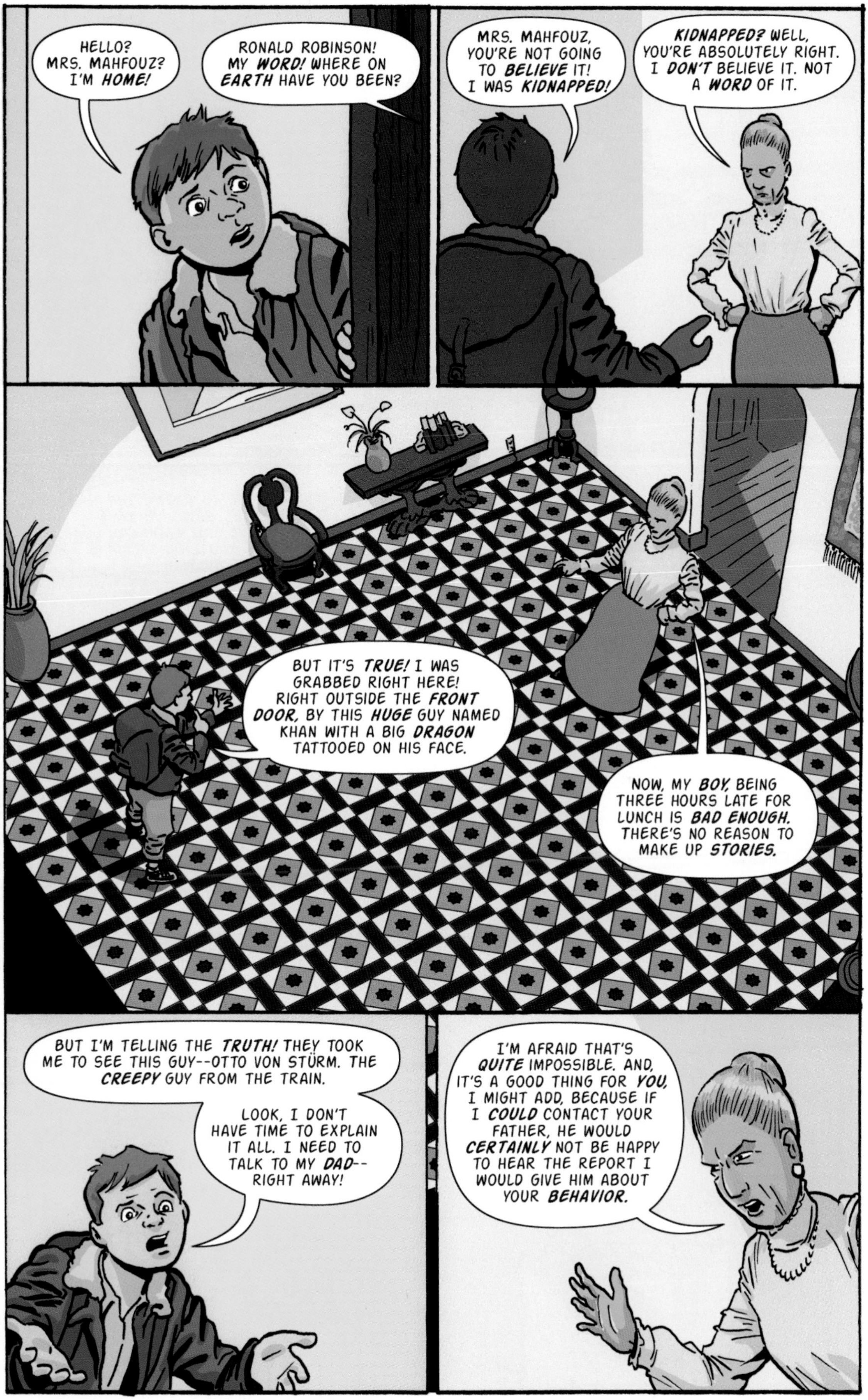
HELLO? MRS. MAHFOUZ? I'M HOME!
RONALD ROBINSON! MY WORD! WHERE ON EARTH HAVE YOU BEEN?
MRS. MAHFOUZ, YOU'RE NOT GOING TO BELIEVE IT! I WAS KIDNAPPED!
KIDNAPPED? WELL, YOU'RE ABSOLUTELY RIGHT. I DON'T BELIEVE IT. NOT A WORD OF IT.
BUT IT'S TRUE! I WAS GRABBED RIGHT HERE! RIGHT OUTSIDE THE FRONT DOOR, BY THIS HUGE GUY NAMED KHAN WITH A BIG DRAGON TATTOOED ON HIS FACE.
NOW, MY BOY, BEING THREE HOURS LATE FOR LUNCH IS BAD ENOUGH. THERE'S NO REASON TO MAKE UP STORIES.
BUT I'M TELLING THE TRUTH! THEY TOOK ME TO SEE THIS GUY--OTTO VON STÜRM. THE CREEPY GUY FROM THE TRAIN.
LOOK, I DON'T HAVE TIME TO EXPLAIN IT ALL. I NEED TO TALK TO MY DAD--RIGHT AWAY!
I'M AFRAID THAT'S QUITE IMPOSSIBLE. AND, IT'S A GOOD THING FOR YOU, I MIGHT ADD, BECAUSE IF I COULD CONTACT YOUR FATHER, HE WOULD CERTAINLY NOT BE HAPPY TO HEAR THE REPORT I WOULD GIVE HIM ABOUT YOUR BEHAVIOR.

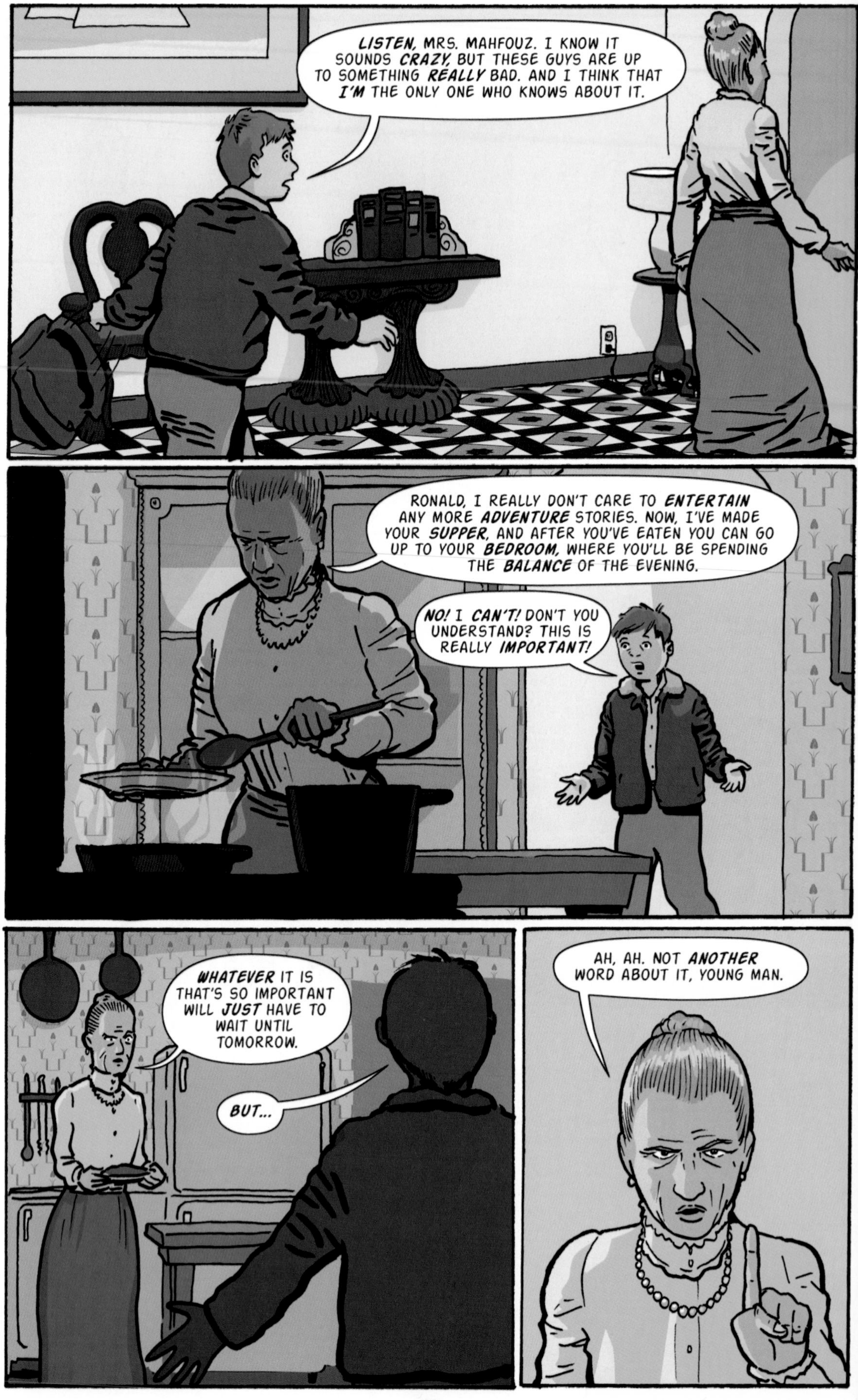
LISTEN, MRS. MAHFOUZ. I KNOW IT SOUNDS CRAZY, BUT THESE GUYS ARE UP TO SOMETHING REALLY BAD. AND I THINK THAT I'M THE ONLY ONE WHO KNOWS ABOUT IT.
RONALD, I REALLY DON'T CARE TO ENTERTAIN ANY MORE ADVENTURE STORIES. NOW, I'VE MADE YOUR SUPPER, AND AFTER YOU'VE EATEN YOU CAN GO UP TO YOUR BEDROOM, WHERE YOU'LL BE SPENDING THE BALANCE OF THE EVENING.
NO! I CAN'T! DON'T YOU UNDERSTAND? THIS IS REALLY IMPORTANT!
WHATEVER IT IS THAT'S SO IMPORTANT WILL JUST HAVE TO WAIT UNTIL TOMORROW.
BUT...
AH, AH. NOT ANOTHER WORD ABOUT IT, YOUNG MAN.

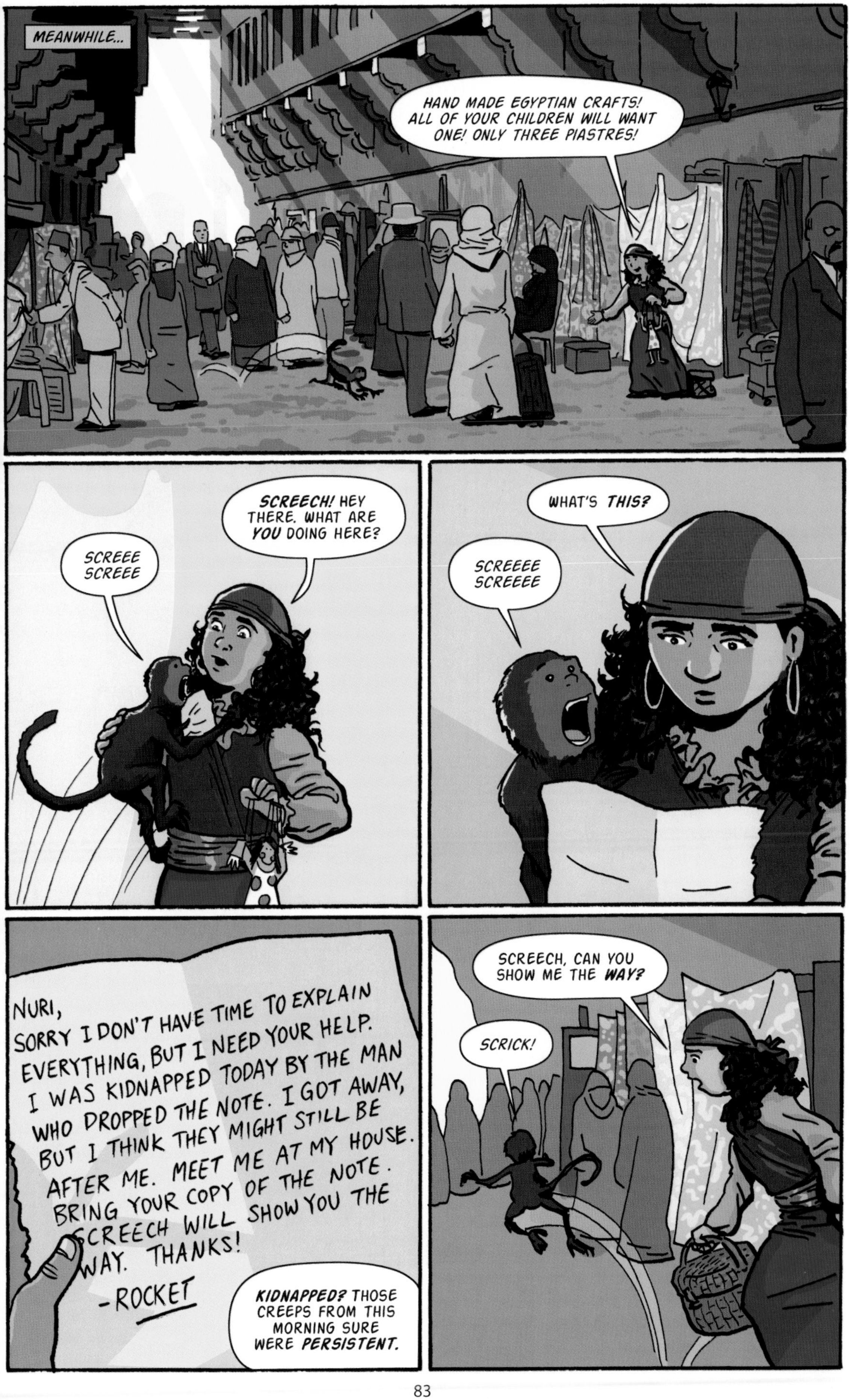
MEANWHILE...
HAND MADE EGYPTIAN CRAFTS! ALL OF YOUR CHILDREN WILL WANT ONE! ONLY THREE PIASTRES!
SCREEE SCREEE
SCREECH! HEY THERE. WHAT ARE YOU DOING HERE?
WHAT'S THIS?
SCREEEE SCREEEE
NURI,
SORRY I DON'T HAVE TIME TO EXPLAIN
EVERYTHING, BUT I NEED YOUR HELP.
I WAS KIDNAPPED TODAY BY THE MAN
WHO DROPPED THE NOTE. I GOT AWAY,
BUT I THINK THEY MIGHT STILL BE
AFTER ME. MEET ME AT MY HOUSE.
BRING YOUR COPY OF THE NOTE.
SCREECH WILL SHOW YOU THE
WAY. THANKS!
-ROCKET
KIDNAPPED? THOSE CREEPS FROM THIS MORNING SURE WERE PERSISTENT.
SCREECH, CAN YOU SHOW ME THE WAY?
SCRICK!

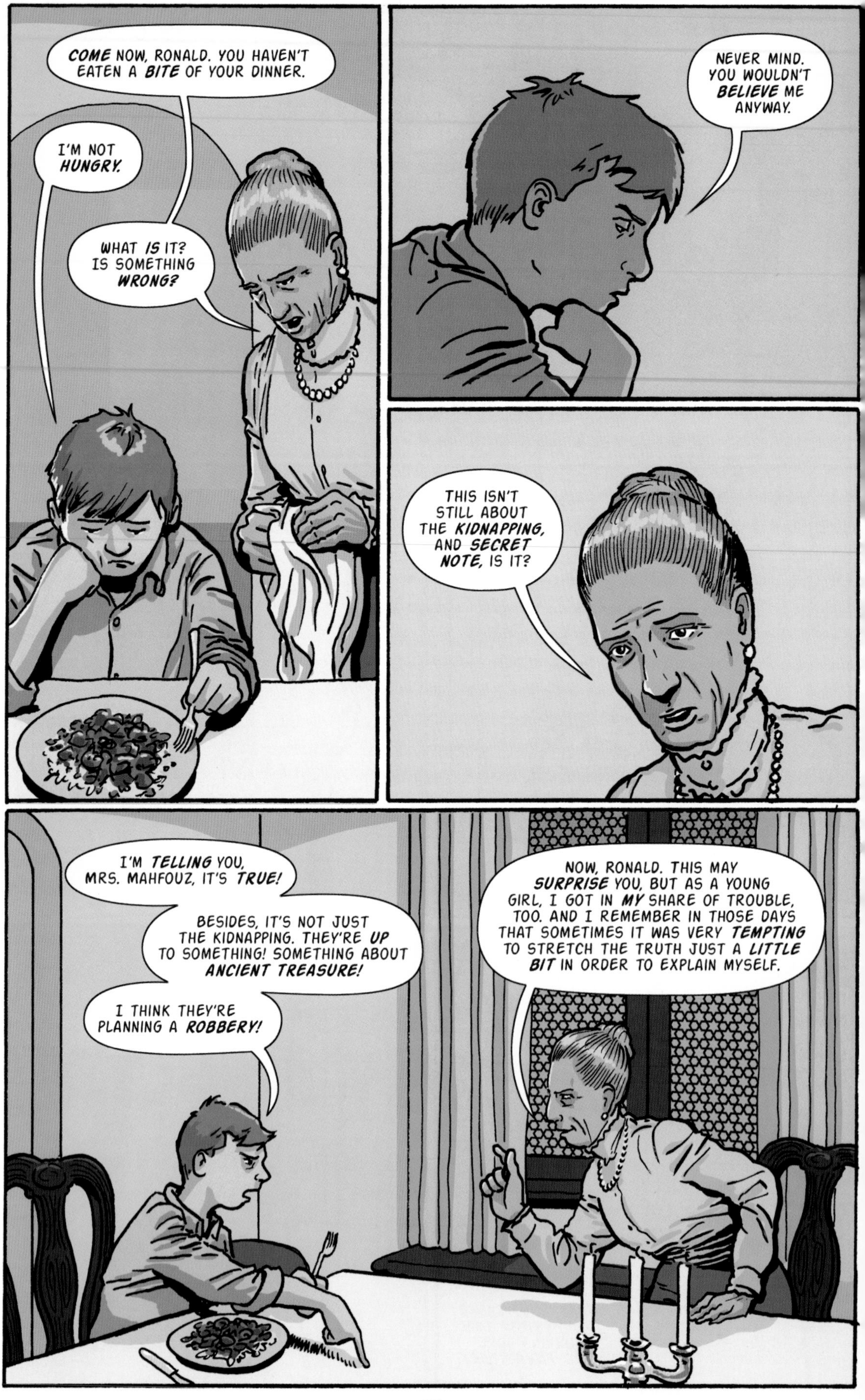
COME NOW, RONALD. YOU HAVEN'T EATEN A BITE OF YOUR DINNER.
I'M NOT HUNGRY.
WHAT IS IT? IS SOMETHING WRONG?
NEVER MIND. YOU WOULDN'T BELIEVE ME ANYWAY.
THIS ISN'T STILL ABOUT THE KIDNAPPING, AND SECRET NOTE, IS IT?
I'M TELLING YOU, MRS. MAHFOUZ, IT'S TRUE!
BESIDES, IT'S NOT JUST THE KIDNAPPING. THEY'RE UP TO SOMETHING! SOMETHING ABOUT ANCIENT TREASURE!
I THINK THEY'RE PLANNING A ROBBERY!
NOW, RONALD. THIS MAY SURPRISE YOU, BUT AS A YOUNG GIRL, I GOT IN MY SHARE OF TROUBLE, TOO. AND I REMEMBER IN THOSE DAYS THAT SOMETIMES IT WAS VERY TEMPTING TO STRETCH THE TRUTH JUST A LITTLE BIT IN ORDER TO EXPLAIN MYSELF.

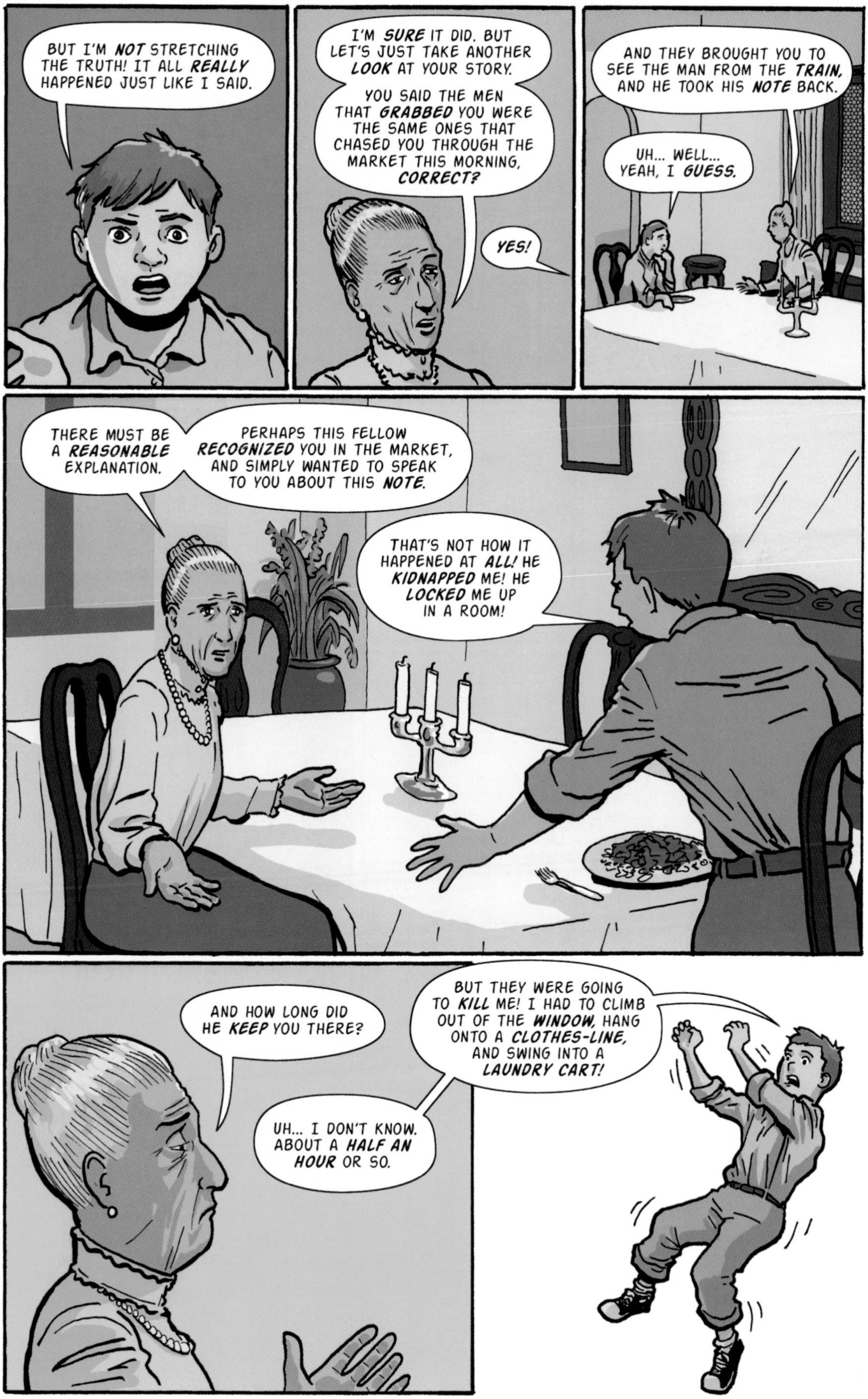
BUT I'M NOT STRETCHING THE TRUTH! IT ALL REALLY HAPPENED JUST LIKE I SAID.
I'M SURE IT DID. BUT LET'S JUST TAKE ANOTHER LOOK AT YOUR STORY.
YOU SAID THE MEN THAT GRABBED YOU WERE THE SAME ONES THAT CHASED YOU THROUGH THE MARKET THIS MORNING, CORRECT?
YES!
AND THEY BROUGHT YOU TO SEE THE MAN FROM THE TRAIN, AND HE TOOK HIS NOTE BACK.
UH... WELL... YEAH, I GUESS.
THERE MUST BE A REASONABLE EXPLANATION.
PERHAPS THIS FELLOW RECOGNIZED YOU IN THE MARKET, AND SIMPLY WANTED TO SPEAK TO YOU ABOUT THIS NOTE.
THAT'S NOT HOW IT HAPPENED AT ALL! HE KIDNAPPED ME! HE LOCKED ME UP IN A ROOM!
AND HOW LONG DID HE KEEP YOU THERE?
UH... I DON'T KNOW. ABOUT A HALF AN HOUR OR SO.
BUT THEY WERE GOING TO KILL ME! I HAD TO CLIMB OUT OF THE WINDOW, HANG ONTO A CLOTHES-LINE, AND SWING INTO A LAUNDRY CART!

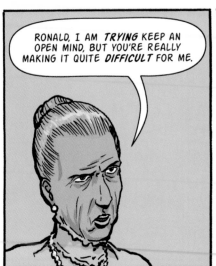

RONALD, I AM *TRYING* KEEP AN OPEN MIND, BUT YOU'RE REALLY MAKING IT QUITE *DIFFICULT* FOR ME.

LOOK, NONE OF THAT *MATTERS* NOW. THE POINT IS, THEY'VE MADE AN *AMAZING* DISCOVERY-- AN ANCIENT, *SECRET* TREASURE. DON'T YOU UNDERSTAND WHAT THAT *MEANS?*

AHH, *FORGET* IT. I CAN SEE THAT YOU DON'T BELIEVE ME. I JUST WISH *POP* WAS HERE. HE'D KNOW WHAT TO DO.

<SIGH>

RONALD, HERE IN EGYPT, WE HAVE A *SAYING.* IT'S AN OLD PROVERB.

"A THOUSAND CURSES NEVER TORE A SHIRT."

WHAT THE HECK IS *THAT* SUPPOSED TO MEAN?

WHAT IT *MEANS,* RONALD, IS THAT COMING UP WITH *WILD,* IMAGINATIVE EXPLANATIONS FOR THINGS WON'T HELP YOU SOLVE THE *SIMPLE* PROBLEMS YOU FACE IN LIFE, LIKE A *TORN SHIRT,* FOR EXAMPLE.

YOU'LL FIND THAT *OFTEN* IN LIFE, THE *SIMPLEST* EXPLANATION IS USUALLY THE *CORRECT* ONE.

SO... YOU DON'T *BELIEVE* ME.

KNOCK KNOCK

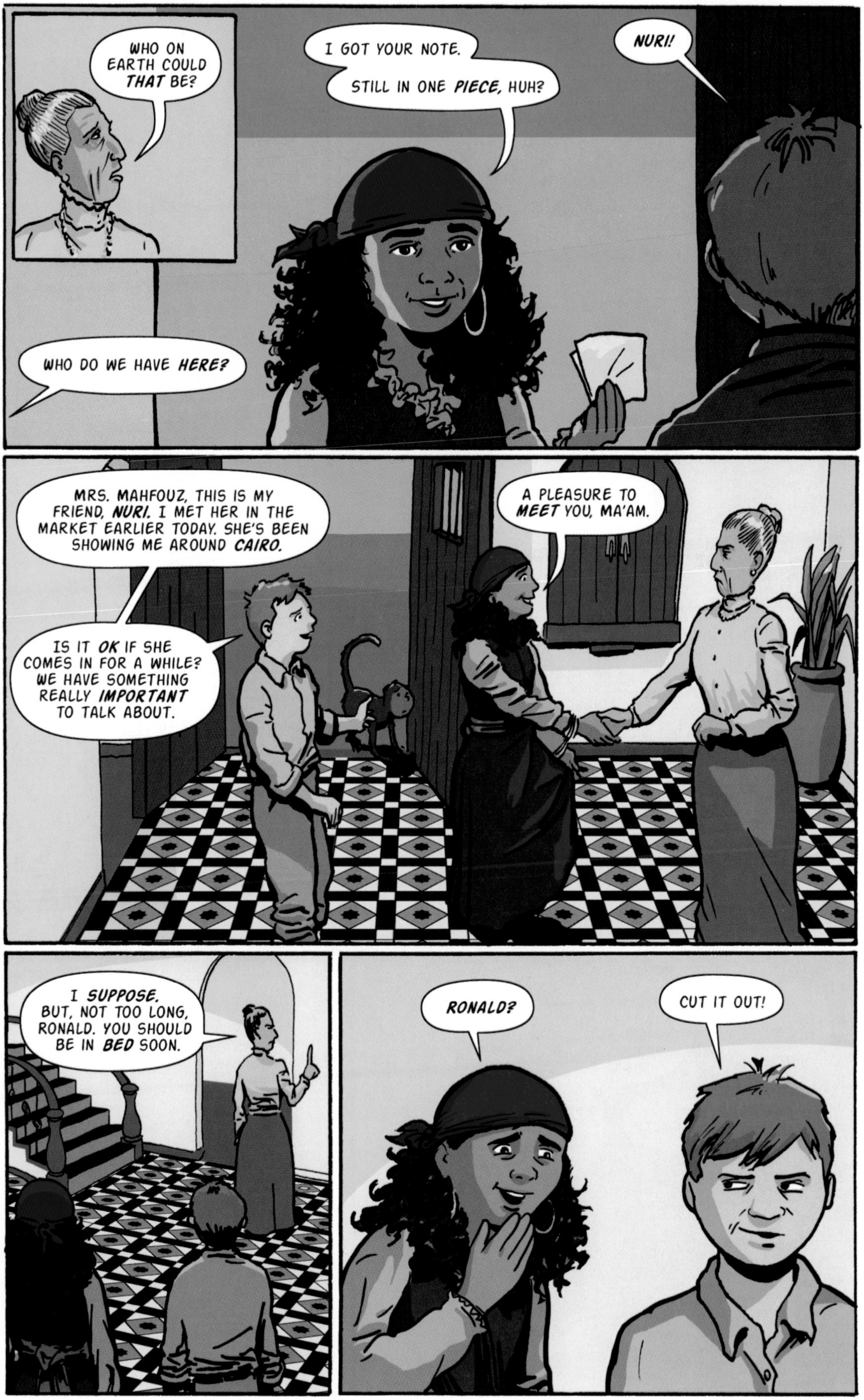
WHO ON EARTH COULD THAT BE?
I GOT YOUR NOTE.
STILL IN ONE PIECE, HUH?
NURI!
WHO DO WE HAVE HERE?
MRS. MAHFOUZ, THIS IS MY FRIEND, NURI. I MET HER IN THE MARKET EARLIER TODAY. SHE'S BEEN SHOWING ME AROUND CAIRO.
IS IT OK IF SHE COMES IN FOR A WHILE? WE HAVE SOMETHING REALLY IMPORTANT TO TALK ABOUT.
A PLEASURE TO MEET YOU, MA'AM.
I SUPPOSE. BUT, NOT TOO LONG, RONALD. YOU SHOULD BE IN BED SOON.
RONALD?
CUT IT OUT!

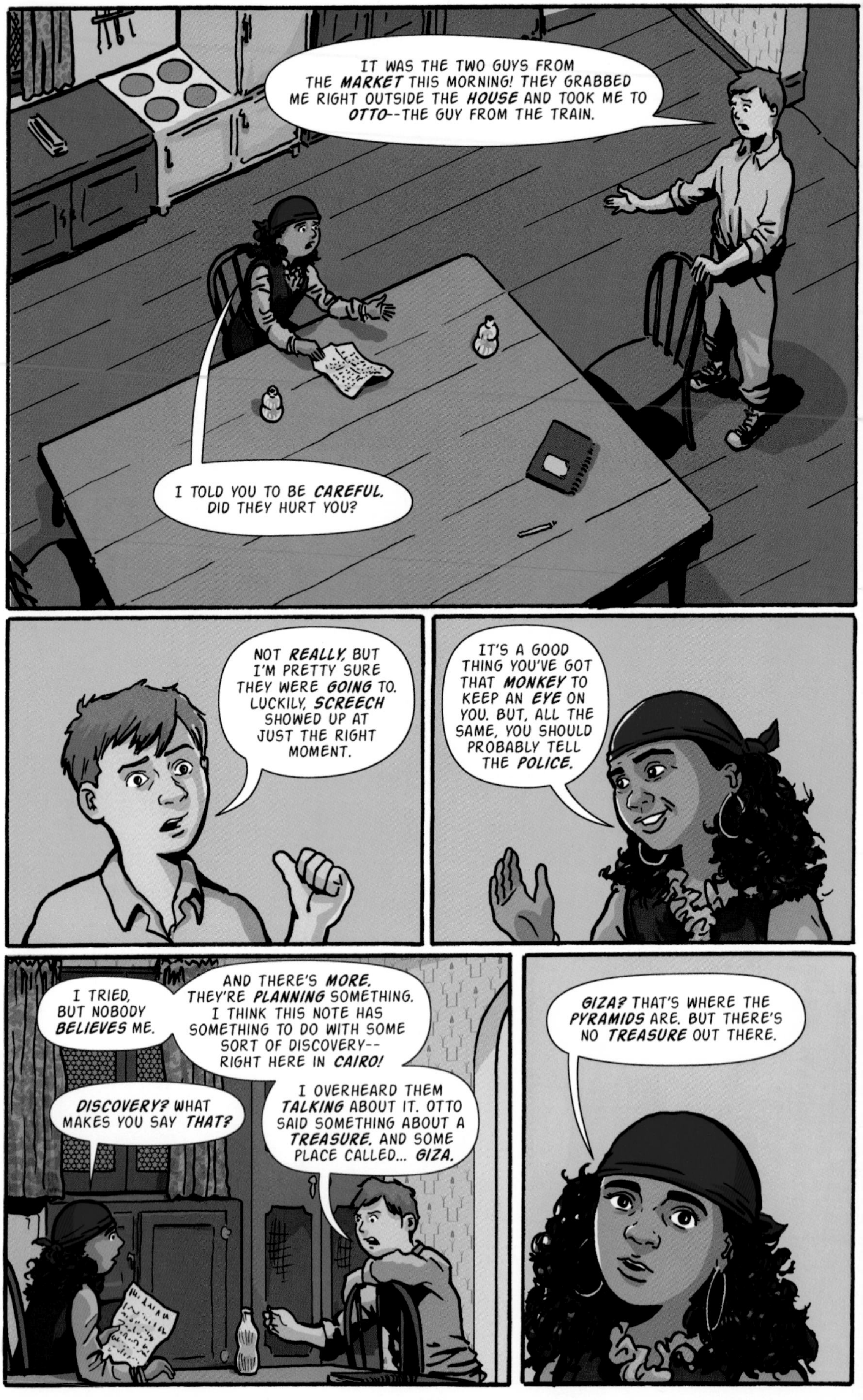
IT WAS THE TWO GUYS FROM THE MARKET THIS MORNING! THEY GRABBED ME RIGHT OUTSIDE THE HOUSE AND TOOK ME TO OTTO--THE GUY FROM THE TRAIN.
I TOLD YOU TO BE CAREFUL. DID THEY HURT YOU?
NOT REALLY, BUT I'M PRETTY SURE THEY WERE GOING TO. LUCKILY, SCREECH SHOWED UP AT JUST THE RIGHT MOMENT.
IT'S A GOOD THING YOU'VE GOT THAT MONKEY TO KEEP AN EYE ON YOU. BUT, ALL THE SAME, YOU SHOULD PROBABLY TELL THE POLICE.
I TRIED, BUT NOBODY BELIEVES ME.
AND THERE'S MORE. THEY'RE PLANNING SOMETHING. I THINK THIS NOTE HAS SOMETHING TO DO WITH SOME SORT OF DISCOVERY-- RIGHT HERE IN CAIRO!
DISCOVERY? WHAT MAKES YOU SAY THAT?
I OVERHEARD THEM TALKING ABOUT IT. OTTO SAID SOMETHING ABOUT A TREASURE, AND SOME PLACE CALLED... GIZA.
GIZA? THAT'S WHERE THE PYRAMIDS ARE. BUT THERE'S NO TREASURE OUT THERE.

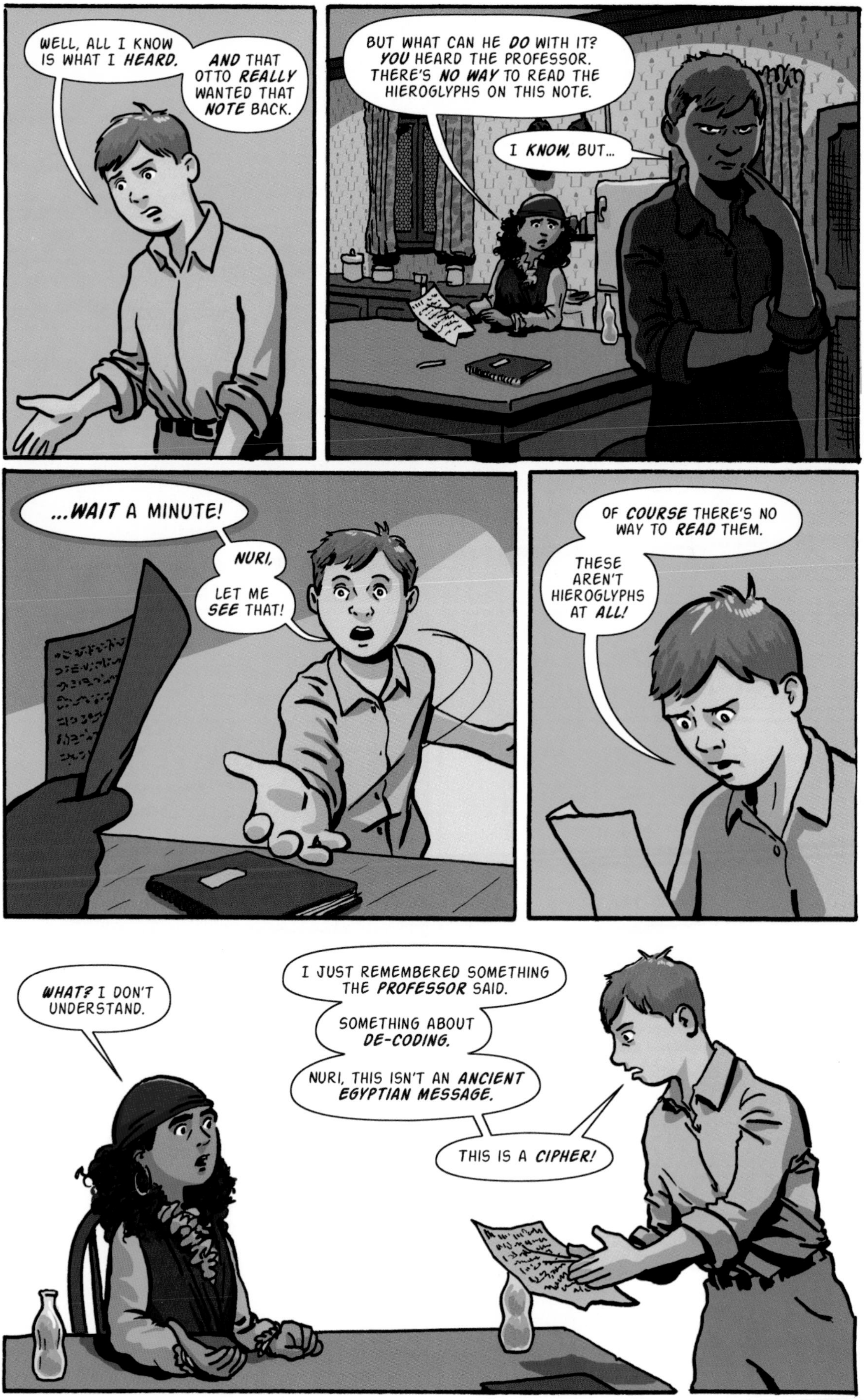
WELL, ALL I KNOW IS WHAT I HEARD.
AND THAT OTTO REALLY WANTED THAT NOTE BACK.
BUT WHAT CAN HE DO WITH IT? YOU HEARD THE PROFESSOR. THERE'S NO WAY TO READ THE HIEROGLYPHS ON THIS NOTE.
I KNOW, BUT...
...WAIT A MINUTE!
NURI,
LET ME SEE THAT!
OF COURSE THERE'S NO WAY TO READ THEM.
THESE AREN'T HIEROGLYPHS AT ALL!
WHAT? I DON'T UNDERSTAND.
I JUST REMEMBERED SOMETHING THE PROFESSOR SAID.
SOMETHING ABOUT DE-CODING.
NURI, THIS ISN'T AN ANCIENT EGYPTIAN MESSAGE.
THIS IS A CIPHER!

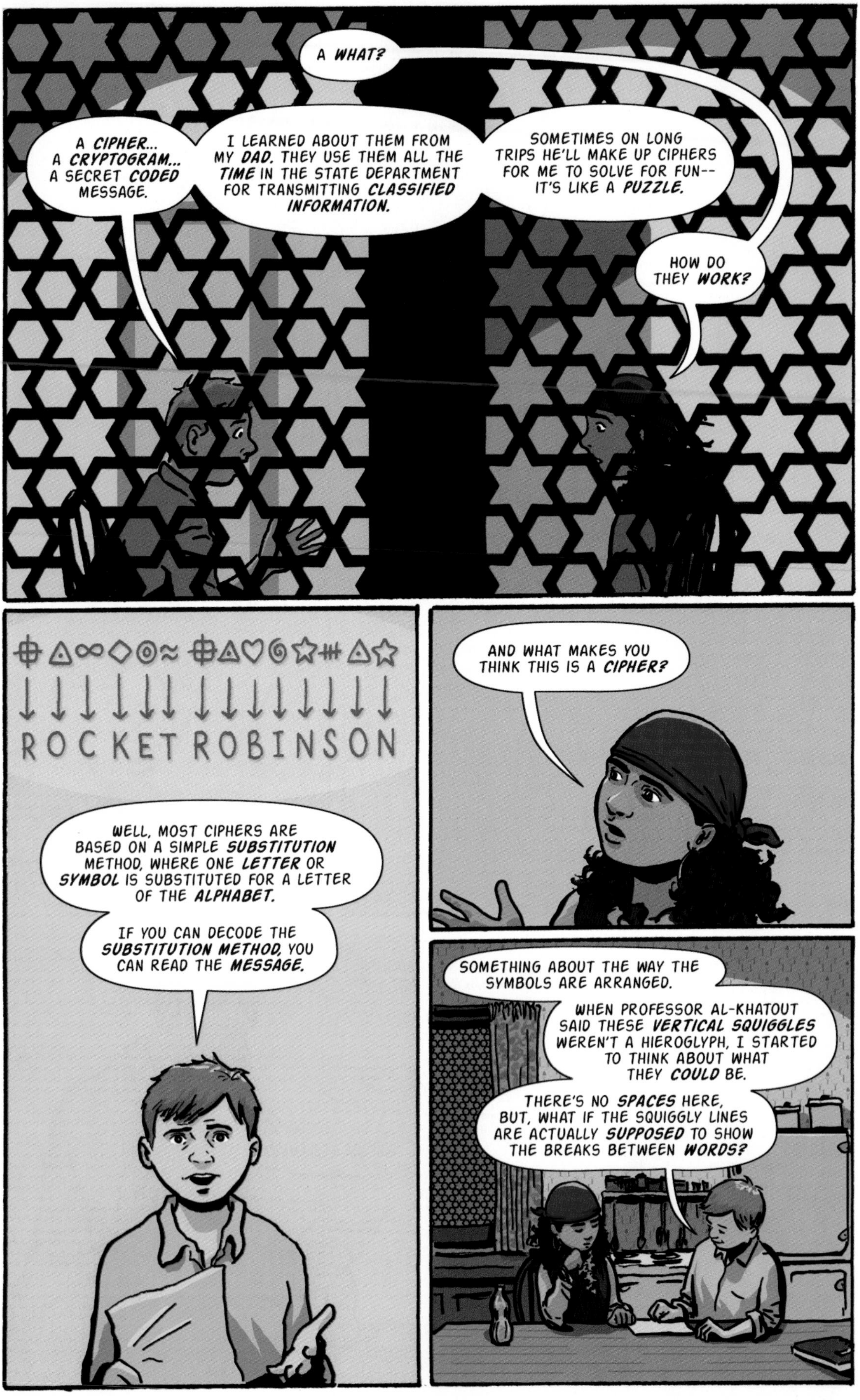
A WHAT?
A CIPHER... A CRYPTOGRAM... A SECRET CODED MESSAGE.
I LEARNED ABOUT THEM FROM MY DAD. THEY USE THEM ALL THE TIME IN THE STATE DEPARTMENT FOR TRANSMITTING CLASSIFIED INFORMATION.
SOMETIMES ON LONG TRIPS HE'LL MAKE UP CIPHERS FOR ME TO SOLVE FOR FUN-- IT'S LIKE A PUZZLE.
HOW DO THEY WORK?
ROCKET ROBINSON
WELL, MOST CIPHERS ARE BASED ON A SIMPLE SUBSTITUTION METHOD, WHERE ONE LETTER OR SYMBOL IS SUBSTITUTED FOR A LETTER OF THE ALPHABET.
IF YOU CAN DECODE THE SUBSTITUTION METHOD, YOU CAN READ THE MESSAGE.
AND WHAT MAKES YOU THINK THIS IS A CIPHER?
SOMETHING ABOUT THE WAY THE SYMBOLS ARE ARRANGED.
WHEN PROFESSOR AL-KHATOUT SAID THESE VERTICAL SQUIGGLES WEREN'T A HIEROGLYPH, I STARTED TO THINK ABOUT WHAT THEY COULD BE.
THERE'S NO SPACES HERE, BUT, WHAT IF THE SQUIGGLY LINES ARE ACTUALLY SUPPOSED TO SHOW THE BREAKS BETWEEN WORDS?

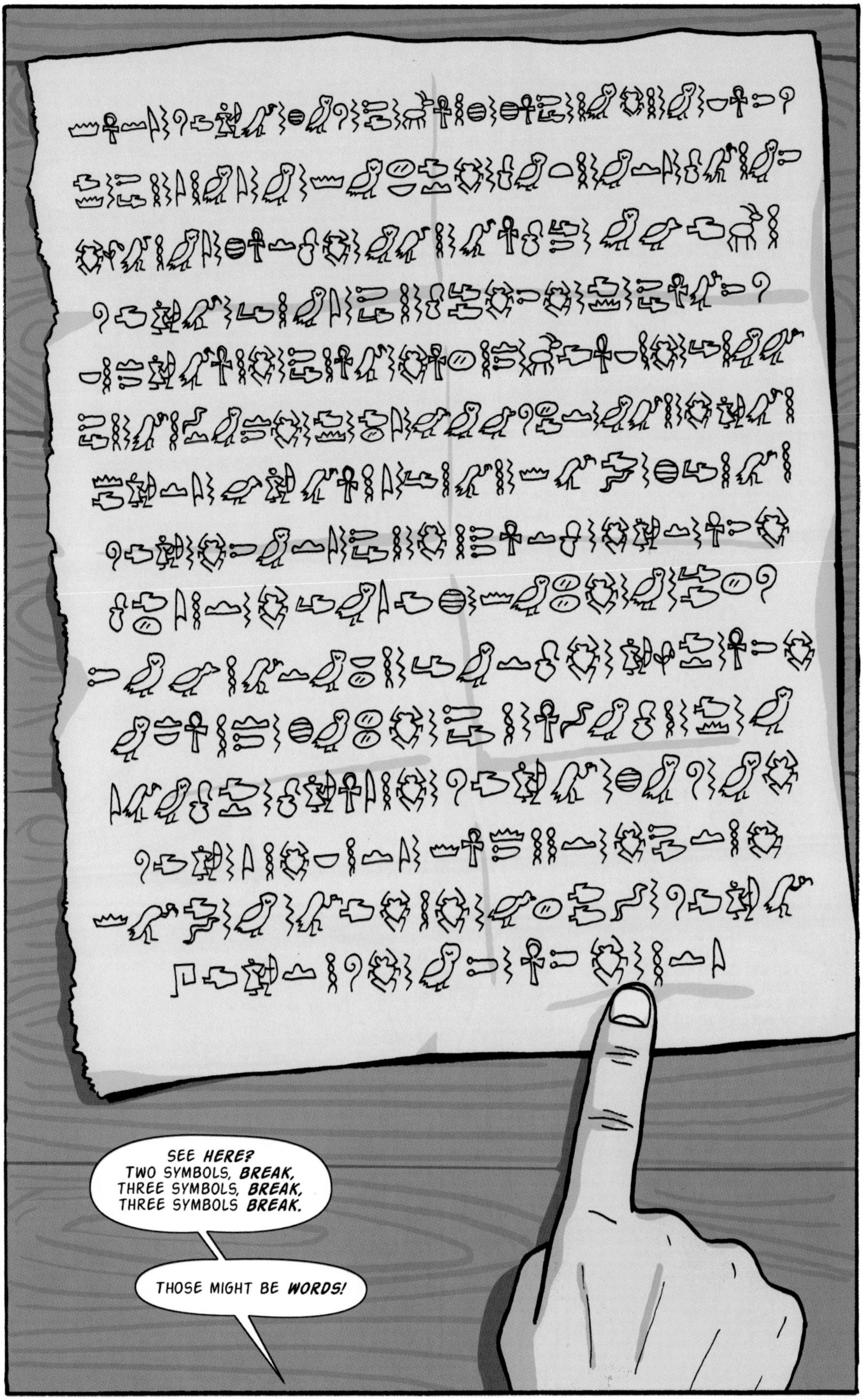
SEE HERE? TWO SYMBOLS, BREAK, THREE SYMBOLS, BREAK, THREE SYMBOLS BREAK.
THOSE MIGHT BE WORDS!

THIS IS WHAT YOU DO FOR FUN?
COME ON. DON'T YOU WANT TO KNOW WHAT THIS MESSAGE SAYS?
SURE. BUT DO YOU REALLY THINK YOU CAN READ IT?
I CAN TRY. WE JUST NEED TO HOPE THAT THE ORIGINAL MESSAGE WAS WRITTEN IN ENGLISH, OR IT'LL BE NEARLY IMPOSSIBLE TO DE-CIPHER.
ALL RIGHT. HOW DO WE DO SOLVE IT?
WELL, LET'S SEE. THERE'S A FEW DIFFERENT TRICKS TO START OUT. IF I'M RIGHT THAT THE SQUIGGLES MEAN WORD BREAKS, THEN WE CAN SEE HERE TWO WORDS THAT ARE ONLY ONE LETTER.
THERE'S ONLY TWO WORDS IN ENGLISH THAT ARE ONE LETTER LONG, A AND I.
= A or I
THE MOST COMMON LETTERS USED IN ENGLISH ARE VOWELS, SO THE SYMBOLS WE SEE THE MOST OF WILL PROBABLY BE THOSE.
= A or I
OTHER VOWELS

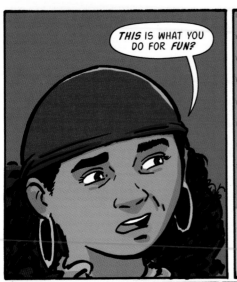

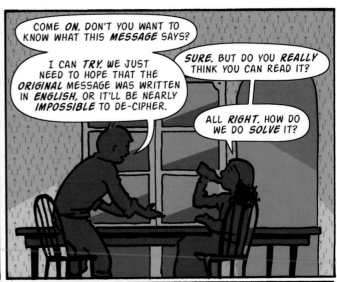

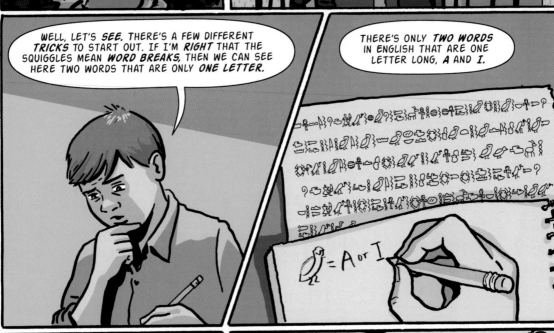

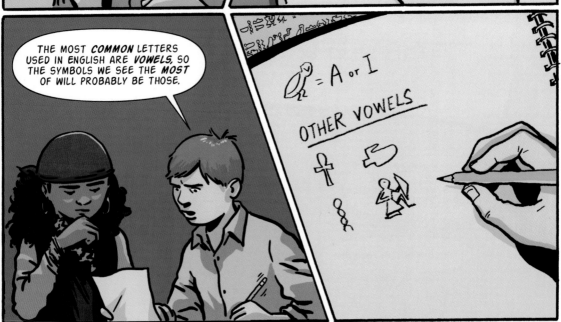

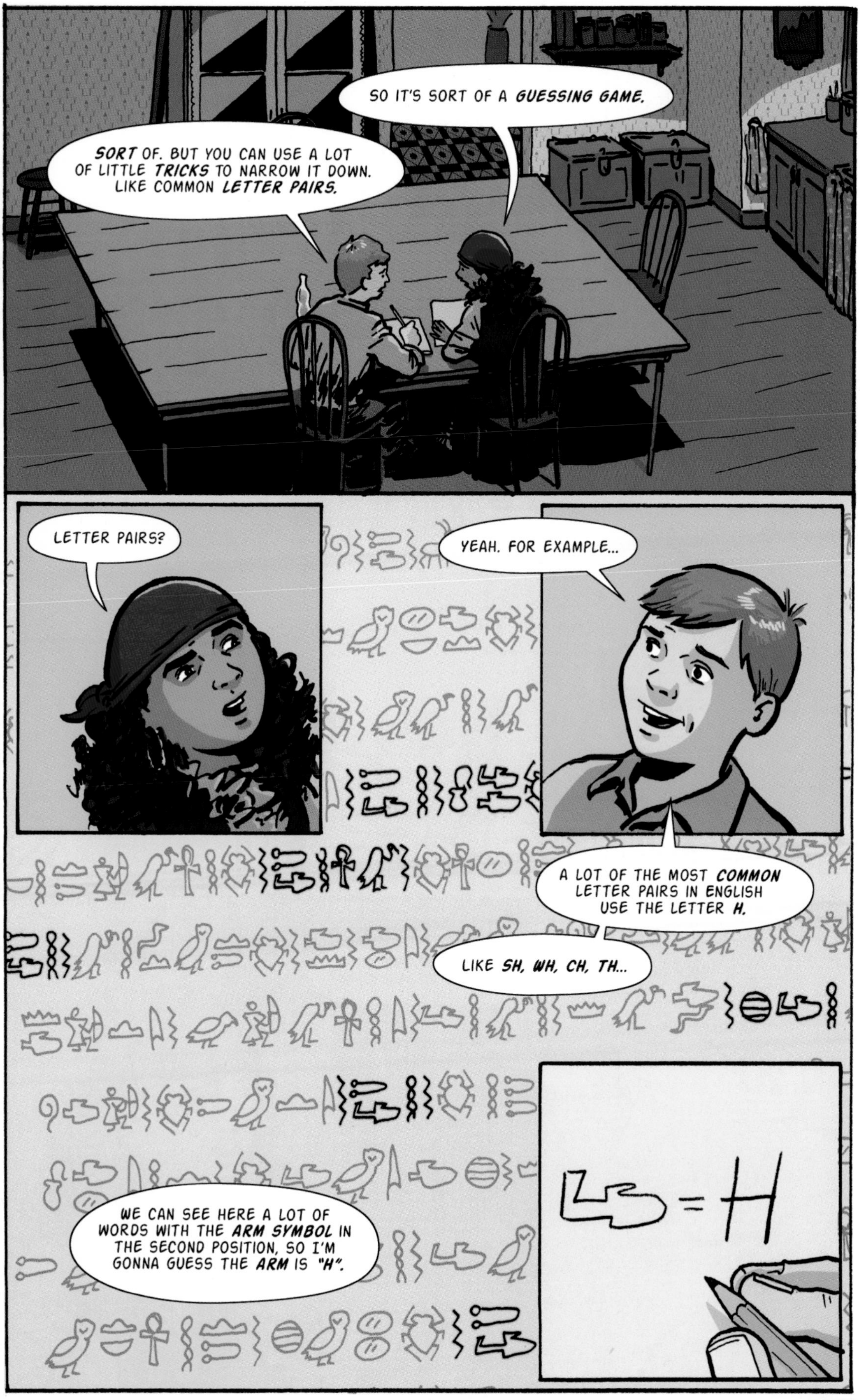
SO IT'S SORT OF A GUESSING GAME.
SORT OF. BUT YOU CAN USE A LOT OF LITTLE TRICKS TO NARROW IT DOWN. LIKE COMMON LETTER PAIRS.
LETTER PAIRS?
YEAH. FOR EXAMPLE...
A LOT OF THE MOST COMMON LETTER PAIRS IN ENGLISH USE THE LETTER H.
LIKE SH, WH, CH, TH...
WE CAN SEE HERE A LOT OF WORDS WITH THE ARM SYMBOL IN THE SECOND POSITION, SO I'M GONNA GUESS THE ARM IS "H".
= H

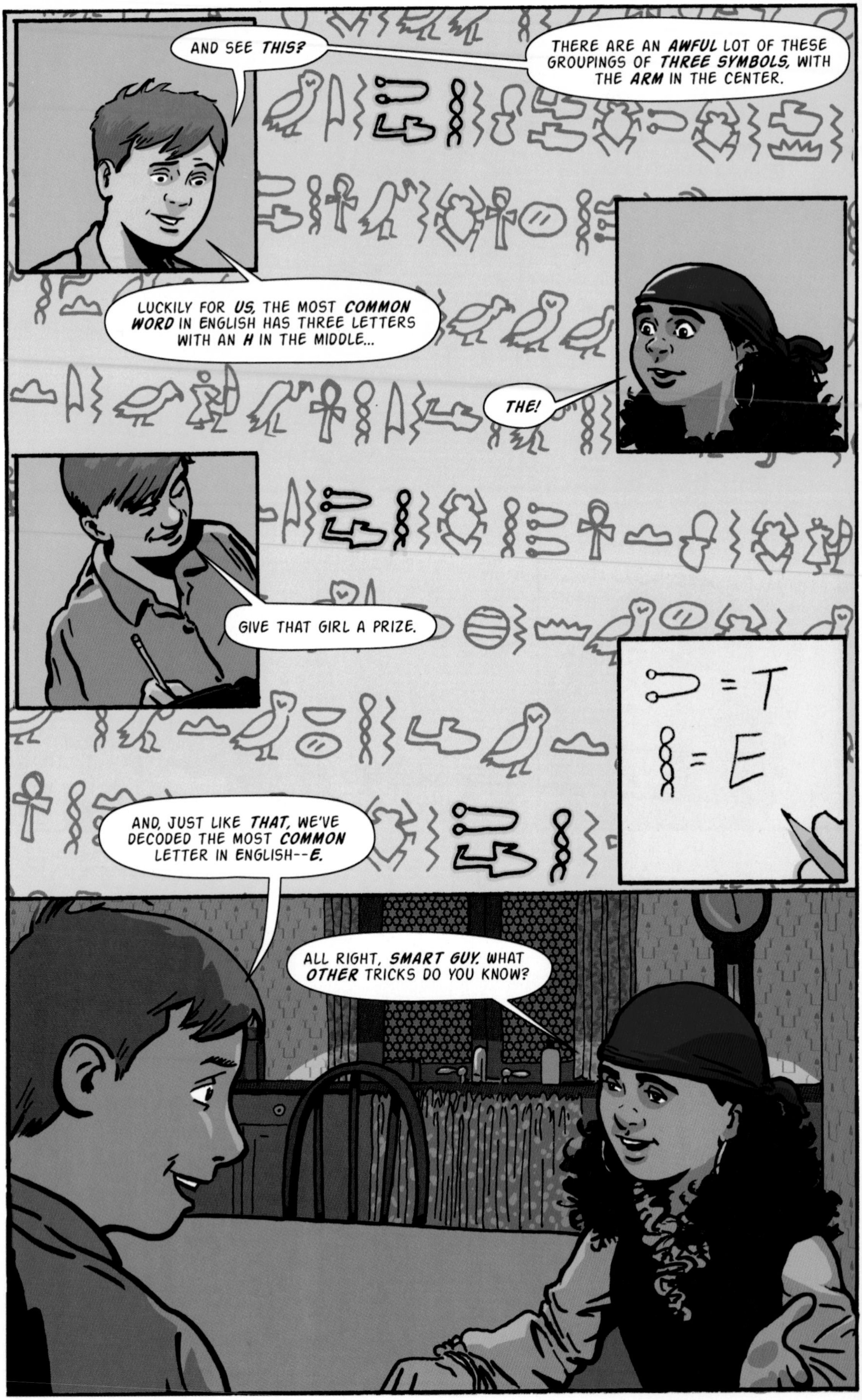
AND SEE THIS?
THERE ARE AN AWFUL LOT OF THESE GROUPINGS OF THREE SYMBOLS, WITH THE ARM IN THE CENTER.
LUCKILY FOR US, THE MOST COMMON WORD IN ENGLISH HAS THREE LETTERS WITH AN H IN THE MIDDLE...
THE!
GIVE THAT GIRL A PRIZE.
= T
= E
AND, JUST LIKE THAT, WE'VE DECODED THE MOST COMMON LETTER IN ENGLISH--E.
ALL RIGHT, SMART GUY. WHAT OTHER TRICKS DO YOU KNOW?

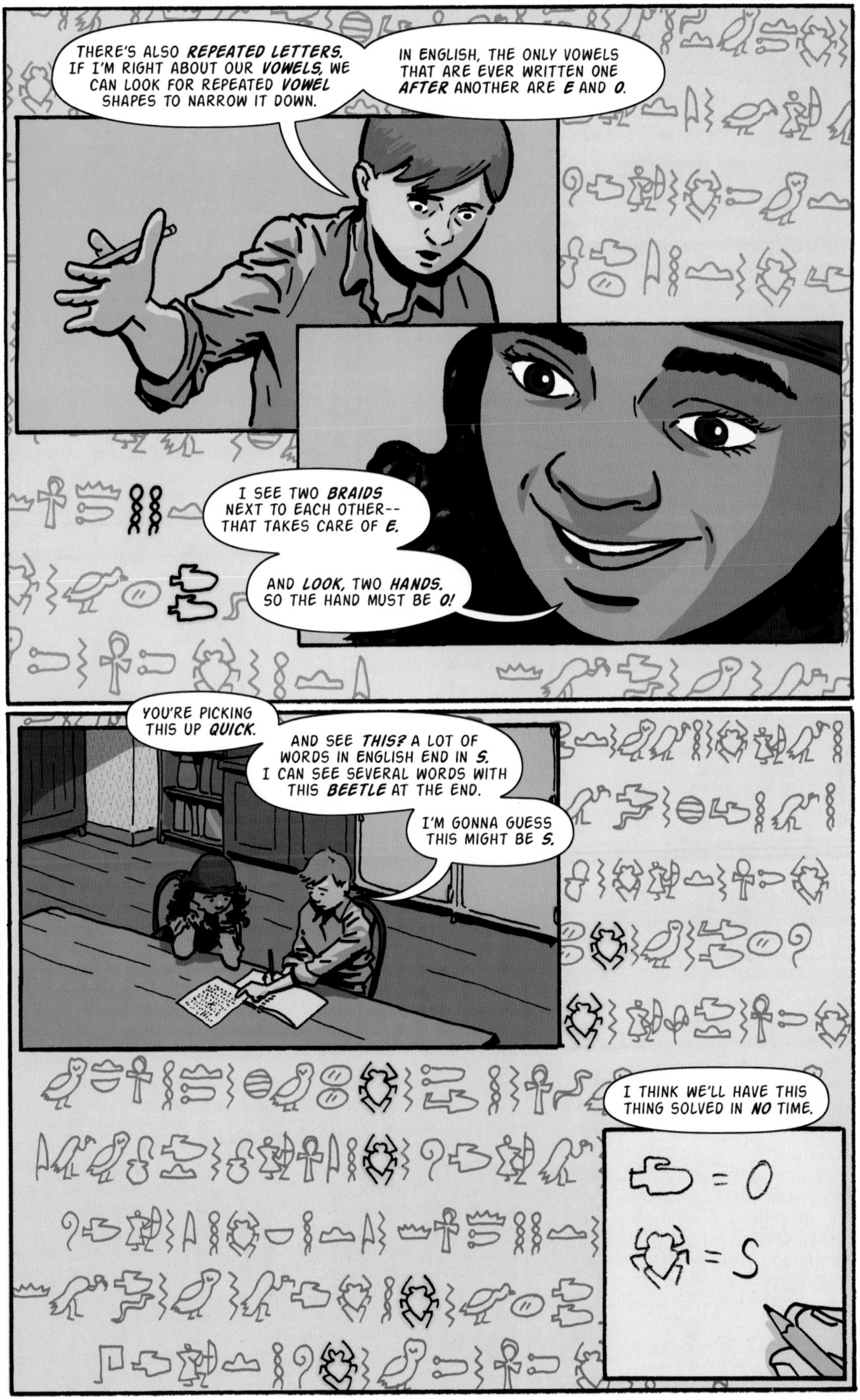
THERE'S ALSO REPEATED LETTERS. IF I'M RIGHT ABOUT OUR VOWELS, WE CAN LOOK FOR REPEATED VOWEL SHAPES TO NARROW IT DOWN.
IN ENGLISH, THE ONLY VOWELS THAT ARE EVER WRITTEN ONE AFTER ANOTHER ARE E AND O.
I SEE TWO BRAIDS NEXT TO EACH OTHER-- THAT TAKES CARE OF E.
AND LOOK, TWO HANDS. SO THE HAND MUST BE O!
YOU'RE PICKING THIS UP QUICK.
AND SEE THIS? A LOT OF WORDS IN ENGLISH END IN S. I CAN SEE SEVERAL WORDS WITH THIS BEETLE AT THE END.
I'M GONNA GUESS THIS MIGHT BE S.
I THINK WE'LL HAVE THIS THING SOLVED IN NO TIME.
= O
= S

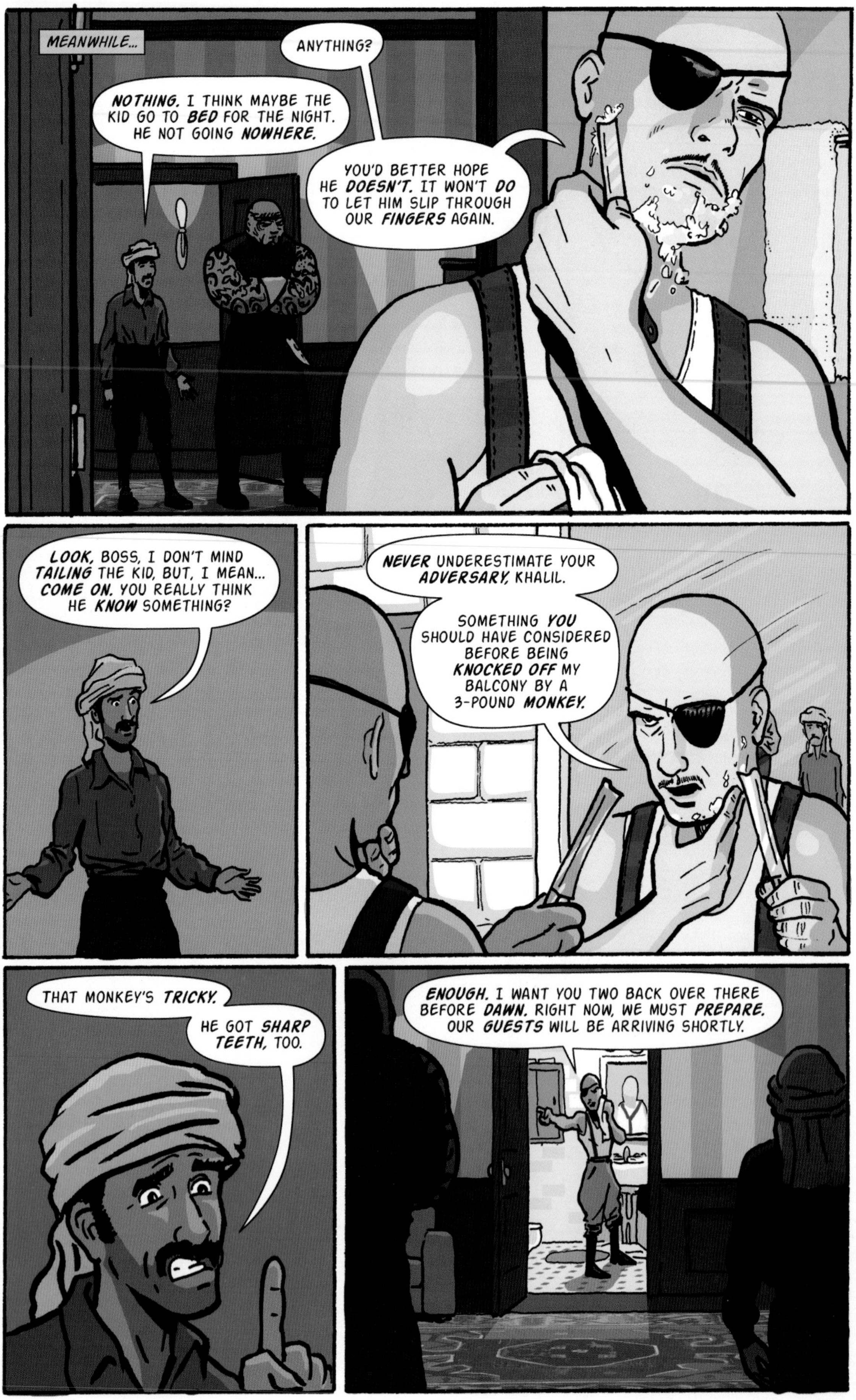
MEANWHILE...
ANYTHING?
NOTHING. I THINK MAYBE THE KID GO TO BED FOR THE NIGHT. HE NOT GOING NOWHERE.
YOU'D BETTER HOPE HE DOESN'T. IT WON'T DO TO LET HIM SLIP THROUGH OUR FINGERS AGAIN.
LOOK, BOSS, I DON'T MIND TAILING THE KID, BUT, I MEAN... COME ON. YOU REALLY THINK HE KNOW SOMETHING?
NEVER UNDERESTIMATE YOUR ADVERSARY, KHALIL.
SOMETHING YOU SHOULD HAVE CONSIDERED BEFORE BEING KNOCKED OFF MY BALCONY BY A 3-POUND MONKEY.
THAT MONKEY'S TRICKY.
HE GOT SHARP TEETH, TOO.
ENOUGH. I WANT YOU TWO BACK OVER THERE BEFORE DAWN. RIGHT NOW, WE MUST PREPARE. OUR GUESTS WILL BE ARRIVING SHORTLY.

MMM... MRS. MAHFOUZ MAKES A *GOOD* KUSHARI. HOW'S THE *MESSAGE* COMING?

WE'RE *REALLY* CLOSE. JUST A *FEW MORE* SYMBOLS LEFT.

SOMETHING ABOUT THIS LOOKS *FAMILIAR.*

_IT_/OE/IHE/_EA_
BO_E/_O_R/HEA_
NT/_OI_S/HEAR
N_/_

IT LOOKS LIKE THAT *LAST* WORD *BEGINS* AND *ENDS* WITH THE SAME LETTER, THIS FEATHER SHAPE...

WAIT! *DEAD!* CITY OF THE *DEAD!*

CITY OF THE DEAD?

YES! IT'S AN AREA OF *CAIRO,* JUST WEST OF THE *MARKET!*

GREAT! THAT GETS US *THREE* NEW LETTERS.

A/CITY/OF/THE/DEAD
/ABO_E/YOUR/HEAD
ENT/_OI_ES/HEAR
OUD/_URI_
EN/SHADO_

SO... LET'S SEE...

= B

= C

JUST A COUPLE LEFT...

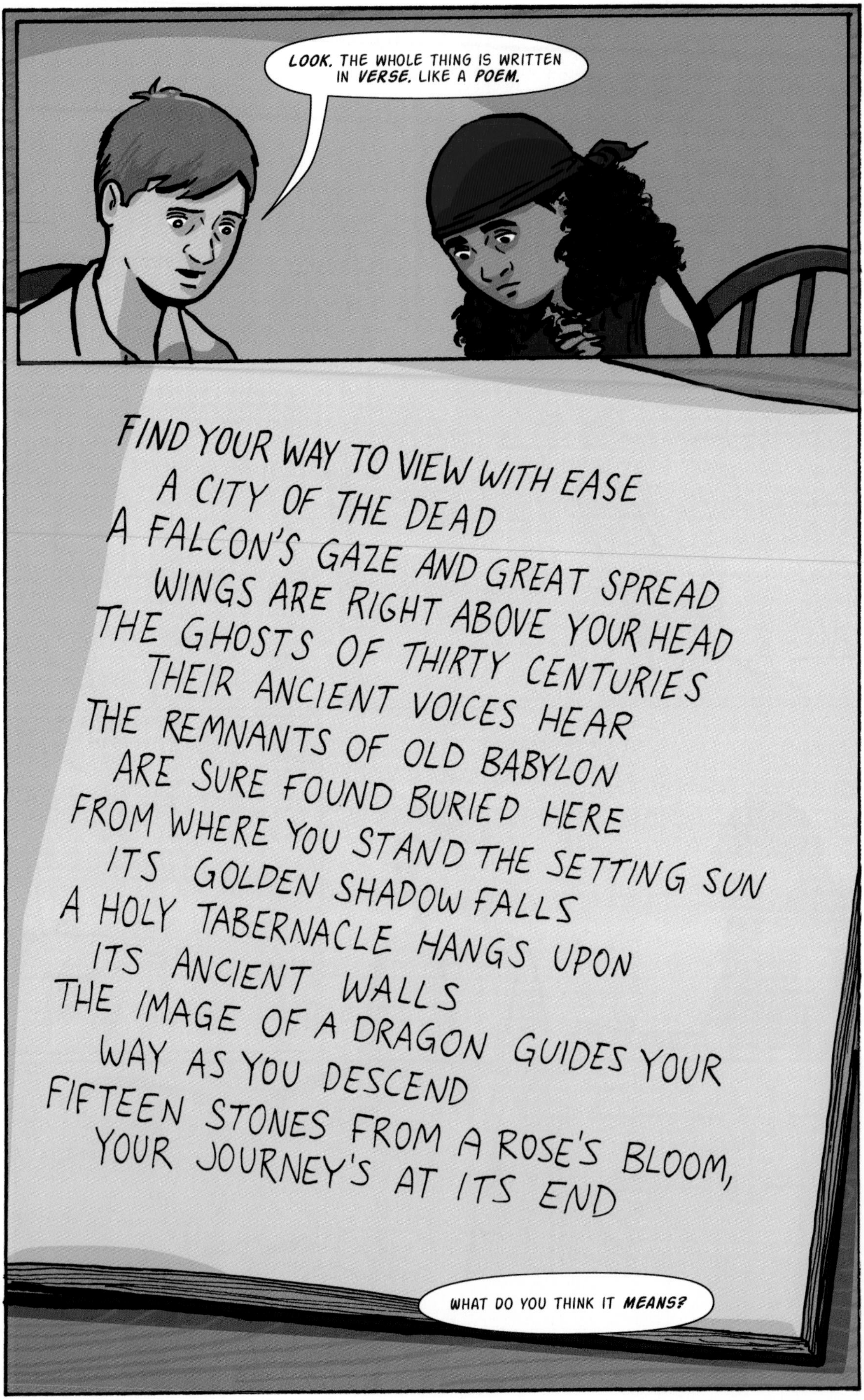
LOOK. THE WHOLE THING IS WRITTEN IN VERSE. LIKE A POEM.
FIND YOUR WAY TO VIEW WITH EASE
A CITY OF THE DEAD
A FALCON'S GAZE AND GREAT SPREAD
WINGS ARE RIGHT ABOVE YOUR HEAD
THE GHOSTS OF THIRTY CENTURIES
THEIR ANCIENT VOICES HEAR
THE REMNANTS OF OLD BABYLON
ARE SURE FOUND BURIED HERE
FROM WHERE YOU STAND THE SETTING SUN
ITS GOLDEN SHADOW FALLS
A HOLY TABERNACLE HANGS UPON
ITS ANCIENT WALLS
THE IMAGE OF A DRAGON GUIDES YOUR
WAY AS YOU DESCEND
FIFTEEN STONES FROM A ROSE'S BLOOM,
YOUR JOURNEY'S AT ITS END
WHAT DO YOU THINK IT MEANS?

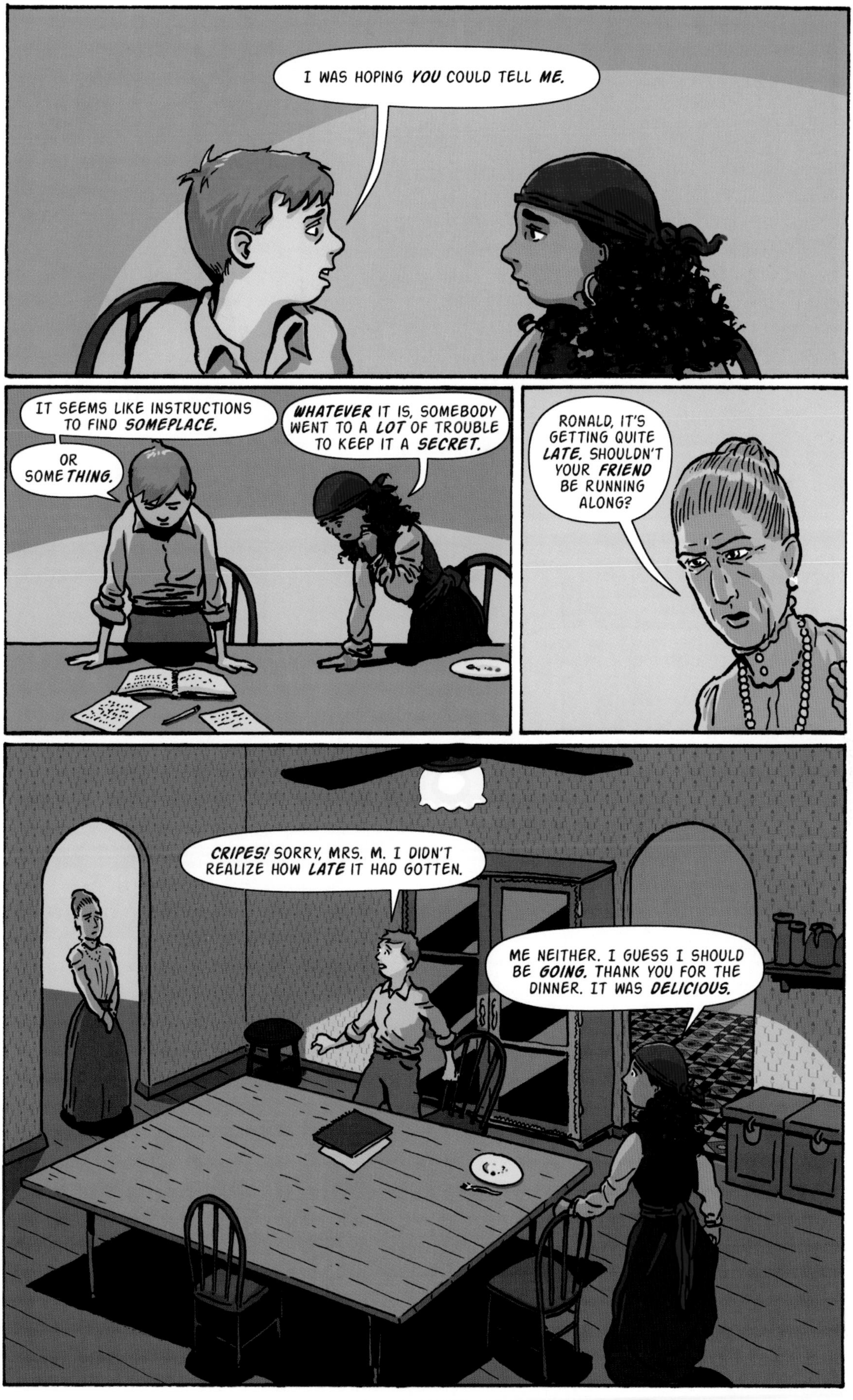
I WAS HOPING YOU COULD TELL ME.
IT SEEMS LIKE INSTRUCTIONS TO FIND SOMEPLACE.
OR SOMETHING.
WHATEVER IT IS, SOMEBODY WENT TO A LOT OF TROUBLE TO KEEP IT A SECRET.
RONALD, IT'S GETTING QUITE LATE. SHOULDN'T YOUR FRIEND BE RUNNING ALONG?
CRIPES! SORRY, MRS. M. I DIDN'T REALIZE HOW LATE IT HAD GOTTEN.
ME NEITHER. I GUESS I SHOULD BE GOING. THANK YOU FOR THE DINNER. IT WAS DELICIOUS.

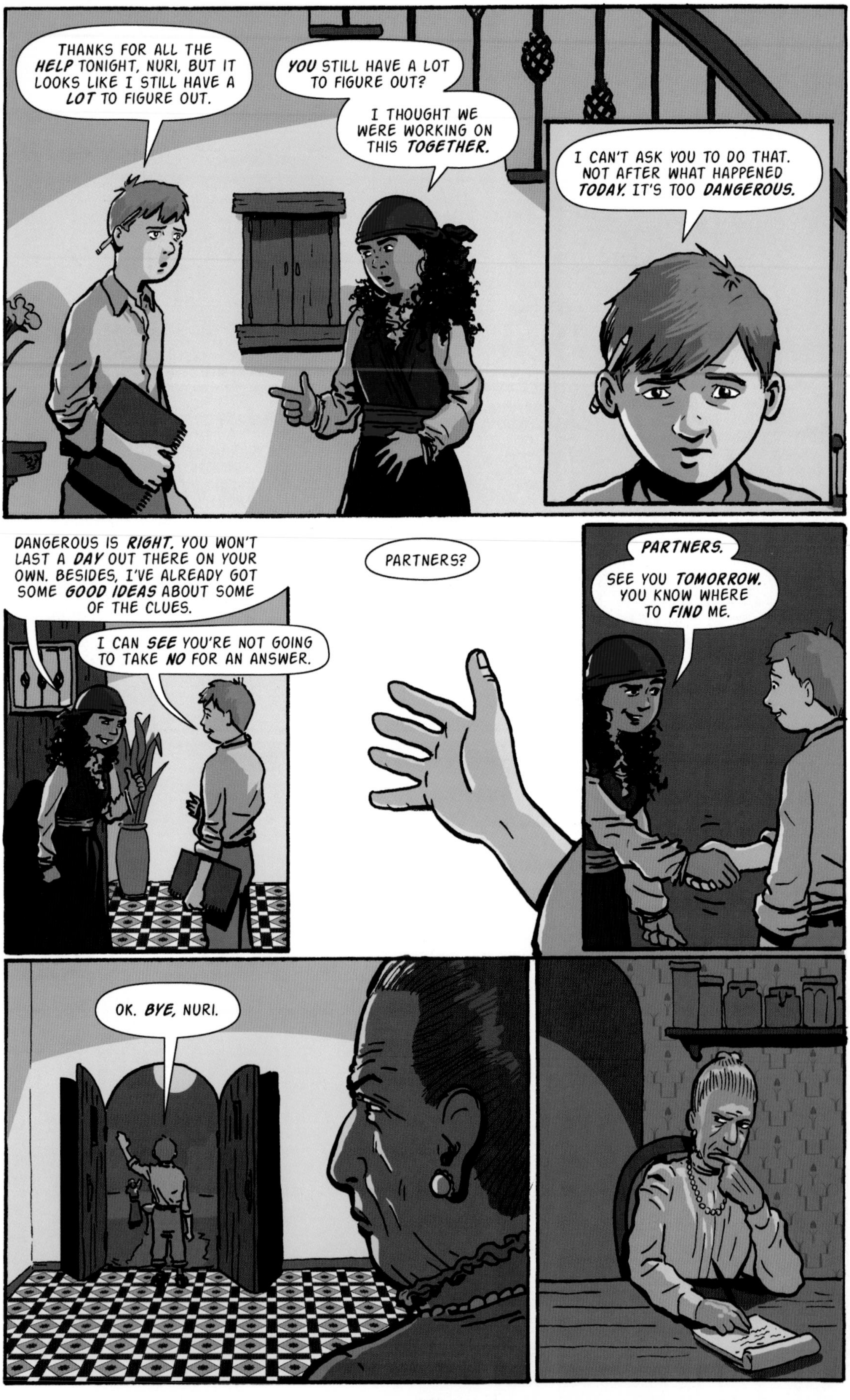
THANKS FOR ALL THE HELP TONIGHT, NURI, BUT IT LOOKS LIKE I STILL HAVE A LOT TO FIGURE OUT.
YOU STILL HAVE A LOT TO FIGURE OUT?
I THOUGHT WE WERE WORKING ON THIS TOGETHER.
I CAN'T ASK YOU TO DO THAT. NOT AFTER WHAT HAPPENED TODAY. IT'S TOO DANGEROUS.
DANGEROUS IS RIGHT. YOU WON'T LAST A DAY OUT THERE ON YOUR OWN. BESIDES, I'VE ALREADY GOT SOME GOOD IDEAS ABOUT SOME OF THE CLUES.
I CAN SEE YOU'RE NOT GOING TO TAKE NO FOR AN ANSWER.
PARTNERS?
PARTNERS.
SEE YOU TOMORROW. YOU KNOW WHERE TO FIND ME.
OK. BYE, NURI.

CHAPTER FIVE

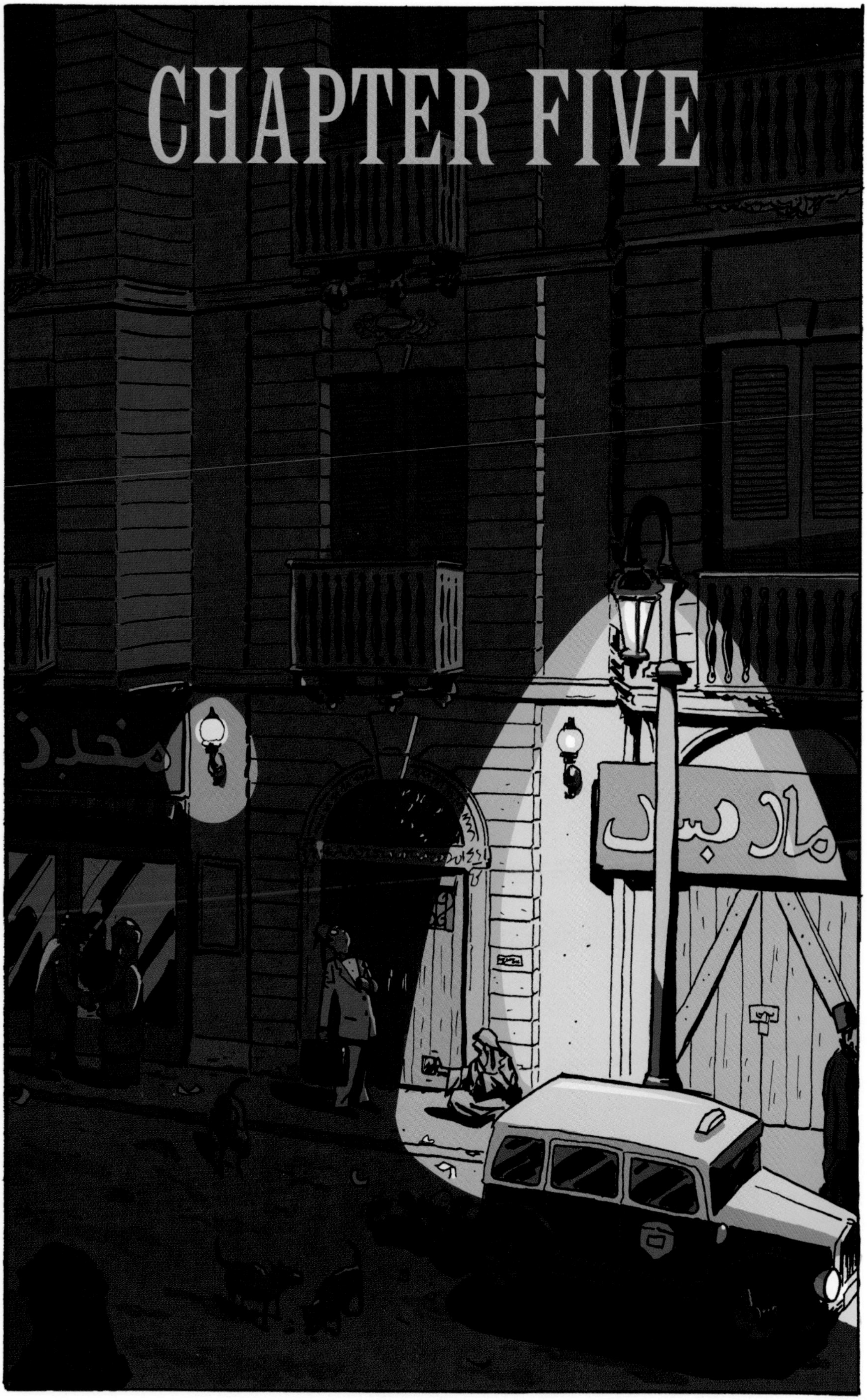

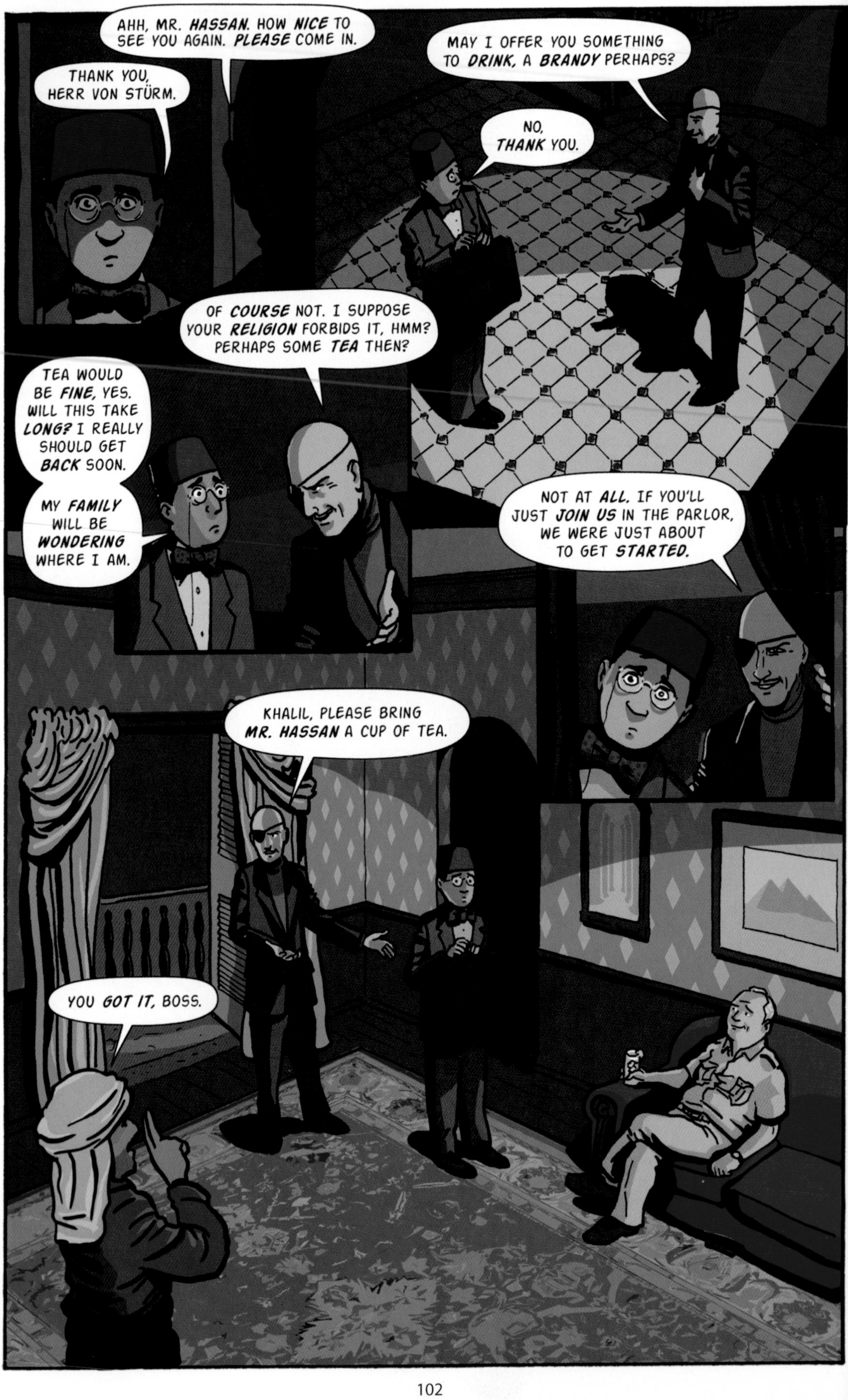
THANK YOU, HERR VON STÜRM.
AHH, MR. HASSAN. HOW NICE TO SEE YOU AGAIN. PLEASE COME IN.
MAY I OFFER YOU SOMETHING TO DRINK, A BRANDY PERHAPS?
NO, THANK YOU.
OF COURSE NOT. I SUPPOSE YOUR RELIGION FORBIDS IT, HMM? PERHAPS SOME TEA THEN?
TEA WOULD BE FINE, YES. WILL THIS TAKE LONG? I REALLY SHOULD GET BACK SOON.
MY FAMILY WILL BE WONDERING WHERE I AM.
NOT AT ALL. IF YOU'LL JUST JOIN US IN THE PARLOR, WE WERE JUST ABOUT TO GET STARTED.
KHALIL, PLEASE BRING MR. HASSAN A CUP OF TEA.
YOU GOT IT, BOSS.

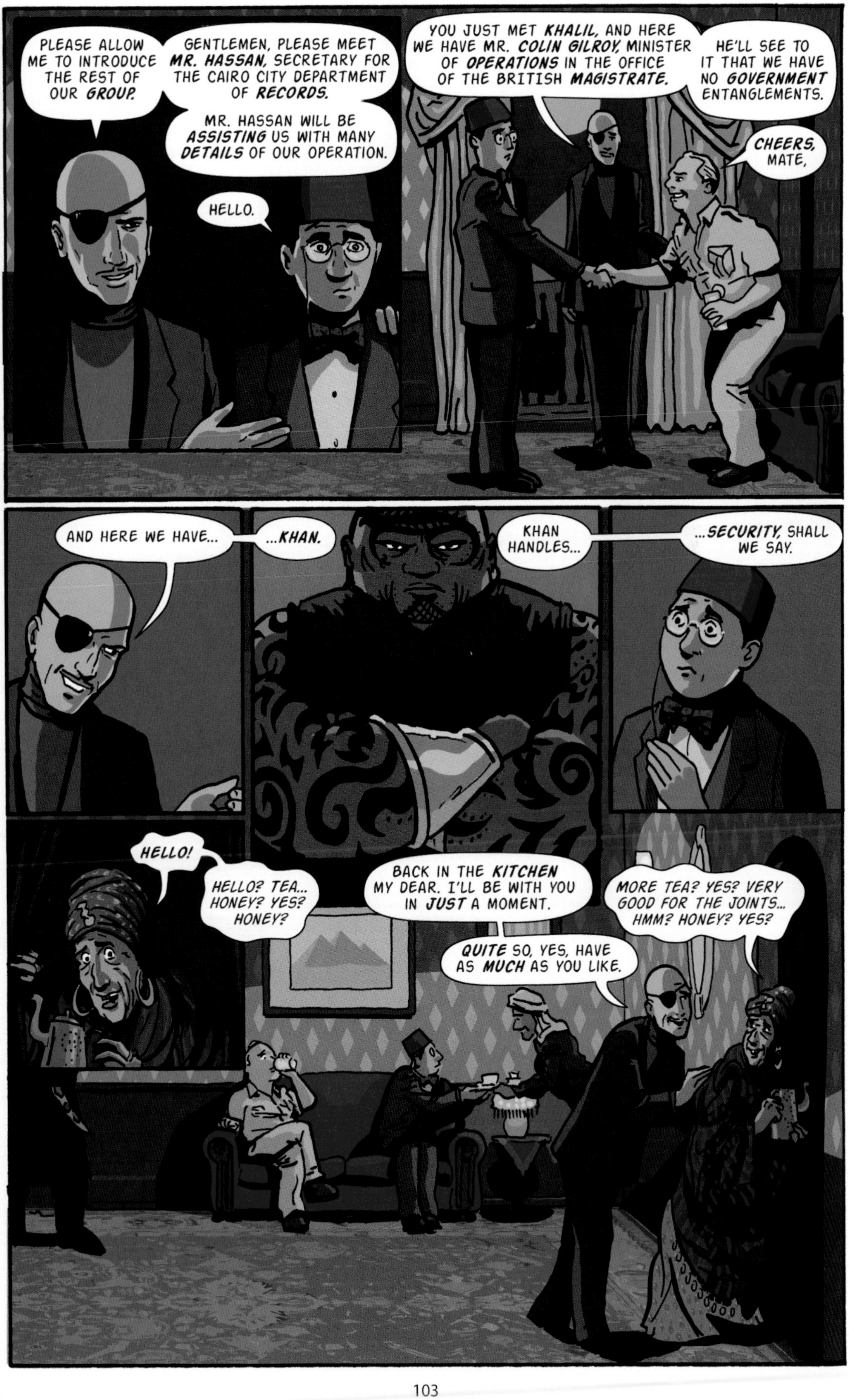
PLEASE ALLOW ME TO INTRODUCE THE REST OF OUR GROUP.
GENTLEMEN, PLEASE MEET MR. HASSAN, SECRETARY FOR THE CAIRO CITY DEPARTMENT OF RECORDS.
MR. HASSAN WILL BE ASSISTING US WITH MANY DETAILS OF OUR OPERATION.
HELLO.
YOU JUST MET KHALIL, AND HERE WE HAVE MR. COLIN GILROY, MINISTER OF OPERATIONS IN THE OFFICE OF THE BRITISH MAGISTRATE.
HE'LL SEE TO IT THAT WE HAVE NO GOVERNMENT ENTANGLEMENTS.
CHEERS, MATE,
AND HERE WE HAVE...
...KHAN.
KHAN HANDLES...
...SECURITY, SHALL WE SAY.
HELLO!
HELLO? TEA... HONEY? YES? HONEY?
BACK IN THE KITCHEN MY DEAR. I'LL BE WITH YOU IN JUST A MOMENT.
QUITE SO, YES, HAVE AS MUCH AS YOU LIKE.
MORE TEA? YES? VERY GOOD FOR THE JOINTS... HMM? HONEY? YES?

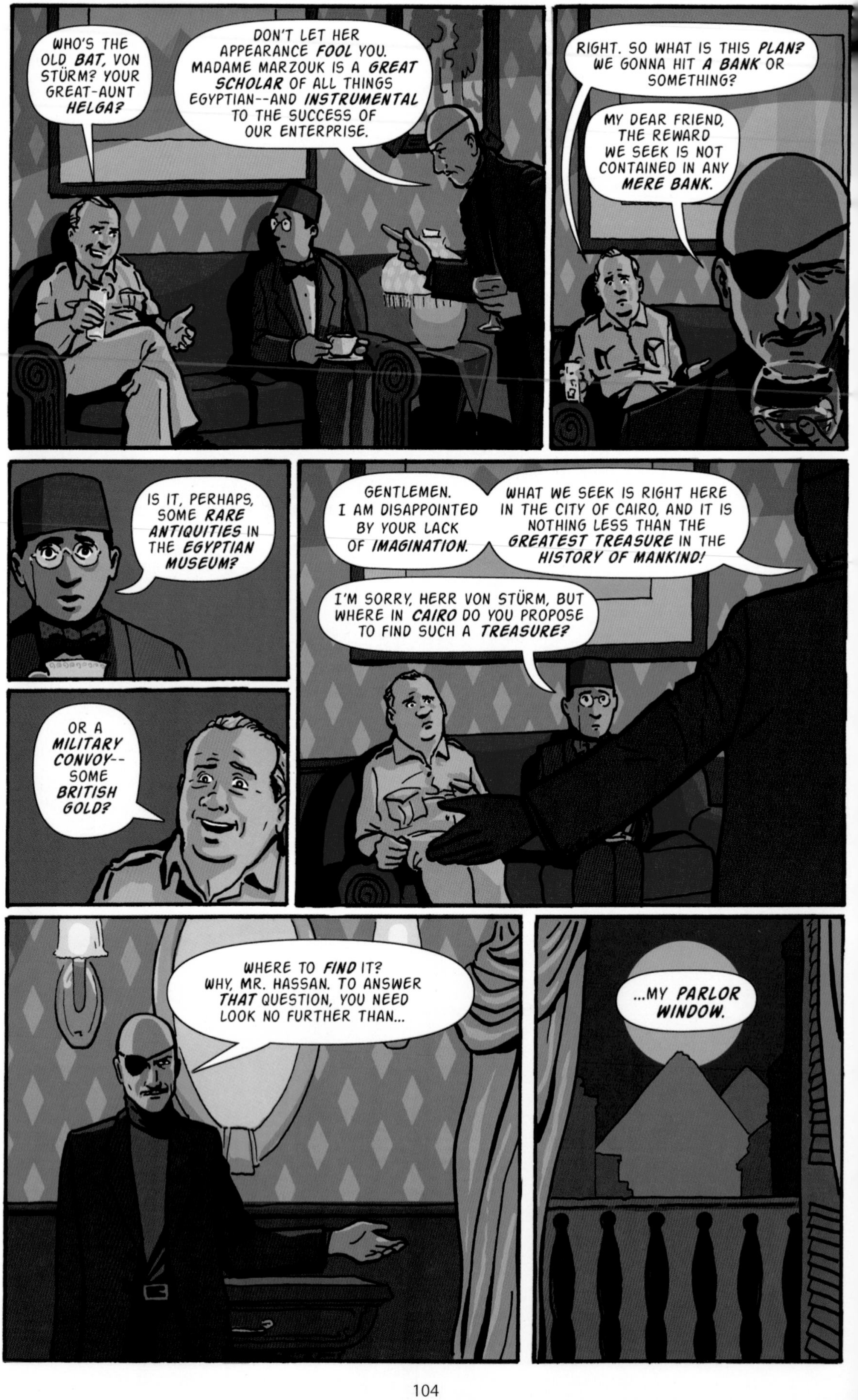
WHO'S THE OLD BAT, VON STÜRM? YOUR GREAT-AUNT HELGA?
DON'T LET HER APPEARANCE FOOL YOU. MADAME MARZOUK IS A GREAT SCHOLAR OF ALL THINGS EGYPTIAN--AND INSTRUMENTAL TO THE SUCCESS OF OUR ENTERPRISE.
RIGHT. SO WHAT IS THIS PLAN? WE GONNA HIT A BANK OR SOMETHING?
MY DEAR FRIEND, THE REWARD WE SEEK IS NOT CONTAINED IN ANY MERE BANK.
IS IT, PERHAPS, SOME RARE ANTIQUITIES IN THE EGYPTIAN MUSEUM?
OR A MILITARY CONVOY-- SOME BRITISH GOLD?
GENTLEMEN. I AM DISAPPOINTED BY YOUR LACK OF IMAGINATION.
WHAT WE SEEK IS RIGHT HERE IN THE CITY OF CAIRO, AND IT IS NOTHING LESS THAN THE GREATEST TREASURE IN THE HISTORY OF MANKIND!
I'M SORRY, HERR VON STÜRM, BUT WHERE IN CAIRO DO YOU PROPOSE TO FIND SUCH A TREASURE?
WHERE TO FIND IT? WHY, MR. HASSAN. TO ANSWER THAT QUESTION, YOU NEED LOOK NO FURTHER THAN...
...MY PARLOR WINDOW.

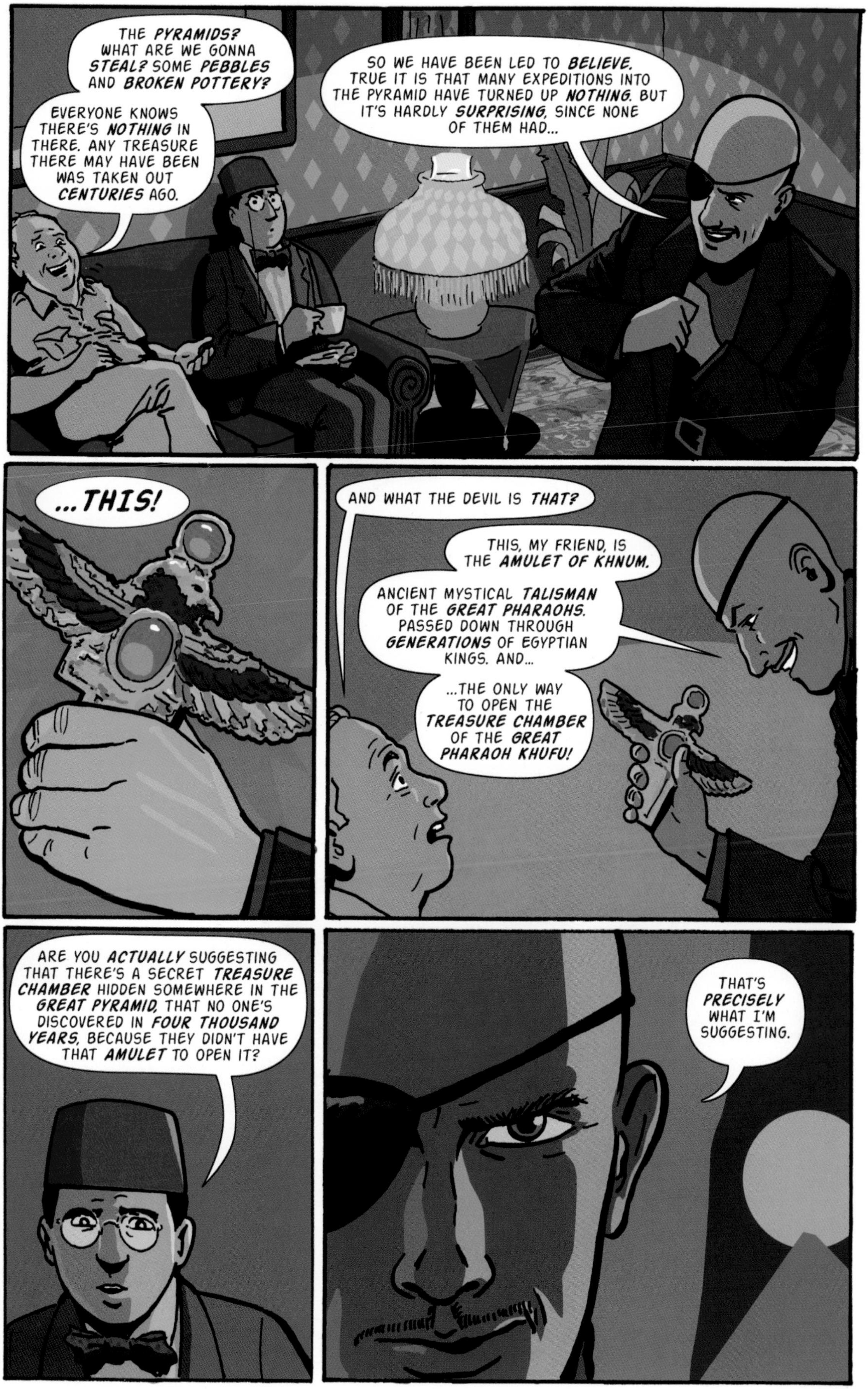
THE PYRAMIDS? WHAT ARE WE GONNA STEAL? SOME PEBBLES AND BROKEN POTTERY?
EVERYONE KNOWS THERE'S NOTHING IN THERE. ANY TREASURE THERE MAY HAVE BEEN WAS TAKEN OUT CENTURIES AGO.
SO WE HAVE BEEN LED TO BELIEVE. TRUE IT IS THAT MANY EXPEDITIONS INTO THE PYRAMID HAVE TURNED UP NOTHING. BUT IT'S HARDLY SURPRISING, SINCE NONE OF THEM HAD...
...THIS!
AND WHAT THE DEVIL IS THAT?
THIS, MY FRIEND, IS THE AMULET OF KHNUM.
ANCIENT MYSTICAL TALISMAN OF THE GREAT PHARAOHS. PASSED DOWN THROUGH GENERATIONS OF EGYPTIAN KINGS. AND...
...THE ONLY WAY TO OPEN THE TREASURE CHAMBER OF THE GREAT PHARAOH KHUFU!
ARE YOU ACTUALLY SUGGESTING THAT THERE'S A SECRET TREASURE CHAMBER HIDDEN SOMEWHERE IN THE GREAT PYRAMID, THAT NO ONE'S DISCOVERED IN FOUR THOUSAND YEARS, BECAUSE THEY DIDN'T HAVE THAT AMULET TO OPEN IT?
THAT'S PRECISELY WHAT I'M SUGGESTING.

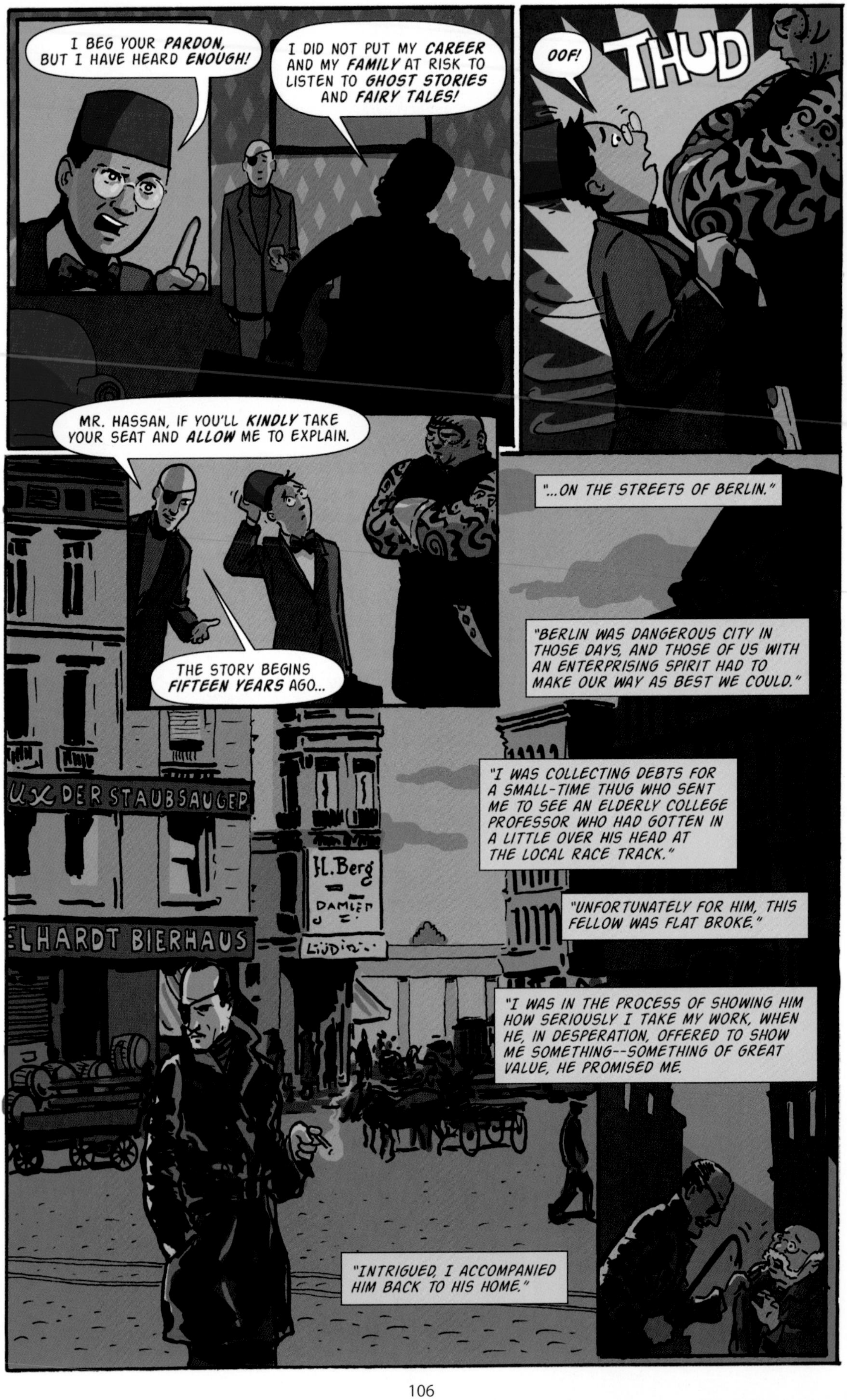
I BEG YOUR PARDON, BUT I HAVE HEARD ENOUGH!
I DID NOT PUT MY CAREER AND MY FAMILY AT RISK TO LISTEN TO GHOST STORIES AND FAIRY TALES!
OOF!
THUD
MR. HASSAN, IF YOU'LL KINDLY TAKE YOUR SEAT AND ALLOW ME TO EXPLAIN.
THE STORY BEGINS FIFTEEN YEARS AGO...
"...ON THE STREETS OF BERLIN."
"BERLIN WAS DANGEROUS CITY IN THOSE DAYS, AND THOSE OF US WITH AN ENTERPRISING SPIRIT HAD TO MAKE OUR WAY AS BEST WE COULD."
DER STAUBSAUGER
ELHARDT BIERHAUS
H.L. Berg
"I WAS COLLECTING DEBTS FOR A SMALL-TIME THUG WHO SENT ME TO SEE AN ELDERLY COLLEGE PROFESSOR WHO HAD GOTTEN IN A LITTLE OVER HIS HEAD AT THE LOCAL RACE TRACK."
"UNFORTUNATELY FOR HIM, THIS FELLOW WAS FLAT BROKE."
"I WAS IN THE PROCESS OF SHOWING HIM HOW SERIOUSLY I TAKE MY WORK, WHEN HE, IN DESPERATION, OFFERED TO SHOW ME SOMETHING--SOMETHING OF GREAT VALUE, HE PROMISED ME.
"INTRIGUED, I ACCOMPANIED HIM BACK TO HIS HOME."

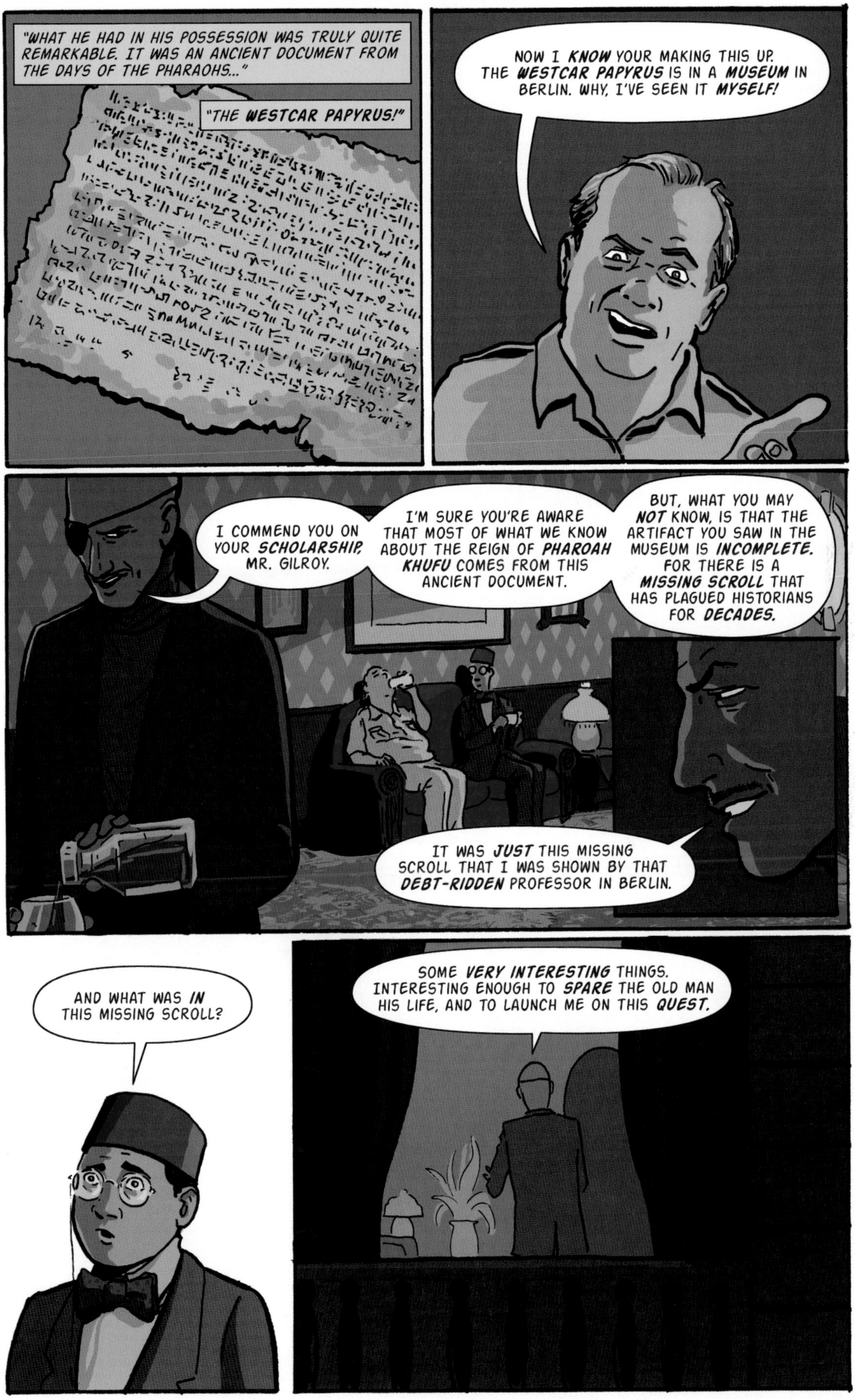
"WHAT HE HAD IN HIS POSSESSION WAS TRULY QUITE REMARKABLE. IT WAS AN ANCIENT DOCUMENT FROM THE DAYS OF THE PHARAOHS..."
"THE WESTCAR PAPYRUS!"
NOW I KNOW YOUR MAKING THIS UP. THE WESTCAR PAPYRUS IS IN A MUSEUM IN BERLIN. WHY, I'VE SEEN IT MYSELF!
I COMMEND YOU ON YOUR SCHOLARSHIP, MR. GILROY.
I'M SURE YOU'RE AWARE THAT MOST OF WHAT WE KNOW ABOUT THE REIGN OF PHAROAH KHUFU COMES FROM THIS ANCIENT DOCUMENT.
BUT, WHAT YOU MAY NOT KNOW, IS THAT THE ARTIFACT YOU SAW IN THE MUSEUM IS INCOMPLETE. FOR THERE IS A MISSING SCROLL THAT HAS PLAGUED HISTORIANS FOR DECADES.
IT WAS JUST THIS MISSING SCROLL THAT I WAS SHOWN BY THAT DEBT-RIDDEN PROFESSOR IN BERLIN.
AND WHAT WAS IN THIS MISSING SCROLL?
SOME VERY INTERESTING THINGS. INTERESTING ENOUGH TO SPARE THE OLD MAN HIS LIFE, AND TO LAUNCH ME ON THIS QUEST.

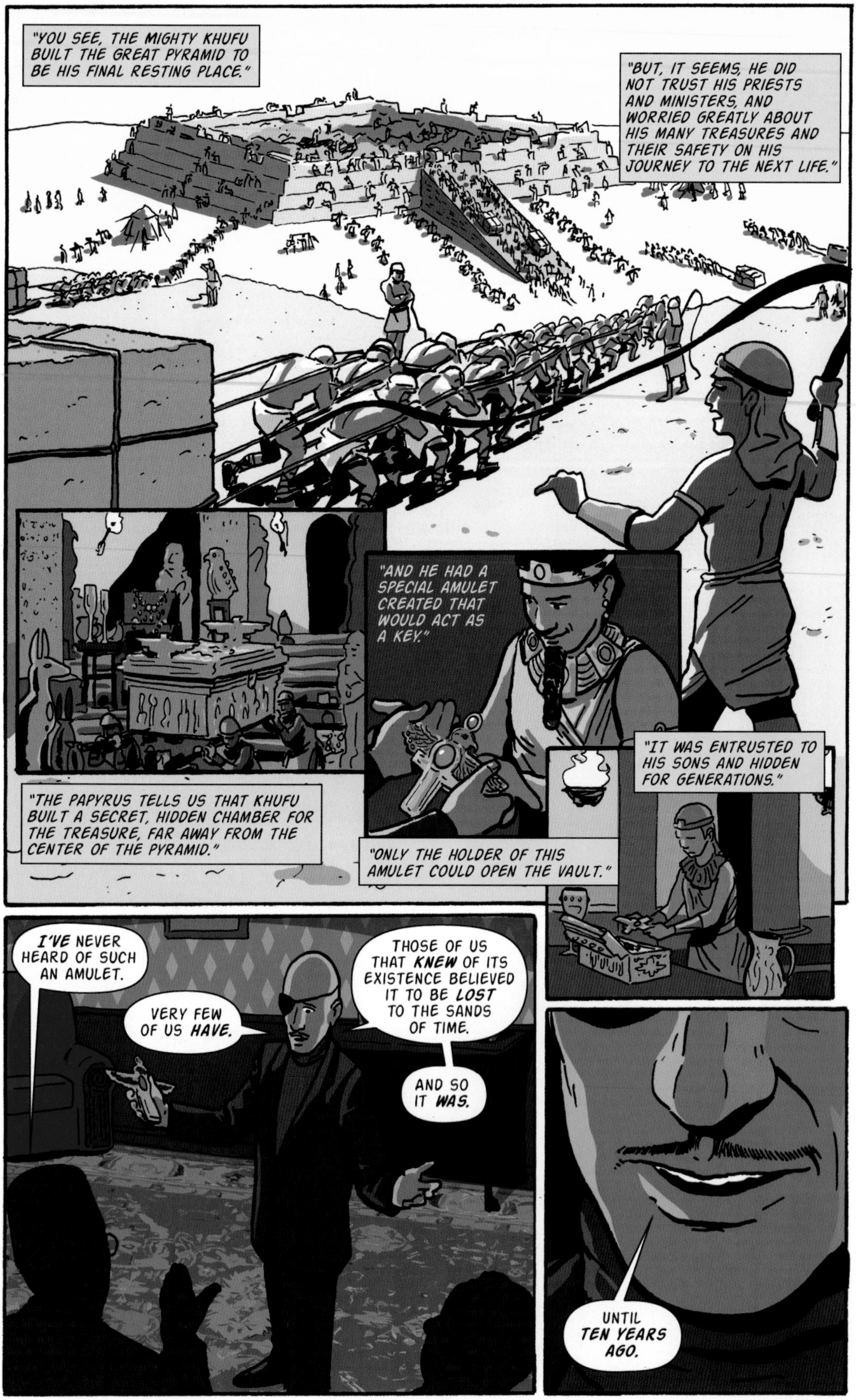
"YOU SEE, THE MIGHTY KHUFU BUILT THE GREAT PYRAMID TO BE HIS FINAL RESTING PLACE."
"BUT, IT SEEMS, HE DID NOT TRUST HIS PRIESTS AND MINISTERS, AND WORRIED GREATLY ABOUT HIS MANY TREASURES AND THEIR SAFETY ON HIS JOURNEY TO THE NEXT LIFE."
"THE PAPYRUS TELLS US THAT KHUFU BUILT A SECRET, HIDDEN CHAMBER FOR THE TREASURE, FAR AWAY FROM THE CENTER OF THE PYRAMID."
"AND HE HAD A SPECIAL AMULET CREATED THAT WOULD ACT AS A KEY."
"ONLY THE HOLDER OF THIS AMULET COULD OPEN THE VAULT."
"IT WAS ENTRUSTED TO HIS SONS AND HIDDEN FOR GENERATIONS."
I'VE NEVER HEARD OF SUCH AN AMULET.
VERY FEW OF US HAVE.
THOSE OF US THAT KNEW OF ITS EXISTENCE BELIEVED IT TO BE LOST TO THE SANDS OF TIME.
AND SO IT WAS.
UNTIL TEN YEARS AGO.

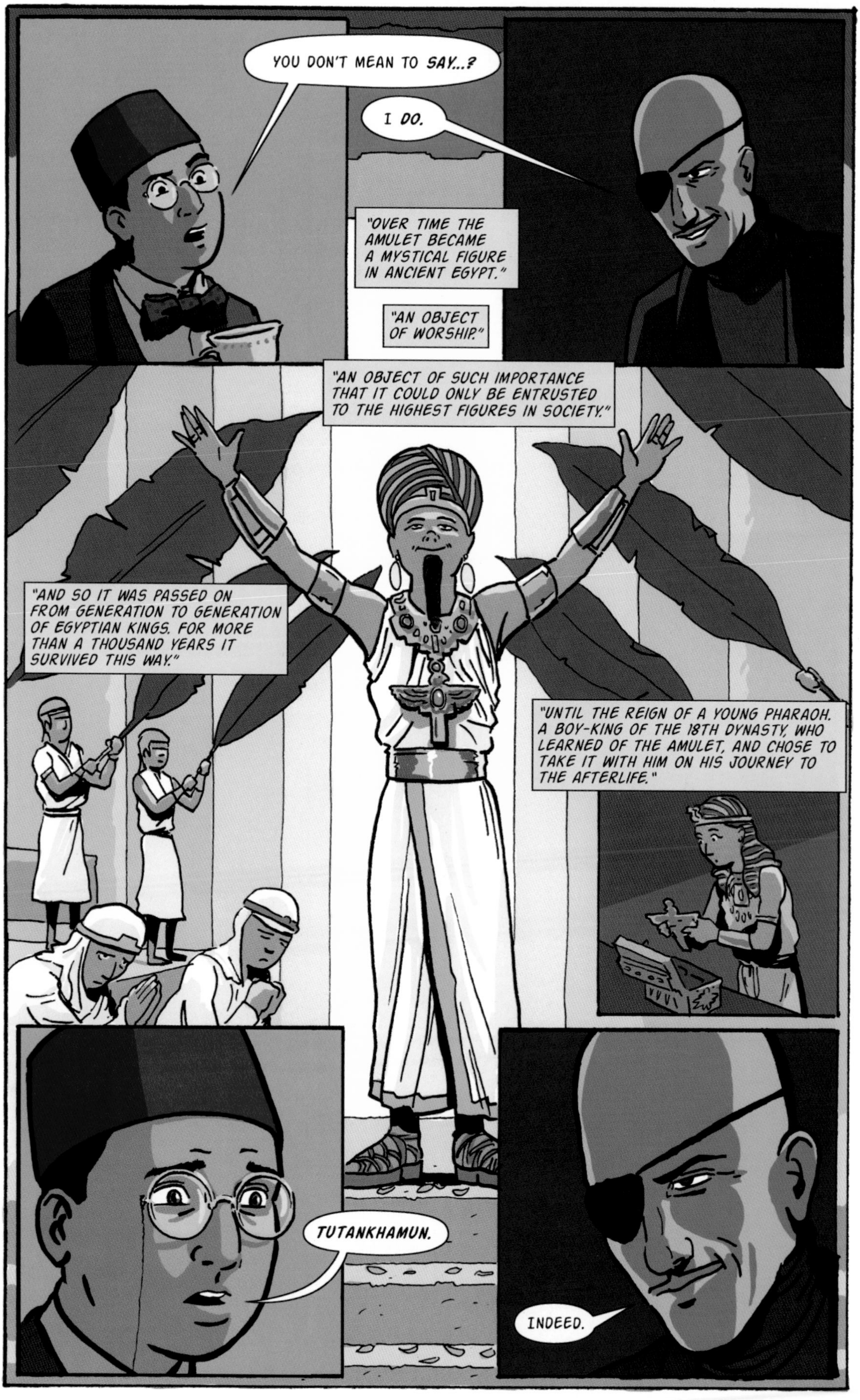
YOU DON'T MEAN TO SAY...?
I DO.
"OVER TIME THE AMULET BECAME A MYSTICAL FIGURE IN ANCIENT EGYPT."
"AN OBJECT OF WORSHIP."
"AN OBJECT OF SUCH IMPORTANCE THAT IT COULD ONLY BE ENTRUSTED TO THE HIGHEST FIGURES IN SOCIETY."
"AND SO IT WAS PASSED ON FROM GENERATION TO GENERATION OF EGYPTIAN KINGS. FOR MORE THAN A THOUSAND YEARS IT SURVIVED THIS WAY."
"UNTIL THE REIGN OF A YOUNG PHARAOH. A BOY-KING OF THE 18TH DYNASTY, WHO LEARNED OF THE AMULET, AND CHOSE TO TAKE IT WITH HIM ON HIS JOURNEY TO THE AFTERLIFE."
TUTANKHAMUN.
INDEED.

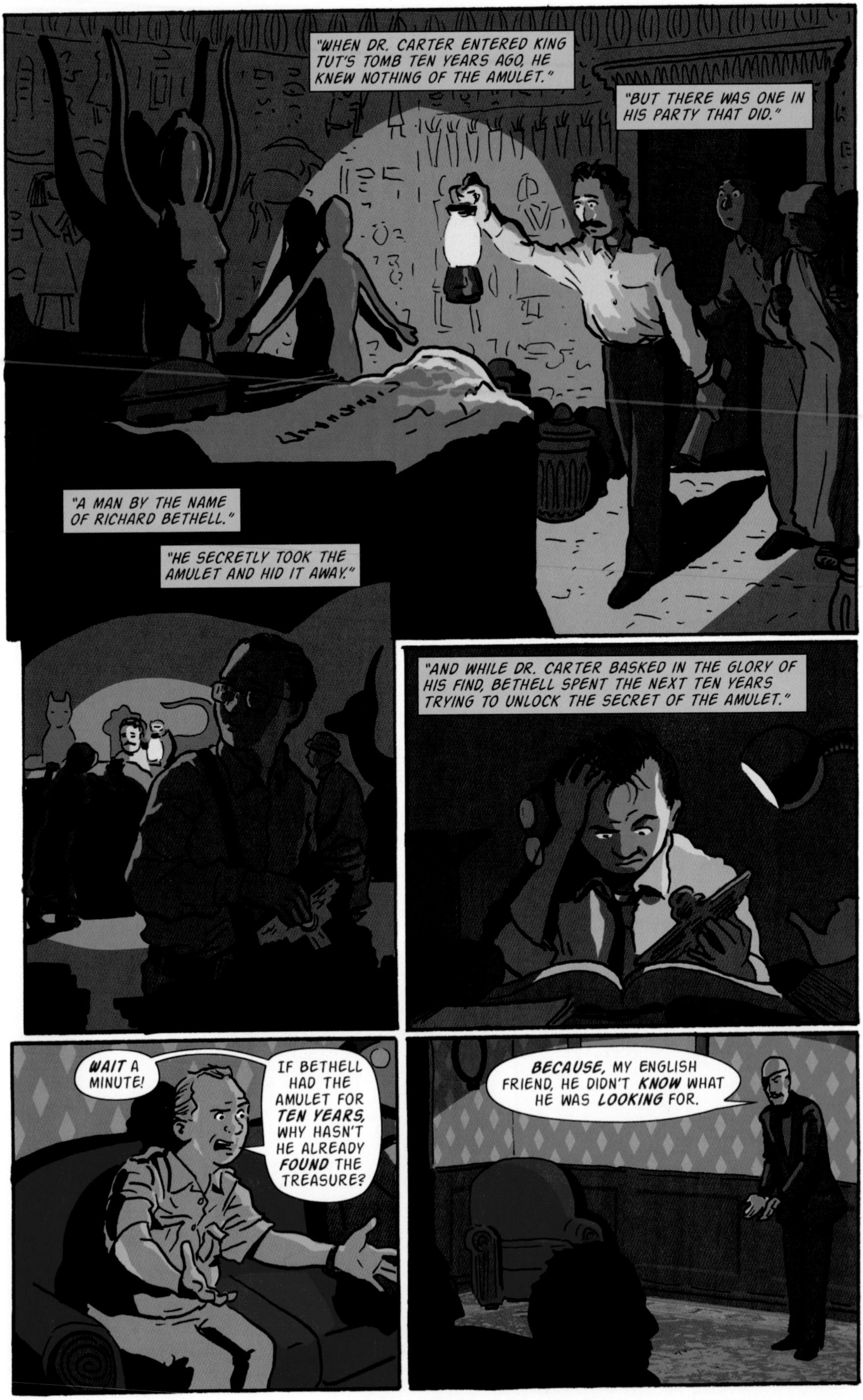
"WHEN DR. CARTER ENTERED KING TUT'S TOMB TEN YEARS AGO, HE KNEW NOTHING OF THE AMULET."
"BUT THERE WAS ONE IN HIS PARTY THAT DID."
"A MAN BY THE NAME OF RICHARD BETHELL."
"HE SECRETLY TOOK THE AMULET AND HID IT AWAY."
"AND WHILE DR. CARTER BASKED IN THE GLORY OF HIS FIND, BETHELL SPENT THE NEXT TEN YEARS TRYING TO UNLOCK THE SECRET OF THE AMULET."
WAIT A MINUTE!
IF BETHELL HAD THE AMULET FOR TEN YEARS, WHY HASN'T HE ALREADY FOUND THE TREASURE?
BECAUSE, MY ENGLISH FRIEND, HE DIDN'T KNOW WHAT HE WAS LOOKING FOR.

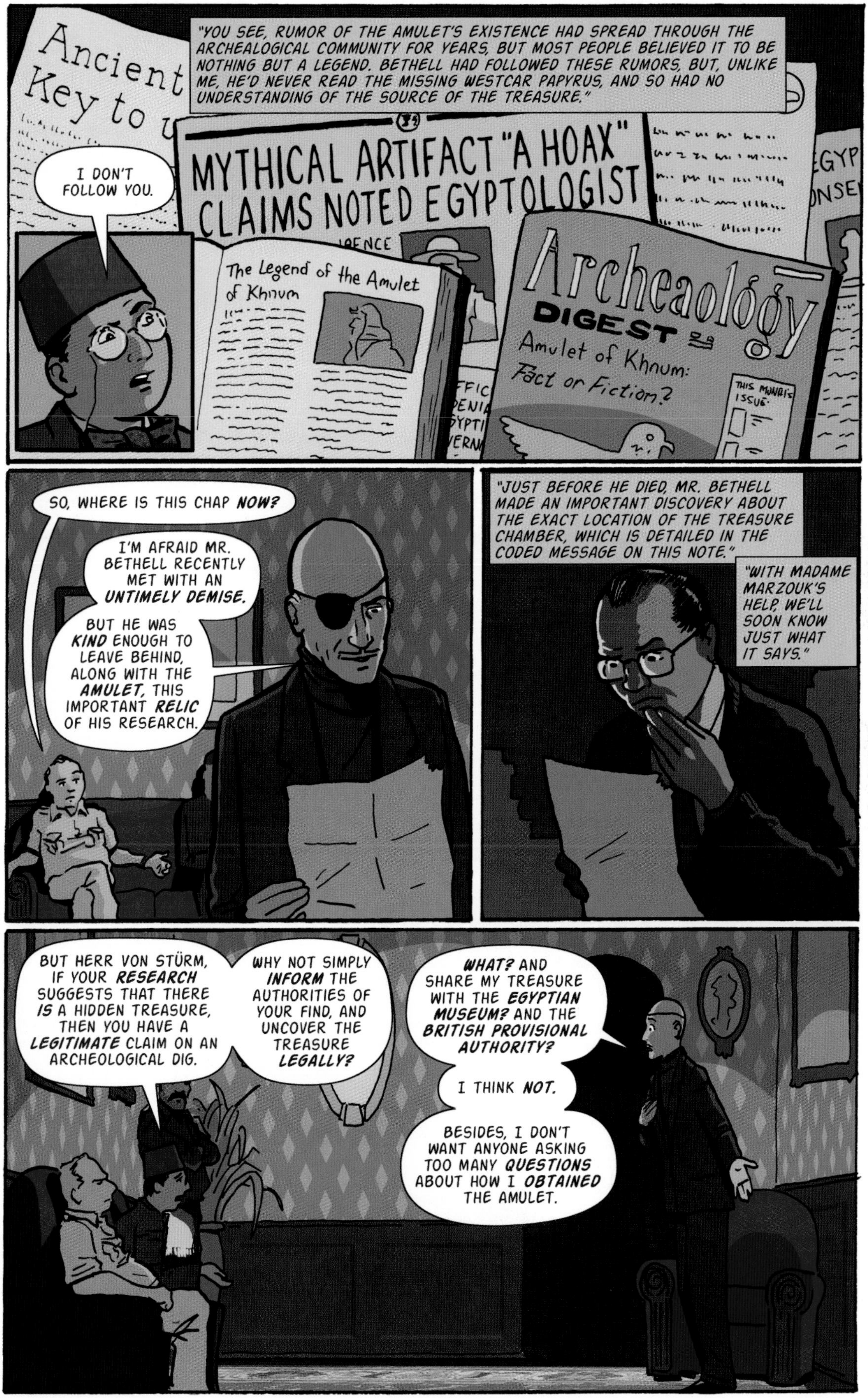
"YOU SEE, RUMOR OF THE AMULET'S EXISTENCE HAD SPREAD THROUGH THE ARCHEALOGICAL COMMUNITY FOR YEARS, BUT MOST PEOPLE BELIEVED IT TO BE NOTHING BUT A LEGEND. BETHELL HAD FOLLOWED THESE RUMORS, BUT, UNLIKE ME, HE'D NEVER READ THE MISSING WESTCAR PAPYRUS, AND SO HAD NO UNDERSTANDING OF THE SOURCE OF THE TREASURE."
Ancient Key to
MYTHICAL ARTIFACT "A HOAX" CLAIMS NOTED EGYPTOLOGIST
I DON'T FOLLOW YOU.
The Legend of the Amulet of Khnum
Archeaology DIGEST
Amulet of Khnum: Fact or Fiction?
THIS MONTH'S ISSUE
SO, WHERE IS THIS CHAP NOW?
I'M AFRAID MR. BETHELL RECENTLY MET WITH AN UNTIMELY DEMISE.
BUT HE WAS KIND ENOUGH TO LEAVE BEHIND, ALONG WITH THE AMULET, THIS IMPORTANT RELIC OF HIS RESEARCH.
"JUST BEFORE HE DIED, MR. BETHELL MADE AN IMPORTANT DISCOVERY ABOUT THE EXACT LOCATION OF THE TREASURE CHAMBER, WHICH IS DETAILED IN THE CODED MESSAGE ON THIS NOTE."
"WITH MADAME MARZOUK'S HELP, WE'LL SOON KNOW JUST WHAT IT SAYS."
BUT HERR VON STÜRM, IF YOUR RESEARCH SUGGESTS THAT THERE IS A HIDDEN TREASURE, THEN YOU HAVE A LEGITIMATE CLAIM ON AN ARCHEOLOGICAL DIG.
WHY NOT SIMPLY INFORM THE AUTHORITIES OF YOUR FIND, AND UNCOVER THE TREASURE LEGALLY?
WHAT? AND SHARE MY TREASURE WITH THE EGYPTIAN MUSEUM? AND THE BRITISH PROVISIONAL AUTHORITY?
I THINK NOT.
BESIDES, I DON'T WANT ANYONE ASKING TOO MANY QUESTIONS ABOUT HOW I OBTAINED THE AMULET.

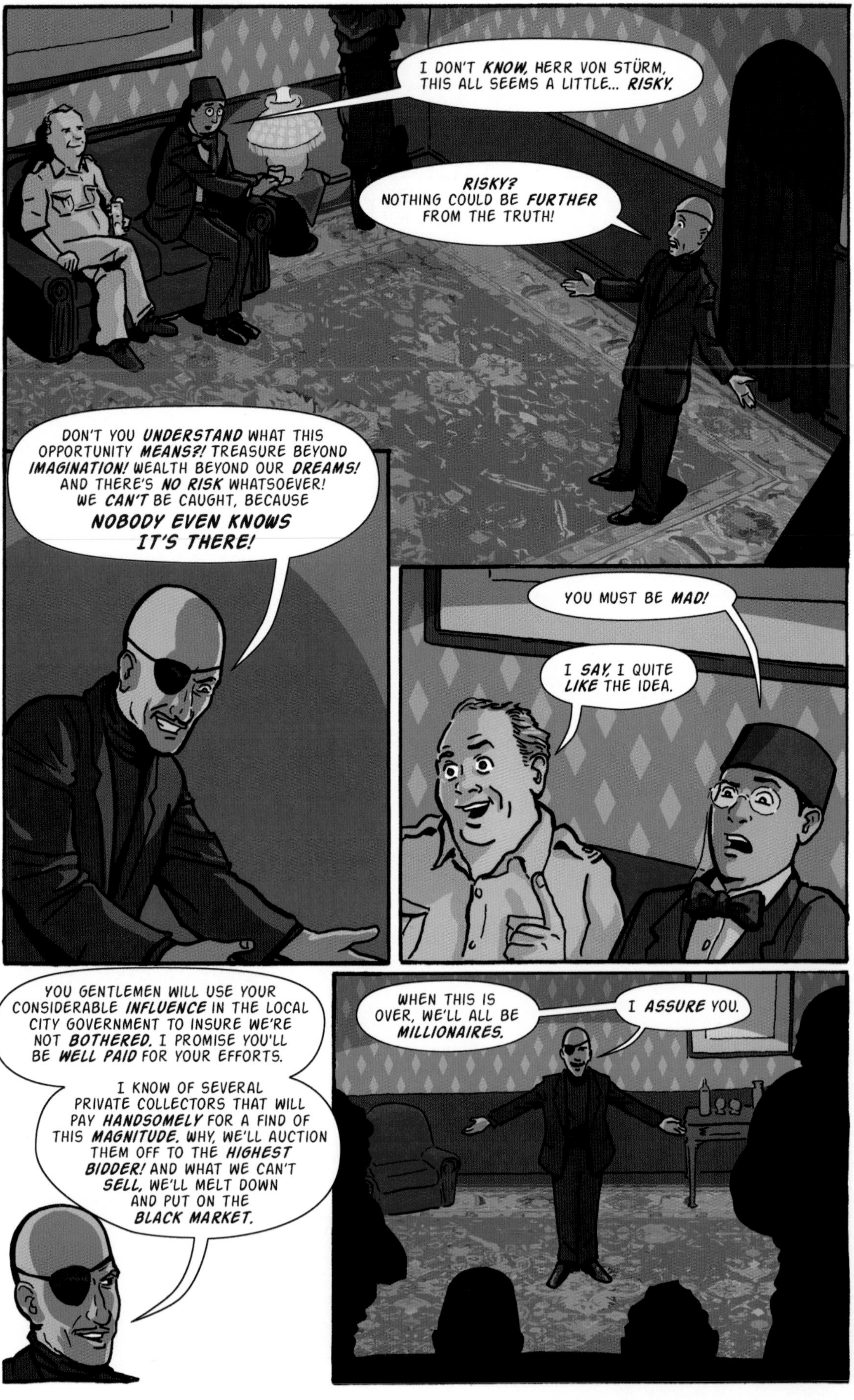
I DON'T KNOW, HERR VON STÜRM, THIS ALL SEEMS A LITTLE... RISKY.
RISKY? NOTHING COULD BE FURTHER FROM THE TRUTH!
DON'T YOU UNDERSTAND WHAT THIS OPPORTUNITY MEANS?! TREASURE BEYOND IMAGINATION! WEALTH BEYOND OUR DREAMS! AND THERE'S NO RISK WHATSOEVER! WE CAN'T BE CAUGHT, BECAUSE NOBODY EVEN KNOWS IT'S THERE!
YOU MUST BE MAD!
I SAY, I QUITE LIKE THE IDEA.
YOU GENTLEMEN WILL USE YOUR CONSIDERABLE INFLUENCE IN THE LOCAL CITY GOVERNMENT TO INSURE WE'RE NOT BOTHERED. I PROMISE YOU'LL BE WELL PAID FOR YOUR EFFORTS.
I KNOW OF SEVERAL PRIVATE COLLECTORS THAT WILL PAY HANDSOMELY FOR A FIND OF THIS MAGNITUDE. WHY, WE'LL AUCTION THEM OFF TO THE HIGHEST BIDDER! AND WHAT WE CAN'T SELL, WE'LL MELT DOWN AND PUT ON THE BLACK MARKET.
WHEN THIS IS OVER, WE'LL ALL BE MILLIONAIRES.
I ASSURE YOU.

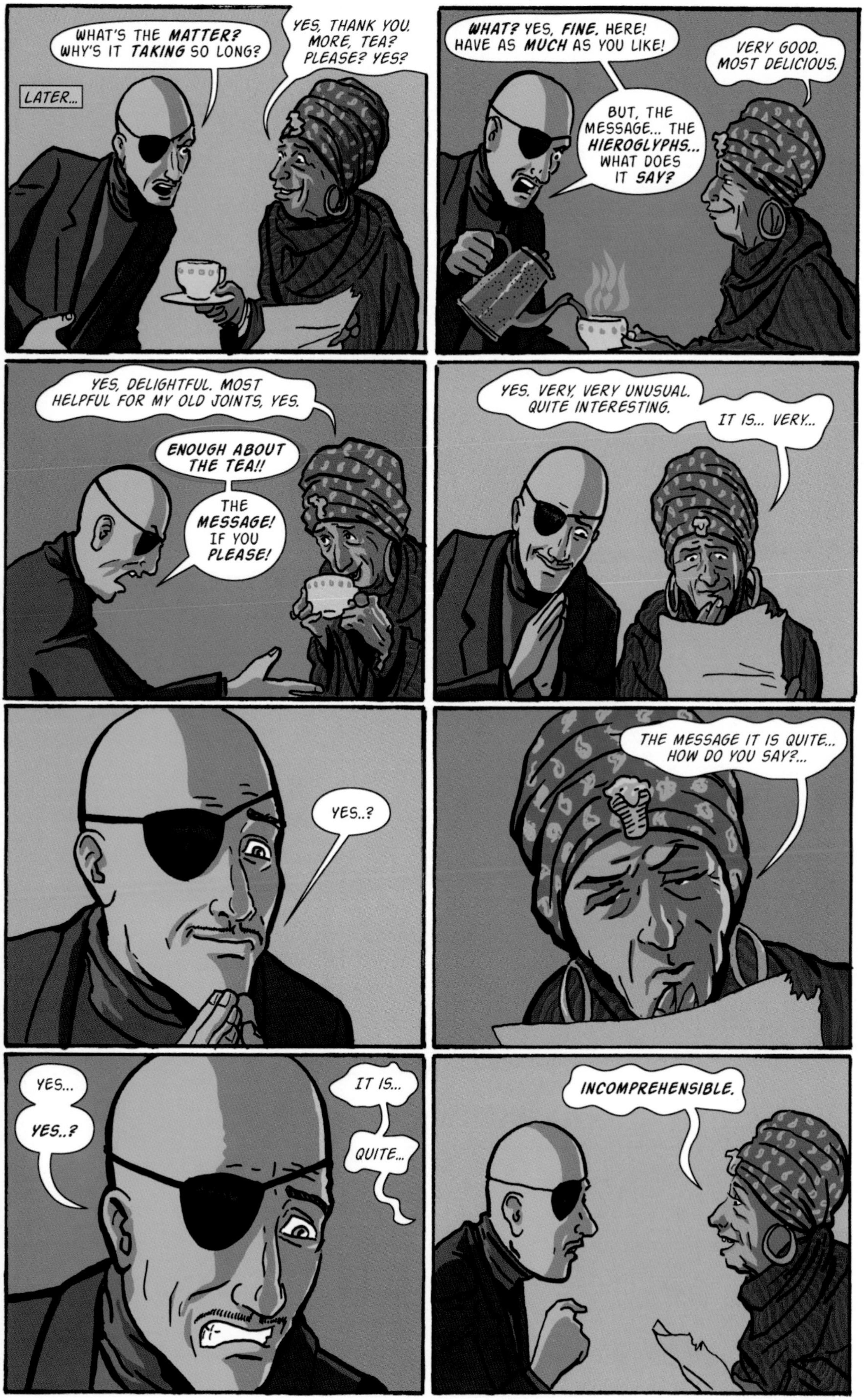
LATER...
WHAT'S THE MATTER? WHY'S IT TAKING SO LONG?
YES, THANK YOU. MORE, TEA? PLEASE? YES?
WHAT? YES, FINE. HERE! HAVE AS MUCH AS YOU LIKE!
BUT, THE MESSAGE... THE HIEROGLYPHS... WHAT DOES IT SAY?
VERY GOOD. MOST DELICIOUS.
YES, DELIGHTFUL. MOST HELPFUL FOR MY OLD JOINTS, YES.
ENOUGH ABOUT THE TEA!!
THE MESSAGE! IF YOU PLEASE!
YES. VERY, VERY UNUSUAL. QUITE INTERESTING.
IT IS... VERY...
YES..?
THE MESSAGE IT IS QUITE... HOW DO YOU SAY?...
YES...
YES..?
IT IS...
QUITE...
INCOMPREHENSIBLE.

I'M SORRY..?

YES. SO... MORE TEA? YES?

WAIT, WAIT!

I DON'T UNDERSTAND.

OH... I AM VERY SORRY. PLEASE, ALLOW ME TO EXPLAIN.

THE WORD INCOMPREHENSIBLE...

...IT MEANS IMPOSSIBLE TO READ.

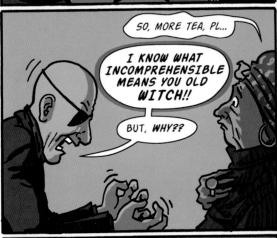

SO, MORE TEA, PL...

I KNOW WHAT INCOMPREHENSIBLE MEANS YOU OLD WITCH!!

BUT, WHY??

THIS MESSAGE... DOES NOT FOLLOW THE CONVENTIONS OF ANY ANCIENT EGYPTIAN WRITING STYLE. IT IS SIMPLY A RANDOM COLLECTION OF MEANINGLESS SYMBOLS.

I AM SORRY TO TELL YOU...

IT MEANS NOTHING.

SO...THANK YOU. YES? MORE TEA?

GET YOUR OWN TEA, YOU ANCIENT WINDBAG!

SMACK

I JUST HOPE THAT BOY IS AS CLEVER AS HE THINKS HE IS.

CHAPTER SIX

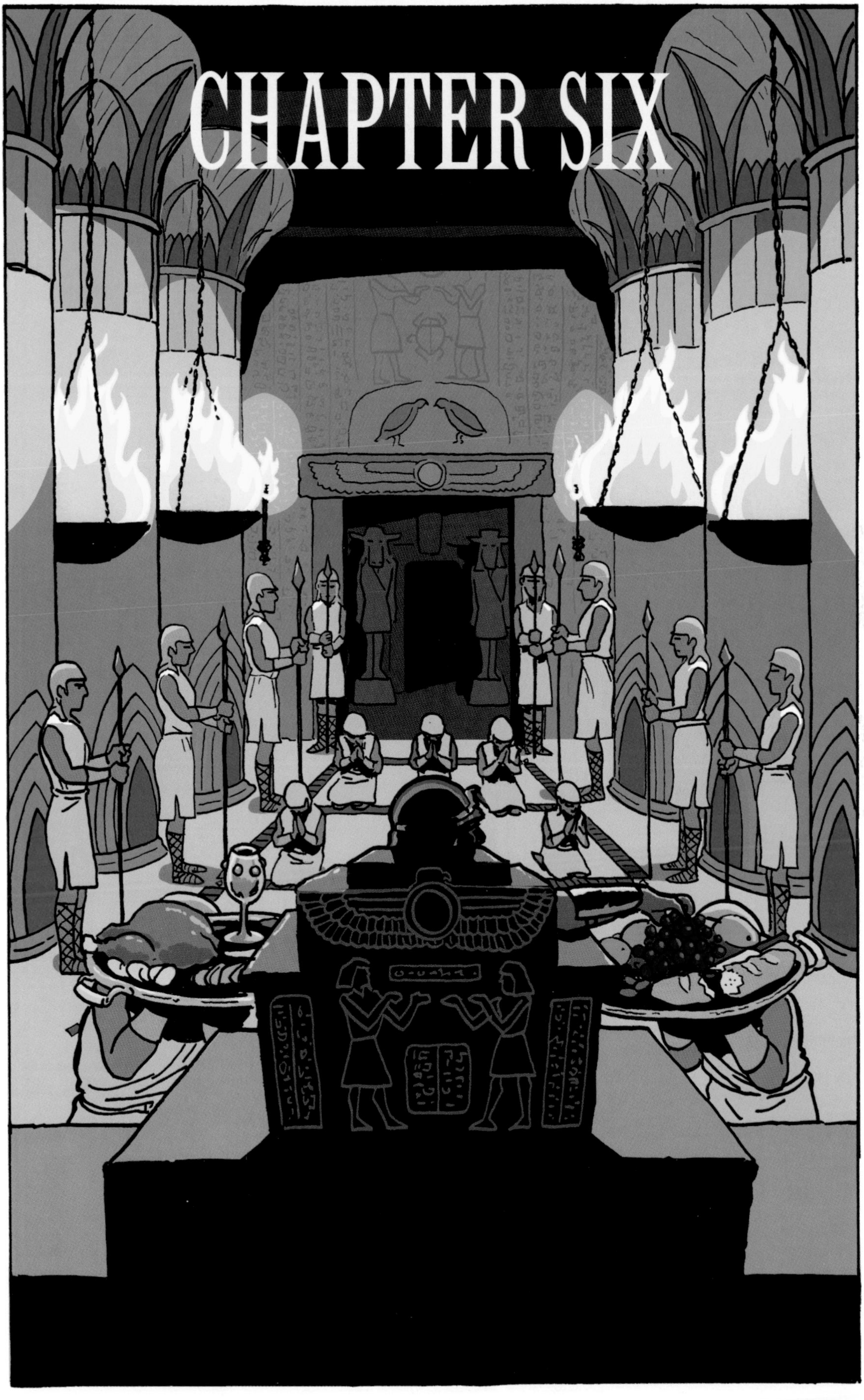

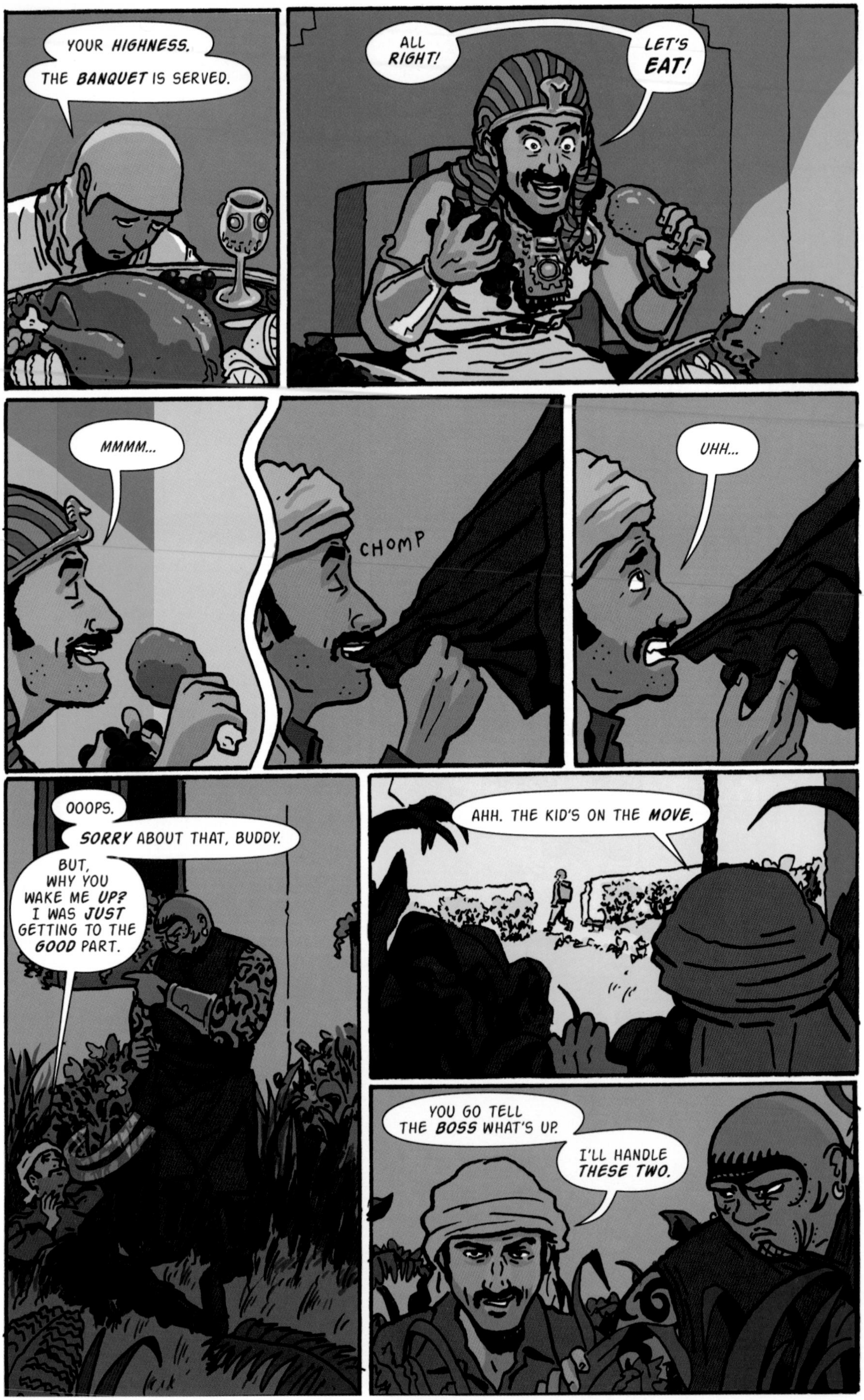
YOUR HIGHNESS.
THE BANQUET IS SERVED.
ALL RIGHT!
LET'S EAT!
MMMM...
CHOMP
UHH...
OOOPS.
SORRY ABOUT THAT, BUDDY.
BUT, WHY YOU WAKE ME UP? I WAS JUST GETTING TO THE GOOD PART.
AHH. THE KID'S ON THE MOVE.
YOU GO TELL THE BOSS WHAT'S UP.
I'LL HANDLE THESE TWO.

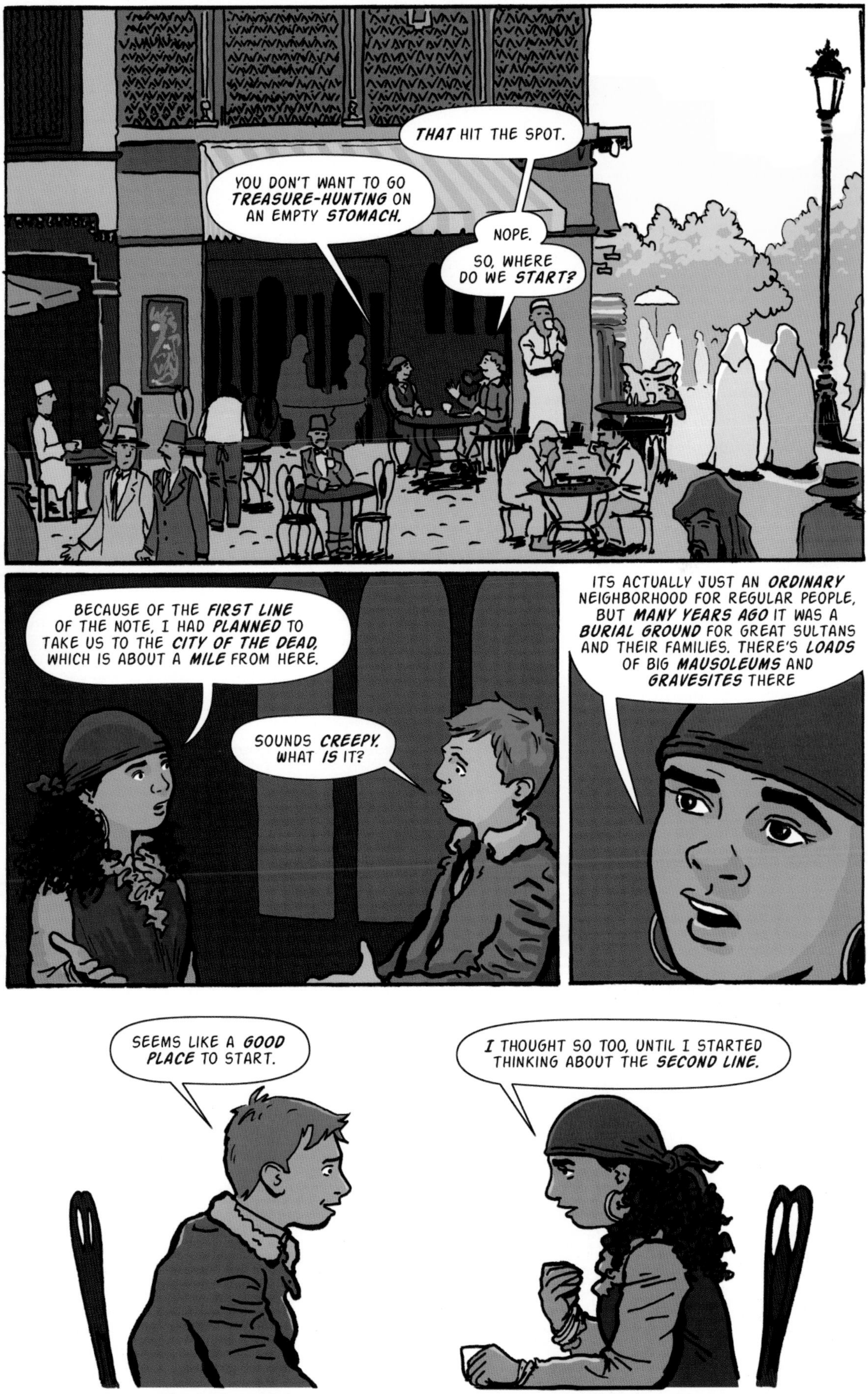

THAT HIT THE SPOT.
YOU DON'T WANT TO GO TREASURE-HUNTING ON AN EMPTY STOMACH.
NOPE.
SO, WHERE DO WE START?
BECAUSE OF THE FIRST LINE OF THE NOTE, I HAD PLANNED TO TAKE US TO THE CITY OF THE DEAD, WHICH IS ABOUT A MILE FROM HERE.
SOUNDS CREEPY. WHAT IS IT?
ITS ACTUALLY JUST AN ORDINARY NEIGHBORHOOD FOR REGULAR PEOPLE, BUT MANY YEARS AGO IT WAS A BURIAL GROUND FOR GREAT SULTANS AND THEIR FAMILIES. THERE'S LOADS OF BIG MAUSOLEUMS AND GRAVESITES THERE
SEEMS LIKE A GOOD PLACE TO START.
I THOUGHT SO TOO, UNTIL I STARTED THINKING ABOUT THE SECOND LINE.

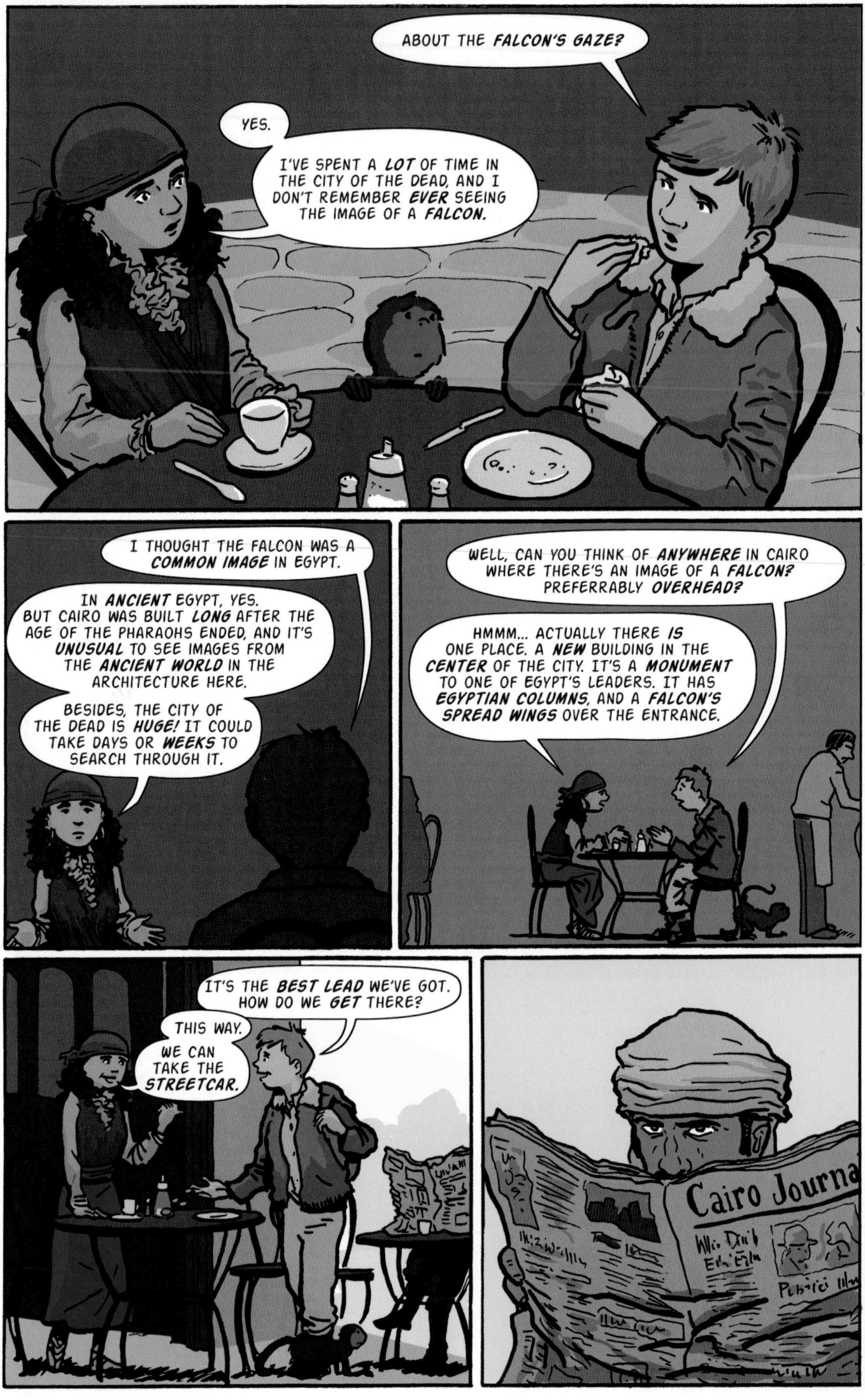
ABOUT THE FALCON'S GAZE?
YES.
I'VE SPENT A LOT OF TIME IN THE CITY OF THE DEAD, AND I DON'T REMEMBER EVER SEEING THE IMAGE OF A FALCON.
I THOUGHT THE FALCON WAS A COMMON IMAGE IN EGYPT.
IN ANCIENT EGYPT, YES. BUT CAIRO WAS BUILT LONG AFTER THE AGE OF THE PHARAOHS ENDED, AND IT'S UNUSUAL TO SEE IMAGES FROM THE ANCIENT WORLD IN THE ARCHITECTURE HERE.
BESIDES, THE CITY OF THE DEAD IS HUGE! IT COULD TAKE DAYS OR WEEKS TO SEARCH THROUGH IT.
WELL, CAN YOU THINK OF ANYWHERE IN CAIRO WHERE THERE'S AN IMAGE OF A FALCON? PREFERRABLY OVERHEAD?
HMMM... ACTUALLY THERE IS ONE PLACE. A NEW BUILDING IN THE CENTER OF THE CITY. IT'S A MONUMENT TO ONE OF EGYPT'S LEADERS. IT HAS EGYPTIAN COLUMNS, AND A FALCON'S SPREAD WINGS OVER THE ENTRANCE.
IT'S THE BEST LEAD WE'VE GOT. HOW DO WE GET THERE?
THIS WAY.
WE CAN TAKE THE STREETCAR.
Cairo Journa

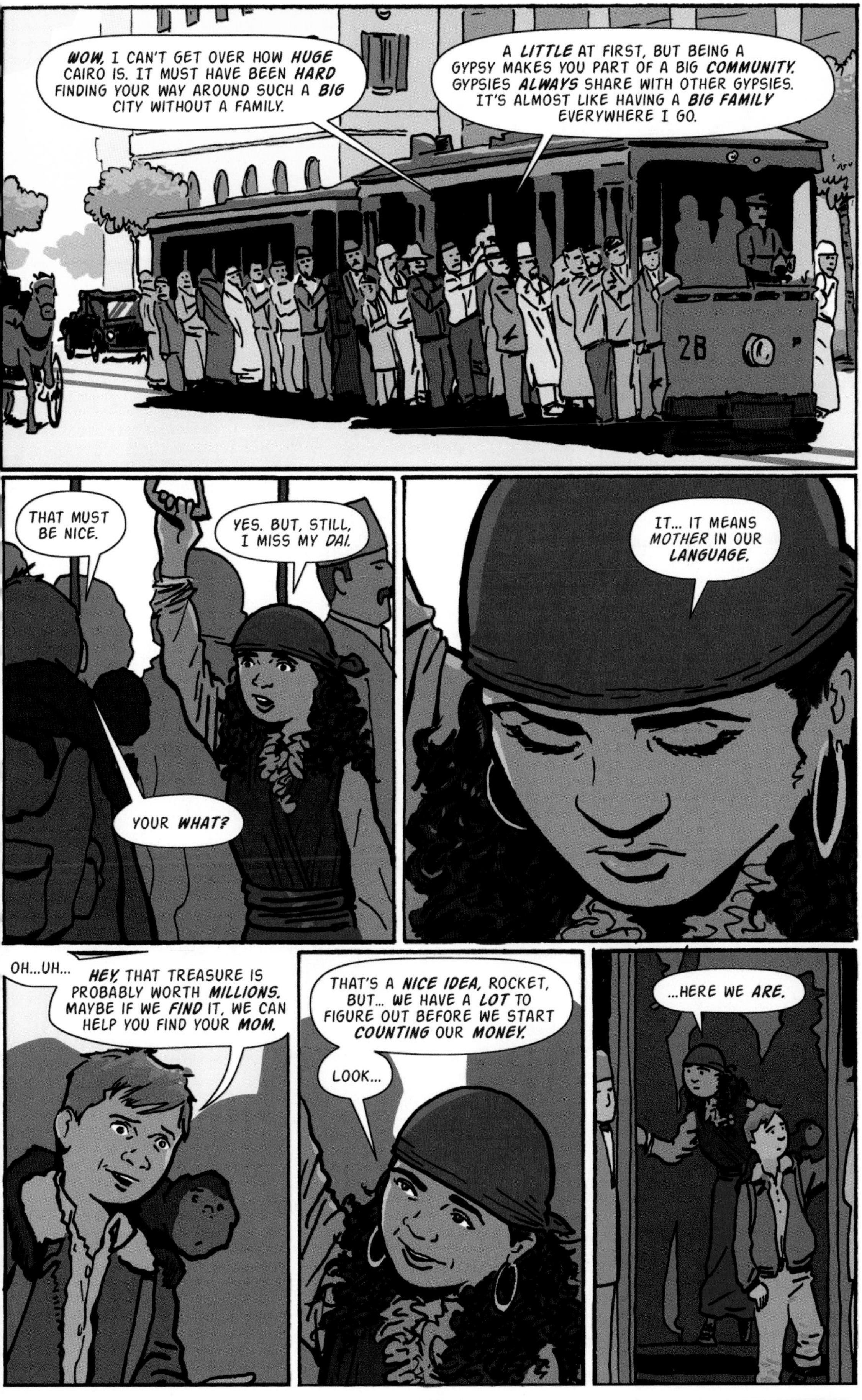
WOW, I CAN'T GET OVER HOW HUGE CAIRO IS. IT MUST HAVE BEEN HARD FINDING YOUR WAY AROUND SUCH A BIG CITY WITHOUT A FAMILY.
A LITTLE AT FIRST, BUT BEING A GYPSY MAKES YOU PART OF A BIG COMMUNITY. GYPSIES ALWAYS SHARE WITH OTHER GYPSIES. IT'S ALMOST LIKE HAVING A BIG FAMILY EVERYWHERE I GO.
28
THAT MUST BE NICE.
YES. BUT, STILL, I MISS MY DAI.
YOUR WHAT?
IT... IT MEANS MOTHER IN OUR LANGUAGE.
OH...UH...
HEY, THAT TREASURE IS PROBABLY WORTH MILLIONS. MAYBE IF WE FIND IT, WE CAN HELP YOU FIND YOUR MOM.
THAT'S A NICE IDEA, ROCKET, BUT... WE HAVE A LOT TO FIGURE OUT BEFORE WE START COUNTING OUR MONEY.
LOOK...
...HERE WE ARE.

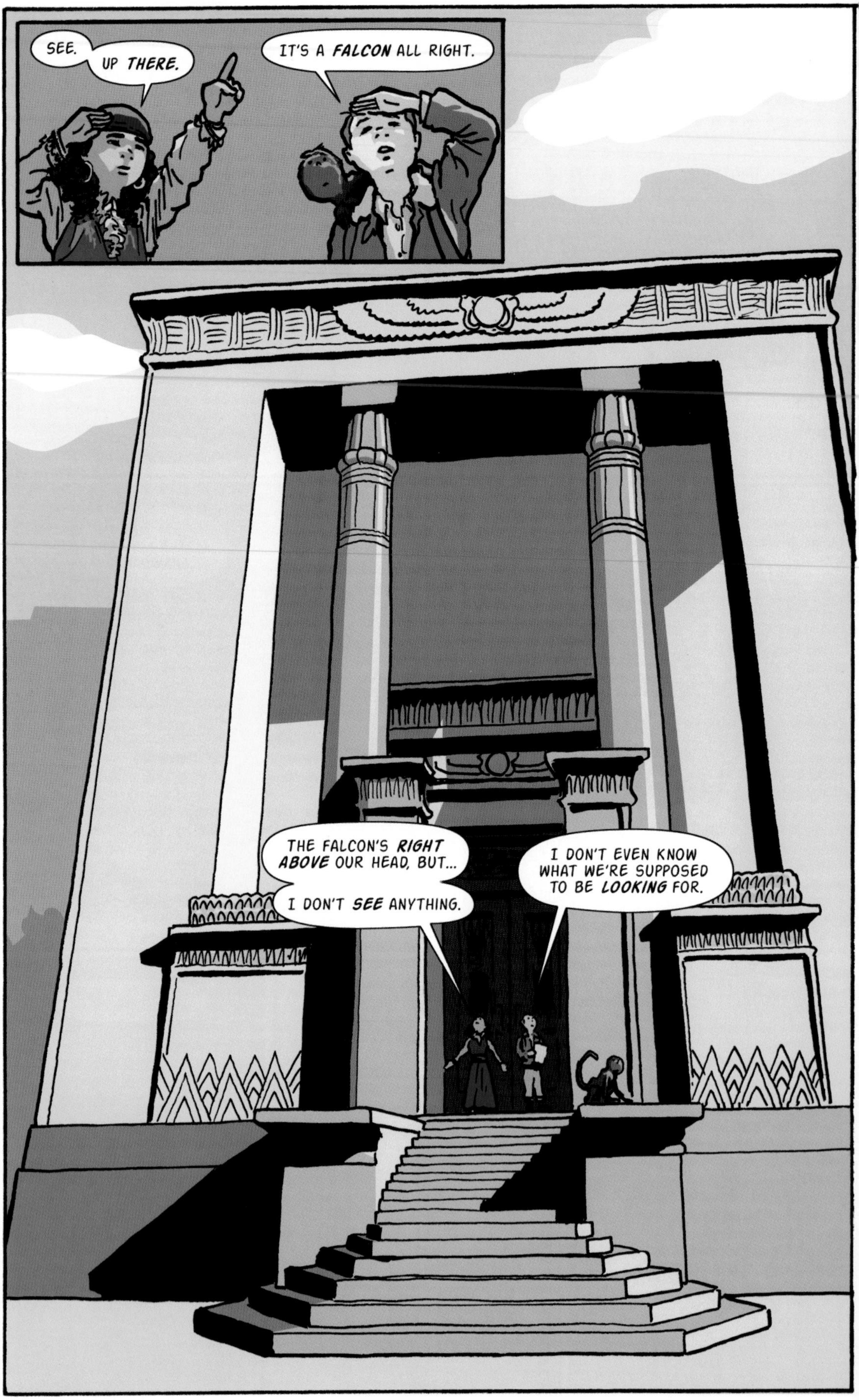
SEE.
UP THERE.
IT'S A FALCON ALL RIGHT.
THE FALCON'S RIGHT ABOVE OUR HEAD, BUT...
I DON'T SEE ANYTHING.
I DON'T EVEN KNOW WHAT WE'RE SUPPOSED TO BE LOOKING FOR.

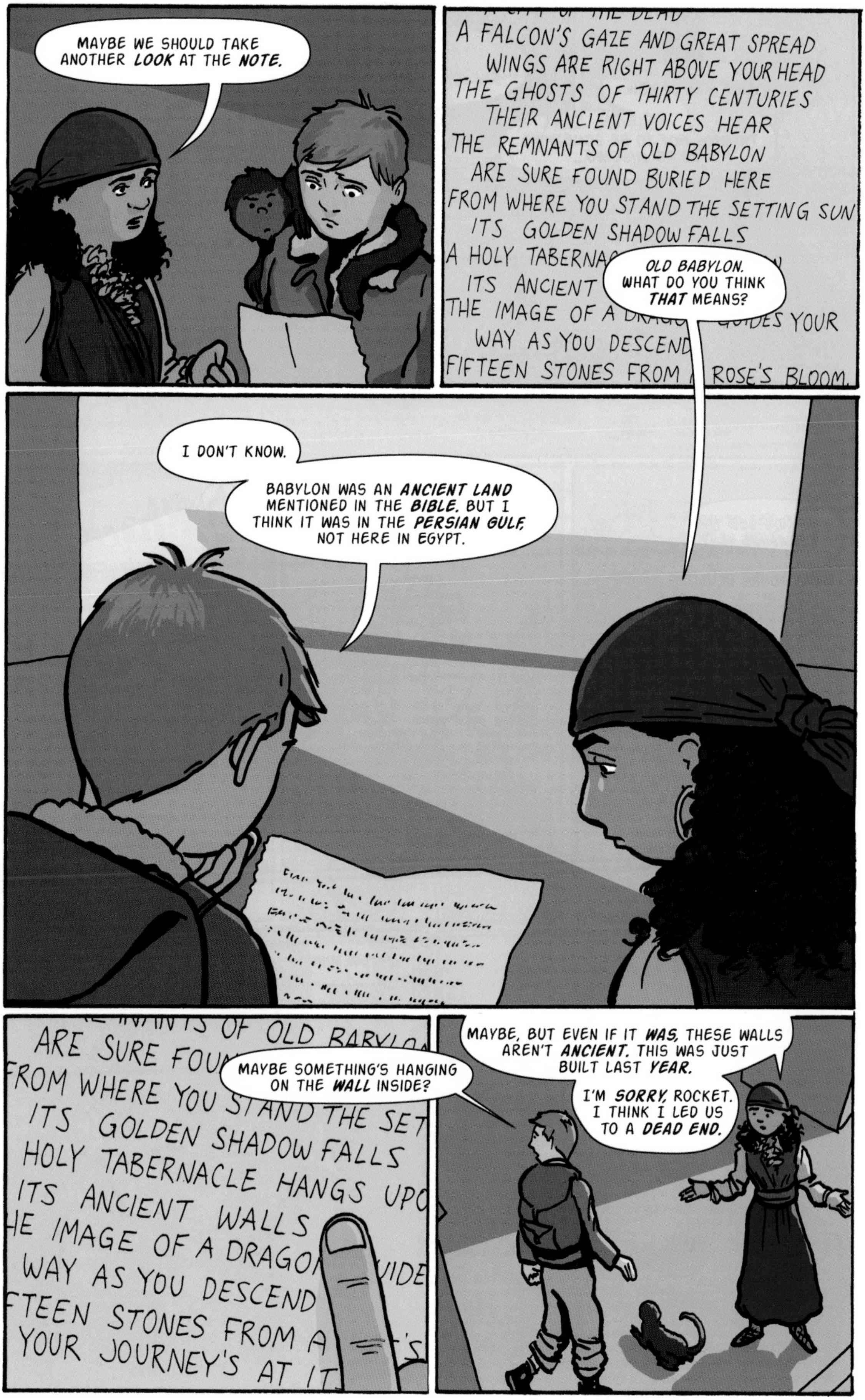
MAYBE WE SHOULD TAKE ANOTHER LOOK AT THE NOTE.
A FALCON'S GAZE AND GREAT SPREAD
WINGS ARE RIGHT ABOVE YOUR HEAD
THE GHOSTS OF THIRTY CENTURIES
THEIR ANCIENT VOICES HEAR
THE REMNANTS OF OLD BABYLON
ARE SURE FOUND BURIED HERE
FROM WHERE YOU STAND THE SETTING SUN
ITS GOLDEN SHADOW FALLS
A HOLY TABERNA
ITS ANCIENT
THE IMAGE OF A
UIDES YOUR
WAY AS YOU DESCEND
FIFTEEN STONES FROM
ROSE'S BLOOM.
OLD BABYLON. WHAT DO YOU THINK THAT MEANS?
I DON'T KNOW.
BABYLON WAS AN ANCIENT LAND MENTIONED IN THE BIBLE. BUT I THINK IT WAS IN THE PERSIAN GULF, NOT HERE IN EGYPT.
ARE SURE FOUN
FROM WHERE YOU STAND THE SET
ITS GOLDEN SHADOW FALLS
HOLY TABERNACLE HANGS UPO
ITS ANCIENT WALLS
HE IMAGE OF A DRAGO
WAY AS YOU DESCEND
FTEEN STONES FROM A
YOUR JOURNEY'S AT IT
MAYBE SOMETHING'S HANGING ON THE WALL INSIDE?
MAYBE, BUT EVEN IF IT WAS, THESE WALLS AREN'T ANCIENT. THIS WAS JUST BUILT LAST YEAR.
I'M SORRY, ROCKET. I THINK I LED US TO A DEAD END.

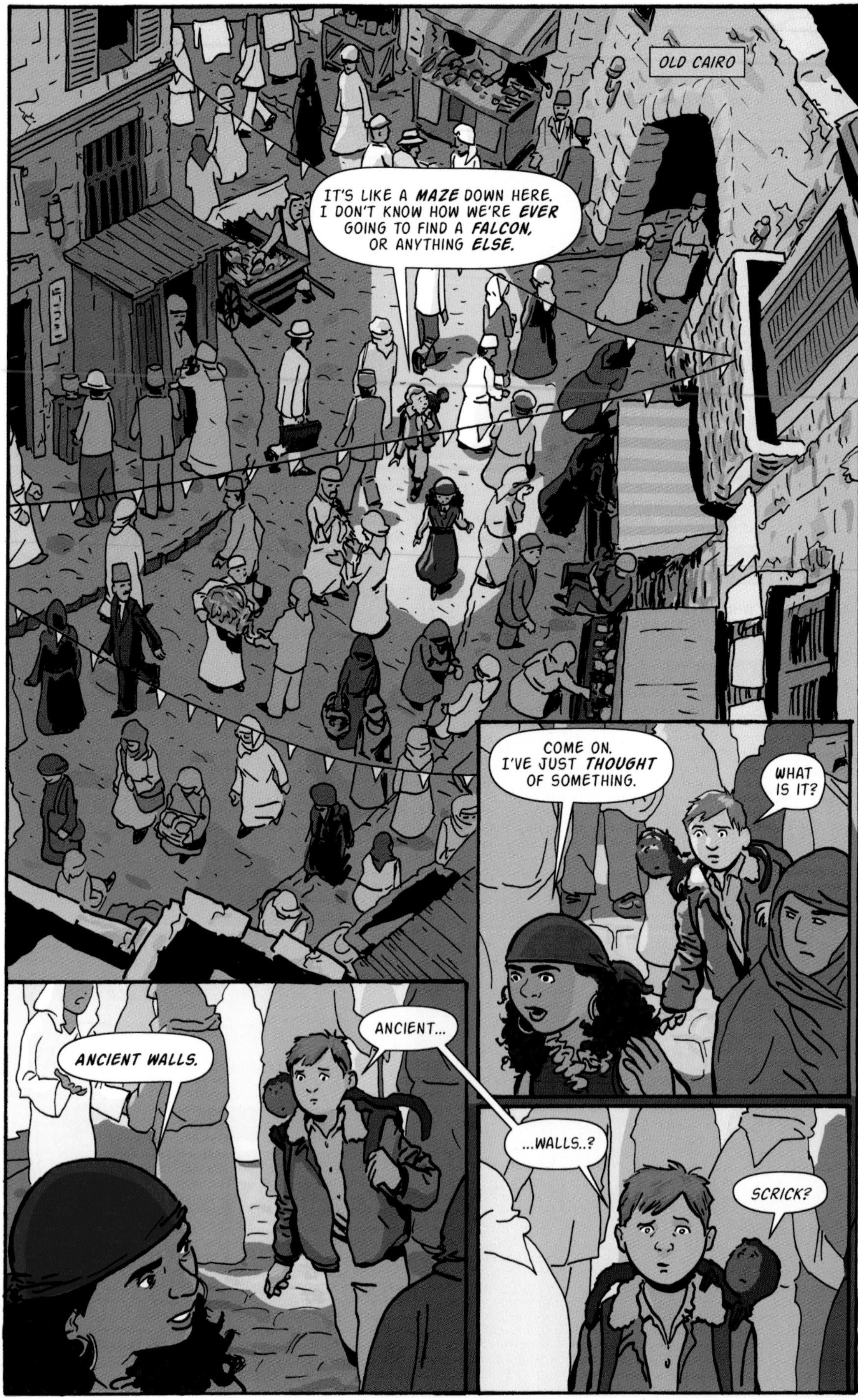
OLD CAIRO
IT'S LIKE A MAZE DOWN HERE. I DON'T KNOW HOW WE'RE EVER GOING TO FIND A FALCON, OR ANYTHING ELSE.
COME ON. I'VE JUST THOUGHT OF SOMETHING.
WHAT IS IT?
ANCIENT WALLS.
ANCIENT...
...WALLS..?
SCRICK?

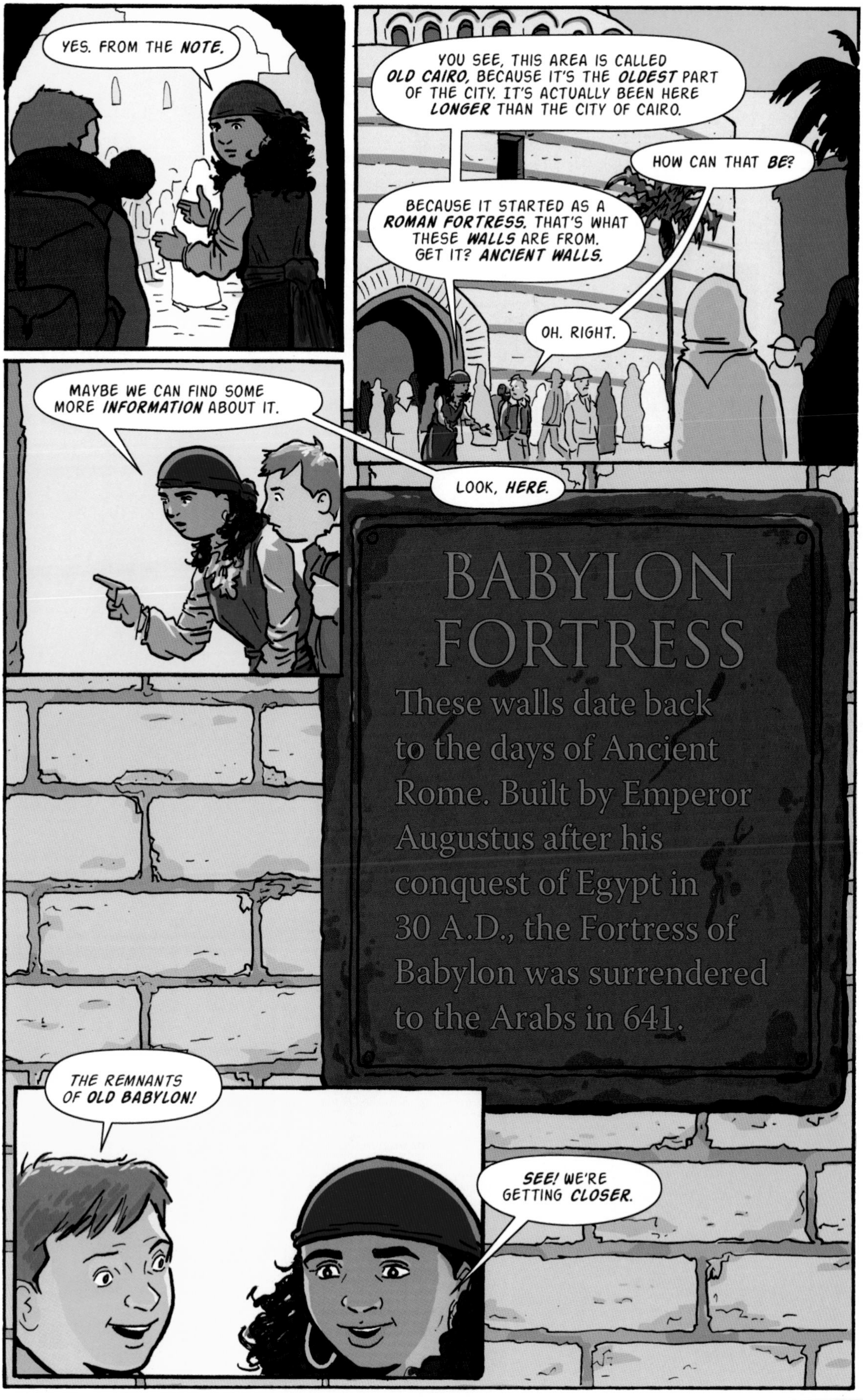
YES. FROM THE NOTE.
YOU SEE, THIS AREA IS CALLED OLD CAIRO, BECAUSE IT'S THE OLDEST PART OF THE CITY. IT'S ACTUALLY BEEN HERE LONGER THAN THE CITY OF CAIRO.
HOW CAN THAT BE?
BECAUSE IT STARTED AS A ROMAN FORTRESS. THAT'S WHAT THESE WALLS ARE FROM. GET IT? ANCIENT WALLS.
OH. RIGHT.
MAYBE WE CAN FIND SOME MORE INFORMATION ABOUT IT.
LOOK, HERE.
BABYLON FORTRESS
These walls date back to the days of Ancient Rome. Built by Emperor Augustus after his conquest of Egypt in 30 A.D., the Fortress of Babylon was surrendered to the Arabs in 641.
THE REMNANTS OF OLD BABYLON!
SEE! WE'RE GETTING CLOSER.

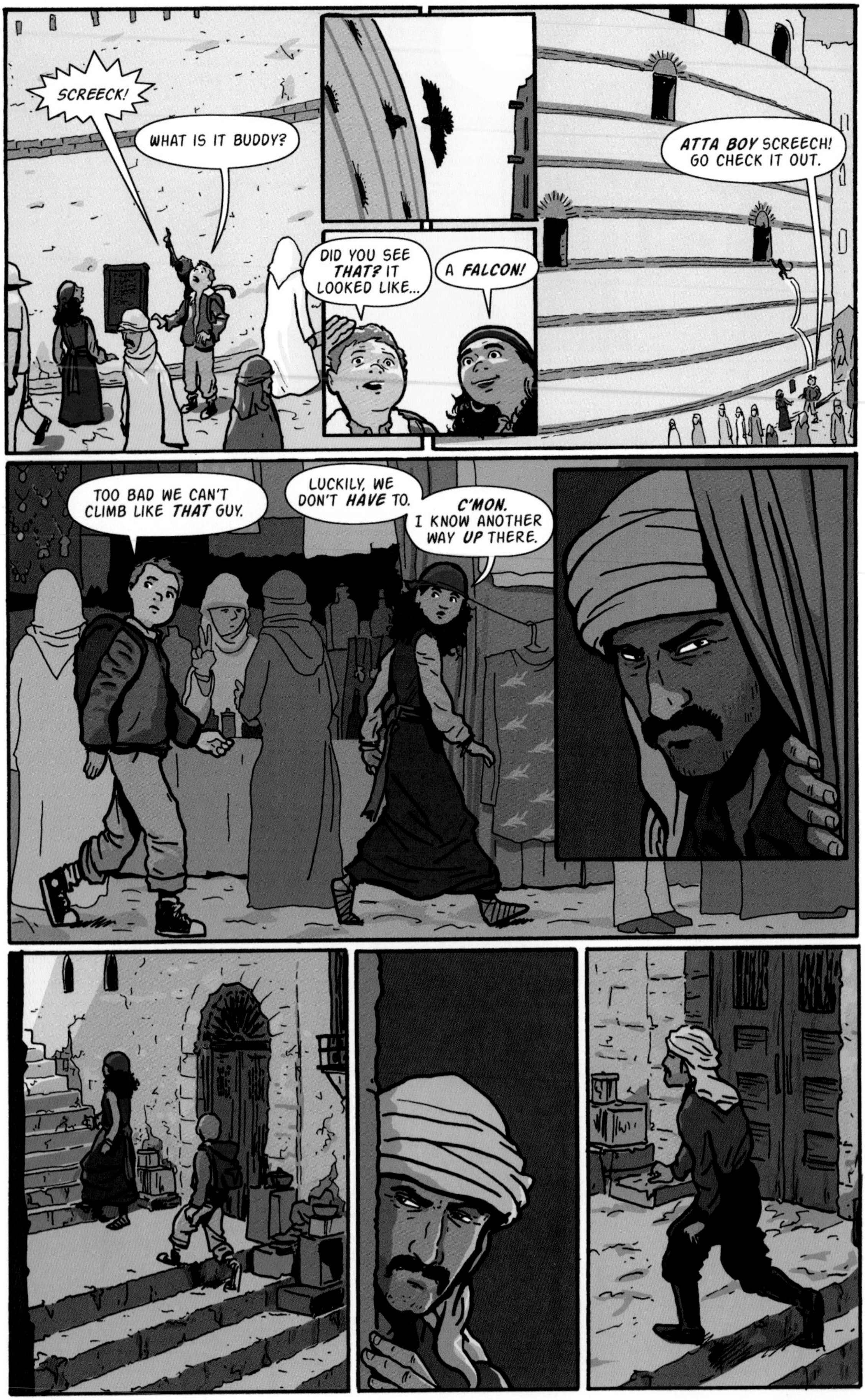
SCREECK!
WHAT IS IT BUDDY?
DID YOU SEE THAT? IT LOOKED LIKE...
A FALCON!
ATTA BOY SCREECH! GO CHECK IT OUT.
TOO BAD WE CAN'T CLIMB LIKE THAT GUY.
LUCKILY, WE DON'T HAVE TO.
C'MON. I KNOW ANOTHER WAY UP THERE.

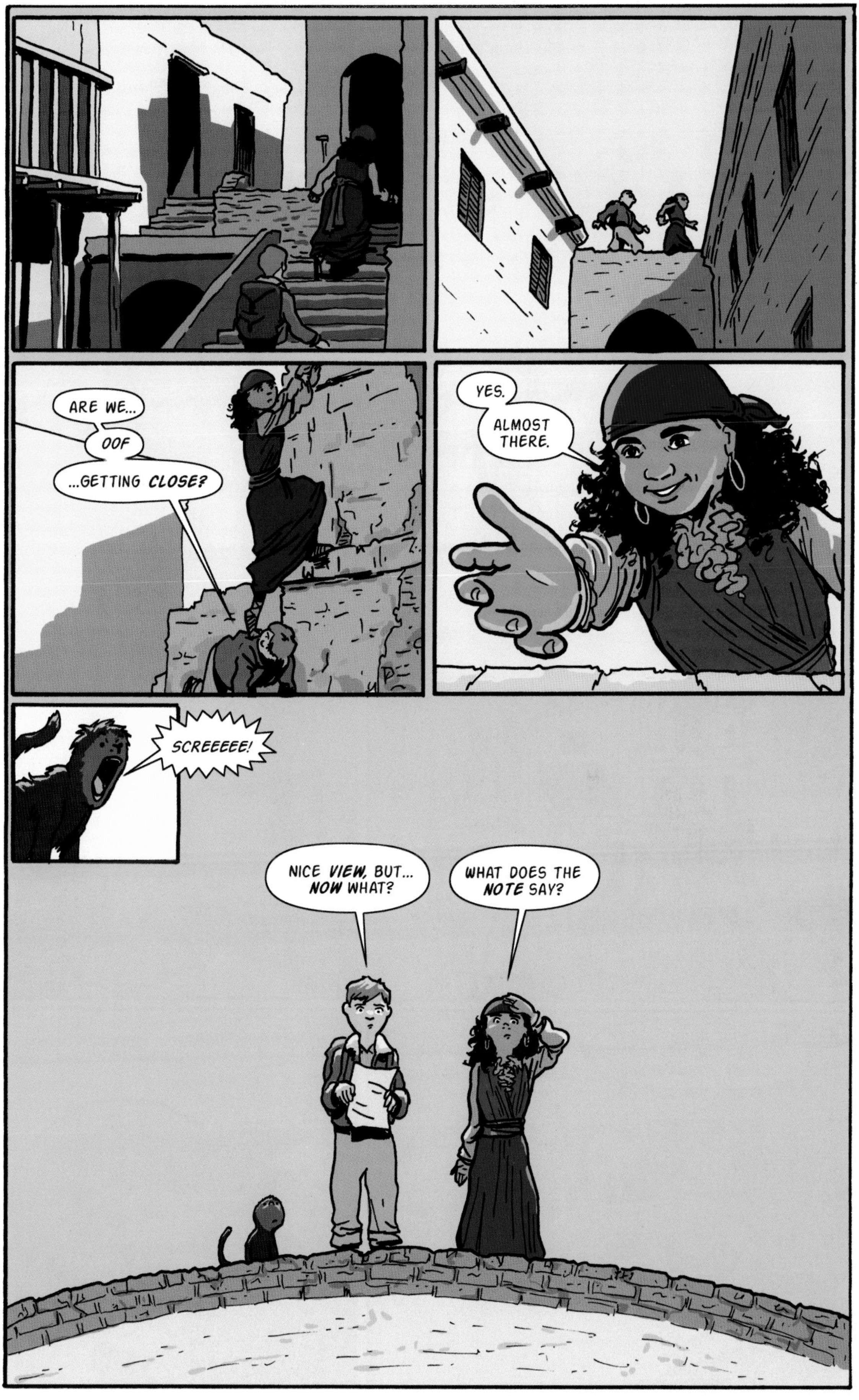
ARE WE...
OOF
...GETTING **CLOSE?**
YES.
ALMOST THERE.
SCREEEEE!
NICE **VIEW,** BUT... **NOW** WHAT?
WHAT DOES THE **NOTE** SAY?

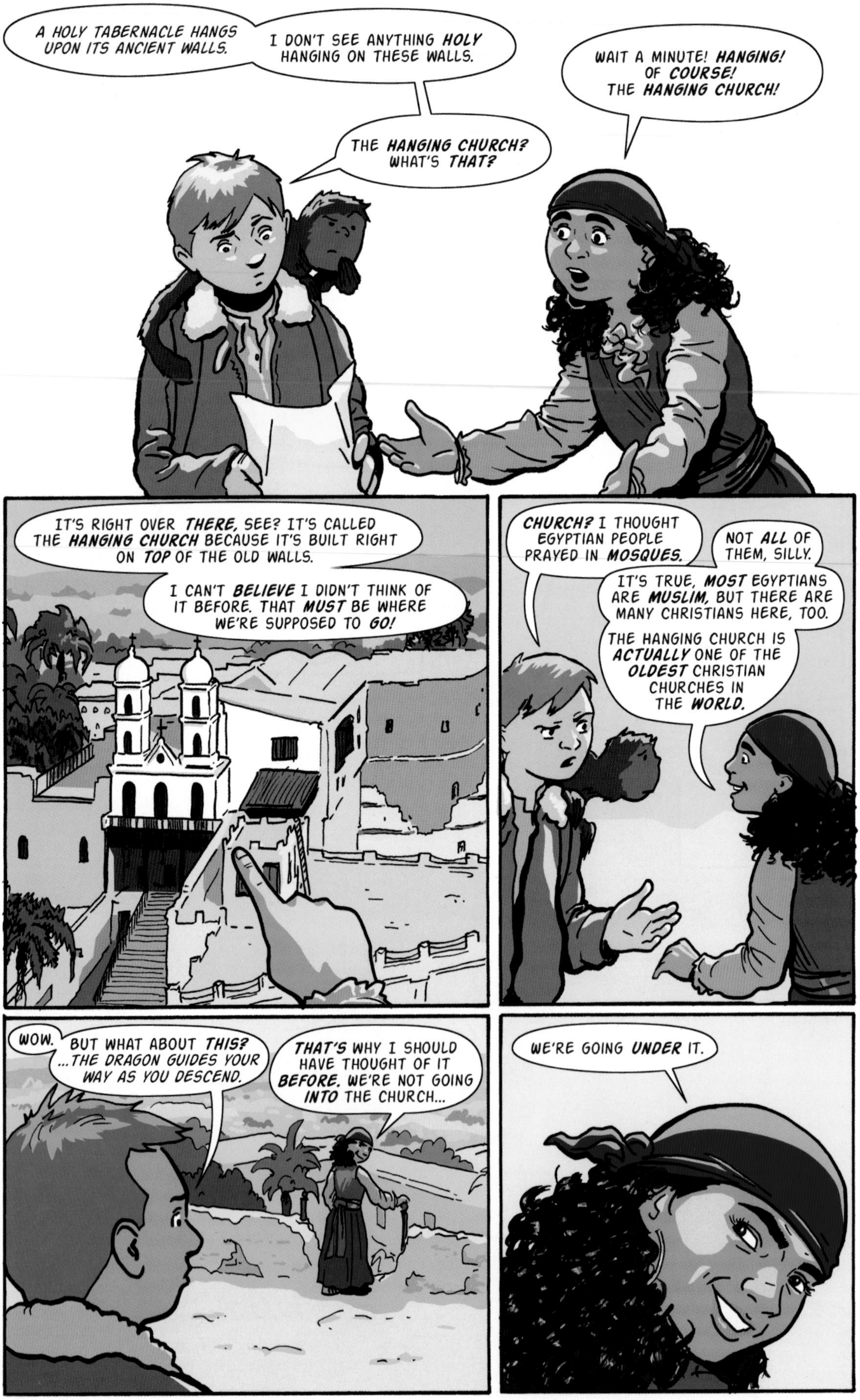
A HOLY TABERNACLE HANGS UPON ITS ANCIENT WALLS.
I DON'T SEE ANYTHING HOLY HANGING ON THESE WALLS.
WAIT A MINUTE! HANGING! OF COURSE! THE HANGING CHURCH!
THE HANGING CHURCH? WHAT'S THAT?
IT'S RIGHT OVER THERE, SEE? IT'S CALLED THE HANGING CHURCH BECAUSE IT'S BUILT RIGHT ON TOP OF THE OLD WALLS.
I CAN'T BELIEVE I DIDN'T THINK OF IT BEFORE. THAT MUST BE WHERE WE'RE SUPPOSED TO GO!
CHURCH? I THOUGHT EGYPTIAN PEOPLE PRAYED IN MOSQUES.
NOT ALL OF THEM, SILLY.
IT'S TRUE, MOST EGYPTIANS ARE MUSLIM, BUT THERE ARE MANY CHRISTIANS HERE, TOO.
THE HANGING CHURCH IS ACTUALLY ONE OF THE OLDEST CHRISTIAN CHURCHES IN THE WORLD.
WOW.
BUT WHAT ABOUT THIS? ...THE DRAGON GUIDES YOUR WAY AS YOU DESCEND.
THAT'S WHY I SHOULD HAVE THOUGHT OF IT BEFORE. WE'RE NOT GOING INTO THE CHURCH...
WE'RE GOING UNDER IT.

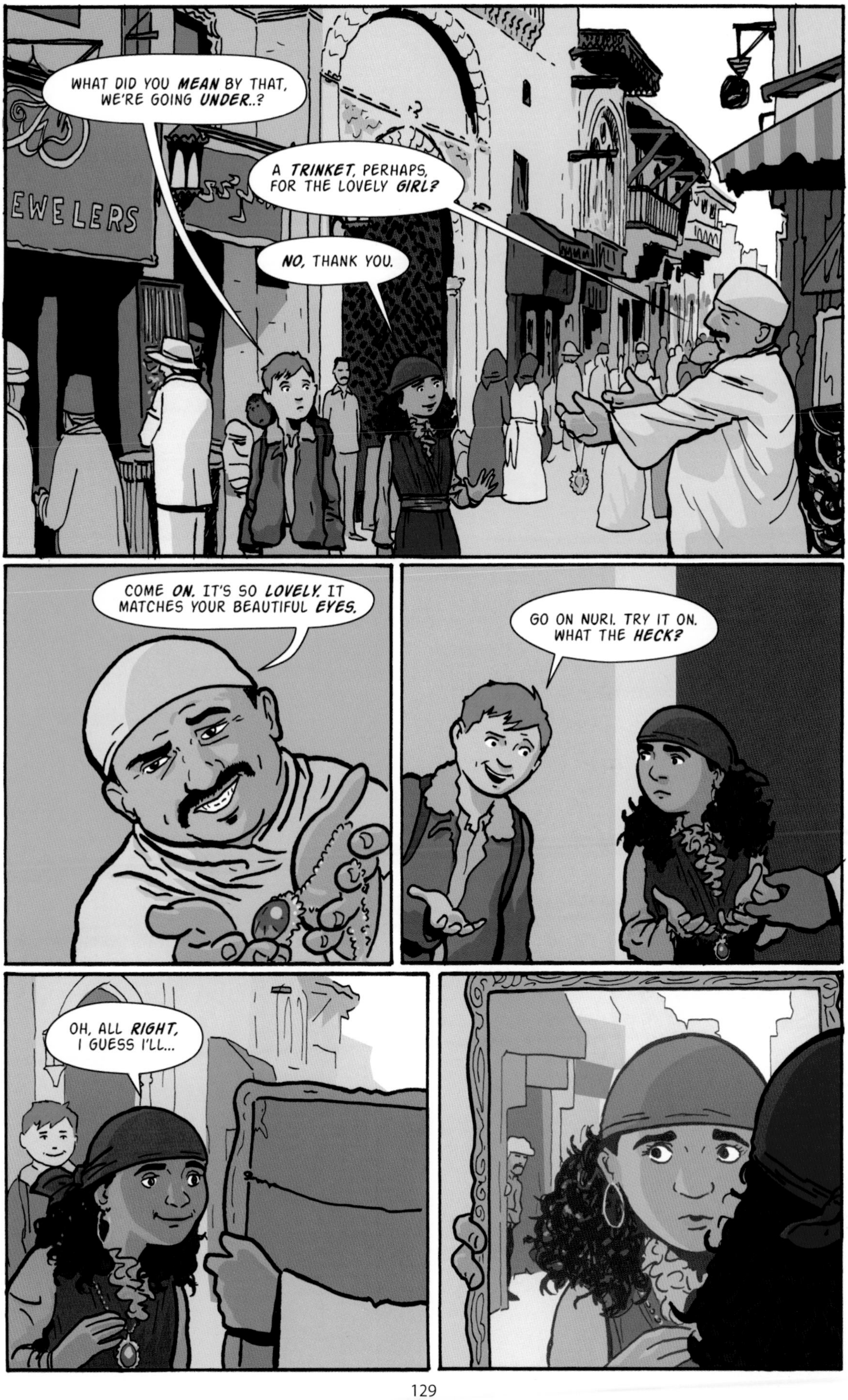
EWELERS
WHAT DID YOU MEAN BY THAT, WE'RE GOING UNDER..?
A TRINKET, PERHAPS, FOR THE LOVELY GIRL?
NO, THANK YOU.
COME ON. IT'S SO LOVELY. IT MATCHES YOUR BEAUTIFUL EYES.
GO ON NURI. TRY IT ON. WHAT THE HECK?
OH, ALL RIGHT, I GUESS I'LL...

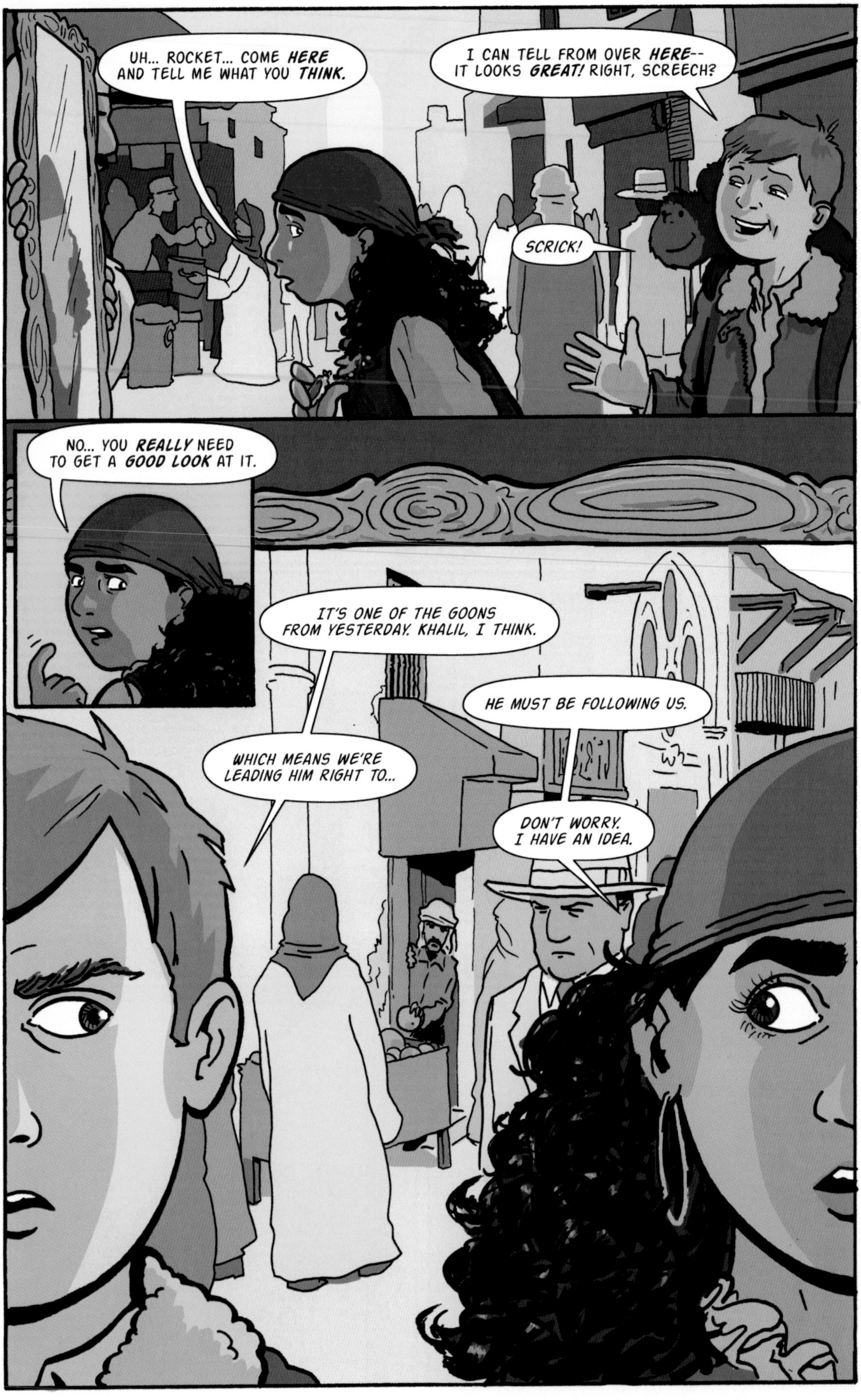
UH... ROCKET... COME HERE AND TELL ME WHAT YOU THINK.
I CAN TELL FROM OVER HERE-- IT LOOKS GREAT! RIGHT, SCREECH?
SCRICK!
NO... YOU REALLY NEED TO GET A GOOD LOOK AT IT.
IT'S ONE OF THE GOONS FROM YESTERDAY. KHALIL, I THINK.
WHICH MEANS WE'RE LEADING HIM RIGHT TO...
HE MUST BE FOLLOWING US.
DON'T WORRY. I HAVE AN IDEA.

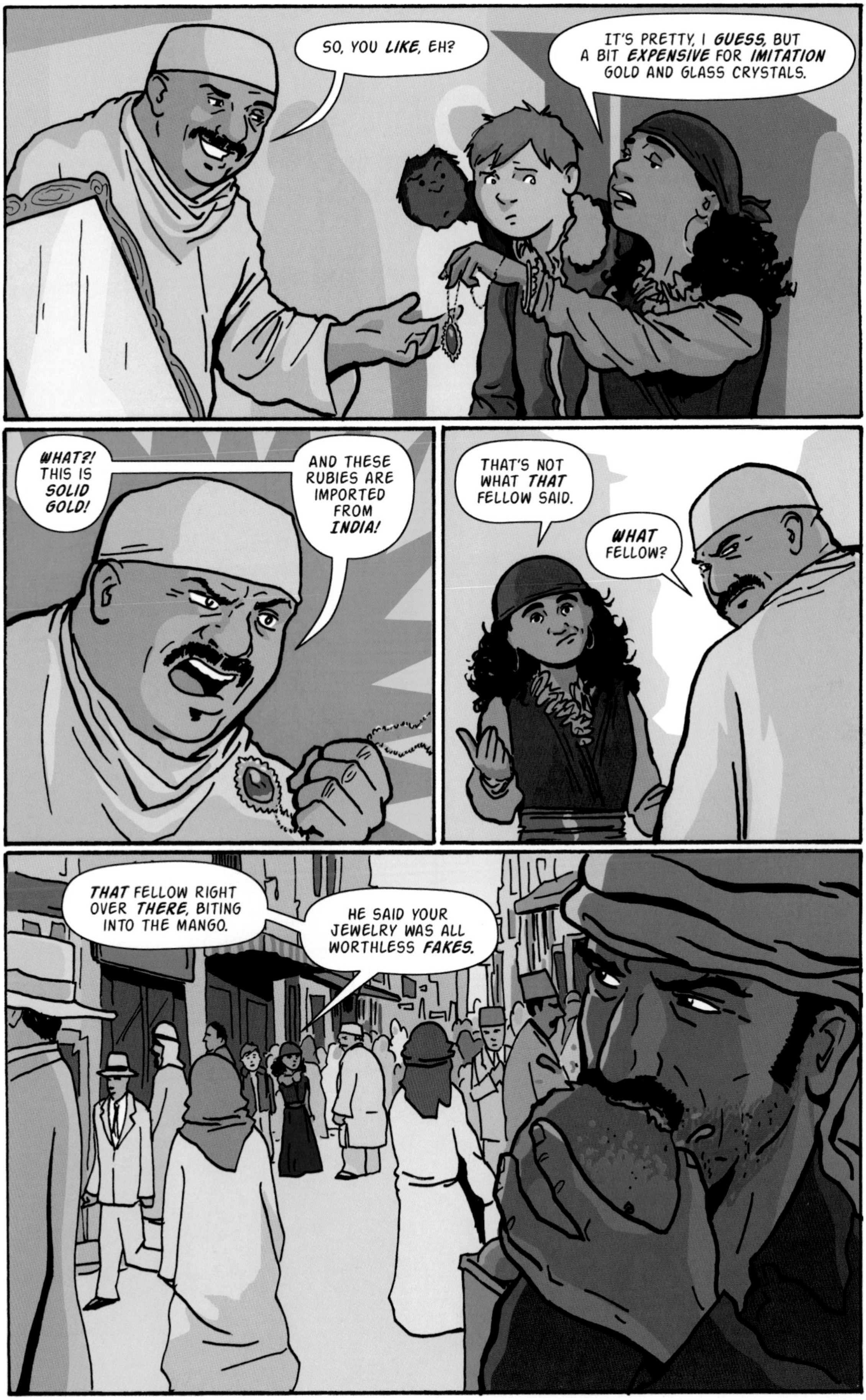
SO, YOU LIKE, EH?
IT'S PRETTY, I GUESS, BUT A BIT EXPENSIVE FOR IMITATION GOLD AND GLASS CRYSTALS.
WHAT?! THIS IS SOLID GOLD!
AND THESE RUBIES ARE IMPORTED FROM INDIA!
THAT'S NOT WHAT THAT FELLOW SAID.
WHAT FELLOW?
THAT FELLOW RIGHT OVER THERE, BITING INTO THE MANGO.
HE SAID YOUR JEWELRY WAS ALL WORTHLESS FAKES.

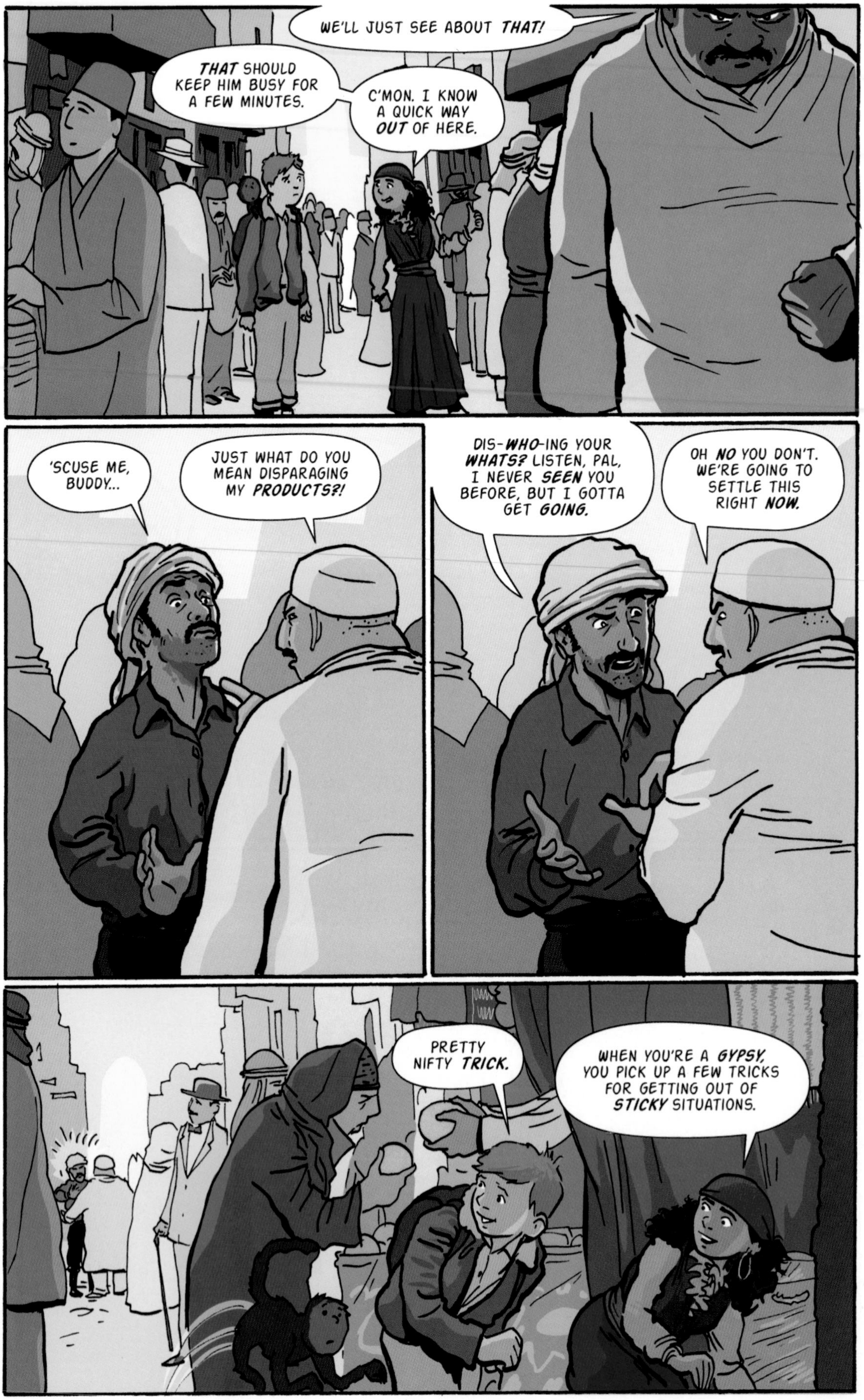
WE'LL JUST SEE ABOUT THAT!
THAT SHOULD KEEP HIM BUSY FOR A FEW MINUTES.
C'MON. I KNOW A QUICK WAY OUT OF HERE.
'SCUSE ME, BUDDY...
JUST WHAT DO YOU MEAN DISPARAGING MY PRODUCTS?!
DIS-WHO-ING YOUR WHATS? LISTEN, PAL, I NEVER SEEN YOU BEFORE, BUT I GOTTA GET GOING.
OH NO YOU DON'T. WE'RE GOING TO SETTLE THIS RIGHT NOW.
PRETTY NIFTY TRICK.
WHEN YOU'RE A GYPSY, YOU PICK UP A FEW TRICKS FOR GETTING OUT OF STICKY SITUATIONS.

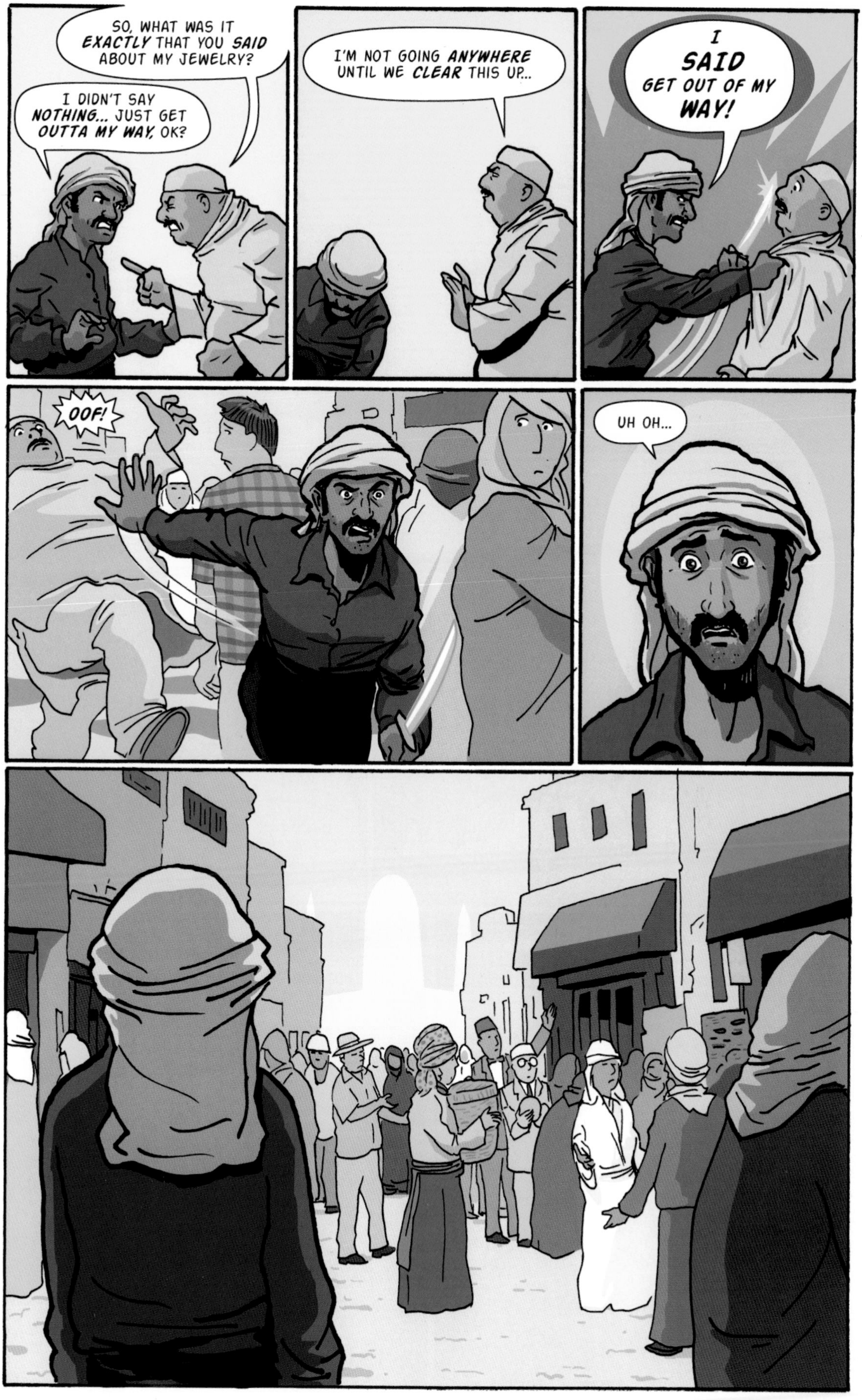
SO, WHAT WAS IT EXACTLY THAT YOU SAID ABOUT MY JEWELRY?
I DIDN'T SAY NOTHING... JUST GET OUTTA MY WAY, OK?
I'M NOT GOING ANYWHERE UNTIL WE CLEAR THIS UP...
I SAID GET OUT OF MY WAY!
OOF!
UH OH...

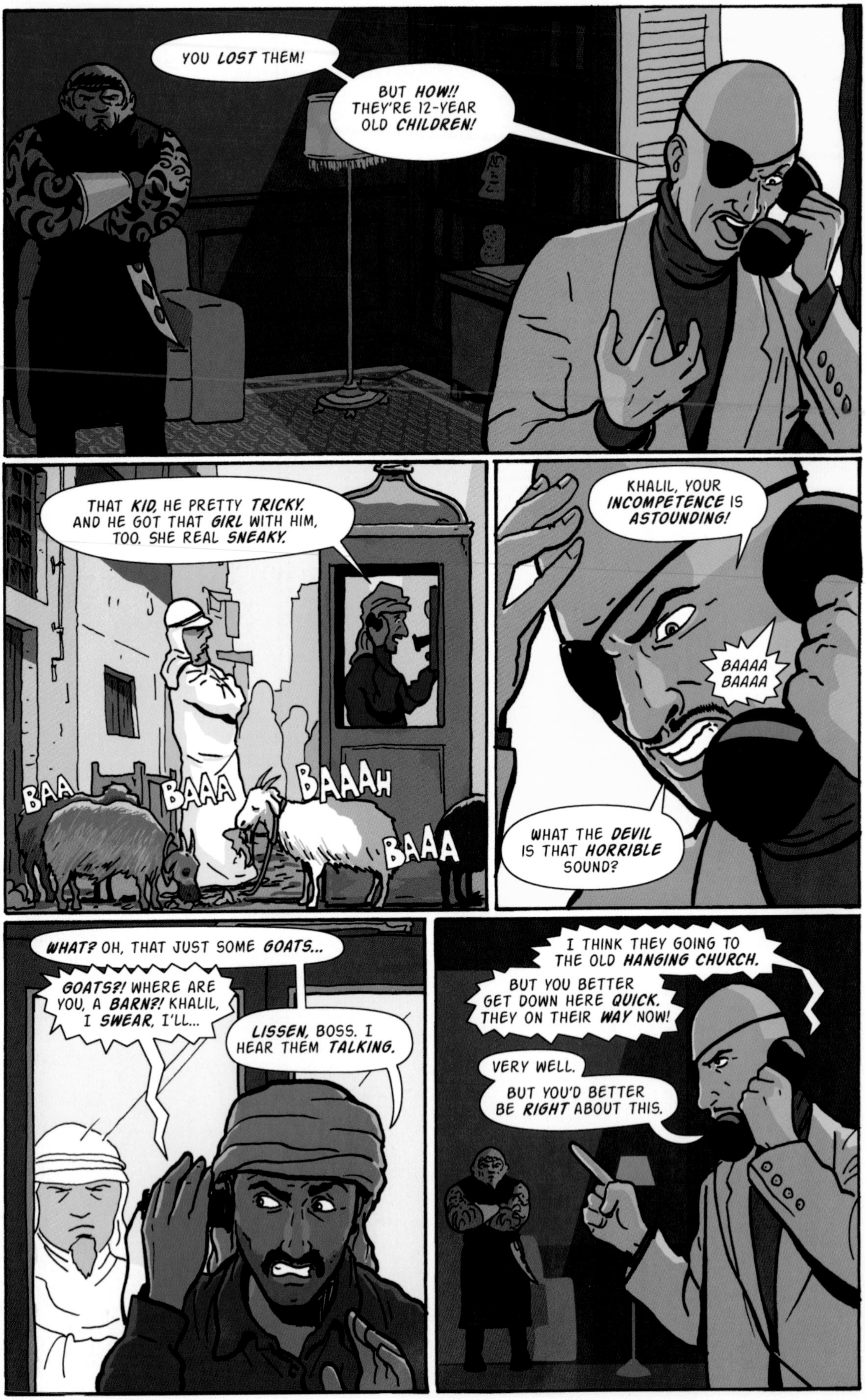
YOU LOST THEM!
BUT HOW!! THEY'RE 12-YEAR OLD CHILDREN!
THAT KID, HE PRETTY TRICKY. AND HE GOT THAT GIRL WITH HIM, TOO. SHE REAL SNEAKY.
BAA
BAAA
BAAAH
BAAA
KHALIL, YOUR INCOMPETENCE IS ASTOUNDING!
BAAAA BAAAA
WHAT THE DEVIL IS THAT HORRIBLE SOUND?
WHAT? OH, THAT JUST SOME GOATS...
GOATS?! WHERE ARE YOU, A BARN?! KHALIL, I SWEAR, I'LL...
LISSEN, BOSS. I HEAR THEM TALKING.
I THINK THEY GOING TO THE OLD HANGING CHURCH.
BUT YOU BETTER GET DOWN HERE QUICK. THEY ON THEIR WAY NOW!
VERY WELL.
BUT YOU'D BETTER BE RIGHT ABOUT THIS.

CHAPTER SEVEN

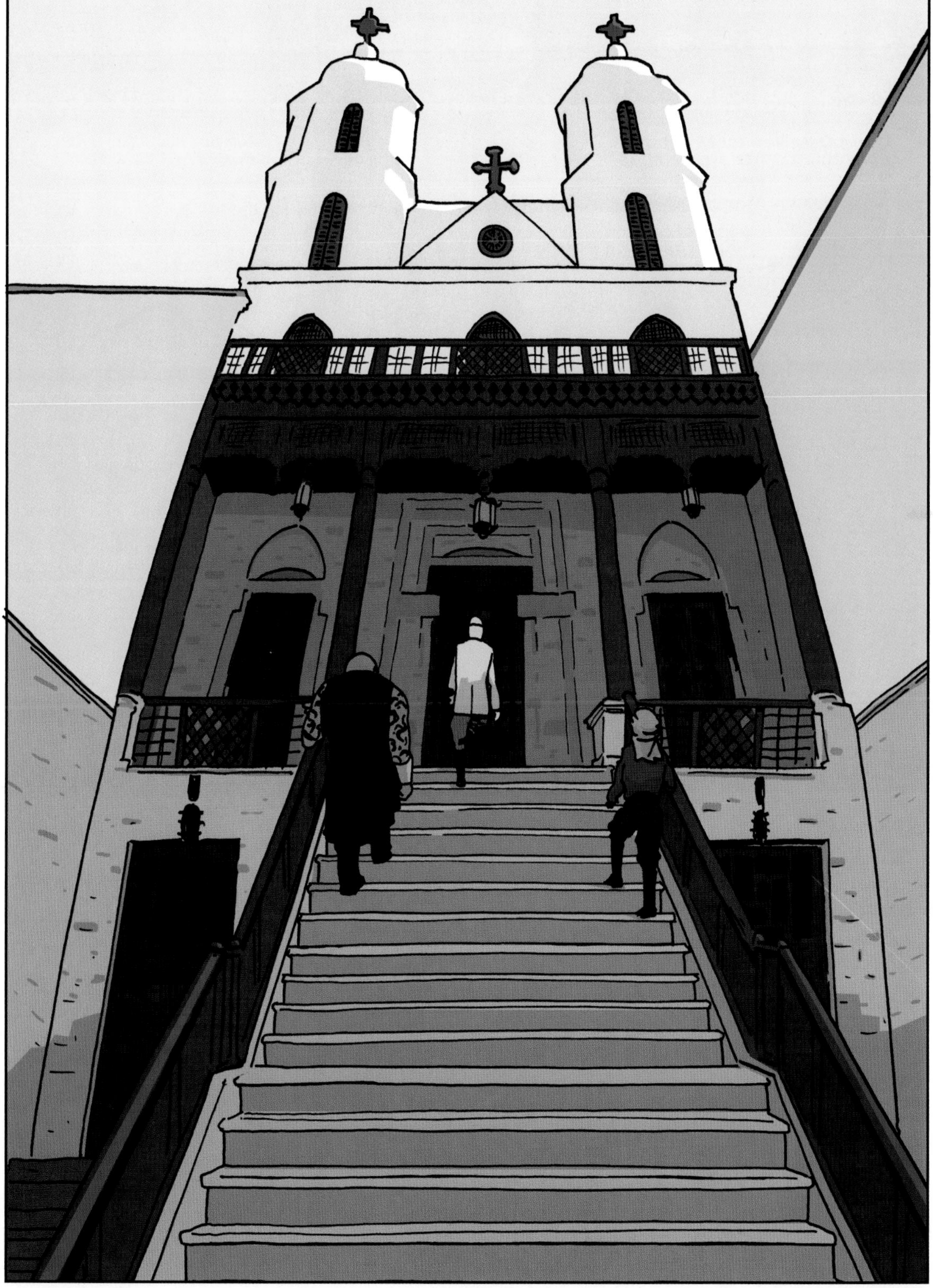

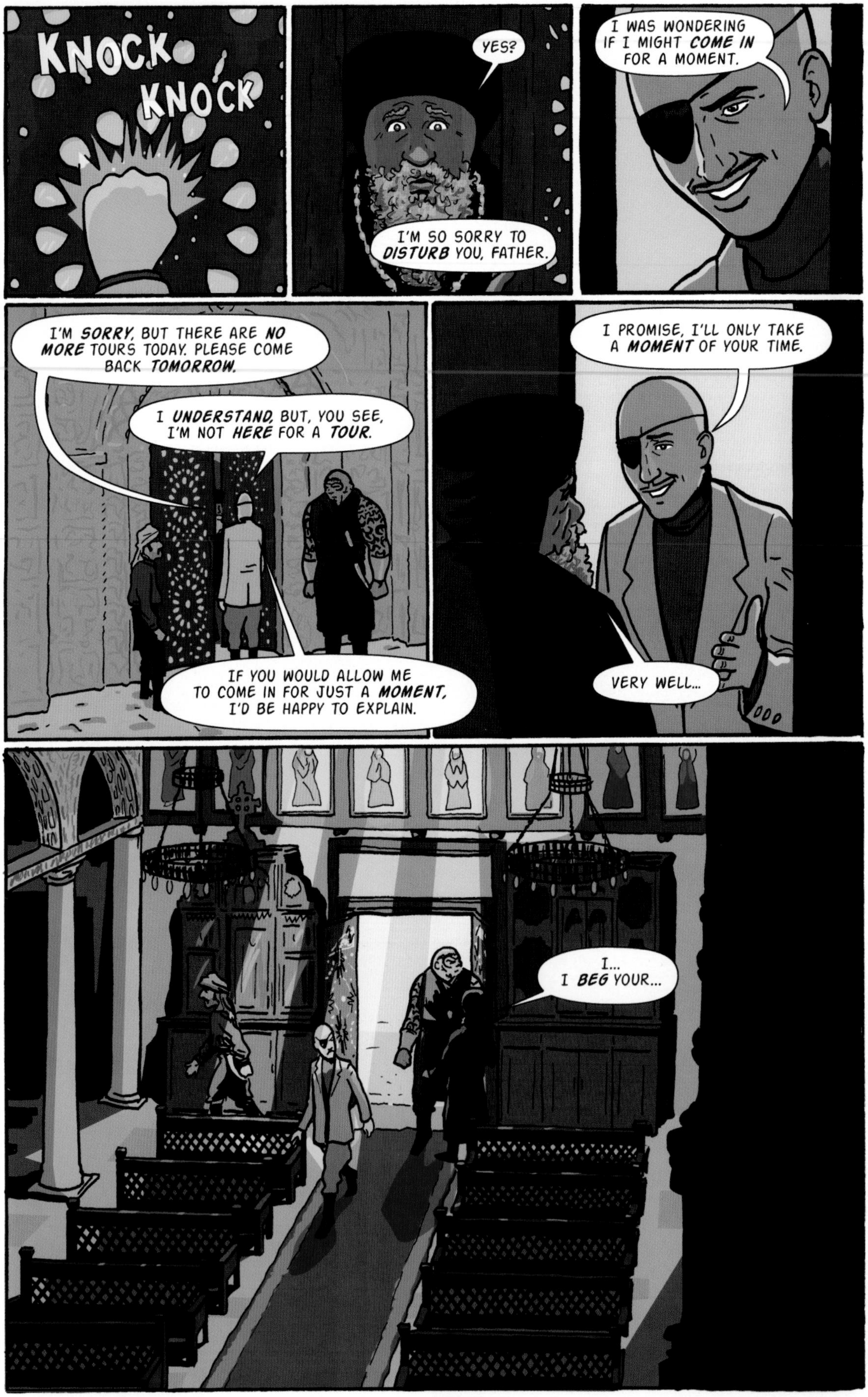
KNOCK KNOCK
YES?
I'M SO SORRY TO DISTURB YOU, FATHER.
I WAS WONDERING IF I MIGHT COME IN FOR A MOMENT.
I'M SORRY, BUT THERE ARE NO MORE TOURS TODAY. PLEASE COME BACK TOMORROW.
I UNDERSTAND, BUT, YOU SEE, I'M NOT HERE FOR A TOUR.
IF YOU WOULD ALLOW ME TO COME IN FOR JUST A MOMENT, I'D BE HAPPY TO EXPLAIN.
I PROMISE, I'LL ONLY TAKE A MOMENT OF YOUR TIME.
VERY WELL...
I... I BEG YOUR...

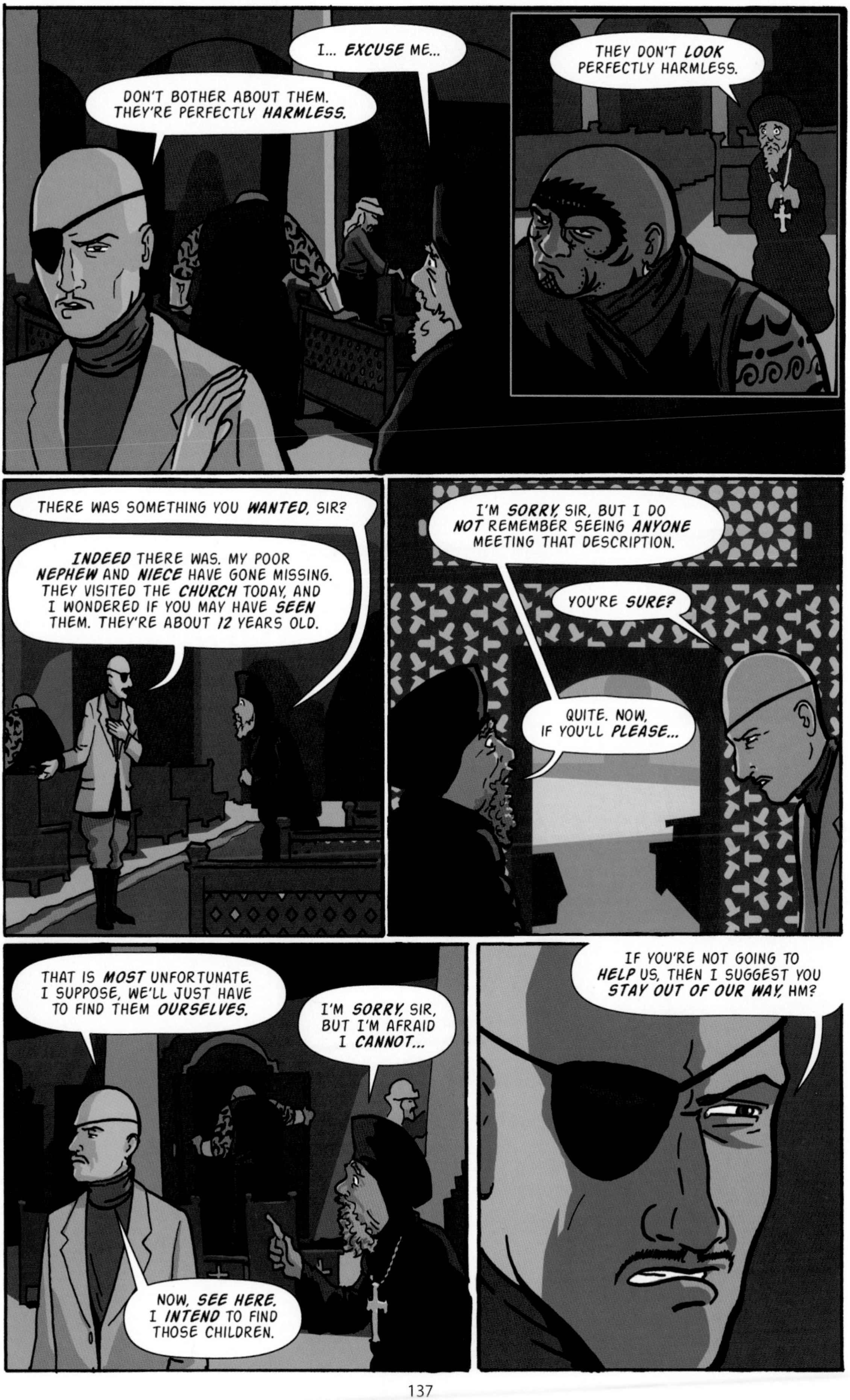
I... EXCUSE ME...
DON'T BOTHER ABOUT THEM. THEY'RE PERFECTLY HARMLESS.
THEY DON'T LOOK PERFECTLY HARMLESS.
THERE WAS SOMETHING YOU WANTED, SIR?
INDEED THERE WAS. MY POOR NEPHEW AND NIECE HAVE GONE MISSING. THEY VISITED THE CHURCH TODAY, AND I WONDERED IF YOU MAY HAVE SEEN THEM. THEY'RE ABOUT 12 YEARS OLD.
I'M SORRY, SIR, BUT I DO NOT REMEMBER SEEING ANYONE MEETING THAT DESCRIPTION.
YOU'RE SURE?
QUITE. NOW, IF YOU'LL PLEASE...
THAT IS MOST UNFORTUNATE. I SUPPOSE, WE'LL JUST HAVE TO FIND THEM OURSELVES.
I'M SORRY, SIR, BUT I'M AFRAID I CANNOT...
NOW, SEE HERE. I INTEND TO FIND THOSE CHILDREN.
IF YOU'RE NOT GOING TO HELP US, THEN I SUGGEST YOU STAY OUT OF OUR WAY, HM?

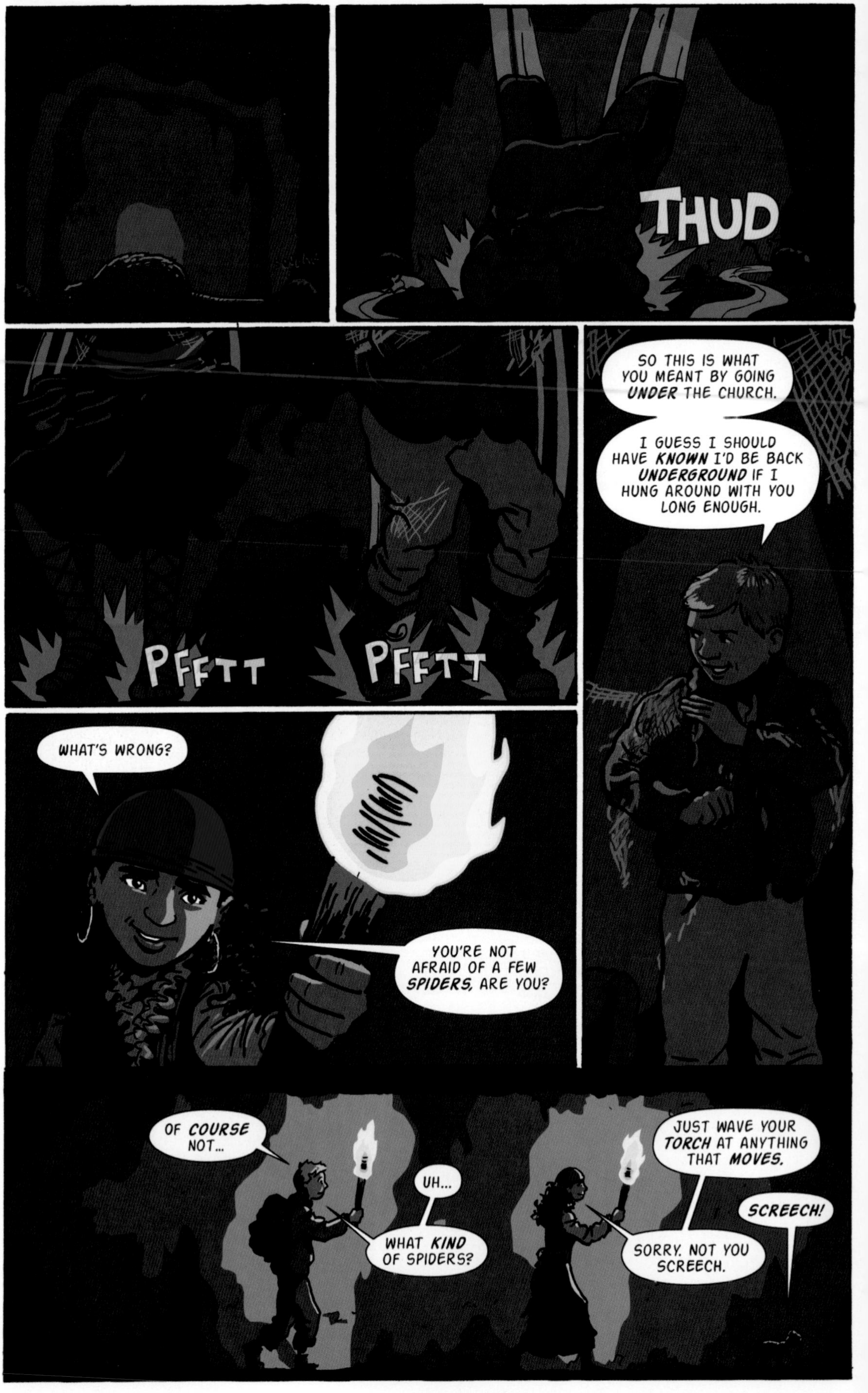
THUD
PFFTT
PFFTT
SO THIS IS WHAT YOU MEANT BY GOING UNDER THE CHURCH.
I GUESS I SHOULD HAVE KNOWN I'D BE BACK UNDERGROUND IF I HUNG AROUND WITH YOU LONG ENOUGH.
WHAT'S WRONG?
YOU'RE NOT AFRAID OF A FEW SPIDERS, ARE YOU?
OF COURSE NOT...
UH...
WHAT KIND OF SPIDERS?
JUST WAVE YOUR TORCH AT ANYTHING THAT MOVES.
SORRY. NOT YOU SCREECH.
SCREECH!

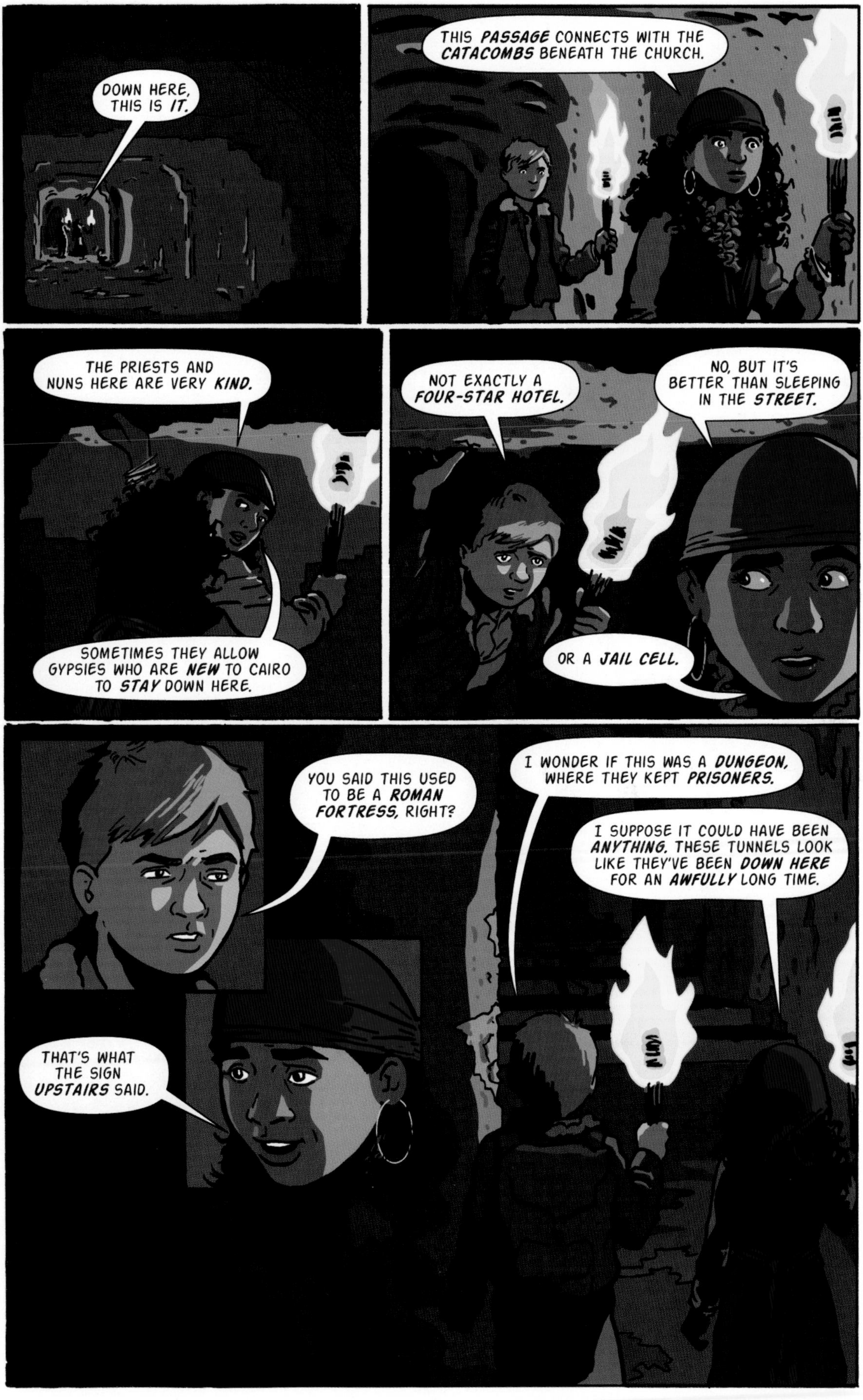
DOWN HERE, THIS IS IT.
THIS PASSAGE CONNECTS WITH THE CATACOMBS BENEATH THE CHURCH.
THE PRIESTS AND NUNS HERE ARE VERY KIND.
SOMETIMES THEY ALLOW GYPSIES WHO ARE NEW TO CAIRO TO STAY DOWN HERE.
NOT EXACTLY A FOUR-STAR HOTEL.
NO, BUT IT'S BETTER THAN SLEEPING IN THE STREET.
OR A JAIL CELL.
YOU SAID THIS USED TO BE A ROMAN FORTRESS, RIGHT?
THAT'S WHAT THE SIGN UPSTAIRS SAID.
I WONDER IF THIS WAS A DUNGEON, WHERE THEY KEPT PRISONERS.
I SUPPOSE IT COULD HAVE BEEN ANYTHING. THESE TUNNELS LOOK LIKE THEY'VE BEEN DOWN HERE FOR AN AWFULLY LONG TIME.

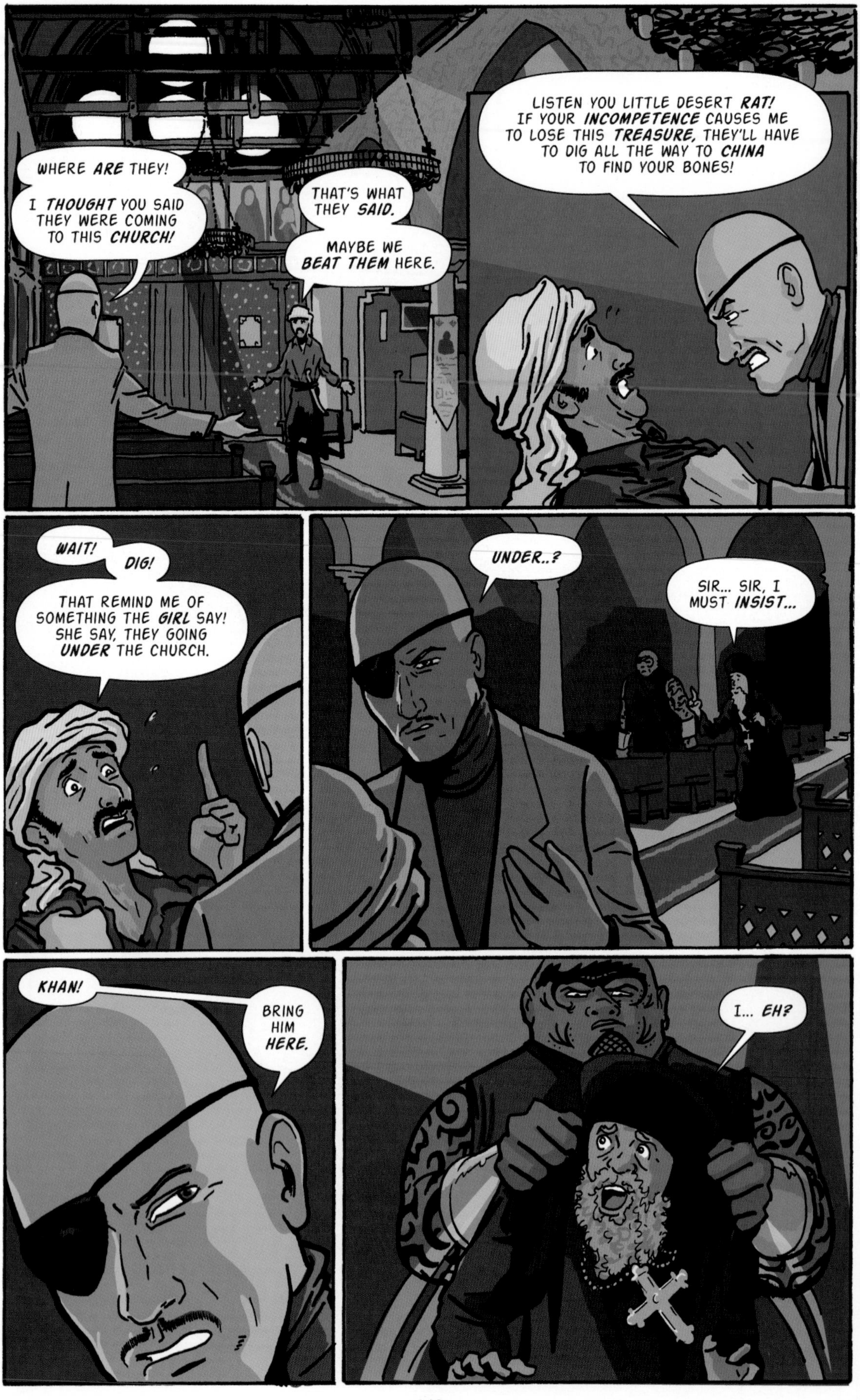
WHERE ARE THEY!
I THOUGHT YOU SAID THEY WERE COMING TO THIS CHURCH!
THAT'S WHAT THEY SAID.
MAYBE WE BEAT THEM HERE.
LISTEN YOU LITTLE DESERT RAT! IF YOUR INCOMPETENCE CAUSES ME TO LOSE THIS TREASURE, THEY'LL HAVE TO DIG ALL THE WAY TO CHINA TO FIND YOUR BONES!
WAIT!
DIG!
THAT REMIND ME OF SOMETHING THE GIRL SAY! SHE SAY, THEY GOING UNDER THE CHURCH.
UNDER..?
SIR... SIR, I MUST INSIST...
KHAN!
BRING HIM HERE.
I... EH?

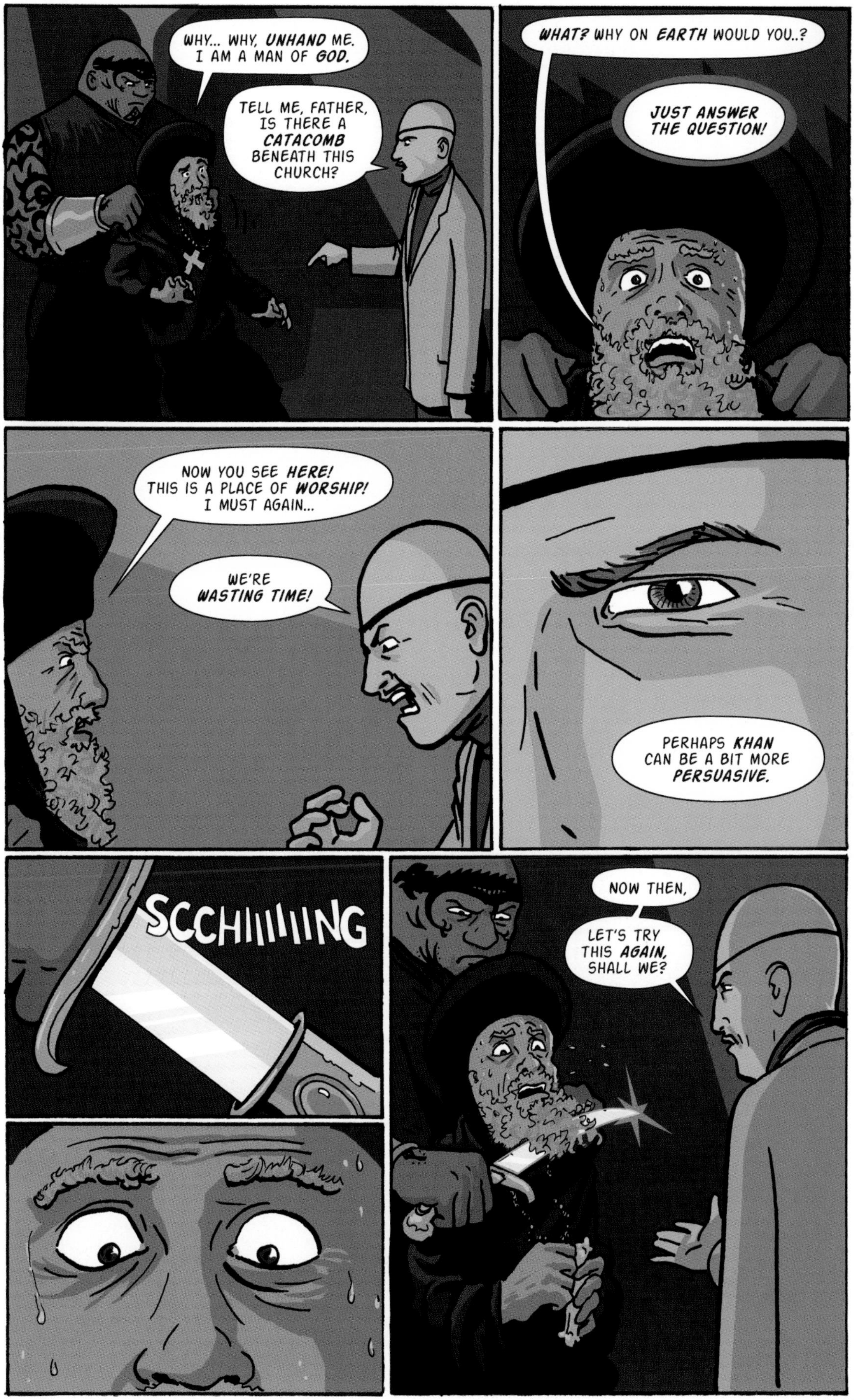
WHY... WHY, UNHAND ME. I AM A MAN OF GOD.
TELL ME, FATHER, IS THERE A CATACOMB BENEATH THIS CHURCH?
WHAT? WHY ON EARTH WOULD YOU..?
JUST ANSWER THE QUESTION!
NOW YOU SEE HERE! THIS IS A PLACE OF WORSHIP! I MUST AGAIN...
WE'RE WASTING TIME!
PERHAPS KHAN CAN BE A BIT MORE PERSUASIVE.
SCCHIIIIIIING
NOW THEN,
LET'S TRY THIS AGAIN, SHALL WE?

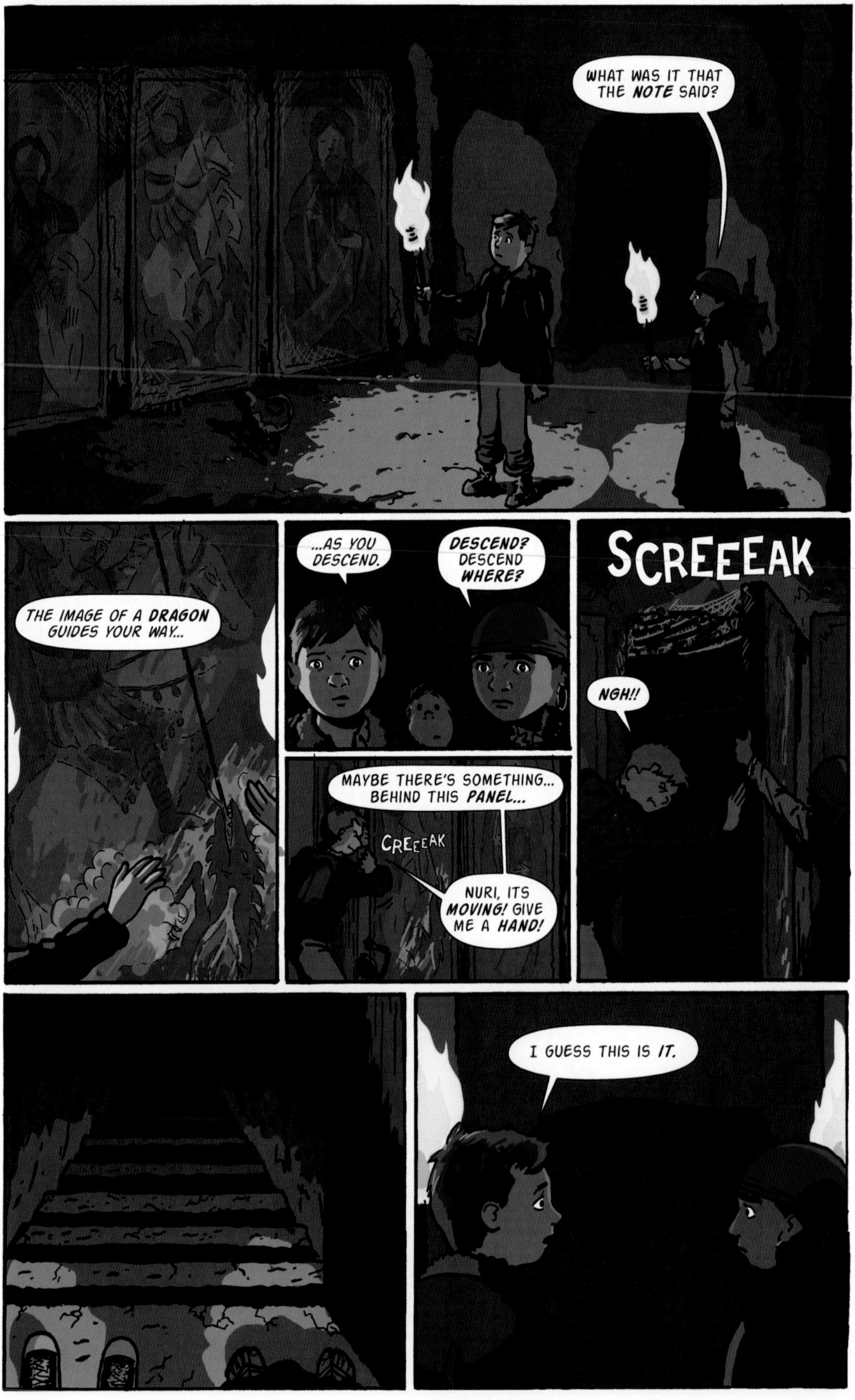
WHAT WAS IT THAT THE NOTE SAID?
THE IMAGE OF A DRAGON GUIDES YOUR WAY...
...AS YOU DESCEND.
DESCEND? DESCEND WHERE?
MAYBE THERE'S SOMETHING... BEHIND THIS PANEL...
CREEEAK
NURI, ITS MOVING! GIVE ME A HAND!
SCREEEAK
NGH!!
I GUESS THIS IS IT.

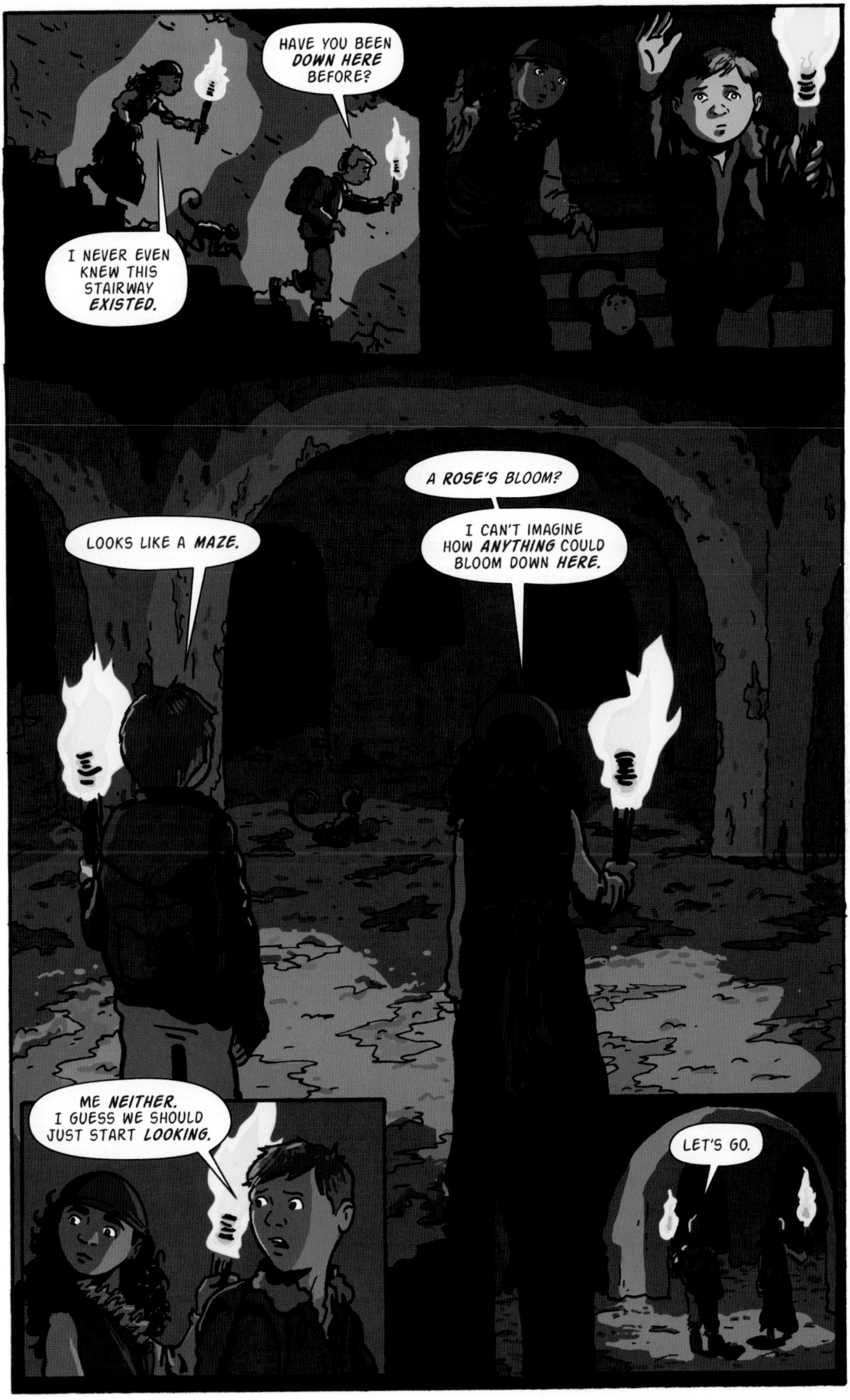

HAVE YOU BEEN DOWN HERE BEFORE?
I NEVER EVEN KNEW THIS STAIRWAY EXISTED.
A ROSE'S BLOOM?
LOOKS LIKE A MAZE.
I CAN'T IMAGINE HOW ANYTHING COULD BLOOM DOWN HERE.
ME NEITHER. I GUESS WE SHOULD JUST START LOOKING.
LET'S GO.

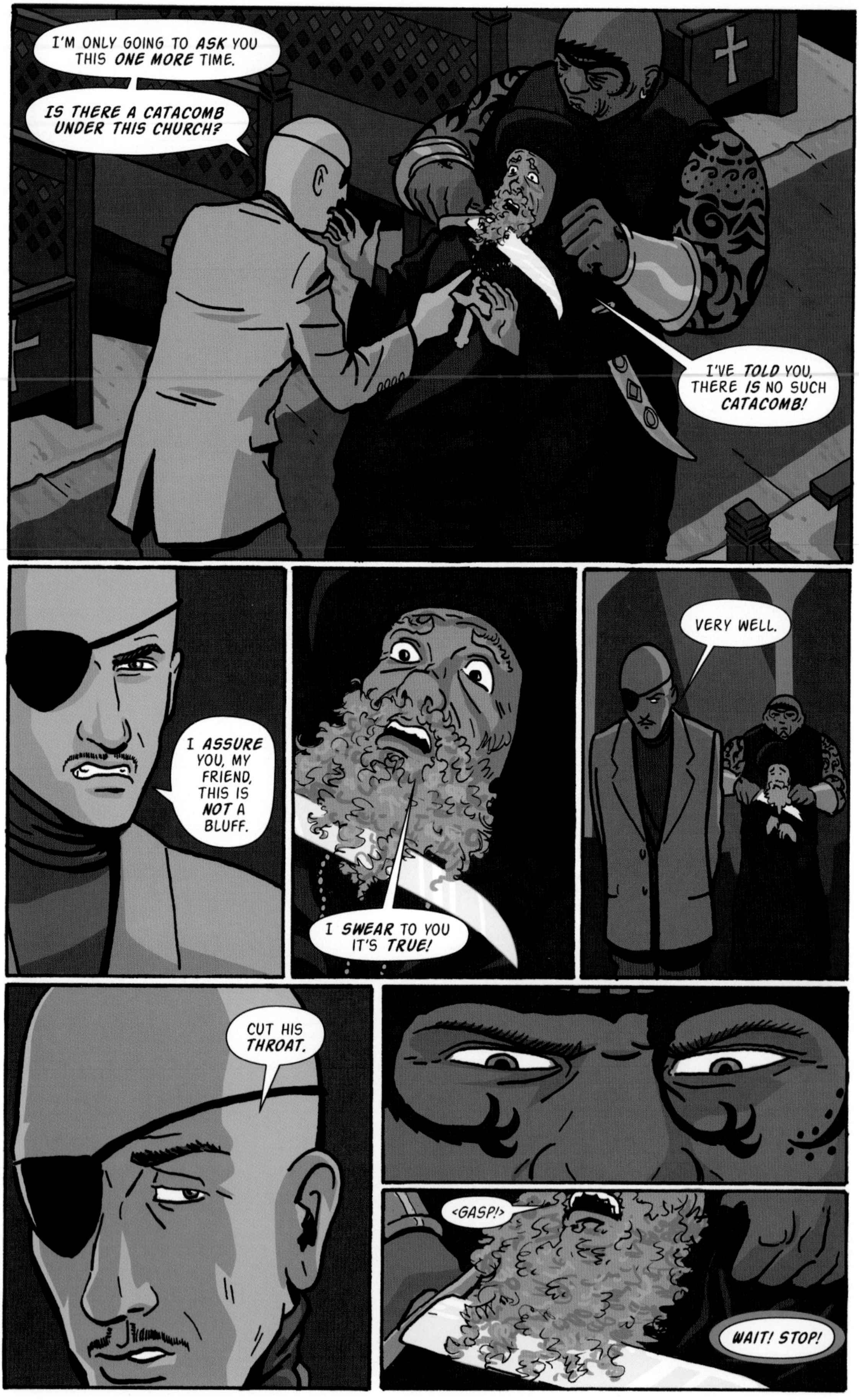
I'M ONLY GOING TO ASK YOU THIS ONE MORE TIME.
IS THERE A CATACOMB UNDER THIS CHURCH?
I'VE TOLD YOU, THERE IS NO SUCH CATACOMB!
I ASSURE YOU, MY FRIEND, THIS IS NOT A BLUFF.
I SWEAR TO YOU IT'S TRUE!
VERY WELL.
CUT HIS THROAT.
<GASP!>
WAIT! STOP!

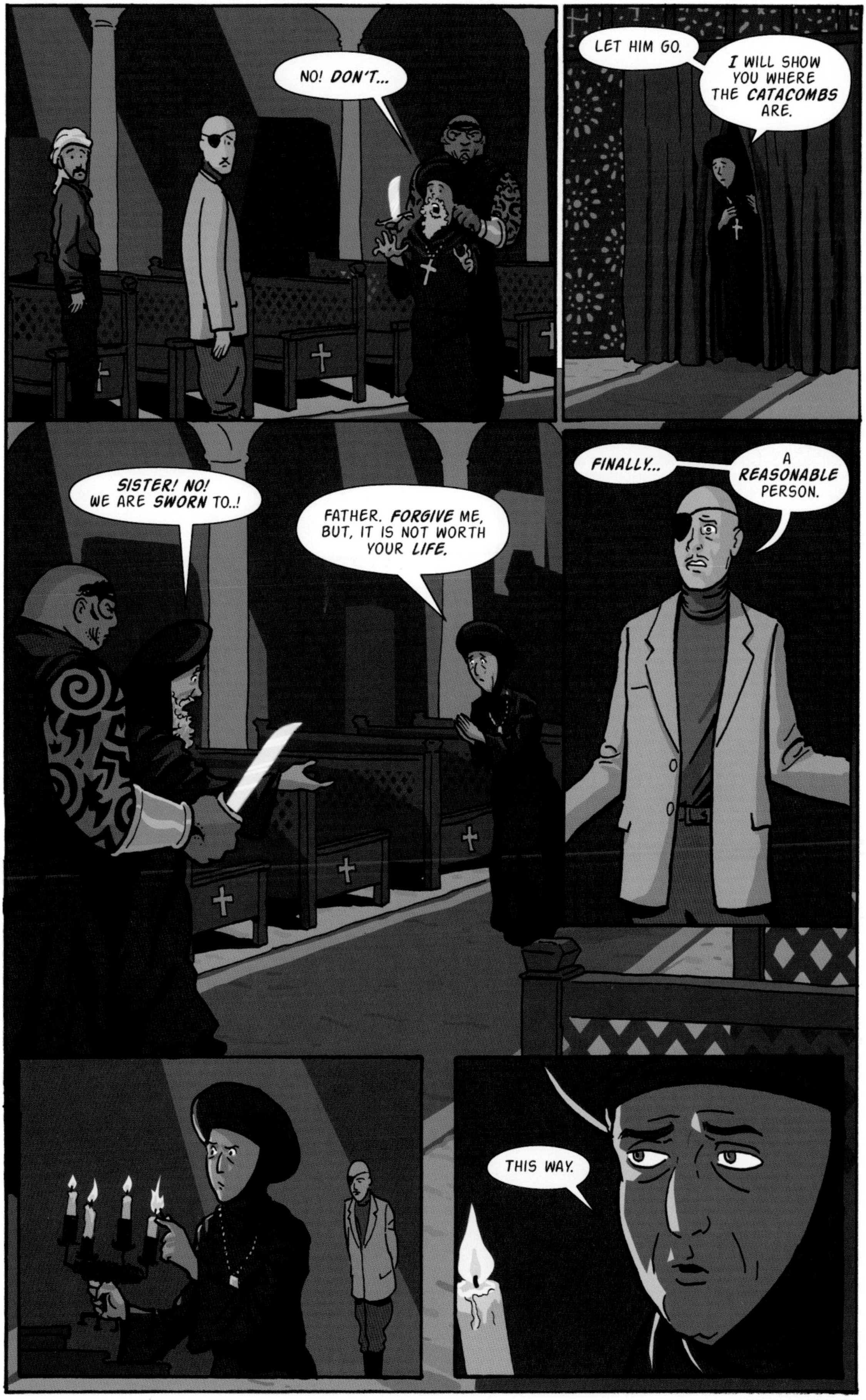
NO! DON'T...
LET HIM GO.
I WILL SHOW YOU WHERE THE CATACOMBS ARE.
SISTER! NO! WE ARE SWORN TO..!
FATHER. FORGIVE ME, BUT, IT IS NOT WORTH YOUR LIFE.
FINALLY...
A REASONABLE PERSON.
THIS WAY.

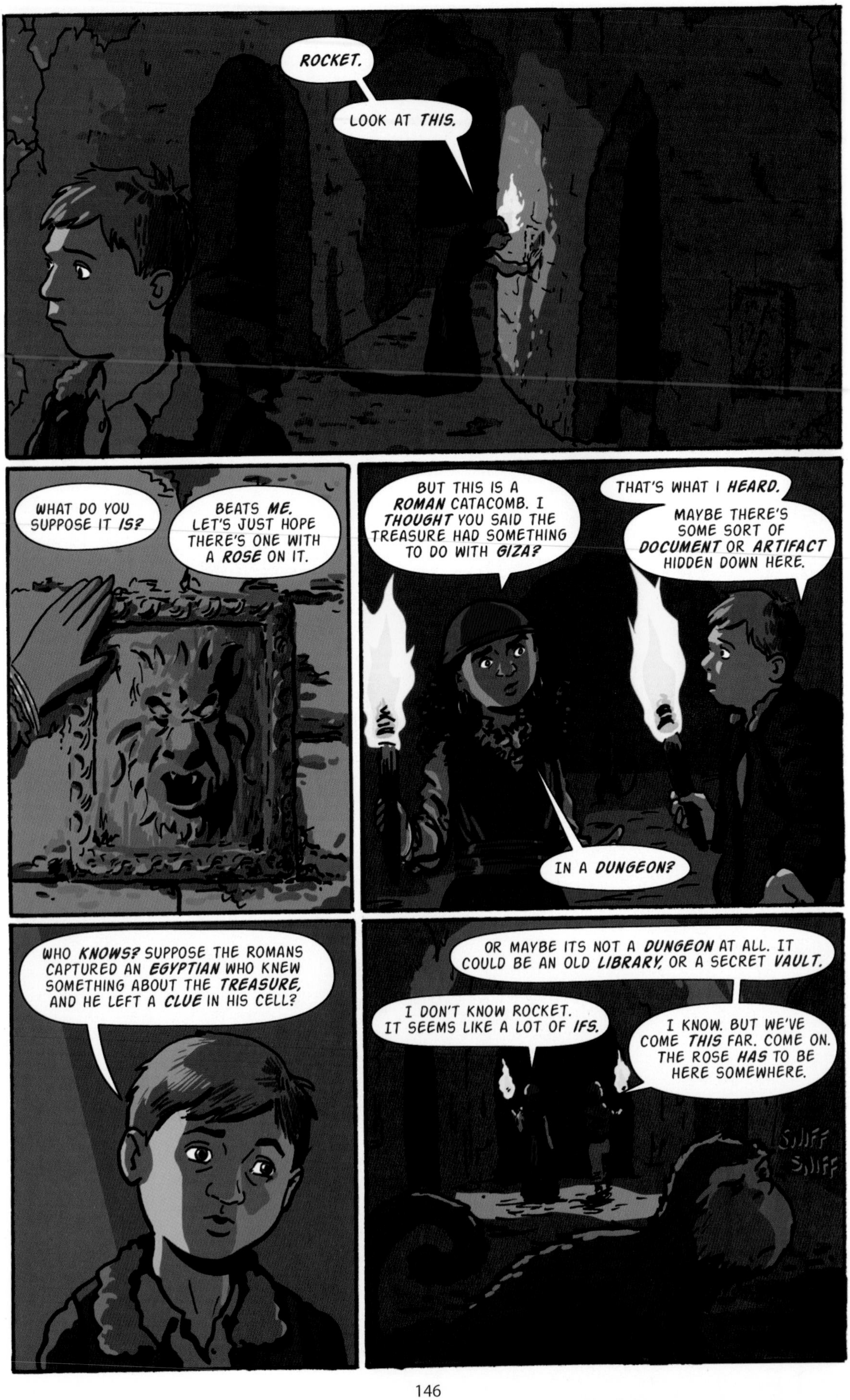
ROCKET.
LOOK AT THIS.
WHAT DO YOU SUPPOSE IT IS?
BEATS ME. LET'S JUST HOPE THERE'S ONE WITH A ROSE ON IT.
BUT THIS IS A ROMAN CATACOMB. I THOUGHT YOU SAID THE TREASURE HAD SOMETHING TO DO WITH GIZA?
IN A DUNGEON?
THAT'S WHAT I HEARD.
MAYBE THERE'S SOME SORT OF DOCUMENT OR ARTIFACT HIDDEN DOWN HERE.
WHO KNOWS? SUPPOSE THE ROMANS CAPTURED AN EGYPTIAN WHO KNEW SOMETHING ABOUT THE TREASURE, AND HE LEFT A CLUE IN HIS CELL?
OR MAYBE ITS NOT A DUNGEON AT ALL. IT COULD BE AN OLD LIBRARY, OR A SECRET VAULT.
I DON'T KNOW ROCKET. IT SEEMS LIKE A LOT OF IFS.
I KNOW. BUT WE'VE COME THIS FAR. COME ON. THE ROSE HAS TO BE HERE SOMEWHERE.
SNIFF SNIFF

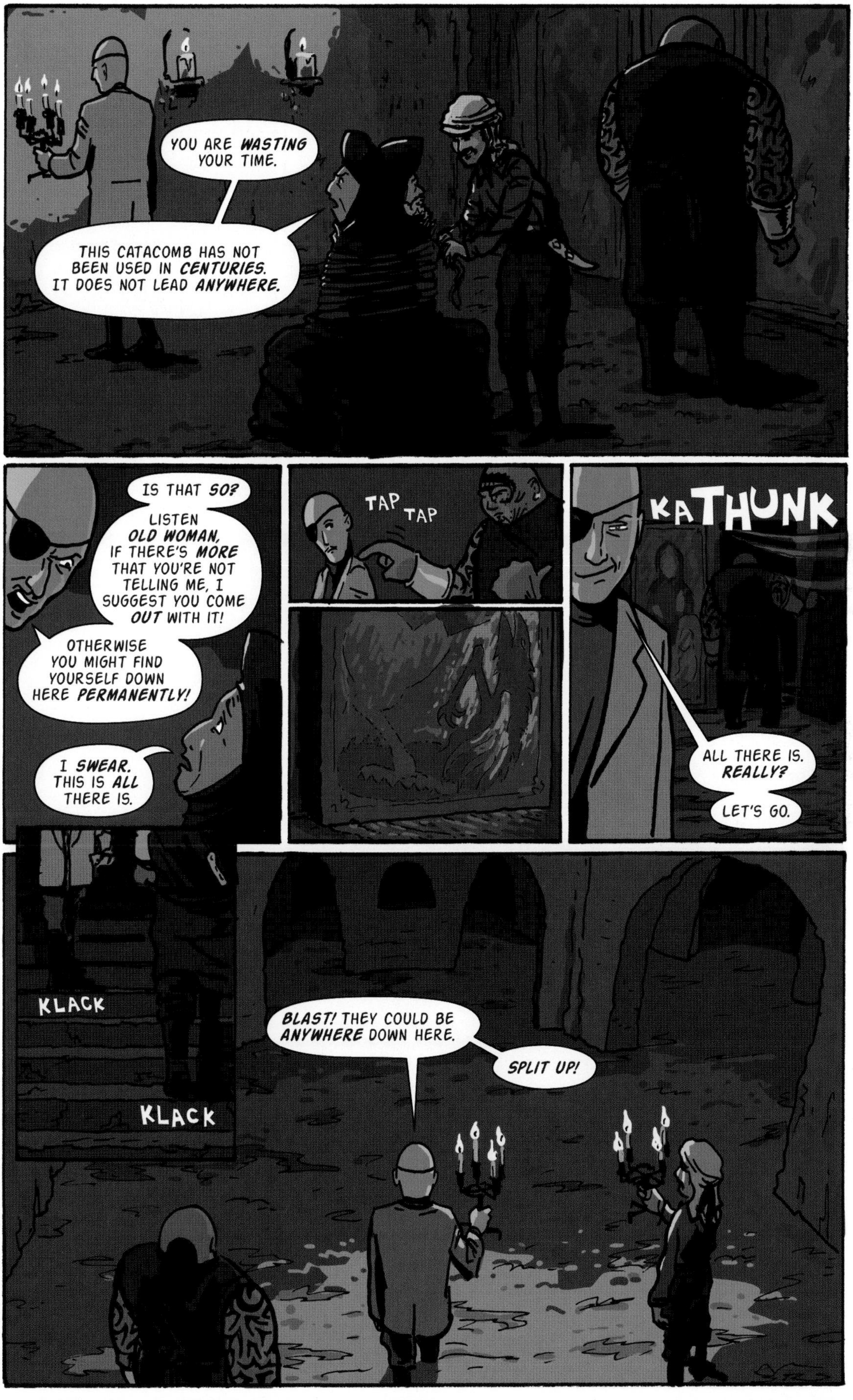
YOU ARE WASTING YOUR TIME.
THIS CATACOMB HAS NOT BEEN USED IN CENTURIES. IT DOES NOT LEAD ANYWHERE.
IS THAT SO?
LISTEN OLD WOMAN, IF THERE'S MORE THAT YOU'RE NOT TELLING ME, I SUGGEST YOU COME OUT WITH IT!
OTHERWISE YOU MIGHT FIND YOURSELF DOWN HERE PERMANENTLY!
I SWEAR. THIS IS ALL THERE IS.
TAP TAP
KATHUNK
ALL THERE IS. REALLY?
LET'S GO.
KLACK
KLACK
BLAST! THEY COULD BE ANYWHERE DOWN HERE.
SPLIT UP!

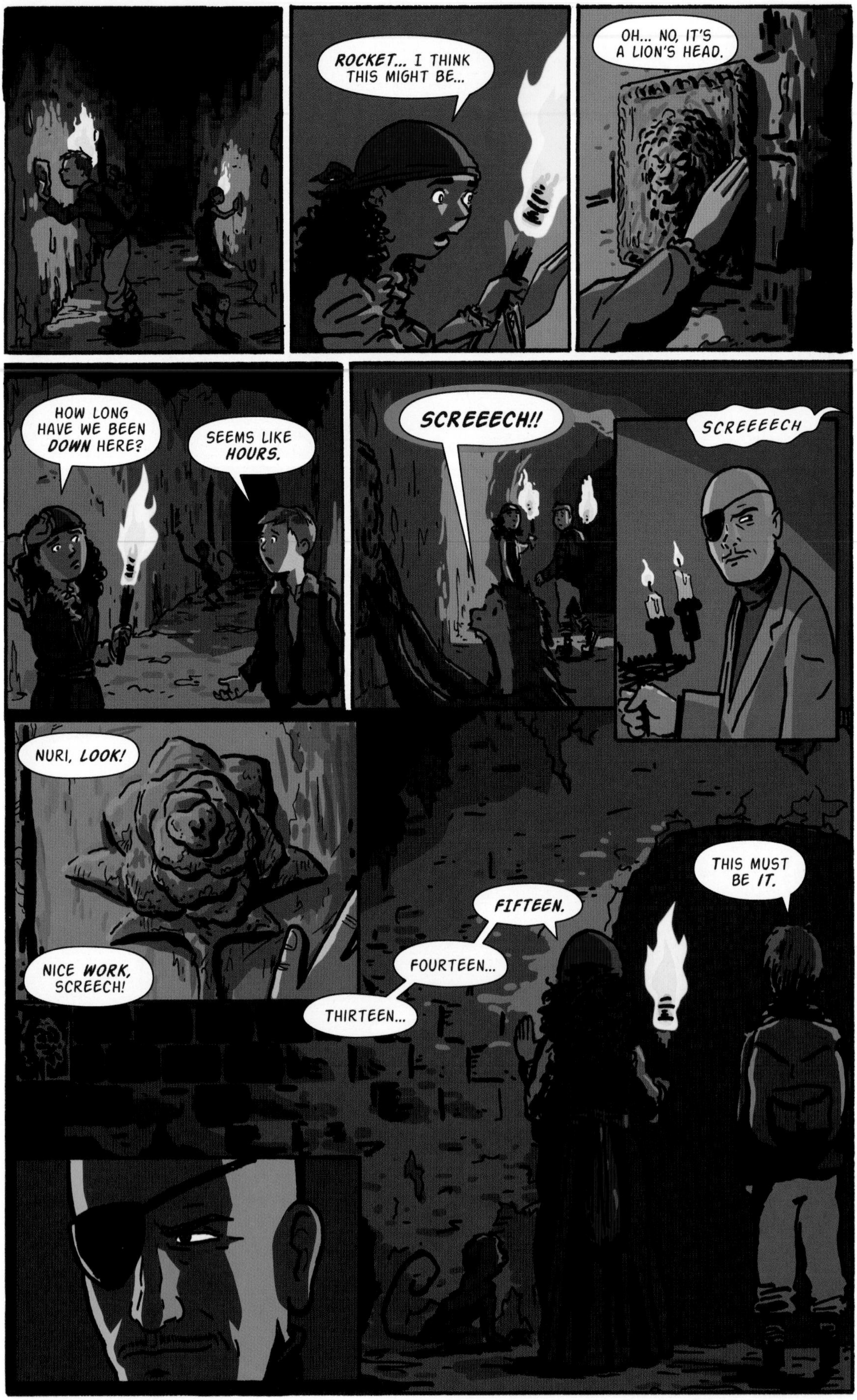
ROCKET... I THINK THIS MIGHT BE...
OH... NO, IT'S A LION'S HEAD.
HOW LONG HAVE WE BEEN DOWN HERE?
SEEMS LIKE HOURS.
SCREEECH!!
SCREEEEECH
NURI, LOOK!
NICE WORK, SCREECH!
THIRTEEN...
FOURTEEN...
FIFTEEN.
THIS MUST BE IT.

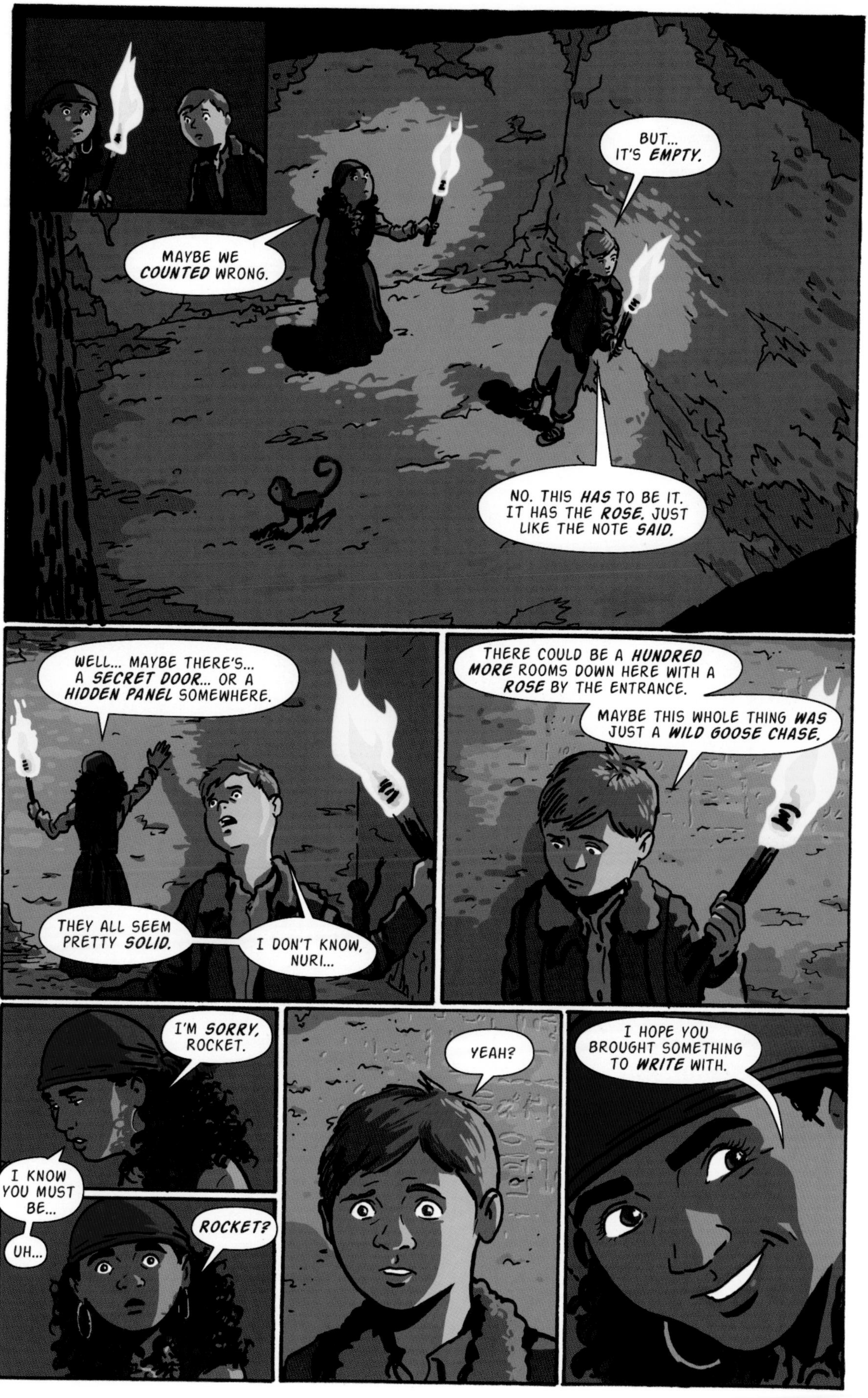
MAYBE WE COUNTED WRONG.
BUT... IT'S EMPTY.
NO. THIS HAS TO BE IT. IT HAS THE ROSE. JUST LIKE THE NOTE SAID.
WELL... MAYBE THERE'S... A SECRET DOOR... OR A HIDDEN PANEL SOMEWHERE.
THEY ALL SEEM PRETTY SOLID.
I DON'T KNOW, NURI...
THERE COULD BE A HUNDRED MORE ROOMS DOWN HERE WITH A ROSE BY THE ENTRANCE.
MAYBE THIS WHOLE THING WAS JUST A WILD GOOSE CHASE.
I'M SORRY, ROCKET.
I KNOW YOU MUST BE...
UH...
ROCKET?
YEAH?
I HOPE YOU BROUGHT SOMETHING TO WRITE WITH.

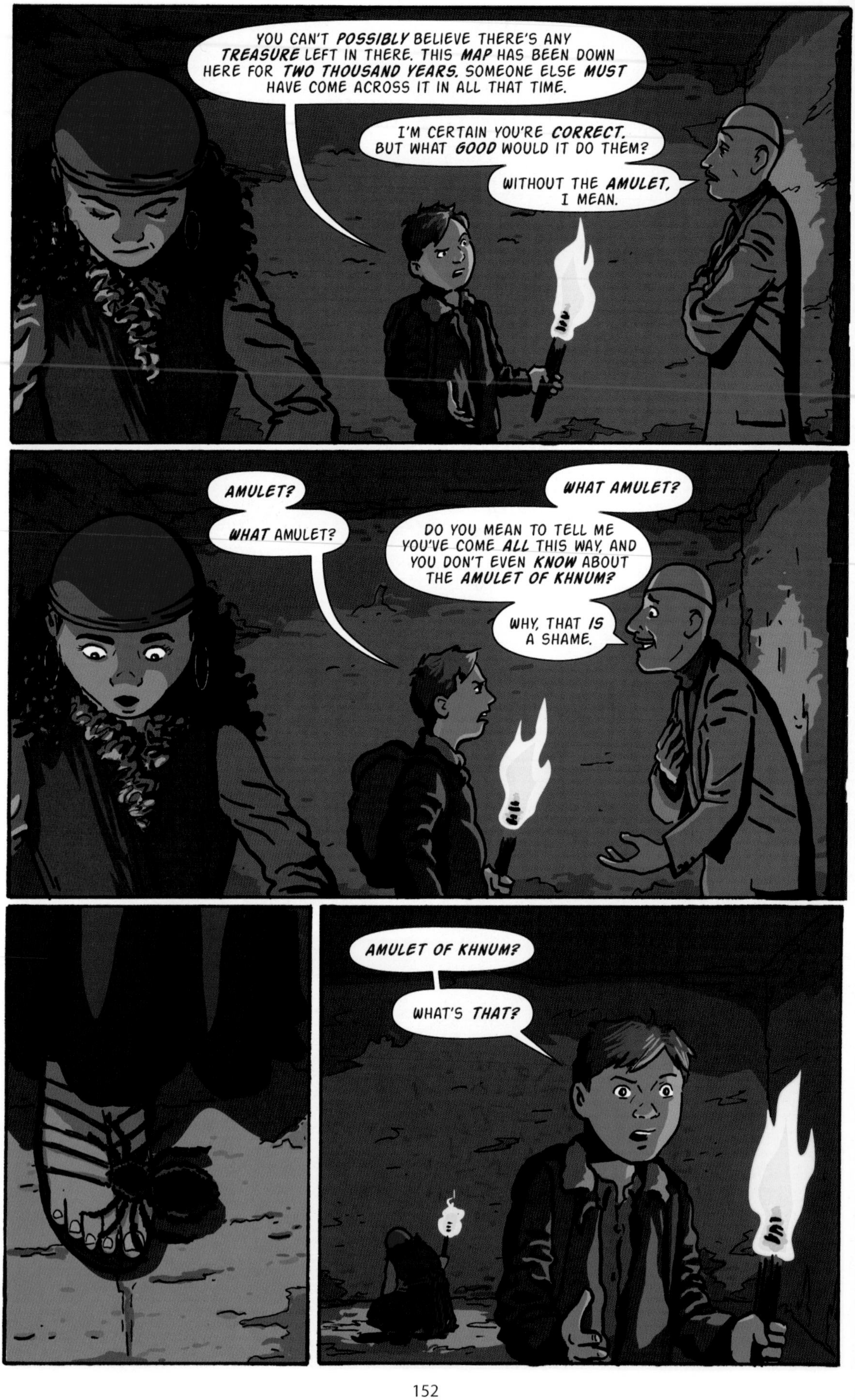
YOU CAN'T POSSIBLY BELIEVE THERE'S ANY TREASURE LEFT IN THERE. THIS MAP HAS BEEN DOWN HERE FOR TWO THOUSAND YEARS. SOMEONE ELSE MUST HAVE COME ACROSS IT IN ALL THAT TIME.
I'M CERTAIN YOU'RE CORRECT. BUT WHAT GOOD WOULD IT DO THEM?
WITHOUT THE AMULET, I MEAN.
AMULET?
WHAT AMULET?
WHAT AMULET?
DO YOU MEAN TO TELL ME YOU'VE COME ALL THIS WAY, AND YOU DON'T EVEN KNOW ABOUT THE AMULET OF KHNUM?
WHY, THAT IS A SHAME.
AMULET OF KHNUM?
WHAT'S THAT?

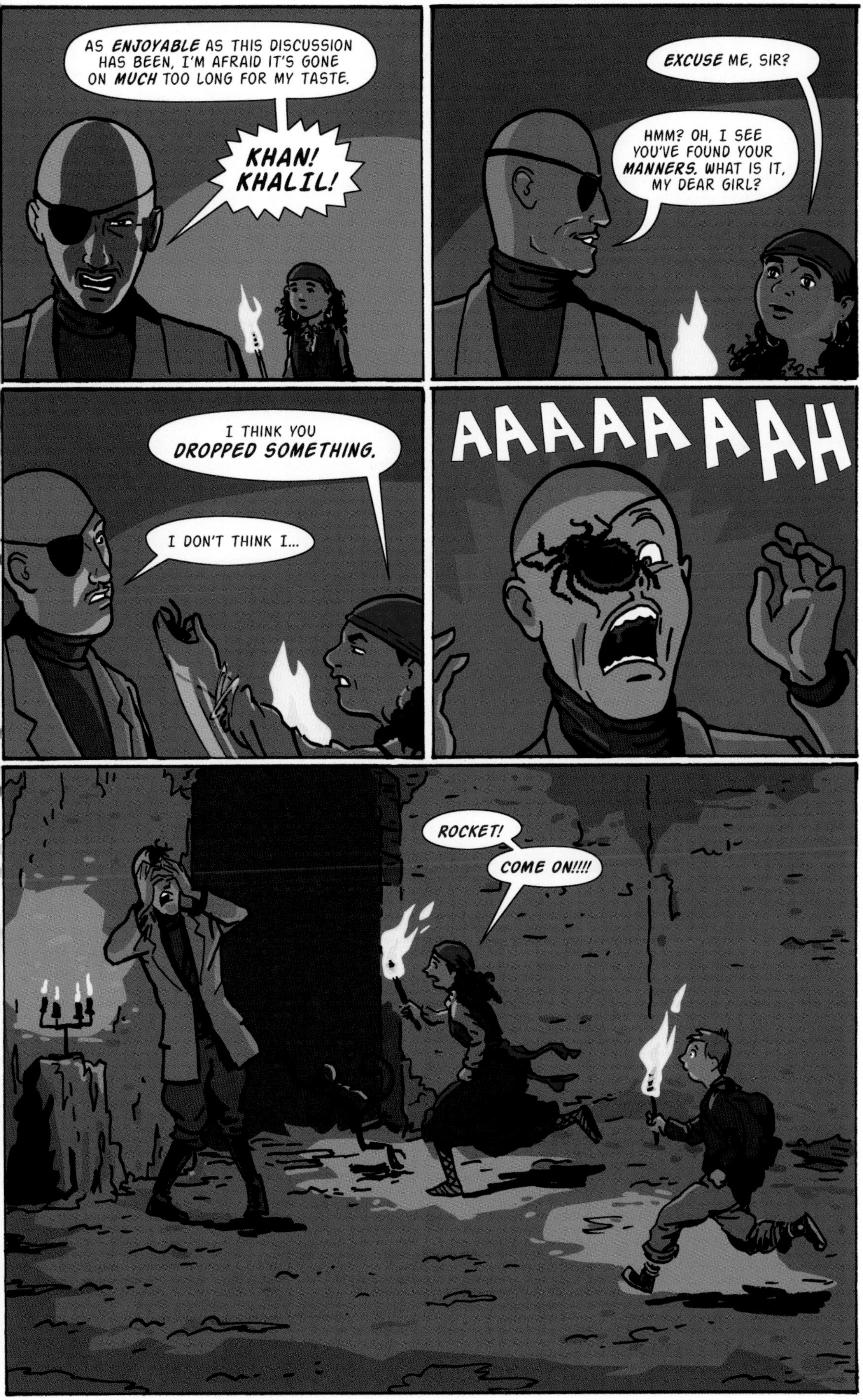
AS ENJOYABLE AS THIS DISCUSSION HAS BEEN, I'M AFRAID IT'S GONE ON MUCH TOO LONG FOR MY TASTE.
KHAN! KHALIL!
EXCUSE ME, SIR?
HMM? OH, I SEE YOU'VE FOUND YOUR MANNERS. WHAT IS IT, MY DEAR GIRL?
I THINK YOU DROPPED SOMETHING.
I DON'T THINK I...
AAAAAAAH
ROCKET!
COME ON!!!!

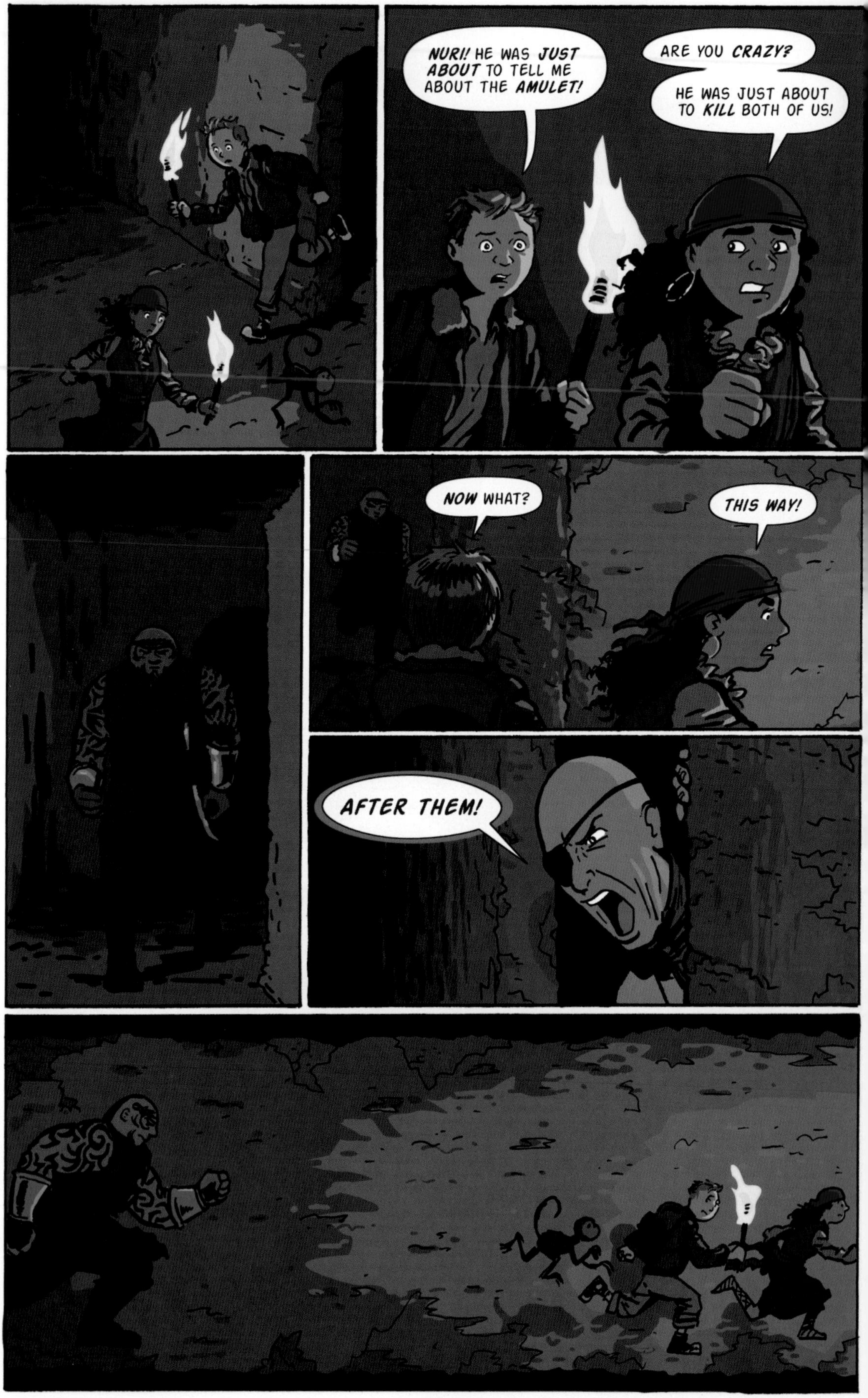
NURI! HE WAS JUST ABOUT TO TELL ME ABOUT THE AMULET!
ARE YOU CRAZY?
HE WAS JUST ABOUT TO KILL BOTH OF US!
NOW WHAT?
THIS WAY!
AFTER THEM!

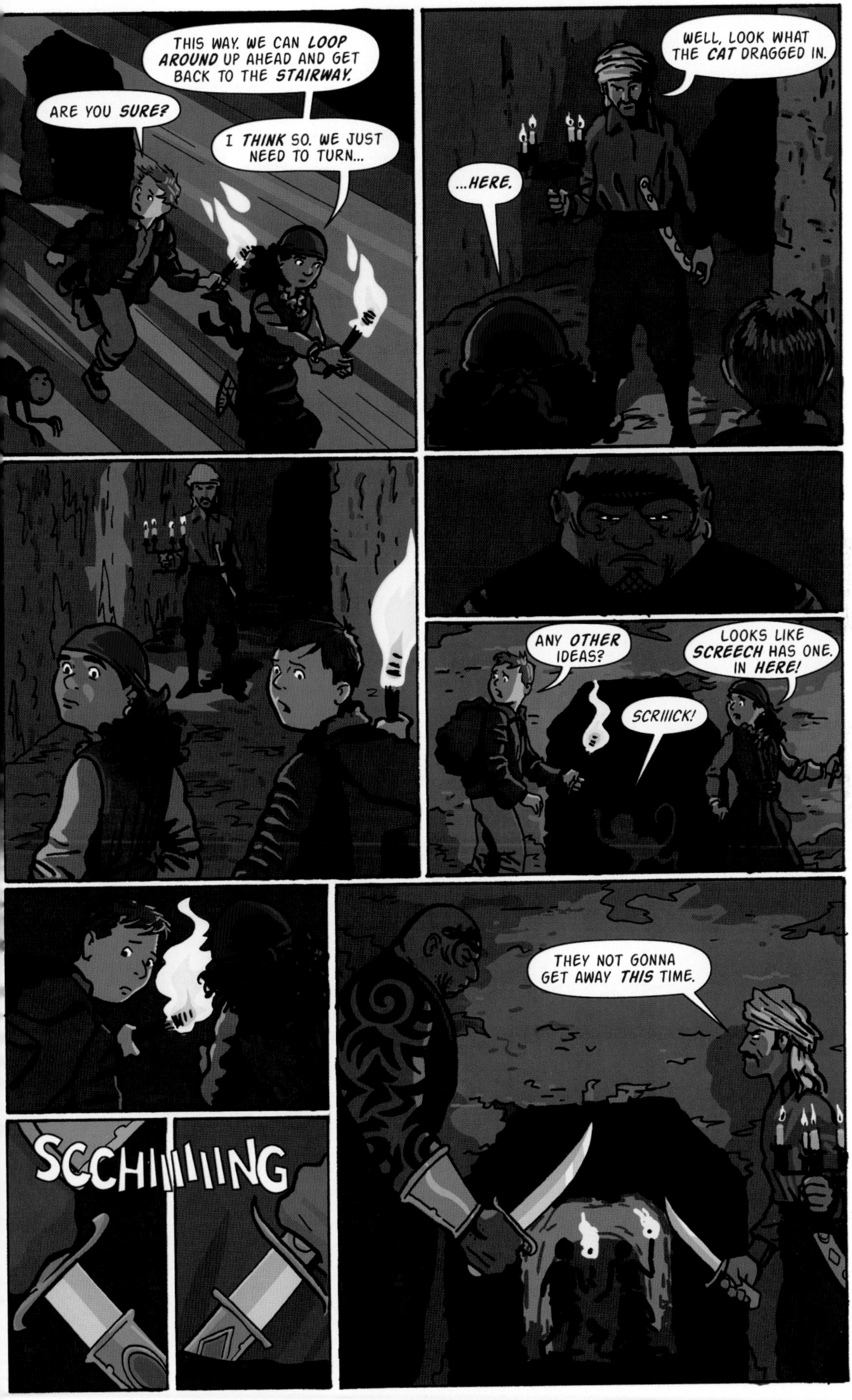
ARE YOU SURE?
THIS WAY. WE CAN LOOP AROUND UP AHEAD AND GET BACK TO THE STAIRWAY.
I THINK SO. WE JUST NEED TO TURN...
...HERE.
WELL, LOOK WHAT THE CAT DRAGGED IN.
ANY OTHER IDEAS?
LOOKS LIKE SCREECH HAS ONE. IN HERE!
SCRIIICK!
SCCHIIIIIIING
THEY NOT GONNA GET AWAY THIS TIME.

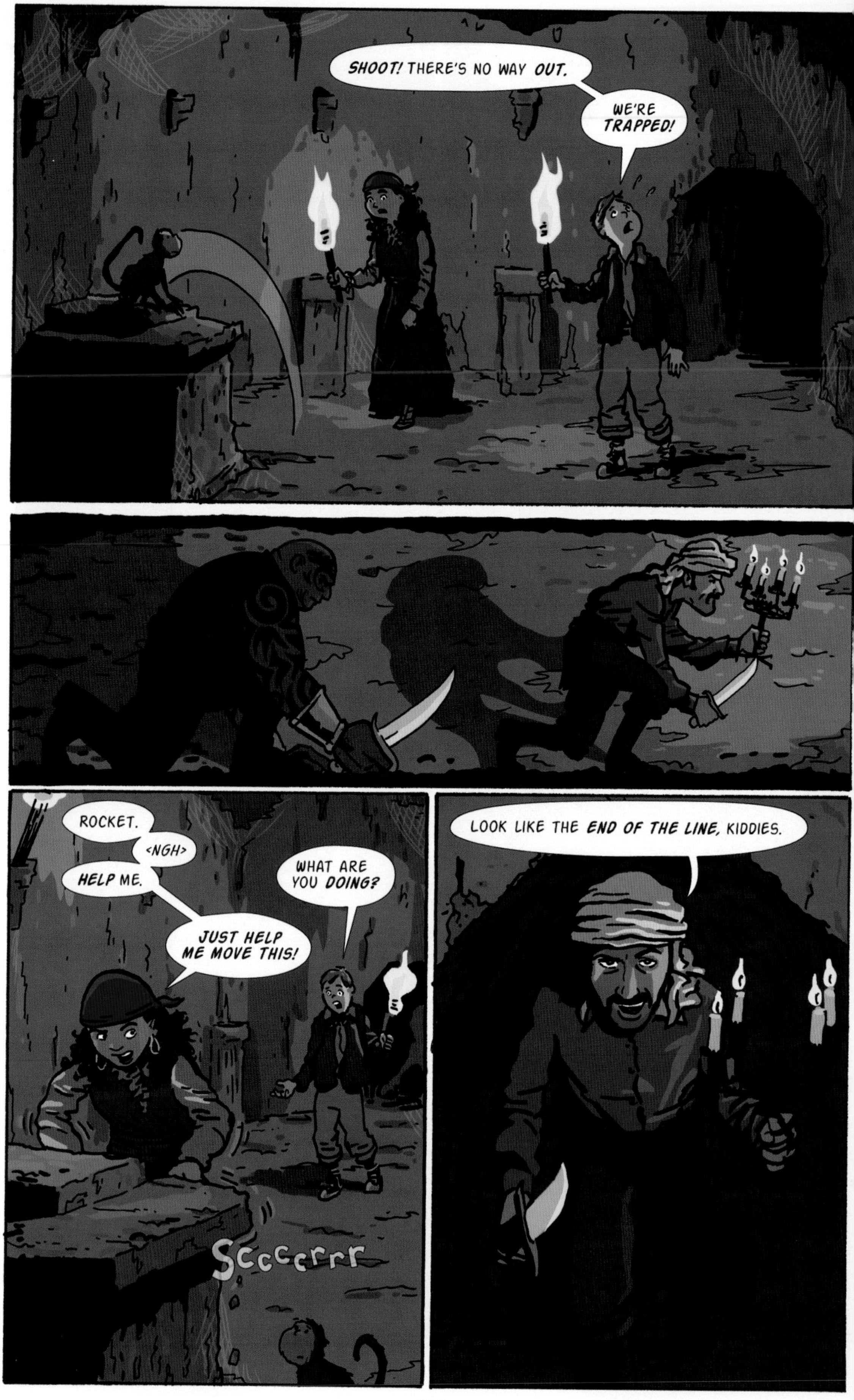
SHOOT! THERE'S NO WAY OUT.
WE'RE TRAPPED!
ROCKET.
<NGH>
HELP ME.
JUST HELP ME MOVE THIS!
WHAT ARE YOU DOING?
Sccccrrr
LOOK LIKE THE END OF THE LINE, KIDDIES.

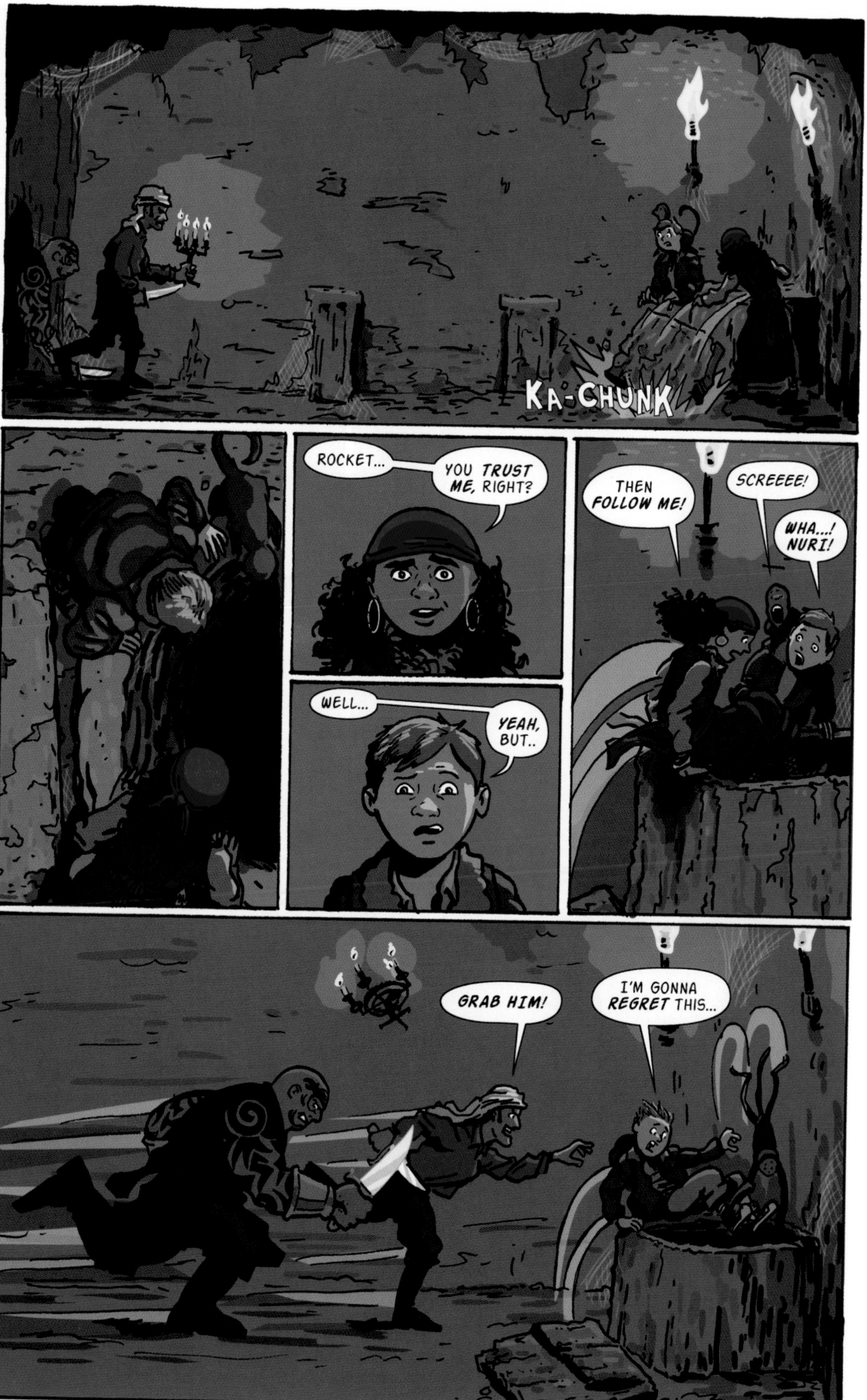
KA-CHUNK
ROCKET...
YOU TRUST ME, RIGHT?
WELL...
YEAH, BUT..
THEN FOLLOW ME!
SCREEEE!
WHA...! NURI!
GRAB HIM!
I'M GONNA REGRET THIS...

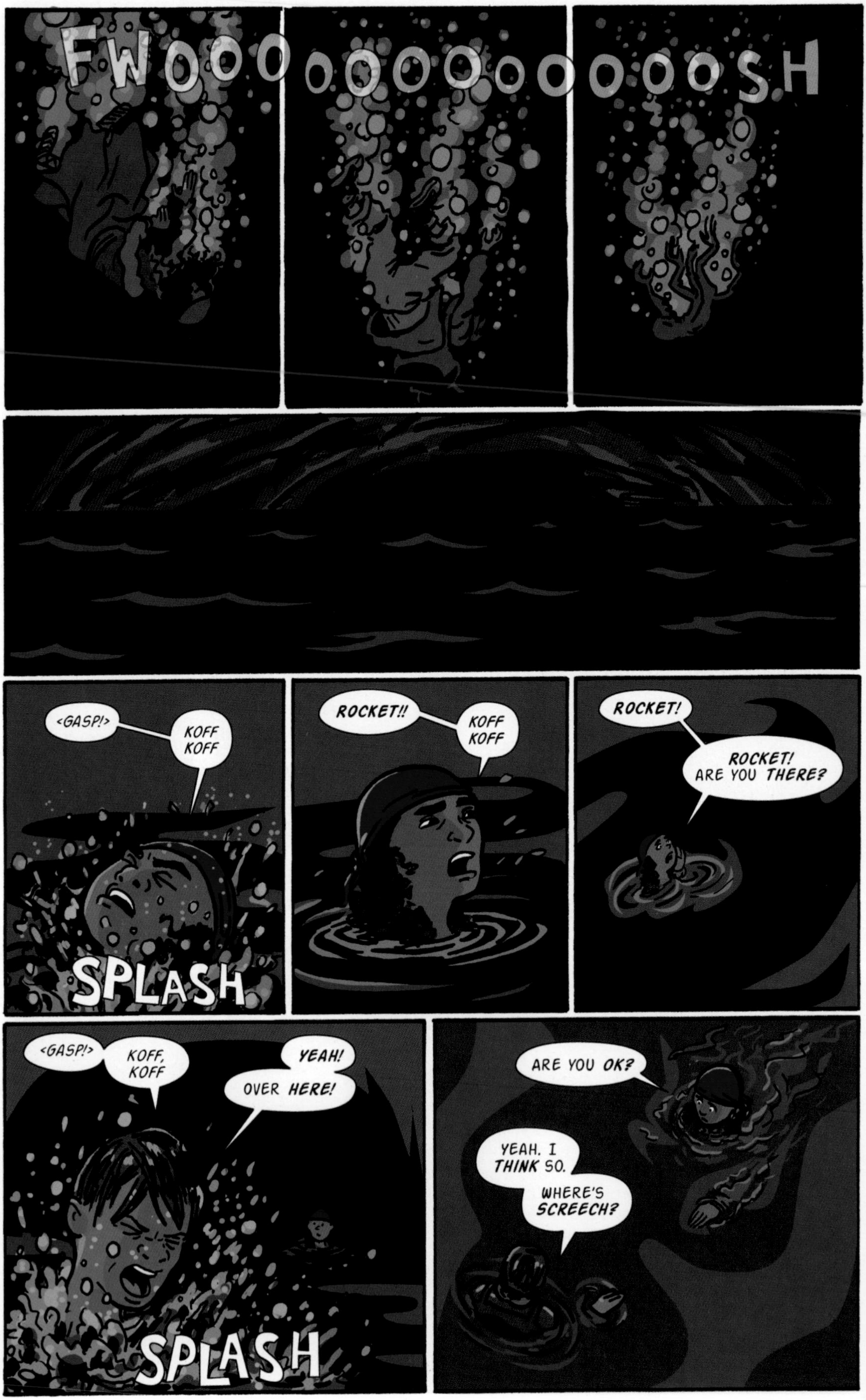
FWOOOOOOOOOOOOOOSH
<GASP!>
KOFF KOFF
SPLASH
ROCKET!!
KOFF KOFF
ROCKET!
ROCKET! ARE YOU THERE?
<GASP!>
KOFF, KOFF
YEAH!
OVER HERE!
SPLASH
ARE YOU OK?
YEAH. I THINK SO.
WHERE'S SCREECH?

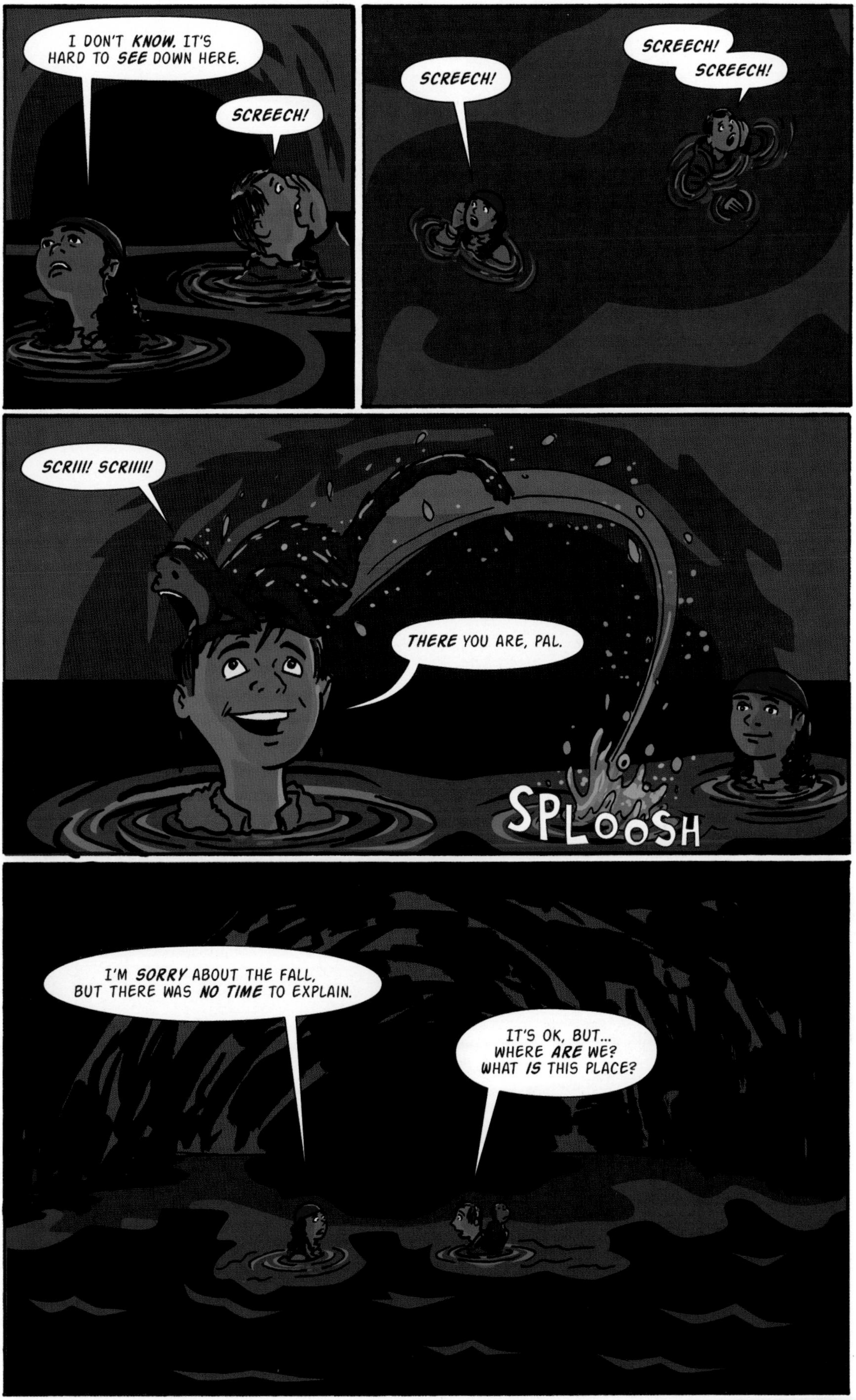
I DON'T KNOW. IT'S HARD TO SEE DOWN HERE.
SCREECH!
SCREECH!
SCREECH!
SCREECH!
SCRIII! SCRIIII!
THERE YOU ARE, PAL.
SPLOOSH
I'M SORRY ABOUT THE FALL, BUT THERE WAS NO TIME TO EXPLAIN.
IT'S OK, BUT... WHERE ARE WE? WHAT IS THIS PLACE?

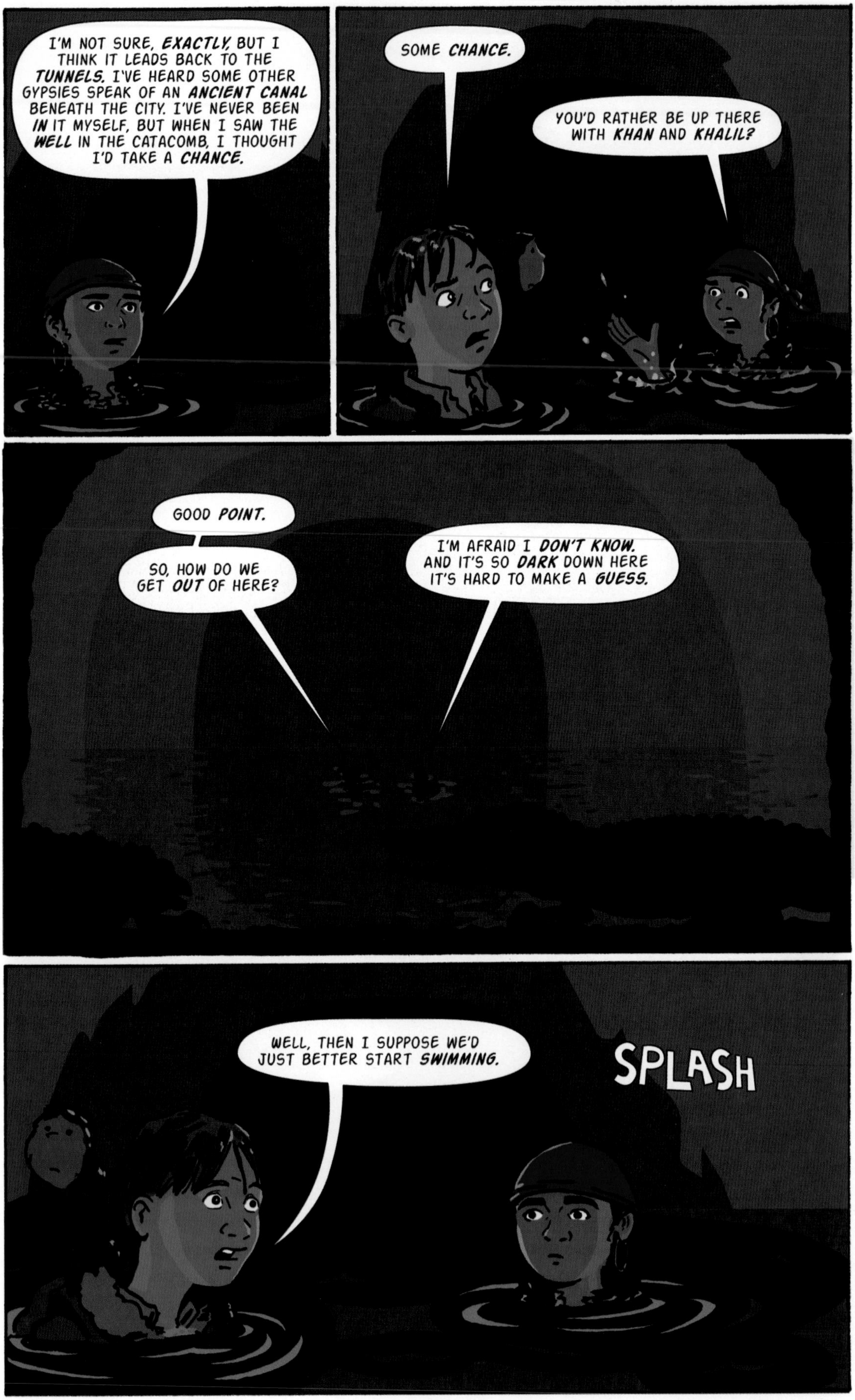
I'M NOT SURE, EXACTLY, BUT I THINK IT LEADS BACK TO THE TUNNELS. I'VE HEARD SOME OTHER GYPSIES SPEAK OF AN ANCIENT CANAL BENEATH THE CITY. I'VE NEVER BEEN IN IT MYSELF, BUT WHEN I SAW THE WELL IN THE CATACOMB, I THOUGHT I'D TAKE A CHANCE.
SOME CHANCE.
YOU'D RATHER BE UP THERE WITH KHAN AND KHALIL?
GOOD POINT.
SO, HOW DO WE GET OUT OF HERE?
I'M AFRAID I DON'T KNOW. AND IT'S SO DARK DOWN HERE IT'S HARD TO MAKE A GUESS.
WELL, THEN I SUPPOSE WE'D JUST BETTER START SWIMMING.
SPLASH

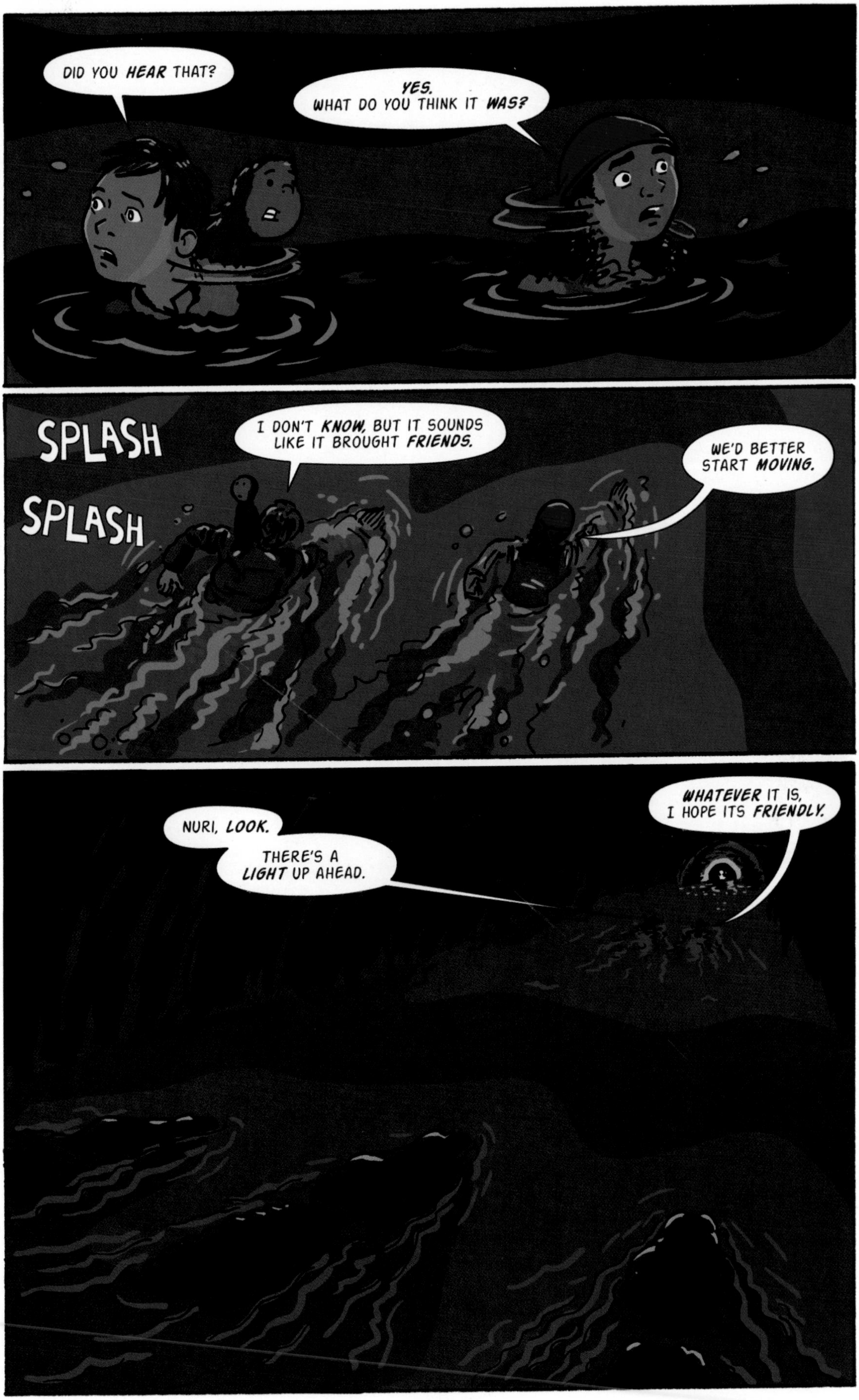
DID YOU HEAR THAT?
YES. WHAT DO YOU THINK IT WAS?
SPLASH
SPLASH
I DON'T KNOW, BUT IT SOUNDS LIKE IT BROUGHT FRIENDS.
WE'D BETTER START MOVING.
NURI, LOOK.
THERE'S A LIGHT UP AHEAD.
WHATEVER IT IS, I HOPE ITS FRIENDLY.

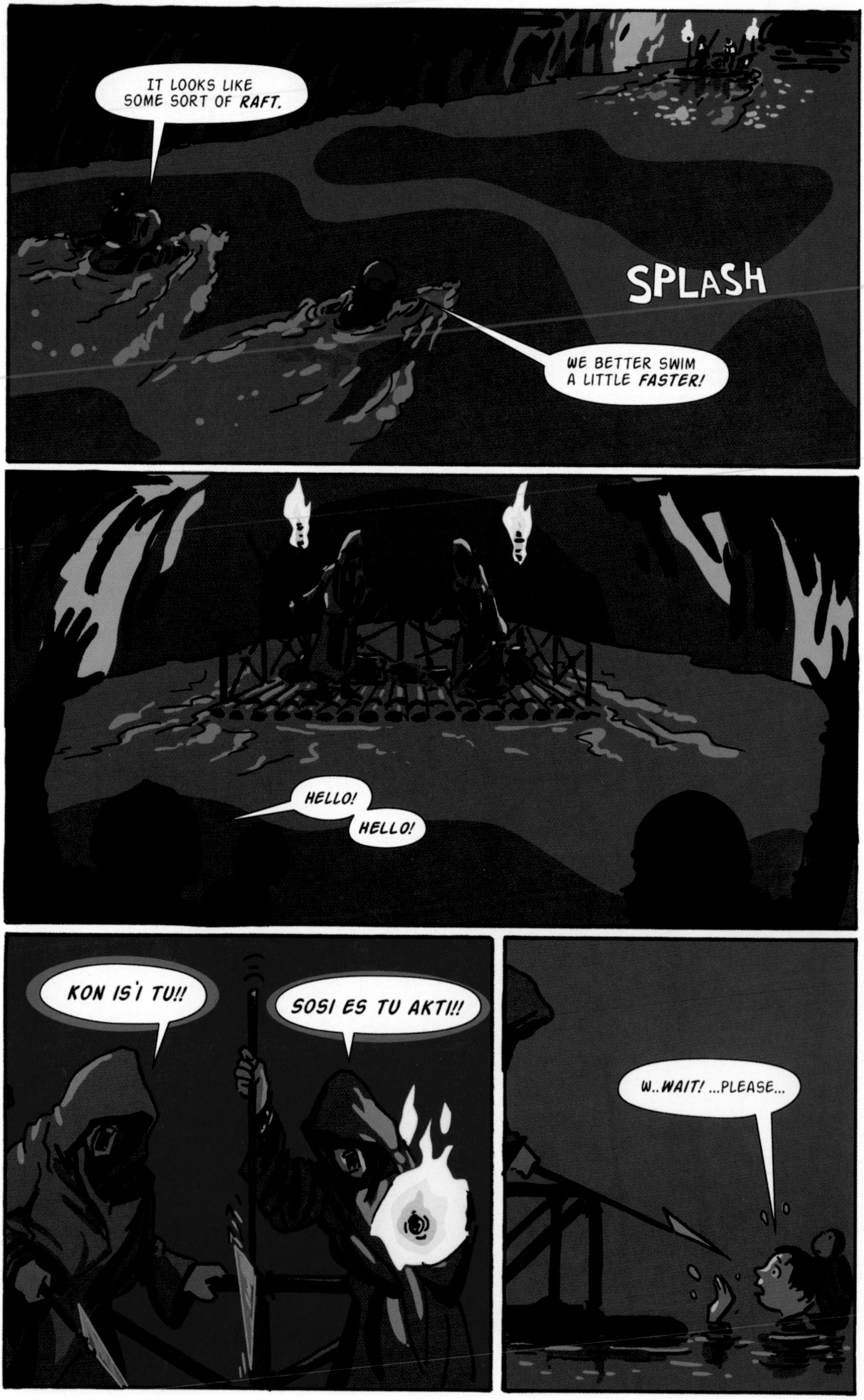
IT LOOKS LIKE SOME SORT OF RAFT.
SPLASH
WE BETTER SWIM A LITTLE FASTER!
HELLO!
HELLO!
KON IS'I TU!!
SOSI ES TU AKTI!!
W..WAIT! ...PLEASE...

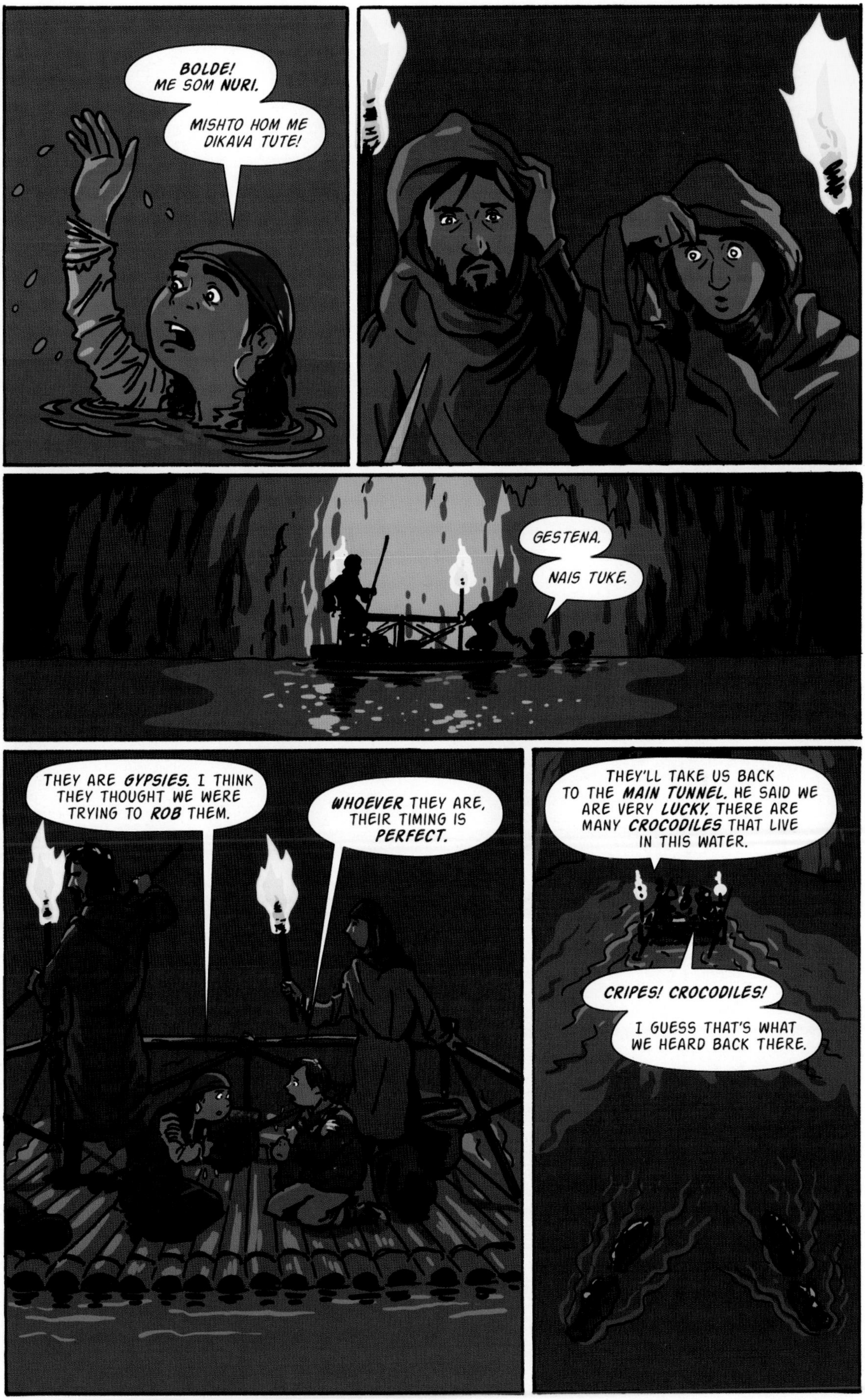
BOLDE! ME SOM NURI.
MISHTO HOM ME DIKAVA TUTE!
GESTENA.
NAIS TUKE.
THEY ARE GYPSIES. I THINK THEY THOUGHT WE WERE TRYING TO ROB THEM.
WHOEVER THEY ARE, THEIR TIMING IS PERFECT.
THEY'LL TAKE US BACK TO THE MAIN TUNNEL. HE SAID WE ARE VERY LUCKY. THERE ARE MANY CROCODILES THAT LIVE IN THIS WATER.
CRIPES! CROCODILES!
I GUESS THAT'S WHAT WE HEARD BACK THERE.

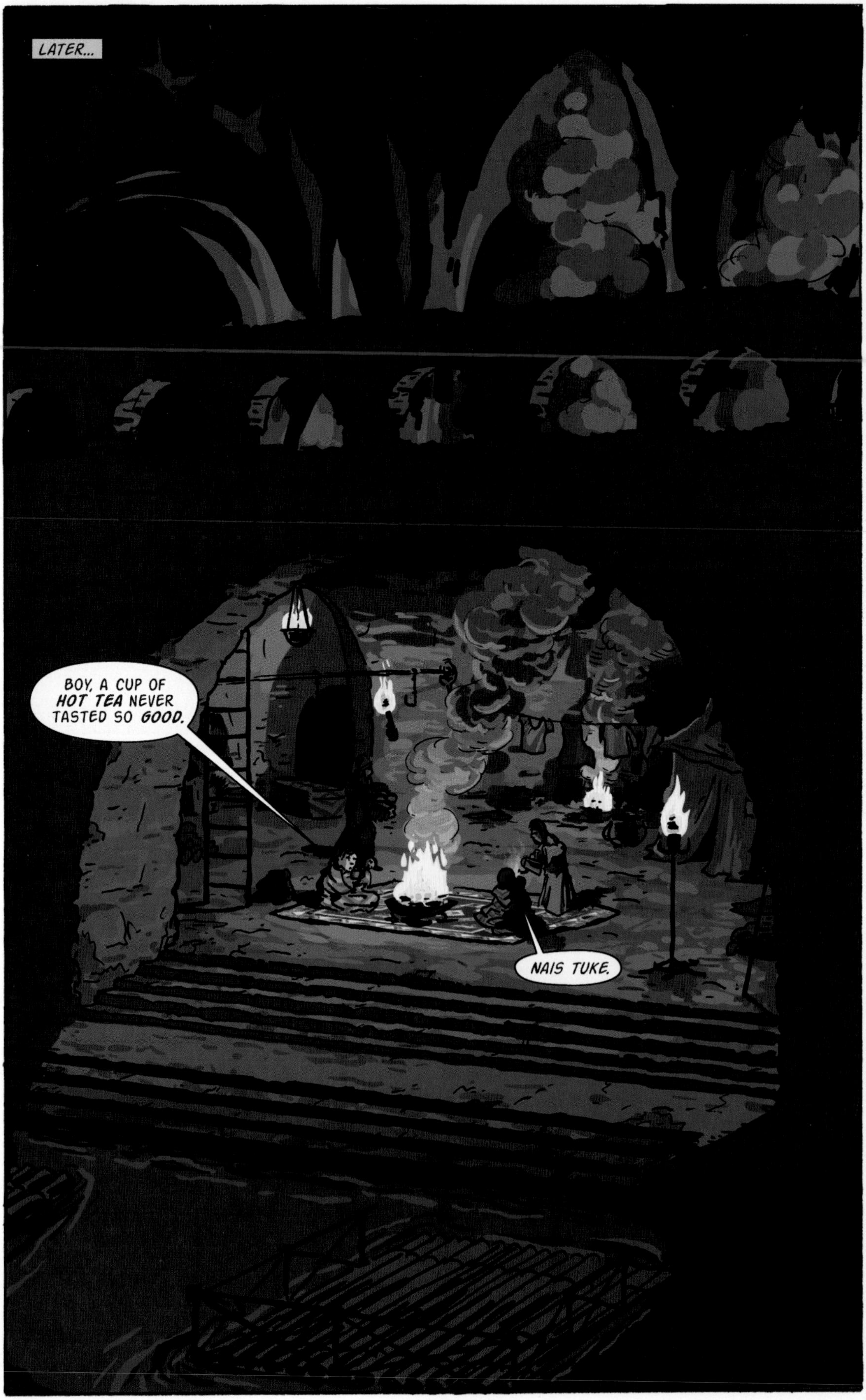
LATER...
BOY, A CUP OF HOT TEA NEVER TASTED SO GOOD.
NAIS TUKE.

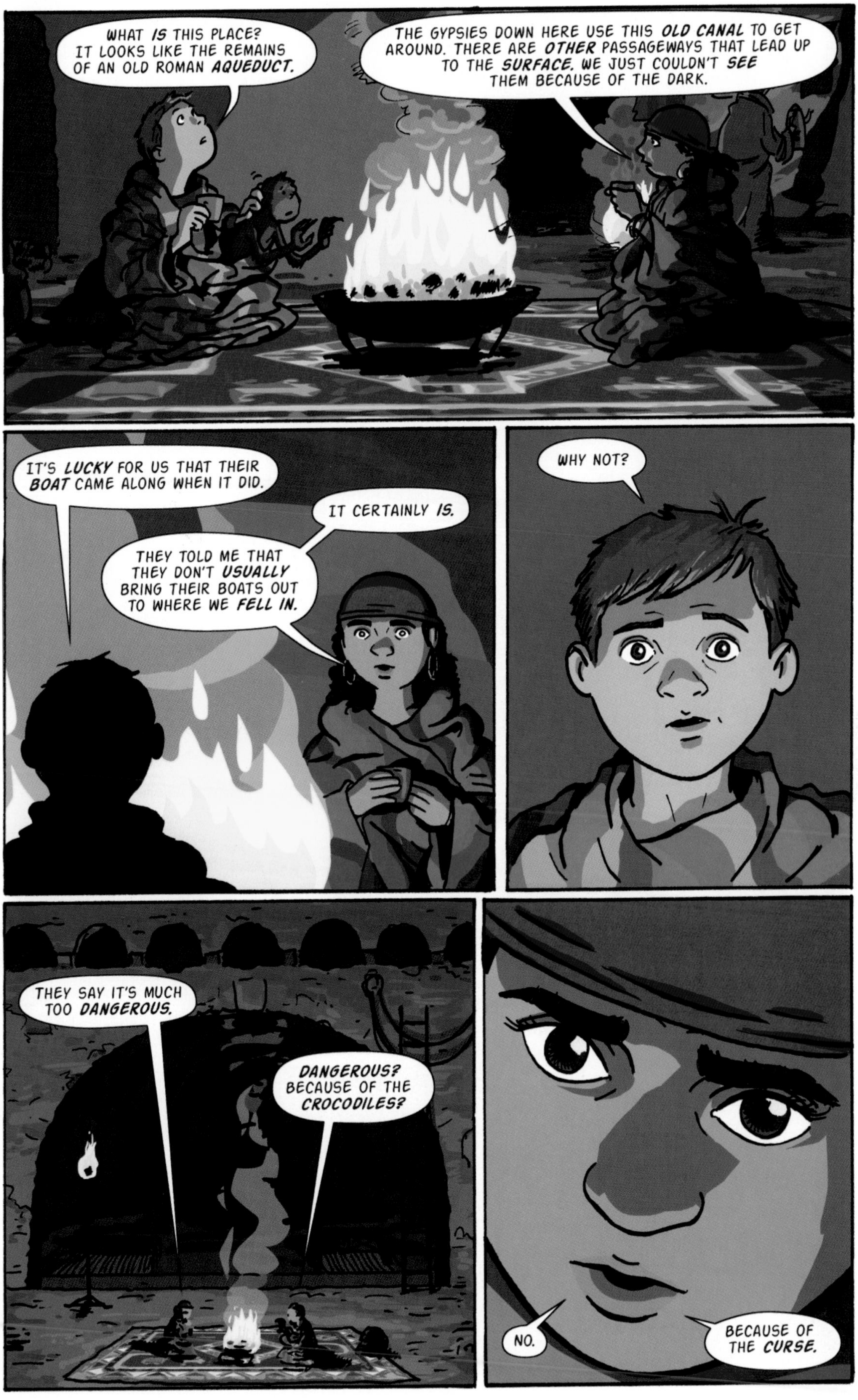
WHAT IS THIS PLACE? IT LOOKS LIKE THE REMAINS OF AN OLD ROMAN AQUEDUCT.
THE GYPSIES DOWN HERE USE THIS OLD CANAL TO GET AROUND. THERE ARE OTHER PASSAGEWAYS THAT LEAD UP TO THE SURFACE. WE JUST COULDN'T SEE THEM BECAUSE OF THE DARK.
IT'S LUCKY FOR US THAT THEIR BOAT CAME ALONG WHEN IT DID.
IT CERTAINLY IS.
THEY TOLD ME THAT THEY DON'T USUALLY BRING THEIR BOATS OUT TO WHERE WE FELL IN.
WHY NOT?
THEY SAY IT'S MUCH TOO DANGEROUS.
DANGEROUS? BECAUSE OF THE CROCODILES?
NO.
BECAUSE OF THE CURSE.

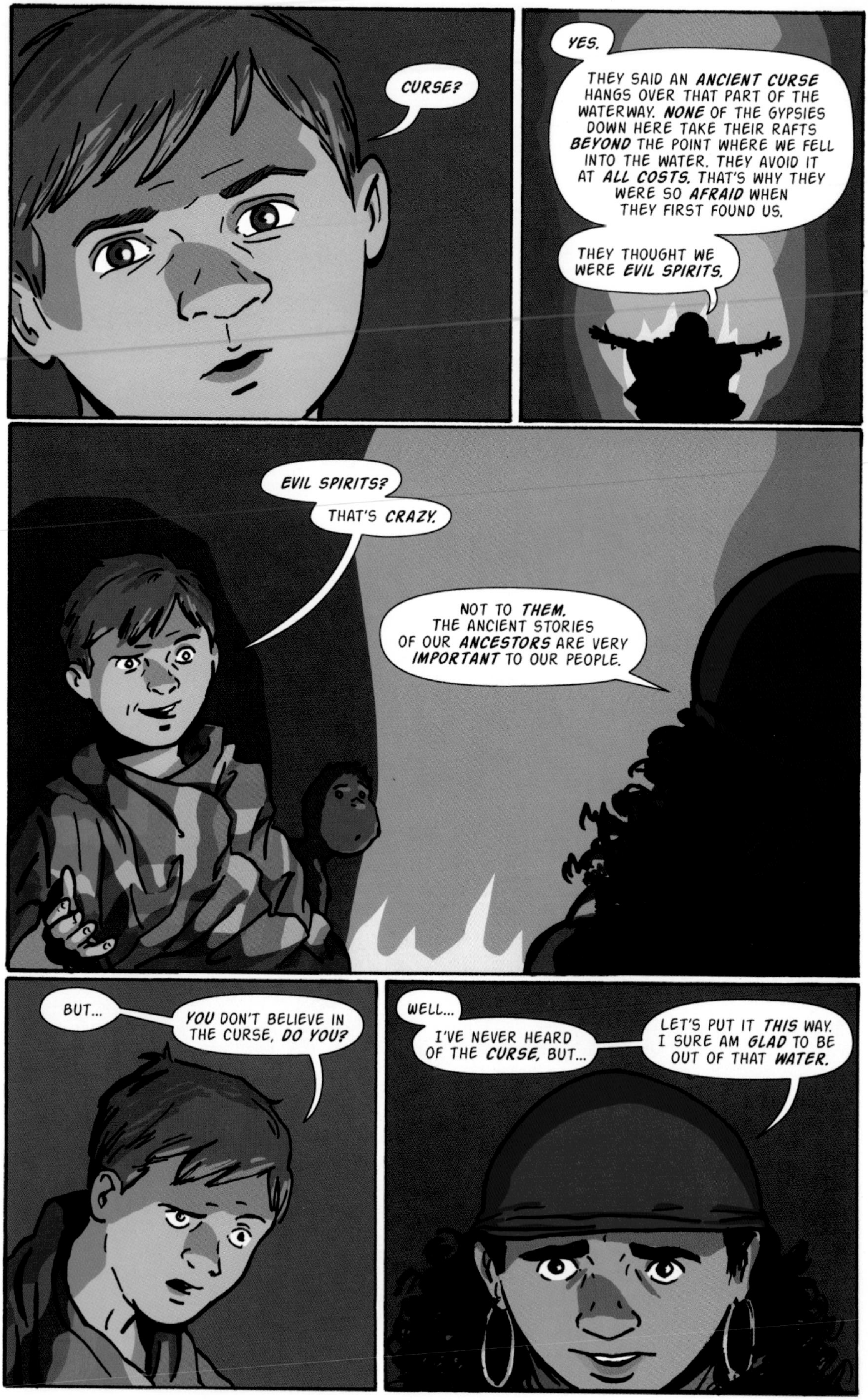
CURSE?
YES.
THEY SAID AN ANCIENT CURSE HANGS OVER THAT PART OF THE WATERWAY. NONE OF THE GYPSIES DOWN HERE TAKE THEIR RAFTS BEYOND THE POINT WHERE WE FELL INTO THE WATER. THEY AVOID IT AT ALL COSTS. THAT'S WHY THEY WERE SO AFRAID WHEN THEY FIRST FOUND US.
THEY THOUGHT WE WERE EVIL SPIRITS.
EVIL SPIRITS?
THAT'S CRAZY.
NOT TO THEM. THE ANCIENT STORIES OF OUR ANCESTORS ARE VERY IMPORTANT TO OUR PEOPLE.
BUT...
YOU DON'T BELIEVE IN THE CURSE, DO YOU?
WELL...
I'VE NEVER HEARD OF THE CURSE, BUT...
LET'S PUT IT THIS WAY. I SURE AM GLAD TO BE OUT OF THAT WATER.

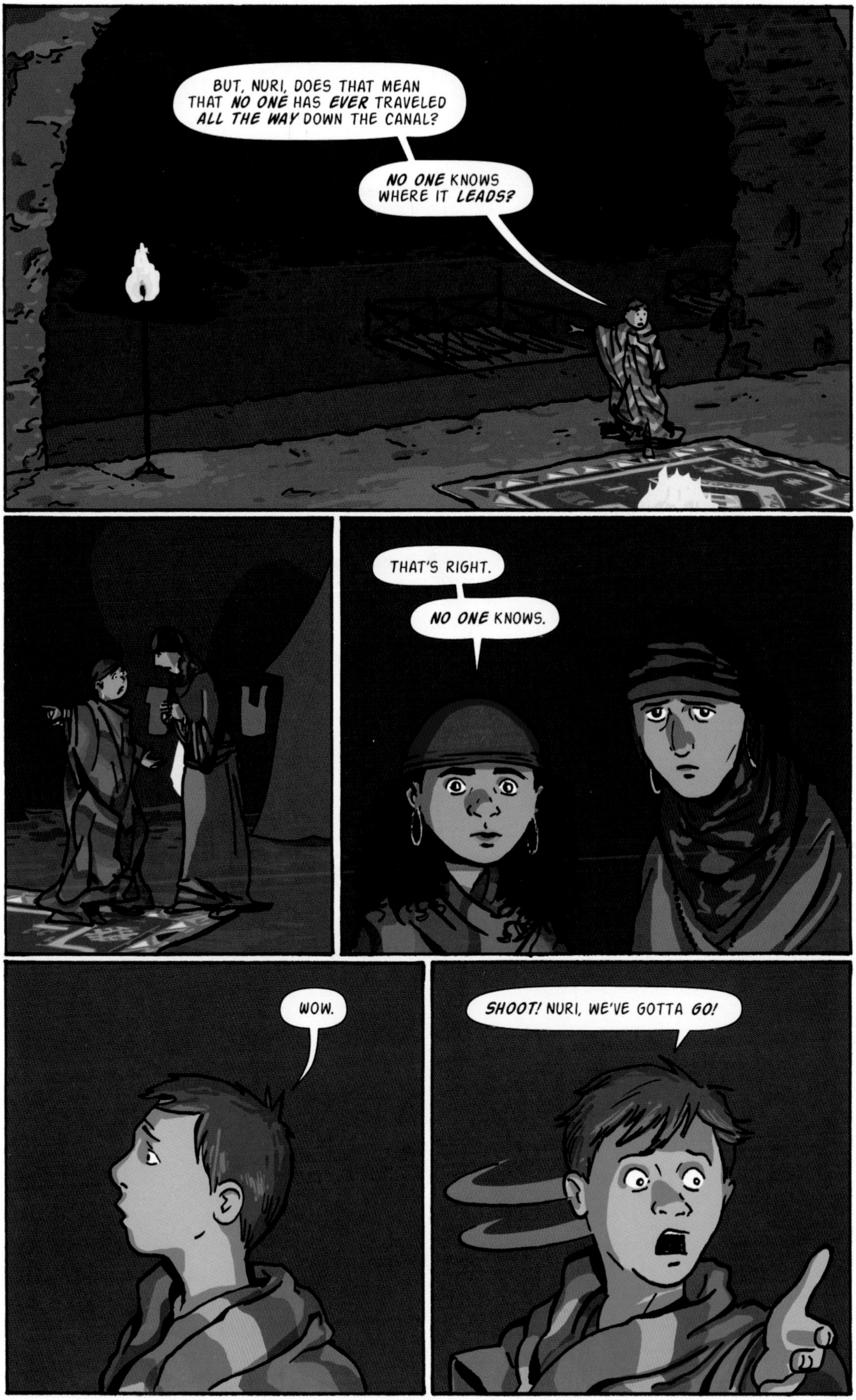
BUT, NURI, DOES THAT MEAN THAT NO ONE HAS EVER TRAVELED ALL THE WAY DOWN THE CANAL?
NO ONE KNOWS WHERE IT LEADS?
THAT'S RIGHT.
NO ONE KNOWS.
WOW.
SHOOT! NURI, WE'VE GOTTA GO!

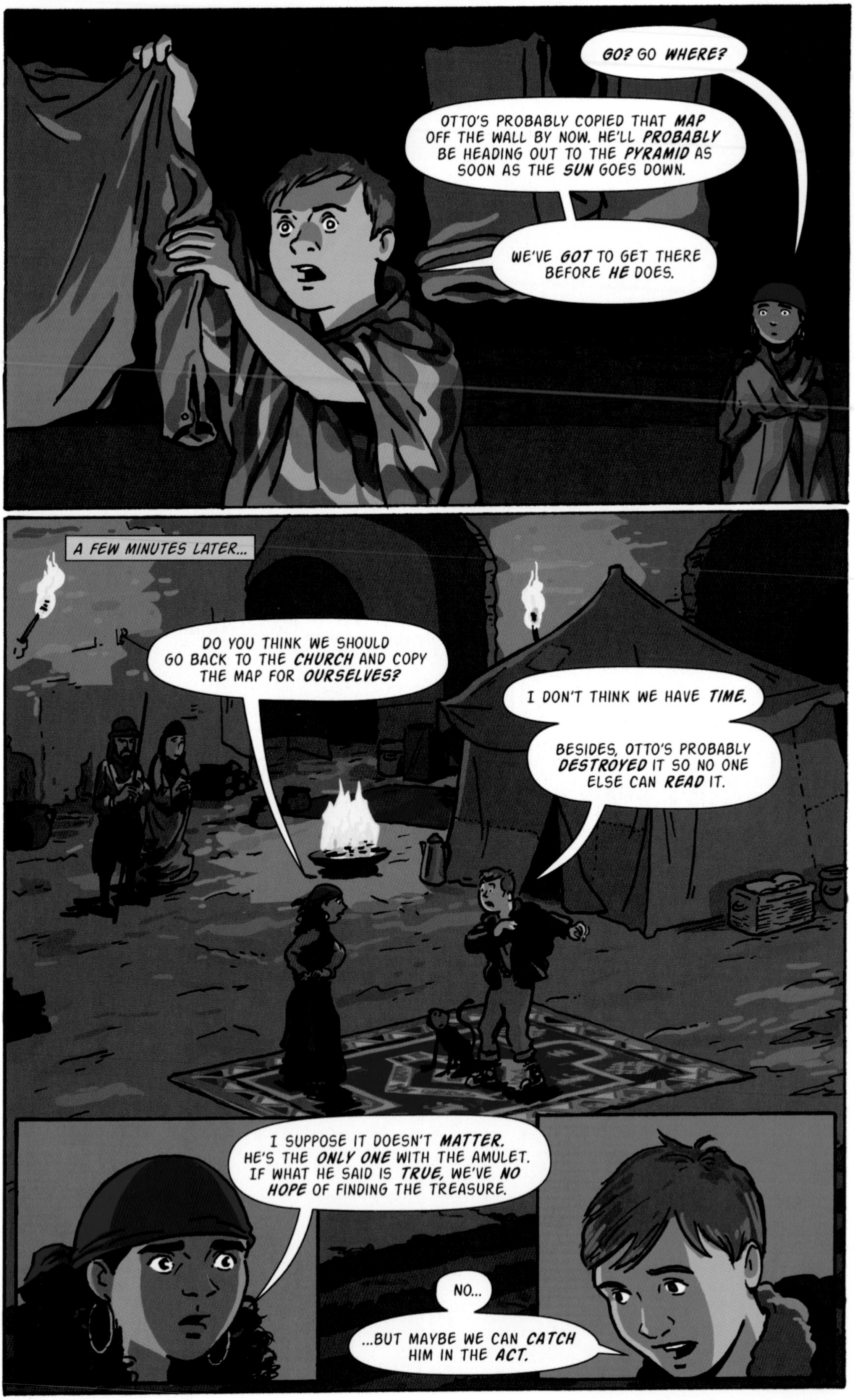
GO? GO WHERE?
OTTO'S PROBABLY COPIED THAT MAP OFF THE WALL BY NOW. HE'LL PROBABLY BE HEADING OUT TO THE PYRAMID AS SOON AS THE SUN GOES DOWN.
WE'VE GOT TO GET THERE BEFORE HE DOES.
A FEW MINUTES LATER...
DO YOU THINK WE SHOULD GO BACK TO THE CHURCH AND COPY THE MAP FOR OURSELVES?
I DON'T THINK WE HAVE TIME.
BESIDES, OTTO'S PROBABLY DESTROYED IT SO NO ONE ELSE CAN READ IT.
I SUPPOSE IT DOESN'T MATTER. HE'S THE ONLY ONE WITH THE AMULET. IF WHAT HE SAID IS TRUE, WE'VE NO HOPE OF FINDING THE TREASURE.
NO...
...BUT MAYBE WE CAN CATCH HIM IN THE ACT.

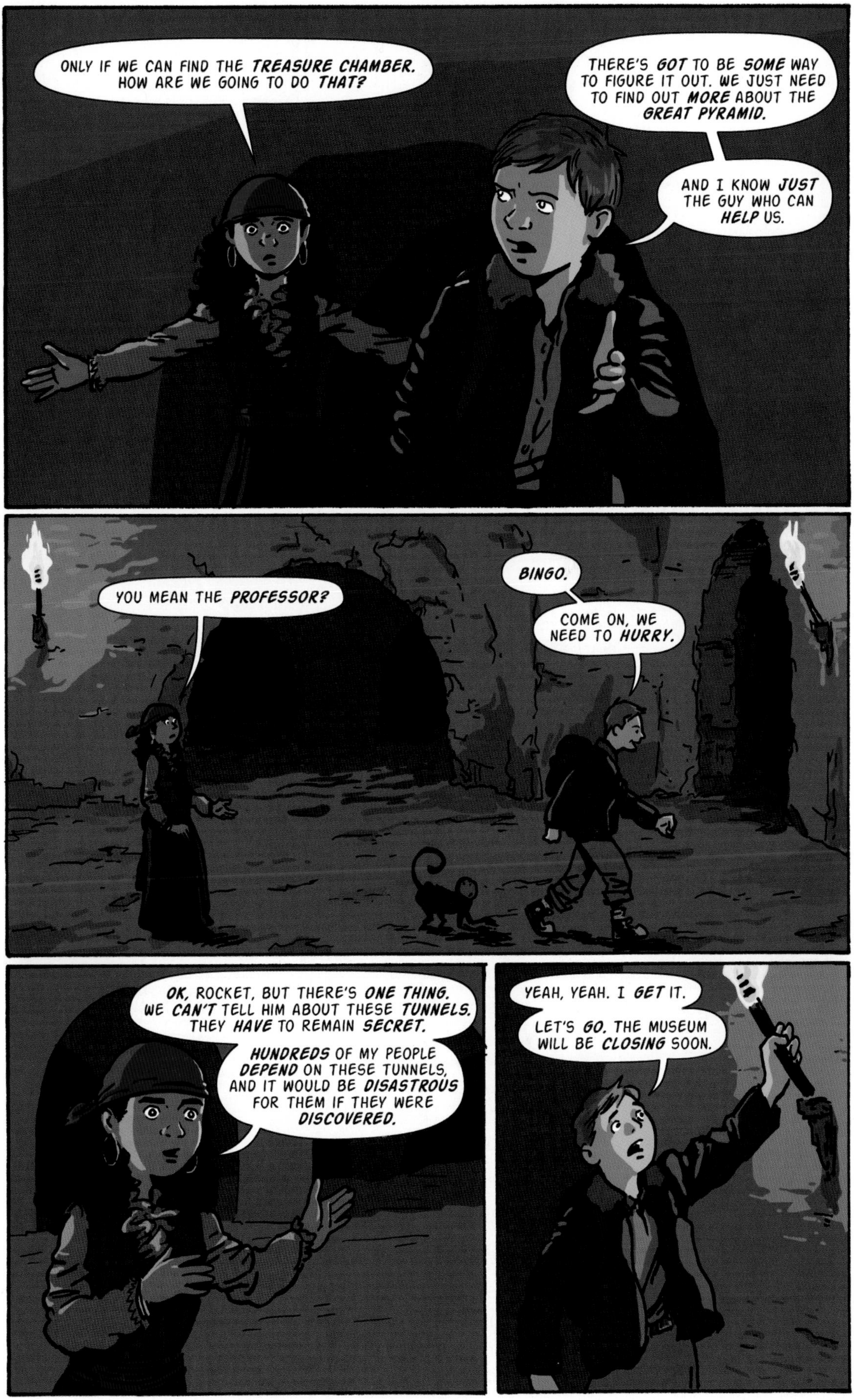

ONLY IF WE CAN FIND THE TREASURE CHAMBER. HOW ARE WE GOING TO DO THAT?
THERE'S GOT TO BE SOME WAY TO FIGURE IT OUT. WE JUST NEED TO FIND OUT MORE ABOUT THE GREAT PYRAMID.
AND I KNOW JUST THE GUY WHO CAN HELP US.
YOU MEAN THE PROFESSOR?
BINGO.
COME ON, WE NEED TO HURRY.
OK, ROCKET, BUT THERE'S ONE THING. WE CAN'T TELL HIM ABOUT THESE TUNNELS. THEY HAVE TO REMAIN SECRET.
HUNDREDS OF MY PEOPLE DEPEND ON THESE TUNNELS, AND IT WOULD BE DISASTROUS FOR THEM IF THEY WERE DISCOVERED.
YEAH, YEAH. I GET IT.
LET'S GO. THE MUSEUM WILL BE CLOSING SOON.

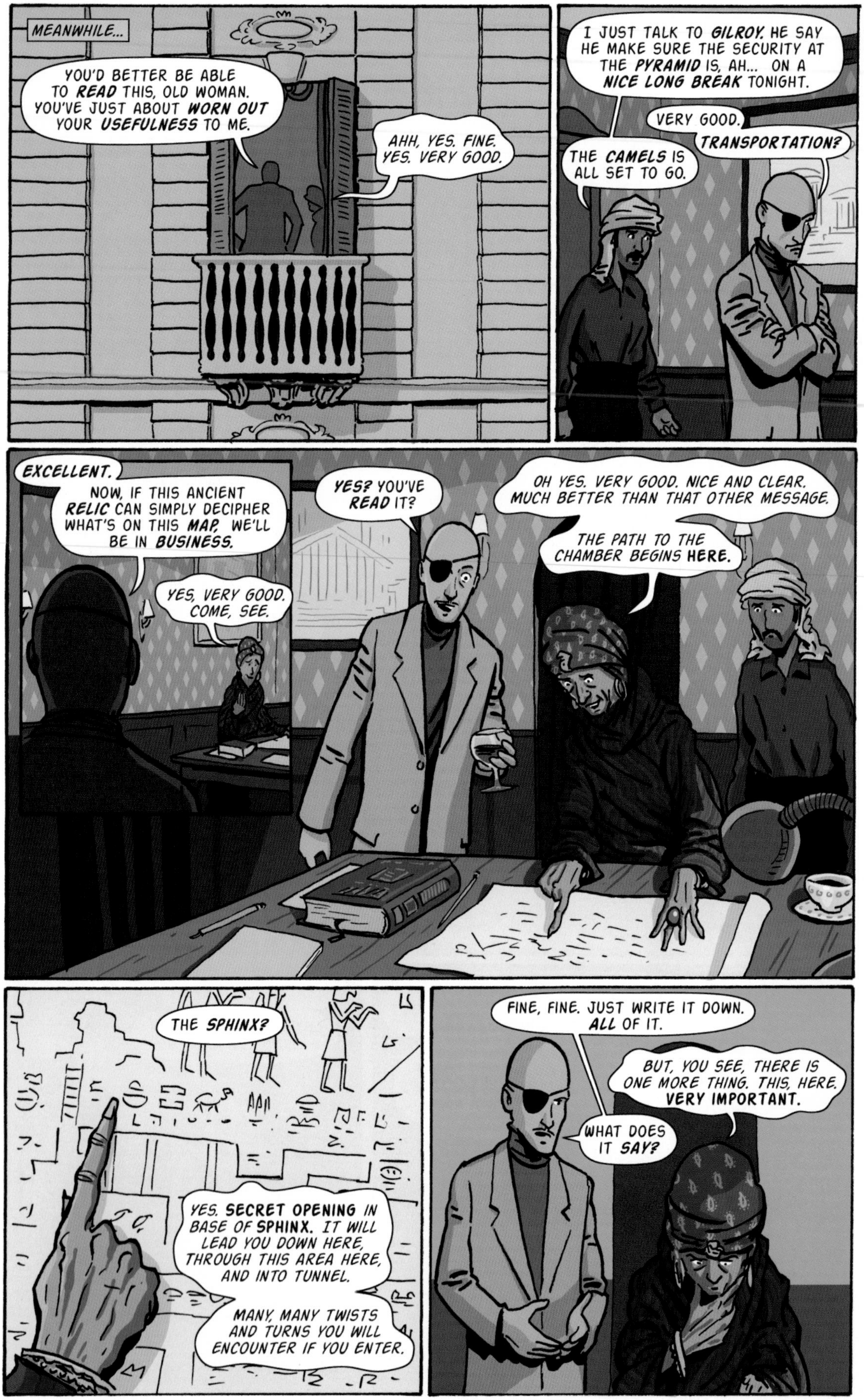
MEANWHILE...
YOU'D BETTER BE ABLE TO READ THIS, OLD WOMAN. YOU'VE JUST ABOUT WORN OUT YOUR USEFULNESS TO ME.
AHH, YES. FINE. YES. VERY GOOD.
I JUST TALK TO GILROY. HE SAY HE MAKE SURE THE SECURITY AT THE PYRAMID IS, AH... ON A NICE LONG BREAK TONIGHT.
VERY GOOD.
TRANSPORTATION?
THE CAMELS IS ALL SET TO GO.
EXCELLENT.
NOW, IF THIS ANCIENT RELIC CAN SIMPLY DECIPHER WHAT'S ON THIS MAP, WE'LL BE IN BUSINESS.
YES, VERY GOOD. COME, SEE.
YES? YOU'VE READ IT?
OH YES. VERY GOOD. NICE AND CLEAR. MUCH BETTER THAN THAT OTHER MESSAGE.
THE PATH TO THE CHAMBER BEGINS HERE.
THE SPHINX?
YES. SECRET OPENING IN BASE OF SPHINX. IT WILL LEAD YOU DOWN HERE, THROUGH THIS AREA HERE, AND INTO TUNNEL.
MANY, MANY TWISTS AND TURNS YOU WILL ENCOUNTER IF YOU ENTER.
FINE, FINE. JUST WRITE IT DOWN. ALL OF IT.
BUT, YOU SEE, THERE IS ONE MORE THING. THIS, HERE. VERY IMPORTANT.
WHAT DOES IT SAY?

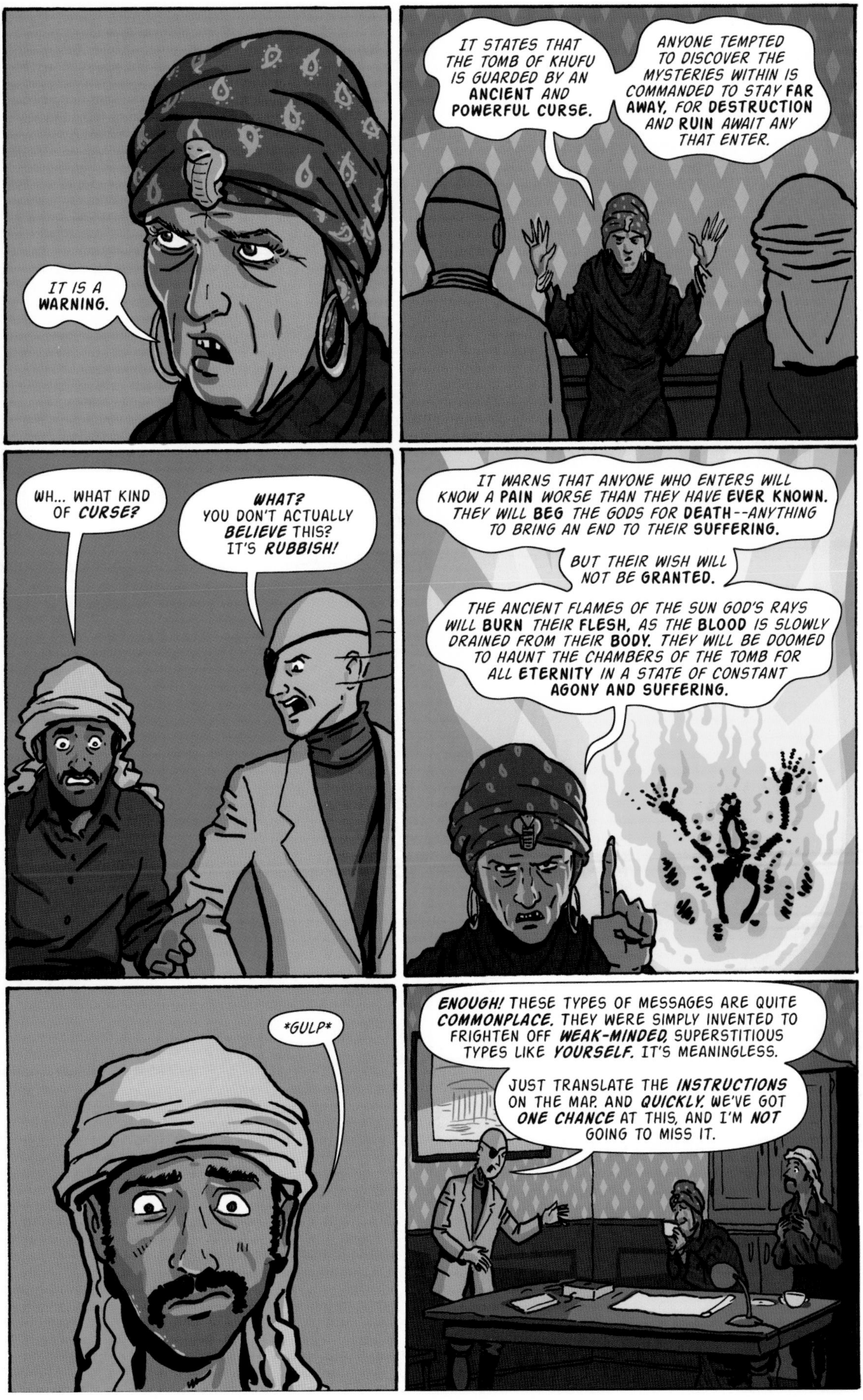
IT IS A WARNING.
IT STATES THAT THE TOMB OF KHUFU IS GUARDED BY AN ANCIENT AND POWERFUL CURSE.
ANYONE TEMPTED TO DISCOVER THE MYSTERIES WITHIN IS COMMANDED TO STAY FAR AWAY, FOR DESTRUCTION AND RUIN AWAIT ANY THAT ENTER.
WH... WHAT KIND OF CURSE?
WHAT? YOU DON'T ACTUALLY BELIEVE THIS? IT'S RUBBISH!
IT WARNS THAT ANYONE WHO ENTERS WILL KNOW A PAIN WORSE THAN THEY HAVE EVER KNOWN. THEY WILL BEG THE GODS FOR DEATH--ANYTHING TO BRING AN END TO THEIR SUFFERING.
BUT THEIR WISH WILL NOT BE GRANTED.
THE ANCIENT FLAMES OF THE SUN GOD'S RAYS WILL BURN THEIR FLESH, AS THE BLOOD IS SLOWLY DRAINED FROM THEIR BODY. THEY WILL BE DOOMED TO HAUNT THE CHAMBERS OF THE TOMB FOR ALL ETERNITY IN A STATE OF CONSTANT AGONY AND SUFFERING.
GULP
ENOUGH! THESE TYPES OF MESSAGES ARE QUITE COMMONPLACE. THEY WERE SIMPLY INVENTED TO FRIGHTEN OFF WEAK-MINDED, SUPERSTITIOUS TYPES LIKE YOURSELF. IT'S MEANINGLESS.
JUST TRANSLATE THE INSTRUCTIONS ON THE MAP. AND QUICKLY. WE'VE GOT ONE CHANCE AT THIS, AND I'M NOT GOING TO MISS IT.

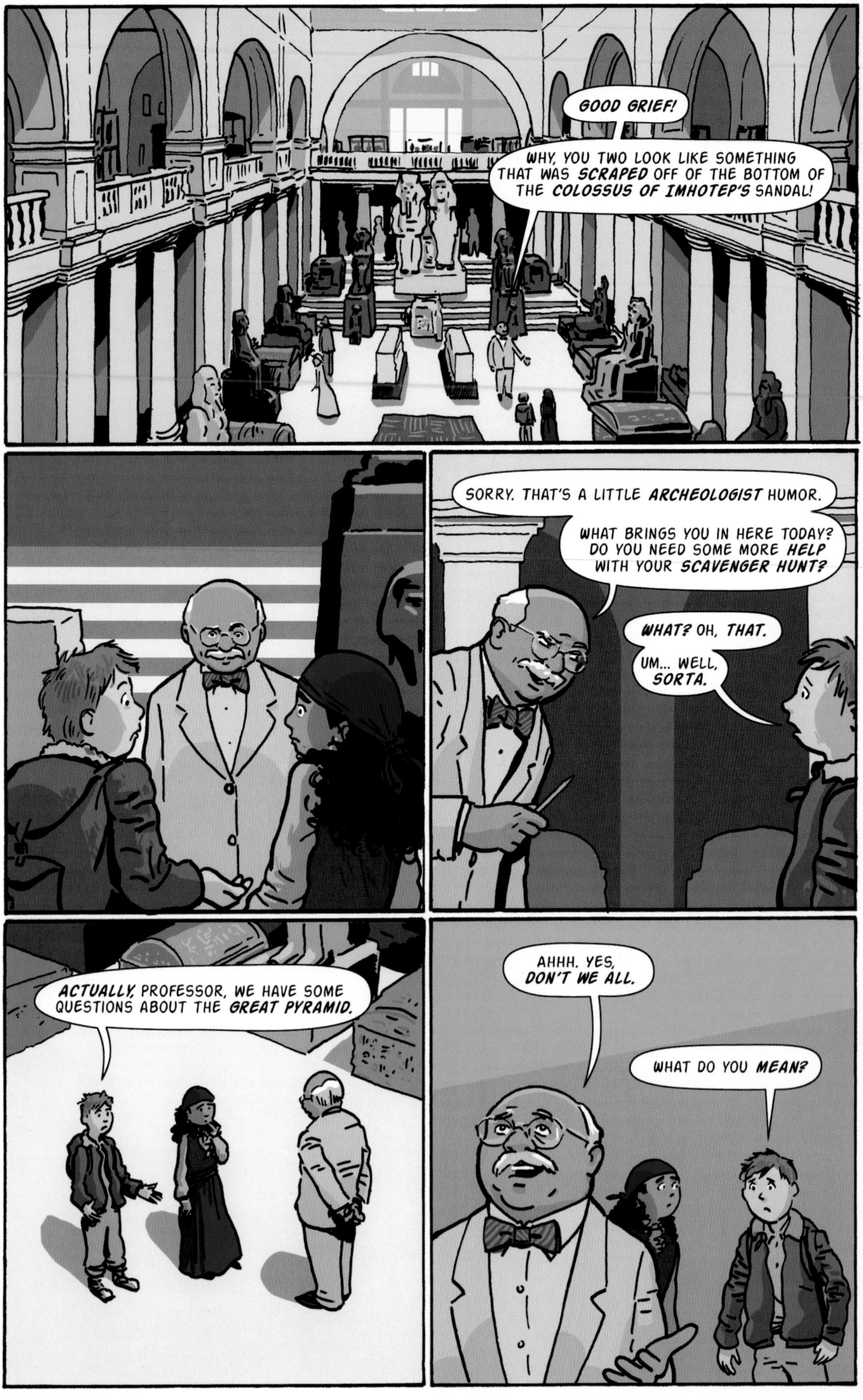
GOOD GRIEF!
WHY, YOU TWO LOOK LIKE SOMETHING THAT WAS SCRAPED OFF OF THE BOTTOM OF THE COLOSSUS OF IMHOTEP'S SANDAL!
SORRY. THAT'S A LITTLE ARCHEOLOGIST HUMOR.
WHAT BRINGS YOU IN HERE TODAY? DO YOU NEED SOME MORE HELP WITH YOUR SCAVENGER HUNT?
WHAT? OH, THAT.
UM... WELL, SORTA.
ACTUALLY, PROFESSOR, WE HAVE SOME QUESTIONS ABOUT THE GREAT PYRAMID.
AHHH. YES, DON'T WE ALL.
WHAT DO YOU MEAN?

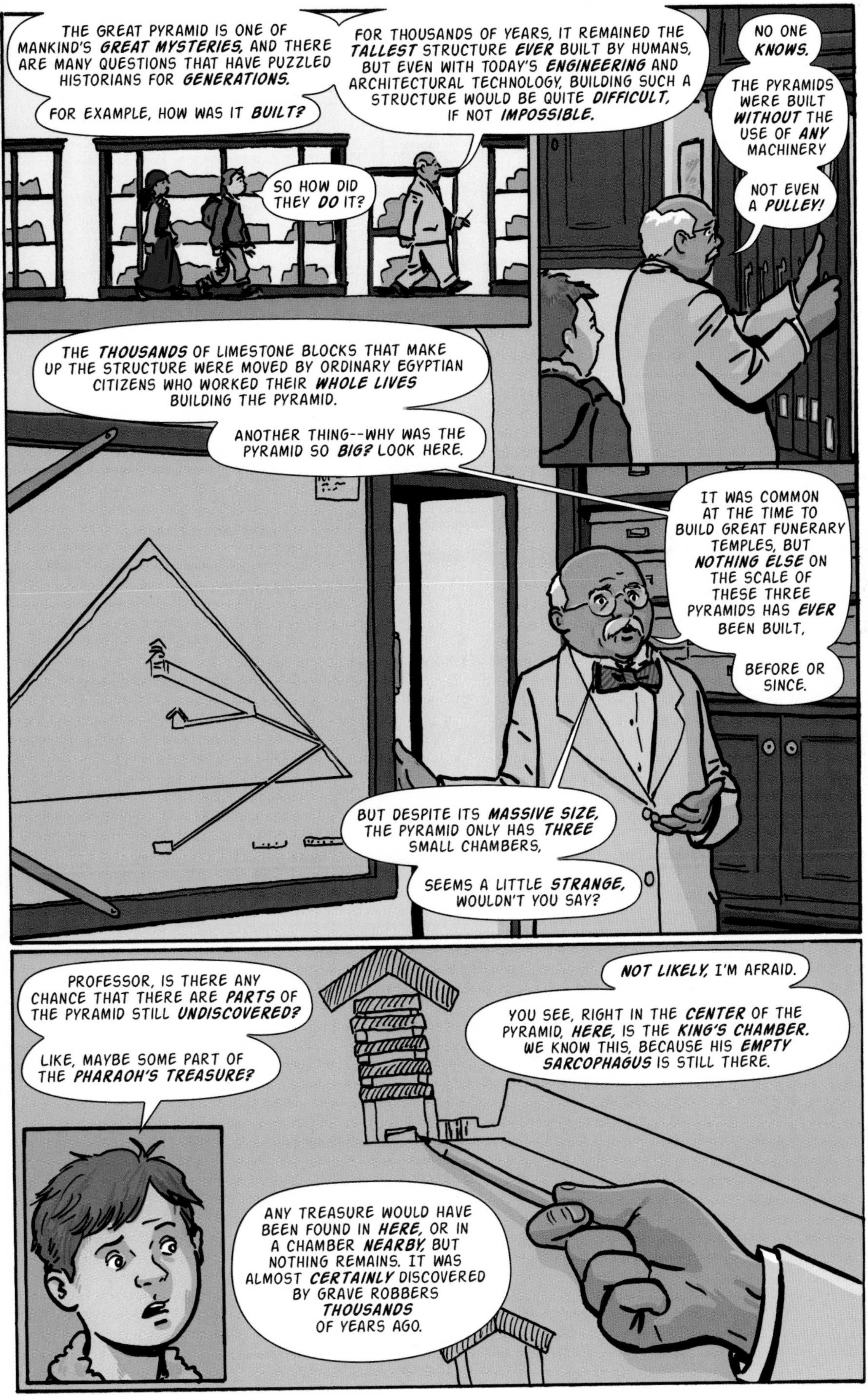
THE GREAT PYRAMID IS ONE OF MANKIND'S GREAT MYSTERIES, AND THERE ARE MANY QUESTIONS THAT HAVE PUZZLED HISTORIANS FOR GENERATIONS.
FOR EXAMPLE, HOW WAS IT BUILT?
SO HOW DID THEY DO IT?
FOR THOUSANDS OF YEARS, IT REMAINED THE TALLEST STRUCTURE EVER BUILT BY HUMANS, BUT EVEN WITH TODAY'S ENGINEERING AND ARCHITECTURAL TECHNOLOGY, BUILDING SUCH A STRUCTURE WOULD BE QUITE DIFFICULT, IF NOT IMPOSSIBLE.
NO ONE KNOWS.
THE PYRAMIDS WERE BUILT WITHOUT THE USE OF ANY MACHINERY
NOT EVEN A PULLEY!
THE THOUSANDS OF LIMESTONE BLOCKS THAT MAKE UP THE STRUCTURE WERE MOVED BY ORDINARY EGYPTIAN CITIZENS WHO WORKED THEIR WHOLE LIVES BUILDING THE PYRAMID.
ANOTHER THING--WHY WAS THE PYRAMID SO BIG? LOOK HERE.
IT WAS COMMON AT THE TIME TO BUILD GREAT FUNERARY TEMPLES, BUT NOTHING ELSE ON THE SCALE OF THESE THREE PYRAMIDS HAS EVER BEEN BUILT,
BEFORE OR SINCE.
BUT DESPITE ITS MASSIVE SIZE, THE PYRAMID ONLY HAS THREE SMALL CHAMBERS,
SEEMS A LITTLE STRANGE, WOULDN'T YOU SAY?
PROFESSOR, IS THERE ANY CHANCE THAT THERE ARE PARTS OF THE PYRAMID STILL UNDISCOVERED?
LIKE, MAYBE SOME PART OF THE PHARAOH'S TREASURE?
NOT LIKELY, I'M AFRAID.
YOU SEE, RIGHT IN THE CENTER OF THE PYRAMID, HERE, IS THE KING'S CHAMBER. WE KNOW THIS, BECAUSE HIS EMPTY SARCOPHAGUS IS STILL THERE.
ANY TREASURE WOULD HAVE BEEN FOUND IN HERE, OR IN A CHAMBER NEARBY, BUT NOTHING REMAINS. IT WAS ALMOST CERTAINLY DISCOVERED BY GRAVE ROBBERS THOUSANDS OF YEARS AGO.

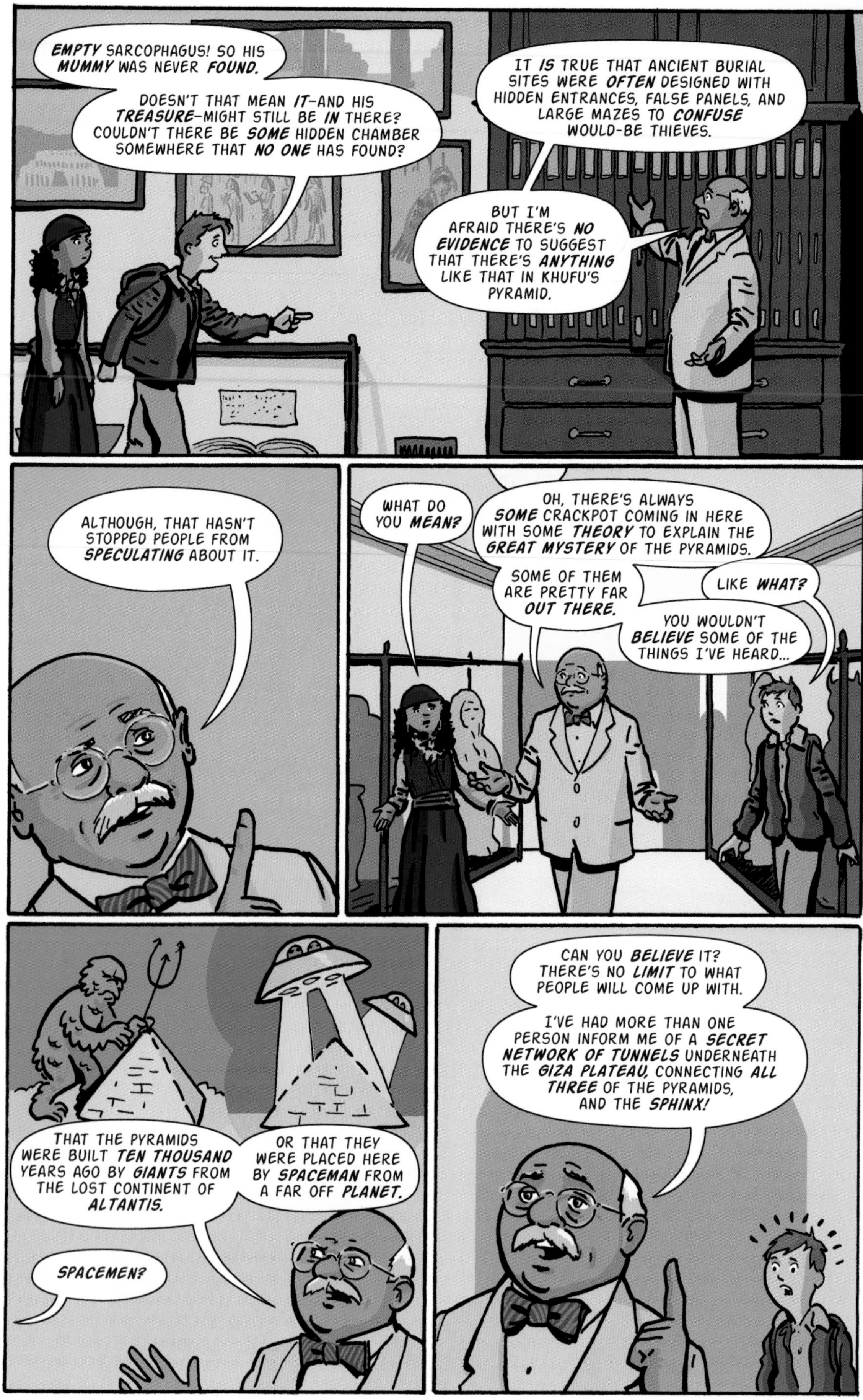
EMPTY SARCOPHAGUS! SO HIS MUMMY WAS NEVER FOUND.
DOESN'T THAT MEAN IT—AND HIS TREASURE—MIGHT STILL BE IN THERE? COULDN'T THERE BE SOME HIDDEN CHAMBER SOMEWHERE THAT NO ONE HAS FOUND?
IT IS TRUE THAT ANCIENT BURIAL SITES WERE OFTEN DESIGNED WITH HIDDEN ENTRANCES, FALSE PANELS, AND LARGE MAZES TO CONFUSE WOULD-BE THIEVES.
BUT I'M AFRAID THERE'S NO EVIDENCE TO SUGGEST THAT THERE'S ANYTHING LIKE THAT IN KHUFU'S PYRAMID.
ALTHOUGH, THAT HASN'T STOPPED PEOPLE FROM SPECULATING ABOUT IT.
WHAT DO YOU MEAN?
OH, THERE'S ALWAYS SOME CRACKPOT COMING IN HERE WITH SOME THEORY TO EXPLAIN THE GREAT MYSTERY OF THE PYRAMIDS.
SOME OF THEM ARE PRETTY FAR OUT THERE.
LIKE WHAT?
YOU WOULDN'T BELIEVE SOME OF THE THINGS I'VE HEARD...
THAT THE PYRAMIDS WERE BUILT TEN THOUSAND YEARS AGO BY GIANTS FROM THE LOST CONTINENT OF ALTANTIS.
OR THAT THEY WERE PLACED HERE BY SPACEMAN FROM A FAR OFF PLANET.
SPACEMEN?
CAN YOU BELIEVE IT? THERE'S NO LIMIT TO WHAT PEOPLE WILL COME UP WITH.
I'VE HAD MORE THAN ONE PERSON INFORM ME OF A SECRET NETWORK OF TUNNELS UNDERNEATH THE GIZA PLATEAU, CONNECTING ALL THREE OF THE PYRAMIDS, AND THE SPHINX!

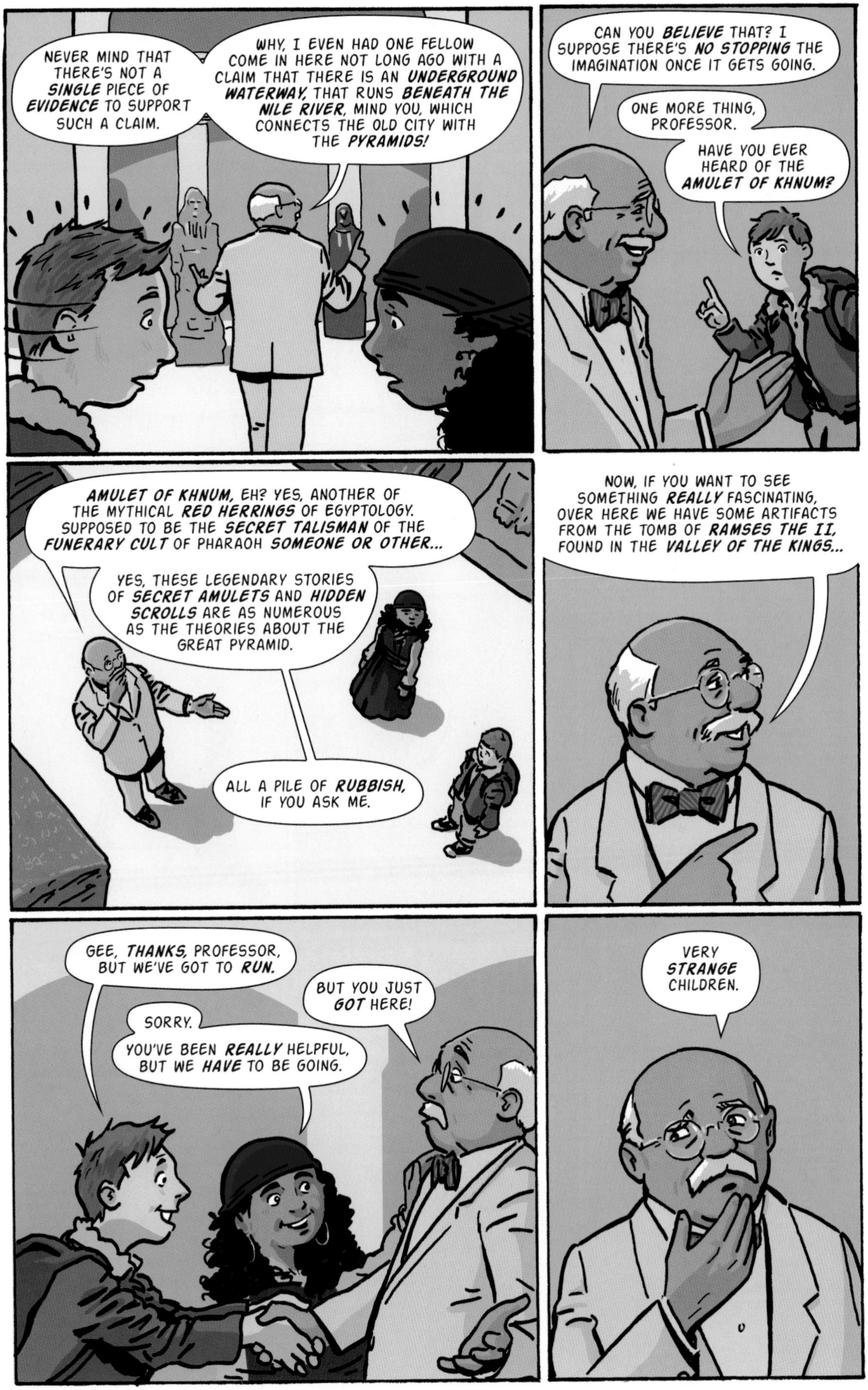
NEVER MIND THAT THERE'S NOT A SINGLE PIECE OF EVIDENCE TO SUPPORT SUCH A CLAIM.
WHY, I EVEN HAD ONE FELLOW COME IN HERE NOT LONG AGO WITH A CLAIM THAT THERE IS AN UNDERGROUND WATERWAY, THAT RUNS BENEATH THE NILE RIVER, MIND YOU, WHICH CONNECTS THE OLD CITY WITH THE PYRAMIDS!
CAN YOU BELIEVE THAT? I SUPPOSE THERE'S NO STOPPING THE IMAGINATION ONCE IT GETS GOING.
ONE MORE THING, PROFESSOR.
HAVE YOU EVER HEARD OF THE AMULET OF KHNUM?
AMULET OF KHNUM, EH? YES, ANOTHER OF THE MYTHICAL RED HERRINGS OF EGYPTOLOGY. SUPPOSED TO BE THE SECRET TALISMAN OF THE FUNERARY CULT OF PHARAOH SOMEONE OR OTHER...
YES, THESE LEGENDARY STORIES OF SECRET AMULETS AND HIDDEN SCROLLS ARE AS NUMEROUS AS THE THEORIES ABOUT THE GREAT PYRAMID.
ALL A PILE OF RUBBISH, IF YOU ASK ME.
NOW, IF YOU WANT TO SEE SOMETHING REALLY FASCINATING, OVER HERE WE HAVE SOME ARTIFACTS FROM THE TOMB OF RAMSES THE II, FOUND IN THE VALLEY OF THE KINGS...
GEE, THANKS, PROFESSOR, BUT WE'VE GOT TO RUN.
SORRY.
YOU'VE BEEN REALLY HELPFUL, BUT WE HAVE TO BE GOING.
BUT YOU JUST GOT HERE!
VERY STRANGE CHILDREN.

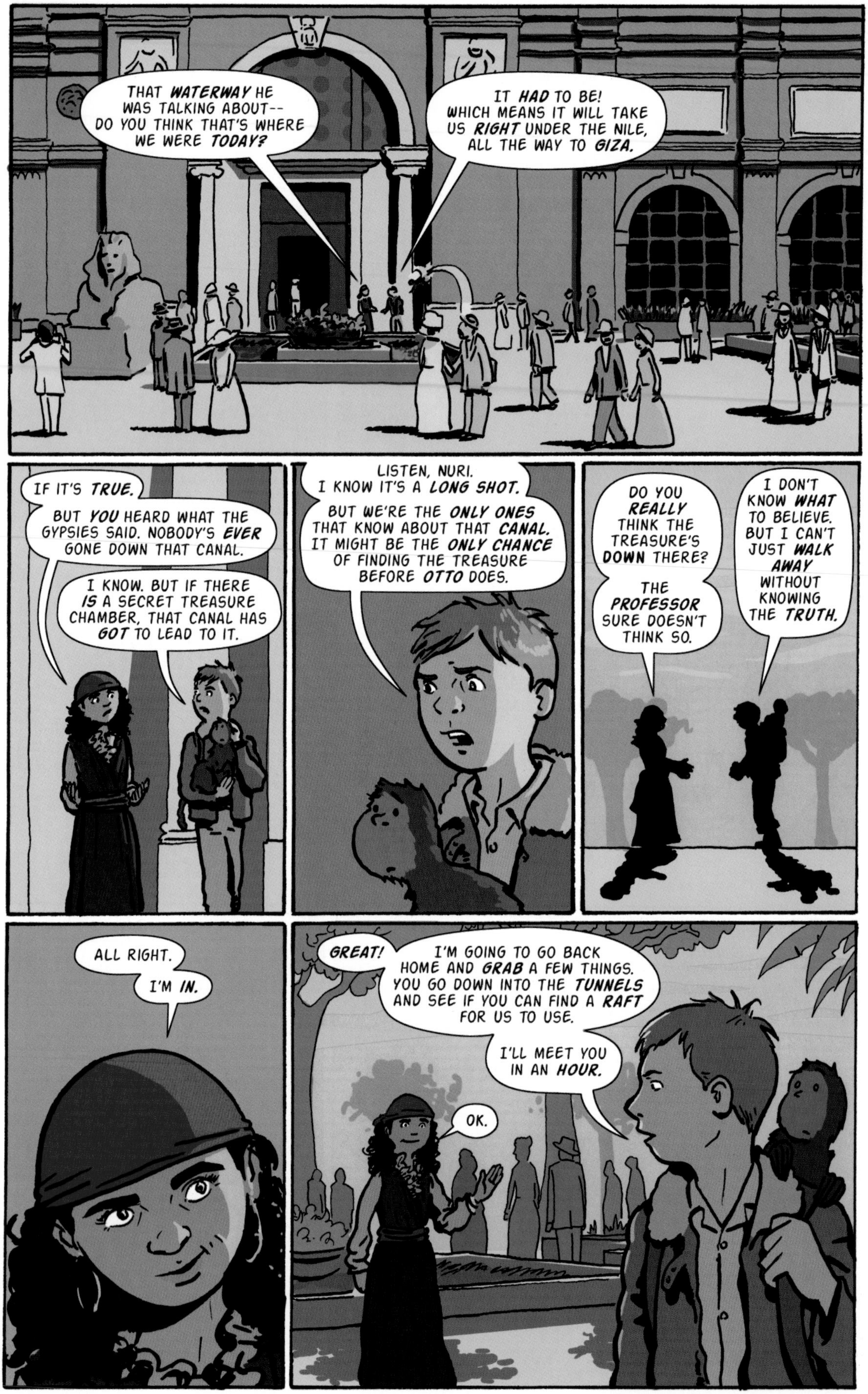

THAT WATERWAY HE WAS TALKING ABOUT-- DO YOU THINK THAT'S WHERE WE WERE TODAY?
IT HAD TO BE! WHICH MEANS IT WILL TAKE US RIGHT UNDER THE NILE, ALL THE WAY TO GIZA.
IF IT'S TRUE.
BUT YOU HEARD WHAT THE GYPSIES SAID. NOBODY'S EVER GONE DOWN THAT CANAL.
I KNOW. BUT IF THERE IS A SECRET TREASURE CHAMBER, THAT CANAL HAS GOT TO LEAD TO IT.
LISTEN, NURI. I KNOW IT'S A LONG SHOT.
BUT WE'RE THE ONLY ONES THAT KNOW ABOUT THAT CANAL. IT MIGHT BE THE ONLY CHANCE OF FINDING THE TREASURE BEFORE OTTO DOES.
DO YOU REALLY THINK THE TREASURE'S DOWN THERE?
THE PROFESSOR SURE DOESN'T THINK SO.
I DON'T KNOW WHAT TO BELIEVE. BUT I CAN'T JUST WALK AWAY WITHOUT KNOWING THE TRUTH.
ALL RIGHT.
I'M IN.
GREAT!
I'M GOING TO GO BACK HOME AND GRAB A FEW THINGS. YOU GO DOWN INTO THE TUNNELS AND SEE IF YOU CAN FIND A RAFT FOR US TO USE.
I'LL MEET YOU IN AN HOUR.
OK.

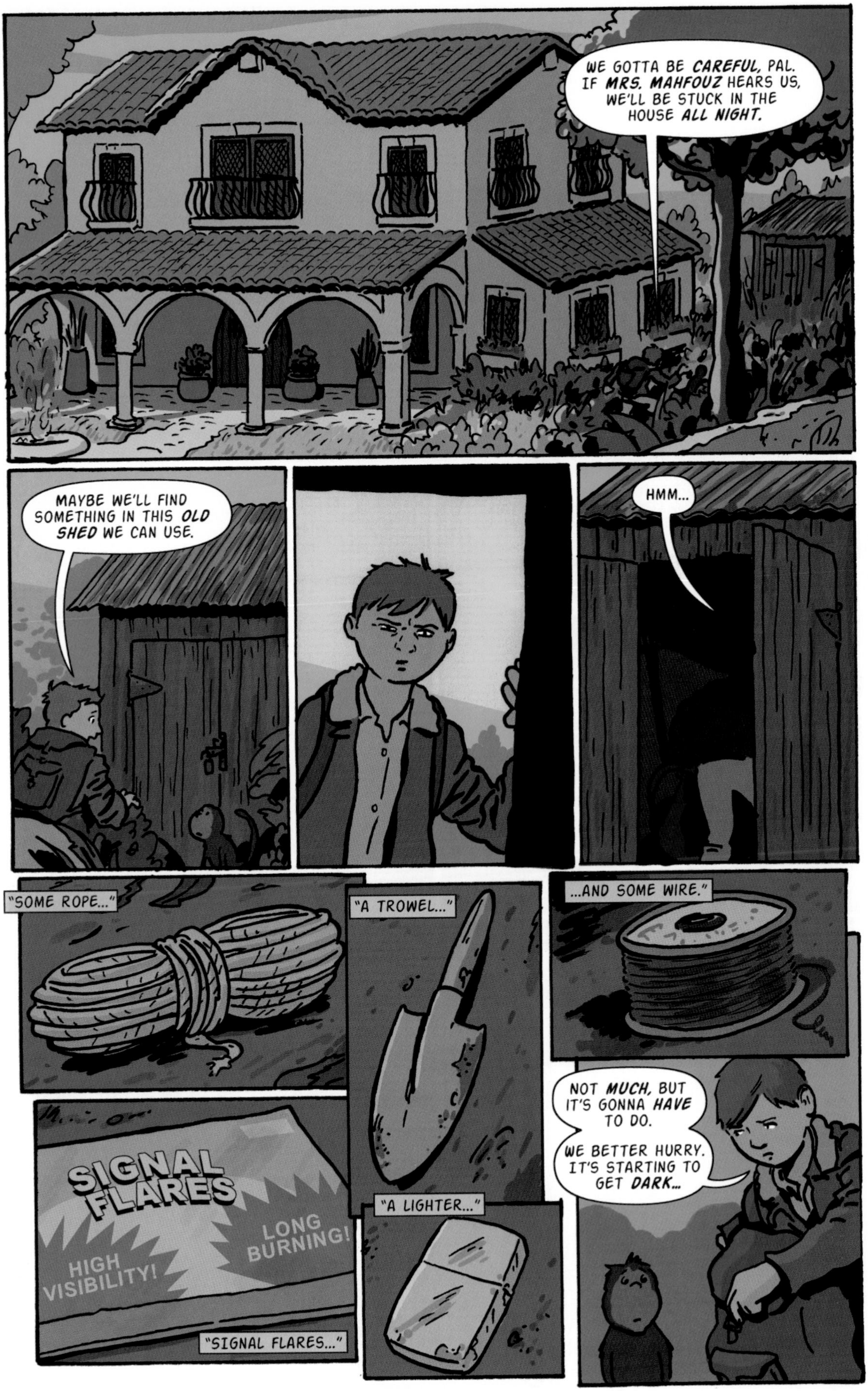
WE GOTTA BE CAREFUL, PAL. IF MRS. MAHFOUZ HEARS US, WE'LL BE STUCK IN THE HOUSE ALL NIGHT.
MAYBE WE'LL FIND SOMETHING IN THIS OLD SHED WE CAN USE.
HMM...
"SOME ROPE..."
"A TROWEL..."
...AND SOME WIRE."
SIGNAL FLARES
HIGH VISIBILITY!
LONG BURNING!
"SIGNAL FLARES..."
"A LIGHTER..."
NOT MUCH, BUT IT'S GONNA HAVE TO DO.
WE BETTER HURRY. IT'S STARTING TO GET DARK...

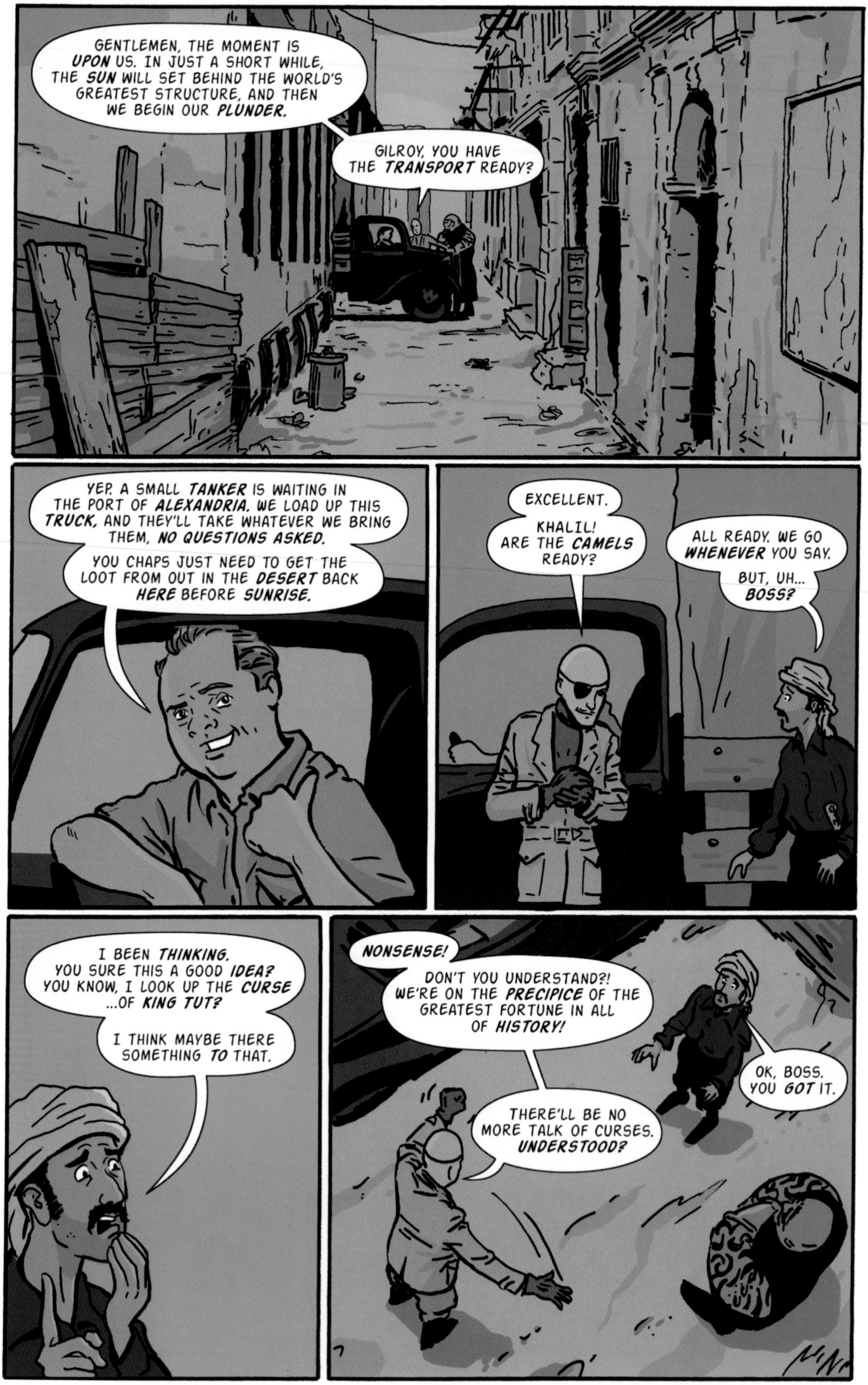
GENTLEMEN, THE MOMENT IS UPON US. IN JUST A SHORT WHILE, THE SUN WILL SET BEHIND THE WORLD'S GREATEST STRUCTURE, AND THEN WE BEGIN OUR PLUNDER.
GILROY, YOU HAVE THE TRANSPORT READY?
YEP. A SMALL TANKER IS WAITING IN THE PORT OF ALEXANDRIA. WE LOAD UP THIS TRUCK, AND THEY'LL TAKE WHATEVER WE BRING THEM, NO QUESTIONS ASKED.
YOU CHAPS JUST NEED TO GET THE LOOT FROM OUT IN THE DESERT BACK HERE BEFORE SUNRISE.
EXCELLENT.
KHALIL! ARE THE CAMELS READY?
ALL READY. WE GO WHENEVER YOU SAY.
BUT, UH... BOSS?
I BEEN THINKING. YOU SURE THIS A GOOD IDEA? YOU KNOW, I LOOK UP THE CURSE ...OF KING TUT?
I THINK MAYBE THERE SOMETHING TO THAT.
NONSENSE!
DON'T YOU UNDERSTAND?! WE'RE ON THE PRECIPICE OF THE GREATEST FORTUNE IN ALL OF HISTORY!
THERE'LL BE NO MORE TALK OF CURSES. UNDERSTOOD?
OK, BOSS. YOU GOT IT.

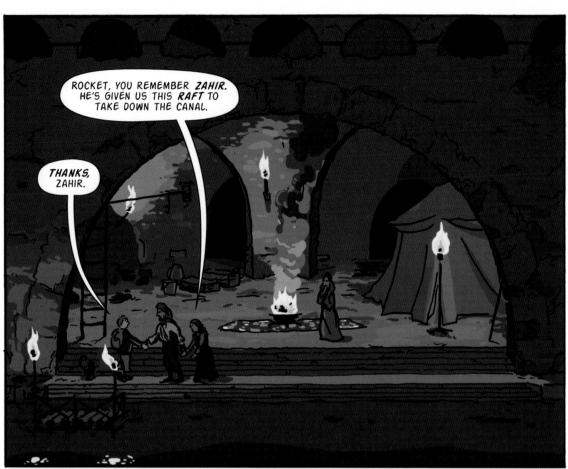

ROCKET, YOU REMEMBER *ZAHIR.* HE'S GIVEN US THIS *RAFT* TO TAKE DOWN THE CANAL.

THANKS, ZAHIR.

UH... KINDA *SMALL,* DON'T YOU THINK?

I KNOW. HE SAID HE DIDN'T WANT TO GIVE US ONE OF THE *BIGGER* RAFTS.

WHY *NOT?*

BECAUSE HE... UH... ...HE DOESN'T EXPECT IT TO COME BACK IN *ONE PIECE.*

⟨PLEASE. I BEG YOU. DO NOT JOURNEY DOWN INTO THE FAR END OF THE CANAL! THE CURSE IS REAL!⟩

⟨IT'S OK. WE ARE READY FOR WHATEVER WE MAY FIND.

I PROMISE, WE'LL BE SAFE.⟩

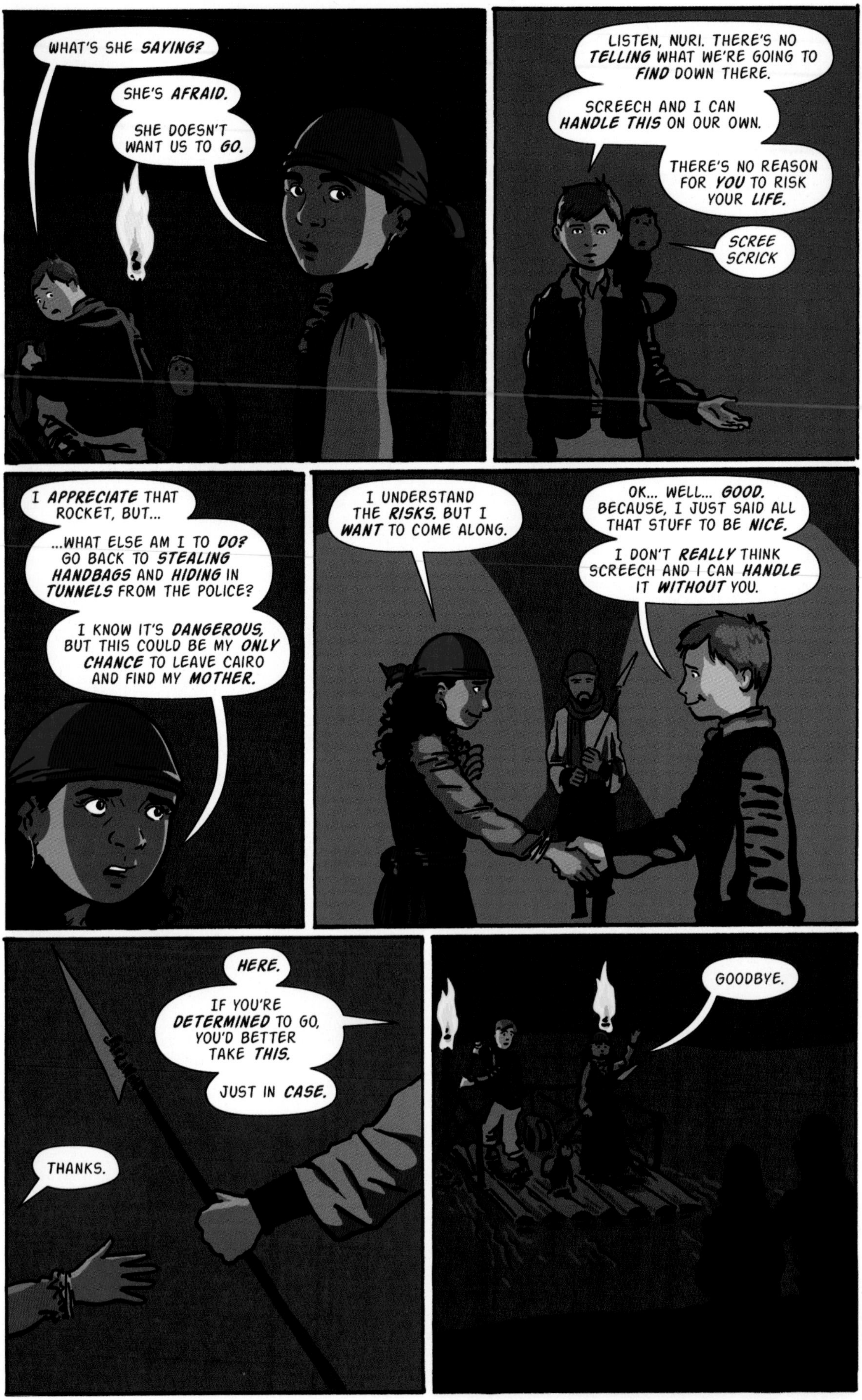
WHAT'S SHE SAYING?
SHE'S AFRAID.
SHE DOESN'T WANT US TO GO.
LISTEN, NURI. THERE'S NO TELLING WHAT WE'RE GOING TO FIND DOWN THERE.
SCREECH AND I CAN HANDLE THIS ON OUR OWN.
THERE'S NO REASON FOR YOU TO RISK YOUR LIFE.
SCREE SCRICK
I APPRECIATE THAT ROCKET, BUT...
...WHAT ELSE AM I TO DO? GO BACK TO STEALING HANDBAGS AND HIDING IN TUNNELS FROM THE POLICE?
I KNOW IT'S DANGEROUS, BUT THIS COULD BE MY ONLY CHANCE TO LEAVE CAIRO AND FIND MY MOTHER.
I UNDERSTAND THE RISKS. BUT I WANT TO COME ALONG.
OK... WELL... GOOD. BECAUSE, I JUST SAID ALL THAT STUFF TO BE NICE.
I DON'T REALLY THINK SCREECH AND I CAN HANDLE IT WITHOUT YOU.
HERE.
IF YOU'RE DETERMINED TO GO, YOU'D BETTER TAKE THIS.
JUST IN CASE.
THANKS.
GOODBYE.

CHAPTER NINE

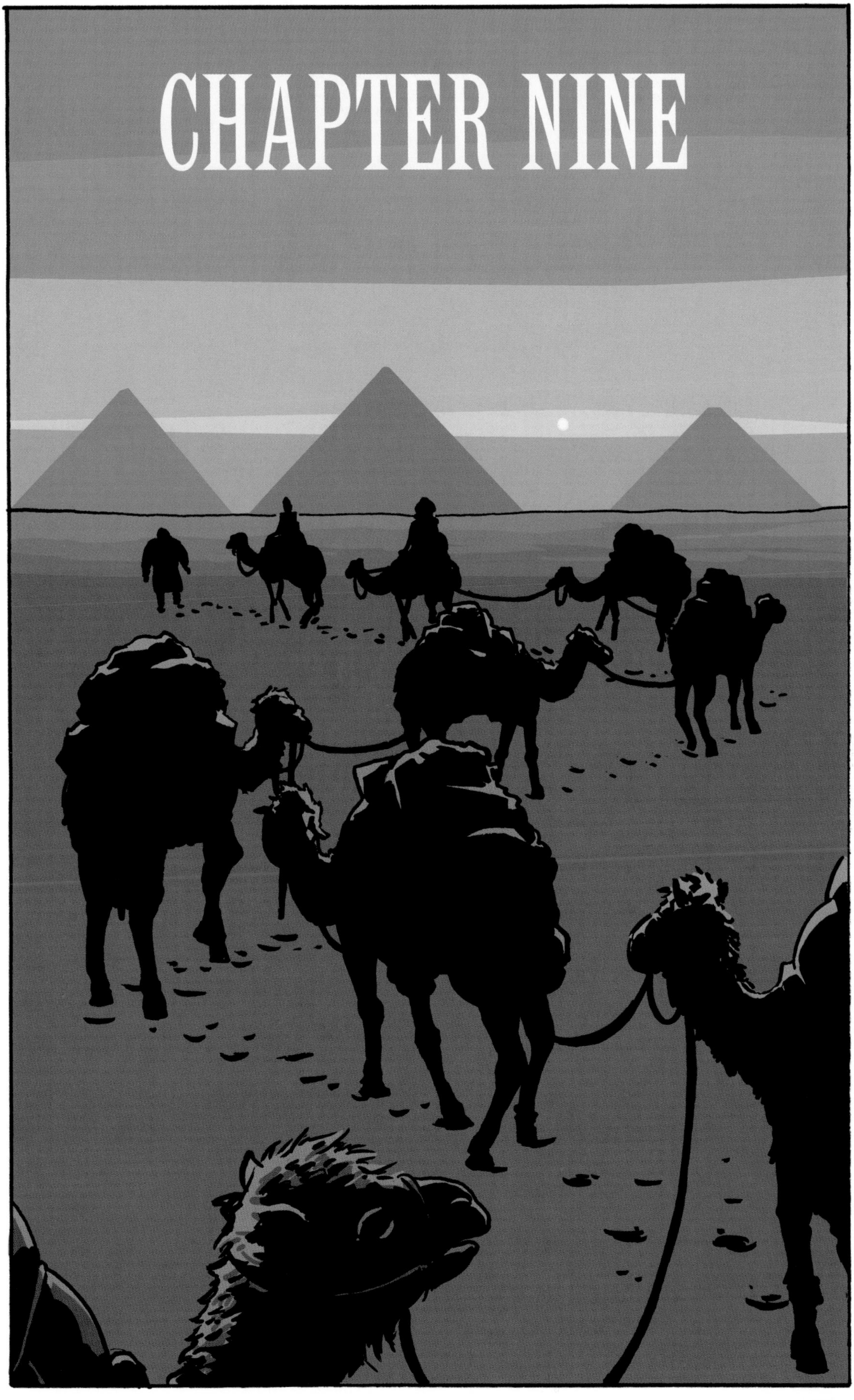

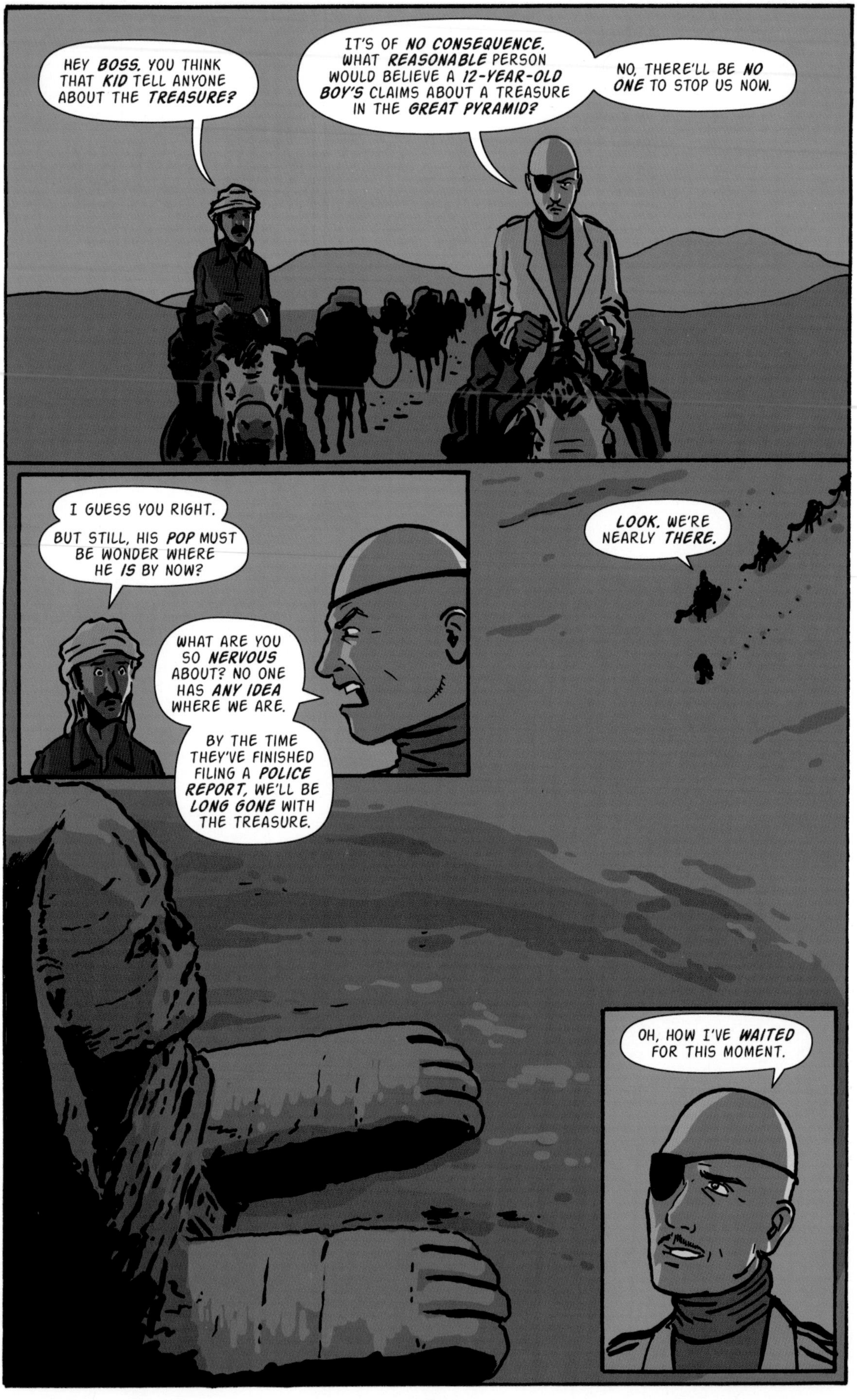

HEY BOSS. YOU THINK THAT KID TELL ANYONE ABOUT THE TREASURE?
IT'S OF NO CONSEQUENCE. WHAT REASONABLE PERSON WOULD BELIEVE A 12-YEAR-OLD BOY'S CLAIMS ABOUT A TREASURE IN THE GREAT PYRAMID?
NO, THERE'LL BE NO ONE TO STOP US NOW.
I GUESS YOU RIGHT.
BUT STILL, HIS POP MUST BE WONDER WHERE HE IS BY NOW?
WHAT ARE YOU SO NERVOUS ABOUT? NO ONE HAS ANY IDEA WHERE WE ARE.
BY THE TIME THEY'VE FINISHED FILING A POLICE REPORT, WE'LL BE LONG GONE WITH THE TREASURE.
LOOK. WE'RE NEARLY THERE.
OH, HOW I'VE WAITED FOR THIS MOMENT.

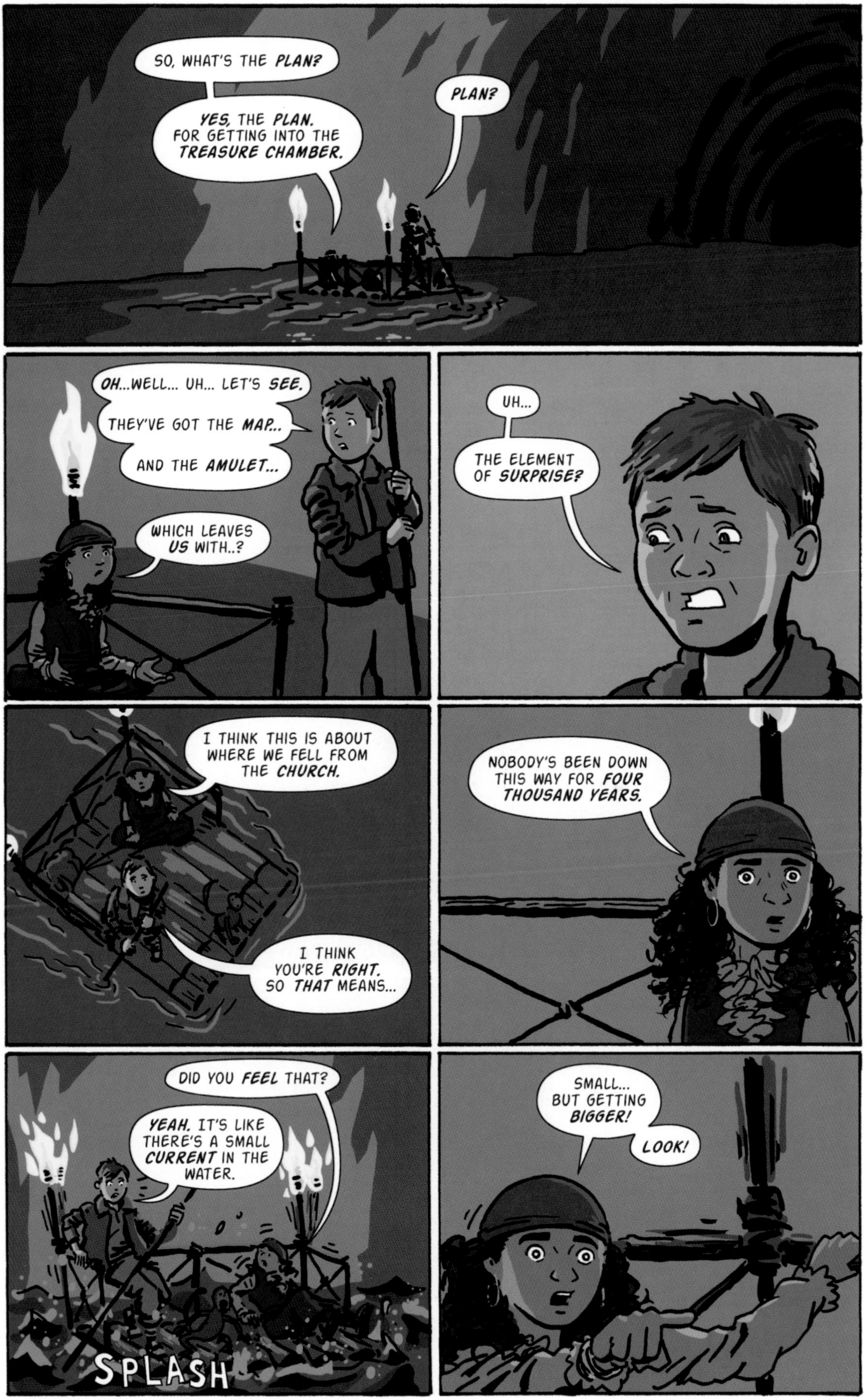
SO, WHAT'S THE PLAN?
PLAN?
YES, THE PLAN. FOR GETTING INTO THE TREASURE CHAMBER.
OH...WELL... UH... LET'S SEE.
THEY'VE GOT THE MAP...
AND THE AMULET...
WHICH LEAVES US WITH..?
UH...
THE ELEMENT OF SURPRISE?
I THINK THIS IS ABOUT WHERE WE FELL FROM THE CHURCH.
I THINK YOU'RE RIGHT. SO THAT MEANS...
NOBODY'S BEEN DOWN THIS WAY FOR FOUR THOUSAND YEARS.
DID YOU FEEL THAT?
YEAH. IT'S LIKE THERE'S A SMALL CURRENT IN THE WATER.
SPLASH
SMALL... BUT GETTING BIGGER!
LOOK!

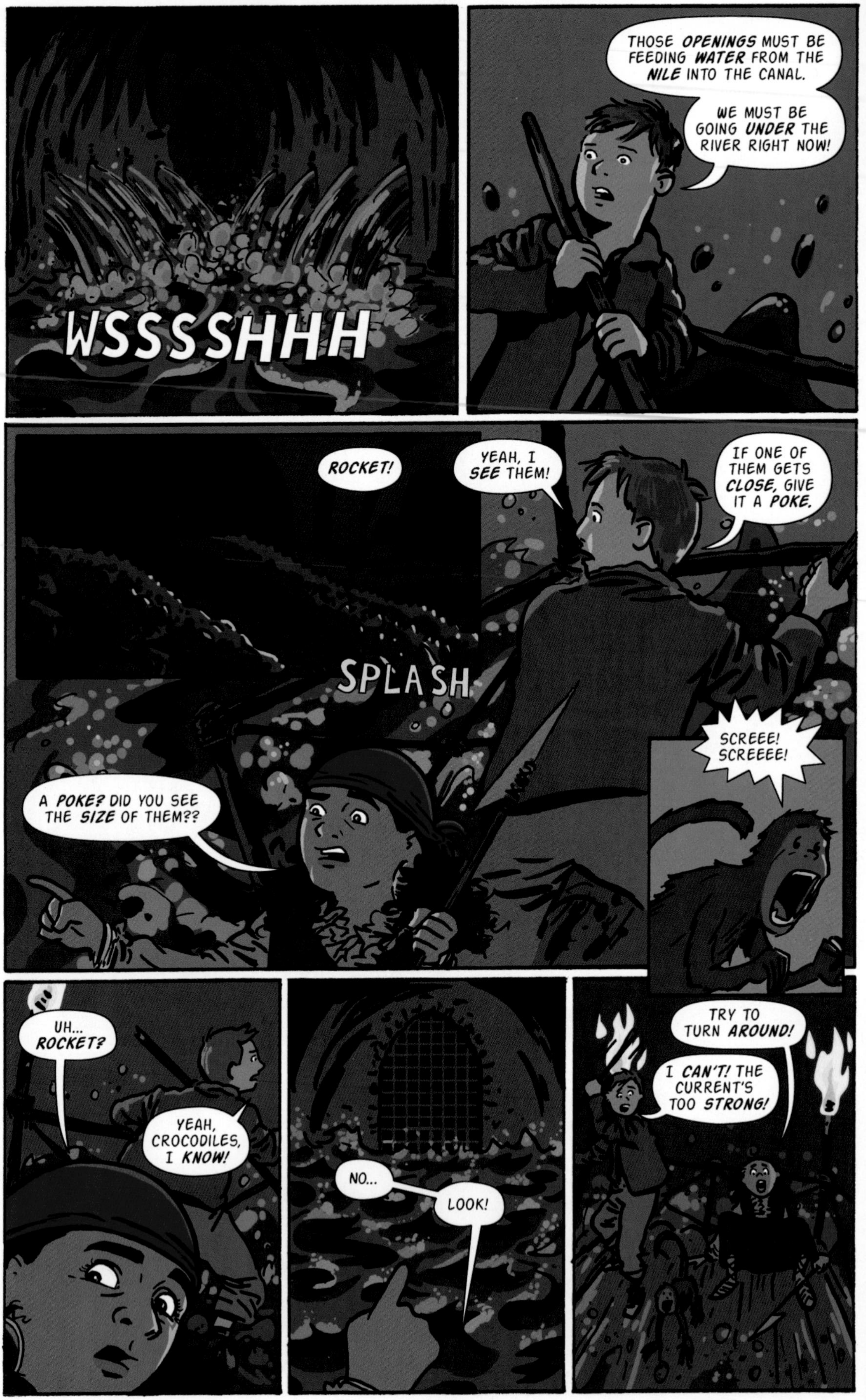
WSSSSHHH
THOSE OPENINGS MUST BE FEEDING WATER FROM THE NILE INTO THE CANAL.
WE MUST BE GOING UNDER THE RIVER RIGHT NOW!
ROCKET!
YEAH, I SEE THEM!
IF ONE OF THEM GETS CLOSE, GIVE IT A POKE.
SPLASH
A POKE? DID YOU SEE THE SIZE OF THEM??
SCREEE! SCREEEE!
UH... ROCKET?
YEAH, CROCODILES, I KNOW!
NO...
LOOK!
TRY TO TURN AROUND!
I CAN'T! THE CURRENT'S TOO STRONG!

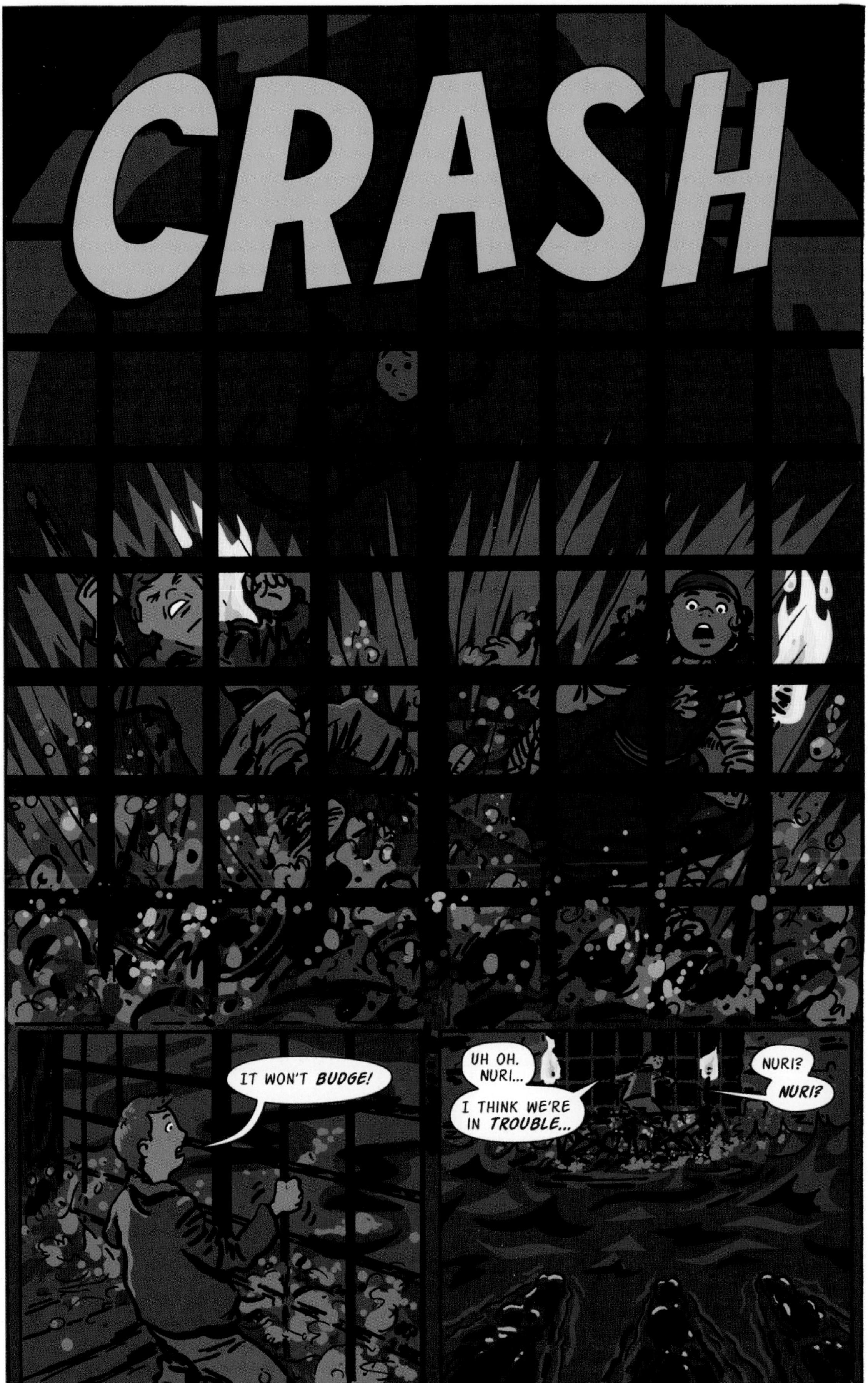
CRASH
IT WON'T BUDGE!
UH OH. NURI...
I THINK WE'RE IN TROUBLE...
NURI?
NURI?

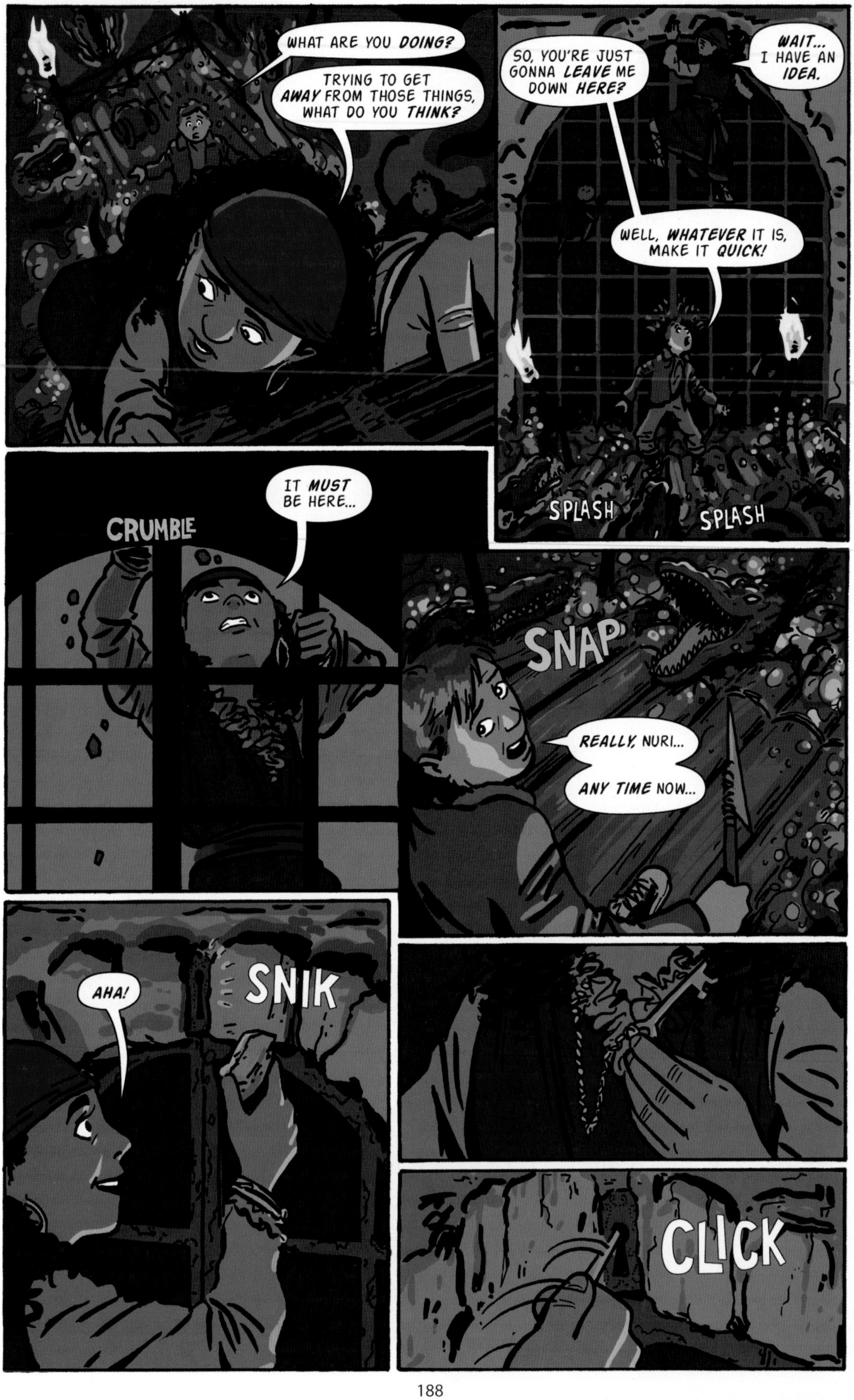
WHAT ARE YOU DOING?
TRYING TO GET AWAY FROM THOSE THINGS, WHAT DO YOU THINK?
SO, YOU'RE JUST GONNA LEAVE ME DOWN HERE?
WAIT... I HAVE AN IDEA.
WELL, WHATEVER IT IS, MAKE IT QUICK!
SPLASH
SPLASH
IT MUST BE HERE...
CRUMBLE
SNAP
REALLY, NURI...
ANY TIME NOW...
AHA!
SNIK
CLICK

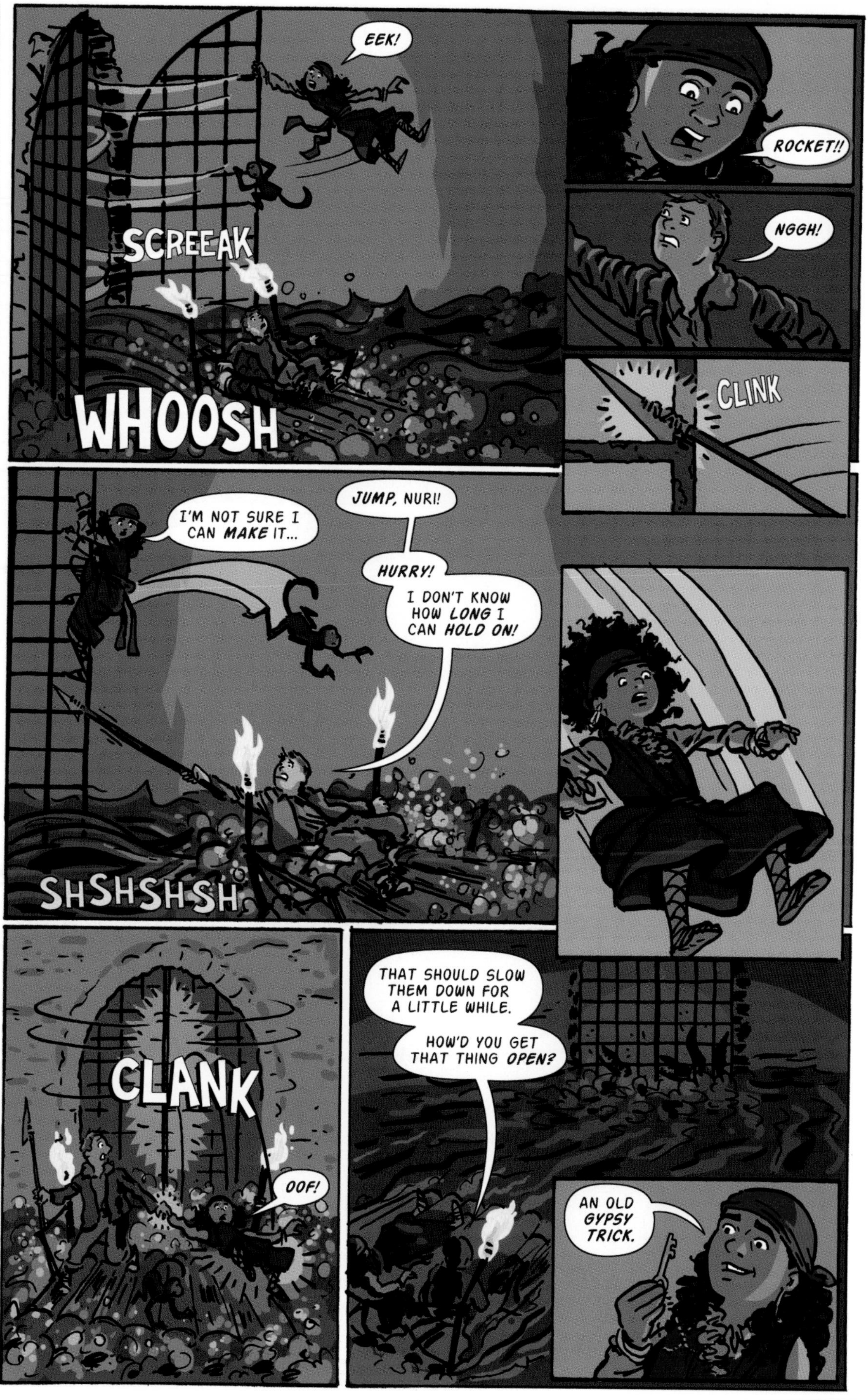
EEK!
SCREEAK
WHOOSH
ROCKET!!
NGGH!
CLINK
I'M NOT SURE I CAN MAKE IT...
JUMP, NURI!
HURRY!
I DON'T KNOW HOW LONG I CAN HOLD ON!
SHSHSHSH
CLANK
OOF!
THAT SHOULD SLOW THEM DOWN FOR A LITTLE WHILE.
HOW'D YOU GET THAT THING OPEN?
AN OLD GYPSY TRICK.

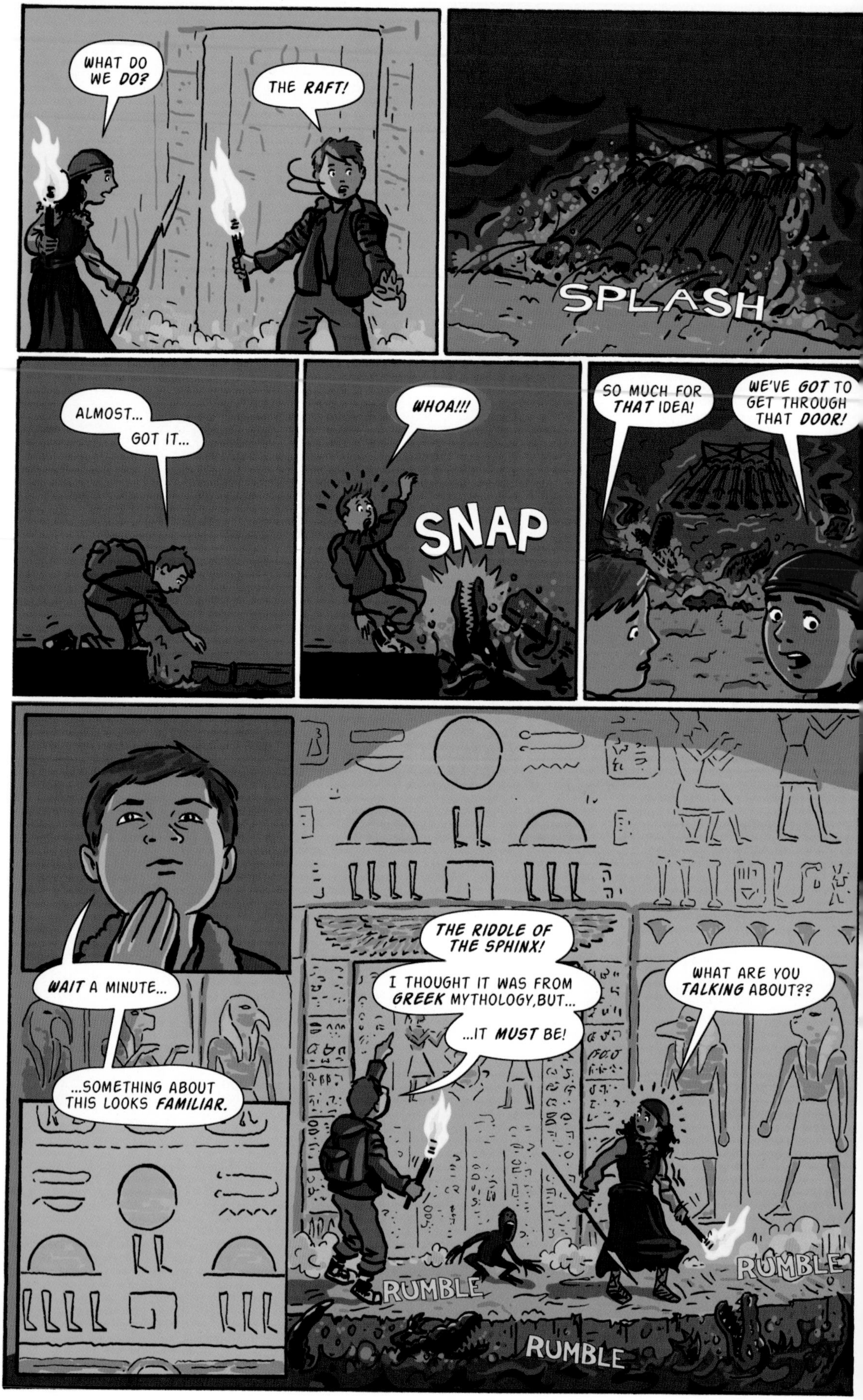
WHAT DO WE DO?
THE RAFT!
SPLASH
ALMOST... GOT IT...
WHOA!!!
SNAP
SO MUCH FOR THAT IDEA!
WE'VE GOT TO GET THROUGH THAT DOOR!
WAIT A MINUTE...
...SOMETHING ABOUT THIS LOOKS FAMILIAR.
THE RIDDLE OF THE SPHINX!
I THOUGHT IT WAS FROM GREEK MYTHOLOGY, BUT...
...IT MUST BE!
WHAT ARE YOU TALKING ABOUT??
RUMBLE
RUMBLE
RUMBLE

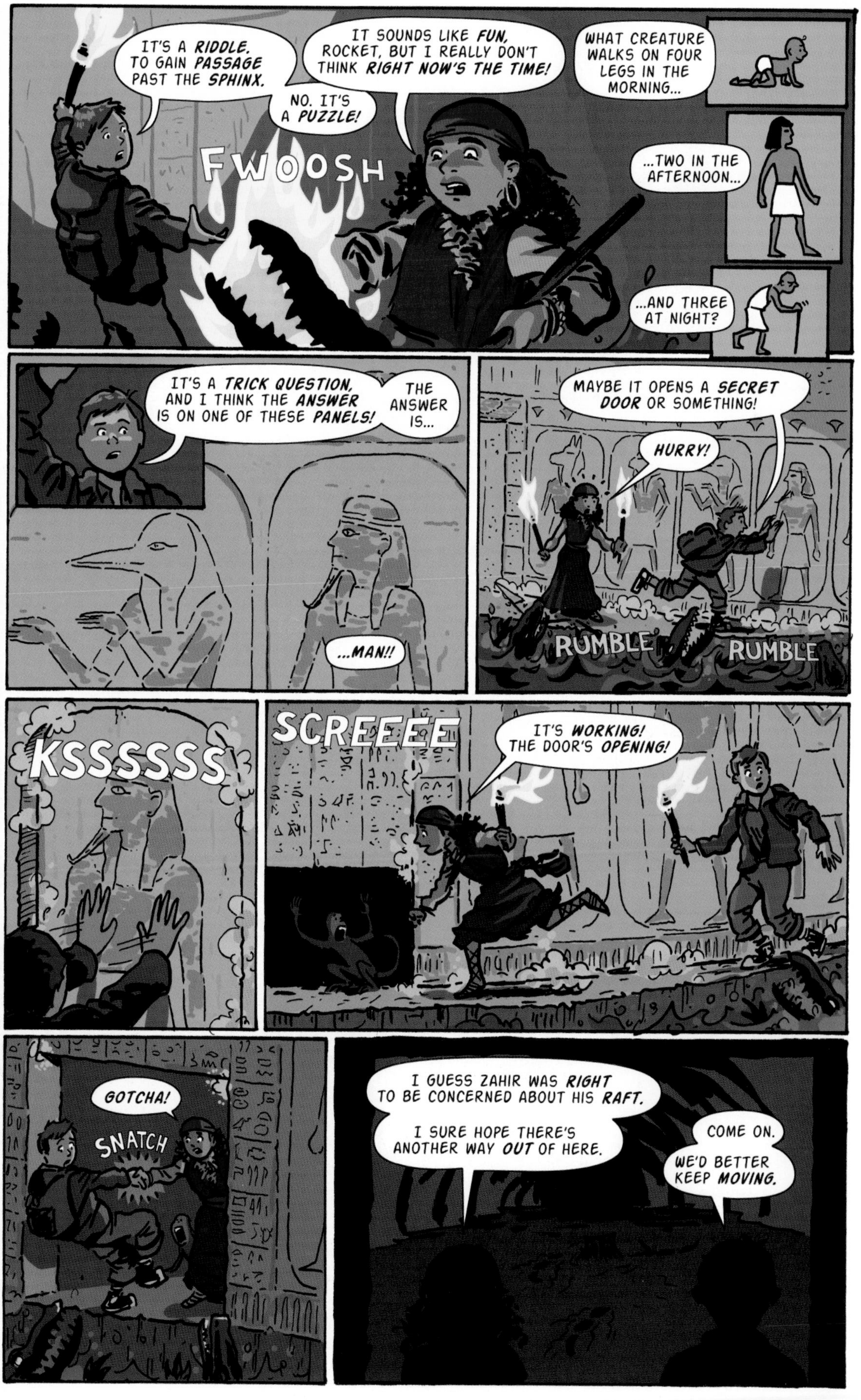
IT'S A RIDDLE. TO GAIN PASSAGE PAST THE SPHINX.
NO. IT'S A PUZZLE!
IT SOUNDS LIKE FUN, ROCKET, BUT I REALLY DON'T THINK RIGHT NOW'S THE TIME!
FWOOSH
WHAT CREATURE WALKS ON FOUR LEGS IN THE MORNING...
...TWO IN THE AFTERNOON...
...AND THREE AT NIGHT?
IT'S A TRICK QUESTION, AND I THINK THE ANSWER IS ON ONE OF THESE PANELS!
THE ANSWER IS...
...MAN!!
MAYBE IT OPENS A SECRET DOOR OR SOMETHING!
HURRY!
RUMBLE
RUMBLE
KSSSSSS
SCREEEEE
IT'S WORKING! THE DOOR'S OPENING!
GOTCHA!
SNATCH
I GUESS ZAHIR WAS RIGHT TO BE CONCERNED ABOUT HIS RAFT.
I SURE HOPE THERE'S ANOTHER WAY OUT OF HERE.
COME ON.
WE'D BETTER KEEP MOVING.

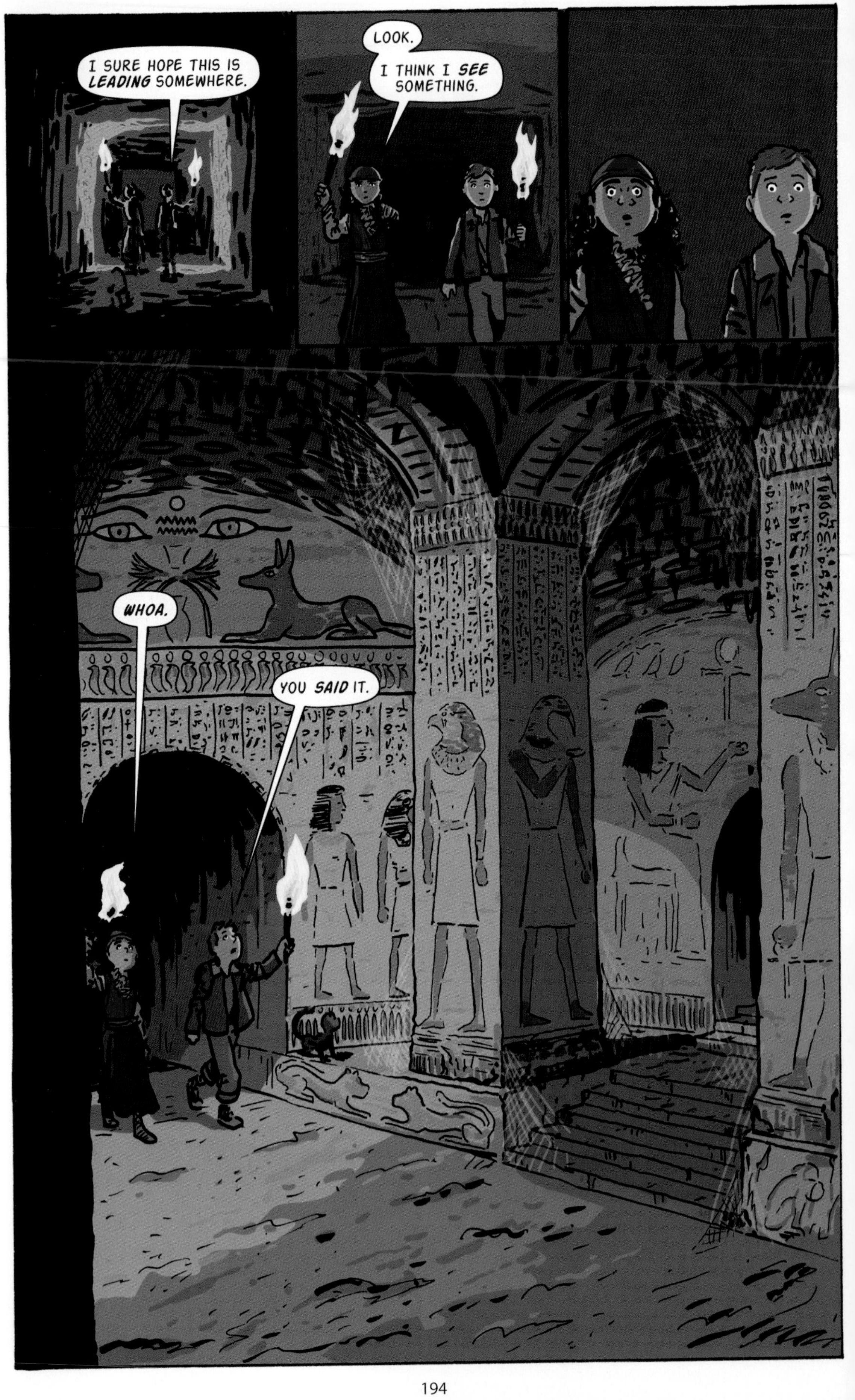
I SURE HOPE THIS IS *LEADING* SOMEWHERE.
LOOK.
I THINK I *SEE* SOMETHING.
WHOA.
YOU *SAID* IT.

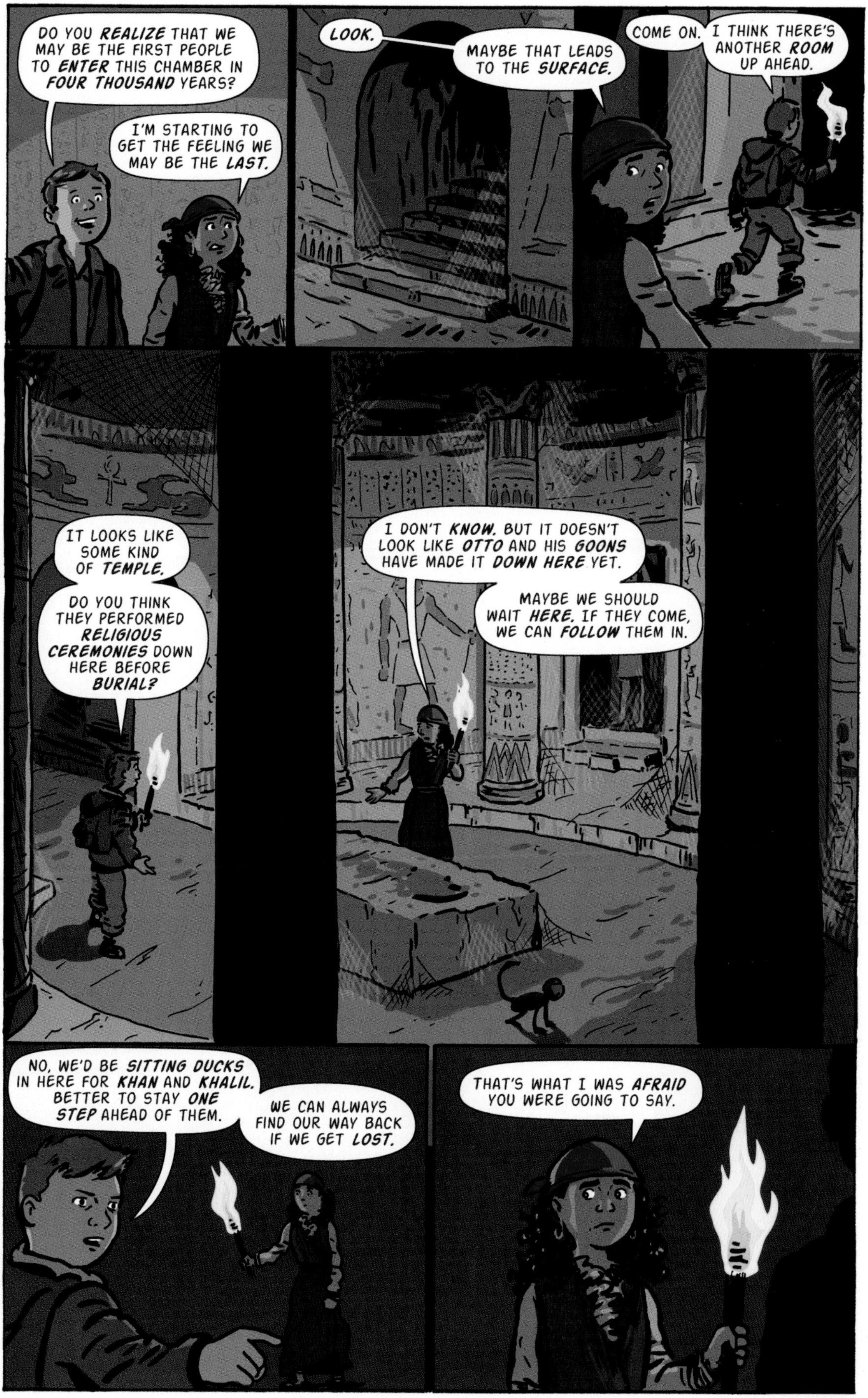
DO YOU REALIZE THAT WE MAY BE THE FIRST PEOPLE TO ENTER THIS CHAMBER IN FOUR THOUSAND YEARS?
I'M STARTING TO GET THE FEELING WE MAY BE THE LAST.
LOOK.
MAYBE THAT LEADS TO THE SURFACE.
COME ON.
I THINK THERE'S ANOTHER ROOM UP AHEAD.
IT LOOKS LIKE SOME KIND OF TEMPLE.
DO YOU THINK THEY PERFORMED RELIGIOUS CEREMONIES DOWN HERE BEFORE BURIAL?
I DON'T KNOW. BUT IT DOESN'T LOOK LIKE OTTO AND HIS GOONS HAVE MADE IT DOWN HERE YET.
MAYBE WE SHOULD WAIT HERE. IF THEY COME, WE CAN FOLLOW THEM IN.
NO, WE'D BE SITTING DUCKS IN HERE FOR KHAN AND KHALIL. BETTER TO STAY ONE STEP AHEAD OF THEM.
WE CAN ALWAYS FIND OUR WAY BACK IF WE GET LOST.
THAT'S WHAT I WAS AFRAID YOU WERE GOING TO SAY.

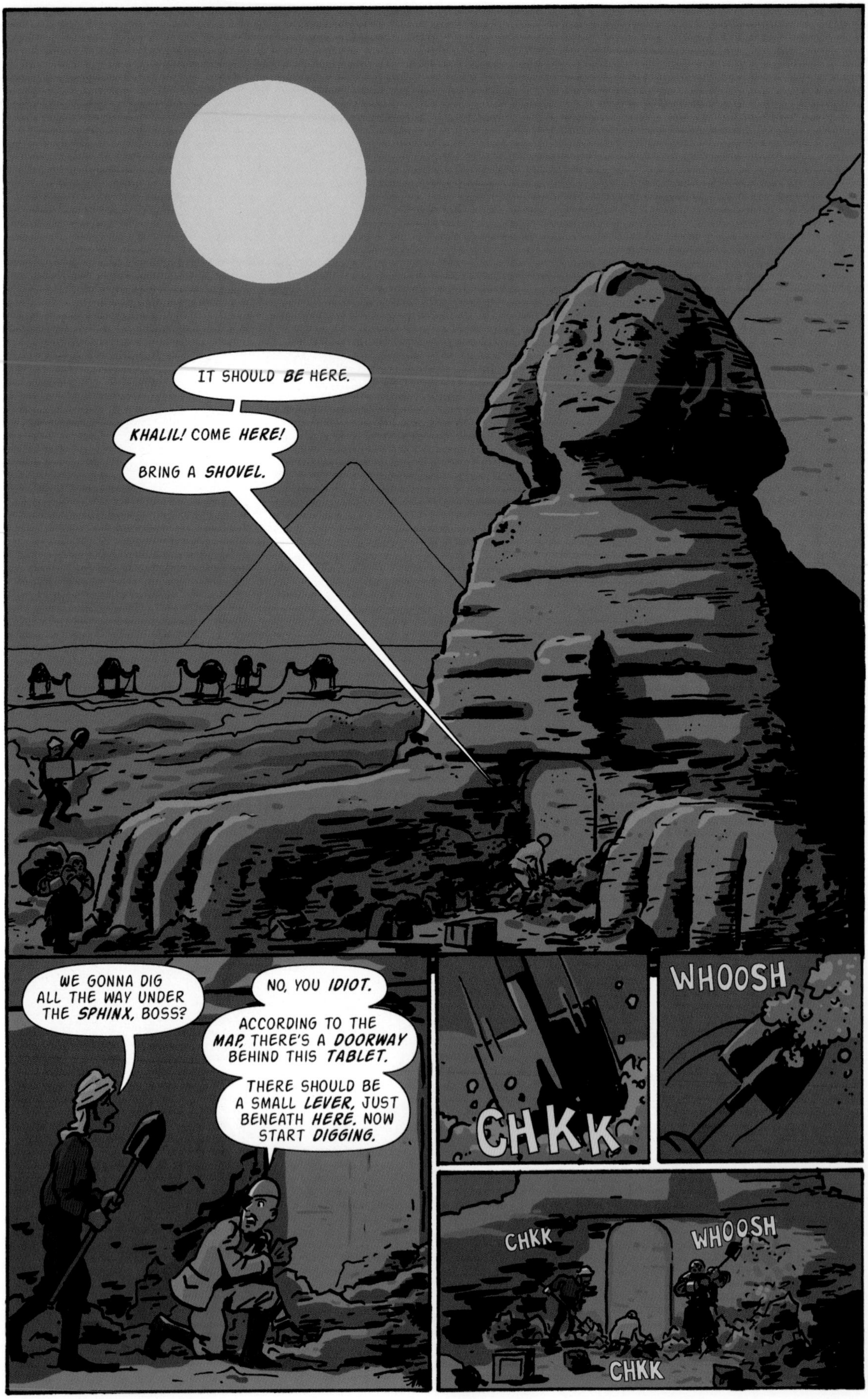
IT SHOULD BE HERE.
KHALIL! COME HERE!
BRING A SHOVEL.
WE GONNA DIG ALL THE WAY UNDER THE SPHINX, BOSS?
NO, YOU IDIOT.
ACCORDING TO THE MAP, THERE'S A DOORWAY BEHIND THIS TABLET.
THERE SHOULD BE A SMALL LEVER, JUST BENEATH HERE. NOW START DIGGING.
CHKK
WHOOSH
CHKK
WHOOSH
CHKK

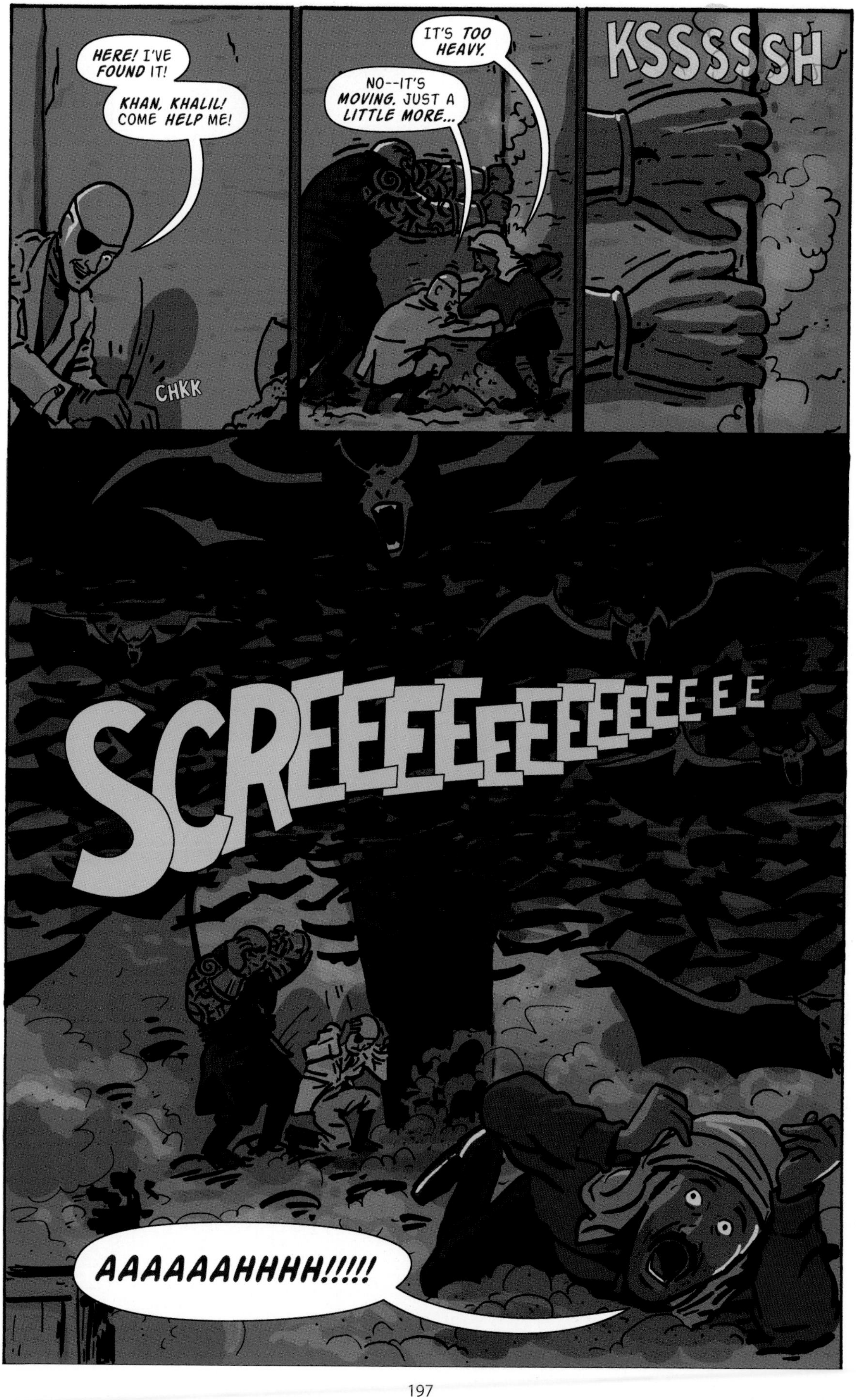
HERE! I'VE FOUND IT!
KHAN, KHALIL! COME HELP ME!
CHKK
IT'S TOO HEAVY.
NO--IT'S MOVING. JUST A LITTLE MORE...
KSSSSSH
SCREEEEEEEEEEEEEE
AAAAAAHHHH!!!!!

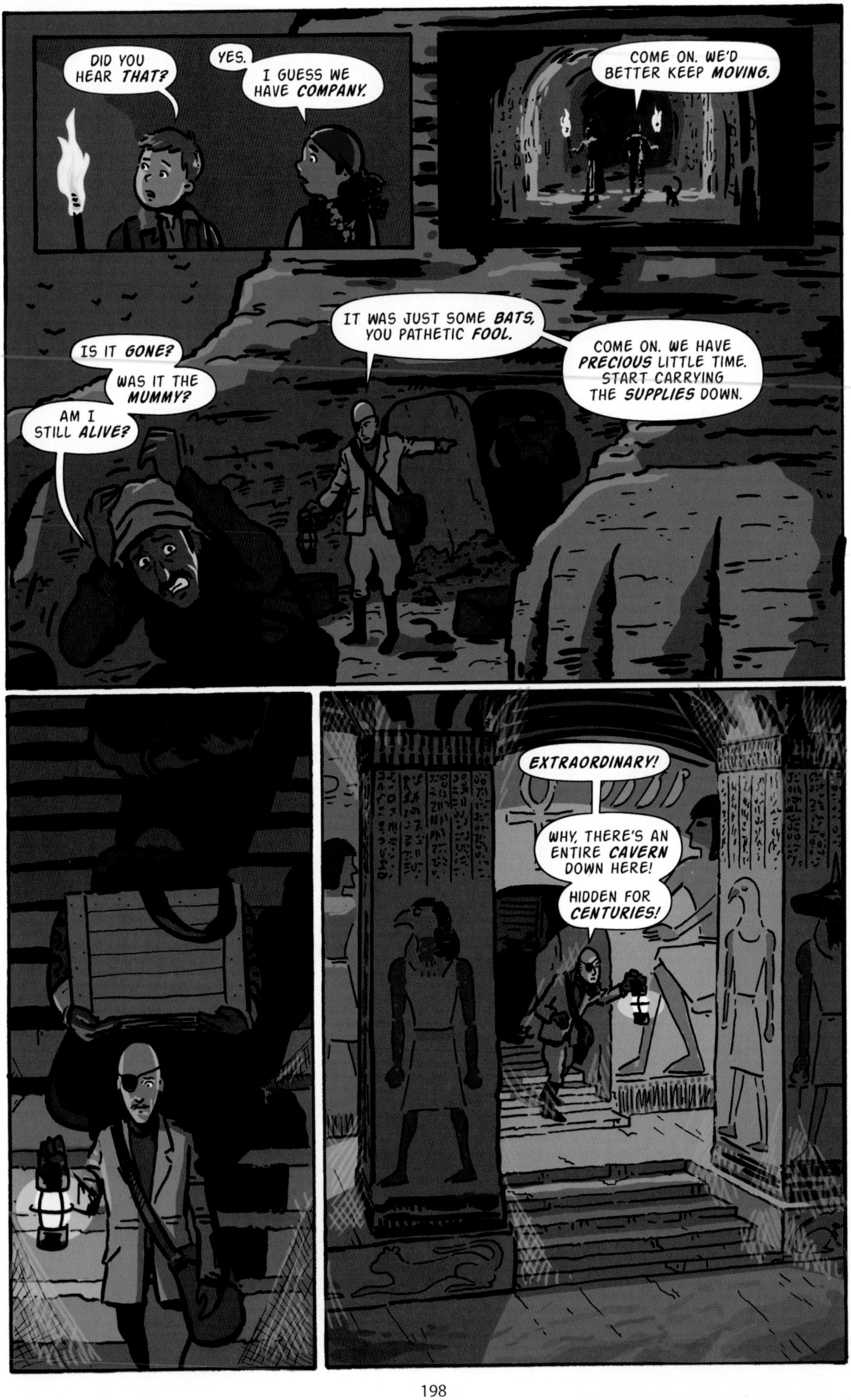
DID YOU HEAR THAT?
YES.
I GUESS WE HAVE COMPANY.
COME ON. WE'D BETTER KEEP MOVING.
IS IT GONE?
WAS IT THE MUMMY?
AM I STILL ALIVE?
IT WAS JUST SOME BATS, YOU PATHETIC FOOL.
COME ON. WE HAVE PRECIOUS LITTLE TIME. START CARRYING THE SUPPLIES DOWN.
EXTRAORDINARY!
WHY, THERE'S AN ENTIRE CAVERN DOWN HERE!
HIDDEN FOR CENTURIES!

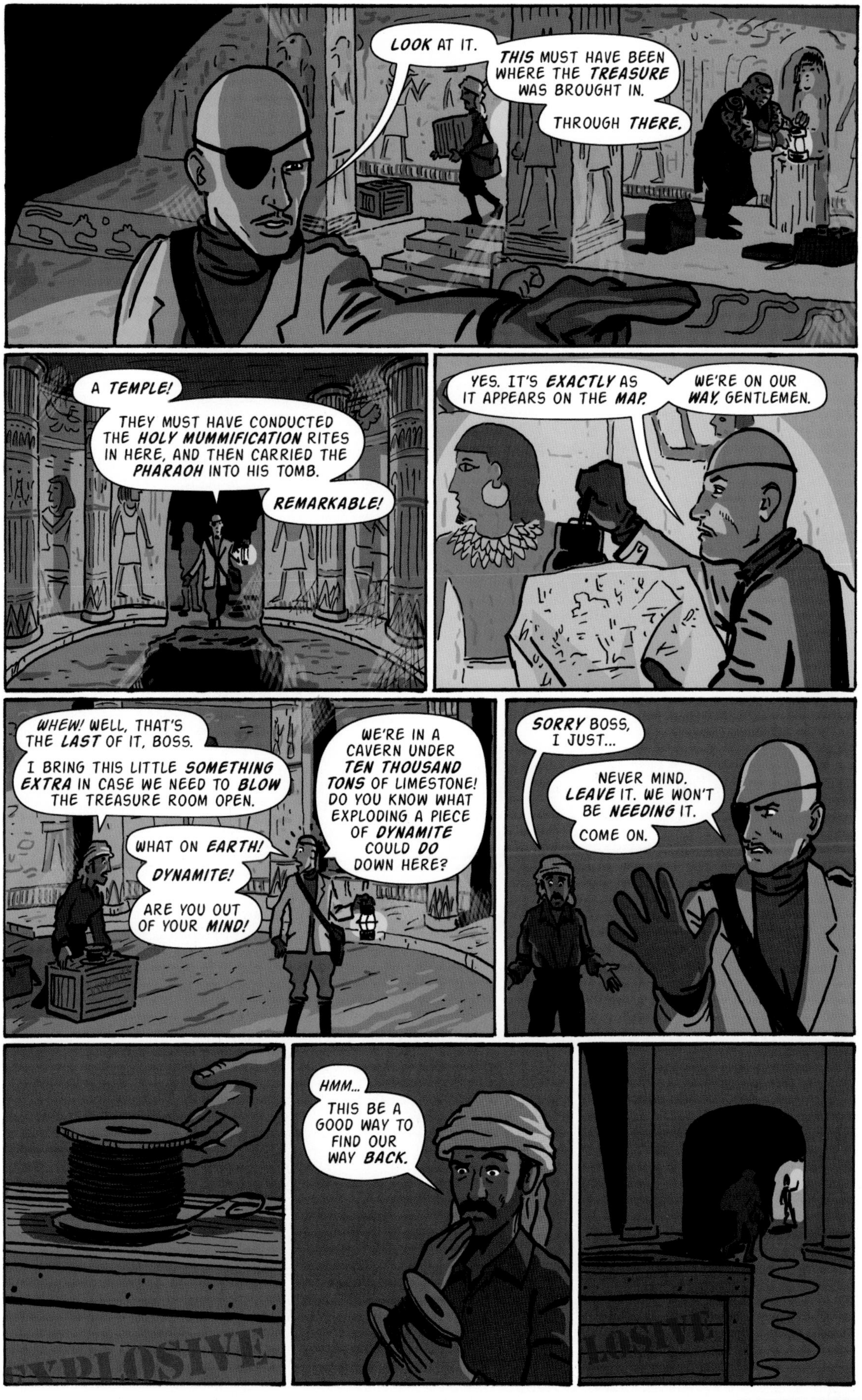
LOOK AT IT.
THIS MUST HAVE BEEN WHERE THE TREASURE WAS BROUGHT IN.
THROUGH THERE.
A TEMPLE!
THEY MUST HAVE CONDUCTED THE HOLY MUMMIFICATION RITES IN HERE, AND THEN CARRIED THE PHARAOH INTO HIS TOMB.
REMARKABLE!
YES. IT'S EXACTLY AS IT APPEARS ON THE MAP.
WE'RE ON OUR WAY, GENTLEMEN.
WHEW! WELL, THAT'S THE LAST OF IT, BOSS.
I BRING THIS LITTLE SOMETHING EXTRA IN CASE WE NEED TO BLOW THE TREASURE ROOM OPEN.
WHAT ON EARTH!
DYNAMITE!
ARE YOU OUT OF YOUR MIND!
WE'RE IN A CAVERN UNDER TEN THOUSAND TONS OF LIMESTONE! DO YOU KNOW WHAT EXPLODING A PIECE OF DYNAMITE COULD DO DOWN HERE?
SORRY BOSS, I JUST...
NEVER MIND. LEAVE IT. WE WON'T BE NEEDING IT.
COME ON.
EXPLOSIVE
HMM...
THIS BE A GOOD WAY TO FIND OUR WAY BACK.
LOSIVE

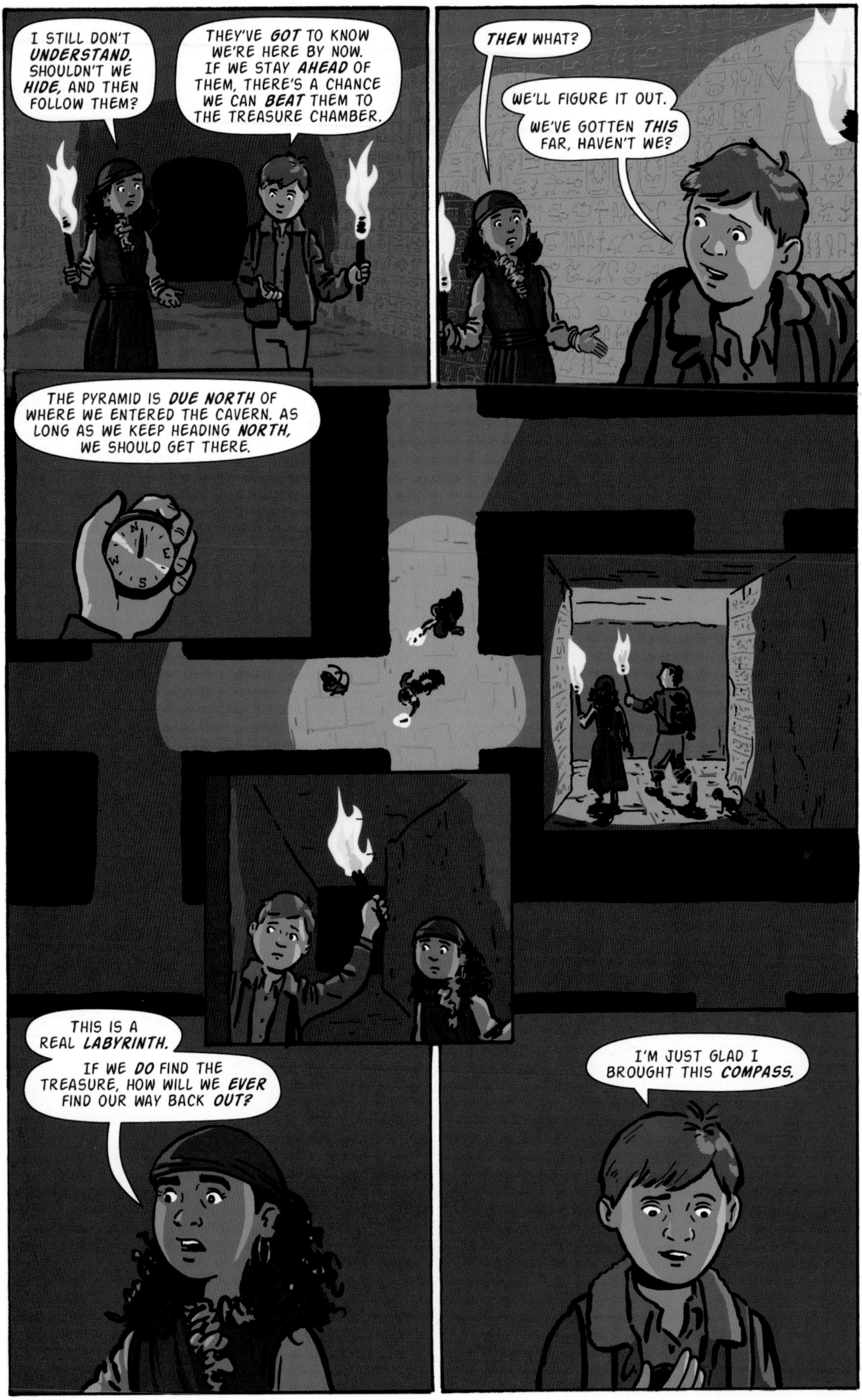
I STILL DON'T UNDERSTAND. SHOULDN'T WE HIDE, AND THEN FOLLOW THEM?
THEY'VE GOT TO KNOW WE'RE HERE BY NOW. IF WE STAY AHEAD OF THEM, THERE'S A CHANCE WE CAN BEAT THEM TO THE TREASURE CHAMBER.
THEN WHAT?
WE'LL FIGURE IT OUT.
WE'VE GOTTEN THIS FAR, HAVEN'T WE?
THE PYRAMID IS DUE NORTH OF WHERE WE ENTERED THE CAVERN. AS LONG AS WE KEEP HEADING NORTH, WE SHOULD GET THERE.
N
E
W
S
THIS IS A REAL LABYRINTH.
IF WE DO FIND THE TREASURE, HOW WILL WE EVER FIND OUR WAY BACK OUT?
I'M JUST GLAD I BROUGHT THIS COMPASS.

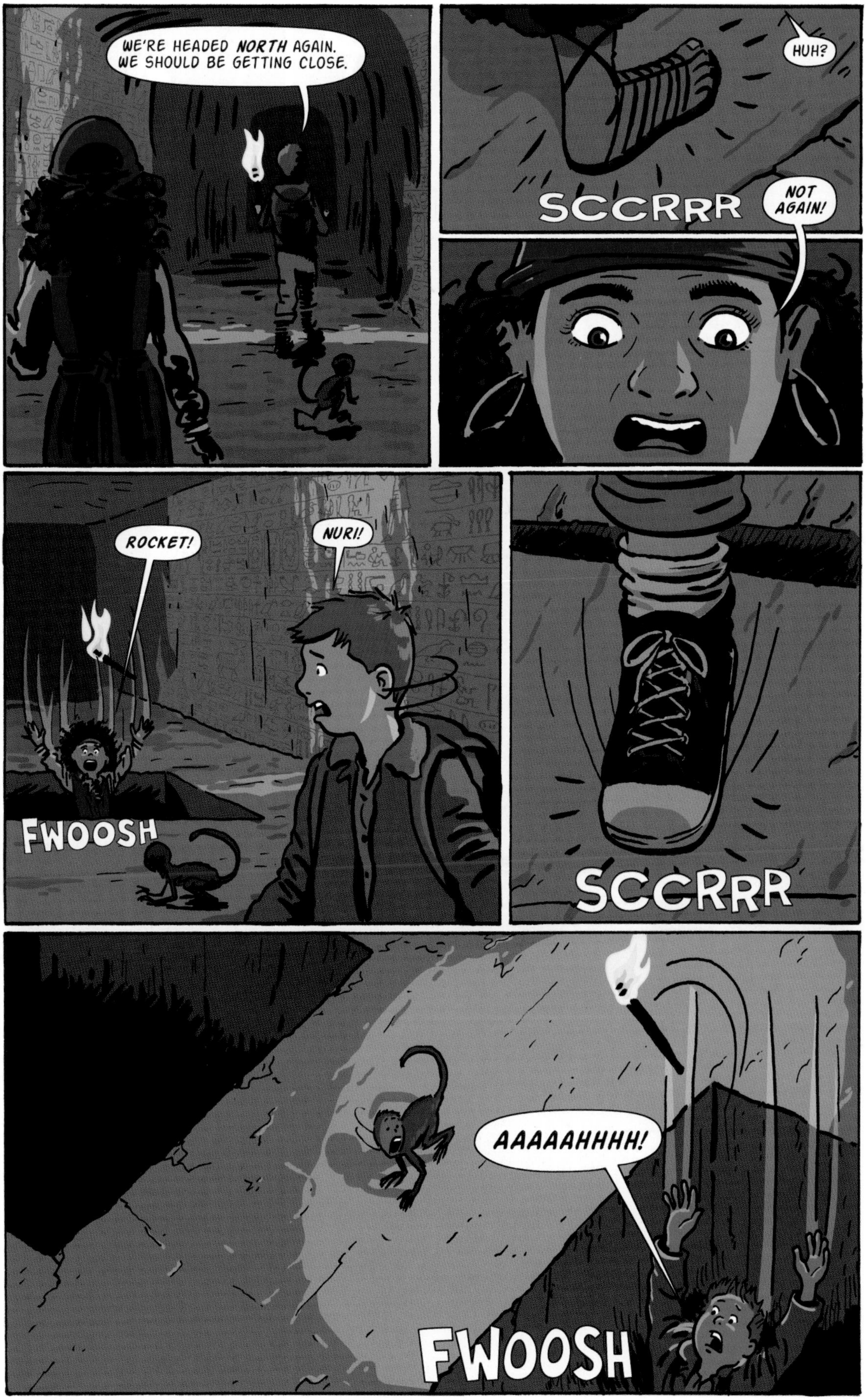
WE'RE HEADED NORTH AGAIN. WE SHOULD BE GETTING CLOSE.
HUH?
SCCRRR
NOT AGAIN!
ROCKET!
NURI!
FWOOSH
SCCRRR
AAAAAHHHH!
FWOOSH

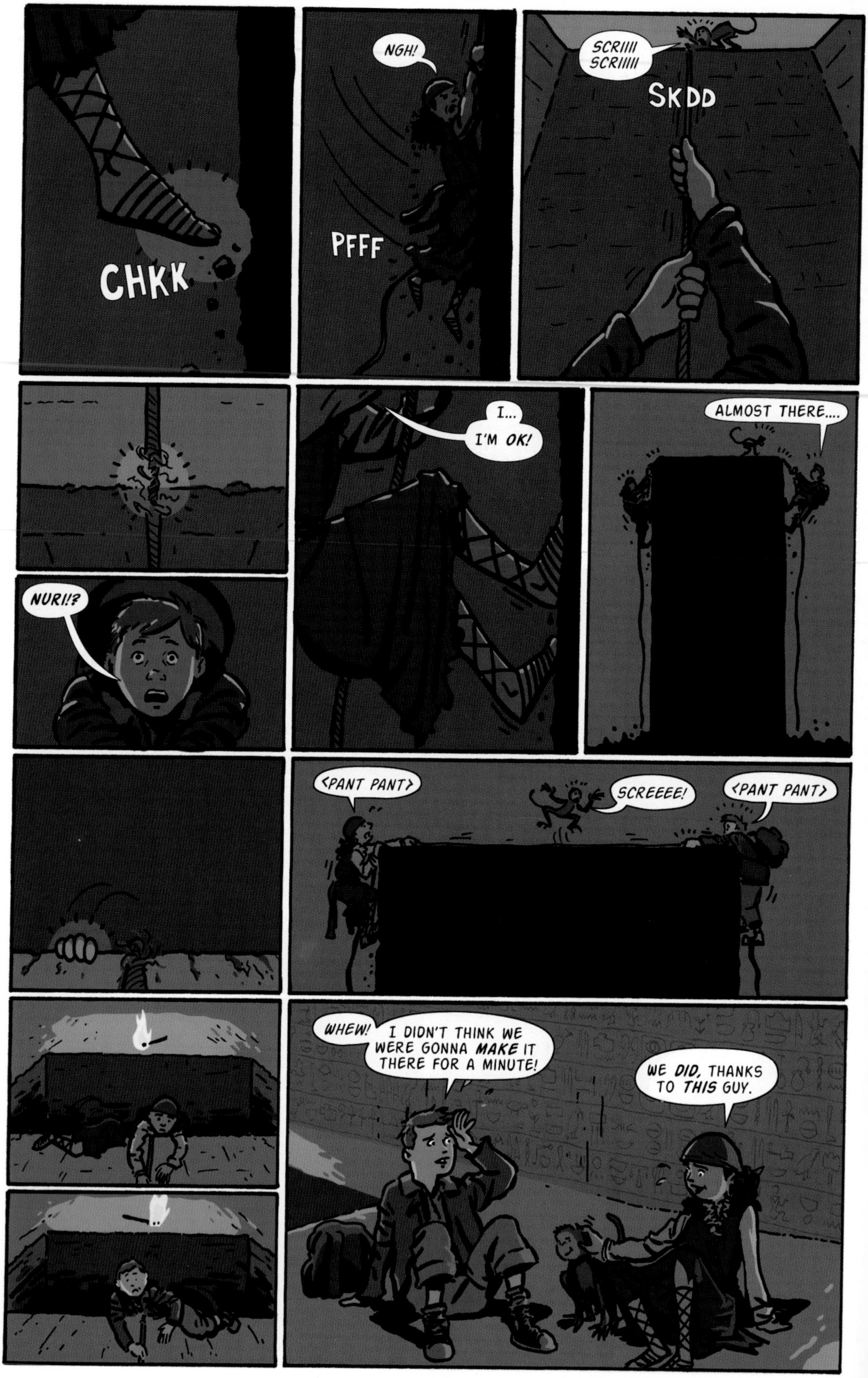
CHKK
NGH!
PFFF
SCRIIII
SCRIIIII
SKDD
I...
I'M OK!
ALMOST THERE....
NURI!?
<PANT PANT>
SCREEEE!
<PANT PANT>
WHEW!
I DIDN'T THINK WE WERE GONNA MAKE IT THERE FOR A MINUTE!
WE DID, THANKS TO THIS GUY.

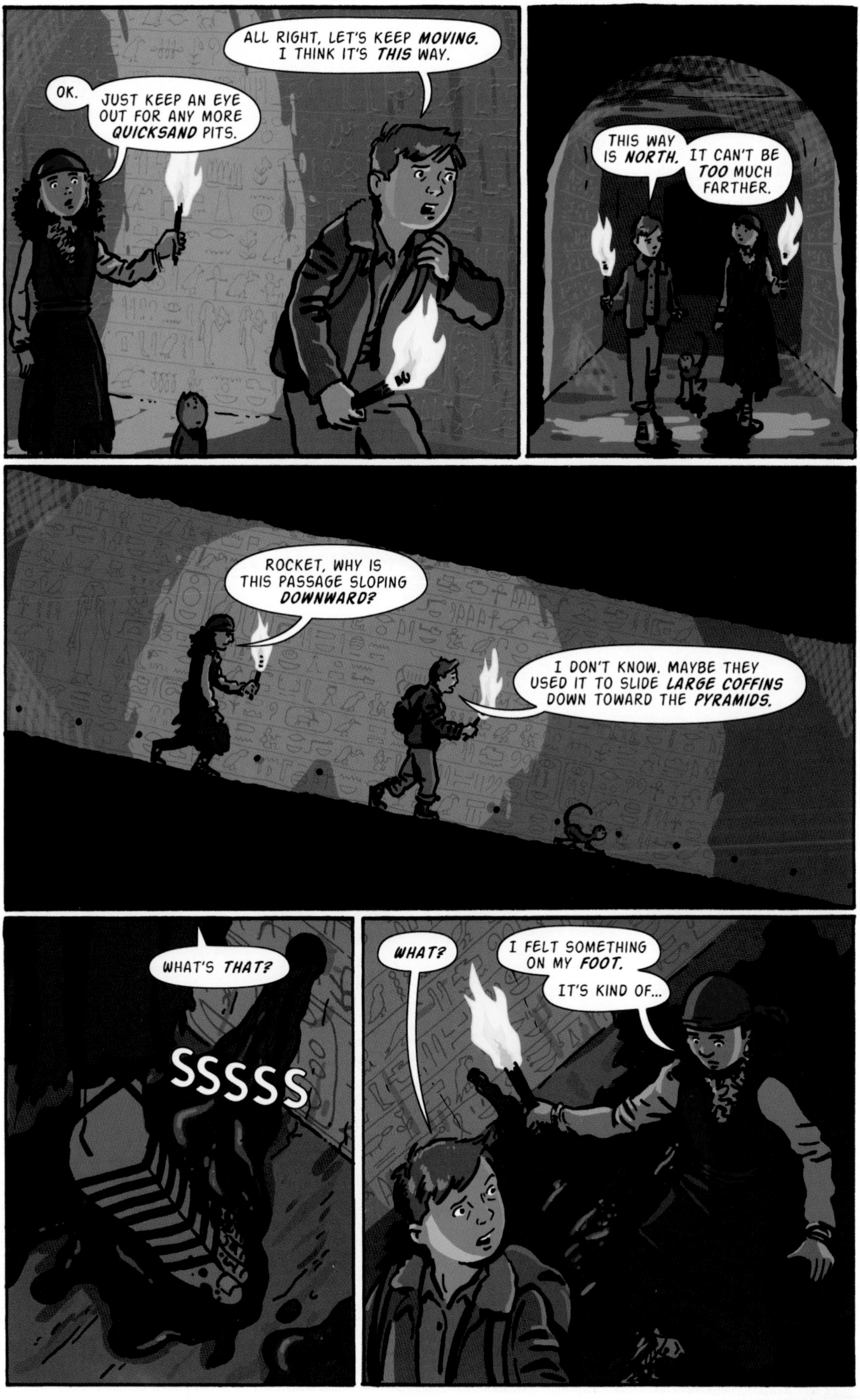
ALL RIGHT, LET'S KEEP MOVING. I THINK IT'S THIS WAY.
OK.
JUST KEEP AN EYE OUT FOR ANY MORE QUICKSAND PITS.
THIS WAY IS NORTH.
IT CAN'T BE TOO MUCH FARTHER.
ROCKET, WHY IS THIS PASSAGE SLOPING DOWNWARD?
I DON'T KNOW. MAYBE THEY USED IT TO SLIDE LARGE COFFINS DOWN TOWARD THE PYRAMIDS.
WHAT'S THAT?
SSSSS
WHAT?
I FELT SOMETHING ON MY FOOT.
IT'S KIND OF...

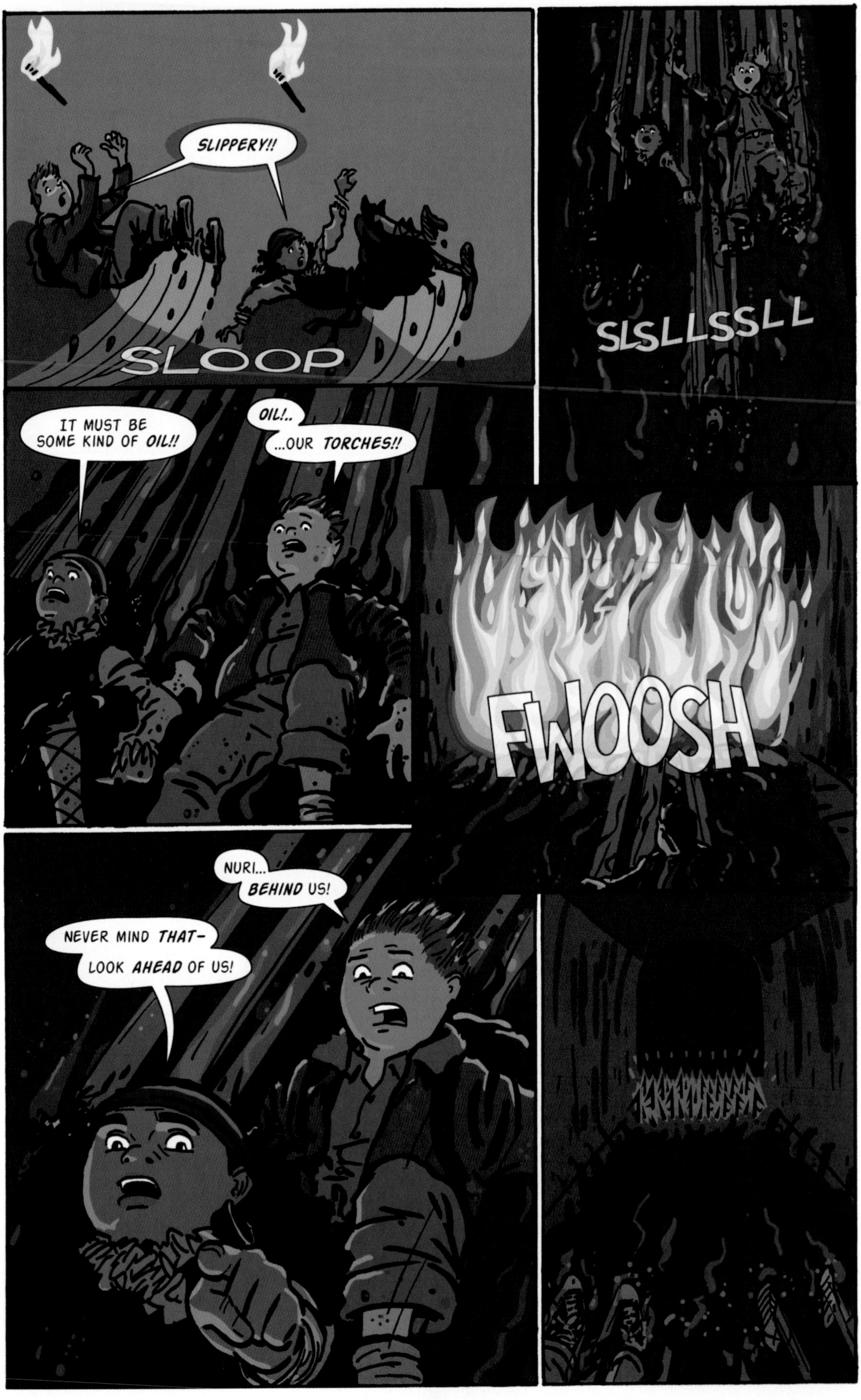
SLIPPERY!!
SLOOP
SLSLLSSLL
IT MUST BE SOME KIND OF OIL!!
OIL!.. ...OUR TORCHES!!
FWOOSH
NURI... BEHIND US!
NEVER MIND THAT— LOOK AHEAD OF US!

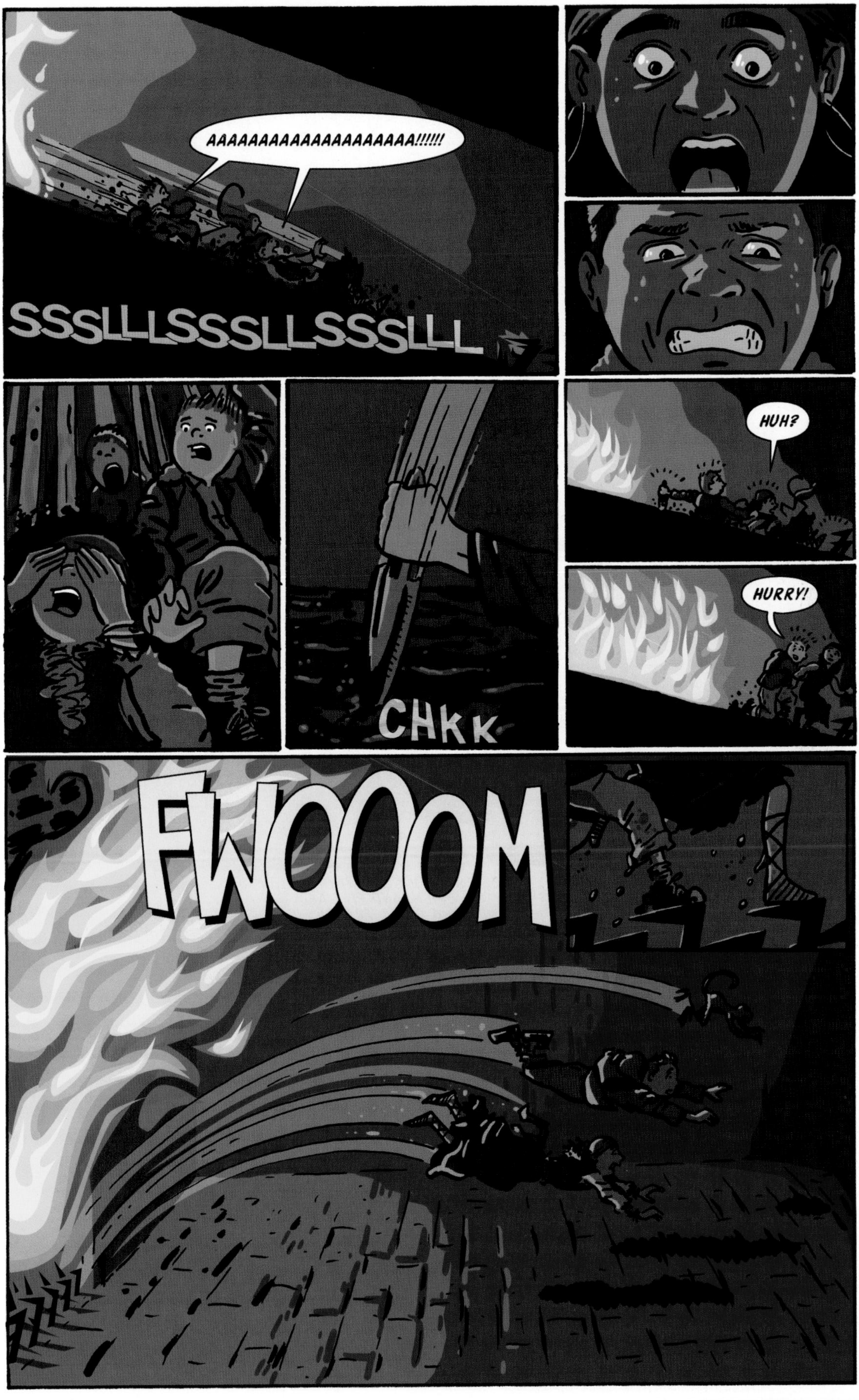
AAAAAAAAAAAAAAAAAAAAA!!!!!!
SSSLLLSSSLLSSSLLL
CHKK
HUH?
HURRY!
FWOOOM

ARE YOU *OK?*

YEAH, BUT I HOPE WE'RE ALMOST *THERE.* I DON'T THINK I CAN *HANDLE* ANY MORE *SURPRISES.*

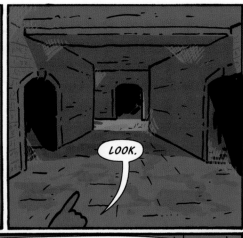

LOOK.

THROUGH HERE WE SHOULD REACH THE *NEOPHYTE'S CHAMBER,* AND JUST BEYOND THAT, THE *ANTECHAMBER,* AND THEN...

THE *TREASURE CHAMBER!*

HOW DID THEY GET HERE SO *QUICKLY?*

THEY HAVE A *MAP,* REMEMBER?

I GUESS THEY TOOK THE PATH WITHOUT THE *QUICKSAND PITS* AND THE *FLAMING SPIKE TRAPS!*

CHAPTER TEN

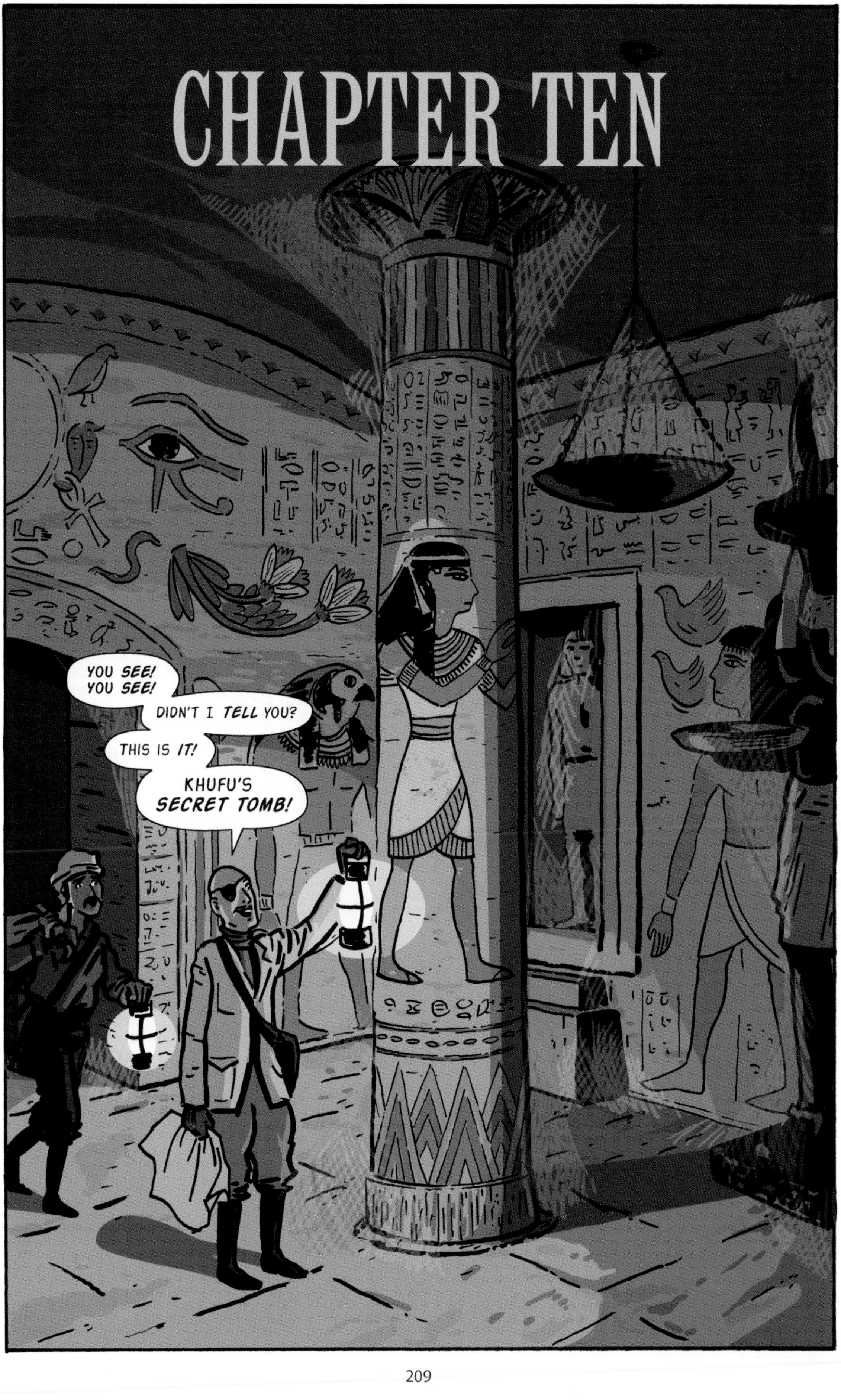
YOU SEE! YOU SEE!
DIDN'T I TELL YOU?
THIS IS IT!
KHUFU'S SECRET TOMB!

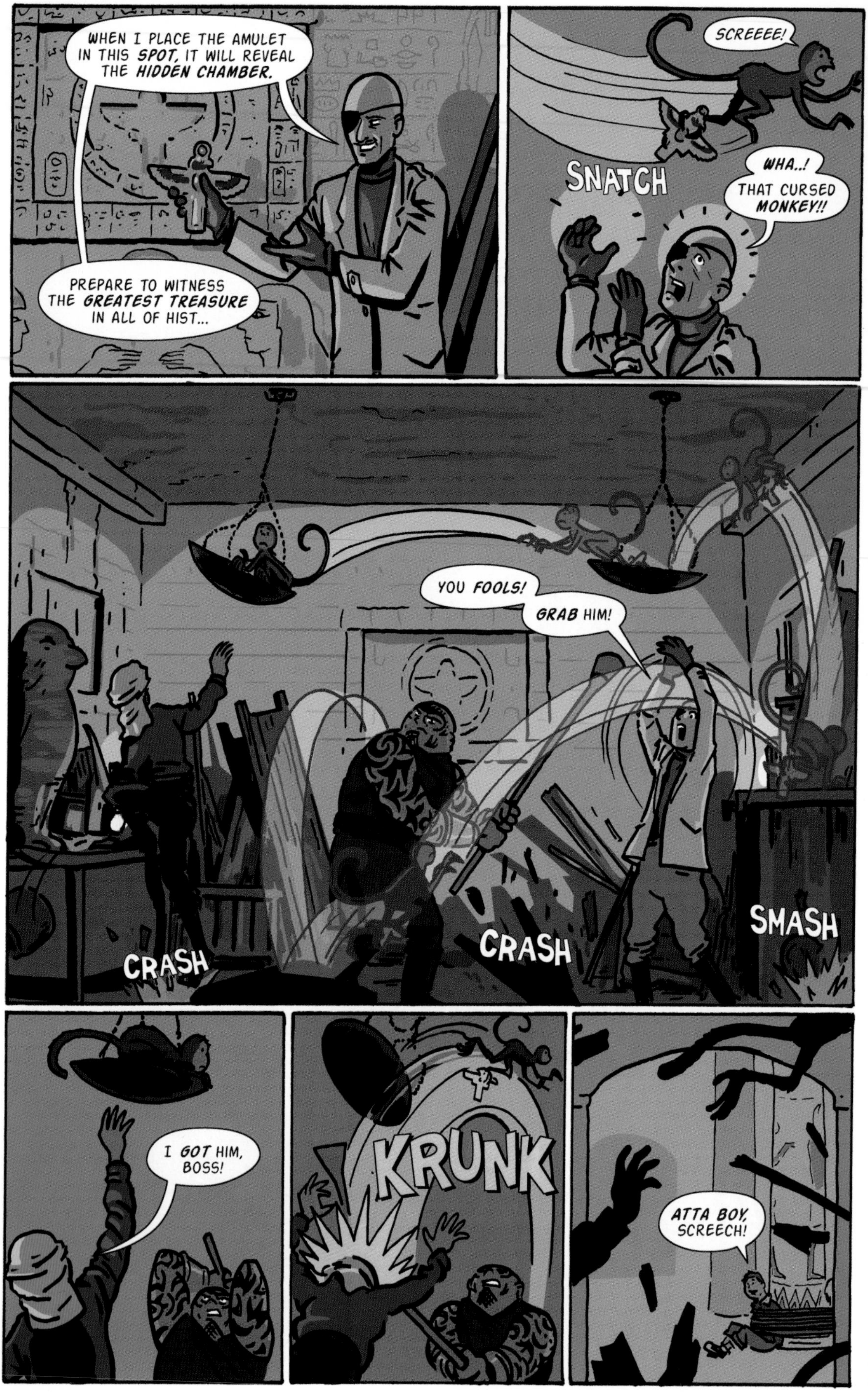
WHEN I PLACE THE AMULET IN THIS SPOT, IT WILL REVEAL THE HIDDEN CHAMBER.
PREPARE TO WITNESS THE GREATEST TREASURE IN ALL OF HIST...
SCREEEE!
SNATCH
WHA..! THAT CURSED MONKEY!!
YOU FOOLS!
GRAB HIM!
CRASH
CRASH
SMASH
I GOT HIM, BOSS!
KRUNK
ATTA BOY, SCREECH!

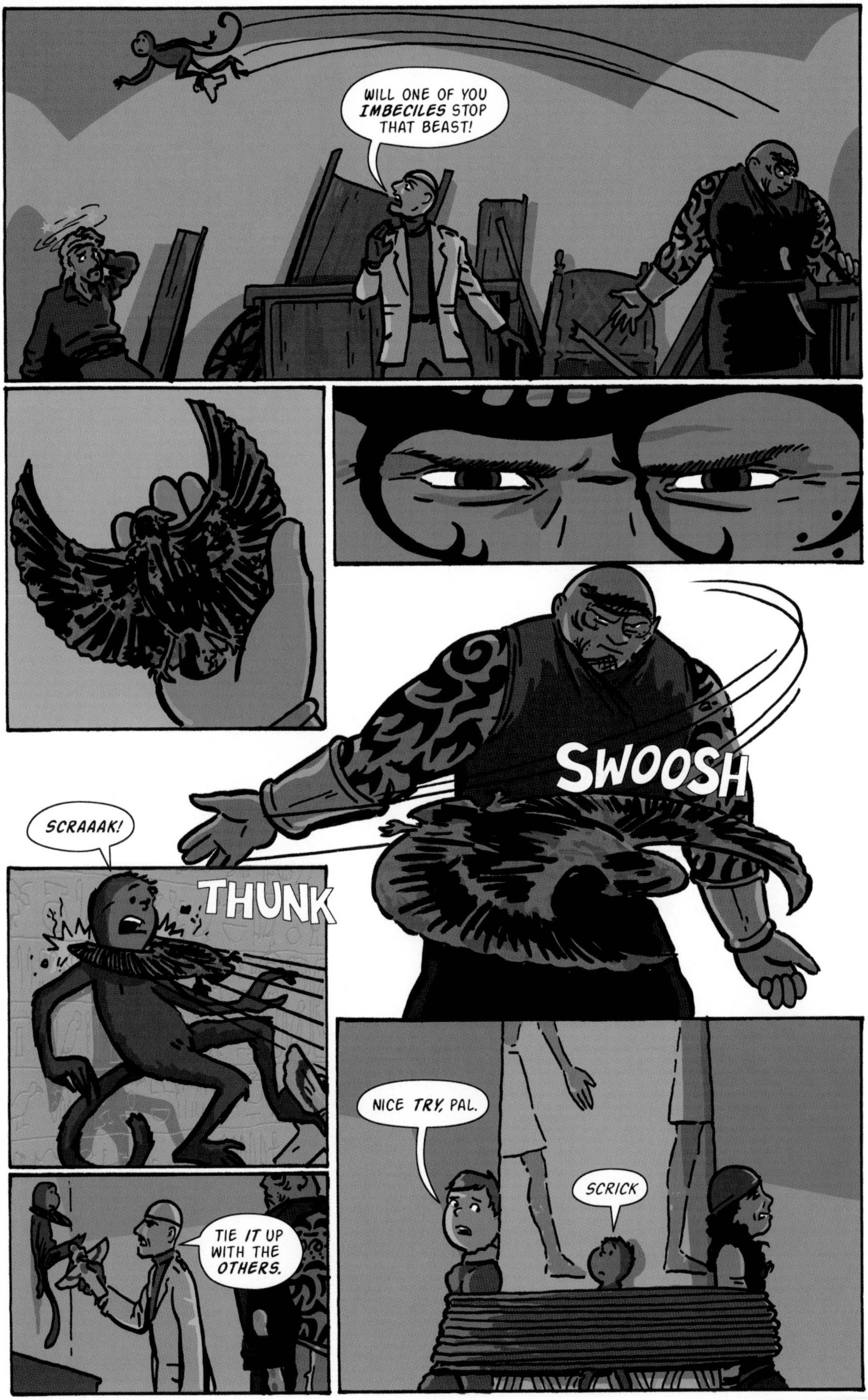
WILL ONE OF YOU IMBECILES STOP THAT BEAST!
SWOOSH
SCRAAAK!
THUNK
TIE IT UP WITH THE OTHERS.
NICE TRY, PAL.
SCRICK

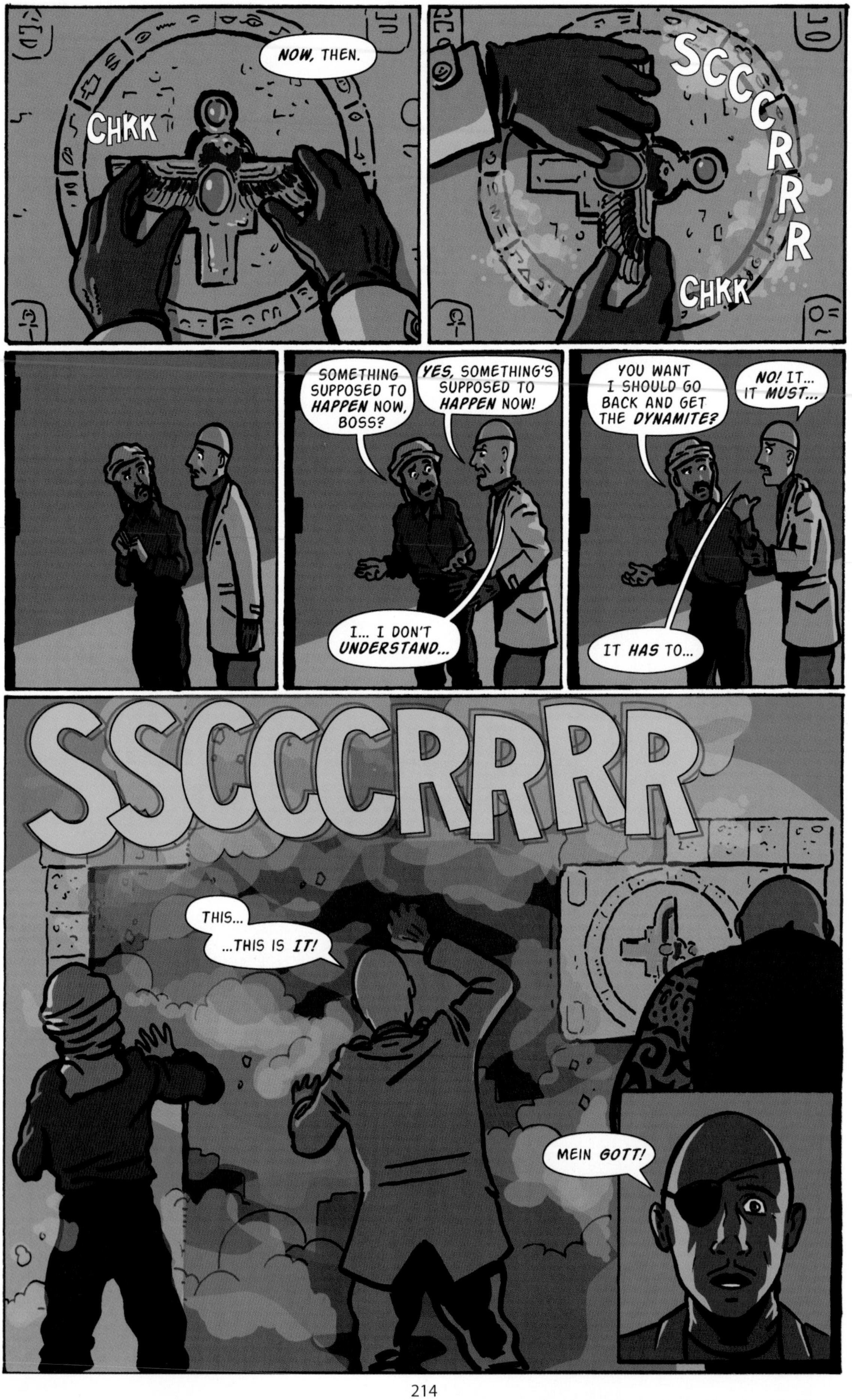
NOW, THEN.
CHKK
SCCCRRRR
CHKK
SOMETHING SUPPOSED TO HAPPEN NOW, BOSS?
YES, SOMETHING'S SUPPOSED TO HAPPEN NOW!
I... I DON'T UNDERSTAND...
YOU WANT I SHOULD GO BACK AND GET THE DYNAMITE?
NO! IT... IT MUST...
IT HAS TO...
SSCCCRRRR
THIS...
...THIS IS IT!
MEIN GOTT!

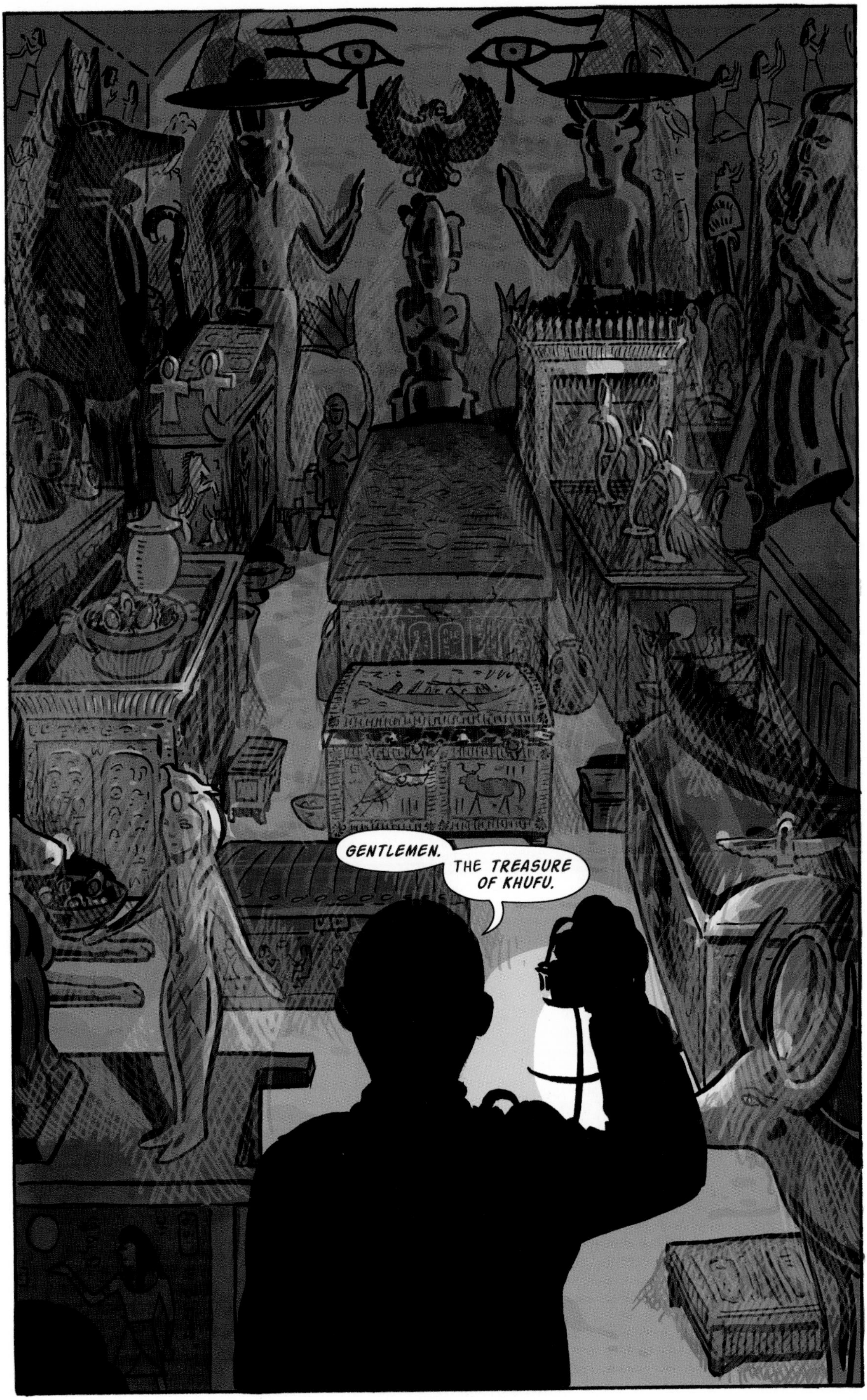
GENTLEMEN.
THE TREASURE OF KHUFU.

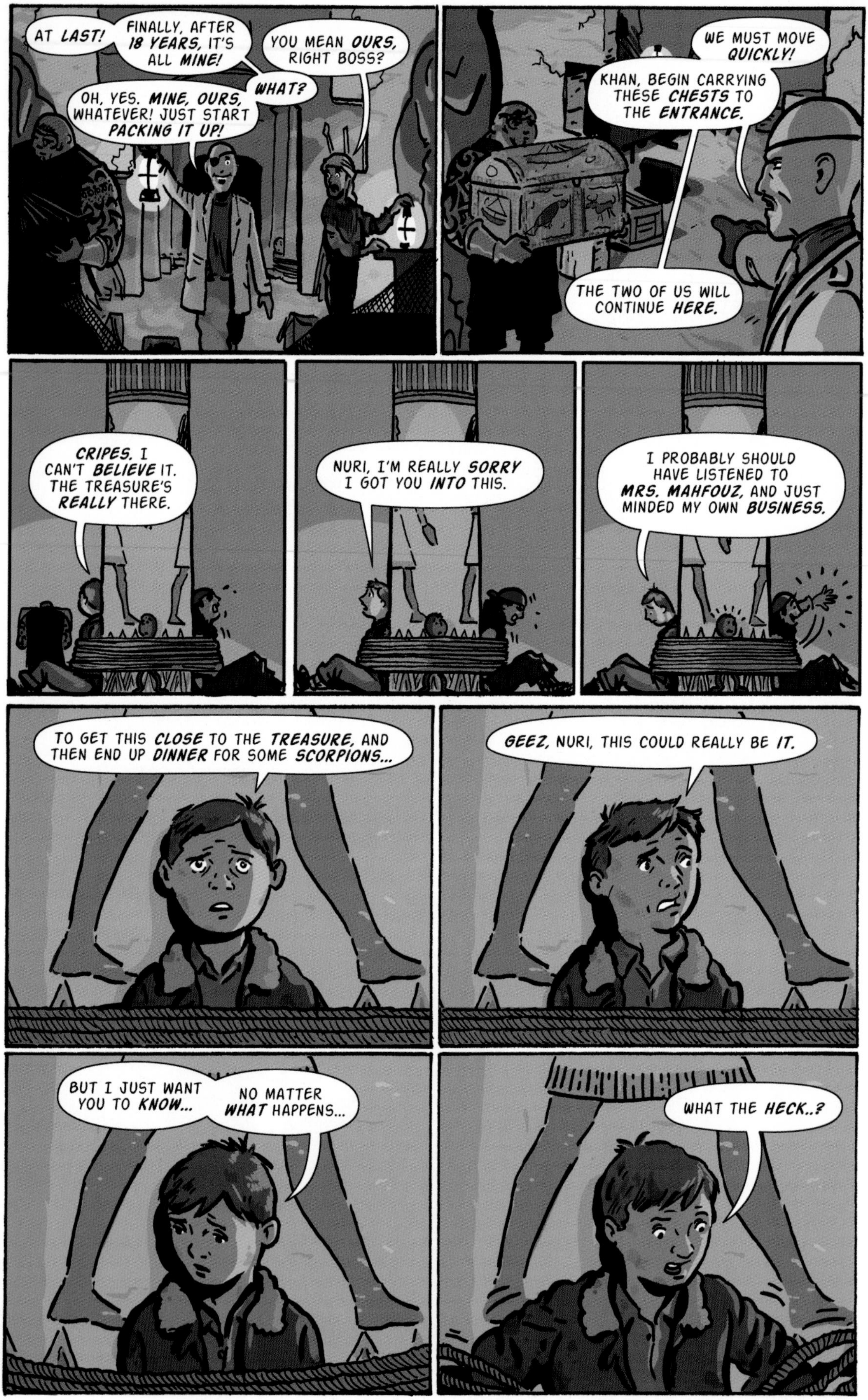
AT LAST!
FINALLY, AFTER 18 YEARS, IT'S ALL MINE!
YOU MEAN OURS, RIGHT BOSS?
WHAT?
OH, YES. MINE, OURS, WHATEVER! JUST START PACKING IT UP!
WE MUST MOVE QUICKLY!
KHAN, BEGIN CARRYING THESE CHESTS TO THE ENTRANCE.
THE TWO OF US WILL CONTINUE HERE.
CRIPES. I CAN'T BELIEVE IT. THE TREASURE'S REALLY THERE.
NURI, I'M REALLY SORRY I GOT YOU INTO THIS.
I PROBABLY SHOULD HAVE LISTENED TO MRS. MAHFOUZ, AND JUST MINDED MY OWN BUSINESS.
TO GET THIS CLOSE TO THE TREASURE, AND THEN END UP DINNER FOR SOME SCORPIONS...
GEEZ, NURI, THIS COULD REALLY BE IT.
BUT I JUST WANT YOU TO KNOW...
NO MATTER WHAT HAPPENS...
WHAT THE HECK..?

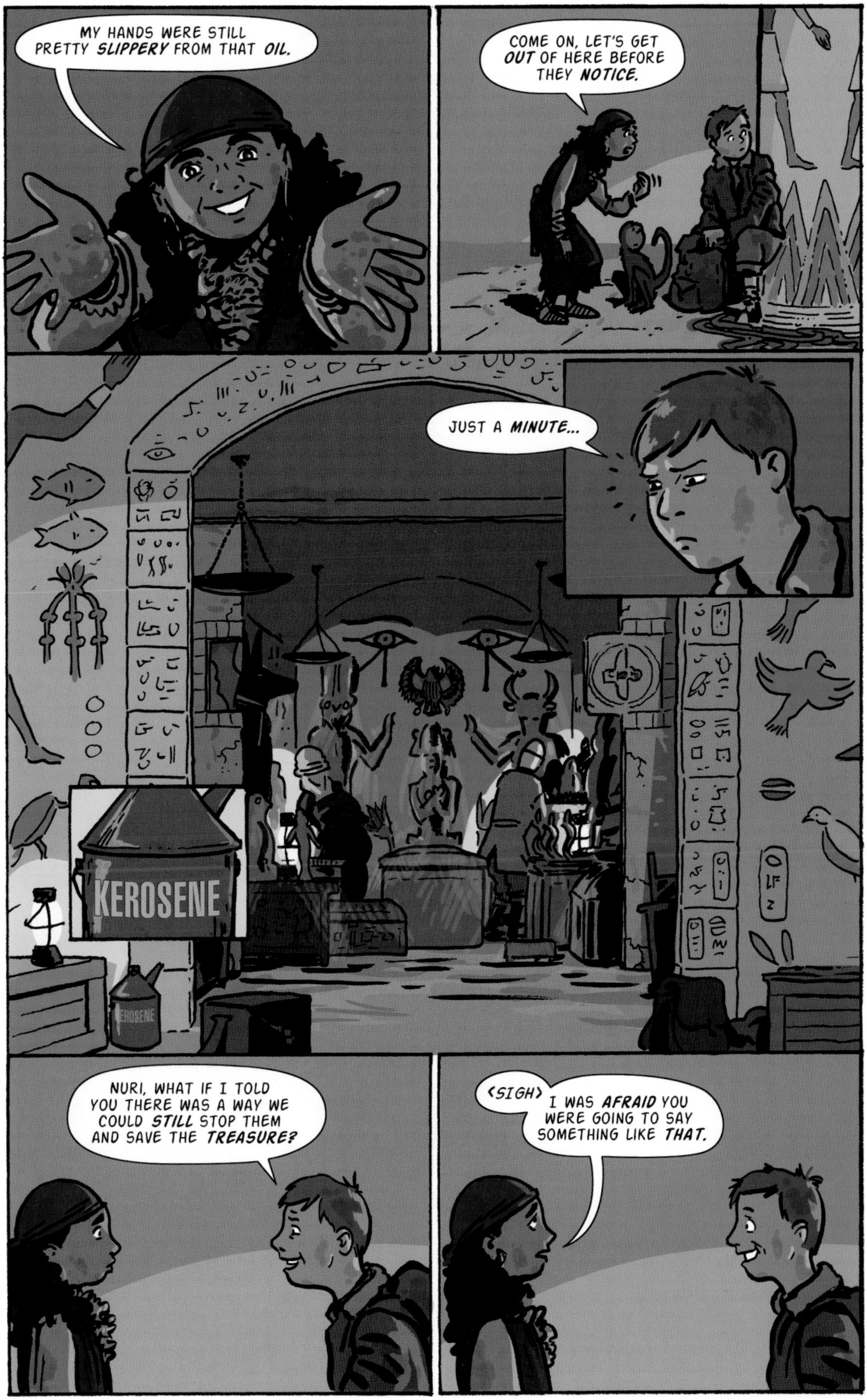
MY HANDS WERE STILL PRETTY SLIPPERY FROM THAT OIL.
COME ON, LET'S GET OUT OF HERE BEFORE THEY NOTICE.
JUST A MINUTE...
KEROSENE
KEROSENE
NURI, WHAT IF I TOLD YOU THERE WAS A WAY WE COULD STILL STOP THEM AND SAVE THE TREASURE?
<SIGH> I WAS AFRAID YOU WERE GOING TO SAY SOMETHING LIKE THAT.

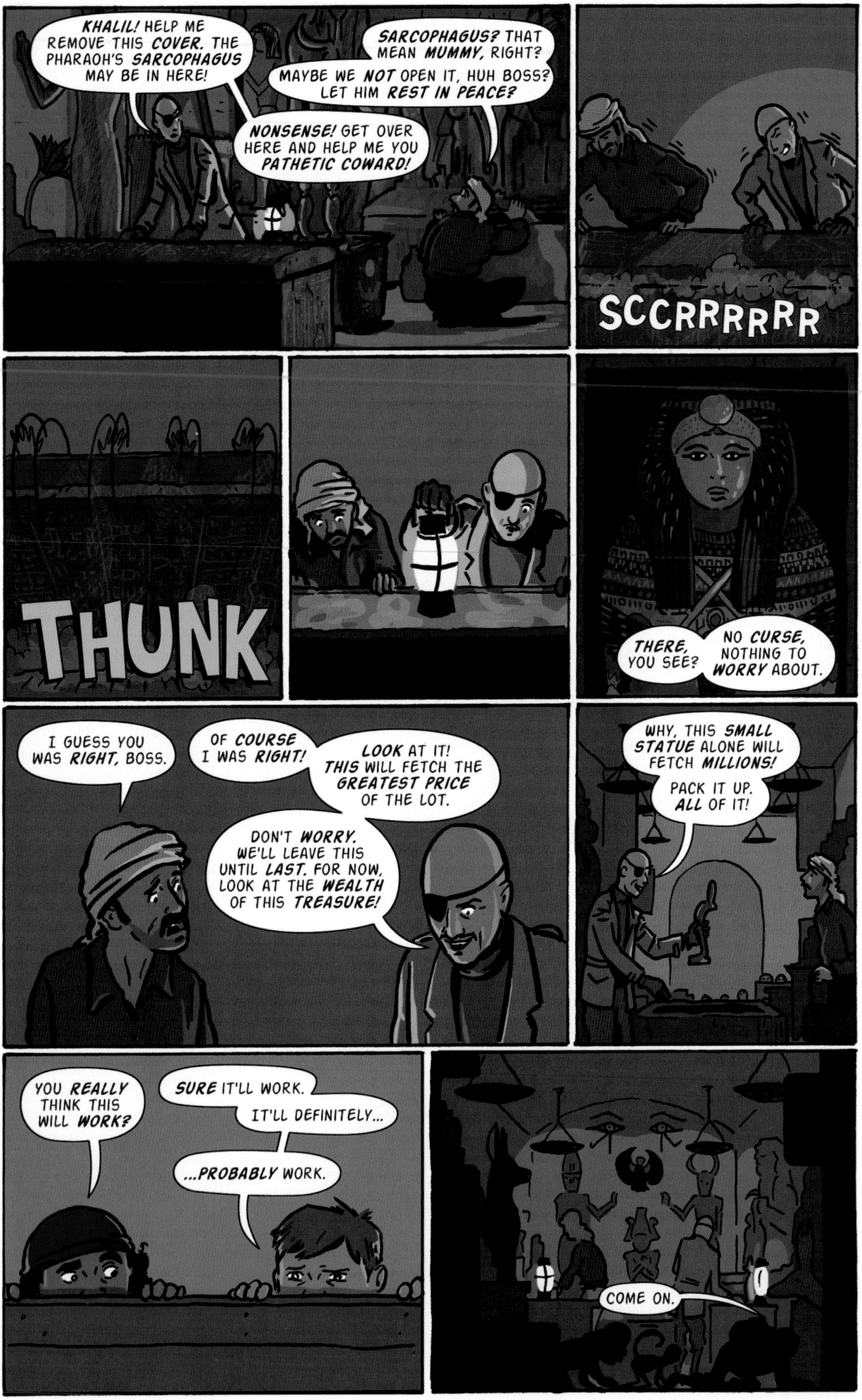
KHALIL! HELP ME REMOVE THIS COVER. THE PHARAOH'S SARCOPHAGUS MAY BE IN HERE!
SARCOPHAGUS? THAT MEAN MUMMY, RIGHT?
MAYBE WE NOT OPEN IT, HUH BOSS? LET HIM REST IN PEACE?
NONSENSE! GET OVER HERE AND HELP ME YOU PATHETIC COWARD!
SCCRRRRRR
THUNK
THERE, YOU SEE?
NO CURSE, NOTHING TO WORRY ABOUT.
I GUESS YOU WAS RIGHT, BOSS.
OF COURSE I WAS RIGHT!
LOOK AT IT! THIS WILL FETCH THE GREATEST PRICE OF THE LOT.
DON'T WORRY. WE'LL LEAVE THIS UNTIL LAST. FOR NOW, LOOK AT THE WEALTH OF THIS TREASURE!
WHY, THIS SMALL STATUE ALONE WILL FETCH MILLIONS!
PACK IT UP. ALL OF IT!
YOU REALLY THINK THIS WILL WORK?
SURE IT'LL WORK.
IT'LL DEFINITELY...
...PROBABLY WORK.
COME ON.

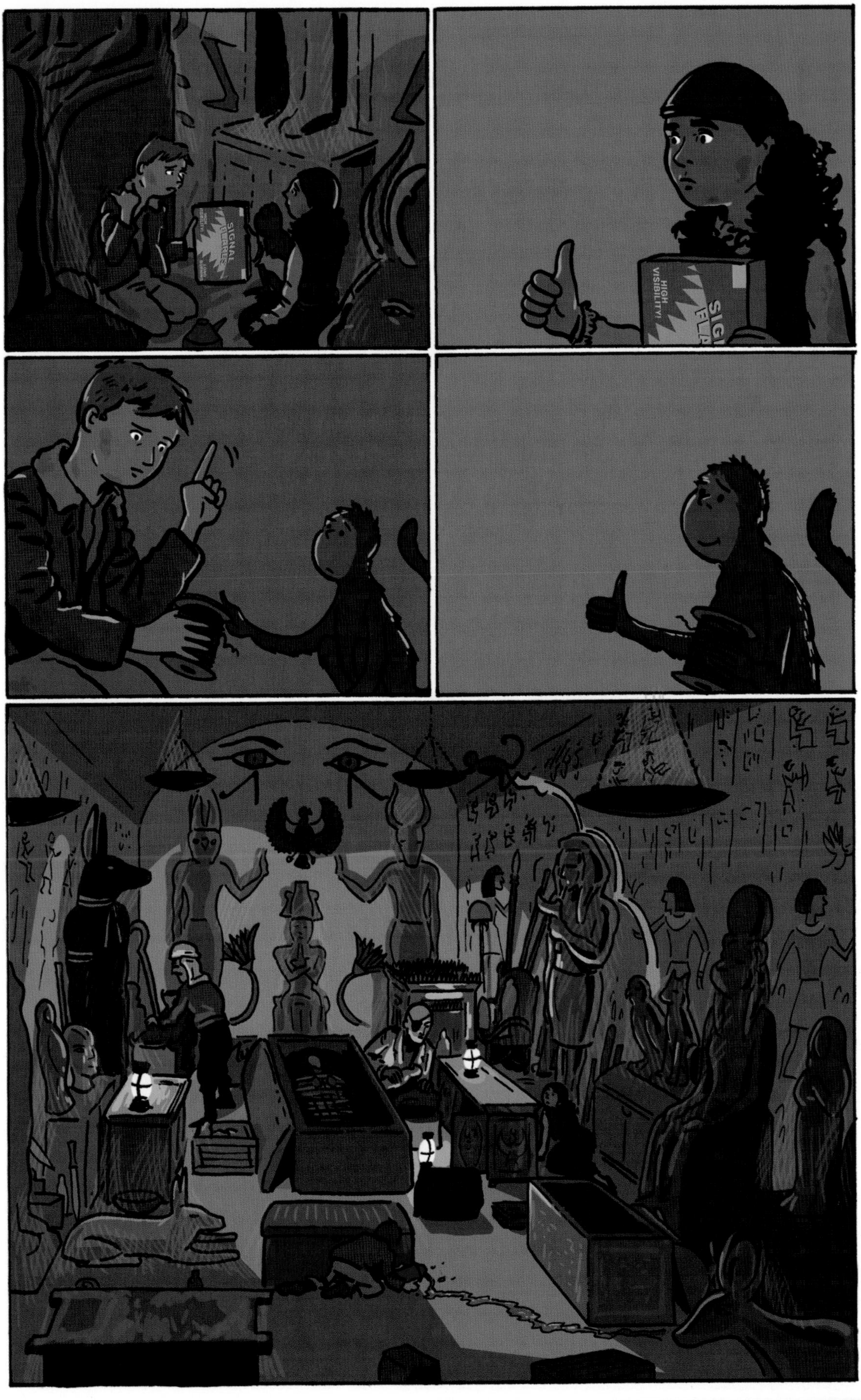
SIGNAL FLARES
HIGH VISIBILITY!

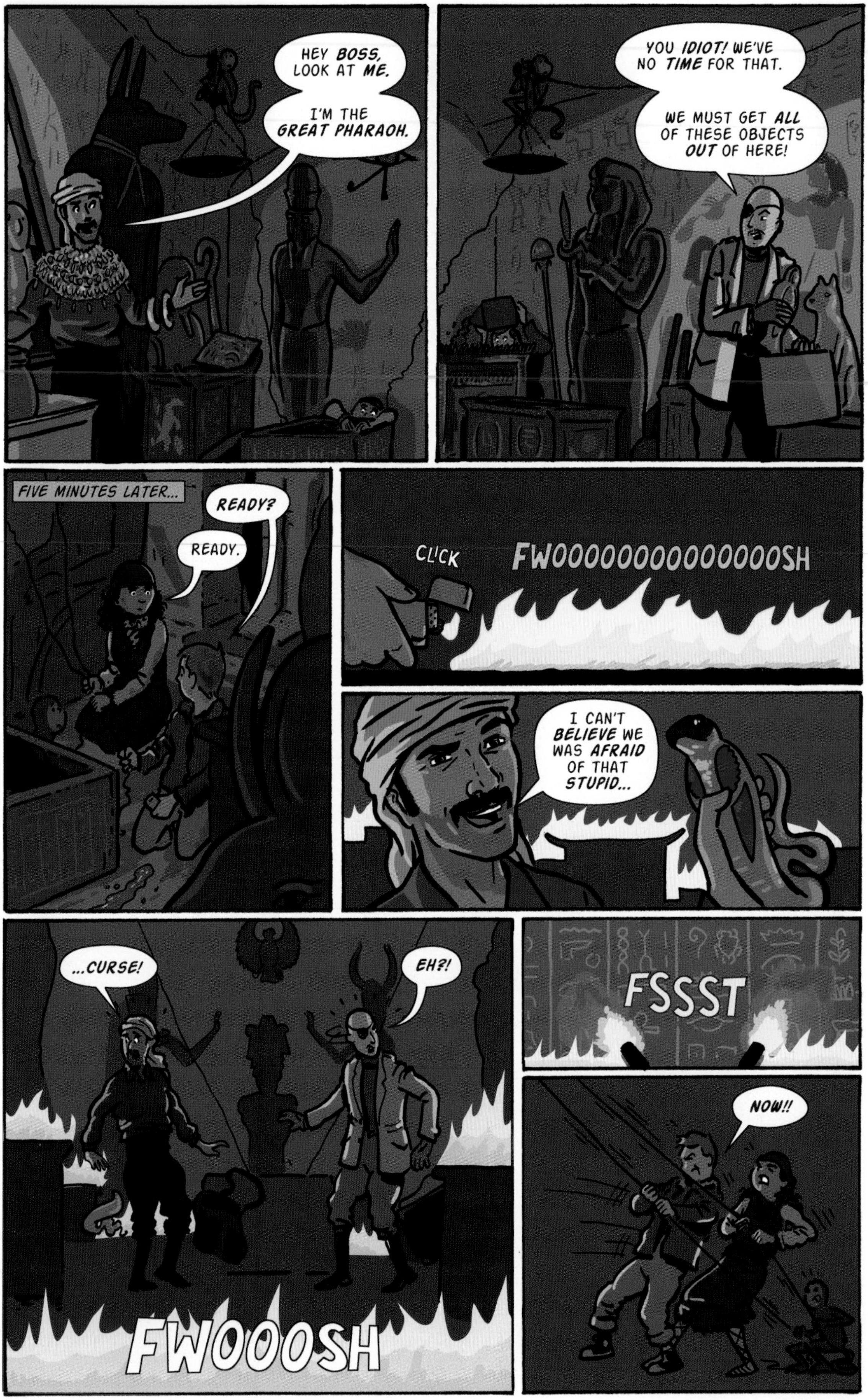
HEY BOSS, LOOK AT ME.
I'M THE GREAT PHARAOH.
YOU IDIOT! WE'VE NO TIME FOR THAT.
WE MUST GET ALL OF THESE OBJECTS OUT OF HERE!
FIVE MINUTES LATER...
READY?
READY.
CLICK
FWOOOOOOOOOOOOOOSH
I CAN'T BELIEVE WE WAS AFRAID OF THAT STUPID...
...CURSE!
EH?!
FWOOOSH
FSSST
NOW!!

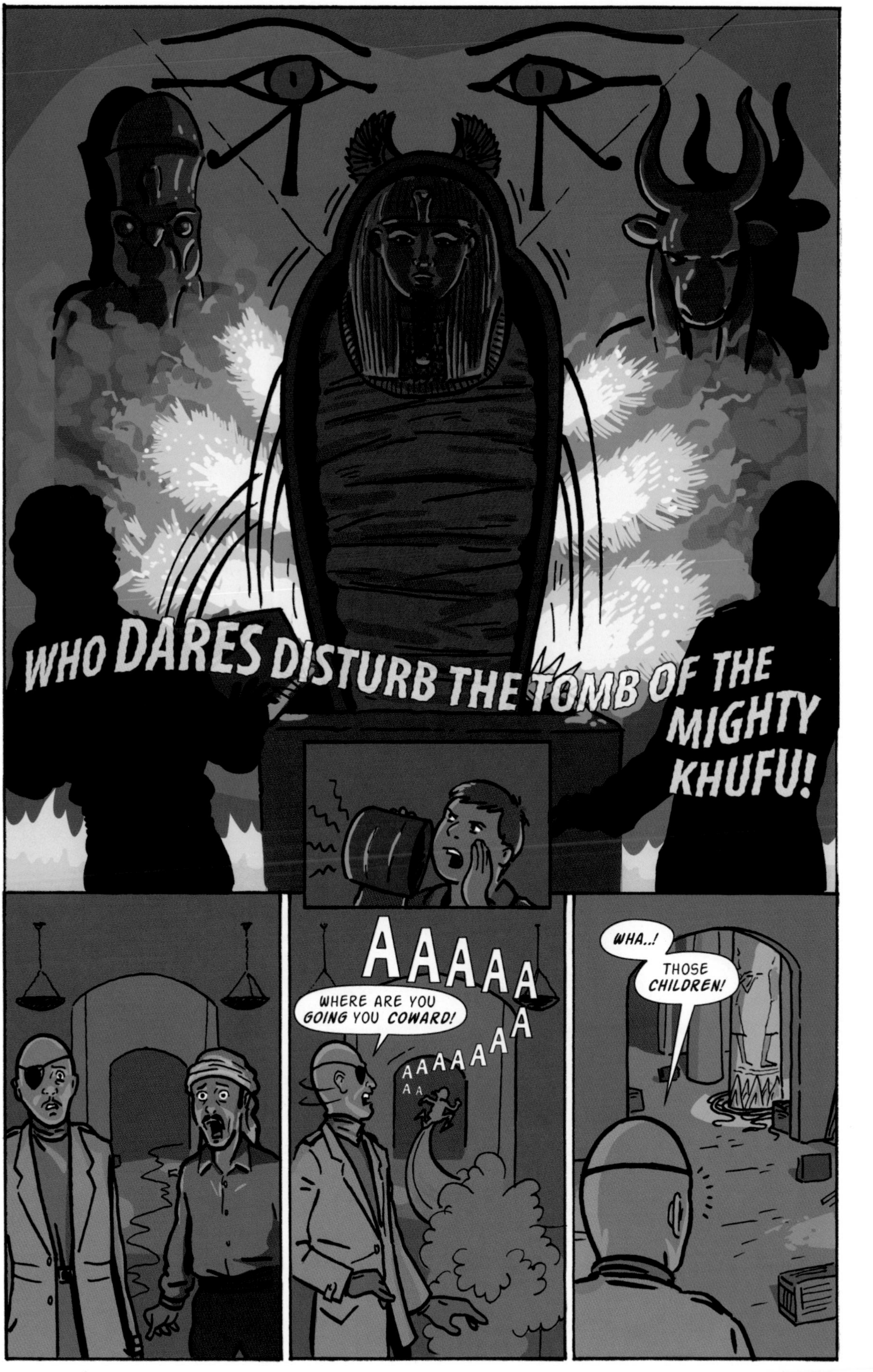
WHO DARES DISTURB THE TOMB OF THE MIGHTY KHUFU!
AAAAAA
WHERE ARE YOU GOING YOU COWARD!
AAAAAAAAA
WHA..!
THOSE CHILDREN!

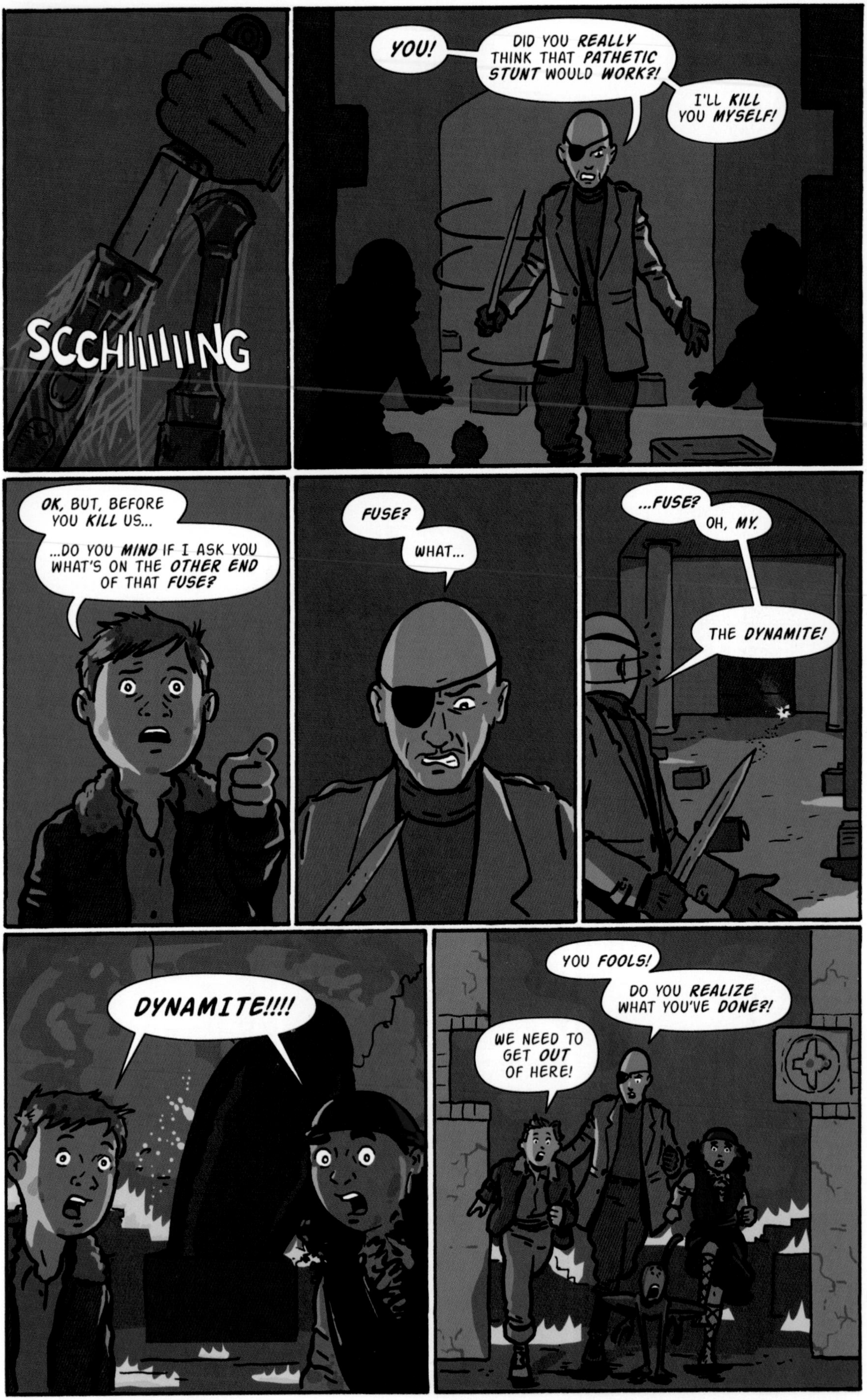
SCCHIIIIIING
YOU!
DID YOU REALLY THINK THAT PATHETIC STUNT WOULD WORK?!
I'LL KILL YOU MYSELF!
OK, BUT, BEFORE YOU KILL US...
...DO YOU MIND IF I ASK YOU WHAT'S ON THE OTHER END OF THAT FUSE?
FUSE?
WHAT...
...FUSE?
OH, MY.
THE DYNAMITE!
DYNAMITE!!!!
YOU FOOLS!
DO YOU REALIZE WHAT YOU'VE DONE?!
WE NEED TO GET OUT OF HERE!

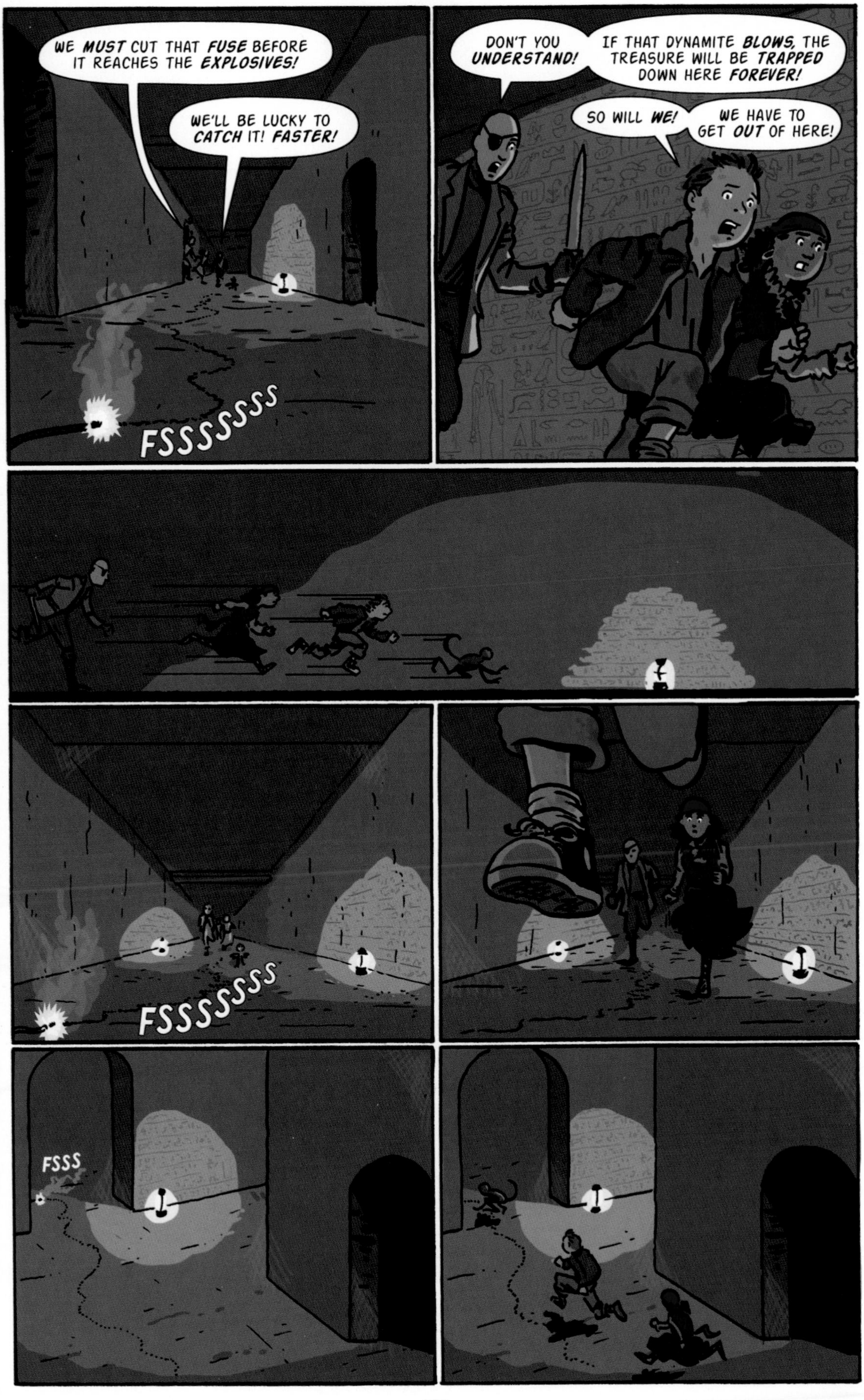
WE MUST CUT THAT FUSE BEFORE IT REACHES THE EXPLOSIVES!
WE'LL BE LUCKY TO CATCH IT! FASTER!
FSSSSSSS
DON'T YOU UNDERSTAND!
IF THAT DYNAMITE BLOWS, THE TREASURE WILL BE TRAPPED DOWN HERE FOREVER!
SO WILL WE!
WE HAVE TO GET OUT OF HERE!
FSSSSSSS
FSSS

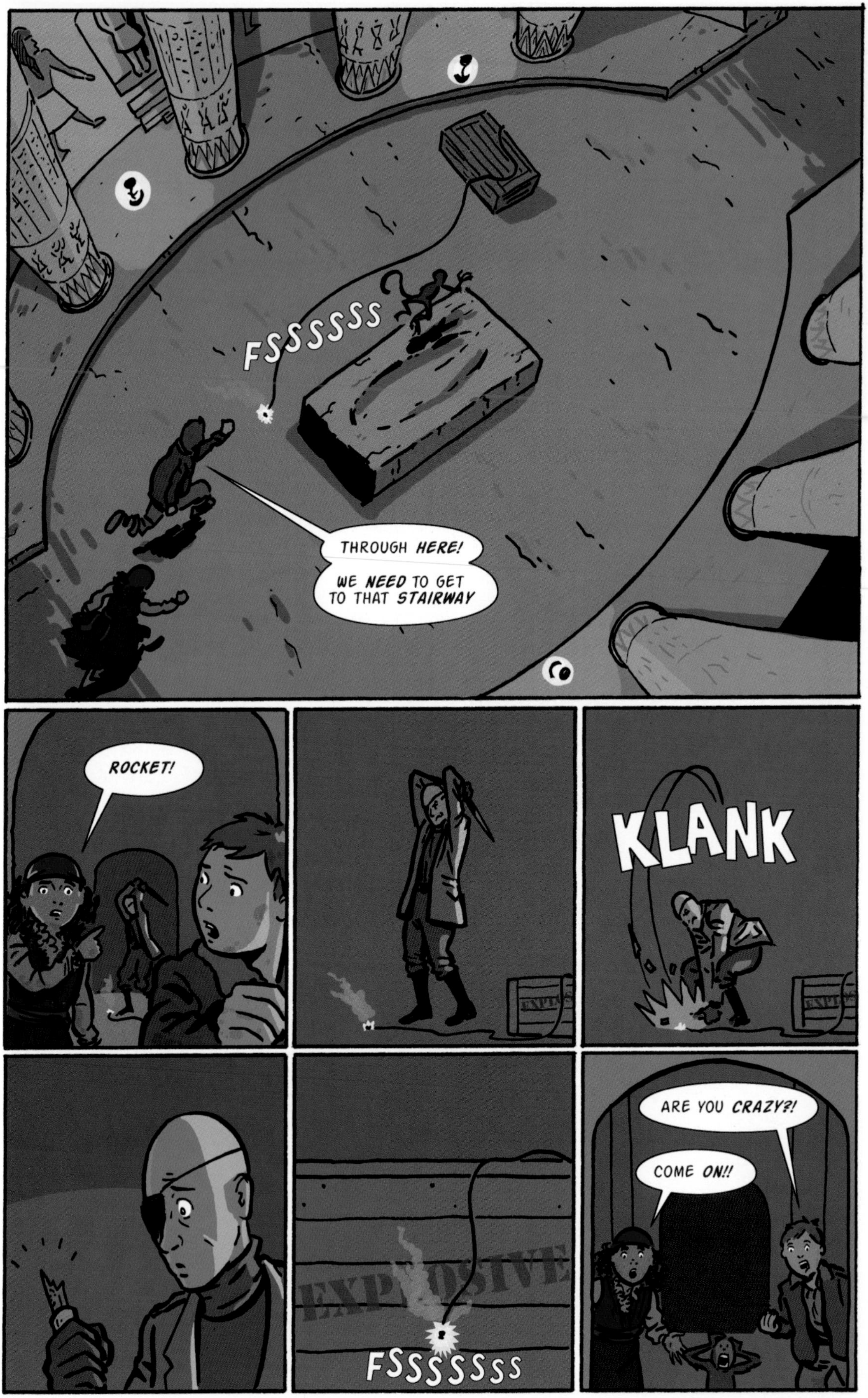
FSSSSSS
THROUGH HERE!
WE NEED TO GET TO THAT STAIRWAY
ROCKET!
KLANK
EXPLOSIVE
FSSSSSSS
ARE YOU CRAZY?!
COME ON!!

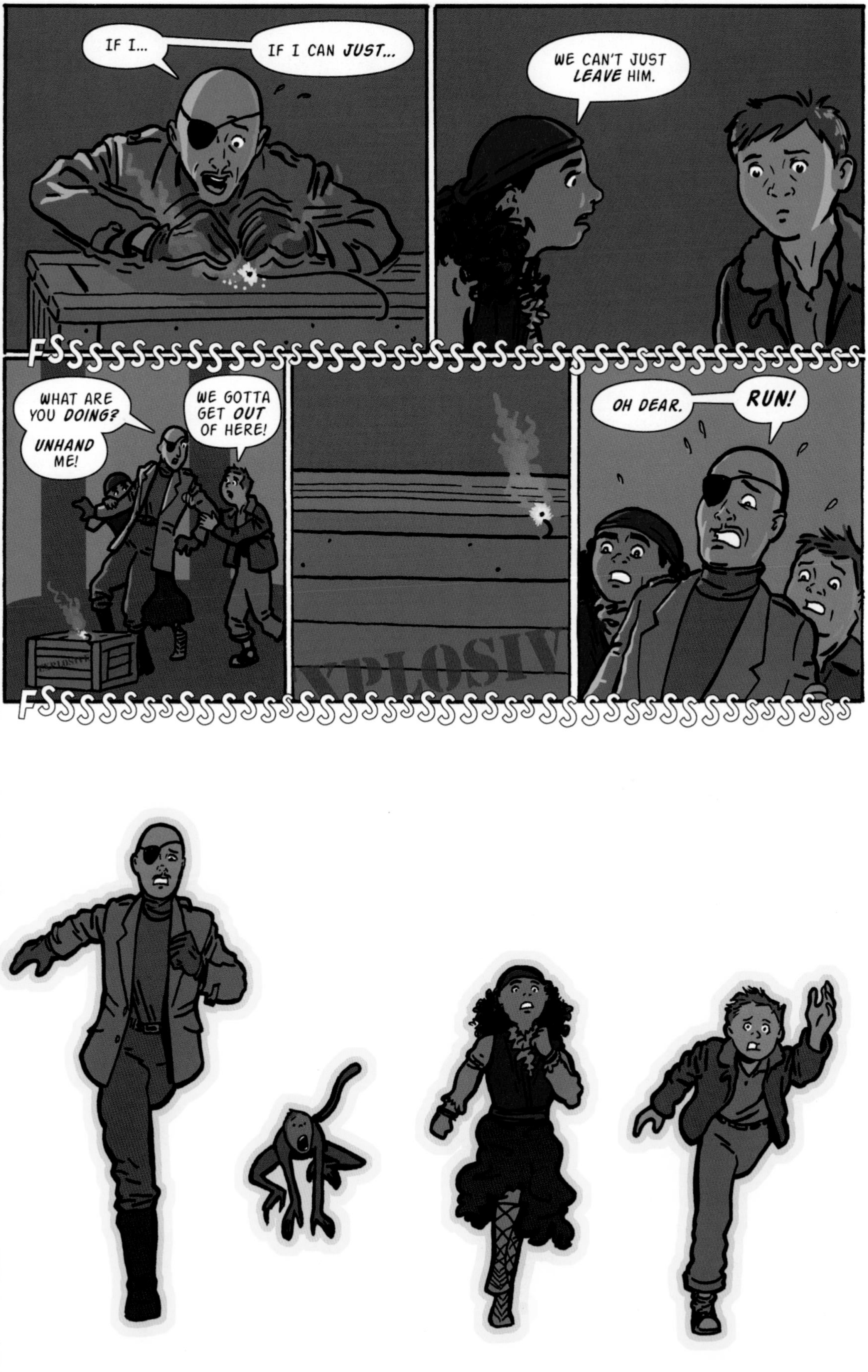
IF I...
IF I CAN JUST...
WE CAN'T JUST LEAVE HIM.
FSSSSSSSSSSSSSSSSSSSSSSSSSSSSSSSSSSSSSSSSSSSS
WHAT ARE YOU DOING?
UNHAND ME!
WE GOTTA GET OUT OF HERE!
XPLOSIV
OH DEAR.
RUN!
FSSSSSSSSSSSSSSSSSSSSSSSSSSSSSSSSSSSSSSSSSSSS

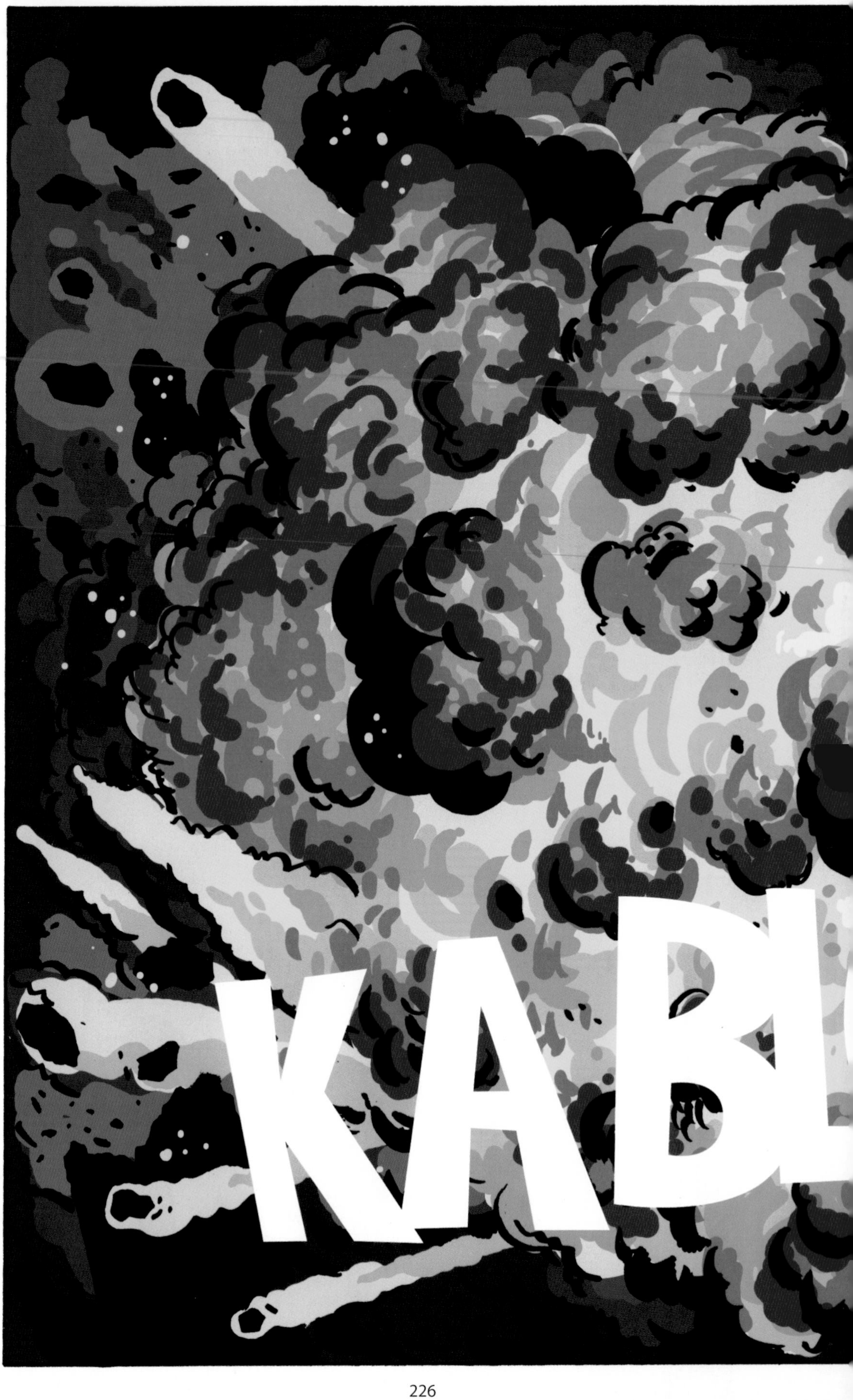
KABL

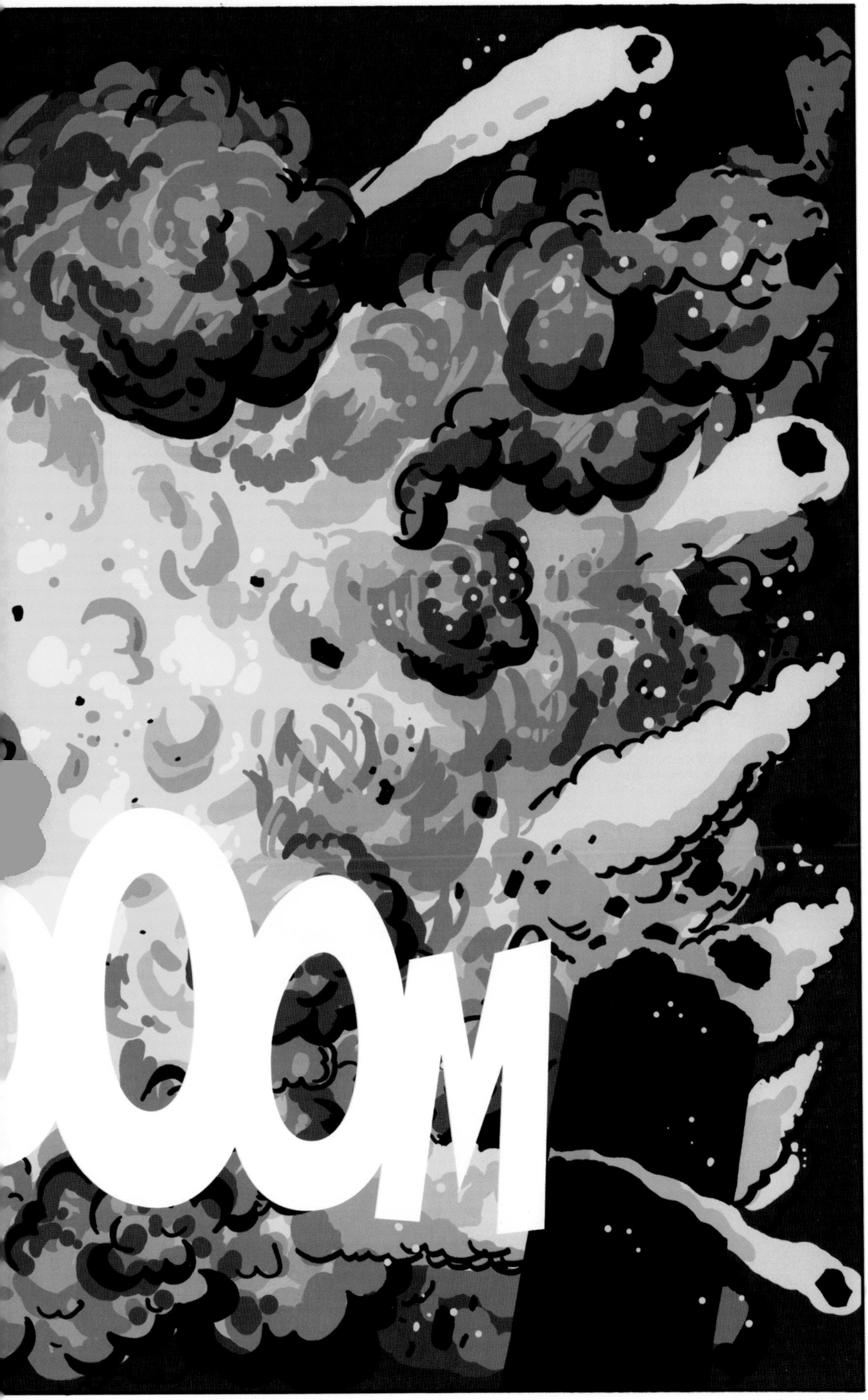
OOM

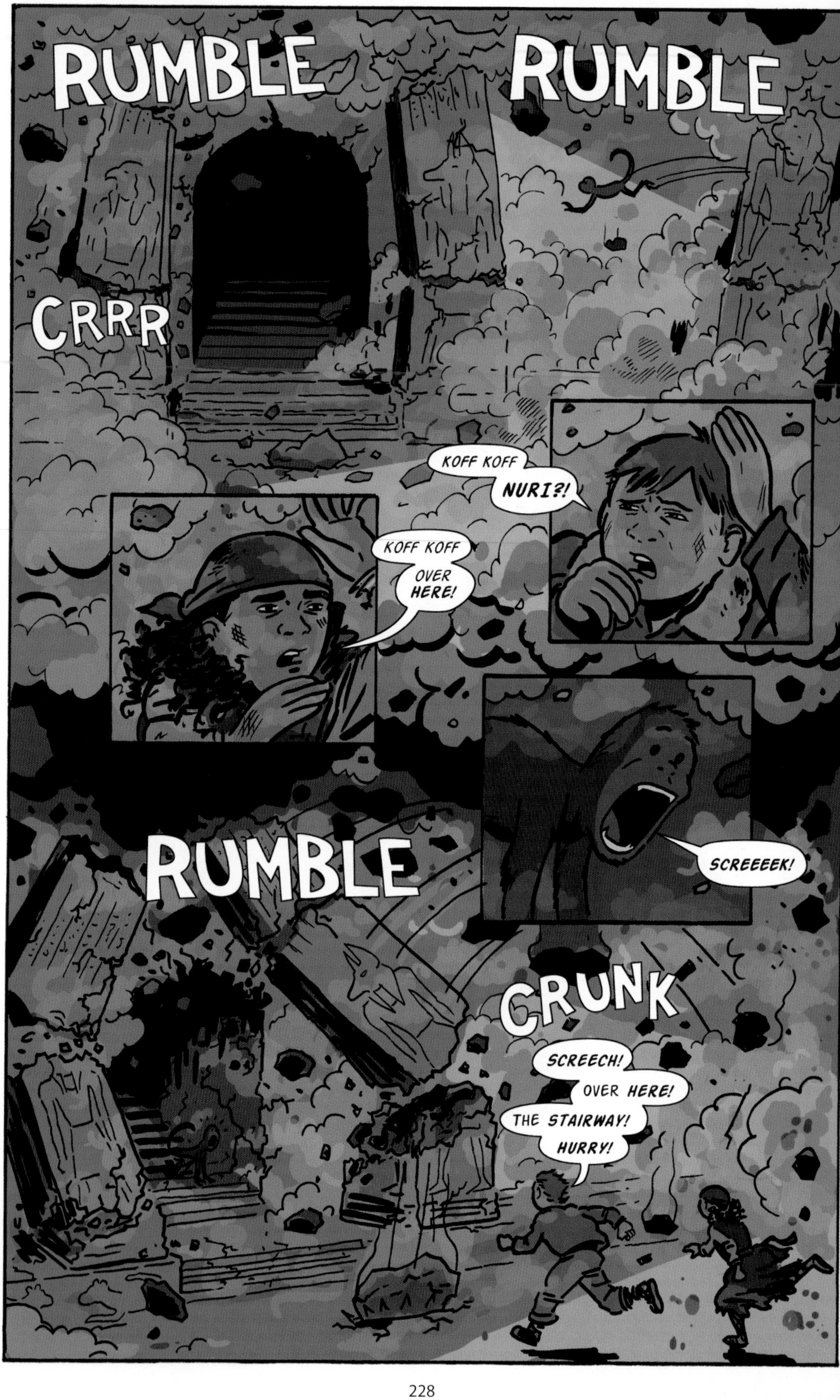
RUMBLE RUMBLE
CRRR
KOFF KOFF NURI?!
KOFF KOFF OVER HERE!
SCREEEEK!
RUMBLE
CRUNK
SCREECH!
OVER HERE!
THE STAIRWAY!
HURRY!

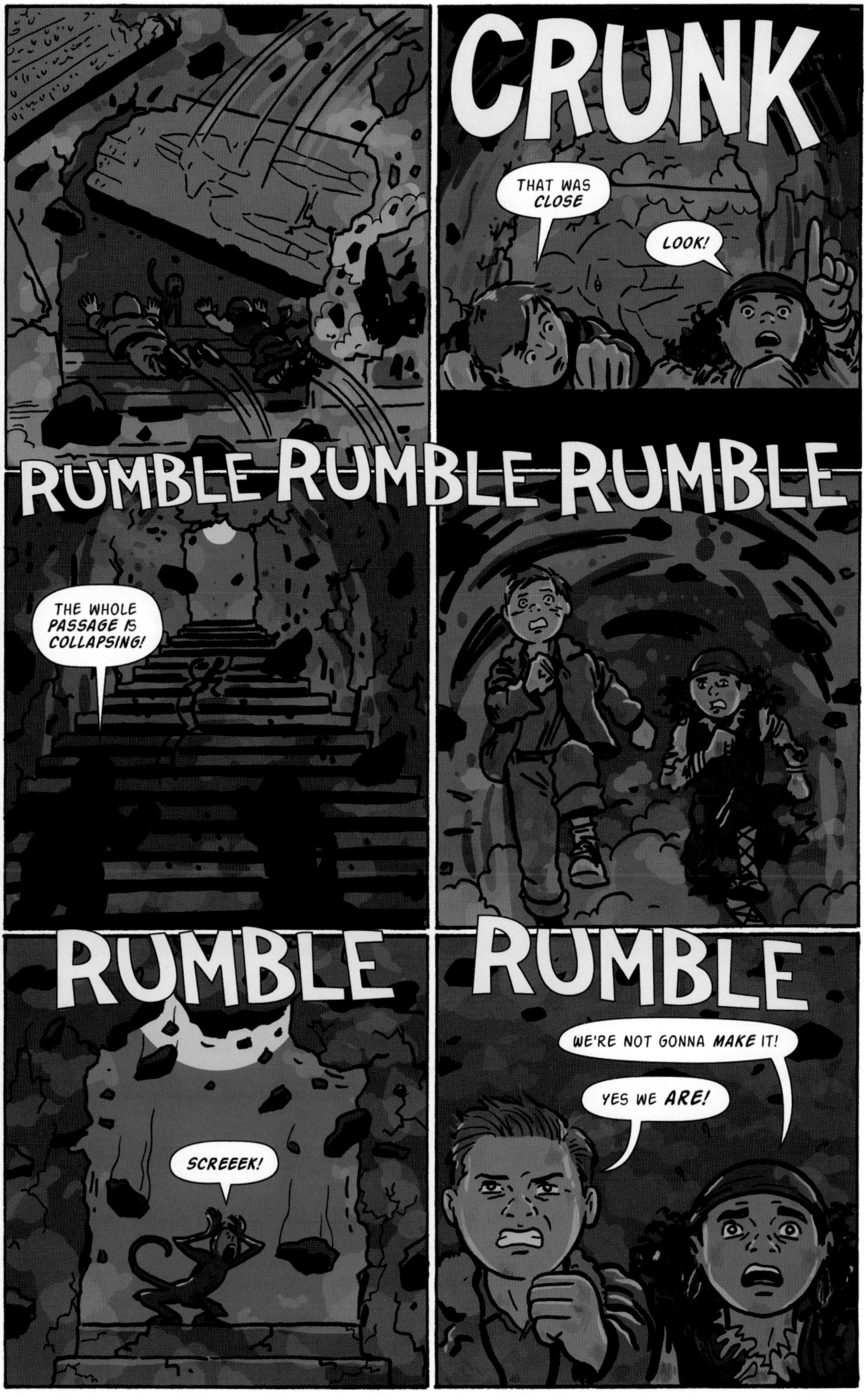
CRUNK
THAT WAS CLOSE
LOOK!
RUMBLE RUMBLE RUMBLE
THE WHOLE PASSAGE IS COLLAPSING!
RUMBLE
SCREEEK!
RUMBLE
WE'RE NOT GONNA MAKE IT!
YES WE ARE!

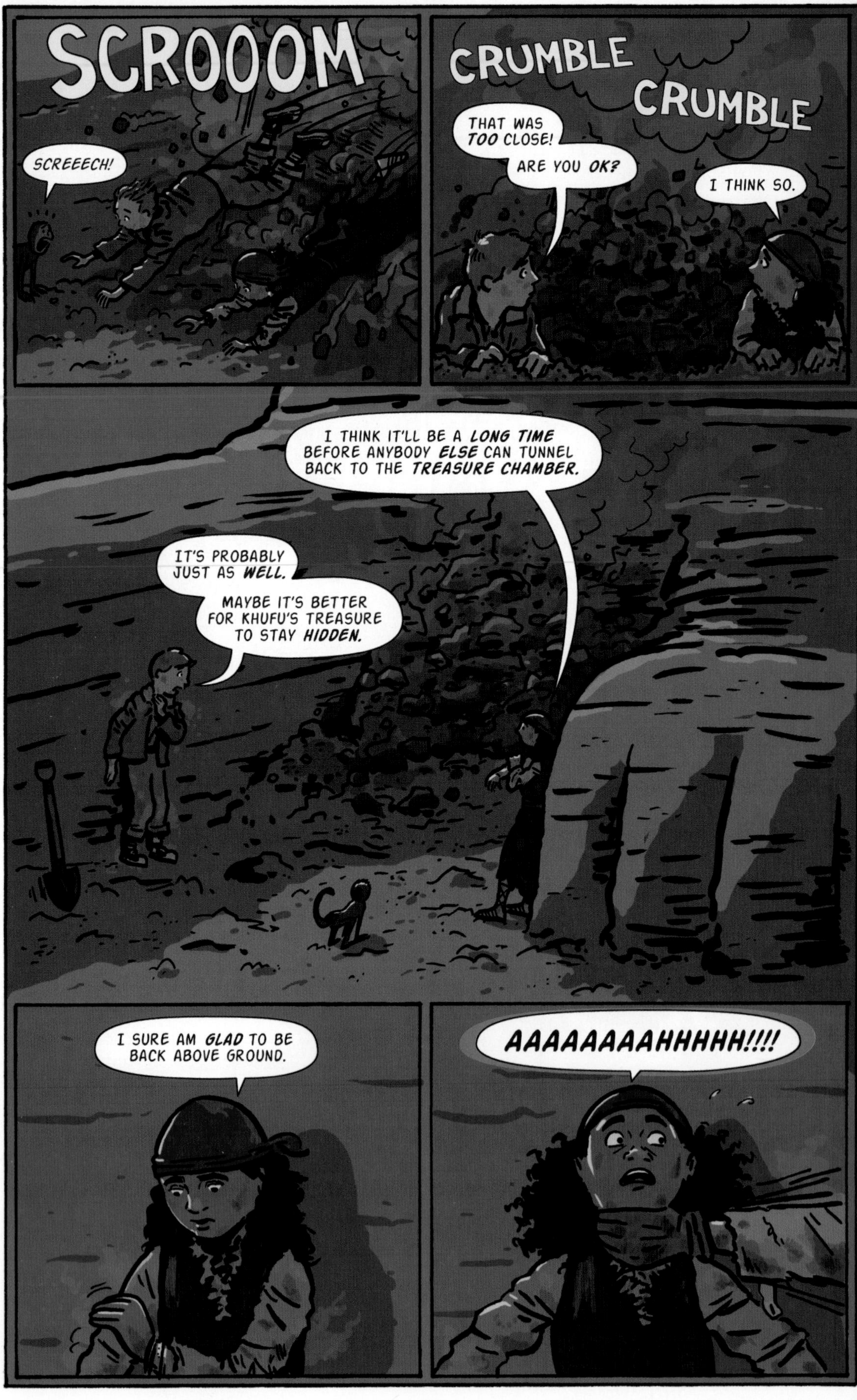
SCROOOM
SCREEECH!
CRUMBLE
CRUMBLE
THAT WAS TOO CLOSE!
ARE YOU OK?
I THINK SO.
I THINK IT'LL BE A LONG TIME BEFORE ANYBODY ELSE CAN TUNNEL BACK TO THE TREASURE CHAMBER.
IT'S PROBABLY JUST AS WELL.
MAYBE IT'S BETTER FOR KHUFU'S TREASURE TO STAY HIDDEN.
I SURE AM GLAD TO BE BACK ABOVE GROUND.
AAAAAAAAHHHHH!!!!

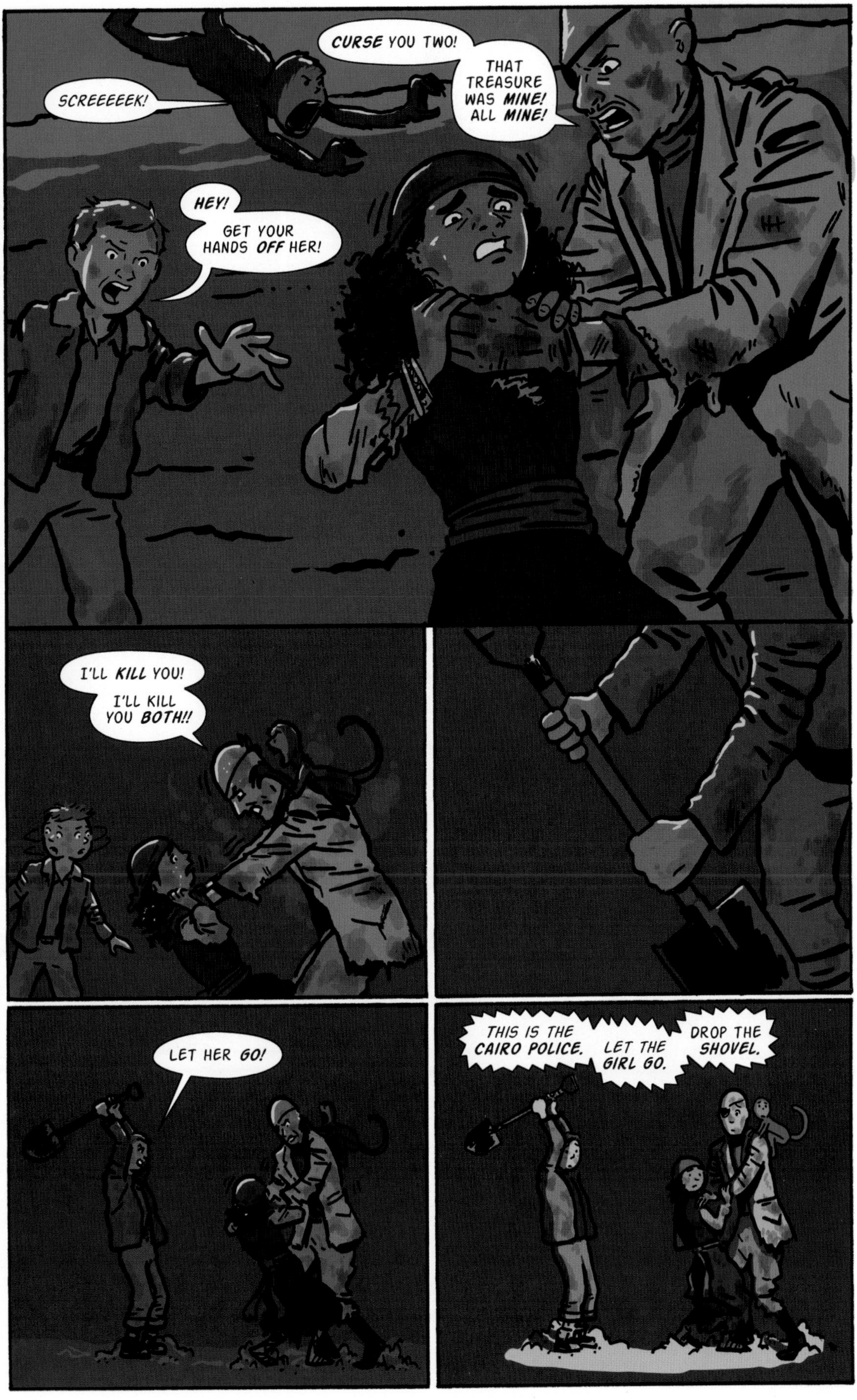
SCREEEEEEK!
CURSE YOU TWO!
THAT TREASURE WAS MINE! ALL MINE!
HEY! GET YOUR HANDS OFF HER!
I'LL KILL YOU! I'LL KILL YOU BOTH!!
LET HER GO!
THIS IS THE CAIRO POLICE.
LET THE GIRL GO.
DROP THE SHOVEL.

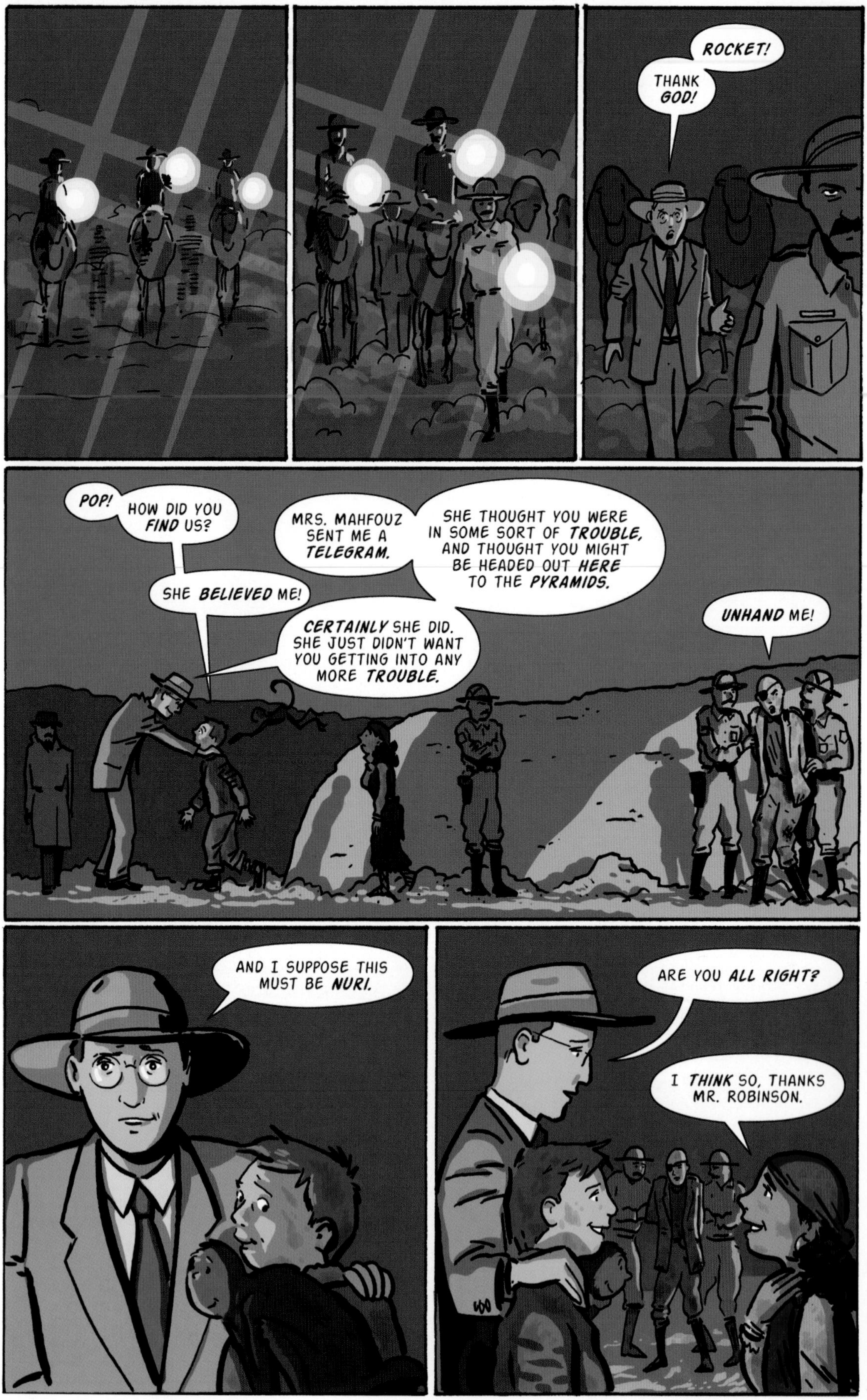
THANK GOD!
ROCKET!
POP!
HOW DID YOU FIND US?
MRS. MAHFOUZ SENT ME A TELEGRAM.
SHE THOUGHT YOU WERE IN SOME SORT OF TROUBLE, AND THOUGHT YOU MIGHT BE HEADED OUT HERE TO THE PYRAMIDS.
SHE BELIEVED ME!
CERTAINLY SHE DID. SHE JUST DIDN'T WANT YOU GETTING INTO ANY MORE TROUBLE.
UNHAND ME!
AND I SUPPOSE THIS MUST BE NURI.
ARE YOU ALL RIGHT?
I THINK SO, THANKS MR. ROBINSON.

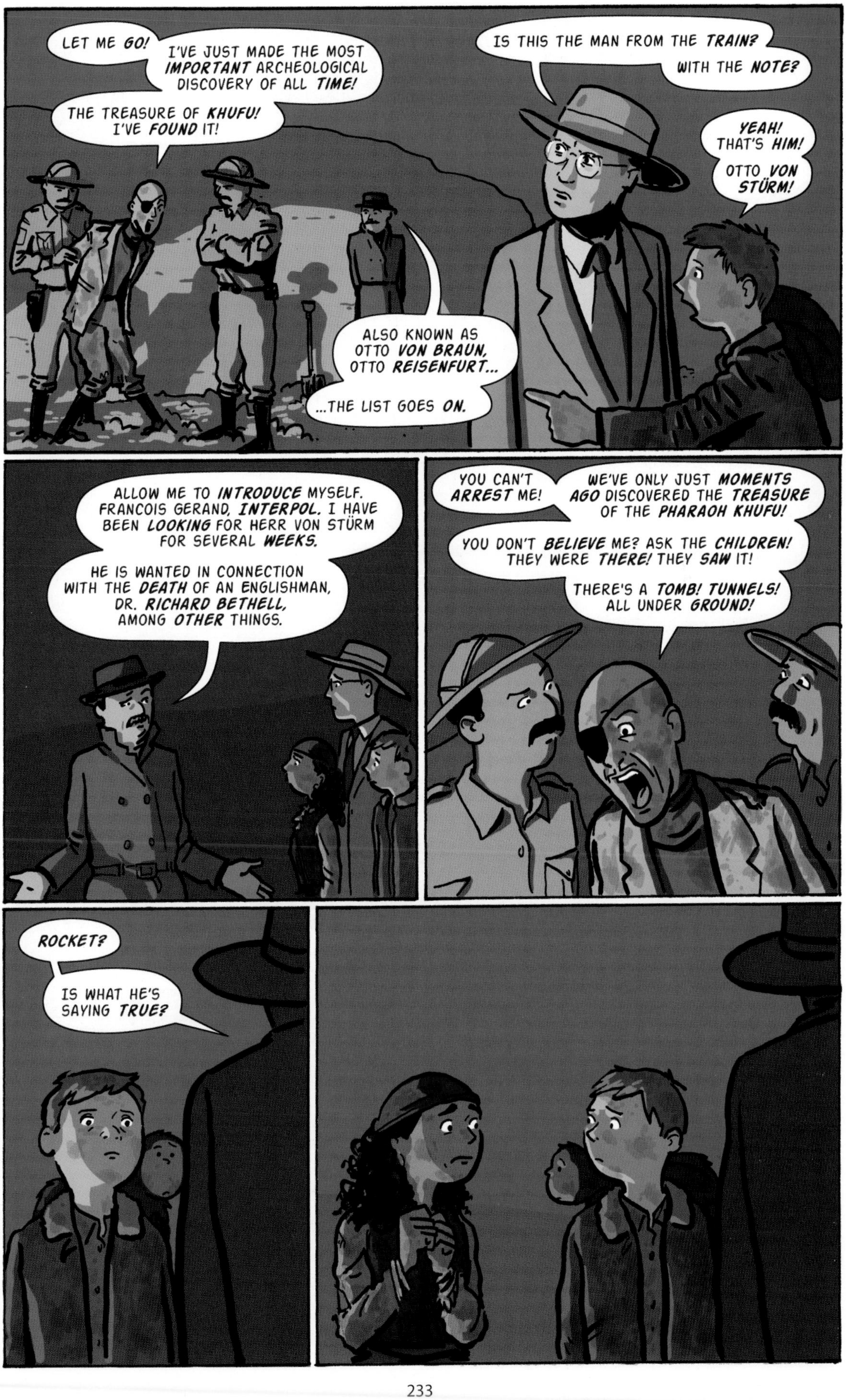
LET ME GO!
I'VE JUST MADE THE MOST IMPORTANT ARCHEOLOGICAL DISCOVERY OF ALL TIME!
THE TREASURE OF KHUFU! I'VE FOUND IT!
IS THIS THE MAN FROM THE TRAIN?
WITH THE NOTE?
YEAH! THAT'S HIM!
OTTO VON STÜRM!
ALSO KNOWN AS OTTO VON BRAUN, OTTO REISENFURT...
...THE LIST GOES ON.
ALLOW ME TO INTRODUCE MYSELF. FRANCOIS GERAND, INTERPOL. I HAVE BEEN LOOKING FOR HERR VON STÜRM FOR SEVERAL WEEKS.
HE IS WANTED IN CONNECTION WITH THE DEATH OF AN ENGLISHMAN, DR. RICHARD BETHELL, AMONG OTHER THINGS.
YOU CAN'T ARREST ME!
WE'VE ONLY JUST MOMENTS AGO DISCOVERED THE TREASURE OF THE PHARAOH KHUFU!
YOU DON'T BELIEVE ME? ASK THE CHILDREN! THEY WERE THERE! THEY SAW IT!
THERE'S A TOMB! TUNNELS! ALL UNDER GROUND!
ROCKET?
IS WHAT HE'S SAYING TRUE?

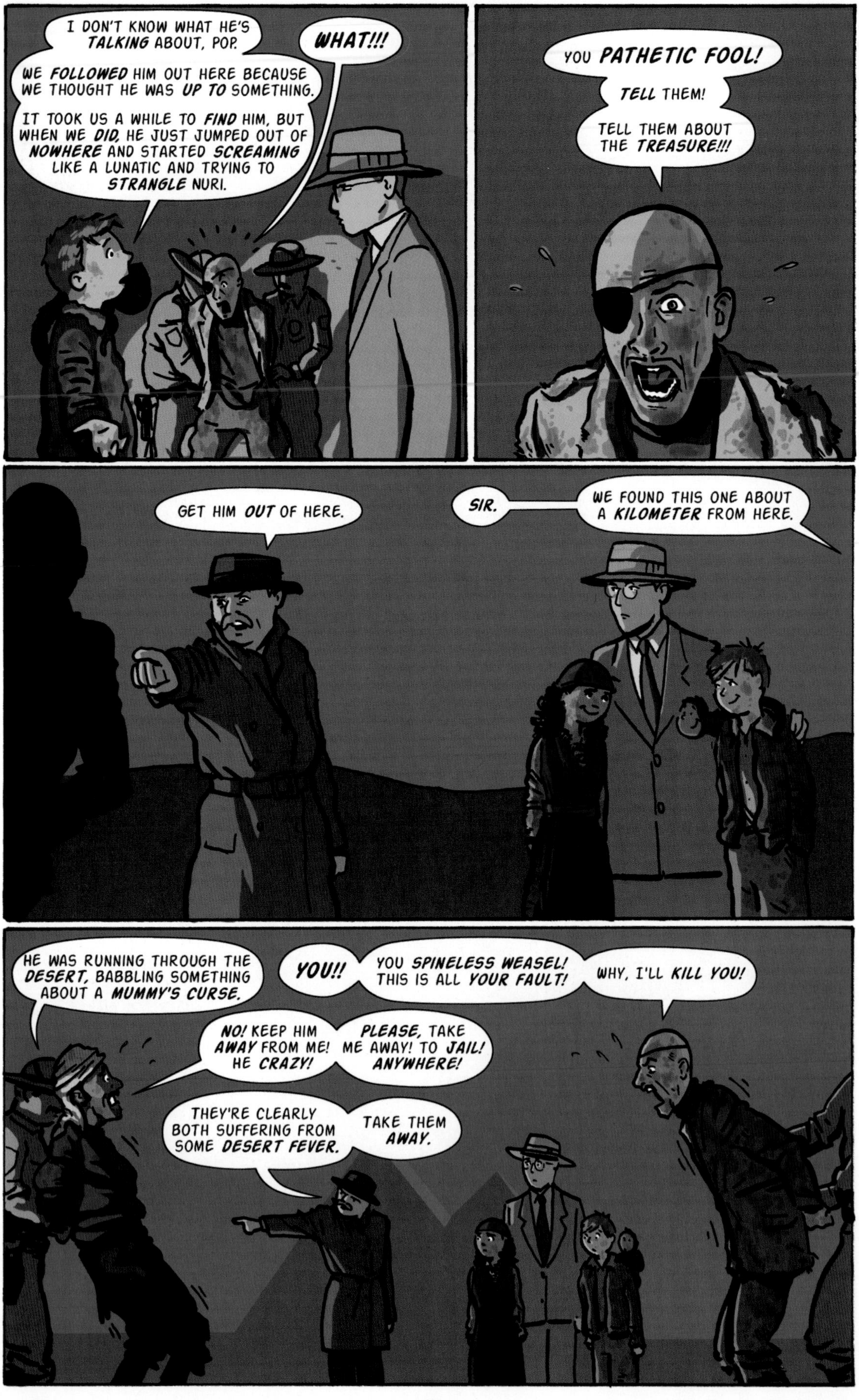
I DON'T KNOW WHAT HE'S TALKING ABOUT, POP.
WE FOLLOWED HIM OUT HERE BECAUSE WE THOUGHT HE WAS UP TO SOMETHING.
IT TOOK US A WHILE TO FIND HIM, BUT WHEN WE DID, HE JUST JUMPED OUT OF NOWHERE AND STARTED SCREAMING LIKE A LUNATIC AND TRYING TO STRANGLE NURI.
WHAT!!!
YOU PATHETIC FOOL!
TELL THEM!
TELL THEM ABOUT THE TREASURE!!!
GET HIM OUT OF HERE.
SIR.
WE FOUND THIS ONE ABOUT A KILOMETER FROM HERE.
HE WAS RUNNING THROUGH THE DESERT, BABBLING SOMETHING ABOUT A MUMMY'S CURSE.
YOU!!
YOU SPINELESS WEASEL! THIS IS ALL YOUR FAULT!
WHY, I'LL KILL YOU!
NO! KEEP HIM AWAY FROM ME! HE CRAZY!
PLEASE, TAKE ME AWAY! TO JAIL! ANYWHERE!
THEY'RE CLEARLY BOTH SUFFERING FROM SOME DESERT FEVER.
TAKE THEM AWAY.

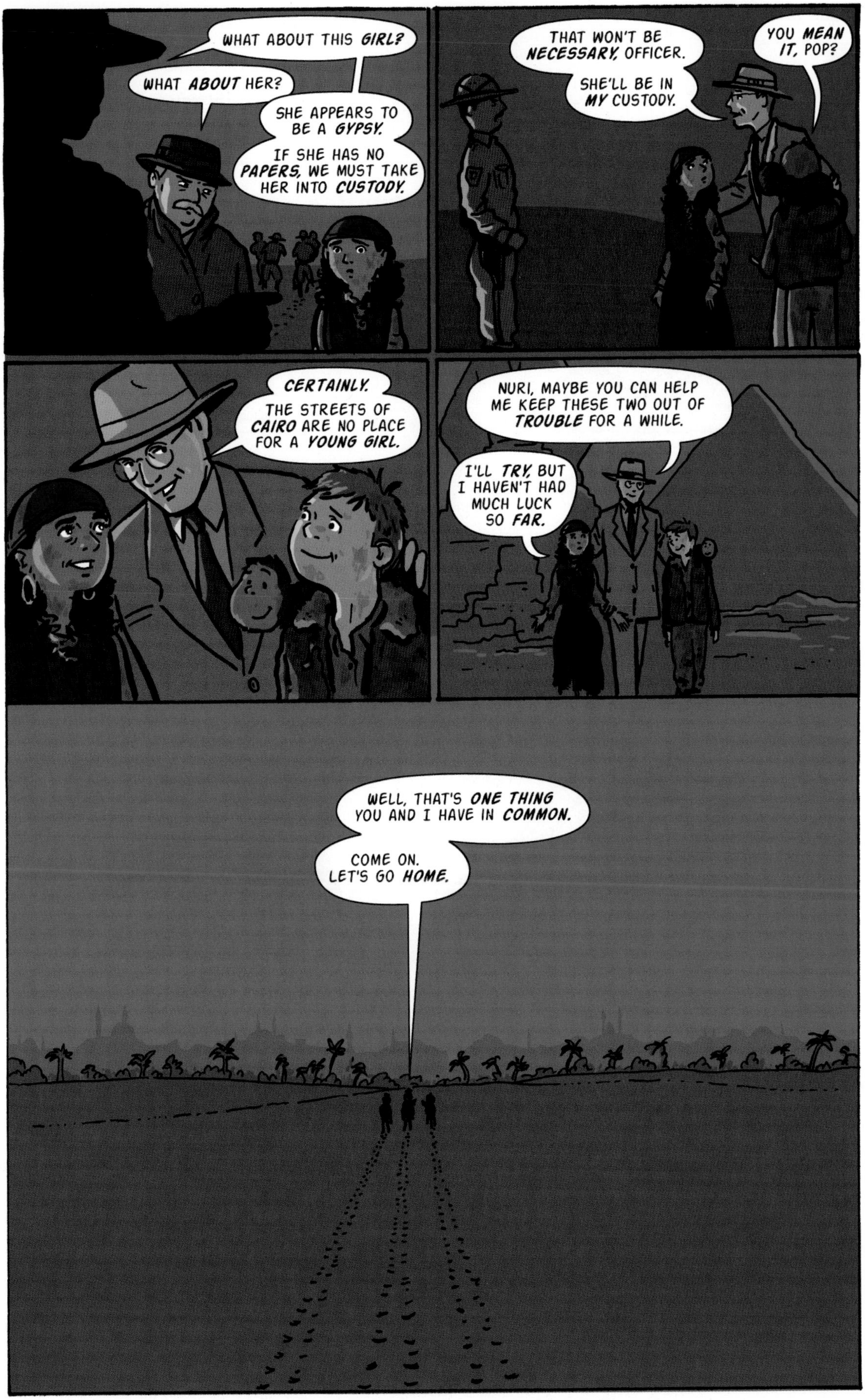
WHAT ABOUT THIS GIRL?
WHAT ABOUT HER?
SHE APPEARS TO BE A GYPSY.
IF SHE HAS NO PAPERS, WE MUST TAKE HER INTO CUSTODY.
THAT WON'T BE NECESSARY, OFFICER.
SHE'LL BE IN MY CUSTODY.
YOU MEAN IT, POP?
CERTAINLY.
THE STREETS OF CAIRO ARE NO PLACE FOR A YOUNG GIRL.
NURI, MAYBE YOU CAN HELP ME KEEP THESE TWO OUT OF TROUBLE FOR A WHILE.
I'LL TRY, BUT I HAVEN'T HAD MUCH LUCK SO FAR.
WELL, THAT'S ONE THING YOU AND I HAVE IN COMMON.
COME ON. LET'S GO HOME.

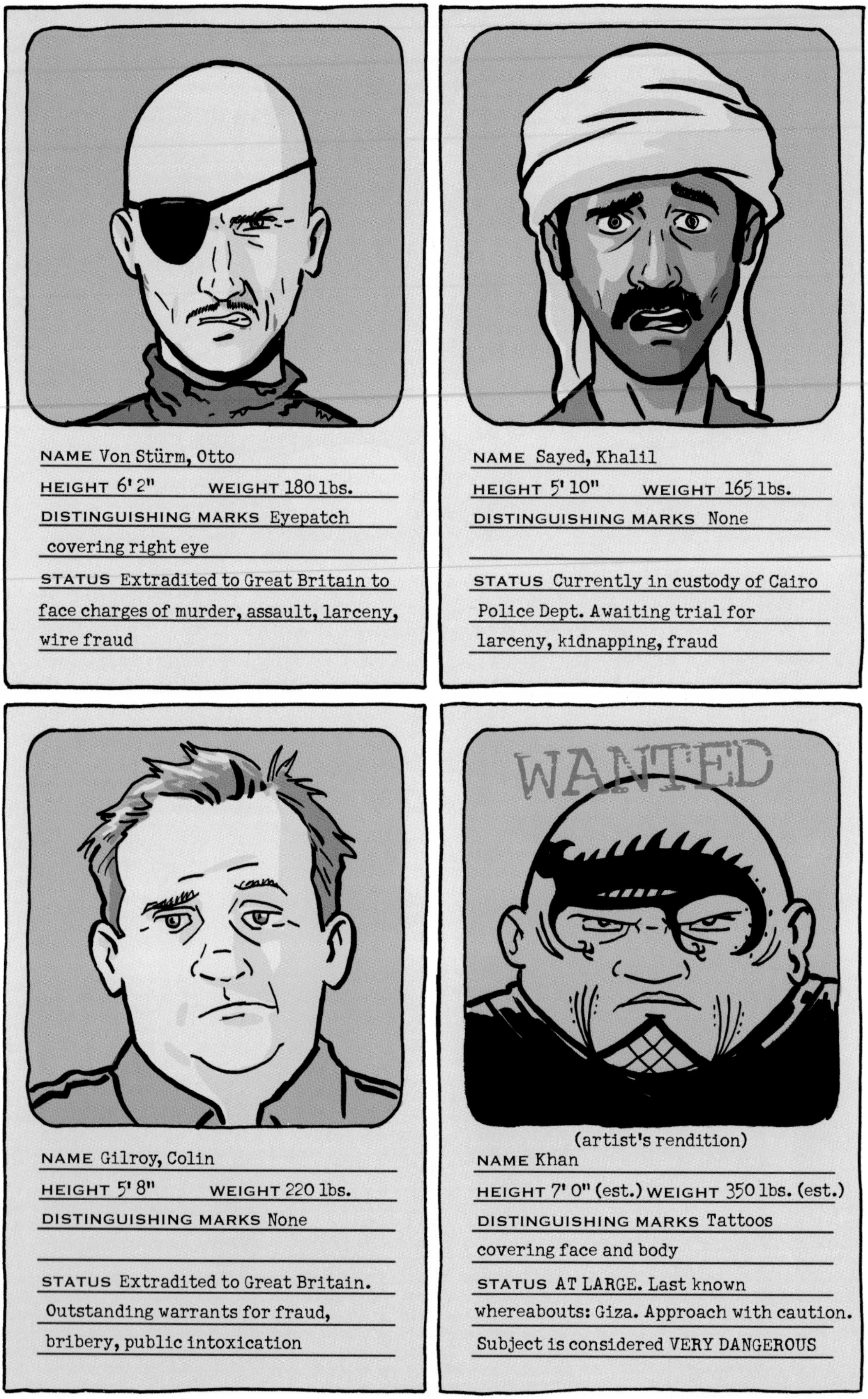
NAME Von Stürm, Otto
HEIGHT 6'2" WEIGHT 180 lbs.
DISTINGUISHING MARKS Eyepatch covering right eye
STATUS Extradited to Great Britain to face charges of murder, assault, larceny, wire fraud
NAME Sayed, Khalil
HEIGHT 5'10" WEIGHT 165 lbs.
DISTINGUISHING MARKS None
STATUS Currently in custody of Cairo Police Dept. Awaiting trial for larceny, kidnapping, fraud
NAME Gilroy, Colin
HEIGHT 5'8" WEIGHT 220 lbs.
DISTINGUISHING MARKS None
STATUS Extradited to Great Britain. Outstanding warrants for fraud, bribery, public intoxication
WANTED
(artist's rendition)
NAME Khan
HEIGHT 7'0" (est.) WEIGHT 350 lbs. (est.)
DISTINGUISHING MARKS Tattoos covering face and body
STATUS AT LARGE. Last known whereabouts: Giza. Approach with caution. Subject is considered VERY DANGEROUS

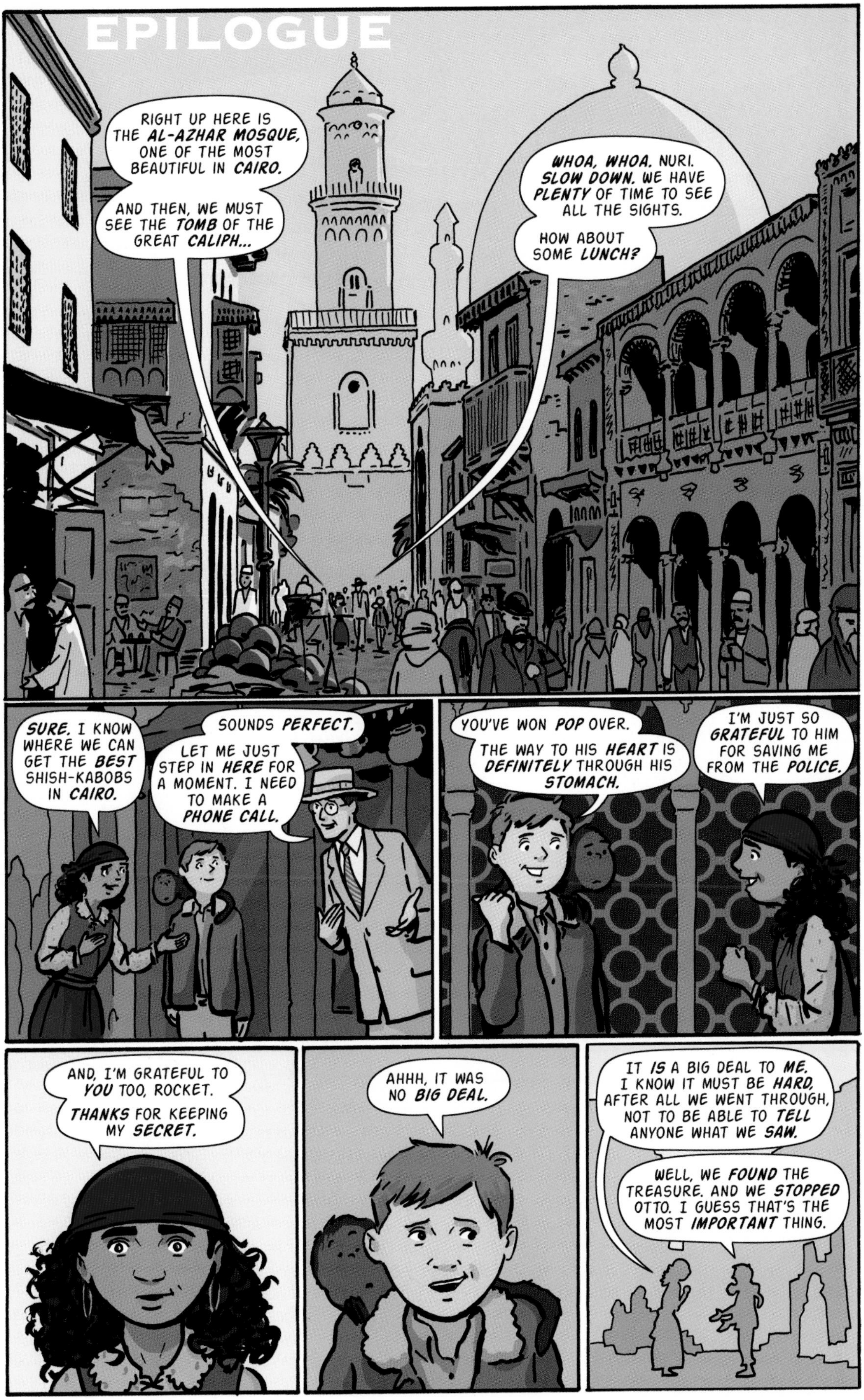
EPILOGUE
RIGHT UP HERE IS THE AL-AZHAR MOSQUE, ONE OF THE MOST BEAUTIFUL IN CAIRO.
AND THEN, WE MUST SEE THE TOMB OF THE GREAT CALIPH...
WHOA, WHOA. NURI. SLOW DOWN. WE HAVE PLENTY OF TIME TO SEE ALL THE SIGHTS.
HOW ABOUT SOME LUNCH?
SURE. I KNOW WHERE WE CAN GET THE BEST SHISH-KABOBS IN CAIRO.
SOUNDS PERFECT.
LET ME JUST STEP IN HERE FOR A MOMENT. I NEED TO MAKE A PHONE CALL.
YOU'VE WON POP OVER.
THE WAY TO HIS HEART IS DEFINITELY THROUGH HIS STOMACH.
I'M JUST SO GRATEFUL TO HIM FOR SAVING ME FROM THE POLICE.
AND, I'M GRATEFUL TO YOU TOO, ROCKET.
THANKS FOR KEEPING MY SECRET.
AHHH, IT WAS NO BIG DEAL.
IT IS A BIG DEAL TO ME. I KNOW IT MUST BE HARD, AFTER ALL WE WENT THROUGH, NOT TO BE ABLE TO TELL ANYONE WHAT WE SAW.
WELL, WE FOUND THE TREASURE. AND WE STOPPED OTTO. I GUESS THAT'S THE MOST IMPORTANT THING.

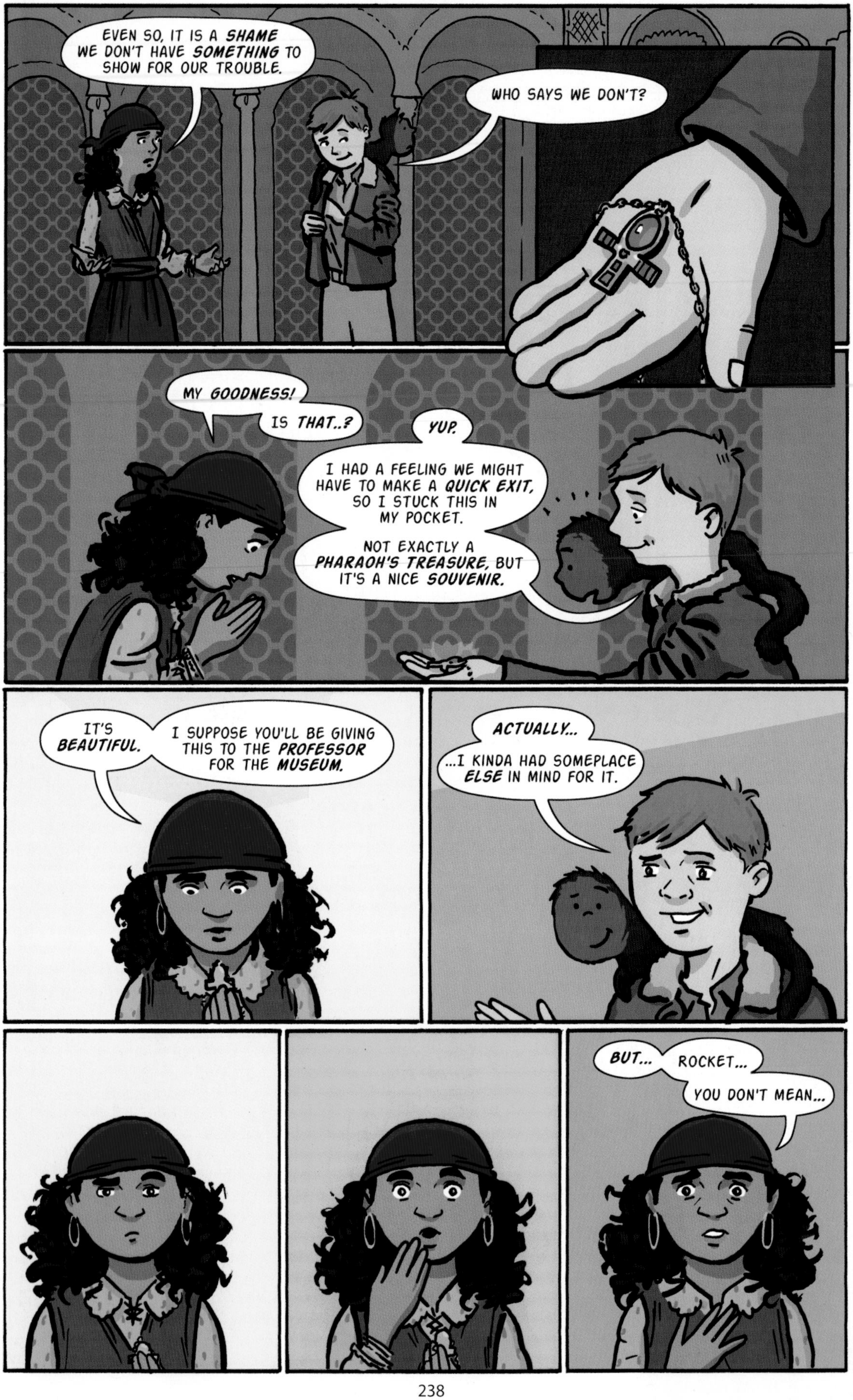
EVEN SO, IT IS A SHAME WE DON'T HAVE SOMETHING TO SHOW FOR OUR TROUBLE.
WHO SAYS WE DON'T?
MY GOODNESS!
IS THAT..?
YUP.
I HAD A FEELING WE MIGHT HAVE TO MAKE A QUICK EXIT, SO I STUCK THIS IN MY POCKET.
NOT EXACTLY A PHARAOH'S TREASURE, BUT IT'S A NICE SOUVENIR.
IT'S BEAUTIFUL.
I SUPPOSE YOU'LL BE GIVING THIS TO THE PROFESSOR FOR THE MUSEUM.
ACTUALLY...
...I KINDA HAD SOMEPLACE ELSE IN MIND FOR IT.
BUT...
ROCKET...
YOU DON'T MEAN...

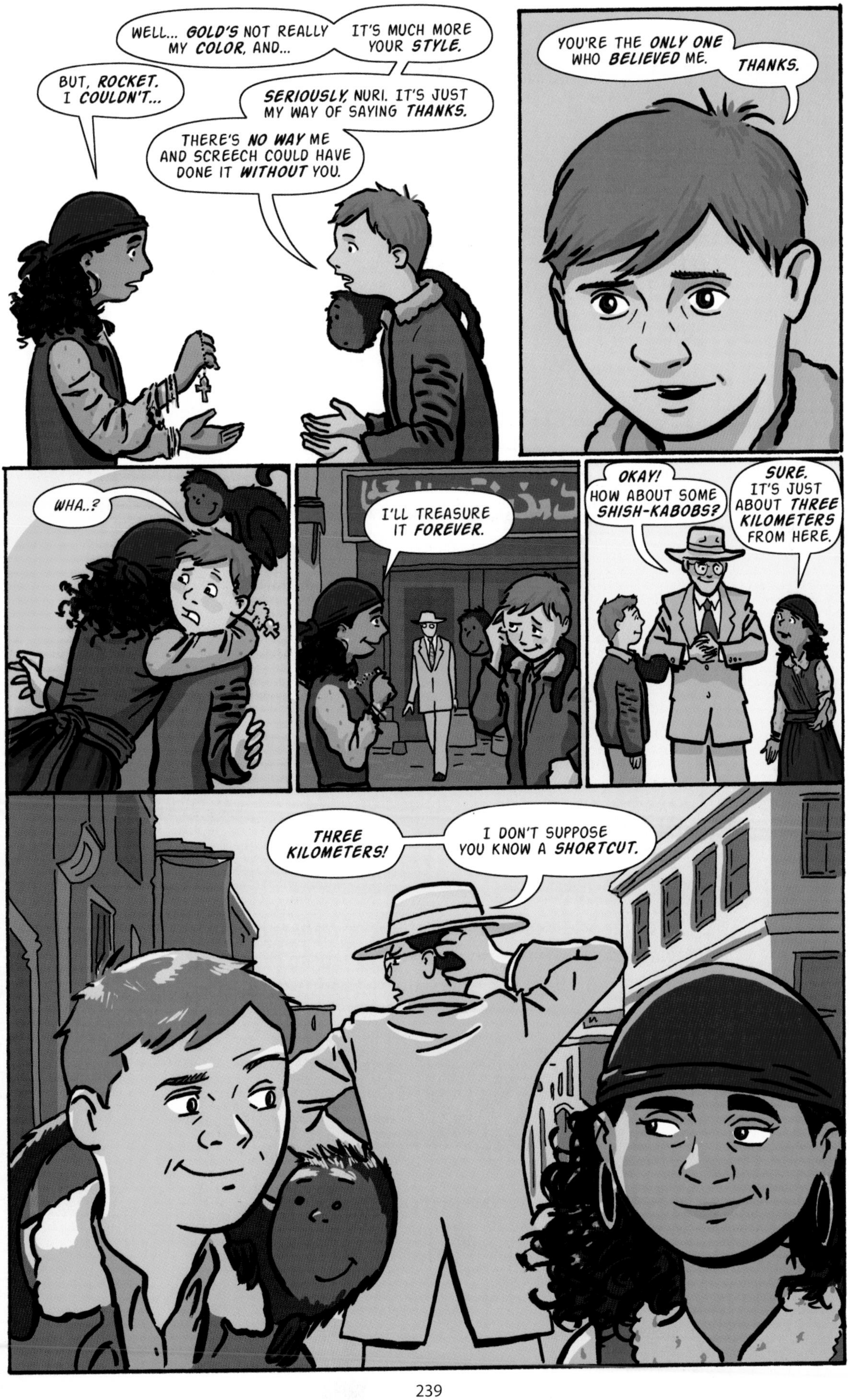
BUT, ROCKET. I COULDN'T...
WELL... GOLD'S NOT REALLY MY COLOR, AND...
IT'S MUCH MORE YOUR STYLE.
SERIOUSLY, NURI. IT'S JUST MY WAY OF SAYING THANKS.
THERE'S NO WAY ME AND SCREECH COULD HAVE DONE IT WITHOUT YOU.
YOU'RE THE ONLY ONE WHO BELIEVED ME.
THANKS.
WHA..?
I'LL TREASURE IT FOREVER.
OKAY! HOW ABOUT SOME SHISH-KABOBS?
SURE. IT'S JUST ABOUT THREE KILOMETERS FROM HERE.
THREE KILOMETERS!
I DON'T SUPPOSE YOU KNOW A SHORTCUT.

ACKNOWLEDGEMENTS

Many thanks to all of the following, without whose generous support completion of this book would not have been possible:

Jordan H. Wachtell and the rest of my Kickstarter backers.

Katie Muhtaris and Kathy Lynch for their invaluable editorial input and content expertise.

Scott Hight Design for design and production support.

And my wonderful family, especially my amazing wife Jennifer Farrington. Thanks for making it possible.

Sean O'Neill
Chicago, Illinois

To order additional copies of *Rocket Robinson and the Pharaoh's Fortune,* find more information, or to stay updated on Rocket's upcoming adventures, please visit:

www.rocketrobinson.com